THE AUTHOR

Margery Louise Allingham was born in London in 1904. She attended The Perse School in Cambridge before returning to London and the Polytechnic for Speech-Training. Writing ran in her family – her father was the author H. J. Allingham – and Margery's first novel (a pirate story called *Blackkerchief Dick*) was published when she was seventeen. In 1928 she published her first detective story, *The White Cottage Mystery*, which had been serialised in the *Daily Express*. The following year, in *Crime at Black Dudley*, she introduced the character who was to become the hallmark of her writing – Albert Campion, the gentle detective who, with his strong-arm colleagues, features in twenty-one of her thirty novels. Reviewing her *Fashion In Shrouds* in the *Observer*, Torquemada said of this remarkable creation that 'to Albert Campion has fallen the honour of being the first detective to feature in a story which is by any standard a distinguished novel'. Her novels heralded, in their day, the more sophisticaed suspense genre: characterised by her intuitive intelligence and extraordinary energy and accuracy in observation, they vary from the grave to the openly satirical, whilst never losing sight of the basic rules of the classic detective tale. Margery Allingham spoke of her self as 'one of the last of the real trained professional writers'. In 1928 she married the artist, journalist and editor Philip Youngman Carter, who designed the jackets for many of her books, and they lived on the edge of the Essex Marshes. She died in 1968.

The Hogarth Press also publishes *The Beckoning Lady*, *Cargo of Eagles* and *Hide My Eyes*.

THE CHINA GOVERNESS

A MYSTERY

Margery Allingham

Why each atom knows its own,
How in spite of woe and death
Gay is life and sweet is breath

ROBERT BRIDGES

THE HOGARTH PRESS

LONDON

Published in 1986 by
The Hogarth Press
30 Bedford Square, London WC1B 3RP

First published in Great Britain by Chatto & Windus 1963
Hogarth edition offset from original Chatto edition
Second impression 1988
Copyright P. & M. Youngman Carter Ltd 1963.

British Library Cataloguing in Publication Data

Allingham, Margery
The china governess: a mystery.
I. Title
823'.912[F]   PZ7

ISBN 0 7012 0635 7

Printed in Great Britain by
Cox & Wyman Ltd
Reading, Berkshire

Contents

*None of the characters in this book
is a portrait of a living person*

The Turk Street Mile

'IT was called the wickedest street in London and the entrance was just here. I imagine the mouth of the road lay between this lamp standard and the second from the next down there.'

In the cold darkness of the early spring night the Chief Detective-Inspector of the area was talking like a guide-book with sly, proprietorial satisfaction. He was a neat, pink man whose name was Munday and he was more like a civil servant than a police officer. His companion, who had just followed him out of the black chauffeur-driven police car drawn up against the kerb, straightened himself and stood looking at the shadowy scene before him without speaking.

They were standing in the midst of the East End on a new pavement flanking a low wall beyond which, apart from a single vast building, there appeared to be a great deal of nothing at all in a half circle perhaps a quarter of a mile across. The great fleece which is London, clotted and matted and black with time and smoke, possesses here and there many similar bald spots. They are cleared war-damage scars in various stages of reclamation. Around the edges of this particular site the network of small streets was bright and the arterial road by which they stood was a gleaming way bathed in orange light, but inside the half circle, despite the lighted windows of the building, it was sufficiently dark for the red glow which always hangs over the city at night to appear very deep in colour.

'The Turk Street Mile has gone now, anyway,' Munday went on. 'A serious trouble spot for three hundred years, wiped out utterly and for ever in a single night by four landmines and a sprinkling of incendiaries in the first raid on London, twenty years ago.'

The other man was still silent, which was something of a phenomenon. Superintendent Charles Luke was not as a rule at a loss for words. He was very tall but his back and shoulder muscles were so heavy that he appeared shorter and there was a hint of the traditional gangster in his appearance, especially now as he stood with his hands in his trousers pockets, the skirts of his light tweed overcoat bunched behind him and his soft hat pulled down over his dark face. The legacy of the last few years which included pro- motion, marriage, fatherhood, widowerhood and the Police Medal, had had remarkably little outward effect upon him. His shorn curls were as black as ever and he could still pump out energy like a power station, but there was a new awareness in his sharp eyes which indicated that he had lived and grown.

'I understand that the district was considered a sort of sanc- tuary,' the Chief was saying. 'An Alsatia like the ancient one be- hind the Strand, or Saffron Hill before the First World War. They tell me there was a recognized swag-market down here.'

Luke drew a long hand out of his pocket and pointed to a thin spire far away in the rusty sky. 'That's St. Botolph's,' he said. 'Take a line from there to the old gasometer on the canal at the back of the cinema over there and you won't be far wrong. The Mile was a narrow winding street and in places the top floors of the buildings almost touched. Right in the middle there was a valley with very steep sides. The road dipped like a wall and went up again. That's why there was no through traffic to clear it. The surface hadn't been altered for generations; round cobbles. It was like walking over cannon balls.' Now that he had recovered from his first astonishment at the sight of the new building which was not what he had expected, he was talking with his usual fierce enthusiasm and as usual painting in details with his hands.

'When you turned into The Mile from this end the first thing you saw was the biggest pawnshop you ever clapped eyes on and opposite, all convenient, was the Scimitar. That was a huge gin palace, built on what you might call oriental lines. The street stalls ran down both sides of the way to the hill and every other one of them sported a strictly illegal crown-and-anchor board. The locals played all day. Early in the morning and late at night by naptha flares. Farther on, round the dip, was the residential quarter. I don't know if that's the term. People lived in caves. There's no other word for them. Have you ever seen a beam eaten to a sponge by beetles? Magnify it and dress the beetles in a rag or two and that's about the picture. I went right through it once for a dare when I was about ten. My mother didn't get me completely clean for a month.' He laughed. 'Oh, The Mile was wicked enough in a way, depending on what you·mean.' He turned back to the scene before him and the enormous new block of council dwellings. The design was some way after Corbusier but the block was built up on plinths and resembled an Atlantic liner swimming diagonally across the site.

'What the devil have you got there?' he inquired. 'A prehistoric "wot-o-saurus"?'

'It's a remarkable building.' Munday was earnest. 'In daylight it takes your breath away. It's as sleek as a spaceship, there's not a hair out of place on it. It's the reason why I've had to disturb you tonight. Mr. Cornish felt Headquarters must be notified at once.'

'Ah, he's the Councillor, is he? The one who's going to get the knighthood for this lot?'

'I don't know about that, sir.' The Chief was wooden. 'I know he's got to raise the money to build five more of these.'

Luke sniffed and surveyed the monster, scored with sun balconies and pitted with neat rows of windows, each one shrouded with pastel colours, blue, pink, lilac, biscuit and lime. A sudden grin spread over his dark cockney face.

'Got the original families in there, Chief Inspector?' he inquired.

Munday gave him a steady glance.

'Not exactly, sir. That's some of tonight's story. I'm given to understand that although it's the primary object of all these big improvement schemes to rehouse the portion of the populace which has been rendered homeless by enemy action, twenty years is a very long time. The new buildings have had to be financed in the ordinary way and the outlay has got to be recovered, so the tendency has been to allot these very exceptional new apartments – they really are quite impressive, Superintendent – to those people who have proved themselves first-class tenants in the temporary accommodation which was rustled up for them just after the war, prefabs and suchlike.'

He came to an uneasy pause and Luke burst out laughing.

'I shan't be asking any questions in Parliament, Chief. You don't have to explain anything away to me. You've got a hand-picked lot here, have you? And that's why this present spot of bother which is only 'wilful damage' has so upset the dovecotes? I see. Come on.'

They set off together down the partially constructed concrete ramp. 'Some of these local government big boys are remarkably like the old-time squires, feudal old baskets!' he remarked. '"Don't hang your bedding out of the window", "Teach the kids to say please, damn them" and "No Singing except in the Bath". I don't like it in a landlord myself. Someone has got irritated by it perhaps? Eh?'

'I don't know.' Munday shrugged his shoulders. 'My informa-tion is that the couple whose home has been wrecked are a sort of show pair. The old boy is finishing his time at the Alandel Branch factory down the road and he's reputed not to have an enemy in the world. The same thing goes for the old lady who is his second wife. I believe there's a temporary lodger, a skilled worker from Alandel's. They got permission to take him in for six weeks' trial and the rent was properly adjusted, so it can't be jealousy on the part of the neighbours. The damage appears to be remarkable and the feeling is that it may be directed against the building itself, the Council that is, and not the tenants at all.'

'Could be. Who have you got out here?'

'A good man, Sergeant Stockwell. I was speaking to him on the phone just before we came out. He thinks it must be the work of a small gang. Possibly juveniles. He doesn't like the look of it but he doesn't see what can be done before morning. However, Mr. Cornish —' He let the rest of the sentence remain unspoken.

'He wants the top brass, does he.' Luke was good tempered but fierce. 'Here it is then. Both of it. We'll go and give him a toot.'

His amused, contemptuous mood persisted as they entered the aluminium-lined passenger elevator which carried them up to the top floor. The convenience and neatness impressed him but the termite-hill architecture made him uneasy.

'It's all very quiet. What's everybody doing behind the fancy drapery?' he muttered, the attempt to muffle his remarkably resonant voice failing disastrously.

'The trouble is on the other side of the building, sir. Top floor. All the doors are on that service side.' Munday sounded defensive. 'It's not quite like a street. A lot can happen without the neighbours knowing.'

Luke opened his mouth to say something acid but at that moment they arrived and he stepped out of the silver box to be confronted by a prospect of his beloved city which he had never seen before.

He stood transfixed before the unaccustomed view of London at night time, a vast panorama which reminded him not so much of the aerial photographs of today but rather of some wood engravings far off and magical, in a printshop in his childhood. They dated from the previous century and were coarsely printed on tinted paper, with tinsel outlining the design. They had been intended as backcloths for toy theatres and were wildly ambitious. The Fall of Rome was included, several battlefields, and even Hell itself complete with steaming lakes and cauldrons of coloured fire. Now to Luke's amazed delight he saw the same glorious jumble of grandeur and mystery spread out below him. He saw the chains and whorls of the street lamps, the ragged silver sash of the river and all the spires and domes and chimney-pots, outlined with a sorcerer's red fire, smudging against the misty sky. It made his heart move in his side.

Munday touched his sleeve. 'This way, Mr. Luke.'

He turned his head abruptly and caught sight of a small crowd at the far end of the balcony. Here again the lighting was dramatic and worthy of the view.

The two open doorways were bright oblongs in the dusk and the shafts from them created a barrier between the crowd and a uniformed man on guard.

As they came forward a square figure in a tight suit advanced to meet them. He stepped delicately like a boxer and everything about him proclaimed that he was Sergeant Stockwell, the inevitable 'good man in charge'. Luke gave him a long experienced stare and moved close to Munday so that he could hear the murmured report. It was made with the mixture of smugness and efficiency he expected but there was an undercurrent of outrage which made him raise his eyebrows.

'The Councillor, that's Mr. Cornish, has taken the old boy who owns the wrecked apartment in to the neighbours next door to talk to him,' Stockwell said. 'His name is Len Lucey. He's a fitter and a good old craftsman with nothing known against him. Before the war he lived on the edge of this estate with his first wife who kept a tobacco and confectionery business – very small. She was killed in the big Blitz. He then married a woman from North London and he had to live over there, travelling across the city to work every day, until he was granted this new first-class flat. His second wife has made a little palace of it by all accounts and that's some of the trouble. She had a sort of fit when she came in and saw the damage. There's a neighbour with her but I've sent for an ambulance. I shouldn't be surprised if she never comes right out of it. I don't blame her,' he added gravely. 'The state of the room shook *me*. I thought at first it was one of the local delinquent mobs but now I'm not so sure. There seems to be almost too much work in it for them, if you see what I mean.'

'It's the farther doorway, I take it?' Luke inquired. 'And the Councillor and the old boy are in the nearest one, is that right?'

'Yessir. The first flat belongs to a much younger couple called Headley. He's a master baker and works at the meat pie factory in Munster Street. He and his wife are nothing to do with this business and they've got the wind up. They're not being unfriendly but they don't want a dose of the same medicine. They've already approached me on the quiet to get everybody out if I can.'

'But they don't want to offend the old squire, eh?' Luke was chuckling with his own brand of savagery. 'Well, well. Let's hope for everybody's sake the poor old lady hasn't taken things too hard or we'll all be in the Sunday newspapers and that won't help anybody get a title, will it?'

Munday started to speak but thought better of it. Stepping forward, he led the way past the saluting constable to the first of the open doorways. There he hesitated a moment, took off his hat politely and walked in, Luke behind him.

The tiny white-painted vestibule which was merely a nest of doors, was as neat a pack as an orange. Any addition, even a rolled umbrella would have been an embarrassment. The two large men were, physically speaking, an insufferable intrusion; they were both aware of it as they stood one behind the other peering into the small sitting-room in which there were already four people, two different kinds of wallpaper, a television set with the picture going and the sound turned off, a magnificent indiarubber plant, a very expensive, very well kept lounge-dining-room suite of contemporary furniture of the 'bundle and peg' variety, three large framed flowerprints and a fierce wrought-iron candelabra. So much high-powered professional 'design' had gone into the apartment that there was no place for anything else and the present drama was suffocating.

For once in his life Luke was taken completely out of his stride. The owners of the flat, large pale young people whose acute discomfort was the dominant thing about them, huddled in a corner, she in an arm-chair and he behind it, occupying at least a quarter of the floor space. The dazed Len Lucey, old and shaking, his very thin neck sticking out pathetically from an extremely white collar, sat at the dining-room table on a spidery chair while before him was a person who had made much larger rooms seem small, a living flame of a man, as passionate and fanatical as Luke himself.

At the moment he was trudging up and down the 'contemporary' rug, his grey hair bristling, his gaunt shoulders hunched and his long bony hands working together as he clasped them behind his back. A more unlikely aspirant for Luke's hypothetical knighthood it would have been difficult to imagine. The superintendent perceived his mistake and began to revise his ideas.

'Councillor Cornish?' he inquired. 'I am Superintendent Luke from the Central Office, Scotland Yard. This is a shock, I'm afraid.'

He was aware of acute eyes, shadowed but intelligent, meeting his own questioningly.

'It's a damn bad thing,' said a pleasant, matter-of-fact voice with a touch of pure steel in it. 'You're going to get to the bottom of it very quickly, Superintendent.'

'I hope so, sir.' Luke was brisk and hearty.

'I know so.' The voice was still pleasant but still completely inflexible. 'You're going to uncover everything about it and then you're going to stop it once and for all before a great project is jeopardized. This estate is called a Phoenix. It's not a municipal venture, it's a social rebirth, a statement of a sincere belief that decent conditions make a decent community, and I'm not having failure.'

Assistant Commissioners are said to use this sort of tone sometimes to senior superintendents, but since there is never anybody else present to overhear it, the theory is not proved. Luke regarded the man before him thoughtfully and cocked an eye at Munday, who was looking at the Councillor with an expression of gloomy contemplation.

'Oo-er!' Luke did not say the word aloud but his lips moved and Munday received the message. For the first time in their entire acquaintance Luke scored a bull's-eye and had the satisfaction of seeing the primness punctured by a sudden ill-suppressed grin.

The Councillor stopped trudging up and down. 'Your sergeant has got a statement from Mr. Lucey,' he said. 'I'm prepared to vouch for the greater part of it myself. I did not spend this particular evening with him, but I can prove that I had his entire life story checked before he was offered an apartment in this new block and I can answer personally for the unlikelihood of him, or his wife, having an enemy. This is a perfectly ordinary innocent citizen, Superintendent, and in any civilized city his home ought to be inviolate. My God, man! Have you been next door yet?'

'No, sir.' Luke was wooden. 'I'd like to visit the flat in the presence of the householder. That's important, sir. If you don't mind.' It was another voice with metal in it and the gaunt, shabby man with the bristling hair looked at him with fleeting curiosity.

'If it's a necessary precaution,' he was beginning.

'No, sir. Just a regulation.' The steel was still there with plenty of butter on top. 'Shall we go? Perhaps Mr. Lucey would lead the way.' Luke flattened himself against the eggshell-tinted wall and the old man was just able to edge past. His frailty was very apparent and as he went by the two detectives caught something of the bewilderment which engulfed him.

He was so small that they towered over him and as they crossed the second threshold and came into his home it was they, the two senior policemen, who caught the full impact of that first unforgettable scene.

A room which had been a comfortable middle-aged home full of comfortable middle-aged treasures, valuable mainly because of their usefulness and their associations, had been taken apart with a thoroughness that was almost tidy in its devastation. Yet at that first glance the one central picture alone occupied their attention. A very neat old woman, still in her good outdoor coat and best beehive hat, was sitting at a polished mahogany table on whose surface there were several scored scratches so deep that a triangular piece of the veneer had come cleanly away, while in front of her, laid out in a way which struck a deep unpleasant chill to the stomachs of the two experienced men, were the entrails of a pleasant old French clock which lay on its back beside them. They were all there; wheels, springs, hands and the pendulum, each torn and twisted out of shape but all arranged neatly in a pattern of deliberate destruction. The old lady herself was not looking at them. Her face was livid and beaded with sweat, her eyes were closed and her mouth had fallen open. Only her weight was holding her in position. Behind her another, much smaller woman, wearing an apron and bedroom slippers but clutching a handbag, peered up at them piteously through gaily decorated plastic spectacles.

'She's gorn,' she said. 'I felt her go. Just now. Just as you came in. The doctor will be too late – won't he?' She seemed to see the little man in front of them for the first time and a bleak expression spread over her face. 'Oh, you pore chap,' she said. 'Don't look, dear, don't look. It was a seizure you see, she never came round.'

'That's right, Dad, come along out.' Luke's glance rested on the livid face which was changing unmistakably before his eyes. The neighbour was right. She was dead. He had no need to touch her. He slid his arm round the old man and swung him gently out into the vestibule. There, with the wide view of the city framed in the open doorway, they stood for a moment like a pair of pigeons huddling on a window ledge.

'You and she came in together and saw the damage, did you?' he inquired gently, still holding the old man to him as if he were afraid he might fall. 'Anyone else with you?'

'Only Reg Sloan. He lodges with us, see?' The old voice was thin and hollow. The significance of the scene had not yet registered upon him. He was still worrying about small things. 'We was allowed to let the room seeing it was empty; we got permission. I told the sergeant. Mr. Cornish knows. Reg got the permit from him. He went to see him – went to see him, I say, called at his house.'

It was like a voice on the wind, something sighing through the rushes. Luke was unnerved by it. 'Take it steady, chum. Get a breath of air,' he said. 'How long has this chap Reg lived here with you?'

'How long? I don't know. Two or three months. Before Christmas he came.'

'I see. Recently. He hasn't been here years?'

'Oh no. He's temporary. He's walking the works and they asked me if I could oblige by putting him up for a few weeks. We got permission, me and Edie did. He got it for us.'

'What do you mean by "walking the works"?' It was Munday. He was half out of the sitting-room door, his hands on the lintels as he leaned forward to speak.

'Well, he was learning the ropes. He came from another firm, you see. It was a business arrangement. He wasn't going to stay.'

'I see.' Luke sounded dubious. 'Where is he now, anyway?'

'I don't know,' The old man looked about him suddenly. 'He went for the police. He went to telephone. We all came in together. We'd been out to have one. Reg liked a chat about old times and we used to go and have a chinwag in the pub. Tonight we all came in together and Edie saw the clock all broken on the table and she's upset because it was her father's. It came from her home. Reg began to swear and went into his room – that's the little one through the kitchen – and he came out almost at once. He said "Stay here, Len. I'll go and ring the police, mate. Gawd, I'm sorry" he said. "I wouldn't have that happen for worlds" he said and he went. Don't you know where he is? Edie likes him. He'll be the only one to pacify her when she realizes her clock's broke.'

'Yes.' Luke glance sharply at Munday. 'What about the neighbour?' he inquired. 'Could she take him along and make him a cup of tea?'

'Yes.' The woman in the decorated spectacles came round the detective like an escaping cat slipping out. 'Yes. I'll see to him. It's the shock, you see. You come along, Mr. Lucey. You'll have a lot to do tonight. A lot of people to see and that. You come and have a sit down and get ready for it.' She put her hand under his arm and eased him away from Luke. 'Make way for us do, there's good people.' Her voice, shrill and consciously preoccupied, floated in above the murmur of the little crowd. 'We want a cup of tea we do. If you want to help there's a woman needed in there. That isn't a thing that ought to wait.'

Luke listened with his head on one side. The brutality made him laugh a little.

'I'm too sensitive altogether for a copper,' he said to Munday, who was looking down his nose. 'It was the lodger's quarrel, then. That's what comes of "walking the works" I suppose. Yet it seems a bit fierce for that sort of industrial dust-up.'

'Fierce? Do you see those chairs?'

The D.D.I. stepped aside to reveal a corner of the room which contained two good dining-chairs whose leather seats had been scored neatly into ribbons with a razor blade. 'Like a joint of pork, isn't it? The carpet's the same. That's no wrecking in the ordinary sense. No joyous smashing up for the hell of it. Just cold bloody mischief.' He spoke with clipped fury and the Superintendent's eyes rested on him curiously.

'I don't like the look of that clock,' Luke said. 'I've got a thing against trick-cyclists and head-shrinkers and all their homework. Let's see the lodger's bedroom. "Off the kitchen," he said. Strewth! That used to be an electric cooker, I suppose?'

They passed through the little kitchen where nothing breakable was left whole and yet where nothing had been overturned haphazard, then on through the farther door leading to the architect's pride, a spare or child's room. It had no space for anything save a bed and a dressing-chest but there was no doubt at all in either mind as they paused in the doorway that here was the centre of the storm.

Everything a living animal could do to destroy and to desecrate bed and walls had been done. Scraps of clothing and the relics of a suitcase made an untidy heap on the narrow strip of floor. A canister of flour from the kitchen had been thrown at the looking-glass and lay like trampled snow over the remains of a decent blue suit with the lining ripped out which lay on top of the ruin of a plastic wardrobe.

On the mirror's clouded surface there was a message written with a gloved forefinger in the kind of printing sometimes taught in schools instead of handwriting.

There were two lines, completely legible and entirely unambiguous, and yet sufficiently out of the ordinary in the circumstances to startle the two senior policemen.

'*Let the Dead Past Bury Its Dead.*' The portentous statement stared out at them, educated and shocking amid the filth. Underneath, in the same careful, clerkly script was a second message: '*Go Home, Dick.*'

Munday stared at the messages, his thin pink face bleaker even than usual in his suspicious bewilderment.

'"Bury its dead"?' he demanded. 'What the hell is this! Who was to know she was going to die?'

'No, that's a quotation. A piece I learned at school. Tell me not in mournful numbers, Life is but an empty dream, and the something or other is dead that slumbers and things are not what they seem. Psalm of Life, Henry Longfellow.' Luke was talking absently, his cockney flippancy unintentional and as natural a part of his personality as his tremendously powerful voice which, even when geared down to a murmur as now, was a rumbling growl which set the shreds of the curtains shaking.

'Someone else has been to school, eh? They didn't teach him much except poetry either, by the look of this room. Poetry and thoroughness, and the rest is the same old uncivilized brute. The same old Turk Street special, cropping up like a symptom of a familiar disease. There's no mystery now about "walking the works" anyhow.'

'What do you mean?'

'"Go home Dick".' Luke's dark face was glowing. 'The chap's name was Reg Sloan. What else can it mean except exactly what it says? "Dick," you old private eye, amateur or professional, go home. The past is dead.'

'Good Lord.' Munday stood staring at him. He had changed colour, Luke noted.

'What's on your mind?'

The Chief Inspector stepped backwards into the kitchen.

'I was thinking of the Councillor. If he gets it into his head that this is an echo from Turk Street long ago, something pre-war, and if he decides that a detective has been employed by someone unknown to dig up dirt about one of his precious handpicked tenants – any of the three hundred and sixty of them – then I'm going to have a job for life, aren't I?'

'That's right,' Luke said. 'Also he's quite an item, this literary character who is so interested in keeping ancient history quiet. Why is he only interested now? What could he want to hide which has only become important after twenty years?'

CHAPTER ONE

The Elopers

IN the expectant greyness which was only just less than the night's dark a cock crowed twice. Instantly, from the rise behind the wayside station a second rooster answered him, and with this unearthly sound, the whole ritual of daybreak began.

In the red sports-car which was pulled up on the lane's verge below the station drive, the two young people who were asleep in each other's arms moved drowsily. The girl's lips were still against the cheek of the young man beside her and she completed the kiss which sheer weariness had interrupted before she opened her eyes. 'Oh no,' she protested sleepily. '*No*. Not morning yet, surely?'

'Julia!' The boy was all over awake at once, his eyes bright as the lids flickered open. He returned her kiss joyfully and glanced down at the watch on his wrist; his forehead crumpled and he sat up. 'So much for our careful planning! We've slept for two solid hours and the train will be here in fifteen minutes. Oh hell! You'll have to go down to the Keep alone. Do you mind?'

'I feel as if I shall never mind anything ever. It may wear off but it hasn't yet,' she said blithely. She was kneeling up on the seat and he put his arms round her waist and hugged her. 'But if I'm to get your car under cover by daylight I'd better go now, which is a bit heart-rending . . . you're sure Nanny Broome really is a hundred per cent on our side?'

'Completely.' His voice was muffled as he rubbed his face against her chest with weary longing. 'I telephoned before I collected you. Anyhow, she's almost my foster-mum. She's always on my side.' He sat up to look at her seriously. 'I gave her the full details. I told her what we had in mind.'

She met his eyes squarely, her own round and grave.

'Was she scandalized?'

'Lord no. She was thrilled to bits.' He shivered slightly. 'And so am I.'

'Me too.' Julia was just visible in the cold light. She was a very pretty girl: not very tall, but slender, with fine bones and hair so dark as to be almost black. Her skin was thick and white and unpainted and her bright blue eyes and determined mouth echoed her father's considerable personality. He was Anthony Laurell, head of the Laurell light engineering empire and youngest self-made tycoon in Britain, and one of the most interesting characters in industry. Julia was just eighteen, warm and gay as a lamb, and every detail of her cared-for, well-dressed appearance acknowledged that she was somebody's very precious only child. At the moment she was absorbed, peering down into the shadowed face raised to her own.

'Your smile is like lace,' she said.

'Lace?' He was hardly flattered.

'Decorative.' She was entirely serious. 'It sort of trims you up and makes you glorious.'

'You're idiotic,' he muttered through his kiss. 'Sweet and certifiable and I love you, I love you. God! I love you. Darling, I've got to catch this dreary train back to London but tonight . . .' His voice broke with a disarming helplessness which pinked them both like a sword. 'Tonight I'll come back and find you and damn everybody else in the world.' He pushed her firmly away and climbed out of the car.

'Timothy.'

'Hello?' He swung round in the fast growing light and she saw him for the first time all over again. He had a rangy body, a distinctive, characterful face, grey arrogant eyes and a wide thin mouth whose lines could curl and broaden like copperplate handwriting. He was twenty-two and all the panoply of masculine physical charm which had earned him a host of admiring contemporaries, even in the Oxford where they both were students, was at its freshest and best. To see all this giddy power and splendour helpless before her was a part of the enchantment which bound her and she caught her breath before it.

'I don't want you to go back to London!'

'Nor do I, lady! But I've got to. I've got to see your old man and have it out with him. His trip to Ireland made it possible for me to get you away and safe here while I talk, but we can't just clear out into the blue.'

'Why not?' She was coaxing. 'Honestly, I don't care any more about anything in the world except being with you. Two months ago I'd rather have committed suicide than upset Daddy or get in the newspapers. Now I just can't care.'

The young man put his hands on either side of her face and looked down at her like a child with a treasure.

'You go on thinking just like that and leave the rest to me,' he said earnestly. 'But I can't face the thought of you and me being turned into a nice Sunday "read" for half-wits. It was foolhardy and inconsiderate of your old man to call the whole thing off suddenly, just when his own invitations to the engagement "do" were out, and he must have known that the gossip hounds would be down on us like a blight. I must talk to him. He can't have so much against me.'

'He hasn't. I told you I don't know why he suddenly vetoed the marriage, but he liked you and he liked your background and was impressed by the degree and the sports record and . . .'

'Then why? For God's sake?'

'It was something to do with a letter he got from Miss Kinnit.'

'From Aunt Alison?' He was staring at her. 'Do you know what was in it?'

'No, or I'd have told you. I only knew it came. I didn't mean to mention it.' The dusky colour appeared in her cheeks. 'She was so nice to me. I thought she approved.'

'She does. She's a funny, cold old thing but terribly kind – after all she and Eustace are my only family and she was delighted about you. They keep teasing me about you being the deb of the year. This must be some completely idiotic misunderstanding. I'll go and put it right. Wait at the Keep and love me.'

From the embankment above there was a clatter as the signal fell and her arms closed round him possessively.

'I'd still rather you didn't go. I'll hold you. I'll make you miss the train.'

He released himself gently. 'Please don't,' he said gravely but with great sweetness, his lips close to her ear. 'You hurt too much.

Too much altogether.' And turning from her he ran up the slope into the half-light which was already throbbing with the noise of the train.

Julia sat listening until the engine had shrieked away into the fields once more and then with a sense of desolation she let in the clutch and drove away through the back roads to where the village of Angevin lay hidden in the Suffolk folds.

She avoided the turning to the single main street of cottages and took, instead, the upper road which wound through the fields to a pair of neglected iron gates which led into a park so thickly wooded with enormous elms as to be completely dark although their leaves were scarcely a green mist amid the massive branches.

The trees grew near to the house, so close in fact that they obscured it from the north side and she had to use the headlights to find the squat Tudor arch which led into the paved yard. As she passed it a yellow-lit doorway suddenly appeared in the shadowy masonry and the angular figure of a woman stood silhouetted within it. She came running out to the car.

'Mr. Tim?'

'No.' Julia was apologetic. 'It's only me I'm afraid, Mrs. Broome. We got held up and I left him at the station. You knew he was going back to London, didn't you?'

'Yes. Until tonight.'

There was an indescribable note of satisfaction in the brisk voice which startled Julia as well as reassuring her, and the newcomer went on talking. 'He told me all about it on the telephone and what he didn't tell me I was able to put together. There isn't much Mr. Tim hides from me.'

It was a strange greeting, neither hostile nor effusive, but possessive and feminine and tremendously authoritative. Julia was only just sufficiently sophisticated not to be irritated. 'What about the car? I don't think it ought to stand out where it can be seen, do you?'

'No, miss, I certainly don't and I've given my mind to that, all night nearly. I think it should go down to the little piggy brick house. I'll show you where.'

She stepped into the empty seat and pointed to an opening on the farther side of the yard.

As she settled down beside her, Julia noticed that she was trembling with excitement, and her round face turned suddenly towards her showed patchy red and white. Margaret Broome was a woman of perhaps fifty, but her coarse hair was still fair and her light brown eyes were bright and shiny as pebbles in a brook. Her gay green cardigan was buttoned tightly across her chest and she folded her arms against the cold.

'It's all overgrown but if you drive slowly you'll make it.' she hurried on. 'I slipped down last evening to make sure we could get in. It's the old summer-house at the end of the View. We used to call it the piggy house when Tim was a baby, after the little pig's house that was built of brick you know.' She was unselfconscious in her nursery talk, matter of fact rather. 'Nobody goes there now. It's too far for anyone in the house but right in front of the windows, so no one's going to hop in there courting from the village. Here we are. See, I propped the doors open. You drive straight in.'

It was a little ornamental temple with a tessellated floor and pillars, designed perhaps as a music-room in some far off Victorian age of extravagance.

The panelled double doors had lost much of their paint but they were still stout and the car lights revealed the usual summer-house miscellany piled in spider-infested confusion against the far wall.

'There,' said Nanny Broome, hopping out with the agility of a girl, 'now we'll shut and lock the doors on it and no one will be a penny the wiser. We must hurry though, because it's nearly light. Come along, miss, stir your stumps.'

The nursery way of speaking flowed over Julia, amusing and reassuring her without her realizing that she was receiving a treatment whose technique was as ancient as history. She hurried obediently, helped to close the doors and then followed the angular figure round the side of the building to the broad, terraced path which led up the slope to the front of the Keep. As she looked up and saw it for the first time from this vantage-point she paused abruptly, and the older woman who was watching her exploded in a delighted giggle. In the pink light of dawn, with the long shafts of sunrise cutting through the mist towards it, the Keep at Angevin was something to see.

At that moment it was a piece of pure visual romance, inspired and timeless. Much of its triumph lay in the fact that it was an unfinished thing. The original family who had begun to build a palace to outrival Nonesuch had died out before they had put up little more than the gateway, so that the actual structure which had come down to posterity retained the secret magic of a promise rather than the overpowering splendour of a great architectural achievement.

Two slender towers of narrow rose-pink brick, fretted with mullioned windows, were flanked by three-storied wings of the same period, all very carefully restored and remarkably little spoiled by the Victorian architect who had chosen to build the summer-house at this magnificent point of vantage.

'How staggering it looks from here!' Julia was almost laughing. 'When I came to the house-party at Christmas we didn't get as far as this so I never saw it from this angle. I know why Timothy calls it his castle.'

'It is his castle.' Again the satisfied and possessive warning note jarred on the younger woman. 'When he was a tiny boy in the war, he and I used to sneak out here in the very early morning mushrooming, and I used to tell him about the knights riding in the courtyard, jousting and saving ladies and killing dragons and so on. He loved it. All the kids have it now on telly,' she added as an afterthought. 'Do you ever see it? *Ivanhoe.*'

'That was a bit earlier, I think. You're a few hundred years out. When was this building begun? Henry the Eighth's reign I suppose?'

'Henry the Eighth! He was nobody to tell a child about!' Mrs. Broome appeared to be annoyed by a fancied criticism. She strode up the path, the patches on her round face brighter, and her eyes as hard and obstinate as stone. 'I'm afraid I wanted my young Mr. Timmy to grow up to be a chivalrous gentleman with a proper attitude towards women,' she said acidly. 'I hope you've discovered that he has one, miss?'

She turned her head as she spoke and made it a direct question. Julia regarded her blankly. 'I love him very much,' she said stiffly.

'Well, I thought you did, miss, or you'd hardly be here now would you?' The country voice was ruthless. 'What I was meaning to say was I hope you've always found him what you'd wish, you having been brought up as I hope you have?'

It only dawned upon Julia very slowly that she was being asked outright whether or no she was a virgin, and her youthful poise wilted under the unexpected probe. The colour rose up her throat and poured over her face, making the very roots of her hair tingle.

'I . . .' she was beginning but once again Nanny Broome had the advantage. Reassured on a point which had clearly been exercising her, she became kindness itself and almost more devastating.

'I see you have,' she said, patting the visitor's arm. 'Of course young people are the same in every generation. There's always the 'do's' and the 'don'ts' and it's only a fashion which seems to put one or the other lot in the front rank for the time being.' And, as if to emphasize her wholehearted co-operation in an enterprise of which she had once been doubtful, she seized the girl's little suitcase and hurried on with it, still talking. 'Sometimes children get funny ideas, but I brought up Mr. Timmy myself, and I didn't think the schools could have done him much harm after that. It's a scientific fact, isn't it, that if you have a child until he's six it doesn't matter who has him afterwards.' Again she gave the little laugh that would have been arch had it not been for the alarming quality of complete faith which pervaded it.

The girl glanced at her sharply under her lashes, and the blurred youthfulness of her face stiffened a little.

'I hope you won't mind me calling you Nanny Broome but that's how I think of you. I've heard it so often from Timothy,' she began, taking the initiative. 'Did you look after him from the time he was born?'

'Very nearly. He was just over the two days, I suppose, and the ugliest little monkey you ever saw. Great big mouth and ears and his eyes all squitted up like a changeling in the fairy tales.' She laughed delightedly and her face became radiant and naïve. 'I've looked forward to saying that to the girl he was going to marry for over twenty-one years.'

Julia's intelligent mouth twitched despite herself. 'And is it true?' she ventured. 'I mean, was he really? Or can't you remember now?'

The elder woman blinked like a child caught out romancing. It was a completely sincere reaction and utterly disarming. 'Well, I remember he was very sweet,' she said, thoughtfully. 'I loved every little tiny scrap of him, that's all I know. He was my baby. I'd lost my own, you see, and he crept right into my heart.' She used the *cliché* as if she had coined it, and the essential side of her nature, which was warm, unselfish and mindless as a flower bud, opened before the girl. 'You see I'd been a nurse in the Paget family over at St. Bede's and I was just on thirty when I met Mr. Broome, who was the head gardener, caretaker and everything else here. He was a widower with five lovely grown-up children and when he asked me I couldn't resist them and all this lovely place to bring them to. So I married him, and my own little boy was on the way when there was all that business before the war – Munich time. The doctors had me in hospital at Ipswich but it was no good. Baby didn't live and I came back knowing I wouldn't have another. So when I was given Timmy to look after you can guess, I expect, young though you are, how I felt. And hasn't he grown up a darling? And now you've come to take him away.' The final phrase was spoken solely for effect and its falseness did not convince even Mrs. Broome herself, apparently, for she laughed at it even while she uttered it and there was no trace of resentment in tone or smile. 'You'll never take him right away,' she added with a grin of pure feminine satisfaction. 'He'll always be my little Prince Tim of the Rose-red Castle in one little corner of his heart. You can see that's true because where did he bring you? He brought you to *me* to hide you. Now you come along and I'll give you a cup of tea.'

They had reached the last terrace as she finished speaking and only a lawn separated them from the tall graceful façade, whose blank windows looked out sightlessly to the estuary two miles away.

'It's all locked up except for my little door.' She took her visitor's elbow and guided her over the damp grass to the narrow entrance from which she had first appeared.

Julia was aware of a small service hall with the stone painted walls and varnished woodwork of the more solid variety of Victorian Gothic mansion, and found herself ushered into a long, narrow room with a very high ceiling. It was yet warm and remarkably comfortable despite a double row of painted waterpipes round the cornice.

'Since the children went and Miss Alison wanted Broome and me to live in the house, we gave up our cottage and I've made us a little flat out here.' Her guide led her over to the window where a modern dining unit complete with pews and a gay blue and yellow plastic-topped table had been installed. 'The big kitchen is nearly forty feet long so there was no point in poor old Broome and me rattling about in it alone. I use the scullery as my kitchen and the butler's pantry has made me a lovely double bedroom and you'd never guess that this was the still-room before the First World War, would you? It's my lounge now and I love it. Excuse me a moment while I see to the kettle.'

She bustled out of the room, arch, affected, enjoying the romantic situation to the full and yet, despite it all, strangely genuine at heart. Julia looked about her curiously. The room reflected its owner to the point of giving itself away. A pile of weekly magazines whose bright covers promised the latest in patterns and notions stood on the old-fashioned dresser, which itself had been treated with white paint. The walls under the festooning waterpipes were hung with a rose-strewn paper and the sky-blue curtains matched the table-top and the washable upholstery of the chair-seats. Home-made black wool rugs broke up the glare of black and yellow linoleum tiles but the 'contemporary' effect was not so much enhanced as debunked by a peculiarly individual type of ornament. The room was full of toys which had been mended and repainted and which stood about in places where knick-knacks would have been more usual. A wooden engine, for instance, enamelled scarlet over its scars, occupied the place of honour in the centre of the dresser, while all over the place there were little newly-dressed dolls and animals, as well as china wheelbarrows and boots holding cut flowers or little ferns.

Julia's white leather coat and silk scarf appeared remarkably sophisticated in this artless setting and Mrs. Broome, returning with a painted tin tray set with multi-coloured china, eyed her with open admiration.

'You look just like what the paper said of you – the one that forecast the engagement,' she announced. '"The leading fashionable young lady of the year", I was so happy I cried when I read that. "A princess" I said. That's what I always promised Mr. Timmy when he was a little tiny boy.'

Julia sat down abruptly, trying not to look dismayed. 'Oh dear,' she said. 'You explain quite a lot about Timothy, Nanny Broome.'

'Quite likely, but not *all*,' The woman spoke with unexpected shrewdness. 'There's nothing like a British Public School and Oxford to mould the clay. Mr. Eustace Kinnit said that when he insisted on sending the poor little chap away to Totham preparatory school. He was only eight and a bit; he *did* look a baby.'

She was talking fast and pouring out at the same time, but as she picked up a steaming cup to hand it to her guest she paused and fixed her hard brown stare on her.

'Tell me, miss, what exactly has your father got against young Timmy? I should have thought my boy had every mortal thing a gentleman could want for his daughter. Looks, lots of money, wonderful brains and education, a place all ready for him in a business which will be his one day, and lovely manners, though I say it myself who taught him. I don't understand your Dad because if we'd been preparing the lad for it all his life he couldn't have been more suitable for you, or that's my view!'

Julia hesitated, and Mrs. Broome nodded her approval without letting up in any way.

'Did something happen to put your father off?' she inquired. 'He seemed willing enough at first, didn't he? He was going to give you a dance to announce it or so *Probe Parker* said in my paper. Then, quite suddenly, he changed his mind and was dead set against it and the column wanted to know why. Quite frankly,

Miss, so do I, and I'm the one who would know if there was anything real to object to.'

The dark and elegant girl in the beautiful clothes sat looking at her thoughtfully and Mrs. Broome watched her.

'You were thinking that too, weren't you, my poppet?' she said with her eyes but she did not venture the question aloud and Julia came to a decision.

'Did you ever meet Timothy's parents, Mrs. Broome?'

'No, miss, I didn't.' She spoke with decision but there was a faintly satisfied, 'just as I thought' expression in the voice. 'I heard Mr. Eustace's and Miss Alison's younger brother had been killed in Spain, of course, but I didn't see much of the family the first year I was married. It was only when I came home from the hospital after losing my baby that I found the family had moved down here because the war was just about to start. When I first married Broome the house was kept as it is now, partly as a show place and partly as a store. The Family owns a gallery of antiques besides having an interest in the big auction rooms. And a lot of the important pieces were very often kept here, as they are still.'

'Yes, I knew that.' Julia was anxious not to intrude. 'I only wondered if you'd ever seen Timothy's mother.'

'No, miss, I only saw the girl who brought him down because London might be bombed. She wasn't a uniformed nurse and not really safe with him, which was why I took over. I always understood that his Mummy had died in childbirth, but with eighty babies in the house you can understand I was too busy to hear much.'

'So many?' Julia's dark eyes widened. 'Miss Kinnit told me at Christmas about the evacuees. On the first day of the war this house was invaded. It was a sort of clearing station, wasn't it, for the district? You must have had a time!'

An expression of such intense happiness that it could almost have been called a radiance transfigured Nanny Broome suddenly.

'Oh! It was wonderful,' she said, fervently. 'I never had a second to think of my own trouble, and then having Timmy without his mother it saved my life it did really!' She paused. 'Your father's very old-fashioned, I suppose?' she said abruptly.

'Father? No, I should have said the opposite.' The girl was out of touch with the trend the conversation was taking. 'Why?'

'I went to the adoption when Mr. Eustace made Timmy his own little son,' said Mrs. Broome without explanation. 'We all went up to the Law Courts in London and into the judges' secret room and it was summer and Timmy was in his first white sailor suit with long trousers although he was only five.'

'*Secret* room?' Julia appeared fascinated.

'Or it may have been "private", I forget.' The romantically-minded lady was unabashed. 'Anyway it was hidden away in the panelling, and all the gowns and wigs and waterbottles and things were about, and I sat in the passage while the business was done. Timmy was wonderfully good so the lawyer told me. We used to play "Judges" after that. I had an old white fur shaped stole that looked just like a wig when you put it round your face. Now, miss, Broome will be up in a minute, so I'm going to take you up to your room. I've been getting it ready ever since I heard a rumour Timmy had got a young lady. I knew he'd bring you here honey-mooning. He always promised me that. "I will bring my bride, Nan, and you shall look after us".' She imitated the small boy with such fidelity that for a second he stood before them, an arro-gant pygmy, packed with authority in a washable white sailor suit.

She picked up Julia's suitcase and turned a smiling face towards her.

'You'd better get some sleep,' she said. 'You won't get much once you're on the run from the reporters. They'll be on to you like ravening wolves, your father appealing for you on the telly like he did last night.'

It took a moment or so for the astonishing statement to register on Julia.

'But that's impossible,' she said at last. 'He doesn't know.'

'Oh yes, he does.' Mrs. Broome was remarkably cheerful about it. 'Parents always know a lot more than children think. They've got an instinct you know, here' – she patted her lean chest deli-cately. 'Anyway I know it's true because I saw it myself when I was sitting up waiting for you. Just after the last news they caught him getting on to an aeroplane to go and look for you. "I wish she was safe at home in bed," he said, and his poor old face was all wizened with worry. I was quite sorry for him even if he has taken a silly dislike to Timmy. "You've made a rod for your back and you'll suffer for it", I said to him and I switched him off.'

The girl rose slowly to her feet. 'My father was coming *home* on an aeroplane last night from a business trip to Ireland . . .' she began.

'Oh, that may have been it.' Mrs. Broome made it clear that she did not care. 'I know I thought that he could go flying to Gretna Green in Scotland, but he wouldn't find you and Timmy because you'd be here, safe in the Bride's Room. Come along, miss, it's quite a way, up on the nursery floor, but it's this side of the turrets.'

She led the way out of the service quarter into the vast house itself. Julia followed her, struck again as she had been on her first visit by the enormous size of the corridors, the endless acres of dark oak ply-wood panelling all looking perfectly new, and the stone staircases which spiralled from floor to floor. Only the windows, whose glazing bars were as finely carved and delicate as if they had been in wood, seemed to belong to the palace which she had seen from the summer-house.

'Wouldn't it have made a lovely school?' said Nanny Broome, only the least bit breathless as they arrived at last in a gallery as long as a skittle alley and looked at the line of mahogany doors all splendidly furnished with brass and cut glass.

'I always call this the Nursery Suite, and there was one time when Timmy was about six and very noisy that we used it for that, but it was always a long way up and lonely. We've never been able to get proper help here, you see, not in my time. It must have been wonderful in Mr. Eustace's grandfather's day. Twenty-three people in the servants' hall and then they thought they were understaffed, or so Broome says. He can just remember the old gentleman. "Like God in tweeds, he was." Broome always says that, though I shouldn't repeat it. Well, this is the room, my dear. We always used to call it the Bride's Room, Timmy and me. We had our own names for all the rooms, but the others were nearly always kept empty except when they were needed to show off a great suite of furniture or some tapestries or something. We had his things brought up to the room at the end there but they were all taken back when Timmy went to school. However, the Bride's Room was always here and kept like this under dust sheets. I've got it all out and pressed all the covers; they're not even yellow, they've kept so well.'

Her hand was on the door knob when she glanced at the visitor. Julia was standing in the long, empty corridor, the clear morning light falling on her from the high windows. There was something about her which was peculiarly lonely and which reduced the cosy chatter to the status of an old wives' tale. A scared look passed over Mrs. Broome's face as she glimpsed reality's fleeting skirt but her resilience was indefatigable and in a moment she was talking away again as happy as a child uncovering a surprise. She opened the door and stood back to let the visitor pass.

'Look, miss!'

There was a long pause as they stood together surveying the scene. 'You can see why we gave it its name? Yet it was made, I believe, for one of Queen Victoria's daughters who didn't get married – or perhaps Mr. Eustace was joking when he told me that. He says some silly things: you never know how to take him. Anyway it's a princess's set of furniture all right, isn't it?'

Julia was silent. The huge square box, parquet-floored and high-ceilinged, had been arranged to display a suite of bedroom furniture designed and made in the halcyon days of the last quarter of the nineteenth century, when modish taste was just due to go clean out of fashion for the best part of the next hundred years.

The half-dozen pieces, all of which were very large indeed, were painted white and carved with festoons of flowers, birds and cupids. To display them the walls had been tinted a vivid blue which had now faded, but the carpet, which had evidently been stored and recently relaid, retained its original turquoise. The bed was the most extravagant piece. Its graceful cane halftester rose high towards the cornice and was so festooned in carved white wood that the effect was positively insecure, as if the great couch were trimmed with icing sugar. A magnificent spread of fine Irish crochet over a blue lining completed a picture of chill grandeur, chaste to the point of being suspect.

'Bridal and pure and oh, I hope you'll be so happy!' Nanny Broome spoke straight from a heart which was coy and warm and unaware of the dismay she was producing. Even when she turned and caught sight of the frozen young face staring from the monstrous edifice in front of her to the horrific intimacy of the double washstand with the green marble top and the waterlily shaped toiletware, she did not comprehend.

'Oh, miss! Don't you like it?' There was reproach as well as astonishment in the question.

'It's very beautiful. Thank you very much for taking so much trouble but the whole room makes me feel rather cold. I don't think I'll stay here now if you don't mind. Is there somewhere else I could change and lie down for an hour or so?'

Julia sounded as if she was aware of being ungracious but had decided she could not help it. Mrs. Broome remained disappointed and deeply mystified. 'It's not *the* room, you know, miss,' she said suddenly. 'This isn't the one the tale is about. That one is on the other floor and right the other side of the house, and even that is not the true one either, because it happened in another house. I wouldn't give you *that*, even though I'd take my dying oath it's never been haunted. There's no ghosts anywhere in the Keep, thank God.' She spoke with tremendous fervency but the chill remained and her round eyes were watchful. 'You've heard all about it, I suppose?'

'No.' Julia was already turning towards the door and the nurse made a move as if to intercept her. Her expression was fearful yet naughty, disapproving yet dying to tell.

'Do you know about Miss Thyrza's chair?' She made the murmured phrase sound comically sinister, like a child trying out a suspectedly wicked word.

Julia heard her but without interest. She had reached the doorway and was almost running towards the stairhead. On reaching it, however, she paused and turned back, re-entering the room just as Mrs. Broome was coming out. Hurrying across the blue carpet, she climbed on to the stone sill and threw open the window pushing back the casements until they were at their widest so that the morning air poured into the room.

'Why, Miss, whatever are you doing? There'll be leaves from the tree-tops, birds and I don't know what flying in. That spread alone is worth a small fortune.'

'Very likely.' There was unexpected firmness in the young voice. 'But I don't think we'll worry about that. Please leave the room like this to air. I may come back here later but just now I should like to lie down somewhere else.'

Mrs. Broome opened her mouth to protest but thought better of it. She was trained to recognize authority when she met it and presently she led the way downstairs again, for the first time looking a little dubious.

CHAPTER TWO

Dangerous Lady

A REMARKABLY ill-tempered-looking old man, as aggressively pink and clean as a baby, wheeled a new barrow slowly across the gravel drive.

As Julia looked down on him from the window of the small sitting-room on the ground floor, the hot midday sun winked off the bright paint of the bodywork and she grinned.

This was Broome himself and his unmistakable resemblance to a Walt Disney dwarf could hardly be entirely unintentional. She wondered if he knew.

Now that she was rested and had fed from the luncheon tray Mrs. Broome had just removed, she had reverted to her normal gaiety. She looked cool in a grey tailored cotton dress with a terra-cotta scarf and shoes and her hair a black silk helmet. She sat on the edge of the table, her small hands, blue-veined at the wrists, folded in her lap. She was very much in love, her mind quite made up.

The morning paper which had been brought to her in triumph with her meal had been folded back by Nanny Broome into a harlequin's wand so that no other news of war or peace should detract from the main story. There was a snapshot of Sir Anthony Laurell across two news columns. He was shown descending from a plane and smiling all over his face, above the caption: 'Tired but On Top; Flying Chairman Settles Strike Threat Yet Again.' The story was a purely industrial one concerning labour disputes in Northern Ireland but it finished with a brief report of the little incident which was all that had mattered to Nanny Broome. 'As he paused to pose for reporters, weary but well satisfied and smiling hugely, one daring correspondent asked Sir Anthony if he knew where his daughter was. This was a reference to the rumour that the engagement expected between Julia Laurell, Sir Anthony's only child, and twenty-two-year-old Timothy Kinnit, heir to the famous Kinnit's Salerooms in Dover Street, will not now be announced. Gossips are blaming Sir Anthony for the broken romance and are predicting much heart-burning from the young people. In reply to the question last night Sir Anthony's smile broadened. "Safe in her bed, I hope to goodness," he said heartily and strode off to his car.'

Julia had explained the significance of the report in some detail as soon as her hostess returned to collect the tray, but without any noticeable success. She was not very surprised therefore when there was a series of furtive little knocks at the door and the good lady arrived in a flurry.

'I told you you were wrong,' she said, her pebble eyes showing white all the way round but her irrepressible smile escaping through the drama. 'They're here!'

Julia slid off the table and took a step towards the window. 'Who?'

'Newspapers, like I told you and you said was so unlikely. Oh, not out *there*.' Mrs. Broome appeared to resent so literal an interpretation. 'Amy Beadle has just telephoned from the Goat and Boot – she's the licensee in her own right and a great friend of mine – she says two different London papers rang up to ask if you or Mr. Timothy had been seen in the village. She told them "no" and then she wondered if I knew anything.'

'What did you tell her?' Julia was developing a very firm way of speaking, coupled with unusually clear enunciation when talking to Mrs. Broome.

'Oh, I was very careful.' An unexpected shrewdness appeared in the shining face. 'I know Amy. If something isn't there she'll make it up. There's only one thing to do with with Amy and that's to look her straight in the face and lie. I said I didn't know why in the world they should want to ring *her*, and if it was anybody's place to know a thing like that it would be mine. I hadn't heard a whisper from London, I said – our exchange is automatic you see, so there wouldn't be a leak there – and I was on the *qui vive* to hear something, but I expected Mr. Tim would take you to Scotland or if they've stopped Gretna Green, to Paris or somewhere like that.'

Julia looked very young again. 'You were very thorough.'

'You have to be with Amy. Which reminds me, miss, if you should see anybody arriving in the drive – I don't suppose you will but you never know – nip straight down this passage here on the left and go into the big door at the end. It looks like an ordinary lock but it isn't quite, there's a little brass catch underneath. Pull that sideways and you'll get into the big drawing-room. I call it the Treasure Room. That's where all the valuables are kept and that's the room I never take strangers into when they call, as they do to see the old historic building and so on. The lock closes behind you and there's the same arrangement inside so you can always get out. It's just a safety precaution. You know the room, it's the one the dance was held in at Christmas.' She paused for breath and was silent for a moment thinking. Presently she took a step forward, laid a shining red hand on the girl's shoulder and spoke with a seriousness all the more impressive because it came from so far beneath the surface.

'I've been thinking about you all the time I've been working about the house this morning, and I do hope you'll understand what I'm going to say,' she began. 'It's very easy to take offence at such time I know, but, miss, why don't you have a betrothal? I know Mr. Timmy and I think I'm beginning to know you. You'd both be much happier. You want to be happy on a performance like this because there's a lot of little things to worry about.'

There was no doubt at all about what she meant or the genuineness of her concern.

'Mr. Lingley, the parson, the Rev-Ben they call him, has known Mr. Timmy for fifteen years and I know he'd like to help.'

Julia was sitting on the table again, her black eyes narrowed and her intelligent face looking so young that its defencelessness was a responsibility.

'I don't quite know what you mean by "a betrothal",' she said. at last. 'It sounds perfect but what is it? Some sort of ceremony?'

'Oh, I think so, miss. You'd have to leave all that to the parson, of course, but you read about it in all the stories don't you? There's an exchange of rings I know. You've got your engagement ring and I can find one for Timmy. There's a lovely big one in the cabinet in the drawing-room – it came from Pompeii, I believe.' It was only the faint upward note, on the final word, an infinitesimal lack of decision in the enthusiastic rush, which conveyed to Julia that there was no real guarantee that Mrs. Broome had any clear idea what she was talking about. In many ways it was a pathetic situation, the treasures at stake priceless and delicate and both women aware of all the facts without comprehending them.

Mrs. Broome was hovering, her eyes hopeful and inquiring.

'I think it's done in church and it's just a prayer and a promise, but the papers aren't signed because you have to have a licence if they are and you're under age, aren't you, miss? What I feel is that it would be a good thing to do because, although it wouldn't be legally binding in a court of law, it *would* be to you two, you being the kind of children you are, and that would make you both much more comfortable. Let me ring up Mr. Lingley and ask him if he'd slip round. I won't tell him why but I know he'll come. He's a very good man. Very kind and conscientious.' She was within a hair's breadth of being convincing in her nursery authority, but at her next step the thin ice cracked. 'Long, long ago the man knelt praying before a sword all night and nowadays they just call it a wedding rehearsal in the newspapers,' she said devastatingly.

Julia caught her breath and laughed until the tears in her eyes were reasonable.

'You're thinking of a *vigil*,' she said. 'I'm afraid that's something quite different. No I don't think I'll talk to Mr. Lingley. Thank you for thinking of it.'

'But he's a good man, miss. A homely practical chap too, even if he does wear a cassock all day. He'd help if he could.'

'I'm sure he would. I did meet him you know, at Christmas. No, let's leave it to Timothy. I'll tell him what you suggest.'

'Ah!' said Mrs. Broome. 'Now I *know* you'll make Timmy a good wife because he's very proud and headstrong and has to be led. I shall hold you to that, miss. You tell him. I'll have a nice supper for him and then you tell him to telephone the Rev-Ben and I'll be bridesmaid.' A sizzling noise from the gravel outside silenced her in mid-stream and they both looked out of the window. A Jaguar had just driven through the arch on to the drive and two men were dismounting almost under the window in front of them.

Nanny Broome took one look at the shorter and darker of the two and flushed scarlet with vexation.

'Oh heck!' she said unexpectedly and managed to make the absurd word shocking. 'Mr. Basil! That's torn it. He *would* come rolling in just when nobody wants him! It's Mr. Basil Toberman. I expect you've heard of him. He's the other side of the business, the black sheep if you ask me. He drinks like a sponge and thinks he's something an angel's brought in. I don't know who that is he's got with him.'

'I do.' Julia was looking apprehensively at a tall thin man who was climbing out of the passenger seat. 'That's Albert Campion. I don't think he *could* be looking for me already, but I think I'd better get out of the way.'

'What is he? A lawyer?' Nanny Broome had drawn the girl back but was still craning her own neck.

'I don't think so. People tell you all sorts of things about him, what he is and what he isn't. You call him in when you're in a flap. Go and head them off while I get under cover.'

CHAPTER THREE

Miss Thyrza's Chair

THE brass lock on the drawing-room door was easy enough to negotiate once one knew its secret and Julia had the satisfaction of hearing the catch spring home as she closed it behind her and entered an immensely tall, gracious room with a polished wood floor dotted with fine, well-worn rugs.

Here the stripped panelling was warmly gold and the pictures, mostly of the English school, were mellow and gentle in the afternoon light. Sepia Delft tiles surrounded the fireplace, their crudely drawn Biblical scenes in faded cyclamen blending with the pinkish pine, while above them, instead of a mantelshelf, there was an archway high enough to form a balcony with slender balusters and a tapestry-hung wall behind. As usual Nanny Broome's pet name for it was extremely apt; there were treasures everywhere including a pair of cabinets in Italian marquetry, huge and splendid things, whose long serpentine glass shelves were covered with porcelain. The general effect was elegant and informed. Glass-topped specimen tables of various periods were scattered among velvet chairs and needlework covered settees and here and there a collector's item, a tiny walnut harpsichord as graceful as a skiff, or a box in stumpwork old as the building itself. The whole place smelled of cedar, probably furniture polish, but pleasant and peppery and very evocative in the slightly airless silence. Through the windows the leaves dancing in the sunlight looked as if they must be making a noise, it was so quiet and still indoors.

The tiles attracted Julia, who had just reached them when she heard the door catch move again and recollected with a shock that at least one of the visitors must know the house quite as well as did Mrs. Broome. There was only one hiding-place and she took it promptly, mounting the enclosed stairs which led up behind the panelling to the balcony. A curtain hung over the arched entrance, hiding her, and she sat down on the second step to wait until they left.

'But the Victorians were tough and very interested in crime.'

She did not recognize the voice and presumed that it was Toberman's. 'Here you are. These are the Staffordshire Murder Cottages and their incumbents. All this collection on the centre shelf.' The aggressive, thrusting voice was not so much loud as penetrating. It reached her so clearly that the hidden girl assumed he must be within a few feet of her. Yet Mr. Campion's laugh, which she recognized at once, seemed much farther away and she guessed that the two men were standing before the china cabinet on the far side of the room.

'Extraordinary,' Mr. Campion said and sounded sincere. She could imagine his expression of innocent bewilderment, his pale eyes smiling lazily. He was not a particularly handsome man as she recalled him but a very attractive one with a strong streak of sensitive interest in his fellow men.

'When you first mentioned the Murder Houses to me the other day I looked them up. It seemed such a macabre idea that I didn't believe you,' he went on frankly. 'To my amazement there they were, illustrated in the text-books; pottery figures representing famous criminals of the nineteenth century and the houses they lived in. I was rather startled in my old-ladyish way. My hat! Imagine looking up from one's fireside to see a replica of George Christie and Rillington Place on the mantelshelf.'

Toberman laughed. 'Perhaps not. But you'd rather like to see Maigret and his pipe, Poirot with a forefinger to his grey cells, or Nero Wolf with an orchid. Taste is swinging that way again. You ought to study this collection, Campion. Eustace will never part with it while he's alive but one day it'll be famous. There's every Staffordshire crime-piece ever made in this cabinet, and that's unique. The Van Hoyer Museum in New York hasn't that very rare second version of Maria Marten's Red Barn over there, nor the little Frederick George Manning – he was the criminal Dickens saw hanged on the roof of the gaol in Horsemonger Lane, by the way —'

'Yet they have Miss Thyrza and her chair?'

'That's right.' He seemed rather pleased about it. 'The only other copy in the world. Eustace's great grandfather, Terence

Kinnit, bought up the moulds and destroyed the whole edition to prevent the perpetuation of the scandal of his murdering governess, but he couldn't resist saving two copies, one for his own collection and one to grow into money to recover what the suppression cost him. As usual his judgement was sound. Miss Thyrza was forgotten and his grandson, that was the present Eustace's father, sold the second copy to the Van Hoyer for the highest price ever paid for a single piece of Stafford.'

'Really?' The quiet man was gratifyingly impressed. 'And the crime happened in this house, did it?'

'The murder? Oh no. Terence moved here *because* of the murder. His restoration of this house took the minds of his neighbours off the other smaller building at the back of the village where the trouble took place. It was pulled down later. Here the lady is, Campion. Drooping over the fatal chair back. How do you like her?'

Tucked away behind the curtain on the staircase, Julia could not see the speaker but she heard the faint twang of the thin glass as the cabinet's doors were opened.

On the other side of the room Mr. Campion was looking over Toberman's shoulder as he took the portrait group from the shelf. It was a typical product of the factory, heavily glazed, brightly coloured and sincerely but ingenuously modelled, so that the overall effect was slightly comic. The chair was a cosy half-cylinder, quilted inside and coloured a fierce pink. The lady, in a long royal blue gown very tight in the waist and low over the shoulders, was draped beside it, her long black hair hanging across her face and breast. At her feet, two indeterminate shapes, possibly children, huddled together on a footstool.

'It has very few flaws and that's unusual for Stafford to begin with,' Toberman said, turning the piece over in his short hands. He was a blue-chinned man in the thirties with wet eyes and a very full, dark-red mouth which suggested somehow that he was on the verge of tears. 'It has a refreshingly direct, modern feeling, don't you think? See the packing needle?'

He pointed to a spot inside the chair's curve where there was a small protuberance. Mr. Campion had taken it for a fault in the glazing but now that he came to examine it he saw the grey blade painted upon it. He glanced up in startled astonishment.

'A packing needle! Was that the weapon? What a horribly practical and homely item. She simply wedged it, sticking out of the upholstery, I suppose? How very nasty.'

'It worked,' said Toberman cheerfully.

'I imagine it would.' Mr. Campion spoke dryly. 'The chair must have become a Victorian version of the medieval "maiden".'

'You could call it that. But the "maiden" was an iron coffin lined with spikes, wasn't it? The victim was pushed inside and the lid shut on him. In this instance there was only one spike, arranged to catch a man just below the left shoulderblade. The needle would be slightly thicker than a hatpin but made of steel and as strong as a stiletto. Either she pushed the fellow on to it from the front, or she went round the back of the chair as he was about to sit down, put her arms round his neck and pulled hard. That was what the prosecution suggested, as a matter of fact.'

'When *was* this fruity little crime?' Mr. Campion continued to be astonished. 'I can't think how but I seem to have missed it altogether.'

'You don't surprise me.' Toberman was disparaging without being actually offensive. 'Experts always develop pockets of ignorance. I notice it all the time. You've got an excuse here, though, because Terence Kinnit was an influential man and was able to hush the business up. There were two or three other sensational crimes in the same year – 1849 – also the young woman wasn't hanged. The jury acquitted her but she committed suicide, so it was assumed that she was guilty after all and the public lost interest.'

Mr. Campion made no comment and there was silence for a moment in the cedar-scented room. Presently Toberman put the group back and his guest stood looking at it through the glass.

'Who are the little creatures in the foreground?' he inquired.

'Those are the cousins. Miss Haidée, Terence's daughter, and Miss Emma, his sister's child. Thyrza was their governess. They were much older than they're shown there; the artist made them small to emphasize their unimportance. Emma was the eldest; she was just on sixteen. Haidée was a year or so younger. Thyrza herself was only twenty. The victim was the music master. He used to ride out from the town once a week and there was an affair. Little Haidée found some letters, nosey little beast. She showed them to her cousin Emma who gave them back to Thyrza. Thyrza got the wind up in case the kid told her mother and tried to get the chap sacked, but without success. All this came out at the trial. The music master had fancied himself as a rural Don Juan and had talked about his conquests, so Miss Thyrza was practically forced to get rid of him or lose both her job and any hope of marrying well. Being an ingenious young woman she set about repairing the upholstery in the visitors' chair with a nine-inch packing needle.'

'Why did the jury acquit her?' Mr. Campion appeared to be fascinated by the far-off crime.

'Oh, I imagine she was young and beautiful and intelligent in the box, you know,' Toberman said. 'She insisted that the thing was an accident and of course, if it hadn't been for the letters and the motive the man had given her by his boasting, it could easily have been one. What a splendidly unhealthy atmosphere there must have been in that schoolroom, eh Campion?'

'Fearful. Why did she kill herself?'

'No future.' Toberman's shrug lent a chill to the statement. 'She came out of the assize court, drifted down the high road, found she had nowhere to go and pitched herself in a horsepond. There was nothing left for her at all, you see. The Victorians didn't waste time and money getting discredited people to write newspaper confessions, and as an ex-employer old Terence Kinnit wouldn't have stirred a finger. Kinnit philanthropy always has an end product.'

The bitterness of the sneer in the hitherto casual voice was so unexpected that it sounded like a snarl in the quiet room. Mr. Campion stared at the speaker through his round spectacles. Toberman laughed, his full mouth disconcertingly unsteady and reproachful.

'I'm the first of my family not to be grateful,' he announced. 'I used to be an angry young man and now I'm a moaning middle-aged one. I'm the last of the Tobermans and the first of them to see the Kinnits for what they must have been all the time – a bunch of natural sharks masquerading as patronizing amateurs.' He broke off abruptly. 'What I need is a drink,' he said. 'Whenever I get unpleasantly sober I clamber up on this boring old hobby horse. The Kinnits are a depressing family. Old Terence must have been typical. He got my great-grandfather out of his particular spot of bother. They used to spell bankrupt b . . . . . . t in those days and he lent his name and a great deal of his money to our Auction Rooms. We remained the auctioneers and the Kinnits kept their amateur status as connoisseurs who did a spot of genteel dealing on the side. That's the Kinnit method; take in lame ducks, don't ask too much about them but make devoted slaves of them ever after. Old Terence hadn't asked for any reference when he took Thyrza on; that too emerged at the trial. She asked very little and he was sorry for her. You can hear every Kinnit who ever lived in that little phrase.'

Mr. Campion turned away idly from the china cabinet and allowed his attention to be caught by a collection of enamelled buttons displayed in a glass-topped table little bigger than a dinner plate. When he spoke his tone was casual but the listening Julia, who had only his voice to go upon, realized that he had at last perceived the opening for which he had been waiting.

'Which gets under your skin most? The patronage or the amateurism?' he inquired with misleading fatuity.

'The ruddy wealth!' said Toberman, speaking the truth and being amused by it. 'Terence Kinnit spent a fortune ruining this place in the biggest possible way – he panelled quite two square miles of wall space with pseudo-Tudor plywood for one thing – but it didn't break him as it ought to have done, because he was able to pay for the lot by instructing us to auction off just a portion of the magnificent stuff he found and recognized in the ruins. The original builders had not only imported their skilled labour from Italy but their "garden ornaments" as well. Classic marbles, old boy, which are now in half the museums in Europe. No one recognized them but Terence. I've never forgiven his ghost for that!' He took a deep breath and his dark eyes were briefly ingenuous. 'And why did he do it in the first place?' he demanded.

'All because some silly little bit he'd taken into his house "out of generosity because she was cheap" had got him into a scandal which had to be smoke-screened. He bought the local folly and turned it into a palace to give the neighbours something else to talk about!' He grinned and his sophistication returned. 'You think I've got a chip on my shoulder don't you? Well, so I have, and let me tell you I've got a cracking great right to it.'

Mr. Campion coughed apologetically. 'I do beg your pardon,' he said hastily. 'I had no idea you felt so strongly. I imagined that as you spent so much time at the Well House that you. . . .'

'Thought myself one of them?' Toberman sounded both irritated and ashamed. 'I do, I suppose, when I'm *not* thinking. I like old Eustace. I ought to. The man has behaved like a rich uncle to me ever since I remember. Both he and Alison treat me as if I were a nephew and I use the Town house whenever I want to. Why shouldn't I? Everybody else has. They've got a South African relation there now. . . . a humourless woman cousin and her female help. I've been "taken-in-and-done-for" like the rest of the outfit and I happen to resent it whilst being too darn lazy to do anything about it. Yet the whole thing is a paradox, because if anyone has a right to inherit from the Kinnits I have. At least I'm not a stray.' Again the bitterness behind the contradictory outburst was quite remarkable. He noticed it himself for he flushed and smiled disarmingly.

'Do I talk too much because I drink too much or the other way round? I never know,' he said hastily. 'We'll go and hunt up some liquor in a moment. There usually is some alcohol concealed upon the premises if one organizes a search. Forgive me Campion, but I'm still reeling under the shock of a discovery I ought to have made twenty years ago. When it came to me the other day I was knocked out, not by its staggering obviousness, but by the fact that I of all people was the one person who knew about it and yet hadn't recognized it in all that time. Hang it all, I saw it happen!'

It was obvious, both to Mr. Campion and to Julia still concealed upon the other side of the room, that he was about to make a confidence and also that it was one he had become in the habit of making recently.

'It was when the rumour first broke that young Timothy had landed the Laurell girl,' he announced devastatingly. 'I don't know why, but that got me down in a very big way. Why should a man who is darn lucky to inherit one fortune suddenly have the nerve to marry another? I was thinking about the unfairness of it all when the blinding truth about that young man suddenly hit me between the eyes. Tell me, Campion, you're a knowledgeable chap, who do you think he is?'

'Eustace Kinnit's adopted son.' Mr. Campion spoke cautiously, but Julia could hear that he was interested.

'Everybody knows that, but you assumed he was also his own natural son, didn't you? Either his own or his brother's, the original Timothy's? Everybody has always thought that.'

Mr. Campion said nothing.

'Well, he wasn't,' said Toberman. 'That's what Eustace let everyone believe, the romantic old so-and-so! That was the view of the whole of London and probably of the boy himself. Certainly that is what my old father thought. He told me about it before he died, as if it was some dreadful family secret, and I believed him, that was the extraordinary thing. I believed him although I was one who knew the truth if I'd been old enough to understand it then.' The expression on his highly coloured face was wondering. 'Imagine that!' he said.

The thin man's pale eyes were misleadingly blank as he turned towards the speaker.

'You suddenly remembered something about Tim Kinnit when you heard of the proposed engagement?' he inquired, leading him gently back to the main subject.

'Yes.' The miraculous enlightenment of the moment of discovery was still fresh to Toberman. 'I was having a drink with someone, Eckermann of the Brink Gallery as a matter of fact. He mentioned the engagement and referred to the adoption and asked me which of the Kinnit brothers the boy really belonged to. I said "Oh, the younger one, the Timothy who was killed in Spain" and Eckerman said "Then young Timothy must be considerably over twenty-two mustn't he?" This foxed me because I knew he wasn't, and for the first time I worked it out and I realized that

Timothy must have been born just about the beginning of the world war, long after the Spanish affair. And then I *was* puzzled because I could recall that year preceding the outbreak. I was ten and my people had the wind up after the Munich fiasco and I was pushed out of London and into the country down here. Eustace was ill. He was in hospital for seven or eight months and then he came down to recuperate. I remember him and I remember the war preparations here, the fire drill and the gas masks and the reception station for evacuees from the East End of London. Alison was in the thick of it – she would be! Eustace, being an invalid, pottered about in the library doing the paperwork and blubbing over the newspapers while I ran loose like a tolerated mongrel pup round his feet. As I was talking to Eckermann the other day I remembered an incident which had meant nothing to me as a child but which was, suddenly, utterly enlightening to my adult mind. The truth hit me like a bullet and I *knew* how young master Timothy, darling of all the Kinnits, Totham, Oxford, heiress-hunter and Success Boy came into the family. He was abandoned here by some slut of a slum mother, Campion. Eustace just scooped him up in a typically arrogant Kinnit way and gave him the name which happened to be uppermost in his mind – "Timothy Kinnit", after his young brother killed in the Spanish war. After all it cost him nothing, and since the whole world was in flames at the time and no one's chances of survival were worth a damn he didn't appear to be risking very much.' All the jealousy and resentment of a lifetime flickered in the small brown eyes as he confronted the other man with the statement.

Mr. Campion's little laugh sounded scandalized.

'Did you actually *say* this to Eckermann?' he inquired.

'I did and I've no doubt he repeated it.' Toberman was defiant. 'I may have told one or two other people as well, and I'm telling *you* now, aren't I? It probably is a silly thing to do but the whole idea has shaken me. I've known it, you understand, I've known it without knowing it all my life. Besides,' he added with an abrupt descent to the practical, 'I don't envisage anybody serving me with a writ for slander, do you? It's true.'

'Wouldn't you have a lot of difficulty proving it?'

'I don't think so.' He was quietly obstinate. 'The fact which misled everybody – the people like my father, for instance – was that the kid had a ration book and an identity card in the name "Timothy Kinnit" long before Eustace adopted him. I remember father commenting on it to Mama, and I remember not being able to understand what the hell they were getting at. It was only when I was talking to Eckermann that I suddenly remembered the incident which explains all that. One day just after the war started I was in the library across the corridor here, sitting on the floor looking at some back numbers of the *Sphere* I'd found, and Eustace was at the desk filling in what must have been the famous "Householder" form of 1939. It was the first census of its kind and it was on the information gathered by it that the identity cards were issued. Once you were on that form you had a right to live in Britain and it was made pretty clear that the converse applied. You were in the services, no doubt, but I wasn't. I remember it vividly.'

Mr. Campion nodded. He seemed afraid of breaking the flow but there was little chance of that.

'Each householder in the entire country had to put down the name of every living soul who slept under his roof on a certain night,' Toberman said. 'That was how the census was taken at such tremendous speed. Eustace had the devil of a job because not only was the place crammed with staff from the London office and their families, but also with official and unofficial evacuees from the East End, the residue of three or four hundred of them who'd been hurried out in the first panic – they nearly all went back afterwards but in those first months the countryside was packed with townfolk all camping in other people's houses. Old Eustace made very heavy weather of the form and insisted that each person should appear before him. They had to come in batches of twelve and he'd stop and explain to each lot how important it all was. It took all day. The evacuee mothers with children came last and when he thought it was all done Mrs. Broome came trotting in with a bundle saying "Don't forget Baby, sir!" And Eustace didn't look up but said "What's its name?" and she said "I don't know, sir. The young lady has gone back to London to get some of her things and I'm minding him. I just call him Baby."'

He paused and laughed. 'I remember that particularly. It was a catch phrase with me after that. "I just call him 'Baby'." Eustace was so wild with her too. He wanted to get the work done. If the child spent the night in the house he'd have to be entered, he said, and "If he hasn't got a name by tomorrow Mrs. Broome, we'll have to give him one."' Toberman's voice died away in the strange timeless quiet of the insulated room and he turned away to look out of the window at the dancing leaves.

'That was it, you see,' he said presently. 'The mother didn't return. Knowing that the kid had got to have papers, Eustace gave him a name to go on with and after that I suppose one thing led to another. I don't remember him after that until he was adopted and going to a prep school. My father was scared of the East coast and packed Mother and me off to Wales.'

Mr. Campion did not speak at once.

'They were exaggerated times,' he said at last. 'Confusing too, especially to a child, but you've got no evidence of this little fantasy, you know. It's not a very. . . . well, a very *good* story do you think? To tell, I mean.'

'I shall tell it if I feel like it.' Toberman's truculence was unabashed. 'One of the enormous advantages of not being a Kinnit is that I can be as "off-white" as I like. I've no code to live up to. I think young Tim is a bore and I think he's had a good deal more than his share of the gravy, so why shouldn't I tell the facts about his origin if it gives me any satisfaction? Everything else has come to him gold-lined and free! The father of that girl of his must be worth a million. A *million*. And she's the one and only child.'

'But you've no proof at all of this tale about him!'

'Ah, but Truth has a way of emerging.' Toberman was ponderous in a besotted fashion. 'Eustace probably won't talk and Alison will back him up, but you can bet your life that Ma Broome would chatter if a newspaper offered her enough money. She must know all about it. There's a rumour that the girl's father has stopped Tim's engagement already. That means that there's a Press story there, and if I go on telling my little anecdote some gossip writer will arrive at the big idea all by himself and come beetling down here with a cheque book. Then we shall get the human angle. *Foundling and Heiress. Who Abandoned Tiny Tim?*' He chuckled at his own joke.

'You're going to hand me the one about it not mattering to any-one in these enlightened times where in hell he came from or who his parents were,' he remarked. 'You may be right, but in my opinion the news is going to shake up the wonderboy himself considerably, and that's the angle which interests me.' He met the other man's eyes and shook his head. 'He's had it too easy,' he added, as if he were passing a fair judgement with reluctance. 'Far too easy altogether.'

Mrs. Broome burst into the room so suddenly that there could be no doubt that she had been listening at the door. She was in a highly explosive state. Her cheeks were bright with anger and her eyes were wet. She came forward across the rugs, moving very swifty but taking very short steps, and she glanced round her for the hidden girl with no subterfuge at all so that both men looked about them also. Julia, who could not see her, did not move and the furious woman turned to Toberman.

'Do you want any tea . . . . Sir?' she said without hoodwinking anybody.

Toberman stood looking at her. He was giggling slightly and wore the sorry anxious expression of one caught redhanded.

'I did say they'd have to offer a lot of money before you'd talk, Broomie,' he said feebly.

Mrs. Broome began to cry and whatever Mr. Campion had envisaged it was not this. Everything he had ever heard about his sex's terror of feminine tears rushed back into his mind in sudden justification. Mrs. Broome was a woman who wept like a baby, noisily, wetly and with complete abandon. The noise was fantastic.

'Be quiet!' said Toberman flapping a hand at her idiotically. 'Be quiet! Be quiet!'

'I wouldn't sell Timmie!' Her extraordinary statement was mercifully incoherent. Her handkerchief was already sodden. 'You ought not to say such things, you ought not to tell such lies, you're jealous of him, you always were. He was lovely and you were always an ugly little thing, and you had that tiresome weakness and I was thankful when you went to Wales.' The incredible words came churning out of the wide-open, quivering mouth in a mass of water and misery. Toberman threw up his hands in terror.

'Shut up!' he shouted at her. 'Shut up! I'm sorry, I didn't mean it.'

Mrs. Broome continued to weep but not quite so loudly. As a spectacle she was unnerving, her face and her drowned eyes red as blood. Both men stood before her temporarily helpless.

'You said yourself that Mr. Eustace didn't look at me.' The words were clear but incomprehensible.

'What the hell are you talking about?' Toberman was near panic and his roughness produced another burst of sobbing.

'You said it yourself!' Mrs. Broome bawled in her rage and grief. 'Of course I was listening! I had a right to if you were going to tell lies about me. You said it yourself, I heard you. Mr. Eustace didn't look at me.'

'When, for God's sake?'

'When I brought Timmy in to him and he asked his name.'

Toberman stared at her stained face. Incredulity and delight were concentrated in his eyes.

'Do you hear that Campion?' he demanded. 'Do you hear what she says? It *was* Timothy! I was right on the bull's-eye.' He seemed astounded by his good fortune. 'She's admitted it. The mother went off and left him and Eustace gave him the first name that came into his head.'

'Oh no, no! That's not what I said. You're putting words in my mouth. Mr. Eustace didn't *look* at me. That was how I knew.' The last word rose to a wail which could not be ignored.

'What did you know?' Mr. Campion's soft authoritative voice penetrated the protective blanket of noise with which she had surrounded herself. Her tears vanished like an infant's and she turned to him with some of her normal gossipiness.

'I knew Baby was either Mr. Eustace's poor dead brother's or his own little son, being slipped home quietly under cover of all the other kiddiewinkies in the house,' she announced, meeting his eyes with a stare of such earnest romanticism that he was set back on his heels by it. 'It was a very terrible *time*, sir, and people were frightened. It stands to reason that if he'd got to give a home from the bombs to all those other children, naturally he'd think of his own flesh and blood.' She sighed, and a shrewder expression appeared upon her tearstained face. 'I daresay it suited him. He may not have known how his sister was going to take to the idea of a baby. Maiden ladies are maiden ladies, you know, some more than others. They're not like us married girls. I knew at once, of course, because he didn't look at me when he asked who Baby was. People never look at you when they're telling fibs, do they?'

She delivered the final remark as if it were a statement of scientific fact. Mr. Campion considered her thoughtfully. She believed, it, he saw, literally and obstinately, and always had. Therefore, since she could never have kept completely silent about anything, this version must be the one upon which young Timothy Kinnit had been brought up. He found he was becoming very sorry for the young man.

Toberman was laughing. 'So the next day when you told Eustace that the mother hadn't returned he filled in the name on the form and Timothy got his ration book and identity card. That's your story, is it?'

'No it isn't!' Mrs. Broome began to roar again. 'I don't talk, Mr. Basil. I was trained as a children's nurse and nurses have to learn to keep little secrets. Where would *you* be if they didn't? Embarrassed every day of your life! You think you've made me say something but you haven't! Times have changed let me tell you. As long as a boy has a home behind him no one's going to ask what church his mother and father got married at. Besides, you're quite wrong about one thing. It wasn't Timmy's mummie who brought him down here!'

'How could you possibly tell that?' said Toberman airily. The man was elated, Campion noted; above himself with gratification.

'A young girl with a new baby. Well of course I could!' An angry blush added to the conflagration already burning in the tear-wet face and Toberman had the grace to appear disconcerted.

'What was her name, anyway?'

Mrs. Broome threw up her hands at his obtuseness. 'If anyone had been able to remember *that* it would have saved a lot of trouble when we came to getting him adopted properly for Totham School,' she said with a tartness which hinted at considerable argument at some time in the past. 'No one who wasn't there at the start of the war seems to be able to remember what that panic was like before the bombing began. *Hundreds* of mothers and babies had been crying through the house. They were all supposed to be labelled but half the tickets had been lost and the babies had sucked the writing off the ones that *were* still fastened. Nine out of ten of the girls wouldn't give their names in case they were asked to pay something, and we were all frightened out of our wits anyhow.' She paused and her devastating streak of commonsense reappeared like a flash of sunlight in the rainstorm. 'If you ask me, it's a miracle dozens of kiddiwiddies weren't left all over the place!' she said. 'But they weren't. Mothers love their babies whatever you may think, Mr. Basil, and so do fathers too. Mr. Eustace knew what he was doing all right but I guessed he didn't want the subject brought up, and nor it was until Miss Alison discovered that the baby I was minding at our cottage wasn't any relative of mine or Mr. Broome's. After that there was a lot of talk in the family.' She dropped her eyes modestly. 'It wasn't my place to know what went on but I believe Miss Alison caused a lot of inquiries to be made. But she came round in the end and little Timmy softened her heart. Of course there wasn't much else she could do,' she added with the now familiar change of mood. 'The raids had started by that time and the whole London district had gone completely. Only dust and litter left, they said. Not a wall standing. They never knew how many hundreds were killed.'

'They found the road he came from?' Toberman pounced on the admission.

Mrs. Broome gave him a warning glance. 'They found the district where the buses which brought the evacuees were *supposed* to start from,' she said stiffly, 'but because of the upset at the time some of them went off early from their garages and never went to the street at all. They just picked up Mummies and babies on the way. Of course I never thought Timmy came in a bus at all. He and his nanna came in a car, I expect, and just mingled with the others, as one might say. That's my idea.'

'It would be! Complete fanciful idiocy! Where was this district? Somewhere in the East End?'

'Hush!' Mrs. Broome glanced round her involuntarily and Toberman suddenly comprehended the situation.

'What *is* all this? Who's here?' He stepped out into the room and looked about him for a hiding place. 'Come on,' he said loudly. 'Come out whoever you are!'

'No, no! Be quiet Mr. Basil. Mind your own business, do. Come along to the other room and I'll tell you. . . . I'll tell you what you want to know.'

'Who is it? This is damn silly! Come out!' Toberman was advancing towards the long window curtains.

Mrs. Broome, who suspected the same hiding place, threw in her ace card to delay him.

'It was Turk Street, Ebbfield. . . . but when they came to inquire about Timmy it was all gone.' She was too late. The man had ceased to listen to her. He had investigated one set of hangings and was advancing upon another.

On the far side of the room Julia slid quietly to her feet and came out from the fireplace alcove.

'Here I am,' she said. 'I'm sorry, but I was trying to get away from you. Does it matter? Hello, Mr. Campion.'

Toberman stopped in his tracks. His smile broadened and his eyes began to dance.

'The little lady herself! You're very like your photographs, Miss Laurell. Well, this is fascinating! It's going to be a better Press story than I thought!'

CHAPTER FOUR

'Above at a Window'

'JULIA? Me.'

Over the telephone Timothy's voice sounded older, more male and somehow more rough than when there was the rest of him present to soften the effect. 'You got the message and you're quite alone?'

'Quite. Completely by myself. What is it? What's happened?' Julia was frightened and the medium did not help her to conceal it. 'You can say anything you like. As soon as you told Mrs. Broome what you wanted she plugged the phone in up here and I think she's sitting on the stairs in the hall keeping guard. What is it, Tim? Is it that you won't be able to get down here tonight?'

He was silent for a moment before he said abruptly: 'Where exactly are you? Where has she put you? What room?'

'Oh I'm not in that white *bedchamber*.' Laughter flickered briefly through the anxiety in her voice. 'I'm in the one your Uncle Eustace has when he comes down on business. It's the little one facing east with the heavenly ceiling and the wall of books behind the couch with eagles' feet. It's utterly secret; we can say anything. The light is out and there's a moon like a new penny pouring in over the fruit trees. I'm on the hearthrug in front of a special fire Mrs. Broome made for us. It's a green wood and it's burning blue.'

'Oh.' She thought he laughed. '"Ash when's green is fire for the Queen." She told you the rest of the rhyme I suppose!'

'"*Ash in its pride, Ash for the bride*"? Yes, she did. She's relentless, isn't she? And very sweet. So gloriously enthusiastic. I think she must have put me in here because of the nightingales. Can you hear them? They're bellowing. Listen. "Eternal passion, eternal pain". . . . Oh darling, darling. What has happened? Tim, you haven't let Daddy talk you out of anything? Tell me. Tell me quickly before I'm sick.'

'I'm trying to.' He was unnaturally controlled. 'Listen. I'm not coming down. Listen Julia. Listen to me before you say anything. First of all, and this isn't the important thing, Fleet Street seems to be on to us. Three papers have telephoned since tea-time. Eustace has had calls too and I've just heard from him that somebody turned up at Well House asking questions. They want to know if it's true that you are at Angevin and if I'm joining you, and if the wedding is on or if we're eloping.'

'Where are you?'

'At your father's house, locked in his study. The key's on my side of course!'

'I see.'

'You don't, you know. It isn't anywhere near as simple as that.' He sounded grimly helpless. 'The newspapers don't matter much. As long as we're apart there's nothing they *can* say. I don't know who gave us away and I don't see why it should be of the faintest interest to anyone, except that everything to do with your father is news. However, that isn't the real point. I've got something more important to say and that's why I'm making all this hooey about the call.'

'You're not making a hooey!' She was fighting with tears. 'If you hadn't telephoned I'd be *dead*. That beastly little man Basil Toberman gave us away. He arrived here this afternoon and found me. He practically told me he was going to tell on us, and the man who was with him, who is a vague, pleasant sort of person called Campion, took him away hastily but I expect he escaped. That's how the newspapers know. I could kill him.'

'Basil? He didn't mean it. He's not worth hanging for. He's just a silly old drunk.' Timothy was uninterested rather than unconvinced. 'He may have let something out. It's a pity he saw you but he wouldn't have the essential drive to become an informer.'

'But Tim . . .' Her voice broke. 'I've been so afraid of something like this happening. I'll get into the car at once and come to London. I think I'll suffocate unless I see you soon. It's looking forward to you so much, I suppose.'

'Be quiet, darling.'

'Why, for Heaven's sake? It's only to be expected. All the books warn one about that.'

'Sweetie! Be quiet. I can't bear it. Be quiet and listen to me. I've something to tell you that's important to me. I've learnt something today which has shattered me. If I know you, you won't care about it one way or the other but I do.'

She could not help interrupting his shaking voice. The snapping fire, the dreaming light streaming in through the window, and the reckless outpouring from the birds, had created an atmosphere which was overpowering.

'You should be here! You should be talking here!'

'I can't! That's what I'm trying to tell you. This thing makes a hell of a difference. You've got to try to understand me, Julia.'

'Are you talking about you being brought here as a baby by some evacuees?' The statement was out before she realized its danger and she went on, clumsily cruel in her helplessness. 'Because if so you're being idiotic. Suppose it was true. What would it matter or what difference could it make to anybody? And if it isn't —'

'*Where* did you hear this?'

The entirely new note in his voice threw her into panic. She was crying as she answered obediently.

'Basil Toberman was telling Mr. Campion and they didn't know I was listening. He seems to have been telling everybody because the penny only just appears to have dropped with him. He's jealous of you marrying someone who might inherit some money. But you mustn't let it matter, you mustn't let anything matter. It's you and me, Tim, tonight and always. You and me.'

'Old Basil! So that's where it's coming from! Your father says he got it from his club a week ago. He wrote Alison and she replied. That's how it happened.' For a moment Timothy had forgotten Julia. The practical mechanism of the betrayal absorbed his attention until dismay overcame him once more. 'I can't believe it of Basil. If he knew, why didn't he tell me years and years ago? We've known each other always.' There was a pause and then he said briefly: 'I'm sorry you should have heard it from him.'

'I didn't exactly.' She was trying to save him. 'It was Nanny Broome who supplied the actual information.'

'Oh God!' The cry came over the telephone. 'It really is true then.'

'Oh, don't worry about it. It happened twenty years ago at least.'

'Does she say it *is* so?'

'Well, she isn't very clear. She never is, is she? But it's obvious.' Julia took hold of herself and began to think again but it was too late. The chemistry by which love kept waiting is distilled to acid had produced its poison on her tongue and touched him. She heard his sigh.

'It was never obvious to me. I just thought I was a bastard.' He spoke lightly and the words were as brittle as icicles.

'Oh don't. Don't. I didn't mean it like that. If I could only see you and hold you. This is like talking to you out of a window. I'll come to London now. Where shall I find you? Tell me, tell me quickly.'

Julia was trying to smother him into warmth again. She was speaking on a single note and the tears were hot in her eyes. 'Wait for me.'

'No. Stay where you are.'

In spite of the discouraging words she was comforted. At least there was contact between them again.

'Are you coming down here tomorrow?'

'No.'

There was silence. 'All right,' she said at last.

'Look darling.' She could hear that he had moved closer to the instrument. 'Julia. Understand darling. Try. It isn't that I've given my word to your father or let him come between us or anything like that, but I've had a hell of a shock and for my *own* sake I can't make any move, or do anything – anything irrevocable until I've found out. It's breaking my heart but I can't, can I? You do understand, don't you?'

'Found out what?' She was appalled to find herself so lonely and out of touch.

'Who I am.' He seemed to find her stupidity extraordinary.

'Isn't it natural? I've been thinking I'm a Kinnit ever since I've thought at all and now suddenly I find I'm not. Naturally I want to know who I am?'

'Does it matter?' Fortunately she was too choked to say the words aloud. When she could articulate she said pathetically: 'To me you're only you.'

'Bless you!' His laugh was unsteady. 'It may take a little time, I'm afraid, but your father and dear old Eustace, who is reproaching himself like someone out of the Old Testament, are joining forces and helping me to get the thing cleared up once and for all. We're all three completely in the picture and they're both on our side. They want us to be happy.'

'Do they?'

'I'm certain of it.' She could hear from his brisk confidence that the thing she had dreaded without recognizing it had happened, and that the energy which she had been promised and for which she was living that night had been diverted from her to meet this new demand.

'And that's why,' he went on quickly, 'I shouldn't mention Basil Toberman to either of them until you're sure he meant it.'

'But I *am* sure. I heard him. He hates you. He wants to do you harm. He's spreading the story about, hoping it'll get in the newspapers.'

'That just can't be true.'

'He said so. I heard him.'

There was a long pause before Timothy said. 'Well, I'd hate Eustace to know that at this moment. He can't imagine why or how the story has got about suddenly like this. He's fond of Basil and doesn't realize what a drunk he is, and if he found out he was spreading it it would hurt him like anything. He'd be ashamed for him too. Leave Basil to me.'

'Very well.' She spoke softly. 'Timothy?'

'Yes?'

'Look, I'm beginning to understand why this matters so much to you but I don't see why my father took the line he did. After all, as everybody knows, he came of pretty homely stock himself and even when mother was alive with all her grand relations he never tried to hide it.'

'Oh, it's not the homeliness! I never met a more democratic man in all my life. He's a great chap. I hope I can have him for an in-law . . .'

'But there's no doubt of that. I'll be of age eventually. Then we can marry anyway.'

'Can we?'

'Oh, Tim . . .' She was panic-stricken. 'But we love each other! Separated we'd be different people. It means all my life. *All my life.*'

'I know.' He sounded as though he did. 'Mine too. There's no question about that. Your father knows it as well as we do but I see his point of view. While you're in his care he's got to be re-assured about essentials. After that it's up to *me* to be reassured. He told me about his sister.'

'Aunt Meg's husband was a nut.'

'He was a hysteric. It wasn't apparent until he was over thirty, but his father and grandfather had finished under restraint. Mean-while the wretched woman was made miserable until she died.'

'But that couldn't be true of you!'

'Couldn't it?'

'No, it couldn't. Don't be absurd. You don't believe it for a moment.'

'Naturally I don't, but I don't expect your uncle did either when he was my age. That isn't the only thing. There are other diseases one doesn't want in a parent. Hideous things that only come out in the kids. And there's other things as well. Tendencies, weaknesses. They may none of them matter, but golly! One wants to know what they are. You do agree to that? You do see, darling, don't you?'

'I see that between them all they've implanted a great doubt in your mind.' she said bitterly. 'I see you've got to know *now*. That's what Basil Toberman's done for you.'

'That's what poor old Eustace thinks he has done for me out of sheer kindliness and romanticism, and it's driving him round the bend. You've got to help, Julia. We've got to keep apart until the

chatter's died down and the papers lose interest. Your father is insistent on that and he's right. I see he's right. You do too, don't
you?'

The appeal produced sudden physical pain in her chest and she
gulped like a child.

'Tim. Tim, listen. This may strike you as being absolutely
crazy but it's an idea Nanny Broome had when . . . when she
thought we were going to spend the night here. I know it's ridiculous and naïve and all that but it would comfort me now. I'd like
it. She suggested we went to the old Rev-Ben and got betrothed —
more than engaged, somehow. It wouldn't mean anything except
to us. Then I'd know that we really were going to marry some
day.'

'Oh darling!' His exasperation came over the wire more vividly
than any other emotion. 'You haven't understood a word I've
said. That's the whole point. Something may emerge which may
prevent me from marrying you or anybody. The chances are remote but I've got to be sure.'

'But whatever you discover, if I still want you —?'

'Then it will be up to me to decide whether I can let you take
the risk. We'll have to wait until we get there. We owe that to
everybody concerned.'

'Everybody concerned!' Her physical disappointment lent her
tone savagery. 'You're thinking of everybody. Your silly uncle
and my father and even Mr. Toberman, but you're not thinking
about me. You're forgetting *me*!'

'My God, girl, don't you see I'm trying to!' His cry was as old
as civilization. 'You may have been disappointed but what the hell
do you think it's been like for me? Don't be silly, darling. And for
God's sake shut up and stay away until I'm human again.'

Julia hung up involuntarily. The movement was as spontaneous as if she had merely turned her back. The sudden breaking of
the link between them was so violent that around her the room
sang and tingled with shock.

She took off the receiver at once but only the continuous throb
of the empty wire greeted her.

CHAPTER FIVE

Off the Record

'THIS place is yet another example of modern jokesmanship,' Mr. Campion remarked as he steered Julia across the splendid marble floor to the dining-room of Harper's Club in Davies Street.

'It's rather like a beautiful Inverness cloak one has inherited. Much too good to hide away, so one wears it instead of an overcoat and pretends it's an amusing new fashion.' He pushed open the mellow mahogany door and they entered a vast Georgian room with a cornice like a wedding cake. 'This was the late Lord Boat's town house,' he went on. 'He had a butler called Harper who was with him for forty years. When old Boat died the title became extinct and Alf Pianissimo, the caterer, bought up the property and rights in Harper. He pensioned him and even had the old man about the place for a while until he drove the waiters up the wall and got Alf in trouble with the Union. At the moment it's very pleasant and quiet and as good a place for luncheon as anywhere. I chose it today because Charles Luke likes it and I particularly wanted to get him here so that he meets you and gets interested in our problem.'

His pleasant voice flowed on as he conducted her to an alcove on the far side of the room where a round table was set for three.

'A superintendent C.I.D. of the Metropolitan Police can find out almost anything on earth if he wants to,' he went on, stowing his long legs under the table and smiling at her, 'but he's hemmed in by protocol. If we go to him officially he has to proceed officially and we don't really want that, do we? – so I thought we might tap discreetly on the back door.'

He was watching her while he spoke and it went through his mind that she was genuinely beautiful with her black silk hair and eyes like blue glass, and that, more rarely still, she was elegant in a puppyish way, naturally graceful and packed with promise. She was uncomfortably young, of course. Still at that most alarming stage when sophistication and naïveté appeared to take turns so that there was no telling what might offend her unbearably or what else, much more difficult, she might take in her stride. He noticed her pretty blue-veined hands. Their short nails were innocent of varnish and she was wearing a ring on her engagement finger. It was a small signet, a schoolgirl's ring. He could see the habitual impression of it on another finger on the other hand. The naïve hopefulness of such a move touched him and reminded him for some reason of something he ought to tell her about Luke.

'He's a rather recent widower, by the way,' he observed. 'It's one of those dreadful stories. His wife made a complete fiasco of having a child. She didn't call for help, and died. The baby girl lived and is being cared for by his old mother who looks after him too. I mention it because it's as well to know these things in case one drops bricks.'

'Of course.' She was looking at him in horror. 'What an extraordinary woman. She was old, I suppose.'

'Prunella? Oh no, not old at all.' Campion was frowning as if he was visualizing someone who had worried him. 'She was in the twenties. The last of the Scroop-Dory's. She had that family's face: high round forehead and hooded eyes like something in a gothic cathedral. I can't imagine how she could have been both so idiotic and so stoic. She didn't want to be a nuisance I suppose, and there was no one there to tell her not to be so silly.'

Julia's youthful eyes were faintly amused by his exasperation. 'Poor girl, anyway,' she said gently. 'Not an awfully suitable wife for a policeman.'

'We all thought not.' Mr. Campion was trying to be non-committal and sounding like every disapproving family friend who had ever existed. 'Charles was in love with her, though. Her death hit him like a bullet.'

There was silence for a moment and the girl shivered suddenly. Mr. Campion was contrite and he began to chatter.

'You'll like him,' he said. 'He talks like a dynamo and does a sort of hand-jive all the time by way of added emphasis, but he's tremendously sound. He's a great natural judge of quality in anything, too. That seems to be a gift all on its own.'

'Oh I know,' she said quickly, grateful for the change of subject. 'Timothy's Uncle Eustace is like that. He's a connoisseur of eighteenth-century pictures, books and silver, but he also seems to know by instinct, or so Timothy says, about modern stuff which isn't really in his province at all and which one might expect he'd rather hate. Do you know him?'

'Not very well. We've met.'

'Have you been to the Well House where they all live?' There was colour in her voice when she spoke about Timothy Kinnit, even remotely. 'It's in Scribbenfields, just not quite in the City. I suppose it was one of the first of the London suburbs and it's frightfully ancient. You'd never expect to find a lovely old dwelling like that in the midst of all those warehouses. I believe there was a medicinal well there once and the head is bricked over in one of the cellars.'

Mr. Campion appeared suitably impressed and she warmed to him. He was very easy to talk to with those long clown lines in his pale face, a natural goon, born rather too early she suspected.

'It was very good of you to agree to help me,' she said abruptly.

'My dear girl, let's only hope I can!' he interpolated hastily. 'Scribbenfields? Yes indeed. The whole place was a noted spa at one time. Jacobean citizens used to ride out the two or three miles from Whitehall to drink the waters and I fancy people still have a vague idea that it's a healthy district. I had a demented client once, I remember, who actually paid a deposit on a small Epsom Salts mine situated, as he believed, under a disused tram terminus in Sheepen Road. An error, it emerged, which was how I came into it! Tell me. When you say "they all live there" whom do you mean? Alison Kinnit, her brother Eustace, young Timothy and sometimes Basil Toberman? Is there a resident staff?'

'No. Not as a rule. Several people come in daily but just at the moment Nanny Broome has had to be sent for from the country to cope. There's a niece of the Kinnits and a help, all staying. They're from South Africa and tremendously wealthy. A child is ill in hospital and they've come to London to see doctors. You remember Mrs. Broome, do you?'

'The woman who wept? Shall I ever forget her?' Mr. Campion fervently. 'It was the first time I ever saw the Picasso painting actually appearing in the very flesh before my bulging eyes. My goodness she was furious with Toberman!'

'Nearly as angry as I was! A beastly, beastly man!'

The loathing in the young voice was savage and Charles Luke, coming up behind her at that moment, caught the full flavour of it.

'Not me, I hope?' he said laughing, as Campion performed the introductions. 'Some other poor fellow.'

Julia regarded him with quick interest. She had expected the size and the heartiness and a certain masculine splendour, but Luke's own peculiar personality, which was catlike, was a surprise to her. He was a proud, lonely animal for all his force and liveliness.

A waiter brought his aperitif, which was a small scotch and soda, and as he sipped it gratefully he sighed.

'Civilized,' he said to Mr. Campion. 'Humanizing.' He described a floating motion with his long hands. 'Cigars and summer days and women in big hats with swansdown face-powder, that's what it reminds me of.' He was entirely unselfconscious and his dark face glowed with energy and pleasure at the picture. It was suddenly understandable how a man with such an unlikely job should take it into his head to marry into the Scroop-Dorys, or indeed any other family on earth if the fever took him.

'I like this pub of yours. I'd like to live here for a couple of weeks every other year.' Although he was grinning he was not entirely joking and his narrow black eyes, which had brows like circumflex accents, were serious as he glanced across at Julia. Something about her had made him gloomy, she was surprised to see.

'And how is the teenage world?' he inquired abruptly, revealing his train of thought. 'All dreams and dance dresses I hope. That's how it ought to be. Something with a future if it's only disillusion. Mine is more homely country and that's in the American sense.' He glanced at Campion. 'Some of the young thugs we're getting in nowadays are dreaming up weapons which would have been thought offside by the Saints and Martyrs!' he remarked and returned to Julia. 'This beastly man you were talking about when I came in? Is this the stern father who won't let you marry the boy friend?'

'Of course not.' She seemed shocked and he smiled at her, amused. 'How much did Mr. Campion tell you on the telephone?' she inquired.

'Almost all, a brilliant *précis*,' murmured Campion modestly. 'What I omitted was the part played by Basil Toberman in resurrecting the tale at this particular time.'

'Do you know he did it deliberately to harm Timothy? He *said* he had.' Julia spoke as though she expected Luke to find the statement incredible and he sat listening to her, his head a little on one side. 'I actually heard him say it to Mr. Campion.'

'How extraordinary!' His lips curled despite himself. 'I'm glad he's the "beastly" bloke, though. I'm sensitive about daughters who don't revere their Dads. My own young woman isn't exactly respectful but she's only eighteen months old.' He was losing his suspicion of Julia, Mr. Campion noted with relief, and his eyes were friendly as they rested on her serious face. 'Well, now,' he said. 'What do you want to know about young Mr. Kinnit's birth? Where his family came from or what has happened to it now?'

'Oh, we know he came from Turk Street, Ebbfield, but the place just isn't there any more. It was bombed to the ground.'

'Turk Street?' Luke glanced at Campion. 'You didn't tell me that.'

'No.' The man in the spectacles was apologetic. 'The information came from what one might perhaps call "other than concrete sources". You haven't met Mrs. Broome the nurse, Charles. She's a delightful woman but as a witness she's a treat of a very special kind. The buses which brought the evacuees from London were thought to have come from the Turk Street area but there's no proof that the boy came from there. Turk Street had a colourful reputation at one time and I thought we'd break all this to you when we saw you.'

Julia glanced from one man to the other.

'I didn't know there was anything awful about Turk Street,' she said quickly. 'Mrs. Broom didn't either. She just remembered the curious name. How awful was it? Vice or crime or what?'

Luke continued to watch her; he was not unreservedly on her side yet.

'It was low class,' he said using the old-fashioned phrase to see if it irritated her. 'Why do you want to know about the young man's family?'

'I don't. Personally, I don't care if they were T.B. infested orang-outangs. Timothy is Timothy to me and nothing and nobody else. It's Tim who seems to have become completely insane on the subject. Father wants to know about the family but Timothy is *mad* to know.'

Luke grunted. 'Why aren't you leaving it to them? You can't hope to suppress anything and if it's there they'll find it as soon as you do.'

She met his thrusting stare steadily. 'I know that, but I want to be prepared and I want to be in it.'

The superintendent seemed satisfied for he nodded.

'Fair enough. He's cooled a little, has he? It happens,' he added apologetically, for the colour had come into her face and a new shininess to her eyes. 'He was all set to elope, poor lad, and got shunted on to a new track suddenly.'

'I know.' Her voice broke, yet she had not looked away. 'But so was I, and *I* wasn't.'

Mr. Campion, who was sitting opposite Luke and following the conversation with some misgiving, was unprepared for his reaction. A spasm of pure pain flickered over his face before he smiled faintly.

'Touché,' he said. 'Well, in that case we'll have to do something about it.' He gave her a wide, disarming grin. 'And it wouldn't hurt us to get a move on instead of asking damn silly questions, would it?'

It was an unusually definite promise from anyone as punctilious as the superintendent, so Mr. Campion led the talk into other channels and the meal ended happily. He was not astonished to receive a telephone call from Luke three or four days later.

'That twenty-year-old inquiry in the Turk Street area,' the superintendent began, the microphone blurring and vibrating under the strain of his voice. 'I haven't discovered very much, but, as I thought, I recollected something fairly recent which might tie up and at last I've had a moment to study the file. You don't read the *Ebbfield Observer*, I suppose?'

'Supposition sustained, chum.'

'All right. Don't let it worry you. There was a paragraph in it a few issues ago which might have interested you and, since it appeared in print, I don't feel I'm divulging any departmental secrets by calling it to your notice. The headline reads "Model Dwelling Outrage. Lodger Identified. Man Understood to Have Left Country". Got that?'

'Yes.' Mr. Campion sounded mystified. 'Model Dwelling refers to that Utility Pile down there, does it?'

'Yes. The idea is to build five more in the same enclosure – they put them on legs like that in the hope they'll make room for each other. About five weeks ago there was trouble there on the top floor. An old couple had their home broken into one night while they were down at the local with their lodger. The place was wrecked in a very big way. When they came in the lodger took one look at the mess and fled after notifying the police by telephone, and the poor old lady had a stroke and died, thereby complicating the issue considerably from our point of view.'

'Oh!' Mr. Campion was interested. 'The "indirect responsibility" question?'

'Is that what it's called?' Luke was not enthusiastic. 'All I know is that the legal bosses have suddenly got excited about any case where the original wicked action produces some extraneous consequence besides the one intended. In this business there was talk of a charge of murder or manslaughter. To me it just means more homework. However, there was considerable pressure put on our D.D.I. He is a Scot called Munday – and he had a local demon on his shoulder as well, in the shape of a Councillor who has to raise the cash to complete the building scheme. This lad wanted everything made sweet just a little quicker than soon. Munday worked like a fiend and finally discovered that the missing lodger was one of the Stalkeys.'

'Really!' Mr. Campion was gratifyingly astonished. 'The detective agency? Is that terrible old gentleman J. B. Stalkey still alive?'

'Talky the Stalker or Stalky the Talker!' Luke's grunt was amused. 'No. He's gone. The angels got him at last – still pontificating no doubt. Joe, the middle son, reigns in his stead and the other two, Ron and Reg, do the footslogging. Reg was the mysterious lodger. He seems to have taken one look at the damage and scarpered. It must have shaken him, because he went right out of the country. He's looking up family connections in Ontario now, according to Joe.'

'What was he doing in Ebbfield?'

'Munday would like to know. He'll be waiting for him at the airport to ask him when he comes home. All we know is that he went round from pub to pub raising the subject of Turk Street in the old days and appeared particularly interested in any family who was evacuated from there to the country in the war. When I saw that in the report I wondered if he was on the same track as yourself.'

'It has a likely smell. What does brother Joe say?'

'Nothing. Joe isn't talking. He's the same old sea-lawyer his father was and he knows his rights. We've got no power over him. He's an ordinary citizen. English tecs aren't licensed, as you know. He says he doesn't know what Reg was doing. He's protecting his client, of course.' He paused. 'There's only one other point which might be of interest and that is, that as soon as the Councillor gathered that the crime might have been committed in protest against an inquiry made by a private investigator he shut down on the whole thing like a piano lid and didn't want to hear any more about it. That was after he'd been badgering Munday on the telephone every half hour.'

'Odd.' Mr. Campion said slowly. 'Has the D.D.I. any theory to explain it?'

'No. But the Councillor has a home and a wife. He may just not want a visit from the same gang of thugs. But if that's it, I'm surprised. He didn't strike me as that sort of bloke. He was more the fanatical sort. The I'll-do-you-good-if-it-kills-us-both type of social worker.' He laughed. 'Well there it is,' he said. 'All I can do at the moment, I'm afraid. I liked the girl. They've got great charm when they're honest, haven't they?'

If he was talking of womankind in general or a type in particular did not appear. He rang off and after a while Mr. Campion took his hat and went down to the East Central District, where in a dusty cul-de-sac there was an unobtrusive door whose small plate announced modestly: 'J. B. Stalkey and Sons, Inquiry Agents. Established 1902.'

He found Joe Stalkey sitting in his father's old chair in an office which had remained carefully unchanged since the founder of the firm had first conceived the idea of a private detective agency having the standing of a firm of family solicitors.

The small room contained one magnificent period bookcase, glazed above and panelled below. It took up all one wall and against its mellow and elegant background Stalkey the Talker had posed and impressed clients for nearly fifty years.

Joe Stalkey had not the old man's florid presence. The slightly harassed expression and deprecating smile so typical of the child of an over-forceful parent had robbed him of authority. He remained a gangling, middle-aged man whose broad features were a little out of alignment, as if they had been drawn by someone with an astigmatism. When Campion came in he looked at him in open astonishment.

'This is a bit of an honour, isn't it?' he demanded, his smile leering. 'I don't think you've been in here in twenty years, have you, Mr. Campion? What can we do for you? Any little chore however small will be welcome, I assure you. Don't hesitate to mention it. As long as it's legal and the money is safe we're not choosey. We can't afford it. We haven't had quite the advantages of some people. Do sit down, won't you? I have at least ten minutes before a client —'

'— Who must be nameless, steps out of a brougham with a coronet on the door,' murmured Mr. Campion with such complete seriousness that he might just have meant it as a compliment.

'You're very obliging. I don't think your father would have been so kind. He never appreciated my style, I felt.'

The man behind the desk was regarding him cautiously. He did not understand him and never had. He suspected bitterly that his incomprehensible success was due to something basically unfair, such as class or education, but was begrudgingly gratified to see him in the office all the same.

'Help yourself,' he said. 'It's all yours.'

Mr. Campion seated himself in the client's chair and crossed his long legs. His hat, his gloves and his folded *Times* newspaper he held upon his knee. 'I wanted to see Reginald,' he said. 'But I hear he's in Canada. I wondered if he could tell me anything about Turk Street twenty years ago.'

The man behind the desk had large cold eyes and their glance became fixed upon his visitor. It rested upon the narrow folded newspaper which Campion held, with an intensity which was noticeable. It was as if he were reading the small type of the advertisements on the outside page.

'Well?' There was nothing even impatient in Mr. Campion's inquiry and he was astonished to see Stalkey's tongue moisten his lips. He had changed colour too, and his fist, which was unusually large-boned, was not completely steady where it lay on the desk-top.

'I'll hand it to you, you've got on to it very quickly.' He spoke without meeting Campion's eyes, letting the words slide out regretfully. 'Ron lost his temper,' he said.

Mr. Campion had no idea what he was talking about but it appeared to be promising.

'Did he?' he murmured. 'That's always dangerous.'

'There's no real harm done.' Joe Stalkey spoke irritably, 'but of course Ron is a big man. He's heavier than I am and ten years younger. The kid put up an astonishing fight but he hadn't an earthly chance and he is in a bit of a mess, I admit it.' His eyes narrowed suddenly. 'Am I making a monkey of myself, by any chance?'

His visitor grinned.

'We appear to have travelled somewhat quicker than sound, if that's what you mean,' he admitted. 'Let me explain myself. I am interested in anything I can discover about a woman and a very young baby who were evacuated from Turk Street to an address in Suffolk on the day war broke out in 1939. I heard today that your elder brother Reg was making the same sort of inquiry just before he went to Canada, and I wondered if we were all working on the same problem and, if so, whether we could pool our resources. For an adequate consideration of course.'

'Damn!' Joe Stalkey was very angry with himself. He had coloured and his hands were nervous.

'You chaps build such a legend about yourselves that one believes it!' he said with unreasonable reproach. 'I didn't see how you could have got on to this morning's shindig, but because it was fresh in my mind I assumed you must have done as soon as you mentioned Turk Street. You're the reason the Central Branch have suddenly got interested again, I suppose? You've stirred them up and they've stirred up the police down there and some wretched detective constable went and leaked to the kid. That's about it. Otherwise it wouldn't have all happened together, would it? A coincidence like that couldn't have occurred otherwise. You coming in here in the afternoon just when Ron had been tackled by the kid in the morning. I was justified in making that mistake.'

The thin man in the hornrims leaned back.

'I'll come clean,' he said. 'I'm not with you at all. Ron is your younger brother, isn't he? He is carrying on Reg's inquiries I suppose?'

'Like hell he is!' Joe Stalkey showed evidence of having a temper himself. 'That isn't our sort of business at all, Mr. Campion. You've no idea what the state of that flat was after the wrecking. I saw Reg before he left for Canada and he was shocked, I tell you. There the message was, you know, written right across a mirror: *Dick, go home!* Like an American film. I don't know what the younger generation is coming to. Stalkey & Sons isn't that kind of concern. Nice neat evidence, clear reports, and if necessary a discreet and creditable appearance in court, that's all we contract for. As soon as we saw what we were on to we walked out and stayed out. Our sort of clients aren't the class to get involved in *violence*!' The final word was invested with unspeakable disgust and Mr. Campion noted the return of an old snobbery new in his time. He was still very much at sea, however, and was debating how to remedy it without being too outspoken when Joe Stalkey went on.

'He says he didn't do it, of course, and he pretends he doesn't know who did. It's gang stuff pure and simple. I think the world is damned; modern youth is quite openly against civilization. Higher education just makes them worse.'

Mr. Campion raised his eyebrows but ventured no comment. Instead he put a cautious question.

'If Stalkey & Sons washed its hands of Turk Street when the flat was wrecked and Reg went to Canada, how did Ron get into the business?'

The flush on Joe Stalkey's unsymmetrical face deepened and his deprecating smile appeared briefly. 'The ass went to get Reg's shoes, can you beat it? As you probably would not know, East End repairers charge a quarter of what one has to pay elsewhere and the work is often much better. When Reg was down there he left a couple of favourite pairs of shoes with some little one-man outfit and told Ron to pick them up for him when he had a moment. Ron is a careful chap and it's just what he would remember, being hard on shoe leather himself. This morning he was going that way so he telephoned to ask if the shoes were ready, found they were, went down there. Of course the kid had been tipped off and was waiting for him.'

Mr. Campion took a long breath.

'When you say "the kid",' he began, 'who?'

'You know quite well who I mean. I mean young Kinnit,' Joe said. 'There's no point in beating about that bush in my opinion. We were acting for his legal guardians. The aunt and father by adoption. Alison and Eustace Kinnit. Actually we dealt with the woman. We were employed by the family before, you see, when they were first trying to trace the kid's identity about fifteen or sixteen years ago. Father handled it on that occasion but it was hopeless from the start. It was just after the war ended and the whole area was still a shambles, records lost and everything. Pa satisfied the court that every avenue had been explored without result and the adoption or guardianship or whatever it was went through and that was that.'

Mr. Campion continued to be dubious.

'You are telling me seriously that young Kinnit was responsible for wrecking the council flat? Have you any proof of this at all?'

'I don't want any. I don't want anything to do with it, and don't forget anything I'm telling you now is off the record.'

Joe Stalkey's face, unattractive to start with, was not improved by an expression of obstinate prejudice. 'Of course he is. Ron reports that he is babbling about having been locked in his college at Oxford at the hour in question, but that only proves he has some useful friends or enough money to employ a few hooligans. What one might be able to prove is one thing but what we know must be the truth is another. Be your age, Campion. Who are you working for? The little lad himself?'

'No. I belong to the other side of the family. I am protecting the interests of the girl friend.'

'Are you indeed? Quite a client!' He was openly envious. 'There's gold in them thar quarters. Oh well, good luck to you. You're welcome to everything we've got – at the right price, of course. Happy to oblige you. But in this particular case we don't want to work with you. We've come out and we're staying out, especially after this morning's performance. That kind is decadent and dangerous. It never pays to take a youngster out of his normal environment and bring him up in something plushy.'

'Do we know what his normal environment was? I thought that was the object of the exercise.'

'We know he came from a vicious slum.'

'Do you? Is that established?'

Joe began to look sulky and his father's mantle showed as far too large for him. The old man had built his business on fact and proof and not on this type of sophistry.

'He went to Angevin by bus with a lot of other people from Turk Street and he was abandoned, which is a Turk Street trick if ever there was one. He's a violent young brute, anyhow.'

Mr. Campion rose. 'I still don't see why you connect him with the wrecking?' he observed mildly.

'You don't think.' Joe was didactic. 'You don't use your head-piece. I'm sorry, but look at it. Who else stands to gain? Who else *cares* if Reg uncovered something about the foundling? As soon as I heard about that message on the looking-glass telling Reg to get out I saw it must be the kid himself. It was obvious.'

'Is that really all you've got to go on?' Mr. Campion sounded relieved.

'It's enough for me.' The head of Stalkey & Sons was ada-mant. 'I don't go in for fancy stuff as you do, Campion. I just see the obvious when it sticks out a mile and I get by all right. Today when the lout set on Ron I was proved pretty right, I think.'

'I see.' Mr. Campion appeared to have no other comment. 'I shall receive a modest account from you, I suppose? Trade rates, I take it?'

Joe began to laugh. 'You've got something,' he conceded. 'The grand manner, isn't it? I'll tell you what. I've been thinking. We might come to something sort of reciprocal in this. You wouldn't like to take the boy off our hands now?'

Mr. Campion stared at him.

'Where is he?'

Joe looked uncomfortable. 'Downstairs in the washroom as a matter of fact. Don't get excited. He's all right but he needed cleaning up of course, and we couldn't very well send him home. There's a funeral there this afternoon, isn't there?'

'A *funeral*?'

Joe Stalkey shrugged his loose shoulders.

'It's in your *Times*, in the deaths there. I thought you were holding it like that to remind me. It's not one of the family, but he felt he couldn't turn up with two black eyes and a cut lip. It's someone employed there. There it is: "SAXON . . . whilst visiting this country with her bereft friend and employer, Geraldine Tel-pher. Interment today in Harold Dene Cemetery, etc.' A gover-ness, I think the boy said she was.'

CHAPTER SIX

Justifiably Angry Young Man

THE washroom under the old building where Stalkey & Sons had their offices had been converted somewhat casually from what might well have been an air-raid shelter and was in fact a wine vault, relic of more spacious days. The ceiling was low and arched, the floor stone-flagged, and the ventilation unsuccessful. The row of wash-basins, installed about 1913, managed to look strikingly modern in the grim surroundings.

There was a rug-covered camp-bed at one end of the cavern and when Mr. Campion entered, Timothy Kinnit was seated upon it, clad only in singlet and shorts. His bloodsoaked shirt was lying on the stones before him and when the visitor appeared he raised his battered face in which only the fierce grey eyes were still splendid.

'Hello,' he said. 'I know you. You're Albert Campion. Surely you're not a part of this outfit of lunatics? Where's that damn fool with my clothes?' He was speaking painfully because of the swelling of his lips but he was not sparing himself. His mood came across to Campion in a wave. He was so angry he was out of himself altogether.

Mr. Campion glanced behind him. 'I appear to be alone,' he said pleasantly. 'Joseph Stalkey has paused to speak to his brother, who is undergoing repairs in the annex. If it's any comfort to you he too has a few souvenirs of the encounter. He was armed, I take it? May I look?'

The young man got up unsteadily. 'My face'll clear up,' he said, reeling slightly as he bent towards a looking-glass. 'But I don't know if there's an actual hole in my skull. It's at the back here, rather low down. Can you see?'

'Yes. Dear me. Wait a minute. Turn to the light, can you?'

The examination was nearing completion when Joe Stalkey came in. Nervousness had increased his restless clumsiness. His big feet splayed awkwardly and his hands and huge wrists were prominent as he walked.

'He's all right,' he said, making it sound as convincing as he could to himself. 'He's all right. That's all superficial stuff. There's nothing to worry about there. These things do happen.'

The man in the horn-rimmed spectacles raised his eyebrows. 'I'm not surprised to hear it if your brother does the family's errands wearing a knuckleduster and armed with a tyre-lever,' he observed mildly.

'It's not a tyre-lever. Just an ordinary, old-fashioned life pre-server; we all carry one.' Joe conveyed that the fact made it re-spectable. 'Be reasonable. A man must have some means of defend-ing himself. Ron expected trouble this morning; don't forget that. He was going back into the area. He realized that the young thugs who would wreck an old people's flat in that peculiarly brutal way merely to warn Reg off an inquiry, would be on the look-out for any return. That's why, when the attack did come, he was ready for it.'

'But there was no attack!' Timothy's explosion was due as much to fury at crass stupidity as to pain and outrage. 'I simply walked out from behind the counter where I was waiting, talking to the cobbler, and asked the man if he was the chap who was making the inquiries about Turk Street just before the war, and if so who was employing him. He went for me with a cosh like a lunatic, and naturally I defended myself.'

'But how did you get here?' Mr. Campion demanded.

'I don't know. I went out like a light – I suppose from this wallop on my head.'

'Ron brought him along in his car,' Joe Stalkey said, avoiding Mr. Campion's eyes. 'He intended to turn him over to the police, naturally, but as it turned out —'

Mr. Campion coughed. 'A wallet happened to slip out of his pocket, spilling an old envelope with his name upon it, no doubt?'

Joe's big washed-out eyes met his own reproachfully.

'Well, things like that do occur, as you must know as well as anybody,' he said testily. 'Anyhow, you can't blame Ron for being nervous. Reg had simply seen the quality of that damage to the flat, and he threw up the case and cleared out to Canada for a rest, remember. So this morning when an attack was made on Ron he was prepared for it. You'll never shake him on that.'

Mr. Campion shook his head. 'No, I don't suppose one ever could,' he admitted. 'What's the matter with Ron? Flatulence? Never mind. Where are Mr. Kinnit's clothes?'

'In the next room. He had a bit of a nose-bleed and they got smothered. Ron took them to discover if anything could be done about tidying them up. So Mr. Kinnit could go home in them, you see?'

Mr. Campion's lips twitched. 'Only too well. The error becomes more apparent at every turn. Ron has my sincere sympathy.'

'I wish you'd all stop blethering and just get me a pair of trousers,' Timothy said wearily. There was something of the helpless dignity of the sick child or the very old man in his appeal. His colour was bad and he was still very unsteady. He stood looking at Joe for a moment, debating his next statement.

'I've nothing against your brother,' he said at last. 'I shan't make any complaint. But I want the answer to my original question. Who was employing you all? Who is trying to find out about me?'

Mr. Campion took the young man by the arm and lowered him gently on to the bed again, and Joe came a step nearer.

'So you knew you came from Turk Street?'

'No. I knew that some evacuees went to Angevin from there. I don't know now that I was one of them. Who was employing your brother?'

Joe Stalkey still hesitated and it occured to Mr. Champion that he was showing uncharacteristic delicacy. 'You're asking us to divulge the name of a client, you know,' Joe protested at last.

Timothy sighed. 'Then there is a client.' He sounded oddly resigned. 'I went to look for Turk Street because my old nurse mentioned that name in front of my fiancée and I got the story out of her. I found a young bobby down there and chummed up with him and he told me a private detective had been chased out of the district for making inquiries. He put me on to the old man who had

had the detective as a lodger and *he* put me on to the cobbler. You say the detective was your brother, so you can tell me what I want to know. Who is employing your family?'

Joe passed one ungainly hand over his chin.

'Well, I don't suppose it'll do any harm, because we're not working for them now,' he said. 'We're turning the whole thing in. It's not our sort of business at all, thank you. As a matter of fact my brother Reg was working for Miss Alison Kinnit and Mr. Eustace Kinnit. They approached us just before Christmas.'

The battered face of the young man on the bed grew slowly dusky red and as slowly drained again. He was sitting forward, his head raised towards Joe's. His eyes were very dark.

'Are you sure Eustace was in it?'

'Of course. I saw him myself. It was my duty to warn them that there was very little chance of us having much success. My father undertook the original inquiry in 1944 or 1945 when the question of regularizing the position of Mr. Kinnit's guardianship arose. My father had to confess failure then and I have to do it again now. I don't think you've got much to worry about, young man.'

The sneer passed clean over Timothy's head. He seemed completely shattered.

'Twice!' he said. 'Get me some clothes for Heaven's sake, there's a good chap, and let me get out of here.'

He got up and staggered dangerously. Mr. Campion caught him.

'I really think you'd better come along with me,' he said. 'There's only one expert I know of who'll get you presentable in a reasonable time. Joe, send your secretary for a taxi and lend us a raincoat.'

They went to Mr. Campion's old flat in Bottle Street. The Police Station which used to be next door had gone and time and rebuilding had changed most of the other landmarks, but the pleasant shabby four-room hide-out remained much as it had always been.

Timothy sat in a faded wing chair before a gas fire, Joe Stalkey's trench coat still covering his bloodstained clothes, and glanced dully round walls cluttered with souvenirs. Although the apartment was only just off Piccadilly, it was astonishingly quiet and somehow remote and even secret in the afternoon.

The sound of a key in the lock of the door was unexpected and Mr. Campion put his head out of the kitchen, kettle in hand.

'Lugg?'

''Ullo?' There was an upheaval in the narrow hall and the panelled wall shuddered. The newcomer was breathless and his accent London at its thickest.

'We have a customer.'

'Reely?' The sitting-room door opened at once and a huge old man whose personality was as definite and obtrusive as an odour appeared in the opening. Even in an era when individuality in dress is a cult, his clothes were noticeable. He was wearing a hard hat of the low round kind favoured by hunting men, and with it a black duffle-coat lined with white. His large pale face and heavy moustache were alive with interest and curiosity. He glanced at Timothy twice; once casually, and then with a long hard stare from small, unexpectedly shrewd eyes.

'I thought you'd bin fightin' at first,' he remarked. 'Knuckle-dusters, eh? Where you been, son?'

Mr. Campion came in and gave him a brief explanation.

'Stalkey!' Lugg was contemptuous. 'It was only 'is name give 'im the idea of being a detective at all. It was a cheap ad for 'im and 'e wouldn't waste it. Any family more kack'anded in their trade you couldn't find. The ole man was nothing but a jaw-fountain and all the children go orf 'alf cock!' He appealed to Timothy. 'Wot a way to treat a client's nevvy. You could 'ave died and then where would they be? Standin' wiv the bill in their 'ands, not knowing where to send it.'

His scorn was magnificent but Timothy did not respond. He sat like a sack, his eyes still dark and shocked. It occurred to Mr. Campion, who was watching him, that eccentrics must be a commonplace in his young life. It was an off-beat age into which he had been born and absurdity as an escape-mechanism had been in fashion for some time now. The youngster's condition worried him a little. He was more shaken than his physical injuries warranted. Suddenly, as if in answer to his unspoken question, the young man glanced up at him and spoke abruptly.

'And who are *you* working for?' he demanded. The question came out brashly and he flushed. 'I'm sorry,' he said. 'I'm not trying to be offensive and I'm helplessly grateful to you. But why are you interested in this tatty old business of my paternity?'

The bitterness in his tone was unmistakable and the older man responded to it involuntarily.

'My dear fellow, don't take it like that!' he protested. 'I'll tell you all I know, which is little enough, in a minute or two as soon as we've got you patched up a bit. Meanwhile, what's all this Joe Stalkey told me about you being due at a funeral this afternoon?'

The sudden flicker of emotion, irritation, or perhaps even unease in the battered face took Mr. Campion by surprise; in an instant it was wooden again.

'No, I'm not due at it,' Timothy said. 'I don't imagine anyone expected me to attend. I said I thought I ought not to turn up to the house in the middle of it looking like this, though, and Stalkey agreed with me.'

'As well 'e might!' Mr. Lugg, who had removed his coat, now took off his hat and thrust it at his patient. 'See that? The idea of this is to pertect yer 'ead from an 'orse's 'oof. If you're goin' to keep stickin' your bonce into trouble you ought to buy yerself one. I'll give yer the name of the place. Now let's see this 'ere depressed area of yours. Keep still.'

He made a long and careful exploration of the damage and finally sighed. 'Yes, well,' he said. 'Ron Stalkey can say 'is prayers. 'E's lucky 'e's not up before the beak for that lot.'

'How bad is it?' Mr. Campion made it clear he was consulting an expert.

'I seen wuss; and in this room. 'E'll live ter break someone's 'eart. Come on into the barroom mate and we'll start the beauty treatment.'

An hour later he was still talking. Timothy, who was looking much more like himself, was wrapped in a bathrobe of his host's while Lugg considered his ruined clothes.

'No,' he said regretfully, turning over the torn and blood-soaked flannel trousers. 'Not reely. Not for a funeral. It would be 'eartless and not quite the article. 'Oose is it? Someone yer know?'

'Hardly at all. She was a stranger. Just an elderly woman staying in the house.'

The young man appeared to be defending himself and Mr. Lugg's bright eyes narrowed.

'Yus?' he encouraged. 'Wot's 'er name?'

'Miss Saxon. I hardly knew her, I'm afraid, but the funeral was announced in *The Times* this morning. Joe Stalkey pointed it out to me. Eustace must have made the arrangements and put the advertisement in automatically. It's just what he would do, of course, although no one knew her over here. She came from South Africa with our – or rather Eustace's – relative, Mrs. Telpher. She was helping her with the child, you see.'

Mr. Lugg managed to convey without offence that he did not see at all and his patient was forced to elaborate.

'Mrs. Telpher brought her child to England for medical treatment. It's in hospital now and Miss Saxon came with them to help. They've been staying in the Well House for about six weeks. I had no idea the old lady had heart trouble.'

The fat man stood looking at him, his large head held slightly on one side.

'She died sudden, did she?'

'Yes. In her sleep last Sunday night. I've been down in Ebbfield most of the time since then.'

'Persooin' your private investigations?'

'Well, yes. You could call it that, I suppose.'

Mr. Campion, who was sitting at a bureau desk in the far corner of the room, heard the interrogation going on mercilessly, and marvelled at his old friend and knave. He pulled no punches in his social skirmishes.

''Ow sudden was it?' he was inquiring with disarming interest. 'Did yer 'ave a ninquest?'

'No. She'd been under the doctor since she came here. Eustace Kinnit called him at once and he gave a certificate.'

'Any reason why 'e shouldn't, son?'

'No. No, of course not. Can I have my shirt?'

Campion felt it was time to intervene. He turned round in his chair and his pleasant high voice cut into the conversation.

'I hope you don't mind,' he said. 'But I telephoned Mrs. Broome at the Well House about half an hour ago and asked her to bring you a change. She should be here at any moment.' He was unprepared for the effect of the words in his visitor. His brows came down and the dusky colour shot over his face. Campion regarded him in astonishment. 'I thought it would be the easiest way,' he said defensively.

Timothy was controlling himself with a visible effort. 'What *is* all this? What do you know about Mrs. Broome? You're very kind, but just who has invited you into this? Aunt Alison I suppose! My God! Who else is involved?'

Mr. Campion leant back and crossed his legs.

'I do apologize,' he said. 'I told you I'd tell you all I know; here it is. I have an old friend whom you know. His name is Anthony Laurell.'

'Julia's father? Oh! I'm sorry. He didn't tell me. I thought he was being perfectly frank with me.'

'I think he was.' The man in the spectacles hastened to prevent any further damage. 'He spoke to me about you quite a long time ago when you and Julia were first going around together. He and I have been friends since we were both up at Cambridge, so it's quite natural for us to gossip about our various interests when we run into each other. He asked me if I'd heard a spiteful little tale which was going the rounds and I had not, but I was interested and so when I received an invitation to Angevin to see some ceramics I accepted. It was there I encountered Mrs. Broome.'

'I see. I'm sorry. How did you know she was at the Well House now?'

'Julia told me.'

'Julia!' His voice quivered. 'Is she pulling strings too?'

'You can hardly expect the poor girl not to be interested.' Mr. Campion spoke with asperity. 'Don't be a fathead. She's in love with you and she's left at the starting post, so to speak. Naturally she's desperate.'

'Do you think I don't know that? And do you think I'm not desperate myself?' The violence of the young man's protest was unexpected. There was a raw force about him which was completely hidden and unsuspected in the normal way. It startled Mr. Campion, since it seemed out of character in one whom he had assumed to be a typical young Oxford success-type.

'The point your old college chum doesn't seem to have confided to you,' the boy continued bitterly, 'is that he has extracted a promise from me not to see or speak to Julia until all this has been cleared up. Moreover he hasn't explained that fact to her yet. Because he knows she wouldn't wear it, I suppose!'

'Why do you?'

'Wear it?'

'Yes.'

Timothy blinked.

'Do you know, I don't know,' he said at last. 'I've been wondering. It's just that in my heart I believe the old buzzard is right, I imagine. I've never believed in heredity consciously before and I don't know that I do now, but I certainly like to know what *is* behind me. Probably I've always been too much aware of everything I thought was there. Now that it's – well, that it's all been altered, I feel like an untethered balloon. I'm afraid that's Mrs. Broome's contribution.'

'Ah.' Mr. Campion perceived the position. 'She need only just hand your bag in. If you don't want to see her, Lugg can simply take it from her in the passage. There's someone coming up now, I fancy. You hear everything in these old buildings.'

'A fac' which 'as bin useful in its time,' said Mr. Lugg as he lumbered out into the narrow hallway, closing the door behind him.

As in many old London houses, the dividing walls were thin, and made of pine panelling, and as the outer door opened the murmur of protesting voices was very audible.

Timothy stood up abruptly. 'That's Julia!'

He pulled the door open and Mr. Lugg, for once completely put out, stepped back to admit two women.

Julia appeared first, looking smartly casual as usual, in a loose grey woollen coat and a heavy multi-coloured silk headscarf. Mrs. Broome followed her, neat in tweeds and beret and tightly buttoned cape gloves. They came sweeping in, feminine and possessive and upset, and filled the whole apartment so that both Lugg and Campion were dispossessed in a matter of seconds and Timothy, his bath-robe wrapped round him like a toga, met the full force of the invasion.

'Oh, *what* has happened to you?' Julia would have flung her arms about his neck but he repulsed her gently. He was relaxed but very much aloof.

'Nothing much. I'm all right. I had a dust up with a bigger boy. That's all.' He turned to Mrs. Broome. 'Did you bring me some clothes?' He gave her no name but added 'Please' as an afterthought.

Mrs. Broome did not look at him. She was more than twice his age but her mood was unmistakable. They were in the midst of a serious quarrel.

'They're in the case,' she said without raising her eyes, her lashes looking long against her weatherbeaten cheeks. 'Everything you could possibly want lugged right across London at a moment's notice by me and the sweetest, prettiest little princess of a girl who's much too good for you and I don't care who I say it in front of.' She flashed a defiant stare at the nearest stranger, who happened to be Mr. Lugg. He was regarding her in pious horror and now stepped back involuntarily. The appealing glance he shot at his employer stirred Mr. Campion to action.

'It is most kind of you, Mrs. Broome,' he said firmly. 'Could I ask you to unpack them in the bedroom?'

'In a minute, sir.' The tremendous authority of the nursery met him like physical resistance. 'There's just something I ought to say first. I'm responsible for bringing Miss Julia. In fact I made her come with me. Before you rang she came to the Well House looking for Mr. Timothy to tell him something. As soon as I heard what it was – I got it out of her, she didn't want to tell me – I said at once that she'd better come up here with me. Some things are serious. Some tales are dangerous and must be stopped. "We'll go and thresh it out once and for all", I said. "And then perhaps he'll stand up for himself and not go condoning every cock-and-bull story told about him. At least he'll know *this* isn't right", I said. I was there and the only thing he did was to open the door and in she fell. . . .'

The final words meant nothing to Mr. Campion and Lugg but their effect on Timothy Kinnit was considerable.

His face grew with fury and he turned on her. 'Nan! Go home at once. I'll talk to you later. Hurry!'

'I won't, you know. Mr. Timmy, Mr. Timmy! It's im . . . *por*-tant!'

There was an ominous gulp on the final word and all three men saw to their dismay the dreadful signs of disintegration: the swimming eyes, the reddening nose, the mouth opening raggedly like a sodden paper bag. Mrs. Broome was about to cry.

Mr. Campion and his henchman stood helpless but Timothy was experienced in such emergencies. He took a step towards the suitcase and inquired softly: 'Did you bring my brown shoes?'

She could only just hear him and the little effort which she had to make in order to catch the words distracted her attention. It was as if they saw the tears actually receding.

'Brown shoes? You don't want *brown* shoes. I brought your blue suit. Black shoes with blue cloth, you know that.'

He did not argue but continued to look disappointed, consolidating the position.

Mrs. Broome's happy, self-assured little smile reappeared like sunshine. 'Only b.o.u.n.d.e.r.s. wear brown shoes with a blue lounge suit, or that is what I was always told,' she said gaily, one eye on the audience. 'Perhaps I'm old-fashioned but it's very nice to have *some* little rules.' And having reduced one school of snobbery to absurdity she returned brightly to the task she had come to perform.

'Well now,' she said briskly before Timothy could stop her. 'That Basil Toberman has privileges because he's almost part of the family, but even so he musn't be allowed to go about saying you helped to kill a poor little old lady.'

If she was striving to capture his attention she succeeded. He stood staring at her, his bathrobe festooned about him, his expression blank with horror.

'What the hell is all this?' he demanded, turning to Julia.

The girl had been sitting on the arm of a couch, her head bowed and her long silk legs stretched elegantly. Now she raised her face towards him, her cheeks flushing red and white.

'Of course that's only half true.' she said frankly. 'I really came round because I wanted any excuse to see you, I suppose, but the story is going about and I do think it ought to be stopped. Ralph Quy rang me this morning and told me that out at dinner in Knightsbridge last night he heard that you'd got in a temper with an old lady from South Africa and shaken her or frightened her or something so that she had a heart attack and died, and that Eustace Kinnit had hushed it all up "as usual".'

'"As usual"? What does that mean?'

'I don't know, Tim. Don't be angry with *me*. I just thought it was a story which ought to be scotched pretty quickly.' She struggled on with an explanation which she found distasteful but important. 'It's silly and untrue I know, but it's being linked with the other business. The inference is that you're reverting to type. You know, like a dog or a tiger or something, all right about the house until it becomes adult.'

'When it has to be put in a zoo.' Timothy sat down heavily and put his hands through his hair. 'This is a little much, isn't it? Did old Ralph convey that Basil was definitely responsible for this item?'

'Well, yes he did. That was what he telephoned to tell me. He told me to warn you that we ought to get hold of Basil Toberman and stop him spreading dirt which wasn't funny any more.'

'As far as I'm concerned it never was.' Timothy was irritated but not as angry as he might have been and Mr. Campion, who was listening to the exchange with tremendous interest, eyed him curiously. His next remark was unexpected. 'Basil is a peculiar chap,' he said. 'He doesn't mean these things he says. He just talks to reassure himself. He means us no harm.'

It was a patron's point of view and highly mistaken, as Mr. Campion knew for a fact. Suddenly he understood that it must be the Kinnit view of all the Tobermans, the grander family's assessment of a 'lesser breed', and for a fleeting moment he caught a glimpse of Basil Toberman's genuine grievance. Meanwhile Timothy was still talking in complete innocence and good faith.

'I'll tackle the old blighter,' he said. 'Don't be too hard on him, Julia. It's just one of those infuriating things. You can't really blame him you see, because in a way it's true.'

'What is?'

'The story. I don't suppose poor old Miss Saxon would have died just then if it hadn't been for me.' He got up abruptly and smiled ruefully at Campion. 'I'll go and dress if you'll forgive me,' he said. 'Nanny Broome will explain all this if you care to hear it. I see I'm not going to stop her.'

Julie was looking at Mr. Campion. 'You do agree that it matters, don't you?' she said earnestly. 'You heard Basil Toberman talking about Tim down at Angevin. He wasn't talking for talking's sake. He meant it. Tim won't believe that.'

'And don't try to make him, Miss.' Mrs. Broome spoke placidly from the other side of the room. She was sitting on one of the few hard chairs the flat contained, in what was once called a "ladylike attitude", both her feet close together and hard on the ground, her thickly gloved hands folded upon her good leather handbag.

'It would break Mr. Tim's heart if he found out that someone really close to him didn't love him,' she continued devastatingly. '"People who really know you always love you if you're lovable". I taught him to believe that when he was the tiniest little boy because I don't like people who are always seeing snakes, do you, sir?' She put the question directly to Campion with a bright smile conveying that she had no doubt of his answer.

The thin man laughed. 'I'm a little afraid of the people who never see them at all,' he said gently.

'Are you?' She seemed astonished. 'I was always taught that if you didn't pull pussy's tail she wouldn't scratch you, and there's a lot of truth in that whatever they say, but of course there are a few horrible boys like Basil and he really ought to be stopped before he does some real harm, which is why we've come, isn't it Miss Julia? We're not just bearing tales, I mean.'

Julia opened her mouth, caught Mr. Campion's eye and ceased to worry quite so much. She returned to Mrs. Broome.

'Tell Mr. Campion exactly what happened when Miss – what was her name? – Miss Saxon fell. Tell him exactly what you told me.'

'*Did 'e lay a 'and on 'er?*' The question, put with earnest interest by Mr. Lugg, who had been forgotten, startled everybody and Mrs. Broome turned to him, scandalized.

'Of course not! That's another thing I've ground into Mr. Tim. Never never *never* hit a lady!'

'Well then, the tale's all cock,' said Lugg, dismissing it. 'Don't worry and don't repeat it. 'E didn't touch 'er and that's the end. Wot did 'appen to 'er? For the sake of the record.'

Mrs. Broome hesitated and he stood watching her, his head on one side, his little eyes very intelligent.

'Start wiv 'oo she was,' he suggested.

Mrs. Broome's radiant smile reappeared. 'Well that was very difficult to find out, although I tried hard enough,' she said frankly. 'She didn't want to be called a lady's maid, you see, and she wasn't a governess because the child was too ill for one. When I was a girl she'd have been a mother's help and liked it, except that she'd have been sixteen and not sixty. "I wonder Mrs. Telpher didn't feel it was too much of a responsibility bringing you with her," I said. "I mean you're quite as likely to get ill on the journey as the kiddie, aren't you?" She didn't like that but I was right, wasn't I?'

Lugg began to laugh in the high teetering way which only escaped him when he was genuinely amused.

'An' she was the one 'oo got 'erself killed!' he said. 'There's justice for you. That's life that is. She'd come from Souf Africa 'ad she?'

'So she said, and you needn't think we didn't get on. She used to talk to me by the hour. She told me all about the diamonds and everything.'

'Diamonds! Now we're coming to something. Where do they come in?'

'They don't. I never saw them.' She sounded regretful and the

childlike streak in her character had never been more apparent.
Her face actually saddened. 'But they're there in the safe deposit.'
she added, cheering visibly. 'Mrs. Telpher put them there because,
as she told Miss Saxon, it wasn't fair to Mr. Eustace to keep them
in the house. They're wonderful. Enormous. If you hadn't known
how rich she is you'd never credit they were real. Miss Saxon told
me that she couldn't think of them without her mouth watering.'

Julia leaned forward.

'Tell them about the kitchen door,' she suggested.

'Yes, well, that is what killed the little lady, dyed black hair,
painted face and all.' Mrs. Broome permitted herself to be kept to
the point. 'Mr. Tim and I were in the kitchen having silly words
about something which after all did happen over twenty years
ago, when he suddenly stopped shouting at me and said, "Nan,
there's someone listening outside that blasted door." It's an old
stone kitchen. We live in an antique up here all right. I wonder
Miss Alison gets any help at all. . . . Anyhow, he leapt across the
matting and wrenched open the heavy old door and there she was
leaning against the other side. So down she came, poor silly old
thing, right down the two steps on to the stones. Mr. Tim and I
picked her up at once but we certainly didn't shake her. She only
said that afterwards to Mrs. Telpher, to take everybody's mind off
her listening at the door.'

'She did not die at once, then?' Mr. Campion appeared fascinated by the story.

'Oh no, thank goodness! That *would* have frightened Mr.
Timmy and me! She waited until she got into bed, poor little dear,
and then she had a heart attack and died and wasn't found until the
morning. The doctor said the fall was quite enough to bring it on
with a heart like hers. She ought not to have taken the job,' she
added earnestly, 'not when there was a child to be considered. She
might have dropped it or frightened it, you never know.'

'When did she tell Mrs. Telpher about the shaking?'

'The night before. She went to bed early, with me fussing
round. Mrs. Telpher was worried, because of course they were in
someone else's house and illness and accidents are a trouble however polite the people are. In the morning it was dreadful when we

knew she was dead. Mr. Tim felt so guilty about pulling the door open and he was worried to death anyhow about the silly evacuee story of Mr. Basil's, which really is the stupidest thing I ever heard, that he went off as soon as he knew from the doctor that he wasn't to blame and he has hardly been home since. He's a very sensitive boy.'

Lugg raised a heavy hand as if to put it on her shoulder, thought better of it and lowered it hastily.

'Wot is stoopid about the evac story?' he demanded. 'Why shouldn't the young feller try to find aht abaht 'is family?'

'Because he's got a perfectly nice family of people he's very fond of and knows all about and takes after by this time!' Mrs. Broome blazed at him in sudden annoyance. 'Why Miss Julia's father wants to upset all that I do not know. Besides, suppose Tim did find a family he seemed to have been born into – I don't think he can, mind you, but suppose he did – then what could that do but mystify him completely, poor boy?'

'Mystify 'im?' Lugg was puzzled.

'Of course. You don't know anything about people by seeing them! I remember a lady coming to inspect St. Mary's Home where I was brought up and seeing us all in our lovely Elizabethan uniforms we were so proud of, and bursting into tears all over us because "it was wicked to dress us like charity children". We nearly crowned her we were so offended. She saw us but she didn't know us, did she?'

Lugg stepped back from her and permitted himself his little high-pitched laugh again.

'You've got it all sorted out, 'aven't yer?' he said admiringly. '"Mum knows best", that's gointer be my name for you! Your young lordship ought'er be dressed by now. You'll all go 'ome together I expeck.' He shuffled out of the room and Julia got up hastily and looked at Campion.

'I don't want to leave it like this,' she began. 'Basil Toberman is doing Tim active harm. He's got to be stopped. If I thought —'

She was silenced in mid-sentence by the reappearance of Mr. Lugg whose face was blank with surprise.

'Gorn.' He announced. 'He went down the fire escape so as not to disturb us. Winder's wide open. Wot's the young feller up to, eh?'

There was a moment of complete silence in the room, broken by Julia's sharp intake of breath. Mrs. Broome swung round upon her protectively.

'Don't take it to heart! It's only because he promised your father faithfully not to see you,' she said so quickly that no one was convinced. 'It wasn't very nice of the old gentleman to ask it but everything's fair in love and war, isn't it? You two have got to stand up for yourselves. You and me must get together, young lady!'

Both Lugg and Campion glanced at the girl curiously to see how she would respond to this somewhat over-direct mothering and they were both surprised. A fleeting curl appeared at one corner of the pale pink mouth and the swimming eyes twinkled.

'Poor Tim,' said Julia.

CHAPTER SEVEN

Ebbfield Interlude

THE highway to the East Coast which ran through the borough of Ebbfield had always been a main road and even now, despite the vast garages, the pylons and the gaily painted factory glass-houses which had sprung up beside it, there still remained an occasional trace of past cultures.

One of these was a fragment of a terrace of early Victorian middle-class houses of a type which had once lined the broad road for two miles on either side. There were three of them left, tall and dark-bricked, with semi-basement kitchens and once-splendid flights of stone steps leading to square porches and fine front doors. The middle one possessed a cast-iron gate with a patch of bald, sour earth just inside it, and a name plate bearing the number 172 and the words *Waterloo Lodge* welded to its serpentine tracery.

It was raining and dark when Timothy Kinnit found the address at last. He was hatless and the collar of his light raincoat was turned up. He was at a splendid age and although his self-assurance was already shaken he ran up the stone steps and pulled the brass knob which he found beside the door.

There was movement inside the house and a light appeared in the transom above his head. The door opened abruptly and a somewhat brusque feminine voice announced: 'Mrs. Cornish.'

Timothy became shyly voluble.

'I'm so sorry to trouble you and I'm afraid you don't know me at all but I was given this address by Tom Tray. He repairs shoes in Carroway Street off the Orient Road. I was hoping that Councillor Cornish could spare me a moment or so?'

His diffidence and pleasant voice appeared to mollify her, for although she did not give ground she turned on the porch light and emerged as a small but stalwart woman in the late forties, still smart and good-looking with bold eyes and a fashionable hair-do. For a moment she regarded him with surprised approval.

'My God, you've spoiled your beauty, haven't you?' she said at last. 'What have you been doing, fighting? I warn you we don't approve of boxing. Come in and I'll inquire if Mr. Cornish will see you. What is it? Youth Clubs?'

'No, I'm afraid it's not.' He followed her into a long, shabby hall which could have belonged to any careless or overworked professional man at any period during the last hundred years. Mrs. Cornish appeared to become conscious of its shortcomings for she frowned at him and said accusingly: 'When one works as hard as we do for the public good one doesn't have time for frills. What did you say you wanted to see the Councillor about? I don't imagine you're from a firm, so I assume you're canvassing. You're wasting time, you know, because every vote the Councillor has on any committee is well thought out *and* discussed, so he's already made up his mind one way or the other and nothing you can do will shift him one iota.'

Timothy found her trick of answering her own questions to the second stage of argument highly disconcerting but he stuck to his purpose.

'It's nothing like that. I merely want to ask him something about Turk Street long ago and —'

'Oh, you're a reporter. Not from one of the local papers, because I know them. Of course! You're the B.B.C. Well, we shall all try to be as interesting as we can.'

'I'm not!' He was trying not to shout at her. 'I'm here on my own account. I'm told that your husband knows more about Ebbfield than anyone else on earth. Some weeks ago a detective—'

'A *detective*!' She gave him a long, suspicious look which he found vaguely unpleasant. 'So you're a detective! I ought to throw you out at once, but you wait in here and if he wants to see you I shan't stop him.'

She thrust him into an airless dining-room in which no one had eaten for a very long time, and left him standing by the large round table which was covered with a faded red serge cloth.

The mahogany sideboard was spread with out-of-date magazines and the pictures on the walls were all of mountains in shabby gilt frames. It was a depressing room and he was still looking about him gloomily when the door shot open once more and the Councillor appeared, his wife behind him.

Timothy was nearly as startled by the man as Superintendent Luke had been on an earlier occasion. He recognized the type at once. His university was full of them; all passionate, dedicated, sometimes wrong-headed men, wedded to an assortment of ideas of which a few were practical. The fire behind his eyes, his long bony wrists and impatient gestures were all peculiarly familiar, but the more disconcerting because he had not expected to find them in the Ebbfield High Road. The other surprising thing about the Councillor was his open dislike of his visitor, who was a complete stranger. Timothy was young enough to be hurt by it. Cornish's nostrils were flexed and when he spoke his tone was contemptuous.

'As I have already told one representative of your firm this morning, the matter is closed,' he said. 'I don't want to hear any more about it. I have the name of your client and that is all I wanted to know when I invited him to call on me.'

Timothy relaxed. 'I'm sorry, sir. You're making a mistake,' he said cheerfully.

'You were directed here by Stalkey & Sons.'

'No, sir. I got your name from the cobbler in Carroway Street.'

'Have you any connection with the Stalkeys at all? Do you know them? Is the name familiar?' There was more force in the probing than the subject warranted and the younger man hesitated.

'I got myself beaten up by one of the brothers this morning,' he said at last.

'Why was that?'

'I don't know. The man set on me out of the air.'

The Councillor stared at him and presently spoke more mildly. 'That's a very dangerous accusation unless you're perfectly sure what you mean by it, my boy.' Without his animosity he was revealed as a pleasant person, a little inhuman perhaps but possessing a streak of dry humour.

'I should hardly have thought that man I met would have hung about long enough to beat up anybody,' he remarked, sniffing a little. 'His brother, who he assured me was working down here on an inquiry, made the most indecently hasty departure from trouble which I ever witnessed. He was literally jet-propelled and all the way to Canada, I believe. What's your name?'

'Timothy Kinnit, sir.'

'*Kinnit!*' The word was an explosion and the lined aesthetic face grew rigid. 'What's this about? Eh?' He turned to his wife. 'Marion, leave me with this young man for a minute or two, will you?'

Mrs. Cornish sat down obstinately.

'I'll wait,' she was beginning, but as he turned and looked at her the colour came into her face and she got up sulkily and went over to the door. 'I shan't be very far away, anyhow,' she said as she left, but it was not clear if the words were meant as a threat or a reassurance.

The Councillor waited until her footsteps had died away before he leaned across the table in an effort, apparently, to be reasonable at all costs.

'Who sent you?' he demanded.

Timothy's irritation began to return. 'I was given your name by the shoemaker off the Orient Road.'

'And you expect me to believe that?'

'I really can't imagine why you shouldn't.'

The Councillor ignored him.

'I think Miss Alison Kinnit sent you,' he said.

Timothy stared. 'Alison? Why should she?'

'You know her then?' The intelligent eyes were shrewdly inquisitive.

'Of course I do. She and her brother brought me up. I live with them.'

'Oh.' He seemed astonished, even a little put out. 'Then perhaps you know a woman called Flavia Aicheson?' He put contempt and dislike into the name and Timothy frowned.

'Certainly I know her,' he admitted. 'She's been around all my life. She's a great friend of Aunt Alison's and a very nice old thing. Has she been making trouble on one of your committees?' He saw that he had scored a bull's-eye as soon as the words were out of his mouth. The Councillor was verging towards rage and colour had appeared on his thin cheeks.

'You're very plausible, very smooth,' he began with intentional offence. 'I'm not a fool, you know, even if I have lived a great deal longer than you have. As soon as I heard a private detective had been snooping along certain lines I suspected something of this sort and I was disgusted, I tell you frankly. For a while I washed my hands of the entire affair but on second thoughts I decided to check and I invited the Stalkeys to call on me. One brother came down this morning and was quite ready to talk, but I only wanted one thing from him and that was the name of his client. As soon as he gave me that I knew I was right. Alison Kinnit and Flavia Aicheson, they're virtually the same woman.'

'Oh but they're not!' Timothy was so exasperated that he laughed. 'They may have the same interests and they're certainly very close friends but they're quite different personalities I do assure you.'

'Are they?' Councillor Cornish conveyed that he was unconvinced. 'You go back and tell them,' he said. 'Tell them they may feel that they're serving the Arts but that I serve Humanity and I am not going to have my life's work tampered with. You can also tell them that if they're hoping to use dirty weapons they should consider their own position very carefully. At least,' he hesitated 'at least tell them not to be so damn silly!'

'I do assure you you're making a great mistake.' Timothy's embarrassment was mounting. He had discovered to his dismay that the personal aspect of his quest was becoming more agonizingly personal at every new encounter, while at the same time the Councillor's accusatory style upset him in an emotional way which he felt to be absurd.

'I came here on my own account because I want to know the things that Stalkey was trying to find out and I thought you might help me,' he said lamely.

'What things? Go on, young man. Put them into words, what things?' There was something savage in the force of the older man's question and his visitor shied away from it.

'Certain – certain aspects of social conditions in Turk Street just before the second war, sir,' he muttered and sounded stilted even to himself.

'*Social conditions!*' The phrase seemed to touch a power centre in the Councillor, who let himself go. 'Don't be a pompous ass, boy!' He used the word in the old-fashioned way with a long vowel, making it even more derogatory. 'Turk Street was a London slum. Your generation doesn't know what that means. You call yourselves "sick", don't you? So do I. You couldn't have walked a hundred yards of the Turk Street Mile in the thirties without vomiting. It turned me up myself and I wasn't a spoon-fed university product.'

He leant further across the table, shaking in his determination to make his point.

'Children crawled over each other like little grey worms in the gutters,' he said. 'The only red things about them were their buttocks and they were raw. Their faces looked as if snails had slimed on them and their mothers were like great sick beasts whose byres had never been cleared. The stink and the noise and the cold and the hatred got into your belly and nothing and no-one has ever got it out again as far as I'm concerned. For God's sake go back to those maiden ladies and get it into their idiot heads that an anthill is less offensive than a sewer.'

Timothy hesitated. The man was making an extraordinary mistake, he saw, and he realized that he was probably the best source of information about the vanished Turk Street remaining in London. Yet he also knew that for some inexplicable reason he could not put up with his open animosity any longer.

The Councillor glanced up. 'What are you waiting for?'

'Nothing, sir.' Timothy was very pale and the damage which Ron Stalkey had done to his face stood out in angry colour on his skin. 'Goodbye.' He turned on his heel and walked across the room, out through the front door and down the steps to the street without once looking behind him.

Mrs. Cornish, who was hovering in the passage, saw him go and she went in to her husband.

'Why on earth did you do that?' she demanded. 'I could hear you from the kitchen. What did the poor boy say to make you so livid?'

Now that his rage was spent the Councillor was a little shame-faced. 'Oh, I don't know,' he said frowning. 'The "holier-than-thou" attitude of that sort of pup always irritates me. A self-satisfied superior approach to matters of taste is infuriating. Those people like the Kinnits and the Aichesons all do the same thing. They look at something which they know nothing whatever about and presume to judge it solely by the effect which the mere sight of it has had on them.'

'Flavia Aicheson,' said Mrs. Cornish. 'That's the mannish old woman who runs the Little Society for the Preservation of the London Skyline isn't it? So that's what he came about. Rather a nice type.'

'I didn't notice it. Those people are up to something. I don't trust them an inch. They're the kind of half-baked intellectuals who never know where to stop. They don't like the look of the new flats. The silhouette is an affront to their blasted eyes, they say. Well, there are alternatives which have offended my eyes . . .'

'Yes dear, not again.' Mrs. Cornish exerted her own brand of force. 'You happened to walk down Turk Street one winter afternoon long ago when you first came up from the country to be Dad's apprentice, and it gave you such a shock that you've never got over it. We know. We've heard enough about it. You weren't there quite half an hour and it's dominated your whole life. It may not have been the utter hell you thought. Anyhow, why take it out on the first presentable youngster who's been to the house for years?'

'Pompous ass!' said the Councillor again. 'He kept calling me "sir" as if I were Methusela. That's all I noticed about him. A useless, opinionated, over-sensitive ass!'

'Oh rubbish,' she said. 'You can't say that. You didn't even let him speak. Do you know who he reminded me of? You at that age. No one was more opinionated than you were, or more over-sensitive for that matter.'

The Councillor stared at her. For an instant he looked positively alarmed. Then he laughed, regretful, even a little flattered.

'You do say the most damn silly things, Marion,' he said.

CHAPTER EIGHT

The Well House

'SEEN it before, sir?' The brisk inquiry from the helmeted figure materializing beside Timothy in the half darkness took him by surprise and he blinked. He had been standing perfectly still, gazing across the broad street at the silhouette of the house which had been his home in London ever since he could remember, and it was as new to him as a foreign land.

He had just walked back from Ebbfield. His interview with the Councillor had had a considerable effect upon him for he was behaving as if a skin had peeled from his eyes. Children first home from boarding school often notice the same phenomenon, very familiar things appearing not different in themselves but as if they were being seen by someone new. He knew of no reason why it should have happened. The front of his mind was satisfied that he had merely had an interview with a difficult old man, but behind it, in the vast, blind, computing machine where the mind and the emotions meet and churn, something very odd indeed seemed to have taken place.

It was a muggy London night and the road which was an inferno in the daytime was now a deserted river, gleaming dully in a dark ravine.

The constable was a regular and had recognized him. It was a lonely beat and he was prepared to chat.

'It's an anachronism,' he remarked unexpectedly, jerking his leather-strapped chin towards the Tudor merchant's mansion which lay, top-heavy but graceful as a galleon, between two towering warehouses on the opposite side of the road. The overhanging latticed windows, one floor up, were lighted and warmth shone out faintly through reddish curtains. But at street level the low iron-bound doors and small windows were hidden in the shadows. 'Completely out of place in a modern world, isn't it?' he went on. 'But it's nice to see it. It's even better than that row up in Holborn they tell me. Is it comfortable to live in, sir?'

'Not bad. Plumbing was put in very intelligently at the early part of this century but the kitchens are still a bit archaic.' Timothy spoke as if the facts were fresh to him and the constable laughed. 'Still, you're proud of it I dare say?' he said.

The younger man turned his head in surprise. 'I suppose I was' he said, but the policeman was not listening. The light from one of the old-fashioned street lamps bracketed on the building behind them had fallen on to the speaker's face and he was startled by the damage.

'Blimey sir! What have you done to yourself? Met with an accident?'

'Not exactly. I had a dustup with a lunatic!' The words came out with more bitterness than he had intended and he laughed to cover it. 'Never mind, officer. All's square now. Good night.'

'Good night, sir.' The man went off as if he had been dismissed and Timothy crossed the road and let himself into the Well House.

There was a small wooden draughtbreak just inside the door with a curtained entrance to the main hall, and he heard Basil Toberman's voice as he stepped through it into the warm, black-panelled room with the moulded plaster ceiling and the square staircase rising up through it. The first thing he saw was a funeral wreath, and the scent of lilies hung in the warm air, suffocating and exotic, and remarkably foreign to the familiar house.

The tribute was very big, nearly four feet across, a great cushion of white hothouse flowers, diapered with gold, and made all the more extravagant by the shining plastic wrappings which made it look as if it was under glass. It lay on the oak table which flanked the staircase and at the moment Toberman was bending over it, fiddling with a card half hidden among the blossom. Mrs. Broome was hovering beside him in a flurry of protest.

'Oh don't,' she was objecting. 'Mr. Basil, don't. It isn't as though it's yours. Don't be so inquisitive, don't!'

'Shut up,' he said without turning round. 'I'm only having a look. The order must have come from South Africa through one of the flower services, I suppose. That's the flaw in these things. There's no way of telling what you're getting for your money.'

'What are you talking about?' she demanded. 'It's beautiful. It must have cost I don't know what!'

'I know. That's what I'm saying. Out there – wherever it is – flowers are probably dear at this time of year. Over here in late spring they cost nothing. I don't suppose anyone, however stinking rich, intended to send to a servant's funeral the sort of wreath which one expects to see the Monarch parking on a War Memorial.'

Nanny Broom sniffed. 'No wonder no one could do anything *with* you,' she observed without animosity. 'Your naughtiness is right in you. Miss Saxon wasn't a servant, and if she had been all the more reason that she should have a nice wreath, even if it did come so late it missed the hearse. I wish I'd had you as a little boy. I'd have scared some of the commoness out of you, my lad. Miss Saxon was a governess and a very intelligent woman with a great sense of humour.'

'How do you know?'

Mrs. Broome silenced him. 'Well, she used to laugh at *me*,' she said and seemed so pleased about it that there was nothing to say.

Toberman swung round on his heel and saw Timothy standing in the doorway. He stood for an instant contemplating the scarred face, his eyes wonderfully shrewd and amused, but he made no direct comment.

Instead he returned to the flowers: 'Wonderfully wealthy guests we have,' he remarked. 'This is how the staff is seen off. How does this appeal to the young master?'

It was a casual sneer, obviously one of a long line. There was hatred behind it but of a quiet, chronic type, nothing new or unduly virulent, and he was taken aback by the flicker of amazed incredulity which passed over the younger man's ravaged face. Toberman was disconcerted. 'What's the matter?' he demanded truculently.

'Nothing.' Timothy's eyes wavered and met Mrs. Broome's. She was watching him like a mother cat, noting the signs of shock without altogether understanding them. She opened her mouth to speak but he shook his head at her warningly and she closed it again without a sound.

'You look like a lost soul,' Toberman said. 'Where have you been?'

Tim turned away. 'I walked home,' he said briefly. 'I'm tired.'

Nanny Broome could bear it no longer.

'Come down to the kitchen, Mr. Tim,' she said. 'I want to talk to you,' and as her glance met his own she formed the word "Julia" with her lips, giving him a clue as she used to do long ago when there was a secret to be told in company and he was a little boy.

Despair passed over the young face and he turned away abruptly.

'Not now, Nan,' he said, looking at Toberman who had found the card he had been seeking amid the lilies and was now transcribing its details into a notebook. He was doing it with that off-hand effrontery which so often passes unnoticed because people cannot bring themselves to credit their own eyes. When a step on the landing above surprised, him, he slid the book into his pocket and patted the covering back into place.

'We were saying how beautiful it is,' he remarked blandly as he glanced up the stairwell. Mrs. Geraldine Telpher, the Kinnit's visiting niece, was coming down, moving quietly and smoothly as she did everything else. She was a distinguished-looking woman in the late thirties, pleasantly pale with faded old-gold hair and light blue eyes, who radiated authority and that particular brand of faint austerity which is so often associated with money. She was wearing a grey jersey suit with considerable elegance, and the way her jacket sat on her shoulders and the trick she had of settling her cuff straight confirmed her kinship with Eustace and Alison so vividly that the others were made a little uncomfortable. Her method of handling Toberman was also startlingly familiar. She laughed at his antics with a mixture of ruefulness and tolerance as if he were a slightly offensive household pet.

'The smell of the lilies is rather powerful,' she said. 'The house is full of it upstairs. Is there somewhere where the wreath could go,

Mrs. Broome? It's a pity it came so late. Perhaps it could be sent to the grave in the morning?'

'I was going to take it myself, first thing,' In her determination to keep in the limelight Mrs. Broome spoke on the spur of the moment and it was evident to everybody that the idea had never entered her head before that instant. 'In a taxi,' she added after the briefest possible pause.

'Perhaps so,' Mrs. Telpher agreed gravely. 'They might not let you take it on a bus but you could try. Anyway it's very good of you and I'm sure she would have appreciated it. She had taken a great fancy to you, hadn't she?'

'Well I should think so, she talked enough to me!' Nanny Broome was "giving back as good as she had got" in an instinctive self-preservative fashion which had nothing to do with reason. The Kinnit trick of making people feel slightly inferior without intending to or noticing that it had been done had never been more clearly demonstrated.

Toberman went on chatting in a determined yet deferential way.

'We were thinking that the flowers must have been ordered from abroad by wire,' he was saying with a little inquisitive laugh. 'The whole wreath is very lush – very grand. The card only says "Love dear from Elsa" but there's a box number which suggests either a P.O. box address, as in South Africa, or a florist's reference.

Geraldine Telpher favoured him with a wide-eyed stare which might have been one of Alison Kinnit's own and shook her head, smiling.

'I imagine it must have come from the family she was with before she came to me,' he said, making it clear that she was humouring him. 'I notified her home and they must have told them. It was the Van der Graffs, I remember. How nice of them. They're good people. You find its size a little ostentatious, do you Basil?'

'Don't make fun of me,' he protested. 'I'm just impressed, that's all. I like lavishness. It's rare. By the way that name – Van der Graff – are they anything to do with the Ivory people?'

'I'm afraid I just wouldn't know.'

'Ah!' he held up a warning hand to her. 'No wicked snobbery. Trade is in fashion. As a matter of fact I was coming to talk to you about that.' He turned to Mrs. Broome and lifted the wreath into her arms, all but hiding her.

'Run along with that to the scullery, Broomie. I shan't stay here tonight, by the way, because I've got to get the late plane to Nice, but I'll be back tomorrow rather late and I'd like to stay then. The room is ready I expect, so you won't have to worry about me.' It was a plain dismissal and Mrs. Broome went, but not defeated.

'Me worry about *you*?' she said from the doorway. 'That'll be the day!'

Toberman laughed and returned to Mrs. Telpher. 'They used to sack them for that sort of remark,' he said. 'I suppose you do now. How wonderful. Now look, Geraldine my dear, I don't know if this is of any interest to you at all but I thought I'd mention it. I'm going to Nice tonight to see a little fourth century bronze which Lagusse says is genuine. I've seen a photograph and it's more than promising. I shall just take one look and come home, because if it's real the only man who has both the taste and the money to buy it is in your country and I've got Philip Zwole flying there on other business and I want to brief him. He'll be overseas for the best part of a month and he'll spend quite a week in Johannesburg, so if there's anything you'd like him to take or any message you'd like to send by him, well, there he is.'

It was a request for introductions and Timothy, who had moved away, turned back irritably.

'I imagine Geraldine can keep in touch, Basil,' he said.

It was a protest and sounded like one and Toberman received it with a stare of reproachful amazement while Mrs. Telpher looked at Timothy and laughed a polite rejection of the whole subject.

'It's very kind of him,' she said. 'If I do think of anything I shall certainly remember the offer.'

Toberman snorted. His dark face was swarthy with blood and his round black eyes were furious.

'Don't be damn silly,' he exploded, turning on the other man.

'Geraldine has just had her Miss Saxon die in a strange country. Presumably the woman had some things which ought to be taken to her home. I was merely offering a service. What other reason could I possibly have?'

'None,' intervened Mrs. Telpher with all the Kinnit tolerance in her quiet voice. 'I do appreciate it. It really is most kind.'

Toberman appeared mollified and bounced again. 'Well then,' he said, 'when I come in tomorrow evening I'll collect anything you want to send and give it to Zwole when I see him in the morning. I can understand you being windy about the poor old thing's family, Tim. You actually knocked her over, didn't you?'

Mrs. Telpher intervened.

'Tell me about the bronze,' she said.

'Why? Are you interested?' His sudden eagerness made her smile and she bowed her long neck. 'I might be,' she conceded.

Timothy left them and went upstairs to the sitting-room whose lighted windows he had seen from the street. It was a civilized, lived-in room, part panelled and part booklined. A vast Turkey carpet with a faded tomato-soup coloured background hid much of the black oak floor, and the remarkable collection of uphol-stered furniture which had comfort alone in common was welded into harmony by plain covers in the same yellowish pink.

Miss Alison Kinnit and her friend Miss Aicheson were sitting where they always did, Alison on one of the angular couches with her feet tucked up beside her and Flavia in a big rounded arm-chair with a back like a sail on the opposite side of the hearth. There was no fire and the wide brick recess housed a collection of cacti, none of them doing very well because of the shade and the draught.

The likeness between Alison Kinnit and her niece Mrs. Telpher was considerable but the twenty years between their ages was not entirely responsible for the main difference, which was one of de-licacy. Mrs. Telpher was a pale, graceful woman but Alison's pallor and fragility were remarkable. Her skin was almost trans-lucent without being actually unhealthy and her bones were as slender as a bird's. She had always had an interesting face but had never been beautiful and now there was something a little frighten-ing in the grey-eyed intelligence with which she confronted the world. Miss Flavia on the other hand was a more familiar type. She was one of those heavy ugly women with kind faces and apologetic, old-gentlemanly manners who all look as if they were John Bull's own daughters taking strongly after their father, poor dears. She was older than Alison, sixty perhaps, and happy in the way that some elderly men who have had great trials and overcome them are happy: quiet-eyed, amused and not utterly intolerant.

It was obvious that they had been talking about Timothy; not because they seemed guilty when he came in but because they were so interested and so clear about who he was and what was happening to him. In the normal way they were apt to be completely absorbed by their own affairs of the moment and these might be literary, charitable or political – one never knew which. The fact that Miss Flavia had stuck to her romantic name all her life said much for her character. Now she turned slowly in her chair and looked at Tim through her glasses.

'Certainly battle-scarred but I hope not woebegone,' she said in her fluting, county voice. 'What does the other fellow look like? Come and sit down and tell us all about it. Shall I get him a drink, Alison?'

'Would you like one, dear?' Alison nodded at him, screwing up her face with mimic pain at the damage to his face. 'We won't. But it's there in the cupboard if you'd like it. Mrs. Broome told us you'd been in the wars. Where have you been? You look awfully distrait.' Her own voice was clipped and academic, and friendly without warmth.

'Down to Ebbfield again,' he said as casually as he could as he seated himself on the edge of the round ottoman which took up a huge amount of space in the fairway between the fireplace and the door. 'I saw a man called Councillor Cornish: he seemed to think that you or Aich must have sent me.'

'And did we?' Alison glanced inquiringly at her friend.

'I don't recall it.' Miss Aicheson's nice eyes regarded him innocently. 'Yet the name is familiar. Is he an Ebbfield councillor?'

'I imagine so. He's responsible for building a block of flats.'

'Oh, of course. The skyline committee, Alison. He's the poor wretched man with the dreadful temper. I remember.' Miss Flavia was delighted. Her charitableness had never been more marked. 'I can imagine him remembering me but I can't think why he should suppose I should have sent you to him. People with chips on their shoulders do get wild ideas, of course. Well, did he help you? What did you ask him?'

Timothy appeared to be wondering and Alison, mistaking his reaction, intervened tactfully.

'Aich is on top of the world. She's had a letter from the Minister.'

Miss Aicheson's red face was suffused with shy pleasure. 'Oh, it's nothing. Only an acknowledgment, really,' she said, 'but it's from White's, not the House, and it's signed, and there's even a little postscript in his own hand thanking me for my "lucid exposition". I'm very bucked. I admit it.'

Timothy frowned. His young body was tense and as he sat with his long legs crossed he tapped on his knee with nervous fingers.

'Is that the Minister of Housing? Is this the Ebbfield business?' Alison's laugh silenced him.

'Oh, no my dear, Ebbfield is very small beer. This is the Plan for Trafalgar Square.'

Miss Aicheson made a happy succession of little grunting noises. 'Ra-ther a different caper!' she announced with satisfaction. 'I expect the over-earnest little men will get their own way at Ebbfield and it can't be helped because that part of London is spoiled already. One just does what one can in a case like that and doesn't break one's heart if one fails.'

'Cornish didn't strike me as being a *little* man.' Tim appeared astonished at his own vehemence and Alison turned her wide grey eyes upon him, surprised also.

Flavia Aicheson waved the protest away with a large masculine hand. 'Very likely not,' she agreed. 'I can't visualize him at all. I only remember how angry he was and how nearly rude, so that all the rest of the conference was on edge with embarrassment. He was over-earnest, though, wasn't he? These dear chaps remember some picture from their childhood, some little injustice or ugliness, and let it grow into a great emotional boil far, far more painful than the original wound . . . Don't let them influence you, dear boy.'

She and Alison exchanged glances and suddenly became utterly embarrassed themselves.

Miss Aicheson made an effort, her face scarlet and her voice unsteady with nervousness.

'This inquiry into your birth is a very difficult and awkward experience for you, Timothy, and Alison and I both feel (although of course we haven't been discussing you, don't think that!) the real danger is of you losing your sense of proportion and swinging violently either one way or the other. Left or Right.'

She was as uncomfortable as a young girl and, since the problem was emotional, quite as inexperienced. The boy got up.

'That's all right Aich,' he said kindly. 'I shan't go Red or Fascist.'

The two ladies sighed with relief. 'Of course you won't,' Miss Flavia said heartily. 'You're far too sensible. Well now, about the investigation: any progress?' She hesitated and a little wistful smile, as feminine and pathetic as any Nanny Broome could muster, suddenly crept over her homely face. 'Don't forget that in one way it could be very romantic and exciting, Timothy,' she murmured. 'I mean – one never knows.'

Alison burst out laughing. Her grey eyes were as hard but also as innocent as pebbles in a stream.

'Dear Aich!' she said. 'Isn't she wonderful, Timothy? She's thinking: "Even the Minister must have been young in 1939!"'

Miss Flavia's colour increased to danger point and she shook her head warningly.

'That's not funny, Alison,' she said. 'Vulgar and not funny at all.'

At once Alison Kinnit lost her poise and became contrite.

'Sorry, Aich,' she said, hanging her head like a delicate child. 'Really truly.'

Timothy went out of the room without them noticing that he had gone.

CHAPTER NINE

The Stranger

Eustace Kinnit was the author of many books and pamphlets on various aspects of the china collector's art as well as being an enthusiastic correspondent on the subject. The small study where he did his endless writing was at the far end of the gallery which ran round the staircase-well on the same floor as the sitting-room. There was a sliver of light under the door as Timothy approached after leaving Miss Alison and her friend, and he stood outside for a moment, hesitating, with an anxious expression in his eyes which was new there. Any sort of nervousness was foreign to his temperament and he bore it awkwardly. Presently he pushed his hand over his hair, stiffened his shoulders, and walked in more abruptly than he would have done at any other time in his life.

Eustace was sitting at his desk in a bright circle of light from the shaded lamp, his pen squeaking softly as it ran swiftly over the page. Timothy, who had seen him in exactly the same position so often and who loved him so well that he had, as it were, never seen him at all, observed him objectively for the first time.

He was a spare, tidy man of sixty or so with a sharp white beard, and a sweep of white hair above a fine forehead. His eyes were like his sister's but more blue and infinitely more kindly and the lines at their sides radiated in a quarter circle. As he wrote his knee jogged all the time. It was a ceaseless tremor which made a little draught in the otherwise still and muffled room. He took no notice of the newcomer until he had finished his paragraph, putting in the final stop with care. Then he put down his pen, lifted his head and removed his spectacles. These were in white gold, made to his own austere design, and were one of his few personal vanities. As they lay on the page they were as typical of him as his signature.

'Hello,' he said happily. 'There you are. It went off very well.

Nothing too barbaric but respectably splendid and decent. I think she was pleased.'

'The funeral?'

'Eh? Oh my goodness, yes! What did you think? I meant Geraldine, too. There's no way of telling what the other poor woman felt about it!' His laugh was schoolboyish and charming. 'Are you all right? I can't see you very well over there. Turn the light on will you? Good Heavens, boy! What have you done?'

Timothy had touched the switch by the door obediently and as the light fell on his face Eustace's horrified reaction to the damage was so completely out of proportion to it that the younger man was irritated.

'It's nothing,' he protested, shying away. 'Only a scratch or two.'

'Not a road accident?' Eustace was speaking of something he was always dreading and fear flared in his voice embarrassingly.

'No, of course not. I merely got a hiding from one of those damn detectives of yours. What on earth made you pick them, or was it Alison?'

'The Stalkeys? I heard something of the sort from the women.' Eustace opened his eyes very wide. 'I can't believe it.'

He spoke gravely, meaning the words literally, and managed to look both so hurt and so completely incredulous that the exasperated colour poured into the boy's face, hiding some of the injuries in a general conflagration. Eustace sighed as if somehow he had been reassured. 'That's much better,' he said unreasonably. 'But you shouldn't make sweeping statements like that. If you attacked the man I suppose he defended himself. They're a very old-established firm and excellent people or we shouldn't have employed them for the second time. Even so I don't know if it was wise. We're only trying to help you, Tim, you know that.'

It was a transparent mixture of prejudice, obstinacy and genuine dismay, and so like him that the young man could have wept.

'Oh scrub it!' he exploded, and suddenly blurted out the one bald question that he had made up his mind never to ask outright.

'Uncle, had no one *really* any idea whatever where I came from?'

Eustace gaped at him in amazement. When his urbanity dropped away from him, as now, he had an innocence of expression which was almost infantile. It was as if the world had never touched him at all.

'But I told you,' he said earnestly. 'I told you, Tim. I confessed it.' The young man watched him helplessly. There was no hope that he was lying. The chill truth shone from him as only truth does shine. 'It was absurd and unrealistic of me perhaps,' he went on, betraying that he was still not entirely convinced of the fact. 'I can see something of that now, but then... ! My goodness! What a time that was! The world was cracking up all round us, you see. Civilization, Beauty, Law and Order, all crumbling like the pillars of a city. You were just a little bundle of helpless jelly, so very vulnerable and appealing. It didn't seem very important what I did. I thought I'd provide for you as long as I could, you know, and there was that thwarted, childless woman so delighted to be able to mother you. I felt I did right afterwards because Alison and I both became so fond of you. I've said I'm sorry, Tim.'

'Don't . . .' the boy put out his hand. 'I'm not ungrateful, you know that. It's only that – I mean, you are absolutely dead sure that I can't possibly be a Kinnit?'

Eustace appeared to consider the remoter possibilities for the first time.

'How could you be?' he inquired.

The utter reasonableness of the question struck Timothy with the impact of a pail of cold water. The final shreds of his romantic swaddling-clothes were washed away and he stood quivering and ashamed of himself for ever clinging to them. It was a moment of enormous danger which anyone in Eustace's position who had a reasonable degree of emotional imagination or experience must have found terrifying, but his protection was almost complete. He reacted in his own way and changed the subject.

'I'm getting on,' he announced, nodding at the written page. 'But it's not easy. There's very little data about Chandler's first factory at Bristol. Oh well, it must wait for the moment. I'm very glad you came in, Tim. I wanted to have a word with you about poor Basil. He *drinks* these days, doesn't he?'

The young man stood looking at him. In his eyes was the half-horrified, half-amused expression with which so many people meet the solution of a lifelong enigma. Eustace the father-figure had turned into Eustace the dear old fuss-pot.

'Basil? Oh, he takes his noggin,' Timothy said. 'It's not serious.'

'Ah, but I understand it makes him *talk*.' Eustace's glance had become frosty and the aesthetic lines in his face were very marked; he had also coloured a little as he always did when he was embarrassed. 'Alison came in here an hour ago,' he said. 'She'd been talking to Nanny Broome – that woman is only up here for a few days and we learn things about each other of which we've been happily ignorant for years! I don't take her too seriously but one thing she is reported to have said worries me very much.' He lowered his voice to a confidential murmur. 'Have you heard an extraordinary story about Basil actually saying – when drunk of course – that you had been *rough* with that poor old woman who died here?'

Timothy frowned in irritation. 'I heard something of the sort.'

'Tim. It's not true?'

'Of course not! Don't be silly, Nunk.' The old endearment from his childhood slipped out without him noticing. 'Even if no one has faced this birth business until now, you can't suddenly decide you don't know me at all! Miss Saxon happened to be listening outside the kitchen door when I pulled it open. She fell into the room and on to the stones. Nan and I picked her up and dusted her down and she went off quite happy, but afterwards she told Geraldine that I had shaken her.'

'And you hadn't?' The anxiety in the tone was wounding.

'No! She was only creating a diversion; she'd been caught listening at a door! Do put it out of your head, it's so unimportant.'

'I don't think so,' Eustace got up from his chair and walked up and down the small room. Something had frightened him.

Timothy found that he recognized the signs but was no longer made afraid himself by them. Eustace was pale and excited and the knuckles of his hands grasping the lapels of his jacket were white.

'It could be most damaging. Most. He's got to be stopped, Tim. He's got to be stopped at once. Where is the silly fellow?'

'He's in the house. He's flying to Nice in the dawn and coming back here to sleep tomorrow night. Don't bother with him. He does chatter and nobody takes any notice of him. Really it doesn't matter.'

'You're wrong. She's dead you see. It makes it very awkward. Very dangerous.' Eustace paused in the midst of his walk and was thinking, his eyes narrowed and his lips moving. 'I'll speak to him,' he said at last. 'Don't you say anything. It's my responsibility. Leave it to me. He must give up alcohol if he can't trust his tongue.'

The younger man turned away wearily. 'I don't care a damn what he says!'

'That's nothing to do with it my boy. Don't you see? I gave Dr. Gross my word that there could be no possible need for a post-mortem.'

'That was a bit god-like of you, wasn't it?'

'Wasn't it?' Eustace's gentle laugh escaped him. 'Something warned me at the time that I was being presumptuous. However, I did it. Gross came over as soon as I telephoned and when he found that she was dead he came in here to me and said something about mentioning the death to the Coroner. Well, I've known him for years, as you know, and rightly or wrongly I dissuaded him. I pointed out that he had attended her so he was behaving quite properly in giving a certificate if he was certain nothing abnormal had occurred, and I took it on myself to guarantee that nothing had. After a certain amount of humming and haa-ing he agreed.'

'Why did you go to all that trouble? Because Geraldine is so rich?'

Eustace looked hurt. 'Tim, that was a sneer!' He shook his head and added with disarming frankness, 'I don't know why one does go out of one's way to oblige Money. It's a funny thing and very wrong but everybody does it. Yet, you know, it wasn't quite that. I think I wanted to save us all embarrassment. Geraldine has trouble enough on her hands with that poor child in hospital.'

He paused and alarm appeared in his kindly eyes again.

'Basil must hold his tongue though. What a stupid man he is! It could be particularly awkward, since the woman was a governess. I noticed that at once.'

Tim looked at him blankly for a moment before he laughed.

'On the principle that the Kinnit family is governess prone?'

'Don't be a fool, my boy!' Eustace actually stamped his foot. 'Use your imagination. Nothing colours a new scandal like an old crime story. In the last century the Kinnits were involved in a Coroner's inquest and a trial which concerned a governess, Thyrza Caleb. The name is not forgotten after a hundred years. It would certainly cause comment if we appeared in a new one now which also concerned a governess. It's obvious. That was why I wrote the announcement for the newspapers myself. I was very careful not to let the name Kinnit appear. "Kinnit" and "governess" are not good words together. We live in an age of mischievous publicity; it's stupid to ignore the fact. Basil must stop drinking and be quiet. I'll see to it myself.' He sat down at the desk again and took up his pen. 'You go and have a good sleep,' he said. 'You're not like yourself tonight.' Tim turned to the door.

'I'm not like anybody, that's the trouble.'

'What's that?' Eustace was looking over his glasses. 'Turn that light down will you as you go. I like just the one lamp on the page. What did you say just now?'

'Nothing of any interest. Good night.'

'Good night, Tim.' He was already writing. 'Don't brood,' he said without looking up. 'And don't forget, not a word to Basil. I'll do that.'

Timothy went out into the passage again and walked round the staircase well to the other side of the house. The door of the sitting-room was closed but he heard Toberman's unmistakable laugh and Miss Aicheson's high hollow voice as he passed it. The rest of the building was as quiet as only London's night-time deserted areas can be quiet. From every side the roar was still audible, but now it came from far away and in the middle there was stillness and the grateful pandemonium quelled.

His own room possessed a staircase of its own which ran up from the end of the right wing where Eustace, Alison and any guests staying the night had bed and bathrooms. It had always been his room and as a child he had been thrilled by the sense of importance and security which the staircase gave him. One entered it through a small door which one could pretend was secret and the stair wound up in a full half turn to the big low room with the uneven oak floor and the tiny washroom and shower built in an oversized cupboard, the panelled bed and the bookshelves filling the wall beside it.

He was so anxious to get to this sanctuary, to shut the door and clear his mind, that he did not notice Nanny Broome who was standing by the passage window, her dark dress mingling with the heavy curtains.

'Mr. Tim?' The voice, almost in his ear as he passed, surprised him and he shied away from her. 'Mr. Tim. I've got to tell you something.'

'Not now, Nan, for God's sake!' The words came out more savagely than he meant and she responded in her own particular fashion. Her eyes flashed and her lips hardened. 'Oh well then, you must find it out for yourself and I shan't take the blame!' she said tartly. 'I'm sorry I wasted my time waiting for you.'

She was not really put out; he could tell that from her voice. She was in one of her slightly naughty and entirely feminine moods, excited and truculent. The threat might mean anything; in his present loneliness he did not care.

He left her without speaking, shut the door of the staircase carefully behind him, turned on the switch which lit the bedroom above and ran up into it, to come to a sudden halt on the threshold. Someone was there, lying on the bed, the shadows of the high foot-board hiding her face. He knew who it was before he went over and looked down.

Julia was lying on her back, her hands behind her head, her eyes wide open and very dark. There was no expression whatever on her face and he got the impression that she was not breathing.

She watched him silently, only her grave eyes, dark with exhaustion from the emotional struggle she had lost, flickering to show that she was alive.

Timothy stood looking a moment and then made as if to turn away from her, his face working, and she put up her arms and pulled him down.

For a little while he let the tide of relief and peace close over him but as the surge rose up in his blood he took hold of himself and pushed her away as he struggled to get up.

'No. Stop it,' he whispered fiercely. 'Not here I tell you. Not in this hole and corner. I won't let you. You're mine as well as your own. We've got something to lose. "With my body I thee worship" and don't forget it, my – my *holy* one.'

'I don't care.' She was shaking and her face was wet against his cheek. 'I was promised. I was *promised*. I can't go on. I can't. Not any more.'

'Be quiet!' He took her shoulders and forced her away from him back against the pillows. 'Listen and for God's sake try to understand. I've just been involved in a sort of . . . *birth*. It has been happening to me all day. I feel that until today I've been in a . . . an eggshell. But all through today I've been breaking out of it. Everything I've ever taken for granted has come apart in my hand. Do you know that even until tonight I secretly believed that somehow it would turn out in the end that Alison *was* my aunt and Eustace *was* my father? Well, they're not. What is more, it must always have been perfectly obvious that they were not. Eustace is a honey, a sweetie, a charmer, but he couldn't be anybody's father. I saw it quite clearly – almost in an off-hand casual sort of way – when I went in tonight. I've known him all my life and never appreciated before what every adult must have felt about him. Julia, don't you see what this is *doing* to me? I'm altering. I'm coming down to earth. I don't know what I'm going to turn out to be.'

She was rigid and the tears were forcing themselves between her closed lids. 'What about *me*? Oh Timothy. What about me?'

'Understand.' It was the ultimate appeal, as young as childhood and as old as the world. 'I must exist. I can't float about unattached and meaningless. I'm a component part. I'm the continuation of an existing story, as is everybody else. I thought I knew my story but I don't. I have been misinformed in a very thorough way. I've got to go on and find out who I am, or I'm unrecognizable even to myself.'

The girl's eyes opened and her hot little mouth was salty as she pulled him to her.

'I'm here. Don't shut me out. I shan't change. I *can't* change. I love you. I'm all love.'

'How do I know?' He was pulling back from her in terror. It was the last question of all.

There was a long silence and then she sat up, suddenly the stronger of the two. 'Well,' she said with the courage of certainty, 'if the rest of the world has changed for you, have I? Look and see. Love isn't love if it alteration finds. That's how you know, I thought.'

It was a gesture of curious generosity. Its blessing flowed over him cool and comforting. He sat down on the bed and held her hands and looked at her and she met his eyes and presently they began to laugh.

They were so engrossed that the clatter of the staircase door and the flying footsteps took a second or so to break through to them, and Basil Toberman was already on the threshold when they first became aware of anything but each other.

For some moments he stood just inside the room, staring like a scandalized frog. His eyes were bulging and his mouth was very red and wet as usual, while they sat blinking at him.

'Do you know the police are downstairs,' he demanded, fixing his pop-eyed stare on Timothy alone. 'They want you to go to Holborn headquarters with them. Apparently the office of the Stalkey Bros. has gone up in flames. It's been a hell of a fire. Four brigades. They don't know if they're going to revive the night watchman. You'd better come down pretty pronto if you don't want them trooping up here. In my opinion, for what it's worth, they've got "arson" written all over them.'

He turned to Julia, truculent and offensive. 'This ruddy young fool is in plenty of trouble as it is,' he said. 'I should sneak out the back way and slide quietly home if I were you. I've got to dash off and catch a plane or I'd offer to take you. Meanwhile I shall hold my tongue until I get back. So make the most of it, my dear. Come down and placate these chaps, Tim. Never say I didn't mean well.'

CHAPTER TEN

Conference in the Morning

SUPERINTENDENT CHARLES LUKE at breakfast in his own home was something to see, Mr. Campion reflected as he sat opposite him in the kitchen of his mother's house in Linden Lea, one of the newest north-west suburbs. It was a very bright room, so clean that it might have been made of highly glazed china, and the wide window looked out on a neat bright garden with white stone paths, smooth green grass, and geraniums all in a row.

In this setting Luke appeared larger and more lithe, darker and more vital even than usual. With his chin freshly shaved, his linen freshly laundered, his crisp, upstanding hair newly oiled and his teeth gleaming, he appeared part and parcel of the whole. Old Mrs. Luke's lifework, a credit to London, the police and a good woman's one pair of hands.

Despite it he was bearing up pretty well, Mr. Campion noticed, wearing the cherishing with good-natured ease, and even now at a quarter past seven in the morning his native cockney exuberance was unimpaired.

'I'm glad you came along,' he said, his eyebrows rising even higher than usual. 'The office is like any other Government Department – not an ideal place to be seen taking an unofficial interest in an old friend's private griefs. It's not a question of the odd snake or so, you understand; just human nature and the requisite spot of common. Here we can say what we like and no harm done. Even Mum is out of earshot.'

Mr. Campion glanced behind him. 'I wondered about that,' he said anxiously. 'I hope I'm not keeping her out of here.'

'Don't you worry!' Luke was amused in his own ferocious way. 'You couldn't do that, chum. Not if you were the Pope. Fortunately she's attending to the baby. That young woman is saving my life mopping up some of her energy.' He reached for a piece of toast and attacked it, including his guest in the campaign with a gesture. 'Well now, as soon as you phoned I got on to Inspector Hodge who is my assistant on nights this week – I don't think you know him.' He blew out his cheeks, sketched in a waterfall moustache with three fleeting fingers, and favoured Campion with a slightly rakish leer, producing by the performance a lightning portrait of someone alarmingly real. 'He's a good chap,' he said. 'Old school cop. All beer, brain and bullockheart. Very comforting to have behind you. Thank you for leaving it till 6 a.m. by the way. The young woman was not so considerate, I have no doubt?'

'No. She telephoned at one in the morning.'

'Frightened stiff I suppose?'

'Upset.'

Luke put his shorn head on one side. 'Does she believe her Timothy could have done it?'

Mr. Campion sighed and his eyes were carefully expressionless behind his spectacles. 'I don't quite know what has happened yet. All I've been told is that the young man was taken to the Thurstable Inn station where he is said to be "helping the police" in their investigation.'

'Ah.' Luke was satisfied. 'I've got a bit more and the rest will come in in a minute. When I rang, Hodge had only got the preliminary. So far it's the simplest case of arson I've ever heard of. Evil without frills. You were at the place yesterday, I believe?' He was more than usually inquisitive, his narrow eyes watchful. 'I hear there's an ordinary, old-fashioned street-door with a letter-box hole in the middle. The typical square job with an iron surround and a flap but no actual box. The mail falls straight on to the mat as it did in grandpa's day. Is that right?'

'I couldn't tell you. The door stands open during office hours and I imagine the postman comes right in.'

'Very likely.' Luke dismissed the point as unimportant. 'Anyway it's a mean entrance. Bare boards and peeling paint and a short flight of wooden stairs leading to the main staircase, just inside. It's an old building which has undergone several conversions in its time. Am I right so far?'

'Yes I think so. My impression has always been that it was a bit pokey, you know. Dark and over-full of the eternal grained panelling. Horribly inflammable, I should think. Where did the fire start?'

'That's it. Just inside the front door. Someone merely posted three or four packets of household firelighters of the ordinary paraffinwax type, the final one of which was alight.' Luke laughed without amusement. 'Brilliantly simple and purely venal. The stairwell acted as a flue with a draught under the door, and the caretaker brewing up in the basement found he'd got five floors of blazing building over his head before he noticed the smell. The door burned in the end but not immediately and there was enough evidence to point to the firelighters. Actually one empty carton was found in the yard.'

'When was this?' Mr. Campion was listening in horror.

'Last night. The alarm went out at eight-thirty-four and the street door would have been closed around six. That's as near as they'd got when Hodge rang. The caretaker is in no condition to talk, but if he followed his normal routine he would have toured the building and wouldn't have gone down to the basement where he was found half suffocated until just before seven. It's too early to say how long a fire like that would take to get the hold it did, but I should say that your lady client's young man must have spent the night telling the boys at the Thurstable Inn station just exactly where he was between seven and eight-thirty.'

The thin man hesitated. 'He was with us in Bottle Street until about a quarter to seven, I suppose,' he said slowly.

'Fair enough.' Luke glanced at a note which he had propped up against a packet of cornflakes beyond his plate.

'Some bright young constable who knows him seems to have leapt forward with the information that he saw him coming home in "a dazed condition" to that house of the Kinnits in Scribbenfields at approximately eight-twenty. He must have been somewhere.'

Mr. Campion did not speak. He sat looking into his coffee cup until the Superintendent laughed.

'What does the crystal ball say?'

'Not enough!' Campion set down the cup and smiled at his old friend.

'I suppose we have to thank the Stalkey brothers for the promptness of police action?' he murmured.

'That doesn't surprise me, does it you?' Luke leant back in his chair, gupped discreetly, and produced a packet of cigarettes from his coat pocket. 'Look here,' he said without looking up. 'I've got complete faith in your judgement and I liked the girl, but while we're in lodge, so to speak, are you quite sure we're on the right horse in this business?'

Mr. Campion's pale eyes flickered wide open. 'It's not a doubt which had occurred to me,' he said frankly. 'Why?'

Luke hunched his wide shoulders and shook his cropped head from side to side with exaggerated uncertainty.

'There's a sort of awful similarity between this arson story and the original bit of bother out at Ebbfield. Both crimes have a frightening streak of modern efficiency in mischief about them. I shouldn't like to explain what I mean in court.' He raised his long hands absently and sketched in the sweeping lines of a full-bottomed wig. 'It's not evidence at all, but if you'd seen the damage done to that flat you'd know what I mean. There's something young and elemental and damn bad in both crimes.'

'I understood Timothy Kinnit had a very good alibi for the Ebbfield affair,' Mr. Campion objected gently.

'So he had" Luke agreed. '"Police-proof" is how it was described to me. They're very clever, these modern kids. They know how to gang up, too, better even than we did.'

Mr. Campion frowned, his kindly face was genuinely puzzled. 'Frankly I don't see your argument,' he said. 'According to Julia he's mad keen to know who he is.'

'Ah, that is what he *says*,' Luke objected patiently. 'That's his story. But it's a new one, isn't it? He's lived over twenty years and he's never tried to find out before, has he? It's the proposed marriage which has set this hare running, don't forget that. As soon as the marriage appears on the horizon – before even the girl's father pops up with his little query – the Kinnits get busy because they know they're going to be asked the awkward question. Detectives are employed, the whole family becomes excited and suddenly the boy makes a move. He does something about it. He makes a secret, rather silly but dramatic action to discourage the searchers.'

Mr. Campion made a sound of protest.

'Why?' he demanded. 'Why do you suppose this? An intelligent educated boy with a good record, good at sport, every future prospect excellent! Why should he suddenly start behaving like a lunatic thug?'

Luke leant further back in his chair and there was a disarming touch of colour in his dark cheeks. He was laughing and a little embarrassed.

'You're a dear chap, Campion,' he said. 'I like you and I like your approach. It makes me feel I'm riding in a Rolls; but sometimes I wonder if you're not a bit too nice, if you see what I mean. Look at it from my point of view. Here is a boy – not a specially bred one, conditioned over the generations to withstand a bit of cosseting like a prize dog – but an ordinary tough boy same like I was, packed with his full complement of pride and passion, and he's brought up to believe quite falsely that he's inherited the blessed earth. Money, position, background, servants, prospects. He's got the lot handed to him on a plate all for being his handsome self. He makes an effort and he's successful as well. Finally he gets the girl he's set his heart on. She's an heiress, a beauty and a social cop. For a dizzy fortnight or so he is the topmost, the kingpin, the biggest orange on the whole barrow! And then, at that very moment, what happens? A ruddy great Doubt as big as a house crops up. Security vanishes and there's a hole at his feet. The people he has known all his life as the corner stone of his existence suddenly start employing private detectives – *detectives* – halfbaked stuffed owls like Joe Stalkey – to go and find out who he, *he* himself, the sacred one-and-only, who he IS? Blimey! Couldn't that send him bonkers? Couldn't it?'

He finished the little oration with one hand outstretched and his eyebrows disappearing into his hairline. Mr. Campion remained looking at him curiously.

'I see what you suggest,' he said at last. 'I do, Charles. I do indeed.'

'But it hadn't occurred to you before?'

'No, no it hadn't. "Conditioned over the generations to with-stand cosseting" is a new conception to me.'

Luke laughed. 'I could be wrong,' he said. 'The kid could be exceptional and tough enough to take the treatment. But also I could be right. It's delicate going. One doesn't know where one is. My advice is play it cautiously and I'm glad we had a chat out here.'

The telephone bell from the shelf behind him cut short his warning and he took the call eagerly. The voice at the other end was a steady rumble and Mr. Campion waited, his fingers drum-ming absently on the brightly printed cloth. When Luke hung up his face was shadowed.

'Hodge has had a word with the D.D.I. and has been at the Thurstable Inn station all night,' he announced. 'The information is that the lad is bloody-minded and won't talk at all, so that's not very promising. He says he was at Ebbfield during the relevant period but won't say why or who he saw there. He merely de-scribes the borough, which is damn silly considering Ron Stalkey had already found him there in the morning. I don't know what he's playing at.'

Mr. Campion hesitated. 'He may be just growing very angry,' he ventured.

'Whatever he's growing it's trouble!' said Luke, drily. 'He's asking for it and the Kinnits are behaving like lunatics. One always finds it with these well-off egg-heads. They must live in space-helmets in the normal way of things! The moment life touches them on the skin they panic and start plaguing absolutely any eminent bird they happen to know personally to "pull strings"!' He pushed his chair back noisily from the table and stood up, six and a half feet of righteous indignation. 'Hodge says that amongst others Eustace Kinnit has telephoned the President of the London and Home Counties National Bank and the Keeper of the Speight Museum of Classic Antiquities in his attempt to find someone of influence to help him get the lad released. Neither of them as much use as my poor old Auntie Glad, and just about as unlikely! The kindest thing you could do, Campion, is to go down there right away and tell them gently to stop being so silly, antagonizing the police!' He paused in full flight. 'Oh and by the way, in the middle of all this a thought occurred to me. How did she know?'

'Who?'

'The young woman. The police didn't get round to the Well House after him until close on midnight and they wouldn't have let him do any telephoning. Yet by one she'd got on to you? How come? I thought there was supposed to be no liaison there on father's orders.'

Mr. Campion appeared interested. 'Odd,' he said. 'But, yes of course, the nurse. Don't forget the nurse, the ubiquitous Mrs. Broome.'

'Ah, very likely.' Luke was satisfied. 'She keeps on cropping up, that woman.'

'That's her way.' Mr. Campion got up as he spoke, and smiled briefly. 'I must apologize for my dubious chums. Thank you for the breakfast, Charles, and all the good counsel.'

He became silent. The door had opened and old Mrs. Luke, who was a force in her own right, came puffing in. She was carrying a baby of eighteen months or so whose arms were clasped tightly about her neck, so that she peered at him over the infant's shoulder. Her arrival was like a train, full of steam and bustle. She was very small and square, with Luke's own narrow black eyes and a ridiculous hair-do, tight and strained to her head and finished with a knob on top.

'I wondered when you were coming to see her, Mr. Campion,' she said reproachfully. 'Men are frightened of babies I know, but she's past that stage now, aren't you, Love?'

The child which, Campion saw, was tall and fair suddenly turned its head and looked at him directly. His heart jolted and dismay crept over him. There it was, just as he had feared, the face again! Prunella Scroop-Dory herself, Luke's lost enchantress, had not had higher arches to her brows nor the promise of a rounder, more medieval forehead.

Mr. Campion had not disliked Prunella for her own sake but for Luke's, and now he pulled himself together hastily and said all the right things with the best grace in the world.

'What is her name?'

Luke grinned. 'Hattie,' he said. 'Her Mum, God bless her, wanted her called Atalanta, which is sweet but silly in a daughter of mine. It was after a character who was always being chased. This is the best we can do.'

Old Mrs. Luke beamed happily at the visitor.

'My daughter-in-law wasn't chased enough,' she remarked. 'A sweeter woman never drew breath but she didn't think enough of herself, being too well trained. That won't happen to you, Love, will it?'

The baby, appealed to, laughed revealingly as infants often do and the startled Campion found himself confronted by Prunella's aristocratic face with Luke's cockney intelligence blazing out of it like the sun in the morning. He went off feeling chastened and secretly apprehensive. It had occurred to him that in fourteen or fifteen years there might well be a personality of considerable striking force in Linden Lea. He put the thought from him; at the moment he had more immediate trouble to contend with. As soon as he was well out of the district he stopped the car at a kiosk and called Julia.

She answered at once, which told him that she had been waiting at the telephone, and her reaction to his cautious *précis* of the news to date was swift and practical.

'I think we ought to see the family at once,' she said. 'I'll meet you at Scribbenfields in twenty minutes.'

'Very well. But are you going to find that embarrassing? I mean – I thought there was a certain amount of pressure to keep you apart.'

'Oh, I'm past all that.' The tired young voice pulled him up and reminded him of the bright, sharp world of his teens in which all colours were vivid and pain was always acute.

'Of course,' he said. 'I'm sorry. I'll be there.'

With a little manœuvring they contrived to meet on the door-step which now, in mid-morning, was in a boiling stream of passers-by, hurrying business people speeding past in a flurry of fumes and dust in the bright haze. Any apprehension which Campion might have felt about their welcome was dispelled by Eustace who opened the door to them himself. After his first blank stare of non-recognition, his face lit up like a delighted child's.

'Splendid!' he exclaimed unexpectedly. 'Hooray! Just the two minds we want on the problem. This is wonderful. We're all up in the sitting-room putting our heads together you know. Putting our heads together!' It would have been untrue and unkind to have suggested that he was enjoying the emergency, but the unaccustomed crisis was certainly exercising emotions he did not usually experience and there was new colour in his cheeks. He led them to the big room with the pink upholstery and the garden of cacti on the hearth. Alison and Mrs. Telpher, the family likeness less acute now that they were together, were talking to a round middle-aged man who wore careful clothes and possessed the solicitor's occupational expression of slight incredulity.

He turned as they appeared and regarded them doubtfully as Eustace made the introductions.

'And this is Mr. Woodfall,' Eustace said. 'He has looked after our affairs for years but not, I'm afraid, in this sort of caper. We're having a little difficulty, Campion. Tim won't ask for a legal representative to be present and Woodfall can't very well force himself on the police, he tells me.' There was the faintest hint of inquiry in the words and Campion met the lawyer's eyes with sympathy. Mr. Woodfall looked away at once.

Meanwhile Alison turned from the open bureau where she had paused in her restless wandering. A fault in a half-written page lying there had caught her attention and she had stooped to correct it in exactly the same way that another type of woman might have paused in a trying situation to put a picture straight. 'I don't know what's the matter with the boy,' she said, replacing the pen carefully in its tray. 'It's so unlike him, to be awkward. You've never found him *awkward*, have you, Julia?'

The query focused everyone's attention on the girl and everybody noticed at the same moment how angry she was. Her face was pale and strained and her eyes were dark with misery. 'I think he may be in a very excited condition,' she said huskily. 'After all, he's had rather a lot to put up with.'

'I suppose he has.' It was Mrs. Telpher speaking from her seat in the corner of the long couch. She was an oasis of calm in the room, sitting there in her quiet clothes, aloof and elegant. 'I don't really know him, of course, and he's not terribly like the rest of the family, naturally. Much more dominant in many ways.' She smiled kindly at Julia. 'A man of action. It stands out, you know. But I don't think he'd do anything capricious would he? He must feel he can manage on his own. Am I right?' She glanced at Eustace, who nodded.

'Yes,' he said. 'Very good, Geraldine. Dominant; that is the word. That's a very good word. I don't see why he's being kept there, though, I really don't.'

Mr. Campion drifted towards Mr. Woodfall, who moved back a little.

'The Stalkey Brothers are being very explicit, I suppose?' Campion murmured the words but Alison heard him from across the room and paused, like some slender bird, her grey eyes penetrating.

'It was I who persuaded Mr. Woodfall to let us employ the Stalkeys again,' she remarked. 'In fact I suppose I started the whole wretched business. Eustace was all for letting sleeping dogs lie and now I realize he may have been right, but I expected that we should have an inquiry from Julia's father and I thought we ought to be ready for it to save embarrassment. I had no idea that old Mr. Stalkey had died and the sons would prove to be so inferior. My recollection of the old man was that he was rather kind and not really too unintelligent.'

'I assure you they are very reliable people.' If Mr. Woodfall had requested her in so many words to cease being indiscreet, he could hardly have made his meaning more clear. He took a fine antique watch from his waistcoat and consulted it and directed a brief smile at the whole company. 'I must go,' he said. 'If the young man should decide to change his mind and answer perfectly proper police questions, don't hesitate to call on me and I shall do the best I can.'

'You're behaving as if you think he did it!' Julia's youth betrayed her and Mr. Woodfall shied like a startled pony before the outburst. He became very severe.

'Not I, young lady,' he said. 'You don't either, I hope?'

'No, I know he didn't.'

'Ah. Was he with you?' He pounced on the idea hopefully but relapsed into gloom again when she shook her head.

'I just know he couldn't have done anything so silly.'

'You're very lucky to be able to speak with such conviction for any man.' He laughed as he spoke, not unkindly but with that little edge of superiority which is cynicism's only privilege, and returned to Alison. 'I must go.'

'Must you? I thought you were staying to lunch.' Nevertheless she moved to the door with him as she spoke, and his laughing protest that he had two appointments before then in his office, and could see himself out, floated back to them from the passage.

'That reminds me, Eustace.' Alison spoke as she came hurrying back into the room and took a large, old-fashioned public house menu card from a drawer in the bureau. It was a dog-eared product, the blanks on the printed folder filled with cramped handwriting in violet ink. 'I always forget to do this,' she went on, 'and they do like it early. Let me see. There's oxtail. Will you like that?'

Eustace smiled at the visitors.

'We used to have the most frightful bothers about meals,' he said with the shy charm which was his most attractive attribute. 'With the vanishing of the domestic it seemed to me that food in the home was destined to be a thing of the past for anyone like myself who is purely an intellectual worker, but I might have known my wonderful sister. Now she merely rings up the *Star and Garter* down the road, and lo and behold we have luncheon on our own table as we always did.' He hesitated and his lips, which looked so pink in his beard, twisted wryly. 'The fare is rather nasty, of course, but one can't help that.'

Alison laughed. She was pink and girlish at his praise. 'Is it the food or the china?' she inquired. 'I shall never know. Those very thick, smeary plates with the smudged blue crest are terribly off-putting, but one can't very well scrape everything off on to Wedgwood, it would get so messy.'

'And cold!' said Eustace. 'And there would be two lots of washing up for someone. Oh no, I think we do very well. Yes. I'll have the oxtail but not peas. I don't like their plastic peas. I shall stick to onions. They do onions very nicely.'

'Eustace has onions every day of his life and with everything.' Alison was still gay.

'Better be safe than sorry!' said Eustace, sounding as if he thought the phrase was original. 'Now. Who is going to join us? You Geraldine, I know, but how about Julia and Campion?'

'And Aich.' Alison was scribbling on a telephone pad. 'Geraldine, you and I will have the plaice, I expect, and Aich will have the joint whatever it is. A great meat-eater, Aich.'

'Thank you.' Geraldine drew her beautifully shod feet up on to the sofa beside her as she spoke. Her Italian shoes suggested wealth more discreetly than any other single item he had ever seen, Mr. Campion reflected. 'What about Mrs. Broome?' she inquired wistfully. 'Doesn't she eat?'

'Nanny Broome does her own catering. She's not with us up here all the time, you see. She won't touch anything cooked outside.' It was evident that Alison saw nothing incongruous in the statement. 'I pay her extra money and she fends for herself.'

'Interesting,' Eustace said with apparent seriousness. 'I don't think she's a vegetarian either. Now Julia, my dear, can I tempt you to a dish of oxtail?'

The girl looked at him with flickering disbelief.

'No,' she said firmly. 'Thank you very much but aren't we going to do something about Tim?'

'I agree.' Alison was jotting down the luncheon order as she spoke. 'But of course there are two schools of thought about whether one *should* interfere even if one knew quite *how*. Eustace found the Police most unco-operative when he went down there last night. And then one doesn't know what Tim's own attitude is. At the moment we're relying on Flavia Aicheson. She's gone down to see the Ebbfield Councillor.'

Mr. Campion heard the news with dismay. 'I don't think the police react very favourably to high-powered pressure from outside,' he began hesitantly.

'I know! And it's not easy to get it either!' Alison's grey eyes met his own. 'People want to help one but they don't feel they ought to. The Councillor, whose name is Cornish, was quite abrupt with poor Aich this morning when she telephoned him. They're old enemies and Aich took a risk in approaching him, but she regards Tim as a nephew and just put her pride in her pocket and went ahead. When Mr. Cornish said he wouldn't go to the Turstable Inn station to speak for the boy she just hung up the receiver and went down to fetch him.'

'But why?' Julia exploded. 'Why upset the police by getting hold of someone who doesn't even want to worry them?'

Alison remained happily unruffled.

'Of course,' she said kindly. 'You don't know, but Tim went to Ebbfield yesterday and saw this man. He happened to mention it when he came in. We're naturally hoping that they were together at the important time. The only awkward thing seems to be that the boy didn't make it clear to Mr. Cornish why he had called on him, and so when this query came up the man immediately wondered if the visit had been made on purpose to manufacture an alibi. He seems to be a difficult person with a highly suspicious mind.'

'Wait!' Eustace spoke from the window where he was standing looking down into the street. 'Here *is* Aich getting out of a cab. Ah yes, she's got the man with her. This must be he. He couldn't be anything but a firebrand councillor could he? Look. Oh! yes, by George! Yes. This is wonderful. Tim is with them. They've got him away. Wait a moment; Mrs. Broome may still be out with that extraordinary wreath. I'll go and let them in.'

CHAPTER ELEVEN

The Councillor

MISS AICHESON was first into the room. She came striding across the black polished boards which were scattered with fine worn old rugs, and the ancient timbers shook beneath her while the dust motes in the shaft of London sunlight, streaming through diamond panes, danced wildly at her approach. She looked tired but triumphant and she turned to Alison for praise.

'Done it!' she announced. 'Tim is on the stairs now. Councillor Cornish is with us, and by the way, dear, I think *all* the credit ought to go to him.

'Oh *splendid*! Quite, quite wonderful, Aich.' Alison Kinnit's emphasis was nearly generous but her glance wandered at once to the menu in her hand and she almost mentioned it, only thinking better just in time as the Councillor, with Eustace fussing behind him, appeared in the doorway.

Here in the Well House Councillor Cornish was still a vigorous personality, but this morning there was a new wariness about him and there was caution in the fierce eyes under the shock of grey hair. His astonishment on meeting Alison for the first time was slightly funny. Her thistledown quality appeared to bewilder him, and if he had actually said that he had expected to see a second version of Miss Aicheson he could hardly have made the point more clearly.

The reaction was not new to Miss Kinnit and she became more feminine than ever, twittering and smiling.

'Thank you, thank you. We are all so very relieved.' Her intelligent eyes met his own gratefully. 'I'm just ordering lunch. You will join us, won't you?'

'I? No, really!' He sounded appalled. 'Thank you very much of course, but I only want to have a word with the young man.' He was preparing to explain further when an interruption occurred.

Tim had arrived. He glanced round the room, caught sight of Julia and walked over to her, his face dark as a storm.

'*Darling*!' he exploded. 'I did so pray that you'd have the good sense to keep right out of this! Why didn't you do what I told you?' He was on edge and his protest was unreasonably savage.

The colour rushed into Julia's face, Eustace made a deprecating cluck, and everyone was startled by the Councillor, who turned on the speaker.

'*Don't* shut her out when she's backing you up!' he exclaimed violently. Realizing his interference was outrageous, he tried to cover it. He smiled at Julia, rubbed his ear and shot a sidelong, slightly sheepish smile at Timothy.

'I'm sorry,' he said. 'Can I meet the young lady?'

It was a direct apology, and Tim relaxed.

'I do beg your pardon,' he said quickly. 'Yes, of course. I'm afraid I was surprised to see her here. Julia, this is Councillor Cornish but for whom I should be in jug, I suppose.'

'Would you? That's what I wanted to talk to you about. Is there anywhere where we could have a word on our own?'

'Yes, of course,' Timothy looked surprised but acquiescent and the unexpected objection came from Eustace.

He came forward, smiling, so smooth in his old-fashioned way that both the Councillor and Tim appeared clumsy beside it.

'You two mustn't shut any of us out,' he said gently. 'We want to hear all about it. We've been sitting here completely in the dark, consumed by a most natural curiosity. I know a little about the fire because I've read the report in the *Telegraph*, but that's all. Why did you decide to keep so silent, my boy? Our solicitor was most anxious to be present at any interrogation. Why didn't you co-operate?'

Tim shrugged his shoulders. He looked tall and big-boned standing there, his face, which was still scarred, pale and stiff with fatigue. He eyed Eustace and laughed. 'Because I was sulking, I suppose.'

'But was that wise?' Eustace was at his mildest, innocently inquiring without a trace of malice.

'No. It was silly. But they made me absolutely furious.'

'You're talking about the police?'

'Yes.'

Eustace jerked his chin up and his neat beard looked sharp.

'They have a very fine reputation,' he said gravely and his eyes were reproachful rather than severe.

'Well, they got my goat.' Timothy was being factual. 'Probably I was in the wrong, but to drag me out in the middle of the night and keep me in a smelly office while two highpowered thugs told me I must know what I'd done, and would I "come clean", for hours and hours on end seemed high-handed.'

'But you could have told them where you'd been.'

'If they'd been polite about it I should have, but they were excited because it was such a damned awful fire. They knew Ron Stalkey had been right about his beating me up, because they could see my face, and so they assumed that everything else he'd said about me setting light to his blessed office was probably true. The whole inference was so insulting and so *silly*, I'm afraid I just wouldn't play.'

Eustace was both hurt and amazed.

'But Tim,' he said. 'You're a civilized, intelligent young man. The police couldn't have behaved as you represent. Not the *British* police . . .'

The young man opened his mouth and shut it again and a sullen shadow settled over his eyes. At the same time there was a smothered sound from the Councillor, and as every-body turned to look at him it was discovered that he was laughing.

Eustace's glance grew cold.

'You don't agree with me?' he said so charmingly and with such disarming diffidence that the unobservant could have been misled.

'Of course I don't!' The Councillor checked himself. 'I mean I'm afraid I don't. I'm inclined to think that the young man has summed up the position pretty accurately. After all, the police are men. Only a nation which can honestly believe that by putting a boy in a helmet it can turn him into something between a guardian angel and a St. Bernard dog overnight could make the British Force what it is today, the worst used, worst paid, most sentimentalized-over body in creation.'

Eustace regarded him with frank amazement.

'Good Heavens!' he said. 'You consider there should be an enquiry do you?'

Something of the same sullenness which Eustace's reactions evoked in Timothy appeared in the Councillor.

'I am not to be drawn,' he said cagily, 'but I feel it might help if this country sometimes ceased to consider the police either through motorists' goggles or rose-coloured spectacles. As it is, ninety-nine per cent of them have chips on their shoulders. Since I don't want my affairs dealt with by chaps who feel like that if I can possibly help it, I keep away from the police as much as I can.' He paused and laughed again. 'If one's forced to talk to them, go to the top. The chaps at the top in the police are all men with something remarkable about them. They've got to be. They're the people who've been through the process without cracking.'

'You amaze me,' Eustace conveyed very nicely that he did not believe a word of it. 'But at the same time I don't see why Timothy *refused to help*. That is the point which mystifies me. I should have said that Timothy was the most courteous and obliging lad in the world. Why Tim? Why didn't you tell them where you had been?'

On the other side of the room Mr. Campion, who had been standing quietly by the window effacing himself with his usual success, began to find the conversation painful. This purely mental approach to what was after all a most acutely emotional problem, at least for Timothy, was getting under his skin and he turned to Geraldine Telpher who was sitting listening, her head bent and her gaze fixed on her folded hands.

'How is the child?' he murmured. 'May one ask?'

He was startled by her reaction. She was taken by surprise and the grey Kinnit eyes which met his own were dilated for an instant. 'I'm so sorry,' he said, embarrassed. 'I shouldn't have asked you so suddenly.'

'Not at all.' She became herself again, calm and intelligent. 'It's very kind of you. It's only that sometimes I find I'm not quite as brave as I think I am. Then I panic. She's just the same, thank you. Still unconscious. This is the second year.'

Mr. Campion was appalled. 'I had no idea. How old is she?'

'Nine. It's tragic, isn't it?' Her voice was intentionally inexpressive and he felt compelled to continue the conversation until she had recovered.

'Where is she? In hospital?'

'Yes. In St. Joseph of Arimathaea's. In a public ward!' Her smile was very wry. 'It's ironic but it can't be helped and she knows nothing. I was told that her only hope was to come to London to be seen by Sir Peter Phyffe. He's one of those dedicated men who won't take private patients and so there she is, poor baby.' She sighed and looked away. 'It was a car accident, her governess was driving.'

Mr. Campion murmured his sympathy. 'You're very convenient here for St. Joseph's,' he said consolingly.

'I know. Isn't it wonderful. Just behind us. That's why I'm so grateful to Eustace and Alison for asking me to stay. They really are wonderful, aren't they?'

Mr. Campion felt himself to be no judge of that point. Alison was still hovering with her alarming looking menu, while on the other side of the room Eustace was quietly persisting in trying to get a rational explanation for Timothy's behaviour.

'You seem to understand the boy rather better than I do, on this occasion at any rate," he was saying to the Councillor, a touch of acidity appearing in his voice for the first time. 'I'm very glad you do and we're all eternally grateful to you for coming forward like this – I won't say "to substantiate his story", but anyway to give him a complete alibi.'

The Councillor looked at him without moving his head. As he had been staring at the floor it was a sharp upward glance through his fierce brows, very characteristic and effective. Eustace paused abruptly, colour in his cheeks.

'I take it that you have?' he demanded.

'I was wondering,' the Councillor said frankly. 'That is why I came here to talk to the young man himself. The Police have let him go for the time being but that hardly means that they've lost interest in him. All I've done is to convince them that he was with me in Ebbfield during the period when the crime was almost certain to have been committed. "Almost" is not "quite" though, and arson is a notoriously difficult business to bring home to anybody. Do you see what I mean?'

'No,' said Eustate testily. 'You are simply telling us that it is a question of the time.'

'No, I'm saying it is a question of evidence. The Police naturally want to make out a case. But if their suspect can prove where he was during the *likely* period for the crime to have been committed, they've got to think again haven't they? They've got to widen their times or find another suspect.'

Eustace sighed. 'I can't believe the police, *our* police, work like that,' he said. 'However, I hear what you say. May I know what you want to ask Tim?'

'You want to know if I did it, don't you, sir?'

The young man who had been standing behind Julia's chair put the question wearily. He looked very tired, standing with his hands in his pockets, the dark smudges across his eyes emphasizing their colour. 'Well, I didn't.' He rubbed his hand round the back of his head and pulled his ear and laughed. 'It was such a damn *silly* thing to do!'

'A wicked thing!' Eustace put in quickly. He was prompting openly, rather as if he were prodding a junior at a business conference when the opposition was not too intelligent.

'But also imbecile.' Tim spoke with sudden affection, his warmth noticeable beside the older man's colder personality. 'For one thing, they're forced by law to be fully insured and the building was patently due for an overhaul. The fire may have saved their lives. No, if I had felt that I wanted to get my own back on the Stalkey Bros., and frankly it never occurred to me, I had only to tell the story to everyone I met. "Fuddy duddy firm of detectives beat up own client in fumbling zeal." It couldn't have done them any good wherever I mentioned it and they could hardly sue.'

'All right!' Councillor Cornish wiped his eyes with amusement. He appeared to be entertained out of all proportion to the joke. 'I take the point. I'm satisfied. Now I want to hear exactly why you came to see me yesterday.'

'I told you. I got your name from the cobbler in the Orient Road. That was before Ron Stalkey came in and we had the dust-up. I was waiting there talking to him for about an hour I suppose. He's a veteran of the 1914 war – a nice legless little bloke who talks and talks with his mouth full of tacks. Do you know him? I imagine most people in Ebbfield do.'

'Yes, I know him. His name is Tom Tray. Did you meet his sister Dora?'

'I didn't see a soul there until Ronald Stalkey arrived. After we started belting each other there was a crowd, of course. I went back in the evening to square up for any damage we'd done in the shop, but Tray was quite happy about it and reminded me that he'd told me to go and see you. So I did.'

'But that means you can prove that you were in Ebbfield earlier than Mr. Cornish here was able to tell the police?' Eustace deman-manded.

'Yes, I know. I told you. I did not set light to the Stalkey Office.'

'Nevertheless,' Eustace was persisting when the Councillor interrupted him in his own house.

'I've got that,' he said to Tim. 'What I want to know is *why?* How did you think I could help you?'

Miss Aicheson could bear it no longer. 'But I explained all that to you when I was persuading you to come down to the Thurstable Inn police station this morning. Otherwise you wouldn't have come, would you?' She spoke from across the room, her voice more flutelike than ever. The Councillor coloured.

'I'd like to hear it from the boy himself,' he protested, making it a grievance. 'Why did you come to see me, Tim?'

His use of the Christian name jarred on the family and the young man himself did not answer at once but stood hesitating. It was a silent tussle between them. The whole room was aware of it.

'Well?'

Timothy shrugged his shoulders helplessly.

'If you've already discussed the story with Miss Aicheson, do I really have to tell it again?'

'About this belated search for your identity?'

'Yes.'

'I see. Having actually seen the squalor of your beginnings you've become violently ashamed of them. Is that right?'

Cornish was trying to be offensive and succeeding. Eustace bristled and Alison made a little protesting sound.

Tim laughed. It was a chuckle of irreverent amusement at the pomposity of the accusation. His eyes narrowed, his wide mouth turned up, and a rare shaft of gaiety which was not a normal part of his everyday make-up appeared for a flashing instant.

'My heart did not leap up when I beheld the gasworks, sir. Since you ask me, no.'

His reaction was a relief to most people present, but the effect of it upon the Councillor was devastating. The man appeared to freeze. He stood rigid for an instant.

'I'm afraid I can't help you,' he said stiffly. 'I was in the R.A.F. by the end of 1938. All we young apprentices were in the reserve. I didn't get to know Ebbfield very well until the war was over. Surely some public records were saved?'

'None,' said Eustace. 'Naturally we looked into that immediately.'

His mind, which was always unhappy and fumbling when emotions of any kind were involved, seized on the purely factual point gratefully.

'It was a tremendous story. I was fascinated when I went into it. When we first inquired during the war the books – ledgers, registers, or whatever they were – had been evacuated and were unobtainable; when we asked again later we were told they had been returned on the very morning before the first great raid which destroyed half the district, and were completely lost.'

'Yes of course. Yes, I remember now. I've heard that in another connection.' The Councillor was still subdued. 'I'm sorry,' he said again, speaking to Tim. 'I can't help. What are you going to do? Shall we expect to see you wandering about the district, looking for clues?'

'Probably not.' Eustace spoke blandly before the younger man could reply. He was smiling in his pleasant adult way and seemed disposed to be philosophical.

'But you can understand the boy's interest,' he went on. 'When one is a child one gathers scraps of information about oneself, little pieces of embroidery from nurses and so on, and one weaves perhaps a rather romantic story until the time comes when cool reason demands facts which are dull and even a trifle drab compared with a tale of fancy, all moonshine and romance.'

The Councillor stared at him. 'Romance!' he exploded. 'My God, if you want romance you must go to reality! The things she thinks up take the shine out of any old invention. I'm sorry I can't help you. If the police need me again presumably they'll contact me, or of course I shall be available to any lawyer of yours. That's really all I can do at the moment. Good-bye.'

He would have left without shaking hands had not Eustace put out his own, and Tim would have followed him down to let him out but there was an unexpected development.

Julia got up and came over. She was smiling politely.

'Councillor, I'm going the same way as you are, and I must go now. We'll go together if you don't mind.'

Tim looked at her in amazement and there was a moment when Cornish hesitated and she stood placidly forcing him to think twice about being rude to her.

'Why not?' he said at last. 'Come along.'

They went out of the room with Tim behind them.

Eustace smiled first at his sister and then at the others.

'A funny fellow,' he said mildly. 'In many ways an extra-ordinary fellow. Did you notice he was so excitable and emotional he was almost in tears at one point? What a char-acter Julia is, too! She got him out of the room in case he upset Tim any further. I like her, she has special courage. Very rare these days.'

Alison looked at the menu in her hand.

'Now I really must make my list,' she said, 'or everything nice will be off. What will Tim have, I wonder?'

CHAPTER TWELVE

The Cobbler's Shop

COUNCILLOR CORNISH paused at a bus-stop and glanced down at his companion dubiously.

He was hatless and the charcoal-coloured raincoat flapping about his bones echoed the tint and texture of his fierce hair and eyebrows, so that he looked like a grey Irish elkhound slinking along silently beside an elegant child of whom he was privately terrified.

He cleared his throat: 'I get my bus here for Ebbfield,' he said.

'I do too.' Julia did not look at him. There was a reckless obstinacy about her which he was trying not to recognize, it frightened him so.

'What are you going to do in Ebbfield?' He fumbled over the words and she moved as the red monster came bearing down on them and made a gesture to shoo him on to it ahead of her.

'I've got business on the way there,' she said and followed him on to the half-empty lower deck.

As the acceleration jerked them into a seat far up in the front, he spoke grudgingly:

'I hear your father is a man of drive. You take after him I suppose?'

'I suppose so,' she said. 'I want to talk to you about Tim.'

'I've told all I know. I've given a statement to the police. He was at my house from approximately seven-thirty to eight o'clock. I've done all I can.' He was keeping his voice down, for a London bus is no place to shout in, and kept looking at her in a kind of horror. She had trapped him, he saw; even a teashop would not have afforded more restraining conditions. He could not storm out from a vehicle jolting and swaying over the ancient stones of Scribbenfields at forty miles an hour.

Julia turned her head and regarded him with an accusing stare.

'It's not that. You think you know who his family is, don't you?'

'I certainly don't! You're off your head, young woman —'

He did not finish the sentence; the need to keep reasonably quiet was hampering him but even so his reaction was unconvincing to himself. He was silent for a moment and she continued to look at him.

'You do, don't you?'

'What makes you think that?'

'Because it's the same family as yours.'

She spoke hastily, and leaning back suddenly in her seat ran her hand up behind her head and brought it down to pull her ear. It was a curious gesture which was very distinctive yet familiar to him.

'I don't do it very well,' she remarked. 'But you and Tim do it all the time, whenever you're embarrassed. You're doing it now.'

'You're mad!' He pulled his hand down from his ear and sat gaping at her. 'That's the most absurd and dangerous accusation I ever heard in my life. I should advise you —'

She sat frowning, looking at him. 'I don't see why you're so excited,' she said, and her innocence becoming suddenly apparent set the ground quaking under his feet. 'Surely you've got *some* relations? Tim is a very nice person. They might be very glad to know.'

'I can't say anything about that.' He felt as if he were shuffling his feet.

'Of course you can't,' she said with enormous reasonableness. 'That's why I wanted to talk to you alone. Haven't you got brothers or sisters or even cousins? You see, I don't know if you know but family characteristics, gestures particularly, are liable to crop up most unexpectedly. I know my father had a Canadian cousin who came over in the army in the war. They'd never met and their parents hadn't met since they were literally babies, and yet the first thing this man did when he came into the house was to push his hair, which was quite short, back over his ears with both hands. No one had ever seen anyone but Daddy do that. It was quite meaningless too, because neither of them had ever worn their hair long, and —'

'You're sure you're right about young Timothy?' he interrupted her gently. 'About the ear-pulling?'

'Oh yes.' She smiled at him with complete assurance. 'I watch everything Tim does. I've seen him do it hundreds of times and so when you did it too I watched you too. Besides, you may not know it, but you smile the same way and the big planes at the sides of your faces are identical. It wouldn't be so extraordinary if you were distant relatives, would it? You both come from the same place apparently.'

'No, I don't come from Ebbfield,' he said woodenly. 'I was born in Norfolk. I came to London as an apprentice. I can't help you in that way at all. If the police want to put him through it again he can call on me. That's as far as I can go.'

'I see,' she said bleakly and continued to ride beside him in silence. 'It's very good of you,' she ventured at last. 'Please don't feel we're not very grateful.'

He grunted and looked out over her dark head at one of the least beautiful main roads in the world; there was mile upon mile of it, a wide-worn ribbon lined with shabby two-storey shops and shabbier open spaces.

'Have you ever been in love before?' He put the question so reluctantly that it sounded angry.

'No. Not really.' She flushed and shot an apologetic smile at him. 'Not with a real person.'

'I see.' He was smiling despite himself. 'And how long has it lasted so far?'

'Oh, ever since I first saw him. It's an "always and forever": one usually knows, I think. Don't you?'

He drew his eyebrows together and sat for a moment framing a question which, when it came, was utterly unexpected.

'You say you watch him all the time?' he began at last. 'Did you happen to be looking at him when he made that damn silly remark about the gasworks? I'd been taking the mickey out of him and he suddenly spiked me with a certain kind of flippancy, with a funny sort of grin on his mouth . . .'

'I know. Like a cat laughing.' He saw to his relief that she had not thought the question in the least extraordinary. 'He doesn't do it often. It's always when someone is being a bit pomp – or a bit grand, you know. That's not like your family surely, is it?'

He laughed briefly. 'No,' he said. 'It's not like my family or me. Not at all.' Once again he looked out at the dismal road and there was water suddenly in his fierce eyes. 'Not at all,' he repeated.

Julia was not listening to him. 'What worries me is that it must be someone,' she remarked. 'Someone really is doing these awful things . . .'

'Setting light to office buildings?'

'Or tearing up old people's homes. You know Tim was asked where he was when that flat down here in the East End was smashed up? We simply couldn't understand it at the time. The police were awfully polite and cautious, and since Tim didn't know then that the Kinnits were employing the Stalkeys to ferret round Ebbfield the questions sounded insane. We'd never heard of Ebbfield. He soon satisfied the detective that he hadn't been out of Oxford that week at all and the man went away.' She paused and sat looking at him with wide-open eyes. 'It must have been the flat-wrecking that the police were investigating though, because it happened about then and the Stalkey who was making the inquiry was staying in it, wasn't he? I only heard about that last night from Tim's old nurse, Mrs. Broome.'

'Where had she heard of it?'

She frowned. 'I don't know. Alison Kinnit, perhaps. But Tim must have heard it yesterday from the Stalkey brother who attacked him. I expect that was the real reason why he was so difficult when the police began to question him again. Being wrongfully suspected of some crime you don't know anything about is all very well if it happens once, but it's rather different if they do it to you twice. It's so frightening. Suppose they pin something on him?'

'When he's innocent?'

'Of course. That's what I'm trying to tell you. Someone is doing these dreadful things. Who is it?'

'How should I know?'

'But don't you?' Her gentle persistence appalled him. 'Can't you think round and see who it might be? Can't you guess?'

'Why should I? What are you talking about?' His voice rose in panic and the old working man dozing on the seat beyond them opened an eye and regarded him with idle curiosity.

Julia sighed. 'I don't know. I'm just at the end of what I can bear, I think. I was sitting there in that pink room, looking round at all those people and thinking how well they all meant and how useless they all were, and wondering who *was* there who could possibly help us. And I looked at you and I thought that you really were awfully like an older Tim and you'd been dragged into the business by a sort of Act of God anyhow, and I felt suddenly that I could *make* you think of something which could give us a lead.'

'Do you know what you're saying?' He was looking at her in a kind of horror. 'Can you hear yourself?'

Tears came into her eyes. 'Oh *don't*,' she said. 'Don't bully. Just try to help.'

The fact that she was strained to a point beyond reasoning, and was proceeding by intuition's reckless compass alone, came home to him. He remained quiet, watching her warily and she returned his stare, her eyes utterly without guile. At last he became convinced that she was only conscious of making a vague but passionately felt appeal for help and he spoke cautiously.

'You're thinking that because I live down here and know the people I might be able to find out something? Is that it?'

'You've got some authority.'

'Suppose I find some suspect and can't prove anything? What do you expect me to do then?'

He had begun to breathe again and it was a return to his normal manner, just a fraction aggressive and unsure.

'But you know what to do.' The protest was inspired. 'You told everybody less than an hour ago. You said the only thing to do was to avoid the ordinary police and go to the very top flight. That's what I came with you to tell you. I know one of them. He's a Mr. Charles Luke, a senior something or other at New Scotland Yard. I've met him and I think you're right and one could tell him anything. He's larger than life but —'

'I know Luke.'

'You do?' She smiled with radiant relief. 'That's miraculous! That's what people mean when they say a thing is "meant". Start thinking who it might be and if it comes to you – and I've got a hunch it will – then you go straight to him. You will, won't you?'

He got up to get away from her and out into the air. There was sweat on his forehead and he stood for a moment swinging on the rail before he bent to take her hand.

'I get off here,' he murmured. 'There's a request stop. Good-bye.'

She held his hand tightly.

'You will try?'

'I will, God help me,' he said and hurried off the bus, leaving her to go on alone to the Ebbfield Market Cross.

It was the next stop; she got down and paused for a moment looking about her. The Old Cross proved to be a Music Hall now used as a box factory, and it lay before her as ornate and derelict as a toy in a dustbin. She was still in that strange mood when hypersensitiveness reaches the point almost of clairvoyance, a direct product of emotional exhaustion in the otherwise healthy. As she pulled her wide blue coat about her, and her eyes, which echoed its colour, wandered over the immediate view, the squalor of the place crept very close.

She was standing in a vast drab circus where five highways met and the heavy transport vehicles rattled and crashed over a patch-work of every known road surface. The filthy pavements were not crowded and many of the shops which lined them were closed, yet the passers-by were all going somewhere, all well fed and gaily dressed but apparently tired out, their eyes dust-rimmed and their skin sallow. It was the lunch hour and the steamy windows of the eating houses, pubs, and coffee bars were like blind eyes. For

London's East End it was a singularly uncosy neighbourhood, neither friendly nor even noisy but hurried and dirty and preoccupied.

The name-plate saying *Carroway Street* above the public house on the nearest corner caught her attention and she set out to walk down it. She was looking for the cobbler's shop without any very clear idea of why she wanted to see it. Her business on the way to Ebbfield had been done.

The road was very long and passed through many phases, none of them particularly attractive, and at one point, having walked for what seemed like half a mile beside a twenty-foot hoarding, she almost lost heart; but presently, as so often happens in London, the whole character of the thoroughfare changed abruptly and it became for a hundred yards or so a village High Street which, although decayed was still a definite entity.

All the familiar shops were there, the gay greengrocers, the coal office, the rather horrible butchers, and the forlorn laundrette looking like some unspeakable peepshow. And then, very much in keeping amongst them, the place she was looking for.

Mr. T. K. Tray's establishment turned out to be unexpectedly alive. It was a double-fronted shop, with one window devoted to the boot and shoe repair business, and the other to newspapers and magazines with a sprinkling of cheap stationery, tobacco and confectionery. There was a panel of small advertisements beside the door and a notice offering an accommodation address.

At the moment it was besieged. A fast-moving queue of chattering women, most of whom appeared to know each other, was forcing its way into the darkened doorway and every so often one of them squeezed back out again and shot away like a bee from a hive, a brightly-coloured periodical in her hand.

The beginning of the queue was a crowd on the pavement, and Julia, who could not pause outside without joining it, found herself sucked into the jostling stream. She gathered that the cause of the excitement was the little polythene packets of detergent being given away with one of the Woman's magazines. They were worth perhaps a penny and each woman was determined to get her due before the supply ran out. As soon as Julia realized that escape was

impossible until she had done the round, she began to feel suffocated. Many of the women were factory workers, their boiler-
suits and headscarves lending them the ruthless cameraderie which
paper hats on an outing lend a charabanc load. They were all in a
hurry, all in ferocious good humour, all hot, and all laughing
aloud. The brutal noise, meaningless as a bird call, reached an intensity which stunned her and she became swallowed up in a whirl-
pool of sound in which scraps of intelligible sentences were few
and all ugly. The uniformed factory women were imitating their
menfolk and swearing as they never did in the normal way when
each was as it were a private person. The trickle of dirty fantasy
threading through the cackle produced a shocking sound which
she had not met before, and which gave her the illusion that there
were no individuals present, only a single merciless personality.

As the queue fed her relentlessly into the dark shop the stale,
sweaty smell of leather and newsprint met her in a wave, and as her
eyes grew accustomed to the shadow she saw the counter embedded in a grotto made of magazines. Her impression was that
there were two figures in the dark cavern behind it and that one of
them was telephoning at a wall instrument hanging amid the
crowded shelves, whilst the other, who was little more than a vast
stuffed bodice swinging there, was handing out papers and packets
with the speed of a machine. As she approached the end of the line
she caught sight for the first time of the half-dozen copies of a
periodical which decorated the shelf on the front of the counter.

'*Oracle,*' it said. '*Oracle. Oracle. Oracle.*'

It was as she was actually looking at the word in supersitious
astonishment that a single intelligible name suddenly leapt out of
the noise.

'Basil Kinnit!'

She heard the words as clearly as if they had been a phrase in the
mother tongue amid a torrent of foreign language.

'*Basil Kinnit!*'

There was no way of telling who had spoken. Either of the two
behind the counter could have said it or it could have come from
any of the brass-lined throats screaming about her.

'Basil Kinnit' said the oracle.

She threw down a sixpence, received her magazine, and sped out into the air. As she came into the light again the nightmare of the shop receded and reality broke over her like morning.

'But there's no such person,' she said aloud. 'No such person at all.'

CHAPTER THIRTEEN

'The Top of the Police'

COUNCILLOR CORNISH'S request for an immediate interview was so unexpected that Superintendent Luke went out of his way to grant it at once and saw his caller in one of the private interrogation rooms. It was a square, austere office where the desk was very wide and very solid. Too wide to lean across, too solid to be turned over. Yet the room was pleasant enough with a view across the grey river.

They had been talking for some minutes and Luke sat prodding the blotting-paper in front of him with a long-suffering pen. He was fascinated and his shorn head was held sideways, his black eyes fixed, and his shoulders, which were so wide in comparison with his narrow hips, hunched as he doodled on the folder.

Councillor Cornish sat back in his chair opposite, his feet together, his hands folded in his lap and his head bowed in the traditional way of resignation. It was not a conscious pose. Luke had been watching him like a cat and had decided that the man was genuine. He was acting under a strong compulsion moving from a sense of duty deeply rooted, and the source of his fanaticism was unveiled. His sense of guilt was temporarily appeased, his truculence gone. He was making his sacrifice completely at peace.

'We shall have to check each point,' Luke said. 'You know that, don't you?'

'I suppose so.' There was no secret complaisance. The policeman was listening for it. "The wallowing martyr", as he called the type, was one of his private hates. He noticed with relief that Cornish was merely regretful.

'Go as easy you can with us all,' was his only request.

Luke offered him a cigarette. 'Don't worry about that, sir. We're not quite as hamfisted as we're said to be. At least we try. Well now, you've spent three hours with this boy and you think he could be yours. Is that your first point?'

'Not quite. I should *like* to think he was mine. That's the danger. But whether he is or not isn't my reason for visiting you.'

Luke nodded. 'I appreciate that. You're merely going on his history as you know it, plus certain likenesses?'

'Yes.'

'And you'd never heard that history – in regard to young Timothy Kinnit that is – until today, when it was told you by Miss Flavia Aicheson while she was persuading you to give evidence on his behalf? You don't think she realized that the history might have some significance for you?'

'Oh no. She merely wanted me to tell the police that he had visited me yesterday evening.'

'And he had?'

'Yes.'

'Do you know why?'

'I didn't know at the time, and this afternoon when he gave me an explanation I didn't believe him, but now since a certain idea has occurred to me I think I do. He told me that the cobbler in Carroway Street had sent him to me.'

'And in view of the likeness between you, you think the cobbler might have done so?'

Cornish smiled. 'You're very shrewd Superintendent,' he said, relaxing. 'Tommy Tray was mending shoes in that same shop when I first came to Ebbfield. He'd lost both legs on the Somme in the First World War and when I first knew him I was about the age which Timothy is now. My first wife and I used the newsagent half of his shop, which was and is run by his sister, as an accommodation address for our letters. My wife lived actually in Turk Street with her only relative, an aunt who was an illiterate, suspicious old woman whom we never trusted not to give us away, so we used the shop very frequently and often went there. I imagine that when Timothy went in recently, asking questions, old Tray noticed something about him which made him send him along to me. It's the sort of thing he would do.'

'Your first wife?' Luke murmured, his pen resting on a note he had made. 'Excuse me, sir. Were you in fact married to her?'

'Yes.'

'It can be proved can it?' Forgive me, but it's as well to get everything quite clear as we go along.'

'I know. I realize too that there is a gap in all the Ebbfield records of about that time, but although Somerset House, even, may not have the details, I can say that I have reason to believe that at least one copy of the marriage certificate is in existence.'

The odd phrase came out softly in the quiet room and Luke's glance kicked upward as if an elusive quarry he had been seeking had suddenly appeared.

'Good,' he said, making the comment non-committal. 'I have this straight now, then. One year before the Second World War, at the time of the famous Munich crisis, when war almost broke out, you were in Ebbfield finishing your apprenticeship to the small tool-making firm of Boxer & Coombe Ltd., which you now own.'

'My present wife and I own it in equal shares. She was a Miss Boxer, her mother was a Miss Coombe.'

'Ah yes. I see.' Luke's pen was busy again. 'In autumn 1938 – that is at the time of the Munich agreement – you were a member of the Royal Air Force Volunteer Reserve and you were called up and drafted to a training camp in Yorkshire. Is that when you married your first wife?'

'No. We married in the first week of July of that year.' Cornish was smiling at the recollection as if he had never thought of the ceremony since it happened. He was remarkably relaxed and the fierce energy which had made him a somewhat uncomfortable companion had disappeared. 'We were "done",' he said, laughing a little, 'in a dusty church in Saracen's Square. I don't suppose you've ever heard of the place. It's all gone now. We turned up very early on the Friday morning just before my summer holiday and we had two witnesses out of the street, a sweep and a milkman. The parson – he sounded as if he had no roof to his mouth, poor chap – had read the banns every Sunday for three weeks, but as he had no congregation no one who knew of us heard him and we got clean away with it without anyone knowing.' His grey eyes were dancing and Timothy, twenty-one and joyous, looked out of them at Luke, who did not recognize him of course. 'Clean away to Southend-on-the-Mud,' Cornish went on. 'A couple of kids, happy as the buds in May.'

'Why did you have to keep it a secret?' Luke was watching him with a half smile.

'The terms of my apprenticeship!' Even at this distance he seemed to find them vitally important. 'Old Fred Boxer, the boss – he was my present wife's father – was more than hot on that sort of thing. Originally he came from my own home village in Norfolk and when my mother was left a widow she sent me up to him to learn the trade. I was bound all right, you never saw such a document!'

'I know. They are tough, those apprenticeship contracts. Did you go into the R.A.F. as unmarried?'

Cornish nodded. 'I had to. Old Fred was backing my papers. Besides, if you remember, nothing like that seemed to matter very much just then. There was no discernible future.'

'How right you are!' Luke's eyes flickered in faint surprise at the recollection. 'Future dubious. That was 1938–39 all right. Funny how one forgets. So you went off to Yorkshire – sent all over the place in the first draught I suppose, as an unmarried man?'

The Councillor continued to smile. 'She followed me whenever she could. She was younger in years than I was, but older in intelligence. A city girl and a country boy, that's what we were. She did the thinking for both of us and I let her.'

'What did she live on? Got jobs I suppose?'

'Yes. Waitress, nursemaid, anything. She was that kind of woman . . . independent, capable and wonderfully gay.' He looked up and made a gesture of resignation which was disarming. 'That's the key to the whole story. That's how it happened and why this boy, Timothy, has knocked me endways. People keep mentioning that he resembles *me*. My God! He not only looks like her but he *is* her. He's treating his own poor little girl now just as she treated me. He's keeping her out of it, suffering all alone. I never understood the bit about honouring one's father and mother so that *one's days would be long in the land* before today. If one respects one's parents' fiascos at least one needn't waste time going over the same ground twice. I didn't know, you see. It never went through my mind.'

'You didn't know she was having a child, you mean?' Luke, whose own experiences were still very close to him, was deeply interested and sympathetic.

'It never entered my head,' Cornish said. 'I was a stupid, ignorant, idealistic young idiot. Perhaps I never believed it worked, or something. I don't know. I left everything to her. As the time must have gone on she wrote instead of coming but as I'd been moved to Scotland by that time I wasn't surprised. She kept saying she'd see me in October, I remember. I had letter after letter full of everything but the important subject.'

Luke's wide mouth twisted. 'Then the balloon went up?' he suggested.

'On the second of September. We were ordered overseas. I sent her a telegram to her aunt's address in the Turk Street Mile and got one back to say she was in St. Saviour's Hospital, Ebbfield. That was the one which got the direct hit from a V2 at the end of the war.'

He moved uneasily in his chair and ran his hand over his head and ear in the gesture Julia had recognized. 'I had an hour, I remember. I didn't know what to do and I panicked. I remember a fatherly old Flight explaining to me patiently that I was on active service and if I deserted I'd be shot. I telephoned at last. I had a lot of help – I was that sort of chap. They got me a line in the end and when I got through to the hospital I didn't know if she'd gone in as Miss or Mrs. and there was a hell of a flap on down there and they couldn't find her. Finally I heard them say Maternity Ward and I didn't understand even then. It meant nothing to me. I was still thinking of a street accident; that's what hospitals spelt to me at that time.'

It occurred to Luke that the man had never told the story before; he could see its reality dawning upon him afresh even while he was talking.

'There was an interminable pause, I remember,' he said softly. 'And the wires were full of voices as if one was listening in to the world, and then they asked if I was the husband, and when I told them I was they said they were afraid they had bad news. By this time the lorries were starting and the Flight was pulling my tunic. "How bad?" I said. "I'm sorry," the voice was kind but sweety-sweet if you know what I mean, "she died peacefully ten minutes ago." I just hung up.'

The eyes which met Luke's were still astonished. 'I just hung up,' he repeated. 'I went out with the Flight and we ran for the transports. It never even occurred to me that there might have been a baby until days later when we were in France.'

Luke did not speak at once and the room which had heard many stories of human insufficiency was silent and friendly.

'What did you hear from the aunt?' he inquired at last.

'Nothing. I wrote her but there was no reply, and when at last I got back a very long time later there was no sign of her or the house. You couldn't even see where it had been. I found out that the whole street had been evacuated soon after hostilities began. The authorities were terrified of the tinder-box areas and they emptied them as soon as they could. There were no raids at first, though, and many people had trickled back by the time the bombs fell so the old lady may have gone with her home. She liked it. It wasn't as bad as most in Turk Street.' He shrugged his shoulders. 'Anyway I never got an answer and the hospital merely referred me to her as the next of kin given. It had been cleared for casualties on the outbreak of war and although they confirmed the death of my wife in childbirth there was nothing on the form about the child.' He hesitated awkwardly. 'I didn't persist, you know,' he said, still speaking with surprise at his own inadequacy. 'I accepted the double death and put it out of my mind like . . . like a sight seen in battle. Things were happening to me by then and I suppose I didn't want to know, either. We were sent to Canada and I came back a navigator. I had a most inglorious war. Having cost the country a packet to train I went out on my first raid, got shot down, and went straight into the bag. It took me two years to get away.' He laughed briefly and shook his head. 'So there you are,' he said. 'That old sissy Eustace Kinnit irritated me this morning. He said something about a romantic tale told to the boy by a nurse. My God! No nurse made up a tale like the real one. Well that's it, briefly. You can guess what happened when I got back, at last. I'd had rheumatic fever whilst a P.O.W. and my heart was gippy.'

'Your old boss was doing essential work and could use you.' Luke hardly made it a question. It was the most natural development, the history of thousands of young men who were early casualties in a war of tremendous movement and change. 'Where were the Boxer & Coombe works then?'

'Out at Epsom. We only got back here after old Fred died in 1948. I'd just married his only daughter Marion, a nice girl. I'd always liked her. She knows nothing whatever about this story, by the way.'

Luke ducked his chin. He looked most discreet and intelligent.

'And that,' he said presently, 'is not all, I take it? Now we arrive at the bit which made you come to see me.'

His eyes were friendly but very sophisticated and they filled with surprise at the other man's sudden reaction.

'Neither bigamy nor blackmail, Superintendent,' Cornish said briskly. 'I think I could have met either of those with less embarrassment. My difficulty is that *I have the son of that marriage complete with his birth certificate* and he's a very awkward young customer, but not I think entirely to blame for what he is – and does. The time has come when I feel I've got to clear my mind about him and so I've forced myself to come to you.'

'I see, sir.' Luke had become remarkably cautious. 'How do you mean "you have him"?'

'I know him. I support him. His name is Barry Cornish.'

Luke recognized the mood behind the abrupt words. It was the confessional state of mind, a phenomenon of human behaviour which never ceased to make him nervous.

'Address?' he inquired.

'I don't know it at this moment but I could find him. At any rate he'll appear at the end of the month.'

'Ah, yes.' The superintendent pulled his jotting pad towards him once more and waited. It was all coming. He could feel the man looking for the best place to begin.

'I first heard of Barry at the end of 1947 when the Trays returned to their shop. They'd been in the West Country all through the war.' The Councillor sounded as if he were dictating and Luke coughed.

'I shan't take it down at this moment, sir,' he murmured. 'Just let it come out as it will. We'll sort it out later. Where were you at that time?'

'In Epsom still. My father-in-law was ill and Marion and I were due to inherit the business and the house where we live now. Our premises had escaped and we were moving the works back to London. I had put up for the Council. I was always keen on social work and the state the place was in made me mad to get at it and see if I couldn't get a better deal for people.' He ran out of breath, coloured, and glanced angrily at the policeman. 'I'm not trying to excuse myself for what I did, I'm only explaining it.'

Luke nodded gravely. 'I understand, sir.'

'Then the boy turned up,' Cornish said. 'I was reached through the Trays as soon as the shop opened again. The only thing which existed to lead to me was the envelope of a letter I had written to his mother at that address. It was in a little cardboard writing folder she had had with her in hospital, tucked in the back. The birth certificate was there and so was our marriage certificate and half a letter written to me.' His voice betrayed him and he pulled himself up savagely. 'Still no mention of the child, even though she was dying, silly girl. Only love stuff and wishing I was with her and worrying how *I* was. Dear God, who'd be young, eh?'

The superintendent's eyebrows drew close together.

'I haven't got this,' he said. 'The child didn't come alone, surely?'

'Oh no, of course not. It was the nuns who brought him.' Cornish was peering at him earnestly through his fierce brows. 'I'd have taken an entirely different line if it hadn't been for them. You must believe that. There's a lot in my life that I reproach myself for, but if they hadn't been there to look after him you must believe me that I'd have done something more than merely paying. I'd have told Marion —'

He broke off and Luke leant across the table, a man of his own age and outlook. 'Look sir,' he said, 'don't worry. I believe every word you're saying. There's only one really impossible thing about the truth and that's how to tell it. The nuns brought the child to you, did they? Who were they, Sisters of Mercy?'

'Nuns of the Good Shepherd. They've got a rather poor but very good place in Crusader's Row, almost into Islington. Do you know it?'

Luke waved him on. 'Wonderful people,' he said. 'How long had they had him? Just tell me the story as it comes . . . start from the first interview. Where did it take place?'

'At Tray's shop. Doris Tray wrote me a note at the works asking me to step down there. When I did she told me how some nuns had come round asking if she knew me. We fixed a meeting and two of them turned up and shewed me a little cardboard attaché-case. It had this writing compendium in it and a broken comb and a strap. That was all. The sisters were very kind. There had been other items in it, no doubt, they said. But when people were poor and tempted things got used up. That was how they put it. They were sweet unworldly women although they appeared to be living up to the knees in sin and dirt and rubble.'

Luke laughed. 'They have a sort of triple glaze,' he observed, 'and as long as they follow the instructions it never wears off, or that's what they taught me when I was a nipper. Had they got the child with them?'

'No. I saw him later.'

There was a shadow in his tone which made Luke glance up at him but Cornish went on without elaborating. 'The story they told me was so damn silly I knew it must be true,' he said. 'It struck a dreadful bell inside me, like first hearing the facts of life when you're a kid. Incredible and ridiculous but inescapably, horribly true. There was a woman who was slightly "sub", they said. They didn't call her that but they made it perfectly clear. She had been a casual, part-time ward-maid at St. Saviour's, Ebbfield at the outbreak of war. The whole hospital had been in a panic getting ready to be cleared for the expected blitz casualties and she was frightened by all the talk. She heard that mothers of newly born babies had been issued with pink tickets, which entitled them to a seat on a bus to take them to complete safety as soon as the warning came. Because she was terrified she stole the suitcase of a patient who had died in childbirth, went down to the crêche part of the hospital or whatever they call it, presented the other woman's credentials and got the baby. Then she went off to join the bus. That was on the Sunday morning, September 3rd.'

Luke sat back in his chair. 'Blow me down!' he said inelegantly.

Cornish met his eyes. 'I know the type of woman, don't you?'

'God yes! A right nit! We breed 'em in the cities. Too little grub, too little air, too much of everything else including noise. The hospital must have accepted her story that she was the next of kin and been pretty relieved to see her if they were clearing the wards for casualties. So she went on the bus with the child and the suitcase?'

'No. Not the suitcase. The little attaché-case I saw had been inside a larger affair containing clothes, I understood. She found this too heavy to carry as well as the child so she left it, if you please, with the porter of the hospital and asked him to have it sent to her own address, which was some digs in Bethnal Green. Are you with me?'

'Utterly.' Luke had given up writing and was in the story himself, on his own ground. 'It's extraordinary how they never vary, that particular type,' he observed. 'Do you know their behaviour is more predictable than a normal person's? They simply move straight on, taking the easiest way every time. That is why they appear to get away with so much. Paths open up before them as they trickle along like water on the ground. The landlady kept the suitcase quite safely, I suppose?'

'She did,' Cornish said. 'That's another amazing part of the story, to my mind. She put it in a cupboard and thought no more about it until five years later when she happened to see the girl again in a bus queue. She'd been in London all the time. The house had stood up to all the raids. Dozens of people had passed through the building. Every sort of commodity was short but still there the bag was, unopened under a pile of junk, exactly as it had been placed when the porter sent it round out of the kindness of his heart. The Nuns of the Good Shepherd reproached me for finding it extraordinary. It was *willed* that the papers should survive, they said.'

Luke was thinking, his brows raised and the long furrows deep on his forehead.

'This evacuees' bus,' he began cautiously. 'where did it go? Suffolk?' The Councillor interrupted him. 'Oh, my dear good chap,' he said, 'don't think that I haven't been wondering about *that* possibility. Ever since that woman Flavia Aicheson – a type I hate on principle – told me the story of Timothy this morning I've been trying to prevent myself regarding it as a revelation.'

'Why?' Luke spoke in astonishment. 'Why prevent yourself? It could so easily be the other half of your story. It's worth exploring, surely?'

'No!' The exclamation was vehement, and at the sound of the tone Luke's experienced ear pricked up and his eyes became wary once more as he recognized the point at which their views were due to separate.

'One could make it fit!' The Councillor said. 'One could want it to fit so much that one could deceive oneself and everybody else. Anyone would rather have a splendid, intelligent, decent, good-looking, honest boy than – well, than what I have.'

The man was lashing himself with a bitterness Luke could just understand but which he was far too old a hand to believe he could cure. 'I haven't told you about Barry yet,' Cornish went on. 'It's the thing I came to tell you and I still haven't brought myself to do it. He's abnormal, Superintendent. It was apparent when he was a child. That was why I felt I couldn't ask Marion to take him into our home and why I left him with the nuns.'

Luke was very serious. The pattern was unfolding before his knowledgeable gaze like the symptoms of a familiar illness before a physician.

'Is he what they call a mongol, sir?' he murmured, his gaze on his notes.

'Not quite. But he's not right. Yet he's not a fool. I wish he were. In some ways he's damnably intelligent. Horribly so.'

Luke sat rubbing his chin. All his training and experience shied at the pitfall which he saw opening before him, and yet his human

judgement told him it did not exist and that the man, however mis-
guided, was at least honest.

'Sons tend to take after their mothers,' he began slyly.

'The ward-maid? Agnes Leach? Of course I've thought of
that.' Cornish dismissed the inference with a gesture. 'The nuns
thought of it. They suspected me and insisted that they brought
the woman while they watched us to see if there was recognition
there. I could have been lying. All the story of my first wife could
have been a fiction. I admit that.'

'No, no sir,' Luke was laughing softly. 'Come. That isn't what
I was saying at all. There's an old English word which isn't often
used nowadays but it's still useful on occasions, and that's
"changeling". Mothers have been known to do that before now.'

'No.' Cornish shook his head with a martyr's obstinacy. 'I've
thought of that. With longing. It would be a nice, easy, soft
way out, wouldn't it? But life isn't like that or I haven't found
it so.'

Luke leant back. He knew he was going to waste his time but
couldn't help having a shot.

'My official life hasn't exactly been what you might call shel-
tered,' he said, 'but I've never found it anywhere near as consistent
as the cynics do. "Surprise, surprise!" That's the message of life in
my opinion. Look here, sir, what makes you think that your first
wife and you would have produced the sort of child you describe
to me? No. Don't answer yet. But then tell me what sort of kid you
would expect this subnormal Agnes Leach to mother?'

The Councillor shook his head. 'You mean very well, Superintendent,' he said. 'I should like to believe you, but aren't you
overlooking something? What sort of chance has a child whose
mother, my first wife, came from the most dreadful of slums (and
believe me, there's nothing in England today to match Turk
Street when I was a boy) and was then, almost on the day after he
was born, thrown to a half-wit, hysterical girl who dragged him
through the countryside in terror? Wouldn't that account for
him, whatever he's become?'

'No sir.' Luke spoke briskly. 'Not if he's what you describe.'

'But don't you think so?' There was a masculine naïveté in the man's face and all the passionate ignorance of the unscientific mind on a deeply emotional subject.

'No sir.' Luke was a father too but also a practical man. 'As long as he was properly fed (and he must have been to survive), not dropped on his head, and kept reasonably warm, it wouldn't hurt him at all.'

'I think you are wrong.'

Cornish spoke simply and his weakness was revealed like a man uncovering a wound. 'It was my fault. I ought to have known the child was coming and I ought to have been there to take over when my wife died. It was a duty I failed in. The R.A.F. was reasonable in such matters. Don't you agree?'

'No sir.' Luke was wooden.

Cornish smiled at him and his mouth twisted.

'You think I'm clinging to a cross,' he said.

Luke's sudden grin was disarming.

'Well, if you set it up yourself it's nothing much to cling to, sir, or that's what the Holy Sisters taught me, but I take it we're not having that kind of discussion. What exactly are you trying to tell me about this boy of yours, Mr. Cornish? You're thinking of the fire and the flat-wrecking, aren't you?'

Cornish looked up gravely and sighed.

'I don't know anything, mind you. But as soon as I realized that the probable reason for the attack on the flat was an attempt to frighten a private detective off an inquiry into the history of a baby evacuated from Turk Street on the first day of the Second World War, I thought of my son Barry. It's the sort of interference which might make him very excited. Agnes Leach keeps in touch with Ebbfield gossip. He would hear about it from her.'

Luke's glance grew bleaker.

'Who did you think had employed the detective?'

'I knew. The police told me. Alison Kinnit. I associated her with Miss Aicheson and I thought she had done it in an attempt to find out something to discredit me.'

'Really?' Luke sounded amazed and a touch of colour appeared in the Councillor's thin cheeks.

'Now I've met her socially I see that's unlikely,' he admitted.

'But you've no idea what she's like in committee: she gives you the impression she'd fight with no holds barred.'

Luke's smile escaped despite himself, but he made no comment.

'When this boy Barry gets excited, is he liable to do dangerous and even criminal things, sir?' he inquired.

Cornish nodded. It was an admission which he had prepared himself to make but he still found it difficult. 'All his life he has been frighteningly awkward. The Nuns of the Good Shepherd passed him on to the Sisters of St. Vincent de Paul who specialize in caring for that sort of case. He became too much for them and he went to some Brothers who wouldn't keep him at all.'

Luke began to understand very clearly. 'Has he got a record?'

'Yes.'

'Oh well,' the superintendent made it sound a relief, 'don't distress yourself, sir. I'll look him up. We probably know more about him than you do. Does he live alone in the normal way?'

'No. I should have felt more guilty still about him if he had, but this Mrs. Leach. . .'

'The ward-maid?'

'The ward-maid, Agnes Leach, has been quite touchingly faithful to him. Through all his vicissitudes she has always been about. Actually I pay his allowance to her, now, so that he keeps it for at least a day or so.'

'And yet you really believe. . . . ?' Luke bit back the rest of the sentence. 'She's good to him, anyway,' he said instead and made a note.

The Councillor had risen and now stood looking at him with a stern dignity which was yet homely enough not to appear absurd.

'You know what you're forgetting, Luke,' he said, using the name as if they were friends for the first time. 'You're overlooking the facts, man. The boy *is* my son. He's got written proof. He's got his papers.'

The superintendent was taken aback. It was an aspect of the situation, a purely legal one, which had indeed escaped him entirely in the emotional problem.

'Who is to judge the age of a youngster?' Cornish asked. 'Is a squinting, backward baby four years or three? Or a gangling teenager twenty or nineteen?' He held out his hand. 'Well, there you are,' he said. 'I shall do what I can for him as I always have. You must be prepared for that, but these dreadful acts of destruction must be stopped. I see that. Look up your files and I'm afraid you'll find him, under "Cornish" alias "Leach". He always uses his own name when he's in trouble. He has his papers, you see?'

As soon as Luke got back to his own room he told his clerk to find Mr. Campion. 'Wherever he is,' he said, 'and get him on the line. Meanwhile I want details of a youngster called Barry Cornish. There'll be a juvenile record if nothing else.'

Twenty minutes later he was talking over the telephone to his old friend.

'Campion, I want to see you right away. Quicker than soon. It's quite a story and quite a development. I think we've got our delinquent. He has a record like a horror-comic strip. Campion?'

'Wait a minute.' Mr. Campion's light voice, which still had its characteristic streak of vagueness, came gently to him over the wires. 'I'm at the Well House. The Kinnit's home you know. There's a bit of a flap on. The nurse I told you about, Mrs. Broome, has just come in with the story that she has again met the woman who brought Timothy to Argevin with the other evacuees all those years ago. What? Oh yes. She says she knew her at once. She was in the cemetery snooping round the governess's grave.'

CHAPTER FOURTEEN

Kitchen Business

'COME, Miss Julia. You sit in the old basket chair while Mr. Tim and I get supper ready. Shall I make you a little fire in the hob-grate and you can pretend you're Cinderella?'

Mrs. Broome's ever-young voice tinkled gaily in the low-ceilinged cavern which was the kitchen of the Well House. As a sample of conversation in the world of today it had to be heard to be believed, and Tim and Julia exchanged secret glances. Julia was still slightly emotional and her eyes were wet as she laughed and turned to look at the carefully restored chimneypiece hung about with iron spoons and skillets.

'You're wonderful, Nanny Broome,' she said. 'I don't think that thing is meant to light though, do you? Eustace would be horrified.'

'Very likely, but he'd get over it. If we put up with all his antique bits and bobs he must give way to us sometimes.'

Mrs. Broome was making noises rather than talking and her glance was running over the details of the fireplace as she weighed up the difficulties of the project.

'I do like a flare,' she said. 'And there are some wine boxes through there we could break up, but it's warm enough with all these pipes. I just want to make you feel at home, miss. After all, as I said to Mr. Tim when you rang up so upset, you've been such a good little girl over all this engagement business we ought to make a fuss of you or he'll lose you.'

'Nan! This will do!' Timothy was embarrassed and, as usual, Mrs. Broome bridled dangerously at any reproach from him.

'You still show you've been fighting, especially when you colour up, young man,' she said spitefully. 'Come along: there are four places to be laid on the kitchen table. We'll give Mrs. Telpher something down here with us, shall we? Poor thing, she won't want to eat alone even if she is so rich! It was a great shock to her losing that little Miss Saxon and she was worried enough before, what with the kiddy-widdy and being so far from home.'

Julia stirred in the creaking chair. She was laughing but yet grateful for the mothering, which was comforting, however absurd.

'I hope you're right that Miss Alison won't mind me coming to stay,' she said. 'I was dreading the evening at home alone but it seems rather an imposition to move in on you when I live reasonably near.'

'Oh, rubbish! Miss Alison always lets me settle little things like that when I'm here. If Mr. Tim wanted to bring a school friend home for a match or the Boat Race he only had to ask me. I do the extra work, you see!'

Mrs. Broome was trotting round the kitchen with her little steps swinging her seat and conveying such ecstatic happiness as could alone excuse her. 'One of these days you'll be the mistress and we shall be the poor old things all very glad that you've got something to be grateful to us for.'

Tim put his arm round her and lifted her gently off the floor. 'Shut up!' he said.

Mrs. Broome squeaked with delight like a musical-comedy soubrette. 'Giving away secrets, am I?' she inquired contentedly. 'I'm always doing that. Never mind me. We must get a tray for the gentlemen. I shall give them theirs in the study. Then they won't come and bother us down here.'

Tim stood for a moment absently caressing his ear lobe.

'Poor Campion,' he said. 'Eustace has frozen on to him as if he was the only spar in an angry sea. I've got a terrific admiration for your father, darling. This deft introduction of an expert instead of bungling about in it himself is masterly.'

The girl looked up quickly. 'I like Mr. Campion, though, don't you?'

'Immensely. I don't know why. He's on our side anyway, perhaps it's that. I'm afraid he's having a depressing day. Alison gave him some dreadful lunch and now he's going to be asked to share Eustace's boiled milk and bickies.'

'No. I shall make him a nice little omelette and he'll eat it with a glass of wine and a roll and butter and like it.' Mrs. Broome was beside herself with happy home-making. 'I shall put a pretty tray cloth on and find a bit of cheese and he'll enjoy it. They're very busy talking about something *I* was able to tell them, Miss Julia.' She was bursting with her news and carefully avoided Timothy's warning glance. 'I happened to go out today and I . . .'

'What about Alison and Aich?' Timothy interrupted her ruthlessly. 'Where are they feeding?'

'Oh, they're going to the Art-Lovers Club.' Mrs. Broome was sidetracked. 'They've got to go to this recital in Wigmore Street you see, because they know the gentleman who's giving it. It's a harpsichord he plays and very rare, but afterwards they're slipping over to the Club to have a hot sandwich and they'll be back at once after that, because of course they're as interested in the the goings-on here as anyone is. You finish this table, Mr. Tim, and I'll slip up to the dining-room pantry and fix the tray and find the wine.' She bustled out of the room but put her head back inside the door immediately afterwards.

'Make him tell you about what I found in the Cemetery, miss,' she said and fled before she saw his reaction.

For once she had misjudged the situation, however, for the instant they were alone they were in each other's arms, too wearily frustrated to care about any mystery save one. Julia lay in the creaking basket chair holding her beloved back from her by his ears.

'Oh God, this is awful,' she said. 'It's like dabbing a burn with cold water, brief peace and then twice as much pain. Look darling, before she comes back, I've got to tell you. I had a sort of extraordinary experience down in Ebbfield at the cobbler's shop.'

'Oh, be quiet.' He pushed his mouth over hers and with his weight upon her edged her back farther into the hard flock cushions sewn into the groaning basket work. The discomfort was a delight to her and the very absurdity of the noise of the chair seemed to add to the pleasure of the sacrifice, but she wriggled away from him at last and struggled on with her story.

'I head someone say *Basil* Kinnit. Do you think . . . ?'

'Basil Kinnit? There's no such person.' He was momentarily interested.

'I know. That's what I thought. But it couldn't be a coincidence because it's an unusual name and anyway Basil's in it, isn't he?'

'Basil Toberman?'

'Of course.' They were whispering without knowing why. Two conspirators, their heads together, their breath mingling. 'He started it all, didn't he? He hates you – he hates us both.'

He was about to protest but changed his mind and began to kiss her again, pressing his forehead hard into her chest.

'It's ridiculous,' he said, suddenly, his head bobbing up like a child out of a cot. 'We want so little, only a bit of peace and solitude, only for a tiny while . . . It's like dying: you only need your narrow bit of earth. Hush —'

They both paused, listening. Someone was coming down the flight of wooden stairs which led from the ground floor to the half-basement in which the kitchen was built at the end of the entrance yard.

Timothy got up and Mrs. Telpher came in quietly and nodded to them. She was aware that she was intruding and regretted it in a mild Kinnit-like way.

'Mrs. Broome tells me we are to have a meal down here,' she remarked, looking about her with the impersonal interest which was so very characteristic of the whole family. 'She is still very excited about her encounter. It's quite an extraordinary chance that she should have found the woman there, of all places. Oh – haven't you told Julia about it yet, Timothy?'

The dark colour came slowly into the boy's face.

'Julia's only just arrived,' he said.

'Oh, I see.' She looked from one to the other with the calmly inquisitive stare which was reminiscent of Alison, and then laughed with a touch of hardness which was not Alison at all. 'I think I should tell her if I were you,' she said. 'It's rather her affair.'

There it was again, the hint of superiority, unaware and unselfconscious, which denigrated the other person's importance in an off-hand, unintentional way. Although he had been familiar with the trick all his life, Timothy could still be flustered by it.

He swung round and addressed the girl who was still sitting in the chair.

'Nan went over to Harold Dene Cemetery to take a wreath which arrived too late for Miss Saxon's funeral,' he said. 'While she was there she ran into a woman whom she fancied she recognized, and afterwards she decided it was the person who brought me down to Angevin when I was a baby. Naturally everybody is rather excited because I suppose there's a very good chance that she is my mother.' He hesitated. 'Nan won't have it, because she didn't take to her. She sounds something of a problem Mum!'

Julia received the full message and made no false move.

'That could be very useful and interesting,' she said slowly. 'I suppose people do recognize each other after twenty years?'

Mrs. Telpher laughed gently. 'One can see how young you are!' she said. 'Did the other woman recognize Mrs. Broome? I shouldn't think she'd changed since the day she was born.'

Timothy looked startled. 'No one seems to have thought of that. I'll ask Nan. She must know.'

Mrs. Telpher sat down at the partly laid table where she managed to look remarkably elegant despite a background of white kitchen fittings.

'She may have made it all up,' she said placidly. 'Not intentionally you know, Timothy. But in a bedtime story fashion. Here she comes. I should like to hear it from her.'

'Everybody wants to hear it from me.' Nanny Broome caught the tail end of the sentence and responded happily as she came softly in, her quick light steps pattering on the stones. 'I should think that Mr. Albert Campion – who isn't nearly so gormless as he looks, let me tell you – took me through it a dozen times. Where exactly was the grave? Where was I? Where was the water tap? Where was the Keeper?'

'The *keeper*?' Julia demanded.

'Well, the man in the peaked cap who was wandering about.' Mrs. Broome was on the defensive. 'It's a very modern place, you know. The same idea as the zoo. Graves not quite graves and cages not quite cages but all lovely paths and gardens. Anyway I spoke to him and asked him the way because he looked as if he ought to know, and he did. There it was, covered with all our flowers. Mr. Eustace's cushion of roses looked lovely. Naturally I was surprised to see a lady kneeling there because she wasn't one of us.'

'A lady kneeling?' Mrs. Telpher's utter astonishment splashed through the chatter like a shower of cold water.

'Well, a person,' said Mrs. Broome, reddening. 'She was stooping if she wasn't kneeling.'

Mrs. Telpher's shrewd eyes began to laugh and Nanny Broome's blush became sulky. 'I said "kneeling" because it was a grave,' she explained unnecessarily. 'I went up softly and, not liking to disturb her in case she was someone we knew, I put the new wreath up against a headstone behind her and went off to get some water. I thought there must be a tap somewhere and I could see the poor tired flowers could do with a nice fresh sprinkle.'

'Had she seen you?' Timothy inquired.

'I don't think so. Not then. But when I came back with a little jam-pot of water – I found one hidden behind the post the tap was on – she was sitting back on her heels looking at the label on the wreath I'd just brought.'

'You mean the card.' Julia spoke absently.

'No I don't. I mean the label.' Nursery authority was very marked and a certain feline streak, directed at Mrs. Telpher, appeared in the narrative. 'I didn't take the wreath out of its wrappings to carry it there, particularly since I was going by bus: so the label was still on it. It was sent "Care of Kinnit" to our address here and there was the name and address of the people who had sent it, too, – somewhere in Africa. Well, this lady – I always call people that because it's more polite – was squatting there reading it. I thought "There's cheek if you like!", so I said "Excuse me, please" and took it away.'

'Is that when you recognized her?' There was still faint amusement in Mrs. Telpher's face.

'No. I shouldn't have known her from Adam. I kept my eyes down you see. I was annoyed with her and I intended to show it.' Nanny Broome conveyed the scene with complete veracity. One could see her, cross and prissy, waggling her bottom, taking her tiny steps, and keeping her eyes downcast so that the lashes were black on her red cheeks.

'I unpacked the wreath and folded the cellophane very carefully for one doesn't want to make litter,' she said virtuously. 'And I set it up in the best place and I said to it "now you lie there and look nice".'

'You actually spoke aloud?' It was Mrs. Telpher again. She seemed fascinated.

'Yes, I did. I always talk aloud to things. It helps me to concentrate. Why, there's no harm in it, is there, Madam?'

She was within an ace of impudence, overplaying her part dangerously. Tim interfered hastily.

'What else did you say?' he inquired. 'Did you speak to the label? Did you, Nan?'

'Why should I?' She flushed so brightly that he was answered.

'Because I know you,' he said. 'What did you say?'

'I only spoke to it as I put it with the rest of the rubbish to go into the litter bin. I said "Well, I don't know, but everyone seems interested in *you*. First Mr. Basil and then a perfect stranger.' Afterwards I did look at her and I was surprised, because I thought "My goodness! I have seen you before!" But I couldn't think where, until I was nearly home.'

'How did she take your delicate criticism?'

'Don't you laugh at me, young man. I couldn't tell you. I didn't stop to talk. I came away. She wasn't the kind of person to get acquainted with. The years had altered her. She was a silly girl in those days – she had adenoids I shouldn't wonder – but she wasn't downright *awful* like she is now.'

'I've lost the thread of all this,' Mrs. Telpher intervened with sudden irritation. 'What did you mean when you said Mr. Toberman was interested in the label on the wreath?'

'Well, he was. He copied it down in his note-book, didn't he? I thought you saw him. You were at the top of the stairs.'

'Really? Was this yesterday evening when it arrived?' She seemed amazed. 'What an extraordinary thing for him to do! I'm afraid I find the whole story amazing. Are you sure you recognized this woman by poor Miss Saxon's grave?'

'Perfectly. Her face came back to me. I told you. I kept thinking about her and then when I was nearly here, "My goodness!" I said. "That's who it was!"'

'Did she know you?'

Nanny Broome seemed to find the question as surprising as everyone else had done. She stood considering and finally made a virtue of necessity, as usual.

'I was always taught it was very wrong to go about wondering what effect one is making on the other person all the time, so I never do. If she did know me she didn't say so, but she did have a silly sly smile on her face, now you come to mention it. It would be funny if she didn't recognize me, wouldn't it? I haven't got any older at all, everybody says that.' She turned away. 'Now I must get on with your meal and hurry. I'm to see the police, Mr. Tim. First you and now me.'

She tossed the small grenade lightly into the conversation and busied herself at the sink. 'Mr. Campion told me,' she said over her shoulder. 'He and Mr. Eustace were full of it when I took the tray up from the pantry. As soon as I've seen to you all down here I'm to slip into a dark coat and go with Mr. Campion to see somebody called Superintendent Luke.'

'Officially?' Julia got the question in before Timothy could speak. Mrs. Broome turned to look at her reproachfully.

'Not quite,' she admitted regretfully. 'I'm not going to head-quarters and I said I'd rather not go to a public house, so I shall meet him out.'

'Why doesn't the superintendent come here?' Tim, fresh from his own experience, was apprehensive.

'He doesn't want to.' Mrs. Broome still talked with her back to him. 'I asked Mr. Campion that and he explained that it's a question of etiquette. So of course I understood at once.'

She bustled out through a door at the back of the room and Timothy looked at Julia, his eyebrows raised.

'What's your chum playing at, do you know?'

'I don't.' She was wary. 'Superintendent Luke is all right only very high-powered. I'm surprised though. I didn't think he'd interfere unless —'

'Unless what?'

'Unless the Councillor talked to him. He conveyed that he might, but I didn't think he'd do it so soon.'

'The Councillor?' Tim spoke in astonishment but did not continue since Mrs. Telpher was watching them with polite interest. Finally, as the silence grew longer she spoke herself.

'Did you want to talk to him or were you just determined to get him out of the house before he drove Eustace out of his mind? I never saw a man so astounded in my life as when you carried him off like that.'

Julia regarded her gravely.

'I liked him,' she said. 'He knows a great deal about Ebbfield. Did you like him, Timothy?'

'I did rather.' He seemed surprised by the admission. 'He's either very human or else he's just a type I happen to know and understand. He annoyed me but I never felt I didn't know what he meant, which is odd because I'm rather slow on the uptake with strangers.'

Julia sat hesitating, her eyes dark with indecision. 'I was wondering,' she began at last and was saved, or perhaps merely interrupted, by a shout from Mrs. Broome somewhere in the back of the building.

'What's happened here? Look at this!'

Both young people hurried out to her, entering first a whitewashed passage of a type which still exists in old London houses, and then on to a square room which must once have been an outhouse before the city had closed not merely round but over it. It was lit by a single bulb hanging from a cracked ceiling and still possessed a flagged floor. Nanny Broome was looking up at the outer wall. Just under the ceiling there were three lunette windows, heavily barred and blacked out in the normal way by centuries of grime. Their bases were on a level with the pavement outside, a narrow way which was several feet lower than the road behind the house.

At the moment, however, a draught of cold, soot-laden air was flowing in freely through the centre window.

'See that?' Mrs. Broome demanded. 'The glass has come clean

out. It's simply gone, unless someone has cut it. Keep away from that Mr. Tim, do, or you'll get yourself filthy.'

Tim had swung himself up by two of the bars and now dropped back obediently, dusting his hands.

'There's no sign of it and the wire netting has gone too,' he said. 'They do sweep along there, though. It serves as a fire escape from the basement of the factory beyond the warehouse next door and has to be kept clear. I expect the netting rotted and the glass fell out and broke and both were shovelled up by the scavengers.'

'In that case they must work funny hours,' Mrs. Broome said, tartly. 'It was perfectly all right at lunch time. I'm in and out here in the mornings but this evening I felt the fresh draught as soon as I set foot outside the kitchen door.'

'What an extraordinary place.' Mrs. Telpher came in cautiously, as if she were entering a cave, and Mrs. Broome frowned.

'It's antique, madam,' she said sharply. 'This is where the famous well was. It's under the floor where that ring is, full of medicine. That's why we can't do anything useful with the room, like making a laundry of it. Someone has been up to mischief with our window, trying to get in, I suppose.'

'Nonsense Nan,' Timothy spoke soothingly.

'No one could get through those bars, they can't be six inches apart.'

'A rat could,' said Mrs. Broome. 'Come along out of here at once and we'll shut the door.'

Julia was uneasy. 'Oughtn't we to report it to the police?'

'I'll mention it,' Mrs. Broome said grandly. 'But as Mr. Tim says, if those bars are no protection a bit of dirty glass certainly wouldn't be. If anyone was hoping to get in there they've been put off. Now all sit round the table please because I mustn't keep the gentlemen waiting.'

On the whole it was a relief when at last, some little time later, they persuaded her to leave them. She tripped lightly up the stairs, her long purple coat wrapped round her and her eyes as bright as if she were going to an assignation. Tim sighed when at last they heard the front door slam.

'Now we can start again,' he said. 'Geraldine, how about another tin of lovely pink soup?'

'Are you still eating? Splendid! We did hope we'd find you still at it.' Miss Aicheson appearing suddenly in the doorway took them by surprise. She was tired but still game and was fussing a little in an old-gentlemanly way.

'The club was shut,' she said. 'I'd been told, too. Alison was quite right. It had slipped my memory completely. So home we came only to find Mrs. Broome on the doorstep being carried off by that pleasant Mr. Campion.' Her smile was disarming. 'I feel certain I can open a tin. You must just tell me what to do, Tim. Alison won't mind as long as we steer clear of onions or red pepper.'

Both young people rose to the occasion. Julia cleared a place and Tim gave up his seat.

'Don't worry Aich,' Timothy said. 'How was the concert?'

'Oh, very good indeed. I'm so glad we went to make two more. Poor Henry Ambush hasn't many friends and he's so talented. It's a very exacting instrument, the harpsichord – on the ear, I mean.'

'Is it?' said Mrs. Telpher mechanically. She had relapsed into her unforthcoming mood and sat relaxed and withdrawn, as if she were out of the circle altogether.

'So this is where you all are!' Alison came flitting in with Eustace behind her. The Kinnit resemblance both between brother and sister and Geraldine Telpher herself had never appeared more marked. They were all mature people, past the age when the family stamp appears unmistakably in the bone structure, and they looked to Julia like three little moulds off the same line, only differing superficially where some celestial paintbrush had been at work.

'Don't worry about us,' Alison sat down in Julia's place beside Miss Aicheson and smiled at everybody. 'Eustace has had his sandwiches and I hardly want anything at all. What have you been eating? Soup and cheese? How very nice. What are you doing down there, Eustace?'

'Looking at this fireplace.' He spoke from behind Mrs. Telpher. 'I come down here so seldom it always takes me by surprise. It's perfect and just as we uncovered it. Every brick quite perfect. A simple ellipse. It's pure fourteenth century, much older than the house, and must have had a big square chimney, long since gone, of course.' He rose, dusting his knees. 'One day Nanny Broome, or some other silly woman, will try to light a fire in it and smoke everybody out. But it's most interesting; this must have been the original ground level, eight feet or more below the street of today. The same period as the Well in fact. Have they shewn you that, Geraldine?'

'I saw the slab over it just now. One of the windows has been broken in there. Julia thought it should be reported to the police.'

'What? A window? Really? Tim, you didn't tell me this? I ought to have been informed at once!' Eustace was already on his way to inspect the trouble, Timothy behind him.

'My dear boy,' his voice came floating back to them. 'we mustn't take any unnecessary risks. These are evil times. There are a lot of unprincipled people about and we have treasures here.'

Alison noticed Mrs. Telpher's expression of astonishment and hastened to explain.

'Eustace is thinking of irreplaceable antiques,' she murmured. 'We don't keep money or jewels in the house. That's why we wrote to warn you to put yours in a safe deposit. We feel it's wrong to tempt people. Any burglar who came here would have to know exactly what he was after or he'd be very disappointed.'

'I see.' Geraldine Telpher inclined her head gravely and everyone was left a little irritated, as if she had disparaged the contents of the house.

'I believe you're right.' Eustace returned to the room wiping his hands on his handkerchief and still talking to Timothy who was behind him. 'The bars are a complete protection but we'll report it in the morning and it must be repaired at once. I can't think it has been done deliberately but —' An expression of dismay spread over his gentle face as a tremendous rattle and thump directly outside the door leading up into the house shook the whole basement.

In the silence which followed somebody outside used a familiar but ugly four-letter word.

Timothy pulled the door open and put his head out.

'Oh, it's you,' he said. 'What's happened?' There was a pause and he glanced back into the room, trying not to appear amused. 'It's Basil. He's slipped down the stairs. Get up, you ass. Are you all right?'

'Ruddy Kinnits!' The voice which was unquestionably drunken sounded tearful. 'This is just the welcome I should expect. I've already been called Basil once tonight – just outside this inhospitable house. I've been asked by a perfect stranger "Are you Basil Kinnit?" What's the answer? That is the question. The answer is no.'

'All right,' Timothy sounded harassed. 'Don't worry about it, old boy, just get up.'

'But I do worry.' The tears were more evident. 'I hate the ruddy Kinnits and all their damned governesses and let me tell you, Wonderboy, I'm in a position to tell them something they don't all know.'

'So you shall, chum, so you shall.' Timothy was speaking whilst expending considerable exertion. 'Just get up and you shall tell us all anything you like.'

CHAPTER FIFTEEN

The Beanspiller

'PUBLIC house nothing! This is a hotel.'

Charlie Luke had never appeared a finer animal in harder condition. His suit might have been buttoned tightly over wood, and he perched on the plush-seated chair in the deserted upstairs dining-room of the Eagle Tavern in Scribe Street, E.C.3, glowing at Mrs. Broome as if she were a plate of cornflakes and he a greedy child on a poster advertising them. Mr. Campion, who was between them, was amused despite his anxiety.

'At lunch-time this room is crowded with solid businessmen but in the evening they've all caught their trains home and it is quiet and comfortable for us to have a chat in, see?' the superintendent was explaining. 'You're being given Royal treatment. I've had them open it up and turn on the lights for us.'

'Not many.' Nanny Broome, smug in her purple coat, glanced up at the spray of bronze wall-lights above the table. They shed a somewhat ghostly glow over the rest of the thickly carpeted room. 'I know it's been used at lunch-time because I can smell spirits and cigars. Still, if Mr. Campion says it's all right I don't mind staying.'

'That's handsome of you, Missus.' Luke was a trifle dashed and his eyes were inquisitive. 'I've invited you to come along because I want to ask you one or two very simple questions You may not be able to tell me anything but there is a chance you could help with an inquiry which is nothing whatever to do with anyone you know.'

'I understand.'

'Do you?' He seemed surprised. 'That's good. I could take you down to the police station and the detectives there could get you to make long, long statements, but I don't want to put you to all that trouble.'

'Why?' She appeared genuinely curious and he caught his breath and let it out in a short explosive laugh.

'Because you're needed at home to do the washing up,' he said and gave Mr. Campion a sidelong glance. 'Would you like a cake with that coffee, Mrs. Broome? No? I'll have a ham sandwich,' he added to the resident manageress who was serving them herself. 'The others will too. Some of those very expensive ones.'

'That's all right, Mr. Luke, don't worry.' The woman, who was tired and motherly for all her spiked heels and diamond ring, set down the coffee tray and waddled off into the darkness.

The superintendent returned to his guest.

'Now I want you to take your time over this so we'll start with something which hasn't very much to do with it,' he began mendaciously. 'Mr. Campion here was telling me that you believe you saw the woman who brought Mr. Timothy Kinnit down to the country when he was a baby, and that to the best of your belief she was in Harold Dene Cemetery this afternoon. Is that right?'

Mrs. Broome smiled at him and presently threw back her head and laughed like a girl.

'I'm not as green as I'm cabbage-looking,' she said. 'You ask me straight questions and I'll give you straight answers. You want to know if Mr. Tim's mummie has turned up out of the blue, don't you?'

Luke blinked, exaggerating the reaction and leaning back in his chair.

'I didn't say anything of the sort.'

'No, I know you didn't, but that's what you were thinking.'

'Was I? You're a mind reader, I suppose?'

'No, I don't pretend to be that.' She was cocky and deprecating at the same time. 'But I generally know what lies behind any question I'm asked. Some people do, you know.'

The superintendent sighed and the wrinkles on his forehead deepened as his eyebrows rose.

'Yes,' he said. 'Some people do – and damn dangerous they are, too! Well then, suppose that is what I wanted to know? I'm not saying it was, mind you.'

Mrs. Broome touched the sleeve of his coat where his wrist lay on the table beside her.

'You're wasting your time, anyhow. She hasn't,' she said reassuringly. 'I told Mr. Toberman that, and Mr. Campion here was listening – as he usually is, it seems. That girl was not the mother of Timothy or anybody else when she came down to Angevin.'

Luke leaned over the table. Cosiness and man-to-woman approach glowed from him.

'It's very easy to make mistakes in a matter like this. I've been taken in time after time. Motherhood is like any other natural thing: there are hundreds of variations of condition.'

Mrs. Broome shook her head. She was sitting up very straight, her cheeks pink.

'I don't doubt that you're a very clever man and that being in the police you've had to get to know a lot of things that aren't a gentleman's business, but you've never had a baby have you? Not personally, I mean.'

Luke scratched his chin but before he could comment she continued:

'Well, I have. More than that, I had just come back from hospital after losing my baby when this girl turned up with Timmy, who was quite new – still on his stalk. That's a thing no one can disguise. Naturally, although I was run off my feet looking after all the other mummies, she was my chief interest because the baby was so young, and I put her to sleep in my little room where we shared the same bed, and all day I was looking forward to talking to her about her confinement.'

'Oh.' A wave of comprehension passed over the superintendent's expressive face. 'She didn't give the right answers?'

'She didn't know anything at all!' Mrs. Broome's contempt and disappointment were as fresh as if she felt them still. 'I spent all the night trying to get some sense out of her and I soon found out she wasn't only a liar but a very ignorant young monkey. Do you know, another woman on the bus had *lent her a bottle* or he would have starved by the time I was there to save him! A wicked, wicked girl!'

'She was pretending to be the mother?'

'Not to me, she wasn't. She soon saw how ridiculous that was. She had had to say she was his mother to account for the pink ticket. She had to have a pink ticket to be allowed on the bus. No. That girl was simply frightened of the bombs. They were her worry, silly little cat! Not a thought for the poor baby. I'd have given her bomb!'

Luke was watching her with the whole of his body.

'After talking to you she ran away?' He could not help anticipating the story.

Mrs. Broome raised mutinous eyes.

'Yes, she did. I knew I'd frightened her but I never expected that. The next morning she vanished. I thought she was hiding so I didn't say anything but looked after the baby. I was so busy and so happy with him that I kept putting off mentioning that she'd gone. Then, when Mr. Eustace practically owned to him, naming him like that, I didn't bother any more. I made up my mind that she was a maid sent down to bring him to me.' She paused and took a defiant breath. 'If you don't believe me I can't help it. But I'm not a liar.'

'No,' said Luke, grinning at her. 'You're not dull enough! I believe you. What about the kid's clothes? I don't suppose they were anything to write home about, but didn't you keep anything? A bootee or a bit of embroidery or anything at all?'

She shook her head. 'The only thing I kept that Timmy had when he came to me was most unsuitable for a baby,' she said. 'It was a cotton head-scarf tucked under his shawl. It was a lovely pale blue. Blue for a boy. It had little jumping white lambs on it and writing made of daisy-chains. "Happy and Gay" it said. All over it. It was just my meat and I've got it somewhere and I'll show it to you, but it wasn't special. There were hundreds of scarves like it in Woolies that year.'

'If you're certain of that, don't bother.' He shook his head regretfully. 'What's your observation like?' He had taken his worn black wallet from his pocket and was looking for something amid the bursting contents. 'This is a curio in itself,' he said to Campion. 'They wouldn't let me borrow the file of course, but the photographic section got me these in fourteen minutes flat.' He produced two small photographs of a woman, one full face, one profile, and handed them to Mrs. Broome who wore the expectant expression of a player awaiting his turn in a quiz game. A single glance, however, wiped everything but dismay from her face.

'Oh, doesn't she look awful!' she said aghast. 'She's not as bad as that, not even now. What are these for? Her passport?'

'You could call it that,' Luke said dryly. 'Is it she?'

'Oh, yes, I can see it's her. They're not as bad as that.'

'Do you remember the name she gave you?'

'She didn't give me any name. If she had I should have remembered it and it would have saved a lot of trouble.'

'Wasn't it on the pink ticket?'

'I had no time for tickets! You have no idea what it was like. We had hundreds of mummies and kiddie-widdies in the house – hundreds! All wanting – my goodness! – all sorts of things.

'What did you call her?'

'Me?'

'Yes, when you were getting down to the intimate details. "Ducky"?'

'No, I should never have said that. I'm very particular how I talk.' She was thinking, casting her mind back as he was persuading her to. 'I'm not sure, but I think I called her "Agnes". She must have told me that was her name if I did. It's not a favourite of mine.'

'All right, don't worry. Have you ever heard of a Mrs. Leach?'

'No. Is that who she says she is?'

The superintendent ignored the question. He was looking at some scribbled notes on a sheet torn from a telephone pad.

'I understand,' he said at last, 'that you told Mr. Campion here that you didn't have a chat with her in the cemetery. It was a chance meeting and although you thought you knew her you didn't place her until you were on a bus coming home. Did any word pass between you at all?'

'None.' With the recollection of Mrs. Telpher's reaction to her habit of addressing inanimate objects fresh in her mind, Nanny Broome was cautious, sticking carefully to the letter of the truth

'I might have said "excuse me" as I passed her to put the wreath on the grave, but nothing more.'

He nodded acceptance. 'You say she was kneeling?'

'I might have been wrong. She might have been just bending, looking at the flowers.'

Luke scratched his clipped black curls. 'What was she doing there at all, do you know? Was she just ghouling about among the graves, or pinching flowers, or what? I mean was this an absolutely chance meeting, do you think, or was she interested in that one particular grave?'

'Oh, of course it was our grave she was looking at!' The idea of any other explanation seemed to astound her. 'I thought "Ah, there's somebody who's heard the talk!"'

Mr. Campion raised a warning hand but he was too late. Luke had heard.

'What talk?' he demanded, looking from one to the other of them with the same suspicious flicker.

'Miss Saxon fell in the kitchen just before she had her fatal heart attack.' Mr. Campion made the explanation carefully. 'She appears to have been listening at a door and when Timothy Kinnit pulled it open suddenly, she fell in. Basil Toberman has been making a point of the incident. He's inordinately jealous of the young man.'

'Oh the tale isn't *true*,' said the irrepressible Mrs. Broome airily. 'I was there and I saw what happened so there's no question about that. Mr. Eustace hushed it up because she was a governess – not because of Mr. Tim.'

'*Hushed it up?*'

'Played it down.' Mr. Campion spoke with more firmness than one might have supposed possible in one normally so casual.

'All right,' Luke conceded but he was still interested. 'Why is he cagey about governesses?'

'Because they had one who did a murder.' Mrs. Broome was enjoying herself. As soon as Luke noticed it he calmed considerably.

'A hundred and twenty years ago,' murmured Mr. Campion testily. 'Miss Thyrza Caleb and her Chair of Death.'

'Oh?' The superintendent was delighted. 'It's the same Kinnit family, is it? We used to have a book of famous trials in the house when I was a kid, illustrated with dreadful old woodcuts. I remember Thyrza with her white face and streaming hair. There was something funny about that story. Wasn't there a postscript?'

'I never heard it,' said Campion. 'I missed the crime entirely. It was new on me when Toberman told me the other day.'

'Oh, no. It's famous in its way.' Luke was still searching his memory. 'She committed suicide, I think.' He shook his head as some of the details remained obstinately shadowy and turned a broadly smiling face to Mrs. Broome. 'Well, anyway, you got it in and startled the poor copper,' he said. 'You're old Bean-spilling-Bertha herself, aren't you?'

Nanny Broome was not amused. As usual when the joke was against her she made every effort to get her own back.

'I've got nothing to hide,' she muttered, jerking up her chin. 'Not like some people!'

Luke's interest was captured despite his better judgement. 'Out with it,' he commanded. 'Who are you telling tales on now?'

'No one. I've got none to tell, but Miss Saxon had. Painting her face, dyeing her hair, listening at doors, and over sixty years old if she was a day! What sort of governess was she?'

'Better than no one,' said Luke, flatly. 'You can't catch me with that sort of stuff.'

'But she had a secret. She was always just about to tell it to me. She'd keep leading up to it and then being put off, or Mrs. Telpher would call her.' Nanny Broome was labouring her points a little. There was a touch of desperation in her bid for drama. 'She told me herself, only the day before she died: "I'm under a great strain" she said.'

Mr. Campion took it upon himself to see that no more harm was done.

'Miss Saxon was driving the car when the accident occurred that resulted in the tragic condition of the child who has been brought over here to hospital,' he said. 'It has been unconscious for two years.'

'Oh Lord!' Luke's sympathetic grimace was lost in Mrs. Broome's amazed reception of the news.

'Oh, so that was it! Well! No wonder she wanted to share a

feeling of guilt like that, and why she seemed more upset about the poor kiddie-widdie even than its own suffering mother.' She paused and added brightly, 'and why she dyed her hair.'

'Eh?' Luke's eyes were sparkling. 'Go on,' he said. 'I dare you.'

'Because she knew she was too old to have been driving the car, of course,' said Mrs. Broome, gathering her gloves and purse. 'And now if you don't need me any longer, sir, I'll be getting back. There'll be some clearing up to do and Miss Julia is staying the night, so I want to pop a nice hot bottle in her bed. Just to comfort her. She's very young and no Mummie.'

Luke got up. 'Very well, be off,' he said. 'Thank you for your help. I don't suppose I shall have to call on you again.'

'Oh, I'm very glad.' Disappointment was evident in every line of her body and her lashes made half circles on her cheeks. 'I shouldn't like to have to give evidence in court.'

'God forbid that indeed!' said Luke, ducking his chin in to his neck. 'Run along, I'll send you a box of chocolates one day.'

She flashed a smile at him which was as gay and provocative as seventeen itself. 'I don't eat them,' she proclaimed, triumphantly. 'I'm slimming.'

The last they saw of her was her seat, wagging as happily as if it carried a tail, as she trotted off into the shadows.

Luke laughed softly. 'It's a crying shame one could never risk her in the witness box,' he observed. 'She's got all the answers. It must have been tremendous fun being brought up by a woman like that. You'd know all the important things about the whole sex before you were seven.'

Mr. Campion put out his hand for the photographs and studied them curiously. They showed a bedraggled sprite of a woman with a slack mouth and huge vacant eyes, who yet managed to convey a hint of cunning. She was unusually dishevelled, he suspected, which was what had so shocked Mrs. Broome.

'What about Agnes Leach's record?'

Luke shrugged. 'She's a type and she has the usual long silly history. Shoplifting, soliciting, minor fraud. Our welfare people suffer from her. They get her job after job and each time she reforms completely for a couple of weeks until something else catches her attention and – whoops! She's flat on her kisser again.'

'I suppose Mrs. Broome did recognize these photographs?'

'I'd take my dying oath she did.' Luke spoke with the conviction of long experience. 'She recognized her in the cemetery and these confirmed it.'

Mr. Campion passed them back. 'What was Agnes Leach doing there? Looking for an address?'

'I should think so. "Looking at the flowers on the grave" suggests hunting among them for florists' labels to me. Somehow or other – almost certainly from Miss Tray at the cobbler's shop – she heard that the young man who was making the awkward inquiries was due at the funeral of someone called Saxon, and that there was an advertisement about it in *The Times* newspaper. No address was given in the paper but the place of burial was mentioned so she went there.' He shook his dark head. 'In my experience it's almost impossible to underestimate anything which Agnes and her associates are likely to know for certain. They snap up bits of unrelated information and make a tale of them. They knew the name Stalkey, hence the destruction of the flat and the fire at the office, but apparently they didn't know the name Kinnit. The chance of Agnes remembering it, if ever she heard it on her brief visit to the country, is remote. She is a simple defective. He, of course, is quite a different caper.'

'Ah,' said Mr. Campion, blinking behind his spectacles. 'At last we come to the dark figure in the wood pile, the lighter of fires and smasher up of flats.'

'Slasher of mail bags and dresses in the cinema, burner of bus seats, and at least three knife attacks on girls who ought to have known better than to be out with him.' Luke spoke without venom. 'He's a problem child,' he added unnecessarily.

'Agnes's son?'

The superintendent leaned back, tipping his chair, and prepared to enjoy himself. 'She says not. To prove it he has a birth certificate and the marriage lines of his parents. An almost unheard-of possession in their vicinity! According to Agnes his name is Barry

Cornish. Certainly his reputed father appears to have done what he could for him.'

'Stap me!' murmured Mr. Campion, who permitted himself un-likely expletives when really shaken. 'So that's it.' He was silent for a moment considering the ramifications of the new position. 'Tell me,' he said at last, 'had Cornish any idea of the true story himself?'

'None at all. He accepted Barry meekly. It was only this morn-ing that Miss Aicheson woke him to tell him a tale about Timothy's arrival at Angevin which was quite obviously the other half of one he had already heard from Agnes's friends about the other boy. Agnes never invents more than she needs, you see. That's the most dangerous thing about her.'

'Yes. It would be. How did Cornish take the discovery that he had been swindled, virtually blackmailed, all these years by some wretched woman who'd pinched his son's papers?'

'He didn't take it,' said Luke slowly. 'He's an honest chap and he realized that Barry was probably behind the violence, so he came to me acting on a moral compulsion. I've got the impression that he's tickled to death with Timothy, who seems to be very like him, but do you know I don't believe he'll ever attempt to own him to disown the other.'

Mr. Campion sighed. 'Poor man,' he said. 'He sees his great sacrifice rejected by the gods and so, no doubt, all the Misses Eumenides let loose again to plague him.'

Luke eyed his friend curiously.

'What a funny chap you are, Campion,' he said. 'I told him that he was clinging to a phoney cross. Also of course he's a perishing official. He can't bring himself to believe that there isn't something sacred about a certificate!'

'Let me get this absolutely straight for the sake of the record.' Mr. Campion was diffident as usual. 'Your suggestion is that Agnes Leach left Timothy with Mrs. Broome but retained his papers?'

'Only by accident.'

'Oh, I see. She left the mother's possessions in a station cloak-room?'

'Better. She parked the whole suitcase on an honest landlady who kept them until Agnes turned up again four years later. By that time Agnes had become baby-prone herself – after her chat with Mrs. Broome perhaps! – and had achieved Barry who was then about three years old. I imagine she dressed him up in anything she could find in the other woman's bag and thought the certificates might fit him since nothing else did, if she called him four instead of three. He was backward, wasn't he? So he could pass for a bit worse. It wouldn't worry Agnes.' His eyes began to dance. 'Anyway I'll bet it was the dear good nuns who looked up the father for her in all innocence once she produced the marriage certificate and told the story of rescuing the baby from the bombs. Agnes has that kind of history.'

Mr. Campion sighed. 'I believe all this,' he said sadly. 'What about Agnes and Barry now? Have they been pulled in?'

Luke glanced at his watch. 'I dropped the word to Munday, the D.D.I. at Ebbfield, who has probably got the boy by this time. His last known address was somewhere in Wandsworth. Sometimes it takes a few hours to locate a chap like that but there's never any difficulty in picking him up in the end.'

'I suppose not. You have some fingerprints from the arson business, haven't you?'

'Nothing very good. They were being treated in the lab when I left. I wanted to get an identification of Agnes from Mrs. Broome off the record, just in case the woman proved to be involved in a criminal charge and so become unavailable for private questioning.' Luke was a little shamefaced about his own consideration and seemed to feel a need to excuse it. 'I never see any point in involving people who have a little front to keep up if it isn't necessary,' he went on. 'I didn't know Mrs. Broome would be so convincing. She might have had to meet Agnes again before she could be sure. As it is, everything is plain sailing. You ought to be able to convince little Miss Julia's papa there's nothing worse than obstinate self-sacrifice in the lad's family, and the poor old Councillor can choose his own bed of nails. Aren't you satisfied?'

'No.' Campion was frowning. 'The thing that's worrying me, Charles, is why didn't she follow her?'

'Why didn't Agnes follow Nanny Broome?'

'Exactly. The only explanation must be that she had already found the address of the Well House and the name Kinnit, presumably on one of the wreaths. She must also have recognized Mrs. Broome. That meeting took place somewhere around early afternoon, leaving plenty of time for Agnes to telephone the news to anyone anywhere. She could have spoken to the cobbler's shop, for instance.'

Luke was listening doubtfully.

'She might,' he said. 'Barry has any intelligence there is between them. He's got a sharp mind in a warped sort of way. You feel he might attack the house because of Timothy?'

'No,' Mr. Campion was gently obstinate. 'I think he might be bright enough to see how many beans make five. Surely the only person on earth who can testify that Timothy was the baby left at Angevin by Agnes Leach at the outbreak of war is Nanny Broome?'

Luke sat up. 'Corblimeah! he said. 'And we've sent her home alone. Let me get on the telephone!'

CHAPTER SIXTEEN

Indictment

ONCE he was seated at the kitchen table with Alison and Miss Aicheson facing him, Mr. Telpher on his left and Eustace on his right, Tim and Julia in the background draped round the basket chair, Basil Toberman passed into a stage of ponderous arrogance.

With his face crimson and his full mouth glistening he achieved a dictator-like appearance, squat, myopic and preternaturally solemn. The Kinnit family were bearing with him in their own peculiar way and sat smiling at him with tolerant superiority, but the rest of the company was suffering.

'The bronze is unquestion – unquestion – unquestionably genuine,' he announced, adding unnecessarily, 'I have said it.'

'So we hear.' Miss Aicheson was almost as red as he was and had never appeared more masculine. 'Don't you think, perhaps, all this could wait?'

'Silence!' Basil had apparently decided to treat them as a public meeting. 'I have just been half across Europe and have flown through the sky with one of the greatest experts the world has ever known. I speak of Leofric Paulfrey of the Museum.'

'Professor Paulfrey!' Eustace was delighted; his face lit up with pleasure. 'Oh splendid. Now that's an opinion which is really worth having. Does he say it's fourth century?'

'*I* say it's absolutely genuine.' Toberman was frowning with he effort of articulation. 'It is a fellow to the Boy Jockey of the Artimisian wreck; in better condition. I am prepared to guarantee that it's by the same man.'

'Are you though!' It was Eustace who spoke but both Alison and Geraldine Telpher looked up with exactly the same twinkling smile of good-tempered derision.

'Laugh! Go on, laugh!' Toberman's thick hand shot out in a gesture which would have been a little oversize in a Pagliaccio 'Laugh your heads off. You can do it today but it'll be for the last time, because I've heard the truth about you and I never keep my mouth shut, do I?'

'My dear fellow, if you've only got the truth about the Bronze it'll be enough for one evening!' Eustace turned the attack gracefully and shot an apologetic glance towards Julia. It was most discreetly done, but Toberman was in the state of over-awareness typical of certain toxic conditions and he pounced upon the girl, noticing her presence for the first time, apparently.

'This is fitting,' he declared with thick theatricality. 'This is Rich. This is Justice. Bride of the Wonderboy meets Family Skeleton.'

'I should hardly call yourself that, Toby.' Tim was juggling with the situation. 'What about a bit of beautiful shut-eye? Shall we go up to bed?'

'No. Certainly and absolutely not. I am not as canned as that.' Toberman began to laugh a little himself. 'I've got something to tell you, Timothy, and when I do you're going to know I'm right just as I knew old Paulfrey was right when he told me. The man was afraid of flying, Timothy. I saw it. I saw it in his eyes and because I was queasy myself, as I always am in the air, I suggested we behaved like reasonable men and drank ourselves out of it and that's how he came to tell me. Otherwise I don't suppose he'd have brought himself to talk to me at all. The man was afraid. He was funky. He sweated. I saw it. To save his face he had to babble out something and because my name reminded him of the Kinnits he babbled out this glorious story.'

'Which was that the Bronze was genuine,' said Mrs. Telpher briskly.

'God!' Toberman regarded her with overdrawn contempt. 'You're a Kinnit and that's typical. That's the first, last and only thing you'd think of. Don't worry, Geraldine, you won't be left out. Professor Paulfrey was very interested to hear that you were staying with your relatives. He knew your late husband by repute, he said, and he knows the Van der Graffs very well indeed. He's been staying with them. But it was your governess he was interested in and so was I, my God, when he told me.' He lurched round to peer at the basket chair. 'Timothy? Do you know what was the really interesting thing about the original Kinnit governess?'

'Basil, you're becoming an abominable bore!' There was an unfamiliar edge to Eustace's voice which jarred warningly on every ear in the room except, apparently, Toberman's own.

He swayed a little but was still remarkably articulate.

'Don't you believe it you silly old Kinnit,' he declared. 'Pay attention my little man. I have news for you. The family secret is out. Miss Thyrza is vindicated. She wasn't guilty, Timothy. She didn't kill the boy friend. It was her pupil, the thwarted fifteen-year-old Miss Haidée Kinnit whose immature advances he'd rejected, who prepared the trap for him. She did the murder and planted the blame, with sweet Kinnitty cunning, squarely upon her more successful rival, the unimportant and defenceless governess. Moreover, there is a very strong supposition that the family knew.'

'Basil! Be quiet! Stop him somebody. Eustace, make him be quiet.' An unexpectedly passionate protest from Alison wiped away any possible doubt of the truth of the story.

Evidently the ancient tale was taken very seriously by the present-day Kinnits. Eustace was shaking with anger, every trace of his normal urbanity gone. Alison was on the verge of tears and for once even Geraldine Telpher seemed startled out of her natural calm. Her face was grey and rigid.

Toberman was enjoying himself.

'Now I can understand why old Terence Kinnit made such a business of hushing up the crime. Why he bought the Stafford-shire moulds and moved house and all the rest of it,' he said happily. 'If his daughter was the murderess the whole thing hangs together and holds water. They'd driven the poor governess to suicide, you see, between them. I don't suppose that worried them. They'd done her a service by taking her in without references, hadn't they? So it was her duty to repay them with her life if necessary. That would be their attitude.'

'Will you hold your tongue, sir?' Eustace when angry was quietly formidable and some of it got through. Toberman began to complain.

'I don't see why you should victimize me,' he grumbled. 'It all came out in a book; Paulfrey told me so. At the turn of the century a book was published which blew the whole gaff. He told me its name. I've forgotten it but it'll come back. *Ten Trials of Yester Year* I think he said. Something corny like that. You'd know, Eustace.'

'Toberman, you're drunk! Oblige me by going to bed immediately.'

'Don't you dare to talk to me like that, old man. Your great grandfather did mine a favour but you haven't bought us body and soul! We're not lackeys!'

'Good Heavens, boy! What utter nonsense. You must be out of your mind. Pull yourself together.'

'I am perfectly sober and I am talking to Timothy. Professor Paulfrey told me that this book which he remembered well was written by a parson who had known Miss Haidée when she was an old woman. When she died she left him a letter confessing the whole thing. He didn't do anything about it but put it in a book when he was pretty ancient himself. He was a damn dull writer and nobody was very interested in Miss Thyrza at that time, but somebody bought up most of the copies of the only edition. I wonder who that was. Your father, Eustace?'

'That will do!'

'Anyway, no one appears to have read the book but a few kids, one of whom was Paulfrey, and the publication passed without comment in the press.' Basil leant back in his chair and began to laugh.

'There's no question that it's true, is there?' he jeered, addressing Miss Aicheson and the two young people. 'Look at them all. Kinnits we have loved. We're all in the same boat, you and me. We're all lame ducks taken in and enslaved by Kinnits because we were cheap. And we all hang about ready to take the buck when it's passed to us.'

Miss Aicheson put a large hand over Alison's slender wrist. 'I shall go up now, dear,' she murmured. 'I can't stand much more of this.'

At the same moment Eustace turned to Tim. The old man was

very white and there was a helplessness about him which was embarrassing. 'It's not true,' he said but without conviction.

'Of course it isn't!' Tim's response, which was furious, swept
the accusation into perspective. 'It's half true, like all Basil's lies.
He's a silly inferior ass and he's tight as a tick. Come on, Basil.
Come to bed, you ape. No more damn nonsense. Up you get.
Come along.'

He left the arm of the basket chair which creaked protestingly,
strode across the room and picked up Toberman in a fireman's lift.
The green strength of his body emerged as an unexpected deliverer
and Toberman made no attempt to resist. They caught a glimpse
of his puffy face and round stupid eyes, solemn and owlish with his
head hanging upside-down, as he was borne away through the
doorway.

The abrupt departure left a tingling silence behind it. Miss
Aicheson settled down again but did not release Alison's arm. 'I
shall wait for a moment or two until he's got him settled,' she
murmured.

'Very sensible, Aich.' Eustace smiled at her vaguely and taking
out his handkerchief passed it over his forehead.

'What a silly fellow,' he said. 'How tiring. An asinine line to
take.' He glanced towards his sister who was looking down at her
plate, her delicate face pale and expressionless. Opposite him
Geraldine Telpher was in much the same mood. She had withdrawn into herself and appeared preoccupied. The light was unkind to her. Beyond her he suddenly saw Julia sitting quiet in the
basket chair, and a frown flickered over his face.

'My dear child,' he said. 'I'd quite forgotten you were here. I'm
so sorry you should have had to listen to all this unpleasant nonsense. Tim will be down in a moment and he shall take you
home.'

Julia was young enough to blush scarlet. 'I'm staying, I think.'

'Really?' Eustace was the last person to be impolite but he was
irritated and surprised. 'Alison? I thought we promised – I mean I
thought that there was an understanding with Julia's father that
the youngsters shouldn't meet just now?'

Alison lifted her head and looked at him blankly. She had been roused out of deep thought and took some time to surface. 'Perhaps there was,' she said vaguely. 'Don't fuss, Eustace.' She turned to Julia. 'Do you know where your room is?'

'No. I'm afraid I don't.' Julia was uncomfortable and the situation was saved by the unexpected appearance of Nanny Broome, pink and pleased with herself and still wrapped in her purple coat. She came dancing in, smiling at them all and talking as usual.

'I just got in the door when the phone went,' she announced, addressing them collectively. 'It was my nice policeman asking if I'd got home safely! I think he felt a little bit guilty that he hadn't minded his manners and sent someone with me if he couldn't bring me himself. Oh, they're terribly busy those two. Talking nineteen to the dozen when I left. Well now, have you all had some nice supper? Where's Mr. Timmy?' She was stripping off her thin leather gloves as she spoke and paused to pull them out and straighten them before she stowed them away carefully in the side compartment of her good handbag.

Eustace scowled at her.

'Miss Alison tells me that Miss Laurell is proposing to stay here tonight. . ?' he was beginning when Mrs. Broome sailed in to the rescue like a hen defending her chick.

'Miss Julia's been asked to stay here sir,' she said firmly. 'Her father's away and it's a big house right across London, so Miss Alison and I put our heads together – didn't we madam?' The interpolation was a warning. 'And we decided the best thing for her to do was to have the little room beyond Miss Aicheson's. It's all aired and ready and I'll just slip a bottle in the bed and she won't know she isn't at home.'

'But I thought we'd promised Anthony Laurell —'

'I'm sure I don't know about that,' Mrs. Broome interrupted him shamelessly. 'All I know is that if Sir Anthony is a proper father, as I'm sure he is or he wouldn't be fussing so, he couldn't care for his daughter to go home through a neighbourhood like this at night. I'm an old woman and I'm nothing to look at –' she seemed a little hurt to hear no cries of protest and her tone became a trifle sharper – 'but even I had quite a little run for it outside here tonight. There are a lot of dark shadows and people coming out of dark corners where there aren't any lamp-posts and pushing against one and whispering things.'

'What things? You silly woman, what are you talking about?' Eustace was testy and exasperated. 'You do talk a lot of rubbish!'

'Ah, but I make you all very comfortable. There's a nip in the air tonight. What about a nice hot toddy?'

'No. We've had quite enough alcohol in this room this evening.'

'Really? I thought I smelled it. Mister Basil I suppose?' She was uncovering the situation with the speed of light. 'Mr. Tim's putting him to bed, no doubt? It's very bad for him, all this drinking. He'll go just like his father, *bang*, one day. Well, we'll all have some nice malted milk. Would you like that, madam?' She addressed Alison, who shook her head without speaking, but Geraldine Telpher looked up.

'I would like a Scotch and soda,' she said. 'May I get myself one out of the dining-room as I go up, Eustace?'

'My dear girl, I'll come and see to it. I'm so sorry. You're so much one of us that I forget you don't know all about our little difficulties. You must have found Basil very upsetting.' Eustace was still flustered and Mrs. Telpher waved him back into his seat.

'I'm sure I can manage,' she said with her faintly commiserating smile. 'He didn't worry me at all. In my life my trials have been rather more specific and he isn't my affair. Poor man, if it's inherited we should be sorry for him I suppose. Goodnight, everybody.'

'Goodnight, Geraldine.' Eustace waited until the door had closed and the murmured blessings ended before he turned on Mrs. Broome.

'You really mustn't say things like that,' he began testily. 'Poor old Ben Toberman may have enjoyed his glass at the end of his days but in his time he was a most intelligent, sensitive, perhaps over-sensitive person.'

Mrs. Broome behaved as she always did when reproved by authority. Her eyes opened very wide and she looked a picture of amazed innocence.

'I didn't know. I always understood he drank like a fishie,' she said earnestly. 'Delirium tremens and everything and everybody talking. Of course I didn't know him at all well. You didn't like him coming down to the country, did you?'

Alison roused herself. 'That'll do, Mrs. Broome. Take Miss Laurell up to her room please. We'll make your excuses to Tim when he comes down, Julia. He may be rather a long time. It's sometimes very hard to get Basil to settle. He's one of those excitable alcoholics. He just won't lie down and go to sleep. Such a bore and so tiring. I'm so sorry this should have happened, my dear.'

It was the most ruthless dismissal a guest could have received. Miss Aicheson tried to soften it with a smile which would not quite come and Eustace held out both his hands in a gesture which was more like an appeal for help than a reassurance of goodwill.

Nanny Broome slipped an arm round Julia's waist and drew her firmly and swiftly out of the doorway so that she was still saying 'good night' as the wood closed behind them.

'Mr. Basil always gets them in a state when he does this.' Mrs. Broome made the confidence as they walked up the broad stairs together to the hall. 'He's so rude and open and that's the thing they can't put up with. They're very civilized sort of people, very covered up.'

It was not the easiest statement on which to comment and Julia did not try. Her own brand of politeness was of the rare long-suffering kind which is at least one parent of serenity. Instead she said simply, 'I don't think I shall want a hot-water bottle. It's very good of you to think of it but I never have one at home.'

'Very well, you can kick it out but you won't go to bed yet, surely?' Nanny Broome paused at the foot of the main flight to look at her in astonishment. 'Poor Mr. Tim hasn't had a chance to see you at all. What with Mrs. Telpher and the ladies he can't have had you to himself for a second, poor boy.'

Julia laughed. 'What had you in mind?' she inquired.

'Eh? Oh, don't you worry about the oldsters.' Mrs. Broome clearly considered herself an evergreen. 'We all have to jolly them along because when they get excited they get tired, and when they get tired they feel poorly and that makes them cross. So I tell you what we'll do.' She broke off abruptly and stood aside to permit

Mrs. Telpher, who had emerged from the dining-room, to pass them. She was carrying a glass and smiled at them before she went her placid way up the stairs.

'I shall get you some milky-drink,' said Nanny Broome loudly to her protégée, adding more softly, 'you sip it in your room and brush your hair, and then when they've all gone to bed, which won't be very long, you and Mr. Tim can have half an hour in the kitchen in the warm.'

'If you think it's all right,' Julia was beginning, but Mrs. Broome was not listening to her. She was looking up the staircase, a thoughtful expression upon her face.

'That was a very dark whisky, wasn't it?' she said. 'Did you see it? I suppose it couldn't have been neat? It was over half a tumbler-ful. I wonder now?' She shook her head and answered her own question. 'No, I don't think so. I should have said she's too much one of *them* to do anything like that. Perhaps she doesn't pour it out herself as a rule and has just overdone it. Yet of course you never can tell. Well, come along miss. I'll lead the way, shall I?'

For the first time she turned her back on the guest and put out her hand to take the baluster rail. The folds of the good purple coat rearranged themselves and the girl stared at them and put out her hand to touch.

'You've torn your coat.'

'I can't have done, it's perfectly new. Where is it?' She turned her head to look over her shoulder and swept her skirts round her, craning her neck to find the damage.

'It's not like that.' Julia sounded frightened. 'Look. Take it off.'

She lifted the soft woollen garment off Mrs. Broome's shoulders and swung it round to face her. The featherweight velour which looked brown in the subdued artificial light had been scored like the crackling on a joint of roast pork. Five two-inch-wide slashes had been made from between the shoulderblades to the hips and the cloth hung like ribbons, showing the silk lining beneath.

Nanny Broome stared at the damage and for once in her life words deserted her. Her face, which was never in repose in the ordinary way, was frozen into a weatherbeaten mask on which her discreet powdering stood out distinctly. The silence in the house was noticeable and the warm family atmosphere had chilled.

'You said some one pushed against you as you came home. Is that where you felt it? On the back, here?' Julia was wide-eyed but still very practical. 'You said some one whispered? What was it? Did you hear?'

'Not really. I thought it was a swear word so I didn't listen. It was a sort of hiss, that's all. Oh miss! This'll upset everybody. We shan't get them to sleep tonight.'

'All the same, we ought to tell the police.'

'Not tonight. I wouldn't go out there again for a fortune. And I wouldn't like anyone else to. My poor best coat! I bought it in Ipswich, I don't know what Mr. Broome's going to say.'

Julia was persistent. 'There's no need to go out to the police station. We'll telephone.'

'Not tonight.' There was an unfamiliar undertone in Mrs. Broome's voice which Julia recognized. The woman was deeply frightened and not particularly by the physical attack. She had perceived that the true danger came from something more serious still, an unclean shadow falling across her bright nursery world.

'I'll telephone tomorrow when it's light,' she said earnestly. 'Tonight we'll just say our prayers and go to sleep. If we get hold of the police now they'll only come round thumping about and up-setting the whole house, which is edgy enough as it is with Mr. Basil drunk. He's still saying awful things about Mr. Tim, I expect.' She glanced round the dark raftered hall and lowered her voice in confidence. 'Tim really didn't touch Miss Saxon, you know, miss. I was there. She died of a sort of fit. I saw her after-wards and I thought "You look as if you've suffocated, you poor old girlie." The blood rushed to her head and smothered her. That's what I'm always frightened of with Mr. Eustace. He looked terrible tonight, I thought. Mr. Basil ought to be muzzled.'

'I could ring Mr. Campion.'

'Do it tomorrow. He'd only tell my nice Superintendent and *he'd* have the place upside down. I know his sort. No one better when you feel like it, but very tiring when you want to go to bed. Oh, my goodness! Now what?'

They both started violently as a commotion occurred suddenly at the top of the stairs.

Basil Toberman, bare-footed and in pyjamas, had appeared on the landing with Tim, looking grey and furious, behind him.

'I am going to get myself a snifter. Go away, Wonderboy. I want a drink. Don't I make myself plain?' Below the bogus authority there was the thin high note of delirium which rings a danger signal in every human ear. Tim seized him and began to heave him back to his room.

'You're not going to drink any more tonight.' His voice, breathless with exertion and lowered in an attempt not to disturb the house, floated down to them in the warm air. 'Oh, for holy Moses sake, man, come back to your bed like a good little bloke. You'll start seeing things if you don't look out. Have a heart, Basil. You're driving me round the bend.'

Another scuffle followed and then a door slammed. Mrs. Broome sighed.

'Poor Mr. Tim! It is a shame just when he particularly wants to get him quiet so that he can come down to talk to you. Mr. Basil is bad tonight. Just like his papa whatever Mr. Eustace says. He couldn't have meant all that, you know. He just likes to hear himself saying generous things. That's all that is.'

'How long will it take Tim to get the man to sleep?'

'Oh, until Mr. Basil's exhausted, I'm afraid.' Mrs. Broome made the pronouncement casually. 'He's had a very long day so he may drop off presently, but I have known him play up for a couple of hours wearing everybody clean out. It's a very long-suffering family you're marrying into, miss.'

'Why on earth do they put up with him?'

Mrs. Broome laughed. 'Oh, it's not only with him, my dear. They put up with the most extraordinary people. They gather them. It's only because they like to be tolerant. I never heard that the older generations were like it but the way Mr. Eustace and Miss Alison go on you'd think they were trying to work off some sort of sin they'd committed.'

The thought flitted out of her head and she gave the little self-conscious wriggle which was so characteristic of her.

'Now I'm not like that at all,' she said happily. 'If I love some-body I'll forgive them, but if I don't I certainly won't. If you put up with people who are awful and you don't even love them then you're encouraging awfulness and nothing more. Well, I mean to say, aren't you? Never mind. Come along and I'll tell you all about my Mr. Luke. He was ever so interested in Mr. Tim and it will be nicer thinking of that than crying out over my poor mauve coatie.'

CHAPTER SEVENTEEN

The Boy in the Corner

THE kitchen smelled warm and airless and the only light came from the small glowing rope across the bright shield of the electric heater which Mrs. Broome had put in the mock fireplace to make it look "like home" for the sweethearts.

The door into the house opened cautiously and Tim put his head in. 'Julia?'

'I'm here in the chair.' They were both whispering and he came round the table, feeling his way cautiously.

'Is he quiet now?' she murmured as he bent over the chair.

'I think so. He keeps dropping off, snoring like a donkey-engine and waking himself up again. Then he thinks he'll go and find a short one for his dry throat! However, forget him. I think he's about had it tonight. Where are you? Oh my God, my darling, where are you?'

'Here. Come on, there's plenty of room.'

He scrambled into the protesting basket, wriggling his shoulder under her and pulling her head into the hollow of his neck.

'Damn this chair! What a thing to make love in! How like Nan to expect us to.' Julia was laughing, shaking the noisy contraption, and he joined her.

'She's keeping the party light,' she gasped.

He began to titter. 'We might as well try to go to bed in an accordion! Don't laugh, don't laugh. "It'll end in tears." I want to kiss you. I want to kiss you. Where's your mouth, woman?'

Julia stiffened. 'Listen.'

The boy craned his neck and they held their breath.

All round them the house creaked and breathed but was still an oasis of partial quiet amid the vast city's endless noise. Yet the only recognizable sounds which came in to them were far-off ones, tugs hooting on the river, the rumble of hidden trains.

'I'm sorry,' Julia whispered. 'I thought I heard him on the stairs.'

'He wouldn't come down here. If he is up again he's streaked off to the dining-room tantalus, in which case there'll be an almighty crash in a minute as he falls flat on his face. He only needs another shot to put him out cold. He's got me down this time. Put him out of your mind.' Timothy settled himself again but the moment had passed, and although he was holding her possessively, rubbing his lips against her ear, she could feel that his thought had wandered from her. She controlled the thrill of panic but it was not easy and she shivered.

'What's the matter now?'

'Nothing. It was only a sort of feeling. Don't you get them? You feel you're waiting, watching for the exact moment when something new is about to begin.'

'Here?'

'No, I wasn't thinking about us for once.' Her cheek was hot on his own. 'I didn't mean an act so much as a turn in the road. You feel that one curl of the pattern is nearly finished and another is just about to spring out of it, and all the people involved are converging to the right spot whether they like it or not. Don't you know what I mean?'

'No,' he said honestly. 'No I don't dig that sort of thing myself but I don't mind you doing it. In fact I rather like it. I'm a bit shaken tonight, though. All that stuff of Basil's in here just now. That was new, you know.'

'About Miss Thyrza? I wondered.'

He moved restlessly. 'It was true, you see.' The whispering seemed to lend importance to the confidence. 'We all recognized it as soon as he said it. Did you notice? It was like suddenly seeing something awful and unmistakable, like blood on the road. The penny simply dropped. Everything one had ever heard or noticed fitted in. I remembered at once, for instance, that there was some mystery long ago about a book being suppressed. A master at school referred to it with an odd inflection in his voice but I never heard the story and it had remained a mystery all my life.'

'But does it matter? Miss Thyrza died well over a hundred years ago.'

'Oh, we shan't have the police in because of Basil's discovery! Now it's you being obtuse, my little muggins. It's rather worse than that, in my opinion, because one spots the basic living sin which the original crime exposed. The Kinnit family *is* what Basil said it was. They do tend to capitalize their charitable acts since they do them for the wrong purpose. They don't keep helping folk for the warm silly reason that they like the people concerned, but for the cold practical one that they hope to see themselves as nice people doing kind things. Alison and Eustace are particularly unfortunate. They know all about this and don't like themselves very much because of it. Basil hurt them horribly. They know they're missing something by being so cold but they don't know what it is. The rest of us recognized that suddenly. Blast Basil.'

'But Eustace is fond of you. Really fond.'

'He is, isn't he?' It was an eager whisper. 'I was thinking that. He's a cold old fish but there is a warmish patch there.' He turned his head and kissed her ear. 'Thank God for you, Lovely. This has been a night of revelation for me. I should have hated it alone.'

'I don't think it's over yet,' she said, creeping yet closer to him. 'Anyone who is loved as much as Eustace is by you must be thawed a bit.' She heard her own jealousy and hurried to disarm it. 'If you're responsible for the thawing you mustn't ever stop. You know that, don't you?'

'Yes,' he said. 'I know that.' She could feel his heart beating under her cheek and her thought followed his own.

'You owe *her* a lot.'

'Nan? Twice as much as everything! She's balmy. She goes through the world like an old butterfly clinging to its wings in a bombardment. They're all she's got so you can't blame her. I say, did you see her coat? She showed it to me just now up on the landing.'

'I noticed it first. It's terrifying. I didn't realize this district was as tough as that. She wouldn't let me telephone the police.'

'I know. She told me. She was still playing the whole thing down just now upstairs on the landing. That means she takes it very seriously indeed. If Nan thinks something is merely naughty she points to it and screams the place down, but once she perceives what she feels is Evil, she hides. She's a type and they drive some people round the bend, but I remember as a kid thinking that God must be fond of her because she took such inordinate delight in "His Minor Works".'

'She's very taken with Superintendent Luke just now.'

'So I gathered. How does he come into the picture? Does that mean underground assistance from your influential Papa?'

'No. I'm afraid that was me. I told Councillor Cornish that if he had any idea who had started the Stalkey fire he ought to tell Mr. Luke and I think he may have done so, but from what Mrs. Broome reports of her interview they don't seem to have talked entirely about the fire. Tim? I've been thinking about Councillor Cornish.'

'So have I, sweetie. That's my true old man, isn't it?'

'Do you think so?' She turned her head quickly, her voice sibilant in the darkness. 'I'm sure you belong to the same family.'

'I think it's a bit more than that. So does he.'

They were silent for a while, lying close in the chair, their heads together and their breath mingling.

'When did you decide about this?'

'I didn't decide at all. It's been sort of seeping into certainty all day. The cobbler was the first person to put the thought into my head. As soon as he heard that I had been evacuated from Ebbfield as a baby he became vehement that I should go to see Cornish. He didn't commit himself but he was extraordinarily insistent. "Let Cornish have a look at yer," he kept saying. "Go and let him 'ave a look!"' He hesitated. 'The likeness really is phenomenal, I suppose? I saw Aich eyeing us very oddly this morning.'

'It's pretty strong. It lies in movements and personal tricks of behaviour as much as in anything else. When you're nervous you clutch your ear in the way he does.'

He caught his breath. 'Do you know I noticed that! He did it when I first saw him and it made me furious. This is horribly dangerous emotional ground, I feel, don't you? I don't like it very much.'

'Are you going to mind if it does turn out to be him?'

'No, I don't think so.' Here in the dark their intimate communion had the quality of complete honesty. 'I'll be rather relieved, I think. I mean I *am* rather relieved. He's the sort of person I know best, anyway. He's an intellectual trying to be practical. He could easily have been a don or a boffin if his training had turned that way. As it is, a lot of that drive of his is being spent on being indignant. I feel I know him frightfully well which is what I resent about him.'

'You're annoyed that you are like him?'

'No. Of course not. I'm very grateful. I do want to belong to someone's line.'

'Why?'

'I told you. When at last I realized that I really was not a Kinnit I felt utterly lost. I felt I didn't know what was coming next and that when it did I might be entirely unable to cope. It wasn't ordinary windiness at all but something subterranean.'

'But you had *me*.'

'Bless you! Of course I had and thank God for it, but this wasn't loneliness. You can see what I mean if you think of this latest business of Eustace and Alison and poor Miss Thyrza. That story has taken over a hundred years already and they aren't at the end of it yet. Our days appear to be "longer in the land" than we are – that's about the essence of it.' He was silent for a time. 'I don't know how *he's* going to react,' he said at last. 'He has a new wife who is not my Mum. It may be that.'

'Which makes him so determined that it shan't be true?'

'Hell! Why did you say that?'

'I don't know. I just thought that he did have some reason. But I don't think it's a low one. It's something he feels rather tragic about.'

'What an extraordinary thing to say! How do you know?'

'Because you sometimes have very strong reasons for not doing something you want to do very much, and when you have you feel tragic about them, and when that happens you look and act as he did today.

'Poppycock! Sorry darling, but that's nonsense. I never feel tragic. Shut up. You're talking rubbish.'

'My arm has gone to sleep.'

'Oh, my dear, I'm so sorry! Is that better? Darling? Julia? What's the matter?'

She had become rigid at his side and he caught her alarm and copied her so that there was no sound at all save the thumping of their hearts.

'A light.' She formed the words with her lips and breathed so softly that they came to him like ghosts.

'On the stairs?'

'No. The other way. Look.'

'What?' It was a moment of superstitious alarm for there was no through way on that side, only the narrow passage and the cellar where the well was.

Julia was holding Timothy, restraining him, her eyes held by the shadows which were black round the inner door. As they waited, their bodies stiff, their necks craned, a clear thin angle of light, wide under the door and narrow as it slid past the ill-fitting jamb, stabbed across the floor, wavered, and vanished.

'It's a bobby who's found the broken window and is shining his torch in,' he said softly. 'I'll go and have a word with him or he may come round to the front and ring. You wait here.'

'No: the light was too near for that. The torch was just outside the door.'

'Impossible. Stay there.'

He stepped softly across the room, opened the inner door a few inches, and stood looking in. Now that the shaft of light was wider it appeared less strong but it still fluctuated, weaving backwards and forwards. There was still no sound whatever.

Timothy remained motionless and after a while an odd quality in his stillness conjured sudden panic in Julia.

She rose to her feet very quietly but the chair creaked and a whisper which was so strained that she hardly recognized it came back to her across the dark. 'Keep still.'

Timothy was too late. She had come up beside him and together they stood staring down the short passage to the open cellar door.

Something black and sinuous was moving above a torch beam directed downwards on the stone with the iron ring in it which marked the well. The figure itself was rooted to a single spot but the pool of light ran round the crevice busily, probing, darting, resting, moving again, while, thrown by the diffused upward glow, a writhing shadow reared across the white wall and ceiling.

As an unexpected confrontation it was shocking because the mind registered it as an impossibility, something appearing in an empty room without an entrance. Julia's little gulp deep in her throat jerked Timothy out of his frozen astonishment. The light switches for the passage and the Well cellar were on the wall just outside the door and he brushed his hand over them.

The cellar was lit by a single swinging bulb which gave a hard yellow light and now the full scene sprang into sight.

There was a harsh slither of rubber on the gritty stone and a soft high whimpering noise, very thin and brief, as the figure scurried back under the high window through which he must have entered. He stood there facing them, still swinging on his strangely rooted feet. Even in full light he was horrific, and that despite his own terror which came across to them like an odour. He was tall and phenomenally slender but bent now like a foetus, seated in the air, knees and one forearm raised very slightly and the whole of him swaying as if he were threaded on wires. He was dressed in black from head to foot in jacket and jeans so tight that they did not permit a wrinkle, let alone a fold, and also – an item which gave him a deliberate element of nightmare – his head and face were covered with a tight black nylon stocking which flattened his features out of human likeness without hiding them altogether. The other factor which was dismaying was that even at a distance he appeared deeply and evenly dirty, his entire surface covered with that dull irridescence which old black cloth lying about in city gutters alone appears to achieve.

Timothy recovered himself first and reacted in the only way left to this century's youth, which has had its fill of terrors. He proceeded to laugh it off. He pointed to the well-head with an expressive gesture, rather as if he did not expect the newcomer to understand words.

'Are you going down or coming up?'

The figure giggled. It was a little snuffling sound, very soft and ingratiating. Also he relaxed and straightened so that the horrible bent quality induced by his sudden alarm was almost lost. He remained on wires however, still rooted to the single spot under the window, still swinging.

'Do you know what's down there? Have you ever had it open?'

It was a soft, lisping voice, very quiet indeed and by no means ill-educated but muffled by the nylon mask. Neither Julia nor Timothy spoke and their silence appeared to worry him. His black stocking mask was open at the top and now he pulled it down, using his left hand. His right was either useless or hidden behind him.

The face which emerged was not reassuring. It was blunt and grey, the nose springing thick and flat from high on the frontal bone of the forehead, whilst his eyes were narrow slits of dark in a tight bandage of tissue. He was not a mongol but there was deficiency of a sort there, and it was not made more pretty by a latter-day hair cut which involved eccentrically long elf-locks and oiled black curls.

Experimentally, his right hand still behind him, he edged forward until he reached the well-stone again and presently he touched it with a long shoe; it appeared to fascinate him.

'There could be thousands of pounds down there. Treasure and stuff like that.' The soft little voice was still off-hand. He was boasting, but in an uncertain way which made the statement half a question.

'What makes you think that?' Tim spoke cautiously, aware of Julia behind him. He could feel her shaking and guessed that the narrowness of the bars across the window above the intruder was causing most of her horror. The fact that the visitor must have squeezed between them was obstrusive and unnerving since it underlined his reptilian quality, which was deliberately accentuated anyway, to a degree which was unbearable.

'It's old, you see?' The lisping, toothsucking accent was very slight but the arrogance was there. 'The house is called after it. I mean to say, that's the ad-dress, isn't it? The Well House. That means it's old, and old wells in the City have been used for more things than water and not only for what you'd think. There's been plagues, you know, and people have been put down quickly with no time to go over them properly. Everything rots but metal. I see you don't read, yourself.'

Elementary academic snobbery was the last thing his listeners expected and it almost touched off hysteria.

'Do you?' Tim asked. He had not smiled but the newcomer took offence. His sensitivity was psychopathetically acute and was almost telepathy.

'Do you mind?' he inquired, rearing backwards but without moving his feet. 'I do as a matter of fact and I've had access to some very remarkable books. You'd be surprised what you can find out in a library. If you've got all the time in the world.' There was no mistaking his meaning or his pride in it and again they were silent and out of their depth. He looked them over consideringly.

'You two work here I suppose, waiting on them upstairs. I should have thought in a house like this they'd make you wear uniforms but that's old-fashioned, isn't it? "Au pair", that's what you are now. That's what they call you. Well, shut up and you won't come to any harm I think. I want to see Basil and I want to see him alone.'

'Who?'

'Basil. You know who I mean. I know he's here. I saw him come in. He's drunk but that won't matter. He'll understand what I've got to say to him if he's paralysed. The girl can slip me up to his room and I shan't touch either of you two. Basil Kinnit. That's who I want.'

'But there's no such person!' The words escaped Julia for the second time that day and the superstitious element surrounding them flared suddenly in her mind, and she put her hand over her mouth because she was afraid of screaming.

Her alarm seemed to reach the newcomer physically as if he had heard or smelled it, for he retreated a yard or so and stood swaying again, not quite weaving but horribly near it. He was also angry.

'You're lying, you're in love with him, you're hiding him.'

He was spitting and whispering and the short syllables were like grit in the fluff of sound.

'Nonsense.' Tim took over. He was puzzled, curious rather than frightened, and his tone was soothing. 'Who is it exactly that you want? Let's get it quite clear. There is no Basil Kinnit. Are you sure you have the name right?'

'Well, yes. As a matter of fact I am.' The newcomer relaxed again and the confidential lisp, soft and ingratiating, returned to his voice. 'I've known his name was Kinnit for a long time, see? But I only got the Basil today. I had to wait for a telephone call.' He conveyed that he considered the use of the instrument to be important and romantic. 'I put a friend of mine on to find out and she telephoned from outside the cemetery and left a message for me at a shop we use for that sort of thing. "His name is Mr. Basil and the address is The Well House." That was the message I got. When I heard that, well, I mean to say it was waiting for me, wasn't it? There was no point in me messing about any longer. So I came round right away.'

'But you must have been here some time. When did you take the glass out of the window?'

He seemed to have no objection to answering questions. His answers were glib and at least partially truthful.

'This afternoon. I've been round here all the time. There's a lot of perching places round here, see. It's made for it and you don't see a bogie. I smoked twenty sitting in a ventilator next door. Twenty. It was a boast. 'Twenty in an afternoon.'

'Why did you wait so long?'

'I always wait. I like to look round. I like to know who comes in and out. It's my business. I'm interested, see? Mr. Basil Kinnit, that's who I want to talk to.'

'What do you want to say to him?'

'I want to warn him to lay off me. I want to teach him not to interfere, see? I don't like private dicks making inquiries into my birth, see? I'm not having no prying, see? And nor is Ag. I've given his bloodhounds a warning and now I'm going to warn him. And you two can keep your mouth shut or you'll learn the same song. . . . Words *and* music.' The final phrase had no meaning but was a threatening series of sounds only, and he repeated them with satisfaction. 'Words *and* music!'

'Why should he want to know about your birth?' Tim's quiet question was yet so forceful that it captured his wayward intelligence and held it on course.

'Because he wants to stop Ag getting the money, see? My Dad slips her a bit, see? As soon as Ag heard about this Kinnit lark it came to her what it was about, see? Ag's not a great intelligence. She's got no mind. She's not with it, really, but she's bright enough over money. She knew what he was after and so she came to me and told me and of course I took it up. Tonight will put a stop to his mucking about round us.'

'Is Ag your mother?'

'No, she's not. She's not. She's not. She never said so and she isn't. She's a friend; she's interested. She does what I say. Like today. She went to the graveyard, see? I told her she'd find the address on a wreath when we couldn't find it in the paper but she went right away. Then she used the telephone.'

'All right. I understand.'

'You don't. You don't understand. You've got no idea. I'm not ordinary, see? Ag rescued me when I was born. I wasn't born normally, see? A lot of famous people aren't as a matter of fact, if you read history and all that. I wasn't quite in the world when a bomb hit the hospital I was in. On the first day of war this was, and my Mum was killed and Ag rushed in and picked me up like a kitten and carried me off all bloody to the rescue buses. Then she had to look after me, she was months going round the camps, until she found my papers and the nuns took over for her and found my Dad.'

'But there were no bombs on the first day of the war. There were no bombs for a year.' Julia made the protest and got the full repercussion.

'That's a lie!'

It was an objection which he appeared to have heard before.

'People say anything but they're wrong and I'm here to prove it anyway, aren't I? I'm not ordinary. I've got certificates. I'm legal.

I've got rights. My Dad and Mum were legally married. In a mucking church. It was a white wedding. Five hundred guests, I believe.
Fancy spending all that on a do. It's amazing!'

'What is your name?' Tim was trying to distract his attention
from Julia.

'You've got a nerve! What's my name? I'm not sure I shan't pay
you for that. That's cheek, that is. That's what they call it in the
posh schools. Cheek. What's my name. Do me a favour! You
must think I'm bonkers.'

'Is it Cornish?' Julia spoke as Timothy thrust her behind him.

He was just in time. The figure made a dart at her and for the
first time brought out his right hand. The sight of it sent them
both back on their heels and their reaction satisfied him. He paused
to enjoy the sensation he was making. Up to the elbow his arm was
a paw furnished with mighty bloodstained talons, a fantastic and
improbable horror familiar to connoiseurs of certain comic strips
and films.

Its realism as far as construction and fit were concerned was
quite remarkable and as convincing as moulded and painted
rubber, inset with a certain amount of genuine monkey fur, could
make it. Only the distinctive convention in which the original de-
signer had worked lent it a merciful artificiality.

Timothy began to laugh. 'We had some of those last term,' he
said. 'Did you get it from the joke shop in Tugwell Street?'

The newcomer forgot his anger and smirked himself. He sat
back in the air again, but intentionally this time, and let his fore-
arms swing upwards from the elbows, his hands flapping.

'Child of the Fall-out', he said and laughed.

The offbeat joke which to any other generation must be indes-
cribably shocking amused them all, albeit a little guiltily, but it
was very shortlived. Flushed with his triumph over them, he
turned his right hand in its ridiculous glove palm uppermost. The
five razor-blades appearing through the rubber caught the hard
light.

Tim leapt straight for him, caught his upper arm and jerked it
backwards. It was a purely instinctive movement so prompt and
thorough that it came as a complete surprise. The stranger's reac-

tion, which was equally spontaneous, almost over-balanced them both. He began to scream in a terrifying, hoarse, but not very loud voice and every joint in his body sagged limply to the ground, so that Tim was left holding his full weight. He let him drop and put his foot on his shoulder while he stripped off the glove. The razor-blades were stitched into a webbing bandage inside it and its removal was a major operation with the quivering, yelping creature writhing round his feet on the stones. When he stopped screaming be began to swear and the stream of filth, in the soft lisping voice, had a quality of nastiness which was out of their experience. Tim turned a furious face on Julia.

'Take these damn things out of the way and put them somewhere safe. Don't cut yourself, for God's sake. You'll get tetanus, they're dirty enough.'

She obeyed him silently, taking both glove and bandage, and disappeared into the dark kitchen.

Left to himself Tim stood back and wiped his hands.

'Shut up and get up,' he said.

The speed with which the creature on the floor leapt to the window high in the wall was as sudden as Tim's own leap at his arm had been, and had the same instinctive precision. Only the bars prevented him from getting away. Their close spacing, which had required a certain amount of negotiation even from one so slender, effectively prevented him from bolting through and he fell back and lay against the wall, hanging limply, a black streak against the grey.

'Get down and turn round.'

The newcomer obeyed. His subservience was more distasteful than his arrogance. He shuffled into a corner and stood in it, letting it support him. His dirty hands hung limp in front of him. His face was wet with sweat and blubber and he smelled like a sewer.

'What is your name?'

'Barry Leach, sixty-three Cremorne Street, The Viaduct, E.'

He gave the information in a stream, clearly the result of long experience, and then paused. A new idea passed over his face as visibly as if he were an infant. 'That's the name I arrange with Ag to give. It's her name. She's Mrs. Leach. We don't give my Dad's name until we have to. It's part of Ag's arrangement, see? We keep him quiet and he pays up. It's Ag's address too. I live with her when I live anywhere, but you know my real name that's on my papers so it's no use hiding it from you. Ag's got my papers. She doesn't show them but she's got them and I read them when I feel like it.'

'Do you ever see your father?'

Timothy was concentrating and much of the youthfulness had left his face so that he looked tired and absorbed. He made a good looking but worried young man, very much a product of the age. 'Does he talk to you?'

'Sometimes.'

'How often?'

'Not as often as he wants. Can't take him, see?'

'Why's that?'

'Well, he's old – we're not the same generation, see. We don't see things the same way. He's got no sense of humour. You've got more humour than he has. It's age, see?'

'But he gives you money?'

'He gives Ag money for me.'

'Why?'

'Well, I don't keep it a day, see. I spend it. I take taxis when I have any money.'

'Taxis? Where to?'

'Oh, I don't know. Anywhere. I like taxis, they make me feel I'm who I am. . . . educated and legitimate and that.'

'I see. Have you ever lived with your father?'

'No. I never wanted to. Ag's right when she's against that. Your soul wouldn't be your own, not with him. He's very rich but he doesn't spend it. He's a do-gooder. It's because he thinks I ought to be living with him, and he doesn't want it because he's got a new wife, that he keeps giving Ag money for me. If you read you keep learning about men like that. Guilty, that's what he is. It suits me.'

'Where do you do your reading?'

'Inside. I get a job in the library, see, because I'm educated. The screws can't read at all. They don't know half the books they've got in those libraries. It makes me laugh and it would you too. You're about my age, aren't you? The old generation is responsible for the next. That's what they think. But it's not true. It's your own generation that lives with you, isn't it? Blaming the bloody old fools doesn't help. I didn't read that, you know. I thought it. I think sometimes. What are you going to do with me?'

'When?'

'Do me a favour! Now, of course. Have you gone soft or something? Push me out, that's what you'd better do. Push me out. You might lose your job if they found us together. I might say anything and you couldn't deny it. I've got a say same as you have. I'm legal. I've got papers, you can't take those away. Can you?'

'Something is happening upstairs.' Julia's voice came in to them from the passage. 'Tim! Somebody is screaming upstairs.'

'No, I don't think I want to.' Tim was answering the boy in the corner. He turned and spoke to Julia.

'The house is aroused, is it? I think we'd better take him with us. He's our pidgin.'

CHAPTER EIGHTEEN

Night-cap

'VERY nice,' said Luke, settling back in Mr. Campion's most comfortable chair. A glass was in his hand, the telephone was on his knee to save him having to get up when it should ring again, and his feet were on the fender. 'This is how I like waiting. We'll give them another half-hour. O.K.?'

His host glanced up from the message he was reading. He had found it on his desk when they had come in to the Bottle Street flat some little time before, and his anxiety to see if it had arrived had been one of the reasons why he had asked Luke in for a night-cap instead of being persuaded to go elsewhere after they had left the dining-room of the Eagle Tavern. It was a long dispatch, written in Mr. Lugg's schoolboyish hand, and had been taken down from the telephone which in England is now so often used for the relaying of telegrams. Mr. Campion had read it without astonishment and now there was a curiously regretful smile on his pale face as he put it into his pocket.

Luke cocked an eye at him. 'Secrets?' he suggested. 'You don't tell us more than you have to, do you, you old sinner? I don't blame you, we've got no finer feelings. Lugg has gone to bed on principle, I suppose? What does he do, a forty-hour week?'

'He says it's nearer a hundred and forty and that if he had a union he'd complain to it, ruin me, and be deprived of the little bit of comfort he *has* got. I could hardly help overhearing you on the telephone just now. They've got Mrs. Leach, then?'

Luke's grin appeared widely, as it only did when he was truly amused. His eyes shone with tears of laughter and his mouth looked like a cat's. 'I don't know why these gormless habituals tickle me so,' he said. 'It's not a nice trait. They do, though. Do you know where she was all the time? In custody at the Harold Dene nick.'

'The cemetery Harold Dene?'

He nodded. 'On a charge of pinching flowers and trying to sell them to the little shop opposite the main gates. The startled proprietor had only just handed an expensive and distinctive sheaf of Arum lilies to a regular customer, who hadn't left the shop above fifteen minutes so he could hardly ignore it, when she brought them in. He asked Agnes to wait while he got some money and nipped out of the back door to find a policeman. While he was away she helped herself to a telephone call and was just hanging up as he returned with a copper. We find 'em, don't we!' He was silent for a moment and sat sipping his drink and looking into the gas fire as if he saw castles there.

'That boy Timothy was lucky,' he observed at last. 'That was his Mum's last throw turned that number up. Some guardian angel looked after him all right.'

He appeared to be very serious, the long waving lines deep on his forehead. 'Remember that tale we heard tonight about the head-scarf? I thought at the time it had the true outlandish ring about it. Little white lambs dancing on a blue field and "Happy and Gay" – *Happy and Gay*! – written all over it in flowers. I ask you, Campion! Think of that poor girl, dying in a hospital which everyone confidently expected to be bombed in a couple of hours. She was married to a nervy, over-conscientious nut who didn't even know he was a father and was away on active service anyhow. Her only relative was helpless and there was no one to mother the baby. So what did she do? She caused the kid to be wrapped in a shawl marked "Happy and Gay" and then dropped off uncomplaining into Eternity. What happened? What you'd think? Not on your nellie! A bird turned up out of the air, a wayward nit, who scooped up the kid as a pink ticket to safety and flapped off with it, to drop it neatly into the empty cradle of the one kind of woman who wouldn't see anything extraordinary about its arrival and who found the message perfectly comprehensible. There you are, a straight answer to a straight prayer.'

Mr. Campion regarded his friend dubiously.

'It's one way of looking at it,' he said. 'There are others.'

'Not if you take her viewpoint.' Luke was unrepentant. 'Locate the true protagonist of each story and straight away you're living in an age of miracles. That's my serious and considered opinion. I see no other reasonable explanation for the stuff I come across.' He laughed and dismissed the whole stupendous subject. 'Munday is wild, I understand,' he remarked. 'There'll be some ruffled plumage to be smoothed down there, I shouldn't wonder.'

'Hadn't he realized that Barry Leach was anything to do with Cornish?'

'He didn't know Barry Leach or Barry Cornish existed. Why should he?' Luke was mildly ferocious. 'One Charles Luke, Superintendent, might have pulled a finger out and recollected something about a small-time problem brat in a totally different manor when the flat-wrecking case first came up, but did he? No, of course he didn't. He'd never heard of the silly twit until this afternoon when he put a query through to records. It's my fault. Cornish is somebody in Munday's area. It might have helped him had he known about this skeleton in his cupboard before. Munday has a grievance.'

'Will he show it?'

'I don't know. It'll be interesting to see, won't it?' As if in answer to his question the telephone upon his knee began to ring and he lifted the receiver.

'Luke,' he said, and brightened visibly. 'Ah. Hello. Your name was on my lips, Chief. How goes it? What? Here? Why not? Mr. Campion won't mind, he may even give you a drink. Right away then. O.K.'

He hung up and made one of his comic faces.

'He'd like to have a direct word with me, *if* I don't mind. Very proper and correct. That'll teach me!'

He was still mildly apprehensive when Munday appeared ten minutes later; and when Mr. Campion, who had not met him before, let him in the thin man was surprised by the newcomer's attitude, which was not at all what he had been led to expect. The correct pink-faced official was neither reproachful towards Luke nor packed with secret satisfaction at the new advantage he had suddenly acquired over the Councillor. Instead he came in with the unmistakable air of a man determined to put a delicate piece of tactics across. His light eyes were cautious and his prim mouth smiling.

'I must apologize for intruding on your hospitality at this time of night, Mr. Campion', he said, with an effusiveness which was obviously foreign to him. 'I've always hoped to meet you but this is an imposition.'

Luke, who listened to him with astonishment, relaxed openly.

'He won't mind,' he said cheerfully. 'Even if he won't tell me what's in his telegram. Now then Chief, what's happening? Have you got the boy?'

'Not yet, Superintendent. But he was noticed by a uniformed man in Scribbenfields this afternoon before the call went out, so he's about there as you supposed. He hasn't been seen since it got dark but the building is being watched and I've had a word myself with the woman Leach.' He shook his fair head. 'A poor type,' he said. 'Not imbecilic you understand, but a distressingly poor type. She admits telephoning the cobbler's shop and leaving a message for Barry Leach with Miss Tray. Just the name and address of the person she thinks was responsible for hiring the Stalkeys, that's all.'

'Did she say how she got it?'

'She got the surname and the address from a label on a wreath, and the first name she learned from something said by a woman she saw by the grave, and whom she thought she recognized as someone she'd met years ago in the country, she doesn't know where.'

'Ah,' said Luke. 'So Mrs. B. did speak. I thought that story of uncharacteristic silence was too good to be true.'

'Probably she spoke to herself, don't you think?' ventured Mr. Campion, who had appreciated Mrs. Broome in his own way. 'Having picked up the habit from *Alice in Wonderland*, no doubt.'

'Alice? That's just about what she is!' Luke was hearty. 'Classic and intended for children. What about this watch on the Well House, Bob? We don't want any more tricks with fire-lighters; that place is full of antique curiosities.'

'So I understand. Some of them human.' Munday could have been joking but his expression of complete seriousness was unchanged. 'I don't think there's any fear of that. I have two good men on it and the uniformed branch is co-operating. We haven't alarmed the occupants yet.' He hesitated and they realized that he was coming to the purpose of his visit. 'I've taken an unusual step which I hope you will approve, Superintendent.'

'Oh yes, what is it?' Luke was highly intrigued by the entire approach. 'What's the matter with you, Munday?'

'Nothing, sir, but I don't know if you quite appreciate the peculiar position of a fellow like Councillor Cornish in a place like Ebbfield.' He took the bull by the horns. 'I've taken the liberty of informing him and he'll be present when we make the arrest. I'd like it. I'd be happier.'

'Do what you like, old boy. It's your baby.'

Luke was sitting up like a cat, his eyes bright as jet bugles. 'I didn't know the local governments had such powers. He can make you a lot of trouble if not buttered, can he?'

For the first time Munday smiled, his thin lips parted in a frosty smirk.

'It's not that,' he said. 'But he has a position to keep up, you understand, and he's at a great disadvantage in being a man of remarkable conscience. Such people are more common in Scotland than they are here.'

'I don't get this at all,'' said Luke frankly, 'but it fascinates me. What are you frightened of?'

Munday sighed. 'Well,' he said, 'let me put it to you this way. Suppose he comes to his son's rescue as he has before, I understand, and he sees him in custody with one or two abrasions on him, perhaps.'

Luke ducked his chin. 'I like "abrasions",' he murmured. 'Then what?'

'Then the father has a great fight with his terrible conscience,' said Munday with granite seriousness. 'Should he make a row with the police, who may have done their duty a little over-conscientiously, thereby calling attention to himself? Or should he say nothing about it and condone brutality for fear of appearing in the newspapers?' He paused. 'I know him. In the ordinary way I have dealings with him once or twice a week. He's an awful nuisance but a good man. Every devil in Hell would drive him to sacrifice himself and we'd all be smeared over the London Press, let alone the local journal, when we could save ourselves a scandal in a nice suburb with a splendid building estate.'

Charles Luke thrust a long hand through his hair.

'I haven't fully appreciated you all these years, Chief,' he said. 'I didn't know you had it in you. So he's coming to see the arrest? That's very sensible. That'll do it, will it?'

'Very possibly.' Munday was wooden-faced. 'But to make perfectly certain of the desired effect I have suggested to him that he brings the probation officer with whom he's had dealings once or twice before, and I myself have taken the precaution of borrowing a C.I.D. sergeant from over on the Essex side. He's a man who knows Barry Leach well and has, in fact, arrested him on two previous occasions.'

'Without abrasions?'

'Without abrasions.'

Luke leant back, his dark face alight with amusement.

'Carry on. It's all in your safe hands, Chief. We'll stay here and leave it to you. It's been a long day!' The telephone bell interrupted him once more and he took up the receiver. 'Luke here.'

He sat listening while the voice at the other end chattered like a starling just out of earshot. Gradually his face grew more grave and there was an unnatural stiffness about his wide shoulders.

'Right,' he said at last. 'The Chief Inspector's here. I'll tell him and we'll come along. Good-bye.'

He hung up, pushed the instrument across the table and rose to his feet.

'Come along, chaps,' he said. 'The balloon has gone up at the Well House. There's no fire but they seem to have had a murder. I'm afraid, Chief, you're going to get publicity after all.'

CHAPTER NINETEEN

Meeting Point

WHEN Timothy and Julia hurried up the staircase to the bedroom floor, where a considerable commotion was taking place, Tim took Barry Leach with him. He had him gripped firmly by the arm, since he felt that it was not safe to let him loose, and he had no immediate idea what to do with him. The captive made no resistance and came not only quietly but in a series of eager little rushes like a timid dog on a choke chain.

The only lights left on in the house were two of the lamps in the candelabra which hung in the stairwell, so that all round them the building seemed ghostly and enormous, a great creaking barn, as they stumbled up the shallow steps among its shadows. Besides the noise from above there was a terrific draught and the night air of the city swept down upon them in a tide.

'It's Nanny Broome,' Julia said breathlessly. 'Shouting out of a window I think. What on earth is happening?'

Eustace asked the same question as he appeared suddenly at his door, the first in the passage down the right wing. He was wrapped in a splendid silk robe and had paused to brush his hair, so that he loomed up neat and pink in the gloom.

'What is all this?' he demanded. 'Is someone ill? Tim, what are you doing?' He caught sight of Barry Leach. 'Good Heavens! Who is that?'

A sudden gust of violent protest in a deep yet unexpectedly familiar voice reached them from the open doorway of a room on the opposite side of the corridor. It was Miss Aicheson. She sounded frightened.

'Be quiet, Mrs. Broome! Hold your damned tongue, woman, and come and help me with him. He's dead, I think.'

'Isn't that Basil's room?' Eustace did not move but spoke to Timothy. 'Isn't it?'

'Of course it is. *Shut up!*' The final admonition was addressed to his captive, who had reared up suddenly like a frightened animal. 'Keep quiet!'

Julia was the first to reach the doorway and she turned on the light switch just inside the room. It had been in partial darkness, only the small bedside reading lamp alight. It was the main spare room and a big one, furnished with Tudor elegance, but now the wall tapestries and the long silk curtains were blowing out across the room like banners, and Nanny Broome, fully dressed but white faced and dishevelled, drew her head in through the window.

'They're coming. I'd been watching them, so I called. The police are coming.'

'Good God, woman, that's no good!' Miss Aicheson was struggling to lift something in the bed, her clumsy hands plucking at it ineffectually. 'Look at this! Come here, somebody. Somebody come at once.'

The new arrivals swept forward in a group and for a dizzy moment stood staring uncomprehendingly.

Something huge and shining lay among the pillows. It was a pool of glistening colour, pink and blue and iridescent in the newly blazing light. At least half of those who came upon it so suddenly were reminded absurdly of flowers, a parcelled bouquet freshly delivered from a florist, until in another instance the evidence of their eyes could be denied no longer and the appalling truth came home to them. They were looking at Basil Toberman's face, flushed pinkish purple and with froth upon his lips, lying inside a plastic bag.

Miss Aicheson was both frantic and embarrassed and for the first time appeared an old maid. She had been trying to tear the bag and now, giving up the struggle suddenly, she pulled down the bed-clothes and threw them aside. The heavy polythene sack designed to store a long dress had been pulled down over Toberman's head. The surplus length, bunched into folds, had been tucked tightly about his neck and shoulders and covered by the blankets. Although he had rolled over, and his knees were drawn up, he was still held securely.

Julia reacted instantly with Timothy a quarter second behind her.

'He's not breathing!' she said. 'Quick.'

He leapt forward and struggled to get an arm behind the heavy shoulders. 'I'll lift him. You pull the bag.'

In the emergency he forgot his captive completely and as his grip on the leather sleeve loosened the stranger slid away like a shadow. He made no sudden rush but melted through the little group and shot out into the passage. No one noticed him go; the entire attention of everybody present was focused on the bed. It was proving a little difficult to get Toberman out. The damp plastic over his mouth and nostrils tended to cling and the material was exasperatingly strong and would not tear. It was several seconds before they had him freed.

'I want to get him on the floor,' Tim said, exerting all his strength to lift the limp figure out on to the carpet. 'If I get above him I can work on his arms. He's got to be made to breathe somehow.'

His authoritative tone pulled Nanny Broome together. Her dramatics ceased and she dropped on to the floor, to help turn the heavy body. Tim took off his own coat and prepared to give artificial respiration. Both she and Timothy were sitting on their heels and the light which hung from the centre of the ceiling shone down directly on the flushed face of the man between them. Presently she bent forward to look at him more closely and, putting out her hand, pulled the lower eyelid down for a moment.

'He's just like she was,' she said to Timothy, but speaking distinctly and clearly enough for everyone to hear. 'I mean that Miss Saxon. She looked just like this but without that froth.'

'My God, woman, what will you say next!' Eustace's voice rose in horror and then ceased abruptly, as from just outside the door and very close to them there was a scream, apparently of pain. At the same moment they all became aware of heavy footsteps flying up the staircase, while from somewhere far below an unfamiliar male voice was shouting instructions.

Meanwhile Miss Aicheson had recognized the voice.

'Alison!' She scrambled round the bed and went blundering across the room to the doorway while everyone else save Tim, who was fully occupied, turned to watch her.

Alison reeled into the room and collapsed in her friend's clumsy arms. She was clad in a little-girl dressing-gown splattered with pink roses, and with her hands held over her face and her sleek silver head bowed she looked pathetic.

'He hit me!' Although her voice was tearful her tone was principally astounded. 'He hit me, Aich! I was just coming out of my room and there he was before me in the passage. I said, "Who are you?" and he hit me and ran away.'

'Who dear, who?'

'Tim! He's got away!' The words escaped Julia, and Eustace, who was dithering midway between both casualties, seized on them.

'Who? Who?' he demanded. 'Who was that man in here? What is going on? How did you all get here fully dressed? What is all this about and who – Good Heavens! Who are you, sir?'

The final question was addressed to a square man in a tight suit who had just stepped daintily into the room.

Sergeant Stockwell gave the scene a single comprehensive glance. He was delighted with himself and confidence oozed from him. He was also sufficiently human to be rather excited.

'I'm the police, sir,' he said to Eustace. 'The lady called to us out of the window. It's all right, we've got him. Somebody called out up here just as we came in and he came streaking down right into our arms. It's all right, he's in custody.'

'Who? Who are you talking about? A burglar?' Eustace was roaring suddenly. His smooth face was damp and he was trembling.

'His name is Leach, sir. At least that is what he's called. But it's all right. You just sit down for a minute while I see the damage.' He thrust Eustace firmly into the arm-chair under the window, turned towards the group on the floor, and dropped down gingerly on one knee. 'That's good work, son,' he said. 'Carry on. I'll get you some relief first thing.' He looked at Julia. 'I wonder if you'd mind, miss? Slip along and tell the uniformed man that he's needed up here urgently. Is there a telephone on this floor?'

'Yes, in my bedroom, just here.' Eustace bounced up again and seized the sergeant by the arm. 'I want an explanation. This is my house and I haven't the faintest idea what is going on. I want information from you.'

'Yes, sir.' Stockwell was experienced. His manner though gentle was remarkably firm. 'But what you want most, you know, whether you realize it or not, is a doctor, and if I can catch our police surgeon before he goes to bed he'll be here in a couple of minutes or so. He only lives round the corner. We must do everything we can, mustn't we? Even if it doesn't look very hopeful. Just lead the way to the telephone sir, please.'

As soon as Julia returned with a constable, Timothy, who was on the point of exhaustion, prepared to give over to him gratefully. The newcomer turned out to be a powerful youngster, fully trained and eager to help, and he stripped off his tunic at once. Meanwhile Nanny Broome was recovering from her initial panic and now seemed anxious to make up for any kudos she might have lost, by exerting her personality to the utmost. She took the policeman's helmet and placed it on a chair, and unfolded his tunic to shake it and fold it up again for him.

'It was lack of air, that's what did it for him poor man,' she said unnecessarily. 'As soon as I saw him I threw up the window and shouted to you. I'd been watching you all from the landing. You were on my mind.'

The constable was not listening to her. One look at the patient had convinced him of the seriousness of the situation and now he went round behind Tim, rolling up his sleeves, and set about making a careful take-over without upsetting the rhythm.

Tim extricated himself and got up wearily, to stand holding on to the bedpost. He was grey with mingled fatigue and dismay and his forehead was wrinkled like a hound's. 'He's like a log,' he said, glancing over at Julia who was watching them helplessly. 'How did he do it?' He bent down and touched the limp body and drew back again. 'Someone has sent for a doctor, I suppose?'

'I think so. They were telephoning from Eustace's room as I came past.' She paused for a moment and the room was quiet save for the steady pumping. 'It's that dreadful colour. It's not quite like anything I've ever seen.'

'He's poisoned himself with his own breath, I think. Something like that. Keep at it for a minute or two, Constable. I'll take over when you want me to.' The constable nodded and continued his exercise, forcing the air in and out of the clogged lungs. Basil Toberman had ceased to be a person. His body had a new and terrible personality of its own, filling the room with its oppressive presence.

The night air streaming through the wide window brought all the far-off street noises which they had not noticed before, and its chill was mixed with a different cold which was settling into them as the first shock passed and they began to think again.

'It's not possible,' Julia was beginning and was interrupted by Miss Aicheson who spoke with sudden petulance from the other side of the room.

'Mrs. Broome, do come here a moment. Miss Alison's face is marked, see? Can you help me to take her to her room so we can at least bathe it?'

The new emergency seemed to have driven Basil Toberman completely out of her mind and she was both tenderly maternal and yet hopelessly shy and ineffectual in her concern for Alison, who might have been mortally wounded she was making such a fuss. The realization that she had no idea that anyone else was hurt occurred to both the young people as Nanny Broome bustled over to help her. She herself had recovered, almost, and her consequential little wriggle as she walked had returned. On the other hand Miss Aicheson appeared to be on the verge of going to pieces; she was at the stage of having to explain.

'I was passing the door on my way to Alison's room with her book when I heard you shouting,' she said hoarsely as Mrs. Broome came up. 'Why did you do that? Why did you call out of the window instead of trying to get the wretched man out of his damned bag?'

Mrs. Broome stared at her and they could see the question presenting itself for the first time. Her answer was spontaneous and clearly perfectly true.

'I didn't know it was a bag,' she said frankly. 'I didn't know what it was. There wasn't a lot of light and I wan't wearing glasses because I don't need them except for reading, and I thought he'd somehow gone like that after all that drink. All liquid and awful.'

It was one of those frank statements of a familiar if idiotic state of mind. 'He didn't look human and I lost my head and screamed the place down. I knew there were police outside and they were real so I called them.'

Julia ceased to listen to her and turned abruptly to Timothy. Her face was pale and her eyes enormous.

'Somebody must have done it to him,' she said. 'I've only just realized it. He couldn't have tucked the bed-clothes round his own neck after —' She left the rest of the sentence in the air.

'It's all right, miss. The man has been taken. We got him downstairs.' The constable spoke without relaxing his steady work. He was breathless and the words came out explosively.

Timothy and Julia exchanged startled glanced and Timothy protested.

'If you mean that chap we brought up here with us, that's utterly impossible.' The constable said nothing but he smiled, and Timothy looked blank.

'I suppose they'll assume he did it,' he began.

'If they do we can alibi him.' Julia dismissed the suggestion. 'Tim! Basil mustn't *die*!'

The young man did not speak at once but looked down at the limp bundle and away again.

'My God, I hope not,' he said earnestly. 'Now we'll know.'

Sergeant Stockwell had returned bringing the doctor, who proved to be a slight man who was remarkably self-important.

He walked over to the group on the floor and after a cursory glance went over to the dressing-table to find a suitable resting place for his splendid leather box.

'Very well,' he said over his shoulder as he unlocked it. 'Now I want everybody out of the room at once please, except the constable. I don't care *where* you go, madam.' He threw the information at Miss Aicheson, who had opened her mouth but not yet spoken and had been about to ask him to look at Alison. 'Downstairs, upstairs, wherever you like as long as it's out of here. I want to try to save this man's life and what I need is space and air. You too!' he added to Julia, who was waiting her turn to move. 'Outside everybody. As quickly as you can. Send me up another man Sergeant, please, and when your inspector arrives tell him where I am.'

'Yes sir.' Stockwell glanced at Timothy and his left eyelid flickered. 'I'd like everybody to come downstairs to the big room on the floor below this one. You lead the way, miss.' They trooped out and the doctor called after them. 'Don't forget my second constable, Sergeant. This man is nearly all in.'

'Very well, sir.' Stockwell spoke heartily, adding under his breath as they reached the passage, 'I'll take one out of the box. They come in dozens.'

'Alison must have her face bathed. He hit her, you see.'

Miss Aicheson turned in her path to appeal to authority and Nanny Broome, who was supporting Miss Kinnit, paused hopefully.

Stockwell was interested and as Tim and Julia went on alone they heard him talking eagerly behind them.

'You mean the man who broke in? He went for her, did he? Did he actually touch her?'

'He did, dear, didn't he?'

'Oh yes Aich, of course, I told you. He saw me and hit out. He was frightened, I think.'

'I expect you were frightened too, miss.' The sergeant aimed to comfort. 'He's an ugly young brute. Just show me where you were and tell me exactly what he did.'

Tim and Julia passed out of earshot. The drawing-room door stood open and the pink light streamed out into the gloom.

'Are you worrying about him?' Julia drew the boy aside for a moment and they stood close together whispering, leaning over the heavy oak balustrade which ran round the stairwell.

'No, but they can't charge him for something he hasn't done. He's broken in and he's almost certainly responsible for Nan's coat and for socking Alison, but they can't say that he's to blame for poor old Basil's condition. Whatever that may be.'

'No, of course not. I wasn't accusing you. I was just asking.'

'Oh! blast everybody.' He turned and kissed her ear, pressing his face for a moment into her warm soft hair. 'What did you do with that horror glove?'

'Hid it. It's in the oven at the back of the mock fireplace. Aren't you going to tell them about it?'

'I'm not going to rush at them with it.'

'Tim! Oh darling! You *can't* feel responsible for him.'

'Why not? He's our age and I caught him.'

'I see.' She was silent for a moment or two and then turned to face him. 'Did you hear Nanny Broome say that Miss Saxon looked like Basil does?'

'Yes I did.'

'What are we going to do?'

'What can we do? Nothing. We're not in that at all. The Basil business appears to be entirely the older generation's head-ache. That's the only thing we do know about it. Come along, Sweetie.'

They went on into the drawing-room to find Eustace standing on the hearthrug before the cacti collection. Councillor Cornish was in a chair on the opposite side of the room, his back was bent, and his long arms were drooping. He still wore his hideous rain-coat and his black hat was on the floor beside him.

Eustace hailed Tim with relief. 'Oh, there you are, my boy!' he said heartily. 'How is Basil? It's not as bad as it looks, is it? He'll come round, I mean? Please God! What a frightful accident to happen! Where were you when all this was going on?'

'Julia and I were in the Well-cellar catching that chap who came in through the broken window. He took the glass out this after-noon, apparently.'

Eustace's kindly face became amazed. He had recovered from his initial shock and his wits were about him again.

'Be discreet, Tim,' he murmured and glanced down at the room towards the Councillor, who was rising as Julia crossed over to him. 'I don't think it could have occurred quite like that, you know. No human being could get through those bars for one thing. Doubtless he was about the house before you found him.'

'He wasn't.' Tim was gentle but adamant. 'We were in the kitchen and he couldn't have reached the cellar from the house without disturbing us. He could get through the bars all right. He could get through a keyhole. Have you seen him?'

'Yes, I have. He and a plain-clothes detective and a pleasant young man who seems to be some sort of welfare officer are all in the dining-room.' Eustace hesitated and presently led the younger man into the window alcove. 'It's Cornish's boy, apparently,' he said softly. 'There's been trouble before, I understand.' He sighed. 'An extraordinary coincidence, don't you think? Just after he was able to help us this morning? I don't mind telling you I'm wondering about that fire. Let's go over. I don't know what your little Julia is telling him about the cellar. We don't want to raise his hopes, poor man.'

As they came up to the two they caught the tail end of an earnest and intimate conversation.

'I hoped so hard you'd go to Mr. Luke.' Julia's voice was as clear as a bird's. 'I'm so relieved. As soon as I heard he'd sent for Nanny Broome I knew that you must have.'

'My dear, be quiet.' said the Councillor. He was a gaunt figure in agony. There was no mistaking his helpless misery. He turned to Timothy and spoke doggedly.

'You didn't hurt him,' he said. 'I'm most grateful you didn't hurt him. Do I understand that he is responsible for something quite terrible upstairs?'

'No, sir. He has done nothing at all since he got into the house except talk to me.'

With exactly the same doggedness Tim was disregarding Eustace's frantic pressure on his arm. 'Julia and I saw the light from his torch when he got into the Well-cellar and after that we didn't let him out of our sight. When we heard the commotion and came up to investigate I brought him with me. We went into Basil Toberman's room together.'

'Basil Toberman? Is that the man who was murdered?'

As the question escaped the Councillor, Eustace made an ineffectual gesture of rejection and drew a long whistling breath. It was as if he had been listening for the word and when it came he had no resistance to offer. He dropped into the nearest chair and sat there like a sack. 'Is he dead?' he demanded.

'I don't know, Uncle.'

'I didn't realize there was any doubt of that.' Cornish was both apologetic and deeply relieved. 'I was misled by something I heard one plain-clothes man tell the other.'

Eustace looked up at Timothy. 'It'll be the end of us if he does die and there's any sort of mystery about it,' he said gravely. 'That scene at supper tonight and everything the stupid fellow has been saying to God knows who on the aeroplane, it'll all come out. All over the newspapers, everywhere, and that will be a quarter of the damage. Once the old stag goes down, you know, the hounds are on him in a pack!' In his mouth the florid simile sounded natural enough but Tim, who was hypersensitive concerning the old man's dignity, snapped at him.

'Then we'll have to dig in and live it down, because there's nothing else we can do.'

'My boy, that's easy enough to say.' Eustace was an odd mixture of despair and a sort of relish. 'Wait until you see Julia's father's reaction. Wait until it touches you personally.'

'But how is Tim concerned? What is it to do with him? He's not a Kinnit.'

Julia's intervention cut clean across everybody's private reservation. She made a terrifying picture of innocent recklessness, interested only in her love. Both older men turned to her beseechingly but Tim was not sidetracked. He put an arm round her and jerked her tightly to his side. 'You be quiet,' he said. 'We can't be bothered with all that any more, darling. We know all we need to know about me. Consider all that settled and done with. Now, if your father says you're to wait until you're twenty-one we'll have to wait and that's an end of it. We shall marry as soon as we can.'

Councillor Cornish hesitated. He seemed relieved to have found somebody of his own weight with whom to deal.

'Do I understand that you can give Barry a complete alibi for the – the happening, whatever it is, upstairs?'

'I am not giving him anything.' Tim had never looked more exactly a younger edition of the man before him. 'I am simply confirming that I was with him while he was in this house tonight. He will confirm that he was with Julia and me. We alibi each other.

On this occasion his word is as good as mine. He has an identity. He told me so.'

The Councillor's eyes flickered under his fierce brows.

'You know about that, do you? I was wondering what I was going to say to you and this young lady about that.' He hesitated. 'Or if I was going to say anything at all.' There was a pause and presently he spoke with a rush. 'He takes his papers very seriously,' he said, and it was as if he was speaking of some strange animal for which he was responsible but which he could never hope to understand. 'They are the only aspect of Law and Order for which he seems to have any respect at all.'

'He takes his identity seriously,' Tim said. 'Naturally. It appears to be all he has.'

It was an extraordinary piece of conversation, momentous and completely enlightening to each participant and yet, to everybody else, almost casual.

Cornish looked at Tim anxiously.

'How about yourself, Son?'

Timothy's glance fell on Julia's sleek head next his shoulder and wandered over to Eustace still sitting hunched and old in his chair. At length he met the Councillor's gaze.

'I've got responsibilities,' he said seriously. 'I'm all right.'

'Mr. Timothy Kinnit?', Stockwell, appearing in the doorway, put the question sharply. He was excited and his habit of swinging on his light feet had never been more evident.

'Here, Sergeant.'

'I see.' Stockwell appraised him. He was behaving as if he felt the situation was a little too good to be true. 'I have the Superintendent and my Chief Inspector coming along. They'll be here in a moment. Meanwhile I wonder if I could ask you to clear up a little question which has come up. I understand from my constable upstairs that you admitted in his presence that it was you who took the man Leach into Mr. Toberman's room?'

'That's right. My fiancée and I took him upstairs with us when we heard the rumpus. We didn't know what else to do with him.'

'I see, sir.' Stockwell was approaching a conclusion as it were on tiptoe. 'Then when you took him into Mr. Toberman's room it was the first time he'd been there, in your opinion.'

'Of course. Doesn't he say so?'

'That's exactly what he does say.'

Tim stood looking at the broad face with the half-triumphant grin on it.

'What's the matter?' he demanded. 'What are you getting at?'

'You've given yourself away, young man, haven't you?' Stockwell, still a little disbelieving at such good fortune, took the plunge squarely, nevertheless. 'It was you who put Mr. Toberman to bed, wasn't it? When he was too drunk to get there himself, let alone into a bag? That's the truth, isn't it?'

The inference, so direct and simple that its enormity became a matter for complicated investigation and endless legal argument before their very eyes, burst in the room like a bomb.

There was a long moment of appalled silence, broken in the end by a voice from the doorway behind the sergeant.

'Oh well, if you're going to be silly and imagine Mr. Tim did it,' said Nanny Broome, irritably, 'I suppose *I* shall have to tell the truth.'

As the sergeant turned slowly round to stare at her, Suprintendent Luke's voice speaking to the constable on duty at the front door floated up to them from the hall below.

CHAPTER TWENTY

Eye Witness

THE reading-lamp on the desk in Eustace's study cast a small bright pool of light on the polished wood, and the reflected glow struck upwards on the faces of the earnest men who stood round it looking down at Mrs. Broome, who sat in the writing chair.

Luke was there and Campion, Munday, and Stockwell, a solid bunch of human heads intent and silent save for the occasional murmur of assent.

For once Nanny Broome had no illusions. She was frightened and completely in the picture. She had no time to be self-conscious.

'We were nearly an hour I should think, me and Mr. Tim, getting him off.' Her voice was very quiet, almost a whisper, but she was keeping to the point remarkably well and they were all too experienced to distract her. 'He'd been up and down, up and down, until he drove you crazy. But he dropped off at last and we tiptoed out into the passage and Mr. Tim went off downstairs to his young lady, and I waited about for a bit in case Mr. Basil woke again. I did one or two little jobs. I turned Mr. Tim's bed down and looked in on Mr. Eustace to see if he'd got everything, He was reading; he always does. Miss Alison had finished her bath; I could hear the waste running. And so I went across the hall to the other three rooms and saw Miss Julia's bed was all right. Mrs. Telpher wanted me to help her close her window which was stuck, and I did that and went next door to Miss Aich but I didn't go in.'

'Did you attempt to?' Luke's tone was carefully lowered to match her own so that there was no physical interruption, as it were, to the flow of her thought.

'Not really. I knocked and she said "All right, all right" in her way, so I thought: "very well". And I didn't disturb her. Then I came back and listened at Mr. Basil's door. He was snoring quite regularly so I went and sat down on the window-bench at the end of the passage and looked out into the street. I sat there for a long time. I often do. It's my seat. I'm not in the way because I'm behind the velvet curtains and the light is up the other end of the passage and doesn't really reach to where I am. I sat looking out at the police for a long time. I thought the plain-clothes chaps were just ordinary men hanging about for a while but presently, when they kept speaking to the copper in uniform and looking about as if they weren't doing it, I guessed who they were and I wondered if Miss Julia could have telephoned them after all.'

'Why should she?'

'Because I'd had my coat cut when I came in after seeing you, Mr. Luke. I told her we'd report it in the morning.'

'Very well.' Luke was holding himself on a tight rein. 'Then what happened?'

'Nothing for a long time. I was wondering if I dare go to bed and leave those two young monkeys up downstairs. You can't really trust anybody at that age. It's not right to ask it of them. Then I heard someone and I peeked out through the curtains and saw a woman come along and go into Mr. Basil's room. I was so angry I could have smacked her because we'd only just got him to sleep, but there was no noise and after quite a few minutes she came out again and went back to her room, and I sat listening with my heart in my mouth because, I thought, "Well, if he's going to start all his tricks again it will be now that he'll begin." There was no sound, though, and presently I got up and listened at his door and he was snoring.'

'Did you go in?'

'No. I only opened the door a foot and put my head in. The street lamps shine into that room. I could see him. He was all right. Sleeping like a great grampus. Poor, poor chap.'

'Don't think of that now. What did you do?'

'I went back to my seat and watched the detectives fidgeting about across the road. A police car came crawling by and one of them went off after it down the side street. To make his report I expect. There was no one else at all about. We don't have many people pass at night although it's so crowded in the daytime. I might easily have gone to bed then but I didn't. I waited to see the detective come back and that was why I was still there when the person came again. I could hardly believe it when I saw her, but she went straight into Mr. Basil's room and she was there five or six minutes. Then she came out again.'

'The same woman as before?'

'Oh, yes.'

'Are you sure you could identify her?' In his effort to keep his voice level and in tone Luke exerted so much strength he set the entire group trembling.

'Well, one never is absolutely sure, not at night, is one? I wasn't sure who it was. I had to satisfy myself. That was why I spoke to her.'

Munday made a little strangled sound deep in his throat and turned it into a cough whilst everybody else held his breath.

'I said, "Is he all right?" I couldn't think of anything else to say. She didn't jump, she just turned round and came up to me. "There are lights on downstairs" she said. I said "I know: it's all right. How is Mr. Basil?" Miraculously Mrs. Broome's urgent whisper had never faltered but, now, remembered indignation interfered with her clear picture. 'She said "I never went in". The cheek of it! "Tim put him to bed", she said. "I never went in." Of course I didn't know then what she'd been up to or I'd have given her something to go on with! . . .'

'Wait.' Luke dropped a hand on her shoulder. 'Take a deep breath.' He was treating her as he treated child witnesses and she responded, obeying him literally.

'I've done that.'

'Right. Now go back. You spoke to her. She answered you. You were sure who it was. When she said she had not been in, what did you do?'

'I stared. "I thought you had", I said. "Good night." Then I sat down again and looked out of the window. She stood there waiting for a second and I thought she was going to explain, but she didn't. She just turned round and went straight back to her room and I stayed where I was, never dreaming he was in that thing.'

'How long before you looked at him?'

'Several minutes.' It was an appalled whisper. 'I sat behind the curtains getting warmer and warmer. My mind was easy, you see. She hadn't woken him the first time and I didn't expect her to do it on the second. I sat wondering why she'd gone in and why she'd been so silly as to try to pretend she hadn't with me actually sitting there, and I almost dozed!'

'Never mind, Keep on the ball. When did you look?'

'After about ten minutes. I'd meant to go down and call the children because they're only young and enough is enough. When I got up I listened at Mr. Basil's door and I couldn't hear him. It was as silent as the grave in there. I didn't think much about it but it did strike me as extraordinary and I wondered if he was lying awake. I opened the door very softly and looked in. The reading lamp was on and there he was, shining like a great pool of water in the bed. I told one of you, didn't I? I lost my head and began to scream and because I knew you were all there outside the window I shouted to you.'

'Because you thought it was a crime?'

'No. Because I wanted help. I don't think of policemen as always having to do with crime.'

'The trusting public,' murmured Mr. Campion under his breath as Luke spoke.

'You'll have to give us her name,' Luke said gently. 'Loyalty and long service and the respectability of the house, all those things are important, but not important enough at this point. Who was it Mrs. Broome? Just the name?'

'It was that old girl who was shouting when I came into the bedroom, wasn't it?' Stockwell could contain himself no longer. 'What's her name? Aicheson? She's pretending to be absorbed by the attack on the old sister of the householder.'

Nanny Broome stared at him.

'Oh no,' she said. 'Miss Aich wouldn't hurt a fly and couldn't without it getting away! No. It was Mrs. Telpher. I should have guessed that without seeing her, once I'd noticed the likeness between Mr. Basil's colour and Miss Saxon's.'

'Mrs. Telpher? Who's she? I haven't even heard of her!' Stockwell was already half-way to the door and Mrs. Broome's unnaturally quiet voice arrested him.

'When you first came over the road who let you in, young man?' she demanded. 'I've been wondering that ever since I came in here. There wasn't anybody else. She must have been going out as you came in. She's bolted. As soon as I spoke she knew she was found out, see? Even if she had been able to get back for the bag before I found him I'd have known she was to blame in the morning when it came out he was dead!'

In the moment of silence while her meaning became clear, there was an abrupt tap on the door and the little doctor came hurrying in, brusque and important.

'I've an announcement,' he said to nobody in particular. 'He'll do. He's just spoken. I don't think the brain is impaired. The last thing he remembers is Miss Alison Kinnit bringing him a drink in bed.'

There was a long silence broken by a deep intake of breath by the Chief Inspector.

Luke shrugged his shoulders. 'That has torn it every which way,' he said. 'Now what? I'm glad he's alive but I wish he'd stopped talking.'

'But it *was* Mrs. Telpher who gave him the drink. That was the first thing I noticed.' Nanny Broome was so excited that she was on the verge of incoherence. 'Miss Julia was with me when we saw her bring the glass upstairs and I mentioned it. I said "She must have half a tumbler of neat spirit there".' She paused and turned to Luke again with one of the sudden outbursts of utter frankness which were her most alarming characteristic. 'That was the real reason why I went to her room when she called me to help with the window. She was taking a long woolly dress out of a plastic bag then. I wanted to see if she really had drunk all that stuff. It's not only that I'm inquisitive, but if I'm to look after the house I must know what's going on.'

'And she hadn't?' Luke pounced on the thread before it got away.

'No. There it was untouched on the dressing-table. She'd put a tissue over it but you couldn't miss it, it was smelling the place out. Later on, when I saw her taking it in to Mr. Basil, I guessed what she was up to. "You're going to make sure he passes right out so there won't be any more disturbances tonight" I thought. "You selfish thing! Serve you right if he gets delirium and the whole place turns into a mad-house." I remember his Papa, you see.'

Luke ignored the historical reference.

'Can you swear on oath it was Mrs. Telpher you saw in the passage and not Miss Alison Kinnit? They're very alike.'

'Of course they're alike! That's what muddled Mr. Basil in the state he was in. All the Kinnits are alike; the family flavour is very strong. Their natures are alike. When she tried to put the whole thing on to Mr. Tim she was exactly like any other Kinnit. I thought that at the time.'

'*When?*' Luke leapt on the flaw. 'When you were speaking to Mrs. Telpher in the passage you didn't know that anything had happened to Mr. Toberman.'

Nanny Broome's innate honesty shone through the clouds of wool.

'No, but as soon as I saw Mr. Basil all glistening like that I realized that whatever had happened to him it must be Mrs. Telpher who'd done it, and that she'd clearly meant to put the blame on Tim. *That's why I screamed and called the police.* I'm not very easily upset, you know. I don't scream for nothing. I usually know what I'm doing. Where would Tim and I be now, let me ask you, if I hadn't screamed and you weren't all here but it had been left to the family to decide what story to tell? I knew she'd have to run because I'd spoken to her and she knew I knew who'd been into Mr. Basil's room. She's got away. Good riddance! I've been thinking she would if I gave her time enough.'

'You be careful what you're saying, Missus!' Munday intervened despite himself. 'The lady hasn't a chance of getting far. Meanwhile, have you ever heard of an Accessory after the Fact?'

'Only in tales,' said Mrs. Broome contemptuously. 'Catch her if you think you can, but don't bring her here near my kiddie-winkies!'

'Who are they?' Munday was beginning with interest, but Luke signalled to him hastily.

'Forget it,' he muttered. 'We've only got one life. Sergeant Stockwell, you ought to have noticed the lady at the door. You put out the call. Wait a minute. She has a child at St. Joseph's. You might try there first. I think we can take it that she's not normal. It's the old psychiatric stuff. There'll be no very definite motive I mean, and. . . .'

'I rather think there is, you know.' Mr. Campion, who had taken no part in the proceedings and who had been forgotten by everybody, now ventured to intervene a trifle apologetically.

'She was the only person who had sufficient motive, or so it seemed to me. Fear is the only adequate spur for that sort of semi-impulsive act, don't you think? Fear of loss. Fear of trouble. Fear of unbearable discovery. Especially when backed by the glimpse of definite gain.'

Luke stared at him.

'"Oh my prophetic soul", your telegram!' he said. 'I might have known! She is not Mrs. Telpher, I suppose?'

'Oh but she is.' Mr. Campion appeared unhappy. 'That is her true name and she is the Kinnit niece. The telegram was a reply to, a routine inquiry I made about her through the Petersen agency in Jo'burg.' He paused, looking awkward. 'It's one of those sad, silly, *ordinary*, explanations which lie behind most criminal acts,' he went on at last. 'I suppose her secret is the most usual one in the world and she hid it successfully from everybody except Basil Toberman, who is the kind of man who spends his life making sure he is not deceived on that particular point.'

Luke's eyebrows rose to peaks.

'Money?'

Mr. Campion nodded. 'I'm afraid so. She simply isn't rich. It is as easy as that. She isn't even badly off, hard up or in straightened circumstances. She is simply not rich. She never has been rich. The deceased Telpher was an accountant but not a financier.'

'But the Kinnit family must have known this?'

'Why should they? There are people who make a habit of keeping an eye on the financial positions of their various relatives, but with others, you know, complete ignorance on the subject is almost a cult. Mrs. Telpher was a distant relative. Distant in miles. The Kinnits were aware of her but not at all curious about her. How the idea that she was extremely wealthy was implanted in their minds originally I do not know. It may have started with some trifling mistake, or be based merely on the simple fact that they are extremely wealthy and she had never let them know that she was not. At any rate, when she had to come to London she found it very easy to make use of them. Her success lay in the fact that she understood them so well. They are all alike. Cold, incurious, comfort-loving and deeply respectful towards money, and yet in an odd inhuman way hospitable and aware of the duties of hospitality.'

'That woman only lives for one thing and that's cash,' said Mrs. Broome unexpectedly. 'If she hasn't got a fortune already her main reason for coming here was to make sure of an inheritance when the time came. You can be sure of that! Don't forget she's the only Kinnit relative except for Mr. Tim and she probably thought he ought not to count, being merely adopted. Her idea was to oust him, take it from me. Meantime, here she got her living free, and Miss Saxon's.'

This prosaic thought, which had been in the minds of everybody present, passed entirely without comment.

Luke was still waiting for Mr. Campion, who finished his interrupted statement.

'The one great risk she took never materialized,' he said. 'No one insisted on visiting the child. Knowing the family she did not think they would.'

'I insisted and was soon told where I got off!' the irrepressible Mrs. Broome put in tartly. 'The poor little mite was "far too ill to see strangers! Doctors' orders." As if a visit from me would hurt a kiddie!'

Luke flapped a silencing hand at her and continued to watch his friend. 'Isn't there a child?'

'Oh, yes, there's a child,' Mr. Campion spoke sadly. 'And its condition is just as she said – silent, incurable, unconscious. A heartrending sight, too terrible for anyone very close to sit and watch for long. Mrs. Telpher is not very close. She is the governess. She was driving when the accident occurred. She was sent by her employers to London with the child and her nurse, Miss Saxon, when every other hope of cure had failed. The child's name is

Maria Van der Graff. She is registered under it at the hospital. Anyone could have discovered it had they thought to ask.'

The story struck the depressingly familiar note with which true stories ring in the tried ears of experienced policemen. No one queried it. It was in the classic pattern of human weakness, mean and embarrassing and sad. The second note, the high alarum, not so familiar and always important since it indicates the paramount sin in Man's private calendar, took most of them by surprise although they had been well prepared.

'Attempted murder,' said Luke. 'She did it to avoid discovery and the failure of her plans, and when she saw she was caught she made a definite attempt to incriminate the young man who stood between her and an inheritance. That covers the present charge.' He hesitated and they waited, the same thought in every mind.

Mrs. Broome's eyes met Luke's.

'If Miss Saxon was the nursie, that was why she was so fond of the kiddie and why she tried to tell me about the diamonds.'

'The *diamonds*?' He was as amazed as if she had attempted to introduce elephants.

'The diamonds in the Safe Deposit,' said Mrs. Broome placidly. 'In the beginning, when Mrs. Eustace wrote in his fussy way and told Mrs. Telpher not to bring a lot of jewellery to the house but to put it in a safe deposit, he put an idea in her head. She invented some diamonds because she saw that he expected her to have some with her, and pretended she'd put them under lock and key. When she mentioned them in front of me Miss Saxon told me – in front of her – that they were so big that she wouldn't have believed they were real if she hadn't known. Well, she did know, didn't she? If they were in service together she'd have known Mrs. Telpher wasn't wealthy. She knew the diamonds weren't real and probably weren't even there. She was on the verge of telling me the joke. We were getting far too friendly, Miss Saxon and me; that was why *she* had to have her head put in a bag! It was aspirin, not drink, that was used *that* time I expect!'

'Quiet!' Luke's big hand thumping on the desk silenced her.

'You open your mouth once more, my girl, and it's you and no one else who'll be inside! Doctor, suppose the gentleman upstairs had died, what would the autopsy have shown?'

The doctor glanced over at him in astonishment.

'Oh, I don't think there would have been any need for an autopsy, Superintendent. It was perfectly clear what had happened to him.'

'Yes, I know, sir. It's a hypothetical question. What would have been the finding if the man had died and the bag been removed and hidden?'

'If I hadn't known? If I had simply been presented with the corpse and not told about the bag?'

'That's it, sir.'

The little man hesitated. 'Well, I don't know,' he said irritably. 'How can I know? There might be any sort of condition which could account for death. We're a bit more complex inside even than a television set, Superintendent. I certainly shouldn't be able to tell that he had suffocated, if that's what you mean.'

'You wouldn't?'

'No. There might be a slight increase in the carbon monoxide in the blood but – no, I couldn't be expected to diagnose suffocation. There'd be no foreign matter in the mouth or windpipe, no bruising, no marks of any kind. No, I should not have thought of suffocation. Fortunately it doesn't arise.'

'Exactly,' said Luke and scowled at Mrs Broome. 'And it mustn't', he said, 'or we'll all be in the bag! Don't you forget it! Chief Inspector, has your sergeant gone to put out that call? Where will you take Leach?'

'Ebbfield, I think,' Munday said seriously. 'We'll sort out the charges down there on the home ground, don't you agree?'

Luke's reply was forestalled by a knock on the door, and the Chief Inspector, who was nearest it, pulled it open to reveal a sleepy-eyed, yet harassed looking young man whom he welcomed with relief. There was a hasty conference on the mat whilst the noises from the excited house swept into them from the well of the staircase. After a moment or so the Chief Inspector turned back into the room and leant across the table to Luke.

'There's a question of a glove which Leach was thou~ have with him. It's missing.'

The doctor snorted with impatience but the superintendent v, very interested. He turned to Mrs. Broome.

'You said you had your coat cut tonight. What did you mean?'

She caught her breath. 'Oh, I wasn't going to think about that until the morning!'

Luke's bright teeth flashed in his dark face and the look he gave her was positively affectionate.

'In case you got frightened of the dark, I suppose? You'll do. Run along with the gentleman at the door. He's not a policeman, he's a probation officer. Tell him everything he wants to know. He's trying to help someone before they break his heart for him, poor chap.'

Mrs. Broome had the final word. She was bustling to the doorway when it occurred to her and she looked back.

'You could have a very nice nature if you weren't so cheeky,' she said and went out, Munday after her.

Charlie Luke, reduced to half-pint size, flushed and turned sharply on the doctor, who was making noises. 'Now, sir?'

'I want to get that man in a nursing home.' The statement was aggressive. 'He won't die now but he's still ill. He's still confused. Some of it may be alcohol, you understand. Professional nursing at this stage is essential.'

Luke stepped back.

'Excellent idea,' he said briskly. 'As soon as possible. You make the arrangements and as soon as the Chief Inspector returns he will make provision for a preliminary statement. Nothing detailed. Just enough to take us through the next phase. We've got to charge the lady when we find her, you see.'

'Of course.' The doctor was satisfied and busy. 'Fortunately there's a telephone in Mr. Eustace Kinnit's bedroom.'

Luke smiled at him without irony. 'Fortunate indeed, sir,' he said cheerfully and turned to Mr. Campion as the man hurried off leaving the door open.

'It could be a long trial, you know,' he said presently. 'She might get away with it on the medico's evidence of Toberman's

an just hear Sir Cunningham cross-exam-
t what she saw on the landing, can't you?
ou like!'

vas still standing by the table, looking into the
ugany.

world is certainly going to hear about the Kinnit family
nd their governesses, alas!' he said at last. 'No one on earth can
prevent that now, I'm afraid. There'll be no more hushing up
Miss Thyrza. She's out of the grave. She wins after all.'

'Murder doesn't hush,' Luke had moved over to the doorway.
'My old copy-book was dead right. *Murder will out.* There's
something damn funny about it. The desire to pinpoint the blame
gets out of the intellect and into the blood. I've known murderers give themselves away rather than leave it a mystery!'

Mr. Campion was thinking along other lines.

'It's very odd how the word "governess" is a guilty one in this
particular history,' he remarked. 'Just before we came in here I had
an account from Julia of the row in the kitchen tonight. Apparently
Eustace Kinnit's father tried to suppress the truth about a governess. Eustace himself went to considerable lengths to prevent the
word Kinnit and the word Governess appearing together. Mrs.
Telpher was responsible for a fearful accident whilst acting as a
governess and she came over here, deceiving her relatives and
bringing an assistant whom she said, quite unnecessarily, was a
governess. To the Kinnits it has become an evil word which is
always accompanied by trouble. Miss Thyrza is not so much a
ghost as their minds playing the goat.'

Luke laughed briefly. 'I know which one frightens me the
most!' he said. 'Mr. Eustace and Miss Alison are going to need
their adopted boy's support. It's a merciful thing he has a sound
young woman.'

He went out into the corridor and when Mr. Campion joined
him he was standing in the shadow by the balustrade.

They paused together, looking down at the curious scene which
the old house presented with its open doors and lighted alcoves. It
was strongly reminiscent of one of the early Netherlandish mystery
paintings; little bright unrelated groups were set about in the dark

and tortuous background of the carved staircase, and its
stages and galleries.

From where they stood they had a foreshortened view of a k
of men below in the hall. Munday was speaking to a constable a
a plain-clothes man down there while a dejected black wand, ben
like a question mark, wavered between them like some spineless
overgrown plant.

On the next floor, through the open doorway of the drawing-
room, they could see Julia talking to Eustace. She appeared to be
comforting or reassuring him, for he was leaning back in one of
the pink sofas looking up at her while she talked, emphasizing her
words with little gestures. It was a very clear scene, the colours as
vivid as if they were painted on glass.

On the upper floor, in the corridor to their right, Mrs. Broome
was showing her coat to the probation officer. She had carried it
to the baluster rail to catch the light from the candelabra, and the
purple folds gleamed rich and warm out of the shadow. Miss
Aicheson, wearing a plaid dressing-gown and carrying a tray with
a white jug and a cup upon it, was coming up the kitchen staircase.
And opposite them, across the well, the doctor, stepping out of
Eustace's bedroom, paused a moment to look across at Luke and
give an affirmative sign.

Mr. Campion was comforted. It was a picture of beginnings, he
thought. Half a dozen startings: new chapters, new ties, new associations. They were all springing out of the story he had been
following, like a spray of plumes in a renaissance pattern springs up
from a complete and apparently final feather.

The murmur of voices from the corridor directly below them
caught his attention. Luke was already listening. Councillor
Cornish was talking to Timothy.

'It was very good of you and I know how you felt,' he was saying
earnestly. 'But if you do happen to know where this glove weapon
is I think we'd better go and pick it up and let the police have it.
We're not the judges, you see. That's one of the very few things
I've learned in the last twenty years. We're simply not omniscient.
That seems to me to be the whole difficulty. We haven't got all the
data, any of us. When we do gang up and make a concerted effort

trial of justice, that's the thing which be-
I see it now, anything we suppress may
thing absolutely vital to the lad's safety or
ve absolutely no sure way of telling, that I can
not predictable.'

wasn't trying to hide anything.' Timothy's young voice,
which possessed so much the timbre of the other was vehement.
'I was merely not rushing at them with it. I didn't want to be the
one who damned him, that was all.'

'Oh, my boy, don't I know!' The older voice was heartfelt.
'That state of mind has dogged me all my life!'

There was a long pause before a laugh, curiously happy, floated
up to the two men by the banisters.

'We may not see much of each other,' the Councillor was saying
as he and his companion began to move away towards the lower
floor, and his voice grew fainter and fainter. 'You're going to have
your hands full with your commitments here, I can see that. But
now that we have an opportunity there is just one thing I wanted
to say to you. It – er – it concerns my first wife. She was just an
ordinary London girl, you know. Very sweet, very brave, very
gay, but when she smiled suddenly, when you caught her unawares, she was so *beautiful*. . . .'

The sound faded into a murmur and was lost in the general
noises of the busy household.

'There's a question of a glove which Leach was thought to have with him. It's missing.'

The doctor snorted with impatience but the superintendent was very interested. He turned to Mrs. Broome.

'You said you had your coat cut tonight. What did you mean?'

She caught her breath. 'Oh, I wasn't going to think about that until the morning!'

Luke's bright teeth flashed in his dark face and the look he gave her was positively affectionate.

'In case you got frightened of the dark, I suppose? You'll do. Run along with the gentleman at the door. He's not a policeman, he's a probation officer. Tell him everything he wants to know. He's trying to help someone before they break his heart for him, poor chap.'

Mrs. Broome had the final word. She was bustling to the door-way when it occurred to her and she looked back.

'You could have a very nice nature if you weren't so cheeky,' she said and went out, Munday after her.

Charlie Luke, reduced to half-pint size, flushed and turned sharply on the doctor, who was making noises. 'Now, sir?'

'I want to get that man in a nursing home.' The statement was aggressive. 'He won't die now but he's still ill. He's still confused. Some of it may be alcohol, you understand. Professional nursing at this stage is essential.'

Luke stepped back.

'Excellent idea,' he said briskly. 'As soon as possible. You make the arrangements and as soon as the Chief Inspector returns he will make provision for a preliminary statement. Nothing detailed. Just enough to take us through the next phase. We've got to charge the lady when we find her, you see.'

'Of course.' The doctor was satisfied and busy. 'Fortunately there's a telephone in Mr. Eustace Kinnit's bedroom.'

Luke smiled at him without irony. 'Fortunate indeed, sir,' he said cheerfully and turned to Mr. Campion as the man hurried off leaving the door open.

'It could be a long trial, you know,' he said presently. 'She might get away with it on the medico's evidence of Toberman's first waking words. I can just hear Sir Cunningham cross-examining Mrs. Broome about what she saw on the landing, can't you? That'll be murder if you like!'

Mr. Campion was still standing by the table, looking into the limpid mahogany.

'The world is certainly going to hear about the Kinnit family and their governesses, alas!' he said at last. 'No one on earth can prevent that now, I'm afraid. There'll be no more hushing up Miss Thyrza. She's out of the grave. She wins after all.'

'Murder doesn't hush,' Luke had moved over to the doorway. 'My old copy-book was dead right. *Murder will out*. There's something damn funny about it. The desire to pinpoint the blame gets out of the intellect and into the blood. I've known murderers give themselves away rather than leave it a mystery!'

Mr. Campion was thinking along other lines.

'It's very odd how the word "governess" is a guilty one in this particular history,' he remarked. 'Just before we came in here I had an account from Julia of the row in the kitchen tonight. Apparently Eustace Kinnit's father tried to suppress the truth about a governess. Eustace himself went to considerable lengths to prevent the word Kinnit and the word Governess appearing together. Mrs. Telpher was responsible for a fearful accident whilst acting as a governess and she came over here, deceiving her relatives and bringing an assistant whom she said, quite unnecessarily, was a governess. To the Kinnits it has become an evil word which is always accompanied by trouble. Miss Thyrza is not so much a ghost as their minds playing the goat.'

Luke laughed briefly. 'I know which one frightens me the most!' he said. 'Mr. Eustace and Miss Alison are going to need their adopted boy's support. It's a merciful thing he has a sound young woman.'

He went out into the corridor and when Mr. Campion joined him he was standing in the shadow by the balustrade.

They paused together, looking down at the curious scene which the old house presented with its open doors and lighted alcoves. It was strongly reminiscent of one of the early Netherlandish mystery paintings; little bright unrelated groups were set about in the dark and tortuous background of the carved staircase, and its several stages and galleries.

From where they stood they had a foreshortened view of a knot of men below in the hall. Munday was speaking to a constable and a plain-clothes man down there while a dejected black wand, bent like a question mark, wavered between them like some spineless overgrown plant.

On the next floor, through the open doorway of the drawing-room, they could see Julia talking to Eustace. She appeared to be comforting or reassuring him, for he was leaning back in one of the pink sofas looking up at her while she talked, emphasizing her words with little gestures. It was a very clear scene, the colours as vivid as if they were painted on glass.

On the upper floor, in the corridor to their right, Mrs. Broome was showing her coat to the probation officer. She had carried it to the baluster rail to catch the light from the candelabra, and the purple folds gleamed rich and warm out of the shadow. Miss Aicheson, wearing a plaid dressing-gown and carrying a tray with a white jug and a cup upon it, was coming up the kitchen staircase. And opposite them, across the well, the doctor, stepping out of Eustace's bedroom, paused a moment to look across at Luke and give an affirmative sign.

Mr. Campion was comforted. It was a picture of beginnings, he thought. Half a dozen startings: new chapters, new ties, new associations. They were all springing out of the story he had been following, like a spray of plumes in a renaissance pattern springs up from a complete and apparently final feather.

The murmur of voices from the corridor directly below them caught his attention. Luke was already listening. Councillor Cornish was talking to Timothy.

'It was very good of you and I know how you felt,' he was saying earnestly. 'But if you do happen to know where this glove weapon is I think we'd better go and pick it up and let the police have it. We're not the judges, you see. That's one of the very few things I've learned in the last twenty years. We're simply not omniscient. That seems to me to be the whole difficulty. We haven't got all the data, any of us. When we do gang up and make a concerted effort to try to get it, as in a trial of justice, that's the thing which becomes most apparent. As I see it now, anything we suppress may turn out to be the one thing absolutely vital to the lad's safety or salvation. We have absolutely no sure way of telling, that I can see. Life is not predictable.'

'I wasn't trying to hide anything.' Timothy's young voice, which possessed so much the timbre of the other was vehement. 'I was merely not rushing at them with it. I didn't want to be the one who damned him, that was all.'

'Oh, my boy, don't I know!' The older voice was heartfelt. 'That state of mind has dogged me all my life!'

There was a long pause before a laugh, curiously happy, floated up to the two men by the banisters.

'We may not see much of each other,' the Councillor was saying as he and his companion began to move away towards the lower floor, and his voice grew fainter and fainter. 'You're going to have your hands full with your commitments here, I can see that. But now that we have an opportunity there is just one thing I wanted to say to you. It – er – it concerns my first wife. She was just an ordinary London girl, you know. Very sweet, very brave, very gay, but when she smiled suddenly, when you caught her unawares, she was so *beautiful*. . . .'

The sound faded into a murmur and was lost in the general noises of the busy household.

Acclaim for
JOSHUA'S BIBLE

A Featured Alternate of Crossings® and Black Expressions™

"JOSHUA'S BIBLE is a wonderful story of the human struggle to courageously stand amid social adversity. Not since Alan Paton's *Cry, the Beloved Country* has there been a more engaging narrative depicting the conflicting social realities within South African culture. Shelly Leanne offers a bold look at life in this context, with broad themes and vivid characterization, challenging each of us to live and to stand with greater conviction."

—Rev. Nolan Williams, Jr.,
coeditor of *African American Heritage Hymnal*

"A very original and literary work...a beautiful love story."
—*Mansfield News Journal* (OH)

"Outstanding...intriguing...This book is sure to garner widespread acclaim."
—*Shades of Romance Magazine*

"What a wonderful novel! This is an uplifting story to be cherished by all readers."
—William Hollinger, author of *The Fence Walker*

"Burning at the heart of JOSHUA'S BIBLE is a radiant spiritual fire...Shelly Leanne has created in her title character a man whose journey is a rich, anguished, and ultimately, a most fulfilling one."
—Sands Hall, author of the national
bestselling novel *Catching Heaven*

"Leanne's rich description and solid plot take the reader through many emotions...The novel leaves the reader longing for a sequel, and inspires a desire to visit the rich, beautiful, and complicated South Africa."
—*ACE Critiques*

Joshua's
BIBLE

SHELLY LEANNE

West Bloomfield, Michigan

WARNER BOOKS

NEW YORK   BOSTON

To
Wilbert Watts, Jr.
The Geigers
The Holloways
Lorelee Dodge
For years of love and support

Published by Warner Books with Walk Worthy Press™

Warner Books
Time Warner Book Group
1271 Avenue of the Americas, New York, NY 10020

Walk Worthy Press
33290 West Fourteen Mile Road, #482, West Bloomfield, MI 48322

Visit our Web sites at www.twbookmark.com and www.walkworthypress.net

Printed in the United States of America

Originally published in hardcover by Warner Books
First Trade Printing: November 2004
10 9 8 7 6 5 4 3 2 1

The Library of Congress has cataloged the hardcover edition as follows:
Leanne, Shelly.
  Joshua's Bible / Shelly Leanne.
     p. cm.
  ISBN 0-446-53032-8
     1. African American clergy—Fiction. 2. Americans—South Africa—
Fiction. 3. Missionaries—Fiction. 4. South Africa—Fiction. I. Title.

PS3612.E237 J6 2003
813'.6—dc21
                                                              2002191023

ISBN: 0-446-69398-7 (pbk.)

Cover illustration by Bernard Hoyes

ACKNOWLEDGMENTS

There are countless people that I must acknowledge for their support. To the many friends I made in my trips to South Africa, who so generously conveyed to me information about the history and culture of the Xhosa, about life in the Eastern Cape particularly in the 1930s, about the history of missionaries in the Eastern Cape, and who gave me detailed tours of King William's Town, Fort Hare, Alice, Ginsberg, East London, Port Elizabeth, and the 39-Steps waterfall near Hogsback. Among those who I wish to specifically thank: Eric Gqabaza, Mzwandile Mangcu, Phumeza Mangcu, Xolela Mangcu, Dr. Vukile Peteni, Dr. Makalima, K.B. Tabata, Evodia Malefane, Snakes Nyoka, Wilmot and Nondwe Magopeni, Songezo Joel Ngqongqo, Mhlobo Zihlangu, Judge Sandile Ngcobo, Drusilla Siziwe Yekela, and Luyanda Msumze. A particular thanks must go to Collin and Angelina Tshatshu, who lived through the forced removals of the King Williams Town area and were relocated to Ginsberg, and to Ms. Biko, Steve Biko's widow who resides in Ginsberg and was generous in taking the time to speak with me.

I would also like to thank several South African leaders who I met in various trips to South Africa in 1994, 1997, and 1999, as I completed a historical work about the relations between African-American political leaders and black South Africans, and whose stories about life in South Africa fighting for a color-blind society helped to inspire this novel. In particular: a special thank-you to former South African president Nelson Mandela, whom I met briefly in my first trip to his country in 1994. A special thanks also to the late Senator Govan Mbeki, for spending so much time telling me stories about his memories of Fort Hare from the 1930s and for showing me around Port Elizabeth. Thanks also to Alfred Nzo and Walter Sisulu, for relaying to me the influence of African Americans and of works such as Booker T. Washington's *Up From Slavery* on their choices in life. Thank you to Archbishop Desmond Tutu for speaking to me at length about the impact of African-American ministers and Black Theology in South Africa.

To the Wanyangus of Kenya: how can I ever thank you for opening your home in rural Kenya to me in the summer of 1988? The beauty of the culture I experienced among the Luo inspired many scenes in this novel, as did the wonderful memories I have of teaching at Shitoto Secondary School.

I express my gratitude to the Transkei missionary who helped inform my writing, Delinda Higgins and to the ministers who have fed my mind over the years, including Reverend Keith Kitchen, Reverend Dr. H. Beecher Hicks, Jr., and Reverend Nolan Williams Jr.

I wish to express appreciation to my many African friends who so generously shared insights about their cultures and their views of Christianity, including Kweku Ampiah, Uche Ewelukwa, Sylvia Kangara, Joel Ngugi, the Otunnu Family, John Okidi, Fungai Rwende, Ndidi Nkonkwo, and Uche Orji. Thank you to the South African and Scottish women who helped me capture cultural facts in the novel as well as I could, including Nonhlanhla (Noni) Jali, Naledi Gush-Nkula, Eileen Anderson and Dominique Kalil.

I would also like to thank the many African Americans who inspired this novel through their work in South Africa. While this work is fictional, it has been inspired by the rich history between African Americans and Africans, including: the black missionaries who served in Africa in the 1800s and 1900s and helped in the effort to build independent schools, Ralph Bunche who had to travel as an "honorary white" person in order to visit South Africa in the 1930s, the AME church that made several African churches a part of their institution in the late 1800s in order to funnel more moneys to help them fund educational institutions and other activism, and to the

African-American women who moved to South Africa to help lead the struggle for freedom in the 1930s.

Of course, I would not be who or where I am today without the steadfast love and support of my family and friends. A special thank-you to Wilbert Harris Watts, Jr., the best husband a woman could hope for. Thank you also to my parents, Barbara Geiger and the late David N. Geiger, and my siblings David, Sandra, Stacia, and Sharon. Thank you to Christine Baker, who has provided such mentoring, love and support, and to Lorelee Parker Dodge, the best friend I could ever ask for. A hearty thank-you must go also to some of my most supportive aunts and uncles, including Mildred and William Geiger, Ann and Alonzo Lewis, Edward Geiger, Sr., Nathaniel Holloway Sr., and the late Ruby Dee Holloway, Thomas and Eunice Holloway, and Joyce and Joe Montgomery. Thanks also to my wonderful family and friends Butch and Tonya Geiger, Derek Geiger, Marty Geiger, Alpha Lavergne and family, Audrey Gross-Stratford, Nat and Veritta Holloway, Ruby Lue Montgomery and family, Carolyn Holloway and family, Patrick Holloway, Sandra Cook and family, Andrew Geiger and family, Thelma Geiger and family, John-nie Scott and family, Geraldine Gegier and family, Yvonne Chang, Julie Taylor, Andrea Chipman, Julie Catterson, Eric Jackson, Ted Small, Sister Helen McCulloch and the wonderful administration of Archbishop Carroll High School, Carolyn Kramer, Helen Corrales, Kevin Dodge, David White and Susan Watanabe, Modupe Labode, Byron Auguste and Emily Bloomfield, the Davis and the Watts families, Richard Newman, Jane Fitch, Rosemary Foot, Barbara Salisbury, Jendayi Frazer, Eric Scheuermann, Robin Teeter, Gary Sutton and family, Laurie Claus, Blair Bowman, Dr. and Mrs. Matthew Jenkins, Juande Blevins, and Averill Pritchett.

I am grateful to the late Professor Armstead Robinson, the Woodson Institute of the University of Virginia, and the Du Bois Institute of Harvard University, for supporting my work and encouraging me to follow this calling. Thank you to my fiction-writing teachers, who inspired me to continue to refine my craft, including William Holinger, David London, Sands Hall, Ms. Starr, and Ms. McMillan. Thank you to Joyce Nagata and Professor Mark Peterson, for inspiring me to excellence. Thank you to the many scholars and writers whose work has helped us remember the beauty of African and African-American history, including professors Chinua Achebe, Robert Edgar, David Anthony, Ronald Walters, and Lerone Bennett, Jr.

Very importantly, a huge thank-you to Denise Stinson and Walk Worthy Press, for the vision, fortitude and commitment to publishing works that glorify God and help to teach African Americans about the beauty of their heritage. A hearty thank-you also to Karen Kosztolynik, my editor at Warner Books, my copyeditor Stephanie Finnegan, and the many others at Warner whose dedicated and outstanding work helped to bring this novel to fruition.

Above all, thank you to my Father God. You know how hard I worked on this. It was truly an honor to write this book.

FREQUENTLY USED
XHOSA WORDS

amakrwala	initiated men
amaqhiya	headdresses
amasi	soured milk
ebuhlanti	cattle pen
ibhasi	bus
ibhuma	initiates' hut
iibhuma	initiates' huts
imifuno	greens
indlu	hut
inyanga	traditional healer
iqhiya	headdress
isibheshu	traditional dress (men)
isihlahla sethemba	tree of hope
izibheshu	traditional dress (men, plural)
izindlu	huts
izipho zothando	gifts of love
kaffir	racial epithet (nigger)
lobola	bride price
masakhane	self-help
muti	traditional medicine
Qamata	Great Spirit
ukholo	faith/hope
ulundi	the horizon
umgidi	initiates' "coming out" celebration
umbhaco	traditional dress (women)

*[A]ll such Negroes are to be absolutely barred
from landing and must remain on their ships
whilst in port. Land borders are also to be
carefully watched to prevent entry and, with
the aid of the Police, a look out should be
kept for the presence of such Negroes about
the towns, both at the Coast and inland, and
enquiry made as to their rights of domicile,
deportation following if that right is not
established.*

*Undersecretary for the Interior
South African Government
15 December 1920*

My servant Caleb,
because he had another spirit with him,
and hath followed me fully,
him will I bring into the land whereinto he went
and his seed shall possess it.

Numbers 14: 24

Now therefore give me this mountain,
whereof the Lord spake in that day.

Joshua 14: 12

CHAPTER 1

It had seemed so real, Joshua Clay thought as he awakened, heart pounding, in the blue-black darkness of his bedroom. It was more brilliant and vibrant and haunting than any dream he'd ever had. He could still feel the dampness on his skin as he'd touched his fingers on the pond's shimmering surface. In his dream, he had bent down before the healing waters, in that spot where he'd knelt a hundred times before. But as he peered at the pond, the image reflecting back appeared brushed in a deeper hue, darker than his own, staring up at the heavens mouthing voiceless words. It was still 1934, still his little piece of nature wedged between two Philadelphia boroughs, and he was still the Negro he'd always been. But staring at his reflection, he'd helplessly tried to understand the motioning of those lips reflecting back on the water, wishing its words would crest in legible colors just above the pond's surface. Instead, that inverted image sank, further still, submerged in a world turned upside down. He'd awoken with his heart racing.

Joshua's cot creaked as he turned onto his back, wrapping his arm behind his neck, trying to calm the dancing shadows of his mind. He rarely remembered his dreams. Why now, with only one day before his departure for Africa? It was everything he could hope for, serving as a missionary there. He would travel to his pond in the morning, Joshua told himself, at the first sign of a brightening sky.

1

He rolled over, willing himself to sleep, but tossed restlessly until that familiar voice sang out in the distance. Faint as a cry from a faraway hill, but soothing as a sparrow, the voice was preceded by crickets chirping freely between shards of porous bark. That shining voice joined their chorus, as if on cue, lending its hopeful tune. Melody and harmony mixing, they synchronized themselves into a soft song that seemed to grow louder as the moon grew fuller, as if when nature shone with all its might, the alto voice carried farther, illuminating all in its path. Though it called from too far away for him to discern its words, everything seemed to stand still in those moments as the bright sounds inched closer, until Joshua could feel his heart beating in tandem with the sounds. *Niya kundinqila, nize nithandaze kum, ndiniphulaphule. Niya kundifuna, nindifumane, xa nithe nandifuna ngentliziyo yenu yonke; ndifumaneke kuni; utsho uYehova. Ndiya kukubuyisa ukuthinjwa kwenu.* Their cadences embedded themselves into the folds of his mind, rocking him gently to sleep.

When he awoke again, he could see faint touches of gray sky through his bedroom's thin curtains. Enough light to see by, he thought. He sighed with relief as he gazed across the room, seeing Uncle Lucius's bed empty. Moving out of his cot as quietly as he could, he trembled in the October morning air, draping himself in a fresh gray sweater and lacing up soft leather boots. This was the him he knew, he thought, as he glanced in the mirror while brushing his raven black hair—the strong chin, the squared shoulders, the eyes that made people stare, as if captivated by something so honest there. Yet the memory of his dream filled him again with unease.

Stepping into the hallway, Joshua heard Lucius's snore rise up in the stillness of the house. Only a board or two creaked as Joshua moved past Lucius, who lay belly up on the sitting-room couch, hugging a Negro history book like a piece of cherished armor. There was a certain peace so early in the morning, Joshua thought, as he made his way through the porch door, gazing up at a sky that was barely more light than dark. With his Bible in hand, he took a moment to take it all in as he looked down the dirt road lined with sleeping houses—one of the best Negro neighborhoods around.

As the wind gently rocked the hanging bench beside him, Joshua's mind flooded with a hundred memories. This was a road always filled during the day with the laughter of Negro children, too young to comprehend the trials life had in store, as they scurried about playing promising games. From this spot overlooking Hope-dale Street, the Clay family would relax on Blue-Law Sundays, giving the Lord His due. Uncle Nate would sit there, puffing his pipe, blow-ing out a cloud of sweet-smelling air, recalling a memory dripping with molasses, telling it with spice-filled words. They would move inside only after daylight receded and the sun had been replaced by the moon. By that time, this street with no lamps would become lit by a kerosene lantern hung on every house or two. "The spirit of the times hangs in them lights," Uncle Nate always said, for the amount of illumination falling on the road always told of their state of affairs. Few lights had been burning brightly in recent years, as purses grew thin and the depression wore on.

As Joshua moved down the dirt road, dust and pebbles stirring gently beneath his soles, he walked more briskly than usual, pulling his collar up to keep warm. This didn't feel like it should, he thought. This morning, he had expected to rise excited, celebrating each last moment with his family. This was everything they had striven for—a Negro minister chosen to go to Africa, to show that Negroes could be trusted with great responsibilities. It was such an honor, everyone said so. But somehow, he couldn't diminish the twisting in the pit of his stomach.

He breathed in the morning's air, enjoying the autumn sights as he turned left onto Anthony Road. The next left would have led to the only paved road in that part of the city, which cut a path straight to the sprawling houses of the white neighborhoods where Uncle Nate tended gardens. But on these special journeys, Joshua always took a right onto a foot-beaten path that had first been forged by two youthful conspirators. As children, he and Darius had jockeyed their way down the undisturbed terrain, to the spot where spiked tumble-weed gave way to green shrubs in moist soil. Joshua passed over that very spot now, as the path veered northward, then dipped down an incline to the spot where a tree had fallen, split in its middle. The sight always brought a smile to Joshua's face, as if that tree marked the end of one world and the advent of another. Its frayed ends were hollowed in parts, spotted with decay and renewal, with young plants poking their fledgling heads through strips of the rotting wood. Every time he passed through this wooden gateway, he'd walk past seven rows of pine trees standing like unrelenting guards, into a cove painted with forty shades of green—a world in which everything had seemed to find its balance and rhythm.

Joshua inhaled deeply now as he took in the sights of this cove, which he and Darius had accidentally discovered. Tiny freckles of fallen rain covered all the leaves and needles, which hung as if with open arms, refreshed, blessed by heaven's drippings, and poised to greet the morning light. Folding his hands into a steeple, Joshua sat on a smooth rock beside the pond's waters. Many times, he had journeyed here and stayed late into the night, looking up at a thousand candles in the sky. Before he had gone to Wilberforce University and even after, when he returned home for visits, Joshua strolled often to this hidden retreat. He'd come to relish the beauty thriving in its every layer—in the crowns of the towering pines, on the pond's face with its lilies outstretched, down beneath the water's surface, where minnows swam. Each time Joshua entered this cove, he shed multiple husks with a glad heart—venerable leader, incisive student, grateful nephew. Stripping down every unnecessary layer, he took long, easy breaths.

In this place, more than any other, he could focus his thoughts firmly, praying, expressing his concerns, listening. His time near the pond—his time to be still—fortified him, producing the strength and wisdom that marked him older than his twenty-eight years. While his classmates would go nervously before congregations, licking their lips, holding their clotted speeches close, and following every word with a pencil, Joshua could square his shoulders up and leave his spot in the pulpit. Walking up and down the church aisles, he'd look his congregation members in the eyes as he delivered his sermons in a thunderous voice. Everyone around him knew he'd been given a gift; they could see it in the way his words kept Shella Perkins from jumping off the Bob Lake Bridge, and in how he'd inspired a congregation to feed the Johnsons well after their house had burned down. Ever since he'd been ordained, expectations had grown large about all he would do, all he could help achieve. And the communities all around him kept bestowing him one great honor after another.

The latest honor, of course, had come in the asking, when Professor James called him to his office shortly before winter break during what should have been his last year at Wilberforce, the Negro college he'd waited five extra years to attend. Joshua had walked into the professor's room, struck as always by the gold-framed diplomas hanging on the dark paneled walls. Professor James had always delivered good news to Joshua when calling him there. As the professor smiled at him from behind his mahogany desk, Joshua had wondered what it would be this time. Taking a seat, Joshua sat up, rolling his shoulders back like Uncle Nate had taught.

"I had a guest yesterday, Josh. A missionary actually." The professor paused, looking at Joshua intensely, eyes dancing. "He wasn't coming to look for recruits, but then you came up at the board meeting."

Joshua remained silent, taking Aunt Hattie Lu's advice to hold still in wisdom if you don't know what to say.

"The whole administration is still so impressed with how you kept those freshers from flaring up too much after that fight down the road," the professor continued.

"I'm glad everything stayed under control," Joshua replied. "We will march on city hall if we need to, but I don't think it will be necessary. Local officials have agreed to a meeting early next week and have already agreed to some of our demands," Joshua could barely hide his smile.

"Everyone understands what you did. You got an even temper—means people respect you, you get things done. You've been a leader at this school for three years now. A more prominent leader than we seen for some time. We're worried what we're gonna do without you here! In any case, this preacher—Reverend Herman Watson—he's got his eye on you now. He was impressed by the stories and wants to speak with you."

"About the students?" Joshua asked quizzically.

The professor remained quiet. A pregnant pause filled the room. "About serving abroad," he finally said, slowly, pride beaming in his eyes.

Joshua thought he'd misheard.

"A missionary, Josh!" The professor smiled broadly, responding to the look in Joshua's eyes. "They want to send you to Africa."

It took a few moments for the words to sink in. A smile painted itself across Joshua's face.

"You know, just like I do, it's rare for white missionary groups to send a Negro to Africa these days," Professor James said. "It's not like it was years ago. Back then, even before they first hired me to teach here, hundreds of Negroes had already traveled to Africa to serve as Christian missionaries with those organizations. But you know the tide turned. Half the newspapers in South Africa been publishing articles sayin' American Negroes have done great harm to mission work there. They think we're all going over there to stir up trouble, to teach Africans to revolt against Europeans. Negroes got no business using the church that way." Professor James shook his head, lost in thought for a moment. "By failing us abroad, those missionaries broke any notion that Negroes could be trusted with great responsibilities—at home *or* abroad."

Joshua nodded. He also had heard the many stories about Negro missionaries sent to Africa, only to be sent back in shame.

"Everybody knows the South African government's got a ban on Negro missionaries to South Africa now. So if Reverend Watson's sayin' he thinks you should go, that's something special. His mission's been havin' a hard time building up a presence at Fort Hare. And with the success of our Negro ambassador to Africa, they started thinkin' a Negro's what's needed there. They think it might make it easier for the Africans to relate—they'd listen more." Professor James stood up and looked out his window at students walking across campus. He looked back at Joshua with mist in his eyes. "All of your work here at Wilberforce has been important, but . . ." His words trailed.

"None of it would compare to successful work abroad," Joshua said quietly, finishing for him.

Professor James nodded, moving in front of a wall-framed commendation letter from the governor, which hung next to a photograph of Wilberforce's president dedicating the school's new building, with Professor James and local white officials smiling on. Joshua could see how much this meant to the professor.

"Of all the reasons why I thought you'd asked me here," Joshua said, "this wasn't among them."

"If you can help show Negroes can be counted on overseas, help make the ways of African natives more acceptable to the world outside—that will help matters here," Professor James said in almost a whisper. He dropped his eyes, tapping his finger on his table. "I know you had ideas about preaching back home after you graduated this year. But this would be an honor for our whole Negro community, Joshua. And for every month you serve in Africa, the mission's benefactors will provide your home church with resources to benefit your community in Philadelphia. Those same benefactors would also give resources to us here at Wilberforce. In these slim economic times, that's a lot." He stopped himself for a moment. "I don't mean to pressure you, son."

Joshua read the professor's expression; the older man looked at him with the face of all those who had been trod on and had spent their lives weathering more insults in order to open doors so that their children might have better. The fluttering in his stomach told Joshua it would be difficult to turn the opportunity down.

"I realize it's a tremendous honor," Joshua said softly. Relief coated the professor's face. Joshua stared out the window for a moment. The idea was only a sketch on a canvas, but it drew him. He'd seen the pictures in magazines of bare-breasted African women with heavy fruit-filled baskets hoisted high on their heads, walking steadily with sweat-sprinkled faces, laboring under a fierce sun. Dressed in rags, with barren feet, they always stared into the cameras with questioning gazes.

"I was close to accepting a position back at my home church in Philadelphia," Joshua said, squinting his eyes. "But I hadn't said yes yet—"

"You'd have to spend a whole extra year here in training—they got special things they want to teach you 'bout reaching out to Africans and how to be a proper missionary. And they'll want you to know a bit more history," Professor James responded, moving near a shelf filled with alphabetically arranged books, from European to

Oriental history. He wiped away a thin coat of dust from one of them, smiling, with that borrowed book between his palms. "Think about it, son."

In the next few days, Joshua did just that. But every time his eyes lit up with the thought of the opportunity, his mind would drift to the troubled times the depression had brought. He could still see the anguished look on Aunt Lu's face as she'd glimpsed swelling lines of jobless Negroes gathering daily outside of the general store, hoping for some work. He remembered her fears as local banks began to fail. He recalled Nate's concern as half the Negroes in town lost their jobs and as he'd watched their neighbors pack their bags, heading south for certain refuge with relatives. Joshua had delayed attending college to work, helping his family bring in money during a tough time; now, bad economic times seemed to loom again. Joshua couldn't bear the thought of causing his family pain. At the earliest chance, he had traveled back from Ohio to talk with his family.

"You know my work's been steady," Uncle Nate had responded, squinting his eyes pridefully, chin raised, when Joshua broached the subject. Lucius and Nate sat side by side in the living room, the two brothers nodding their heads in agreement for a change. "That shouldn't be somethin' you even think 'bout . . ."

". . . and you know my work's even more safe than Nate's," Uncle Lucius continued as if speaking with the same breath. "They need more ships over in Europe to build back up after the Great War, and America's building her own fleet up. They need us Negroes for them jobs even the whites won't take."

"So don't be thinkin' of stayin' on our account," Nate said firmly. "Some of the worst of the bad times is over anyhow, Josh. President Roosevelt's been sayin' that on the radio, and I believe him." They pursed their lips, their eyes more filled with pride in his accomplishments than Joshua could ever remember. Their words lifted Joshua's spirits. He knew money had trickled into their house regularly, even after the depression had begun to hit fiercely, but he had still needed to hear those words.

Joshua replayed their words in his mind now as he inhaled the pine-scented air and glanced at the cove's beauty. He always seemed to see things more clearly here before the placid waters. It had always been that way, even back when Darius was still alive. Joshua could remember his cousin so vividly, and could still picture him as a teenager, dancing a jig as he hopped from stone to stone over the pond's most shallow waters. His adolescent laughter had graced the cove as he leaped, arms spread for balance, trying to make it to the next smooth rock. Missing time and again, Darius would dip his foot into the water, his laughter becoming punctuated with "Ah, man! Ma's gonna get me!"

Remembering their time here, Joshua found his heart filled with so much love and so much sadness, too much of both to comprehend. They had been like the gum and the bark, steadfast companions. Deferring to his seniority, Joshua always followed Darius a few steps behind as they combed every inch of their hidden land. Darius, seven years his elder, would sit on a stump and give Joshua lessons here, his imagination teeming with determination as he'd tell tales of how he'd help change things for black folk—as if they could be changed and others simply hadn't tried hard enough. To any notion that it wasn't possible, Darius would puff out his lip and shake his head side to side. His dreams were aimed high, his words laced with conviction. Joshua remembered it all so clearly, even though he'd seen Darius grow five years beyond that youthful age to the soldier he'd become. With a restless soul, a thick chest, and a strong nerve, Darius had shaved his hair low and waved, with a broad grin, as Uncle Nathan drove him to the train station and to his service.

Joshua sighed. This was a large part of his unease. Darius. Everyone in his family was still mourning his loss. And every time Lu looked at Joshua lately, she seemed to fear what would become of Joshua on his own sojourn. With the thick pine scents all around him and a soft wind caressing his skin, Joshua's guilt and doubts loomed again. The silence suddenly seemed to grow louder as the day's first rays crept through the lowest pine branches, calling Joshua's eyes back to the pond. Sprinkling the still water with steady beams, the sun's rays spread like tiny footprints making their way slowly, then scurrying, touching every living thing. The whole cove seemed ablaze in yellow, bright like blooming daisies. With God's handiwork so brilliant around him, Joshua sank to his knees, losing himself in a soulful prayer.

Heavenly Father, I come before Your throne of grace and mercy, and I ask You to guide my steps. I understand the honor I've been bestowed, as I've been chosen to serve in Africa. To whom much is given, much is required, and I thank You, Lord, for this opportunity. I understand there are those who believe a Negro is not worthy of such responsibility, that a Negro cannot spread Your Word and bring the backward and the unrighteous to You. I pray, Father God, that You help me to show them that they are wrong, by giving me the strength to stand tall with my mission in South Africa. I know there are others who distrust the intentions of my mission, who do not believe that Negroes can work with whites toward any common good. I ask that You ease their hearts: give my aunt Lu peace as she thinks of my journey and assure my uncle Lucius that the intentions of those who are sending me are to glorify You, and for no other purpose. Give me the strength to succeed. Watch over my family. And please look after Shantal while I am away. I understand my family wishes me to marry Shantal. I ask, Father God, that You guide my actions. Help me, through all of my works, to glorify Your name. These in Your Son's name I pray.

As he prayed, his concerns slipped away, leaving such peace. Joshua sat back on the rock, happy to have time to reflect on his journey. He cradled his Bible between his palms, tracing his finger around its binding, which was worn and tearing, and across the mud stains on its hard covers. He rubbed his fingers gently over those mud stains, looking closely at those marks from the Carolina riverbanks, still visible after all of these years. Touching them always sent a chill through him, knowing they marked the very spots where his grandfather's blue-black hands had once touched this Bible. His family still recited the tale proudly—how Joshua's grandfather, a slave, would gather with other slaves beneath the cover of darkness, kneeling down beside the river. There, under the stars, the blue hills and river beside them, they would pray with all their hearts and souls to God for freedom, for hope, for the future. These mud stains always caught Joshua's eyes, drawing him back in time. He could practically see the sight, as the few slaves who could read lifted that Bible up to the night's silver light, finding inspiration in its Word. *That's faith,* he thought to himself as he moved his finger over the mud stain. *To kneel in your midnight hour, Bible in hand, praying to the Lord to set your chains free, and to believe so fully that your prayer would be answered—that's faith.*

He parted the Bible's pages, his brow knit, meditating on the Word, considering it deeply, taking the time to be still. He seemed to hear that distant voice again. He'd come to feel such peace every time he'd hear that singing. At times the sound was so faint it seemed no more than the breeze rustling sweetly, music sent to soothe his soul. At other times, its words seemed formed fully, echoing in his mind like chimes in the wind.

There had been too few moments like this in the last year, as his mission prepared him for his journey abroad. With the extra classes led by his mission's teachers, the trips to meet wealthy benefactors, and the long list of dos and don'ts to memorize, he'd had so little time to be still. He closed his eyes, his soul filling with peace as that faint voice called forth a song.

Soon the sun's rays grew stronger. Joshua wiped a hand across his brow. He glanced up at the sun, positioned high in the sky. He hadn't realized he'd been here so long. Everyone would be wondering where he was. As he began to retrace his steps back up the hill, it pierced him, causing him to pause—a fear as real as the blood in his veins. He couldn't understand this deep sense of unease and why it hadn't gone away. But he had no more time to ponder the churning inside. In that moment, he hoped with all his heart he'd be able to whisk those feelings away.

CHAPTER 2

"What happened to you?" Shantal laughed, her shining eyes drawn directly to the mud circles around Joshua's knees as he walked through the porch door, nearly out of breath after walking quickly back from the pond. She perched herself up farther in the living room's cushioned chair, trying to read his expression.

"I can't give away all of my secrets," Joshua joked, pulling a chair next to her, taking her hand as he sat down.

The clanking of cast-iron pots drew his attention toward the kitchen, where he could hear the muffled sounds of his aunts behind the closed door. There was something very peaceful about this day's rhythm. The house bustled more vigorously than usual this Saturday, with the feel of Christmas Day. Everyone busied themselves preparing for Joshua's last supper before he departed. He could see the tables and piano had all been polished to a shine, and the smell of grits and fried salmon cakes lingered in the air, gently mixing with the aroma of scalding milk. The smells wrapped around him like a welcoming hand. Reverend Watson would be joining them for dinner, and he could tell his aunts were preparing quite a feast.

Joshua caressed Shantal's hand. He was happy to see her smiling for a change. In the last few weeks, her spirits had seemed so downcast. He knew what was on her mind. As she searched his face, he shifted in his seat, trying to find the words to tell her what he needed to. He was relieved as Lu interrupted, moving on thick ankles into the nearby dining room, placing a pot on the table.

"Thank you for going to such trouble to prepare a big meal," Joshua said to Lu, who stared at his muddied pants, her full lips thinning.

"You only got so many pairs to take with you," she said sternly, nodding at the mud on Joshua's pants.

"Yes, ma'am, I should have been more careful," Joshua said, studying her face. With every day his trip drew nearer, her coolness toward him grew.

"We just want our young man to dazzle them when he goes abroad," Aunt Alma said, trying as always to soften Lu's words as she moved to the table to set down another bowl. She gave Joshua a balmy smile.

"You best change clothes so I can wash them for you," Aunt Lu said, moving a feather duster to clean the dining-room chairs.

Joshua touched Lu's arm as he left to change.

"Is there anything I can do to help with preparations?" Joshua asked when he returned a few minutes later, wearing as usual a pressed shirt, neat trousers, and dress shoes, which made Lu proud. Lu paused her dusting, the fat under her arms jiggling faintly as she moved toward him, taking his muddied garment.

"Just set yourself down and focus on gettin' ready to go," she said in a whisper.

Shantal readily put her book down and joined Joshua in his bedroom as he settled down to finish packing. She flopped down on the bed across from him. Any other time, Lu would never have allowed this. It was one of "Lu's Laws." Young ladies were to go nowhere near the men's room. Lu said girls who wanted to break that rule deserved a special name. She'd enforced her law especially strongly every time Darius's admirers had flocked to their house on Sundays, smiling broadly and evoking unwelcome reminders that Lu's sister Cherene—Josh's ma—hadn't had the common sense to keep away from a man's room. His ma had gained entrance to college, a first for her family, but hadn't understood what her own mother had meant by "watch your p's and q's and don't take any wooden nickels." As it turned out, that advice wasn't specific enough. Seven months after she'd left, his ma returned from college with her belly bulging so largely it shamed her whole family. The only good thing that came out of it, Lu always said, were that her baby sister returned home and Joshua was born. But that sort of foolishness would only happen to their family once, Lu insisted. Ever since then, Lu's Laws had multiplied. But just then, Lu passed Joshua's room glimpsing Shantal sitting there carelessly with her arms stretched in back of her. She didn't say a word.

Joshua kept quiet as he dug into the battered trunk from Ohio on the floor, pulling out a bundle of clothes and his Bible, handing them to Shantal to hold as he repacked a smaller suitcase. Shantal set his Bible aside and handed him his clothes piece by piece as he refolded them into the smaller hard-backed suitcase. Her eyes darkened as she bit her lip, gathering her words.

"Christa Rae's cousin went to Africa and came back in ten months. Said he couldn't stand the filth and the bugs," she finally managed.

"Christa Rae says a lot of things, most of which have only half a grain of truth to them," Joshua responded plainly as he removed a thin band from around the stack of letters Shantal had written to him over the years, aligning their edges. He knew Shantal was trying to pick a fight. He had invited her to meet his family and spend time in Philadelphia, thinking that it would make his departure easier. It had only seemed to make matters worse.

"What she said got truth to it—Africa ain't the same as it is here. Just the livin' alone . . ."

He inhaled deeply, standing to wipe a thin coat of dust from a gift box he lifted from the drooping mantel. "I don't want these to get lost," he said, raising the letters. "They'll be more safe here." He gently placed them inside the red-lined box. Shantal tensed her lips.

"It's gonna be real different there. You seen them magazine pictures—" she said.

"What are you trying to tell me, Shantal?"

"Don't be getting all huffed, I'm just trying to warn you."

He took a deep breath, keeping the frustration from his tone. "I need for you to wish me well in this. You know it's important," he said, folding his sweaters more deliberately.

"You packing like you ain't never coming back, that's all. I saw all them lists when we was back in Ohio. If it was just a little while, you wouldn't be so careful. I thought you told me that it wouldn't be long and you'd be back for me."

Joshua heard Shantal's worry seep from somewhere deep inside. He'd never seen her so uncertain, and he felt so ashamed to have caused this. The bed creaked as he sat down beside her, looking at her intensely. His family had seemed to make up their minds quickly, long before they'd met her. Most of them seemed satisfied with two bare facts: She came from a "good" family in South Carolina with long ties to his own, and she had made it to college. Just right for a preacher's wife. Only Lu had seemed a bit less certain after meeting Shantal. "Too hard-headed." That's what he'd heard Lu mutter under her breath. But that was the quality that enticed Joshua the most— she had such a determined spirit. The other young men at Wilber-force had been fixated on Candy Dandridge, whom they'd deemed the prettiest new lady at school. But Shantal caught his eye the minute she walked into the freshman mixer dressed in a pink dress, with pumps to match.

To the other young men, Shantal may have looked ordinary in every way, but there was something in the way she walked as she strolled along with self-assurance. And there was something also in how she focused on meeting the other new women at the mixer, not on trying to ingratiate herself with the men, that kept Joshua look-ing in her direction. They soon became a familiar sight around campus—he with his hair patted down and suspenders fastened neatly; she always dressed in something sunny, with her hair pressed and curled under. Back home, the news that Joshua had a girlfriend spurred a lot of talk—everyone had been waiting.

"You found yourself a woman yet?" Alma had asked him jokingly at Christmastime during his sophomore year. The whole family chuckled, just as they had the previous year when Joshua had returned home for winter break. Lucius, planted in the middle of the living-room couch, had kept reading his book. Lu hadn't even both-ered to look up from her knitting. But this time, Joshua didn't answer. Only the thud of snow sliding in a clump to the ground from the ledge outside broke the room's silence. Everyone fell still as the meaning of Joshua's silence and his crooked smile sank in. They burst out laughing.

"Oooooooooh, it finally done happened!" Aunt Waneda said. "Some girl finally got his attention."

Nate nearly choked on his pipe, while Lucius bellowed, "Darius broke hearts for years—we could never even get you to look at a girl. Head in the books! I knew it was bound to happen one day!"

They knew, as did Joshua, that Shantal had to be someone special. And she was. He'd never seen such a doubting look in Shantal's eyes as now, with her hands knotted in her lap.

"You know I promised I would send for you if conditions were right," Joshua said as gently as he could, taking one of her hands in both of his.

"And what conditions would those be?"

Their eyes lingered and Joshua's lips parted, but he couldn't find the words. He would never speak an untruth to her, not even to put her at ease. She pulled her hand away, lips dipping. He couldn't respond at first.

"Shantal." He sighed. "I don't know what Africa is really like. Maybe I won't adjust well. Maybe I'll be like Christa Rae's cousin and be back here in six months." He tried to joke, but she didn't crack a smile. "Or maybe I'll find once I'm there I can make a difference. Reverend Watson and Reverend Moore could ask me to stay on. That may be what life has in store for me."

"And if that's the case?"

He stood back by his suitcase, frowning as he packed more clothes. "I promise I'll write you often, and once I get to Africa, we can think about where we fit in."

Shantal's eyes grew full, her lips narrowed. "I'll go fix us some water," she said, holding her voice steady as she got off the bed. He started to ask her not to leave, but she quickly disappeared down the hallway.

"I think Reverend Watson is here!" Alma shouted as she scurried inside from the porch. Joshua felt a tug inside. He put down the papers he was sorting in his room and moved out to the porch, his heart filling as he followed Nate's gaze down the street, toward the clangor of an automobile inching closer with starts and stops, dust floating behind it in rounded clouds. The car's driver slowed before each home on the left, poking his head out of his window trying to find numbers on houses that had few. *This marks the beginning,* Joshua thought as a broad smile stretched across his face. Reverend Watson had probably never visited the home of any Negro before. This was a sign, a good sign of change. Nate looked at Joshua with such pride.

"Is that him?" Shantal asked as she walked toward the porch steps, returning finally from a long walk.

The smile on Joshua's face disappeared. "That's him," he said, his thoughts on her as he noted the red tinge in her eyes. He knew she'd been crying.

"Better clean myself up a bit," Nate said as the shiny blue Ford made its way closer. He was already dressed in his Sunday slacks, but he left anyhow, giving Joshua a moment alone with Shantal.

"I didn't mean to upset you," Joshua said softly after Nate walked inside. He paused. When Shantal straightened the steel in her back like that, he knew better than to say more. She walked past him into the house. He hoped they could talk at length before he left on his journey.

His spirits lifted again as he moved to the edge of the yard, the Ford finally pulling in front. "Good to see you, sir," Joshua said, barely hiding the hope under his words as he stood next to Reverend Watson's car. "We're so glad to have you here. I hope you didn't have a hard time finding our house."

Reverend Watson straightened out of the car, seeming ill at ease for a moment as he shook Joshua's hand. Noticing neighbors staring from their porches at him, Reverend Watson curled his lips into a deliberate smile. "I'm glad to be here, son." He offered sincerely as he turned back to his car and brought out a small frosted cake.

Joshua's voice cracked slightly as Reverend Watson handed it to him. "Thank you, sir." There was something touching about the quaintly decorated strawberry cake, its strong scent telling him it was fresh from the baker. It was a small gesture, but so important and so reflective of the man Joshua had come to know.

Uncle Nate walked back outside, greeting Reverend Watson with a clasped shake and warm words. Joshua smiled, knowing the greeting was heartfelt. They made their way inside, where the air was vibrant with the savory scent of a well-cooked ham and gently rising corn bread. A smiling Jesus caught Reverend Watson's eye from His position in the center of the living-room wall. Reverend Watson took a moment to admire the framed photos that cluttered every other inch of free living-room wall, the glasses of which had all been cleaned to a shine. His eyes lingered on the many pictures of Darius that formed a shrine on top of the piano.

Nate motioned Reverend Watson to the couch, which sat undraped for only the third time in years from its plastic cover. Joshua quickly peered into the kitchen. Waneda, Alma, and Lu each stirred over a different pot. A crowded kitchen had always been their sign of pride—over the years, each of them had proudly dripped lard and precise seasonings over their own cast-iron pots, baking in the flavors as they slowly blackened those pots over low flames.

"The reverend just arrived," Joshua said, smiling broadly.

Alma's bright-eyed expression matched Waneda's smile, but Joshua's disappointment stirred as Lu only nodded, her eyes still cast down. She would always fall silent whenever anyone mentioned white folk. She'd acted that way long before Darius was killed, ever since the well-funded white school nearest them refused to let Darius attend. She'd acted that way all the more after Darius died in the Great War. Lu never uttered a writhing word, not even a sour phrase, but whenever someone brought up white folk, her lips tensed up with a bitter thought, like she was consciously not saying something—something mighty full of hate. Her spiteful hush could fill a room with a silence that spoke a thousand words. "Reverend Watson is a good man," Joshua whispered, responding to Lu's frown.

Alma removed her apron, touching Joshua's arm as she motioned Joshua to follow her back into the living room. "Reverend Watson, sure good to have you here with us today," Alma said with a smile that made Joshua proud as she extended her hand. Waneda greeted Reverend Watson the same as he settled into his seat across from Nate and Joshua, clutching a glass of lemonade. Joshua was so happy to see Reverend Watson in their home. Reverend Watson finally remembered to take his hat off, revealing dark hair brushed with silver tones. He stared at them from behind thick spectacles. There was something in the brownness of his eyes that was as gentle as his movements and his voice. Joshua waited to see if Reverend Watson would guide the conversation.

"We're all very happy you were able to come share a meal with us before I depart." Joshua filled the silence.

Reverend Watson seemed to search for something to say. "Oh," he sat up, fumbling to retrieve a thick envelope from his coat pocket. "I brought these for you. These are your papers of endorsement," he explained with a smile.

Joshua's curiosity piqued as he unfolded the stack of papers. "Everyone thought very highly of you, Joshua. Your endorsements were glowing. This is the first time you've seen them all?" Reverend Watson asked.

Joshua nodded as he turned through the pages slowly, noticing the typewritten letters from his home church in Philadelphia. A warm feeling stirred inside as he ran his hand over each letter from his home church's ministers and deacons, each testifying to his commitment to the church and his work among the congregation. His eyes welled as he read their words. Their endorsing signatures were scrawled high and pressed hard, proudly embossed on the pages. He turned through another set of letters, handwritten by his missionary organization's U.S. leadership. A letter from Reverend Watson lay among them. Joshua's eyes were full when he looked up.

Reverend Watson had a twinkle in his eyes, and nodded at Joshua's expression. "While you're abroad, keep those papers with you," Reverend Watson said with a level of concern that surprised Joshua. "You might need to offer proof of your occupation when you are en route or once you've landed." His tone made Joshua feel there was much he wasn't saying, but Lucius came in from work before he could probe further. Walking as always with his chin up, always looking poised to tell the next joke, Lucius pursed his full lips, then curved them into a lively smile, shaking Reverend Watson's hand.

They all chatted for a while, sharing a laugh as Nate teased that he'd one day frame those endorsement letters, hanging them right across the wall from Jesus.

Alma called everyone into the snug dining room just then, as she came out of the kitchen carrying the ham she'd just carved into thin slices. One by one, Alma, Waneda, and Shantal brought more food in, proudly holding the steaming pots with thin rags, gingerly, as if carrying purses full of the finest gold. There was so much more to this dinner than just a meal with Reverend Watson, Joshua thought. The effort they'd put into it moved him. Within a few minutes, everyone had claimed a seat before the steaming bowls. Alma set one more bowl in front of Reverend Watson, who tensed at her touch as she patted his shoulders to welcome him again. If Jesus is watching this, Joshua thought, his lips would be curving downward around now.

"I'd ask Reverend Clay to pray," Lu said proudly, "but we should say a special blessin' for Joshua. Alma, you'd like to bless the food?"

Joshua winced. She should have asked Reverend Watson. His lips thinned as his anger stirred faintly. She wouldn't have done that to a black minister. With bowed heads, everyone touched hands, forming an unbroken circle.

"Deah Lord," Alma began, "we want to thank You for puttin' all this food on this table here, lettin' us feast on this day before Joshua leaves us. We thank You for wakin' each of us up to be here this mornin' so we can give thanks and eat a proper dinner to see him off. We know that You got great things in store for our Joshua, and we thank You for that, Lord. And we thank You for bringin' the Reverend Watson all this way to be in this home with us to share in our celebration of Joshua's service."

Reverend Watson seemed touched by her words.

"Reverend Watson, would you also like to bless the meal?" Joshua asked. The shimmer in Reverend Watson's eyes told Joshua that he hadn't taken offense at Lu's action. He smiled and added a short blessing, then looked around curiously as everyone paused for a moment with their forks and knives clutched anxiously in their hands.

"You just wait now," Lu warned Lucius, who could barely keep from dipping his fork into the collards.

"*The Lord is my Shepherd, I shall not want,*" Nate said as he began the family tradition. He turned to his right, puckering like he'd just sipped wine and was passing a precious chalice to his right.

"*Thy Will be done,*" Lu added, taking her turn.

"*Lo, I am with you always, even until the end of time,*" Alma said with passion in each word as she turned to Waneda.

"*The Lord is my light and my salvation; whom shall I fear?*" Waneda observed as Shantal wiped her hands nervously on a napkin a couple of seats away.

"*The Lord is the strength of my life; of whom shall I be afraid?*" Lucius said as he turned to Shantal beside him.

"Why don't y'all come back to me," Shantal whispered, eyes dropped, looking as if her mind had gone blank. Joshua felt heat rush to his cheeks as Lu made an incredulous sound, before reaching back to a small shelf, pulling out a Bible and placing it down hard in front of Shantal.

"If we sit here waitin' on Shantal to find a verse, the food gonna turn to ice!" Lucius joked. Waneda couldn't help chuckling.

"Y'all hush now, ain't nothin' funny. This girl can't remember one line out of that Book!" Lu said.

"That's 'cause you're making her nervous," Alma chided.

Joshua inhaled deeply as Shantal turned the Bible pages back and forth. "I'll go," Joshua said, as Shantal gave him a grateful nod. "*Jesus said, 'I am the gate,'*" Joshua said, emphasizing each word slowly with a wisdom in his tone that made everyone sit still. "*'Whoever enters through me will be saved. My sheep listen to my voice; I know them, and they follow me.'*" Joshua turned to Reverend Watson beside him, who looked at him with smiling eyes, as if Joshua's intonations had brought fresh meaning to the words.

"*Let your light so shine before men,*" Reverend Watson said with a passion that matched Joshua's, "*that they may see your good works, and glorify your Father which is in heaven.*"

They turned back to Shantal, and Joshua held his breath. "*Blessed is the man that walketh not in the counsel of the ungodly,*" Shantal finally said, reading a verse Joshua knew Lu'd already underlined in that Bible. Shantal traced the words with a finger, trying to make no mistakes as she read. "*He shall be like a tree planted by the rivers of water that bringeth forth his fruit in his season.*"

"Amen," they all said at once, and the pots began their trips around the table. Alma cut the first loaf of corn bread in two and passed it around the table. Reverend Watson fixed himself a modest plate and spooned the candies yams toward his mouth first. Joshua could see his eyes gleam as the cinnamon and brown sugar melted over his tongue. No one spoke for a while as they focused on the onion juices sliding in their mouths from the crevices of the collards, the peppery flavors of the chicken in thick gravy, and the tang of the ham. Gladly, they each seemed to eat history whole. Lucius swallowed each bit of heritage with a smile, licking his fingers with an extra smack. Reverend Watson lost his hesitancy quickly, enjoying flavors that seemed new to him. What a sight to take in! Joshua hoped every moment of this would remain etched in his mind. Soon enough, though, a distance in the silence grew, everyone uncertain of what to say.

"Reverend Watson spent a great deal of time with me in Ohio during my year of special studies, telling me about our mission and how we are expected to help bring African natives to God," Joshua said to his family. "I've told them how much the extra year of training at Wilberforce should come in handy with the work in Africa," he said to Reverend Watson, who nodded.

"You been down there to that place before?" Alma asked Reverend Watson, her eyes wide with fear.

"Many times," Reverend Watson answered, "but I have never lived in Africa; I've only visited some of our missions." His tone was toilsome, as if he were reluctantly crossing a frail bridge.

"We all heard stories 'bout them jungles and them monkeys and diseases. Rituals and voodoo killings," Alma said. "Joshua says he'll be fine, but I heard them stories one too many times to be thinkin' he's right."

"You heard them stories from *who*?" Lucius asked curtly, a familiar annoyance tingeing his tone. The room fell silent as every Clay family member moved their eyes toward Reverend Watson, who didn't seem to notice they were holding their breaths as they looked nervously back to Lucius. Joshua could feel their collective thought: *Please don't say that the white man's been intentionally spreading all those lies!*

Lucius let out a loud breath, measuring his words. "She be hearin' *nonsense* from folk who got reason to be tryin' to make us think Africa ain't nothin' but jungles and monkeys and witch doctors," he finally said coolly, spitting out a chicken bone. "I read other works—got that book out there," he said, pointing the chicken bone toward a crisp book straight from Harlem in the living room, "'bout old cities and castles they found out there. Ain't sayin' none of them Africans ain't backward, 'cause we seen them magazine pictures same as you, but they ain't *all* backward. Even the ones that need a little teachin' 'bout dressin' still smart as a whip."

"How you know they smart as a whip?" Alma asked.

Joshua held his breath, knowing what was coming.

"He *said* he read a book," Waneda replied in a pointed tone, always defending her brother.

"Can't tell nothin' like that from no book!" Alma retorted.

"You ever read that book?" Waneda said.

"What you tryin' to tell me?"

"You talkin' 'bout somethin' you ain't never bothered to look at. He said it's in the book!"

Joshua barely stifled his laughter as he watched Reverend Watson, who looked like he was viewing a familiar sight and could barely contain his own laughter. *Every family must have bickering relatives like this,* Joshua mused to himself.

"I'll be *safe,*" Joshua cut in, trying to assure them. "The whole point of my journey is to bring civilization to the Africans. But I won't be in physical danger. I'll write often so that you'll always know that."

The room was quiet for a moment.

"Well, with all them lynchings down South, Joshua's probably much safer over there than here," Lucius said.

Joshua's heart sank as the whole room froze.

Alma's eyes welled. "Our boys went off to fight in the War. We read all them articles 'bout how they traveled by foot 'cross France to fight them Germans, walking till the soles of their boots was split open, how they slept in them ditches two men to a blanket, going without food some days if the rations was low, and then they came under fire." Her pain was palpable. "We seen them stories about the heavy shellin' and all them Negro soldiers killed for this country. You think it done any good, changed any minds?"

"What was it for?" Waneda echoed.

Joshua frowned as Lu dropped her eyes, like she always did when they were tearing up. Her bitter hush began to fill the room.

"This isn't the Great War, Aunt Alma," Joshua said, frustration in his tone.

The room was silent for a moment, no one knowing what to say.

"There are great things in store for Joshua with our mission," Reverend Watson finally said gently. "Joshua is a leader now." He whispered, pausing until Alma nodded. "You needn't worry. We will look after him well." He said those words in a tone that sealed the subject.

CHAPTER 3

Reverend Watson left for the evening just after the sky dimmed to a dusky blue. Joshua sat on the hanging porch swing, rocking gently in the cool air. His thoughts drifted to the drive he'd soon make with Reverend Watson to the ferry dock in Jersey. *Finally,* he thought, after a year of special missionary training, *the day of departure is nearly here.*

"You know you had that Shantal cryin' up a storm?" Nate said loudly, interrupting Joshua's thoughts as he stood in the porch door-way, pipe in hand. Joshua's stomach turned, knowing he had some explaining to do. He just hoped no one was within earshot.

Nate sat directly next to Joshua, silent at first as Joshua kept his eyes focused on Hopedale Street. Nate was always slow to anger or to utter any stern word. Even on the rare occasions when he grew mad, he'd narrow his eyes, taking another long smoke of his pipe before speaking out measured words. But now Nate seemed intent on staring Joshua down. Joshua felt the intended pressure, but he waited for Nate to say something as he looked down Hopedale Street, watching the kids playing a vibrant, defiant game even now as he gathered his response.

"When was she crying?" Joshua asked.

"She came walkin' down that hallway," Nate said, pointing with his pipe toward the bedrooms, "stiff and choking on them tears. Went into the washroom, back of the kitchen, and all I heard was her sobbin'. I tried to ignore it right for a spell, thinkin' I know what you done, but she was crying so hard, got me scared! Had to go in there to make sure she was all right and I put my arm 'round her, but she couldn't stop that sobbin'. She just gone on crying like a baby." Nate shook his head, running a finger over the carved notches in his pipe. Those ridges had been forged in the pipe's handle by Nate's father, who'd sit in his old age on their Carolina farm, describing grim plantation days and speaking with brightness of the future. Nate struck a match and cupped his hand to light the pipe's bulb, puffing out a cloud that drifted up like a soft-winged dove. Joshua glanced toward him, noticing the rough skin and his graying sideburns, which framed such a round, honest face. He was a man of no pretenses. He always seemed to smell like soil, as if it became lodged beneath his nails as he tended the lawns across town. There was such a simplicity and humbleness about him. Nate was as close as Joshua had ever come to having a father, and he always had a way of putting Joshua at ease. Every morning, Nate rose at 6:30, hitching a hammer with calloused hand through one rung of his grease-spotted overalls, tying a handkerchief filled with flat nails to another. He'd go out to work whistling, lips pulsing as he blew his tune deliberately—as if to say that life was hard but he was winning, because in spite of his rough path he was still singing a sweet song. There was no one Joshua admired more.

"She told me it ain't got nothin' to do with you two, and I promised her I ain't gonna say two cents 'bout it to you," Nate said, looking at Joshua, expecting an answer.

"I won't tell her you mentioned it," Joshua said quietly.

"What you tell her, you ain't gonna marry her?" Nate finally asked in a quiet tone, with a hint of accusation.

"I didn't tell her I wouldn't marry her," Joshua responded. "I just didn't say anything about marriage at all." He met Nate's gaze directly, surprised he wanted to tell Nate that he had intended to propose to Shantal this week. He quickly shook the impulse away. If he said that, he'd have to explain why he hadn't done so. Nate wouldn't understand. Everyone thought he'd been happy with Shantal over the past years. And he had been, that's why he was so confused by his own hesitation. It was probably all of the changes, preparing to go to Africa, he told himself. He waited for Nate to admonish him.

Nate puffed out another lungful of sweet air. "What time you said that preacher gonna be here tomorrow?"

"Nine o'clock," Joshua answered, perplexed by the quick change of subject.

Nate lowered his eyes, seeming to read Joshua's mind. He tapped his pipe against the side of the porch swing, as lightly as he might have tapped a gavel—a few sure knocks that centered his tobacco in its bulb.

That's it, no lecture? Joshua stared at Nate.

"We sho' gonna miss you, Josh," Nate said. "All of us, even Lu."

Joshua's throat went dry. Lu had barely said a word to him in the past few weeks.

Nate looked away to the distance now. "Lu ain't been saying much about your trip away. She might be silent as a rounded hedge-hog, but she ain't lookin' forward to havin' you so far away, even if it's an honor," Nate said, answering a question in Joshua's mind. "Done broke Lu's heart, losing Darius," he said quietly, his lips tense. "Darius was a part of her, her only child. Wanted more, but there was complications. Always acting like she failed me, but I never felt that way. One was plenty, and he sure was a son." The hanging bench creaked a bit as Nate shifted. "She blames the white man for that. Says the white man's the one who put the gun to his head and pulled the trigger real slow. Lot of anger in her 'bout that."

It was hard for Joshua to hear the pain in Nate's voice. He couldn't respond.

"You may not realize how much Lu loves you too. Felt your spirit was too fiery, is all. Don't think it was a matter of her loving Darius more 'cause he was more her flesh and blood. You is too, a nephew who's like a son, and she never loved you no less. Thought you needed a different sort of lovin', though. She was stern with Darius, but she felt she had to be stone hard with you. Brimstone and fire for some folk, she always said, and with your spirit, you was what she be talkin' 'bout. Be honest, can't say I think she was entirely wrong 'bout that!" He chuckled. "Slippin' out in the night to let all the chickens out of Gram's pen 'cause you thought they should be free to roam the world like God's children—we couldn't even find half of 'em the next mornin'! You sure caused yo' mama some mischief!"

They shared a laugh. Joshua flashed an embarrassed half smile. Joshua's family never let him forget the many moral crusades he'd waged as a child.

"But Lu sure do love you," Nate said, looking Joshua in the eyes. "And if she ain't sayin' much of nothin', it's 'cause she feelin' like she losin' you too. Second son going, may not be comin' back. Can be hard on mothers."

It was just like Nate to say those gentle words. Joshua nodded toward Nate, but he still wished Lu would find a way to show some enthusiasm for his trip abroad.

Alma joined them on the porch just then. Joshua wished she hadn't interrupted—there was so much he'd wanted to say to Nate, who simply gave him a warm smile and looked away. They each sat wordlessly, taking in the peaceful night.

"I'll go finish getting packed." Joshua excused himself after a while, hoping to finish soon so he could relax with his family for the rest of the night.

It was only a short while before Joshua finished packing a brown sack with his books and papers, then the hard-backed suitcase with his clothes, ordering them by color. He had to stretch far across the bed to get his Bible from where Shantal had moved it. He smiled as he set it like a crown at the top of his sack, where it could be the first thing he took out in the mornings, and the last thing he tucked away at night. He heard Uncle Lucius call everyone into the living room just then.

As Joshua walked toward the living room, he glimpsed Lu through her cracked bedroom door. With her curtains drawn tight, a framed picture of Darius pulled close, she sat silently in the rocking chair that Nate had cut and buffed to a shine for her. Pressing her feet together on the unvarnished floor, she barely rocked. Her lips were pursed in a frown as she knit a gold sweater, straining to see her handiwork in a single candle's light. It pained him, the motion of her hands as she guided the needles so morosely, as if spreading gel from an aloe plant over an open wound.

He realized just then that her hands were the first thing he envisioned when he thought of Lu; not her face, but her hands. Aged and worn from years of picking tobacco as a child in Carolina, her hands had helped birth two babies when the local midwife fell sick.

Perfectly manicured despite their wear, they always found their way around a bar of homemade soap, scrubbing with vigor to produce foaming dishwater. Those same hands had scoured every inch of his body until he turned six, whenever he'd stayed in Lu's home. During his summer visits, Lu took over the mothering duties for his ma, giving her baby sister a rest. Soaping Joshua down, Lu'd cleanse every inch of his body. At ages one through four, he found it almost fun. By ages five and six, words forming an objection always lingered on Joshua's tongue as Lu told him to strip down and get in the tub. Her hands would wrap around his viny legs, anchoring him in place so she could wash him well. Had he been a bit more brave and a bit less scared, he would have spoken those objections. But embedded in the motions of Lu's hands were the words, spoken curtly, "You better keep hush, now." And so he did. There was something in her steadfast grip and the sureness of her strokes that assured him it was okay for her to see him that way.

Those same hands would wrap around a dark splintered yard-stick, the one she took everywhere she went when he was a child. The ruler was always there, moving with the motion of her right foot, a constant "Sign of Law—Lu's Law." One wrong move and those thirty-six inches came down hard anyplace they could find—on Joshua's thigh, on his hip, on his behind as he ran to avoid another strike. "If you colored in this world," Lu'd always call out, "you gotta work twice's hard, be twice's good, be twice's careful." No son of hers, she'd go on to declare, would go out into the world giving anything less than his best, or acting in any way other than proper.

She probably sat around during her free hours splintering that yardstick herself, he used to think. Long ago, he could have imagined her sitting down, sweeping a cutting knife against the wood to shave it rough, making sure it never went smooth through loss of splinters on someone's behind. And when he was young, the sight of her hand on that ruler sent him running.

"Come say hi to your aunt Lu," his mother would prod him when Lu visited their little boarding room from time to time. His ma would inevitably drag him from his hiding place beneath a table or cot.

Even if Joshua said hello loudly, Lu'd reply sharply, "I didn't hear you."

"She can't hear you," his mother would echo, thrusting Joshua toward Lu. "Give your aunt Hattie Lu a hug!"

The smell of the grits and bacon that lingered on Lu's dress would grow stronger as she'd lean over, with her yardstick still glued to her palm, to offer Joshua a distant, rigid embrace. Never tight enough to let him feel the full touch of her flesh. He'd only feel the stiff press of her one-piece plaid cotton dress. But the image of Lu with her yardstick had matured into one that evoked Joshua's gratitude. Lu's Law had been like an extra spindle on a potter's wheel, shaping him, putting ample cinder in his foundation, always demanding excellence, never mediocrity, fueling his desire to achieve. But Joshua lacked that understanding at age seven, when he received word that his mother had died.

His mother's death came as a shock to the whole family. It had all begun with the cold sweats she began to suffer late at night, which were followed with small lumps she'd felt nestled at the base of her neck. Joshua would visit her at the colored hospital, and she'd stroke his hand, singing softly. As her health got worse, his ma refused to eat, insisting angels were feeding her, as she reached into the air to caress their invisible faces gratefully. Joshua learned later that his ma soon began to call the names of relatives who'd died years before, claiming she could see them. And on her last day, her face glowed with a great brightness in the moment she passed on. A shine so radiant that Lu and Alma thought for a moment she was getting well. And then, with a smile, she was gone.

Joshua had only responded with childish understanding. He had been around to hear Lu planning the funeral—what kind of casket, what hymns to sing, what dress they should put her in. His mother might have died, but Joshua only understood that there would be no more hugs to wish him good night, no more night songs sung softly in soprano. Worse than that was when Uncle Nate told him to whom he'd been bequeathed. "Lu always wanted herself another boy anyhow," is how Nate had explained it.

Alma and Waneda thought Joshua wasn't getting much sleep in the days after his mother died because he was upset by her loss. That too, but what burned in his mind late into the night were thoughts about his likely fate with Lu. Joshua couldn't stop thinking through scenarios. One of those splinters would get lodged inside his leg—expand and explode—and he'd also be gone for good. All scenarios ended the same way. When Nate came to prepare Joshua for the move to his new home, Joshua whispered his concerns.

"I like the color blue. My favorite suit is the blue one. I only got two, but I like the blue one better," he uttered urgently.

Nate stared at him blankly.

"When I went with Ma to the church down the street, I liked the hymn they sung, 'Chariot Swingin' Low.' I imagine a big swing, like that one Johnny Tether's got. That hymn's my favorite one, best one I can remember."

Joshua grew sad as Nate looked off into the distance, seeming to dismiss his words as nonsense. "*The Lord is my Shepherd,* is nice, and I like dark wood," he tried again.

Joshua thought his efforts had been lost. He learned years later that Nate had quietly chastised Lu. "You got this boy so scared he's plannin' his own funeral!" That explained why, when Joshua first arrived and peered into his new home, with its daisy print curtains pulled close to keep it cool from the hot summer sun, he saw a quick flash of white as Lu smiled, a real smile, as her smell of grits and bacon moved with her to open the door. Nate had worked on Lu long enough that she greeted Joshua with a nice hug. And for the first time Joshua could remember, her hand was free of her yardstick when he walked through the door.

Lu even sat him down on an unveiled living-room couch, serving him homemade lemonade in a special cup rimmed with red flowers, the ones they only used on special occasions. Joshua sat in the parlor, licking his lips after a few sips, the lemonade so fresh he could taste the rind. Nate and Lucius sat across from him, welcoming him in his new home, while fourteen-year-old Darius stood behind them, secretly making funny faces, flicking his wrist to mimic Lu hitting at them with her ruler, moaning silently and rubbing his bum like it was smarting. Darius mouthed a silent, hardy laugh as Joshua's eyes welled.

Joshua looked at the motion of Lu's hands now as she rocked faintly and the candlelight flickered against the picture of Darius. It pained him to see her anguish. "You think the reverend will be here on time in the mornin'?" she asked lowly after Joshua knocked lightly on her door.

"I would expect so," Joshua said. "Are you going to join us?" he asked as he motioned down the short hall to the living room. She looked up wordlessly, then turned back to the sturdy design in her hands. He had expected as much.

Joshua took a chair next to Shantal as Nate and Alma retreated inside from the porch and sat across from Lucius. The sky was now black, the scent of lantern oil drifting into the air as Nate placed another lantern beside the sofa.

Lucius burrowed himself into his usual place in the middle of the couch, licking his fingers to pry the crisp pages of his latest history book apart. Lucius might be far-fetched in his dreaming, Joshua thought, but his pride in Negro history was truly admirable. He always came home with something new to share, having mulled over the meaning of a magazine article or two with club members at Liberty Hall. From the corner of his eyes, Joshua saw Lu slip quietly into a chair at the edge of the room and he smiled to himself. He caressed Shantal's hand, shifting his chair closer to hers. He pretended not to notice as Shantal pulled away.

Lucius held up the book's slave ship sketches as the lantern flickered, curved silhouettes dancing on the walls. "Our forebears sailed across the Atlantic," Lucius began in a low voice. "They were forced across that sea, chained to each other at the wrists. Chained to each other at the ankles. *Pinned* down in a dark and cold place, stinkin' with the smell of human waste. Mold and dust clinging to the ship's walls. Urine and vomit matted on the damp floor. The *stench* of fear piled up high. The perverted music of them rattlin' chains creakin' into the darkness."

The intensity in his voice caused Joshua's heart to beat faster. Waneda and Alma stopped sipping their homemade ginger ale. For the first time in months, even Aunt Lu looked up from her knitting to listen.

"No windows. No light. No hope. Nothing but the haunting sounds of chains wiping against the metal bars that held them captive," Lucius continued. "In the lowest level where the cargo's kept—a living hell on earth. Imagine them there, in a three-masted ship, movin' up and down, high and low, with the rhythm of the sea, the waves poundin' darker than night. They came from different tribes, spoke different languages—couldn't talk to each other to console one another. Couldn't understand each other's words. They could only look at each other and stretch out their bonded fists offerin' a comforting stroke. Can't you imagine the fright, the fear, the *pain* in their cries in the dark. They couldn't understand each other's words, jus' the meanings of those high-pitched wails. How alone, how alone." He shook his head. Somehow the darkness in the room grew deeper.

"Many chose not to make it," he said, waving his hand in the air. "They jumped off the boat if they found the chance, into the sea. Others threw their own babies over. Some was dumped if the ship wasn't sittin' right enough in the water, if the boat seemed too heavy. Black skin. Dark skin. Their lives were judged to be worth nothin' more than the price they'd command on the auction block. Babies plucked from their mother's breasts and sold out to the highest bidders. No more family. Freedom sinkin' down to the bottom of the sea." Lucius seemed lost in his own words as he dropped his eyes, shaking his head again.

"Think how strong you'd have to be," he said, looking straight at Joshua. "Think how strong! To survive *that*—a livin' hell on earth." After a few moments, Lucius tapped his fingers on the low wooden table before him, a steady knocking, and he looked up with intense eyes. "And now, our Joshua will be traveling that same passage, in reverse!"

A chill shivered through Joshua as Lucius's voice cracked faintly, the triumph in his tone made smiles curve at everyone's lips. They all looked at Joshua as if he were taking all of their hopes and dreams with him. Joshua felt so humbled.

They chatted on into the night, sharing laughs after Lucius had finished. What they talked about for those many minutes after, Joshua couldn't recall, he was too lost in his own thoughts. He promised himself again he'd make them all proud.

Nate soon lightened the mood, reciting his own story about his journey with Lu from South Carolina to Philly, the one he jokingly called the "Latter Passage." They'd all heard the story a hundred times, enjoying it with every telling. Joshua smiled as Nate talked on, relishing the familiar warmth of his family. Nate soon waved his hand over his checkerboard, challenging one person after another to a game.

"I can see Joshua already," Lucius teased later in the night, flopping his arms around, "up there on the top deck playin' shuffleboard and sippin' tea with some Englishman." Laughter filled the room.

"Not very likely on a goods ship." Joshua chuckled along with them.

The whole room suddenly fell quiet, a stunned silence descending over them. Lucius's smile vanished and the phonograph needle started sticking, playing the same Duke Ellington jazz stanza over and over. Lucius reached across the sofa, lifting the needle from the vinyl, hushing the music's strident notes. The silence was complete.

"They're sending you on a *goods* ship?" Aunt Alma asked in disbelief.

"I knew there'd be something," Shantal whispered. "I knew it."

"How can they do that?" Lucius's voice cracked.

Joshua couldn't wipe the surprise from his face. "My mission sends all its missionaries to Africa on goods ships," he said, glancing over at Nathan, at whose request the Mt. Canaan deacons had agreed to write the required reference letters. Mt. Canaan, his home church, had proudly endorsed Joshua's selection as a missionary. Just one week earlier, Joshua had stood near the Mt. Canaan pulpit; Nate was beaming beside him as the whole congregation rose in applause, honoring Joshua's achievements as a minister. The congregation had looked at Joshua just like Nate and Lucius had, as if Joshua represented everything they'd dreamed about for their children and their children's children. Joy filled that church as the congregation sang one song after another. It was only a few minutes before Mrs. Jones was in the aisle swinging her arms and stomping her feet to the music, raising her hands to God and casting her head back down as she stomped harder. Several other women joined her, caught in the spirit, lifting up their skirts a few inches to move more freely. The joy in that place! But now, the cold indignation on Nate's face took Joshua aback.

"It's not important that we travel on a fancy ship," Joshua said, trying to reassure them. "It's considered a misuse of money. I didn't take offense when they told me I'd be sailing on a goods ship."

Only the sound of turning pages broke the room's silence as Alma leafed through her Bible, pulling a folded paper from between her favorite Corinthians chapters. She looked down at the unfolded sheet. "I had imagined you on something like this," she whispered, almost to herself, as she stared at it. She held it out toward Joshua with a frown.

Joshua smoothed the sheet between his fingers. It was one of the popular Cunard Line ads from *National Geographic*. COME TO SOUTH AFRICA, it read, with a European woman wearing a one-piece swimming suit boldly designed without a skirt to cover her thighs. She was relaxing in a beach chair under an umbrella, with a luxury liner leaving a port in the background. How long ago had she tucked this in her Bible? Where had she even found a *National Geographic*? Every time Lucius saw one in the house with its pictures of bare-breasted Africans, he tossed it out.

"As far as I know, my mission sends all their missionaries to Africa on goods ships," Joshua said, trying to keep his tone level. "They're equipped with passenger accommodations—no one's going to have me lying on the floor between two crates of wool." He tried to joke. "It's in the best interest of the people we're going to serve— save money and you have more to work with when you land. We live well enough once we've landed, everyone has said so."

They weren't convinced.

"It's just not what we was expectin', that's all," Nathan remarked, clearing his throat, his brow still furrowed.

"I'm sure it'll be just fine," Alma soothed, recovering. She squeezed her eyes, bracing herself. "So what does your ship look like if it don't look like that one?" she asked.

Joshua hesitated. He didn't actually know.

"Like one of Marcus Garvey's ships, I bet," Lucius volunteered, as if anything associated with "Back to Africa" would be all right.

Alma arched her eyebrows in a question.

"A little beat-up," Nathan clarified cynically as Lucius sent him a steel glare from across the room.

When Joshua finally made his way to sleep, only Lucius and Nathan were still sitting in the living room. Joshua put on a nightshirt and nestled into his cot, hoping he'd sleep well so he'd be rested when Reverend Watson returned in the morning to drive him to the ferry landing.

This is it, he told himself, excitement tugging inside. He listened to the muffled sounds of Lucius and Nate, feeling the gentle comfort of family around him again. It had taken a little while for the room to perk back up. They were so worried about him and the goods ship. He rubbed his hand over his brow—perhaps he should have foreseen their concern. He promised himself again that he would succeed, showing his family that whites could be trusted, and showing whites that a Negro could be counted on. The weight of his responsibilities overwhelmed him again—the high expectations of his work in Africa, Lu's fears, Shantal's desires. He closed his eyes, searching for the peace his morning trip to the pond had brought for a while. "Thank you, Lord," he whispered, "for this wonderful family and for this opportunity. I know You are with me and I hope to serve You well."

He opened his eyes in the room's darkness, turning on his side. His eyes rested on the portrait of Marcus Garvey that hung over Lucius's empty bed. He lay still for a moment as he looked at that portrait. So many of the tales Lucius had told about Garvey's dreams came flooding back to him, making him smile. Lucius, the grand storyteller. He'd relayed to the family on so many quiet nights all the grand details of Garvey's dreams—to build a world in which Negroes enjoyed prosperity, respect, and dignity and made their own way as doctors and mayors and scientists. If they couldn't have it in America, Lucius had repeated the words of Garvey, then they should be willing to go back to Africa and build that world of opportunity there. And there he was, in a photograph that served as Lucius's daily reminder—Marcus Garvey dressed like royalty, wearing his dark skin like pride, the center of a long automobile procession that had paraded down the streets of Harlem. Joshua closed his eyes. He'd miss all of his family so much, but perhaps in some odd way, he'd miss Lucius and all his dreaming the most. He whispered another prayer and lay still.

At that moment, he heard that familiar voice calling out again in the distance. A soft alto, it sang this time a cheerful song, sucking out the marrow of each phrase as the words danced across its tongue and leaped out into the world. The wind seemed to blow the words fuller as they floated like balloons lifting ever higher. Like a cool wind with rhyme, the whispering night carried to Joshua words he still did not know. It soothed him, the doubtful shadows in his mind settling again, leaving him with welcome anticipation. He listened to the song's determined rhythm as the voice sang with a crescendo, crescendo, again and again. Through the trees nearest the window that Darius once claimed as his own, the gentle sound drifted; the voice paused every now and again to take a deep breath and then sang out again, until the pulse of Joshua's heart and the beat of its tune became one. *Ezam izimvu ziyaliva ilizwi lam, ndibe nam ndizazi, zindilandela; mna ndizinika ubomi obungunaphakade; azisayi kutshabalala naphakade; akukho namnye uya kuzihlutha esandleni sam.*

CHAPTER 4

The ferry sailed straight toward the bustling, singing part of town as it forged a catty-corner path across the mighty Hudson. Joshua's heart lifted—the journey was real now, he thought, as he glanced back from the deck to see Reverend Watson fade to a dot on the Jersey shore, hand still waving as he disappeared into the landscape. It took Joshua's breath away as he neared New York's soaring pillars, which scraped high against a bright blue sky. As he disembarked, everything around him buzzed. A crowd of newspaper boys shouted out, trying to sell their latest editions. Thick scents filled the warm air as street vendors turned beef slabs on open grills. Automobiles everywhere honked. *New York City!* Joshua could hardly believe it. It was just as Darius had described. This must be how Darius had felt, he thought, when he moved here to experience the Negro Renaissance. It felt odd to retrace his cousin's steps.

Joshua joined a line of white men, waiting in turn for a taxi, moving slowly to its front. Joshua soon stood by himself, hand held out, trying to flag down a ride. Each empty black cab that passed reminded him of the source of Lu's hate. What a contrast with the drive from Philly, Joshua thought, his temper stirring a bit. He and Reverend Watson had chatted easily for hours about their families, about religion, about their ministries. There was a certain shine in Reverend Watson's eyes when Joshua had turned to take his bag and head toward the docked ferry, which rocked gently with the rhythm of the waves. What would Reverend Watson say if he could see him now? Finally, a taxi stopped a few feet from him, its driver reluctantly accepting Joshua inside.

Joshua pulled his directions from his pocket, reading the name of the pier to the driver. His anger at the driver's curtness quickly disappeared as he sat back, taking in the views. Driving toward his goods ship, they passed yachts tied to the docks and crowds gathered before luxury liners waving tearful good-byes. After another mile, the crowds thinned, the streets narrowed, and the landings grew bare except for bleak cranes loading crates onto the many rows of goods ships. Emotion swept over Joshua as he stepped from the cab with the *Amissa* towering before him. Moored firmly to a gray platform coated with lime green mold, the ship sat high in the waters, its cold steel cut at harsh angles, an imperial crest emblazoned onto its side, and its funnels topped with gold. It was a little beat-up, just like Nate predicted, but not as badly as Alma had feared. Its keel and the V of its bow were rusted, but to Joshua it seemed to glisten as if christened with a thousand bottles of the finest champagne. With the sun's shimmer on the water, the fresh scents of the sea, and waves tapping lightly against the hull, Joshua's senses were ablaze.

He walked in the shadow of the sprawling steel, past thick ropes tied to the bollards, the entire ship's length. Sitting nearly seven stories high, the ship stretched over fifteen houses long—the whole length of Hopedale Street. Joshua wondered how many men it had taken to cast and ply so much metal. When he finally reached the stern, he looked out at the Atlantic, which stretched wide and deep to the horizon.

Joshua's heart raced a bit when he finally stepped on board, making his way down several cold stairwells and a dimly lit hallway. He looked around the ship after dropping his bags in his cabin. When he returned an hour later, a dark portly man was planted firmly on the left bunk, with his feet hanging two inches above the floor. He held up a wooden block to the portal's light as he carved it gingerly with a file. He focused his attention squarely on his handiwork, chiseling notches as if engaging in a high art, shards of wood piling near his other pieces of handiwork—a sculpted ship, a two-story home, a church. Behind him, bits of uncrumpled paper, each with penned words, were stuck carefully to the wall. The man smiled to himself, knowing he was a sight to behold, with a sextant, large map, and book about the seas strewn beside him.

The man finally looked up with a start as Joshua moved to the opposite bunk. "I guess you're my cabin mate!" He grinned broadly, offering Joshua an outstretched hand. "I'm Marvis."

"Reverend Clay," Joshua said, chuckling as he sat down in the cool cabin.

"Reverend!" Marvis let out a hoot, pushing up the edge of his cap. "It's Reverend Joshua T. Clay, isn't it?" Marvis grinned again, pointing to Joshua's suitcase where Nate had written "Joshua T. Clay—Handle with Care."

"What the *T* stand for, Toussaint?"

Joshua laughed, assuming that was a joke. "My family wasn't that bold."

Marvis dipped his chin and rolled his eyes slowly. "Don't tell me you're named after *Booker T. . . .*"

Joshua squinted his eyes and sat down on his bunk. This was much like talking with Lucius. "No, I wasn't named after Booker T."

"What you goin' to Africa for?" Marvis asked.

"I'll be serving as a missionary."

"Now ain't that something," he said, pausing his carving, pushing back on both elbows. "I sure didn't expect to see no Negro missionaries going to Africa again anytime soon, after y'all caused such a stir all them years ago."

"Only a few did," Joshua said a bit defensively.

"Heard it was more than just a few," Marvis said, narrowing his eyes. "I used to hear those mission heads fussin' up a storm 'bout it when they traveled over."

The ship let out three penetrating horn blows just then.

"Come on!" Marvis said, heading out the door. "Can't miss this!" He prodded Joshua until he reluctantly followed, stopping only once he'd clasped his hands on the ship's top ledge. Joshua joined him, feeling the deck's cold rusted bars beneath his palms. Marvis waved a hand toward the pier, bidding farewell to an imaginary crowd as if he were riding on a luxury liner. "Good-bye!" he shouted with a roar of laughter.

Joshua closed his eyes and shook his head faintly. This would be a very long boat ride.

Two tugs eased the *Amissa* slowly to deeper waters. Standing on the top deck, Joshua could now see that each of the ship's three funnels stretched as tall and wide as a single home. As the ship's engines roared, black clouds billowed through the funnels, followed by beautiful white ones, then majestic black ones again. The fifty tons of steel moved out to sea. As they picked up speed, Joshua could still see the glittering landscape of Manhattan, where ship hands unloaded bullion bars, jewelry, fabric, and woven rugs, while others waited to load mechanical gadgets and books. As they moved faster toward the horizon, one twig of a street, crowned at its top with a low-lying church, caught Josh's eye. That church looked so lonely, as the tall buildings nearby leaned in, crowding it on their common foundation.

"That's where all them men been jumpin' to their deaths," Marvis said, following Joshua's gaze up Wall Street. "And that's where you and I ain't had no relatives pass!" Marvis pointed as they floated past a majestic-looking castle where Europeans stood, holding the hands of their young children: As they passed Ellis Island, heading out to sea, Joshua's heart raced. It seemed to be happening so fast! Joshua turned and squinted in the moist wind, hoping his last glimpses of America would remain carved in his memories. He knew he'd remember what he saw as he gazed back—the blue ocean, the stately tiers of towers, and Lady Liberty standing as tall as any nearby building, her face to the horizon with that still flame clutched in her steadfast hand.

———

Joshua had expected a restless weeklong ship ride before the first port of call in Lisbon, with nothing to do each night but read more about Fort Hare and his mission. Instead, Marvis greeted him each late night, sitting back on his cabin bunk and staring at Joshua. Dark-skinned and bug-eyed, his tensed-up lips were a proud pink, as if he'd spent too much time sucking tobacco. Stout and pudgy, he wouldn't be able to run a mile, but he walked with a kick in his step, a certain flouting to the world in every stride. Joshua couldn't tell his age. From all of his adventures, you'd think he must be a hundred. And he kept his version of history surrounding him, like a teacher before his chalkboard. Each night, Marvis would take down one of his bits of posted paper from the wall, reciting its penned word and lecturing Joshua for hours. Or he'd explain the little wood minia-tures he was carving. Then he'd tell stories about his women, the ones he loved. He always looked for a black one, Marvis explained. Black black black, the deepest darkest black.

With those big eyes and prideful posture, he reminded Joshua of the picture of Marcus Garvey that Lucius had hung on their bedroom wall. Marvis looked like he'd practiced making that exact expression, the one painted across Garvey's face as he sat in the back of a black convertible, parading through a street lined with onlookers, a red-green-and-black flag draped across the automobile. Garvey's eyes had danced, his coat adorned with medals, his confidence piled as high as his presidential hat. Marvis seemed like the staunchest of Garvey's followers.

In the evenings, Joshua shared meals in the mess hall with Marvis, always making sure to leave just before the other men slumped down in their chairs, their bellies swollen with fried fish, preparing to throw down cards and drink thick beer. Joshua relished the time after dinner because Marvis would stay with the others, giving Joshua precious time to himself on the deck or reading in his cabin.

"You left these out," Marvis said sharply after dinner on the seventh night, when Joshua returned from the deck. Marvis dangled a stack of carefully clipped articles just above the floor, like trash, an incredulous look on his face.

"They all like this?" Marvis asked, picking one out and tossing the others aside as he ghurred up and spat. He stuck more tobacco under his tongue, scrunched up his nose, and started reading out loud. *"The responsibilities of a Native graduating from Fort Hare are onerous and demanding,"* Marvis read. *"By rising so far above the level of his peoples, this educated Native must demonstrate he is worthy to keep the company of his white counterparts, who welcome him into the realms of civilization.*" Marvis made no attempt to hide his contempt, holding up his tin again, ghurring up and spitting another thick wad. "So, you gonna try to help prove Africans is worthy of the company of whites?"

"Fort Hare is the only university in the region that's willing to educate natives, and it accepts African students from all the countries in the area—Uganda, Zanzibar, Rhodesia. I'm not sure what you're criticizing." Joshua was defensive again.

"There's a lot I'm criticizin'. You sayin' that mission ain't got no problem with sending a Negro preacher?"

"They've chosen me."

"Without any fuss about it?"

Joshua raised his eyebrows. He couldn't answer that without conceding Marvis was right, in part. *Negro preachers haven't got any business in Africa, far as I'm concerned, but Reverend Watson here's got it in his mind that because of the color of your skin you can help us succeed.* That's what Reverend Moore, the mission's U.S. representative, had said curtly, traces of his Southern accent still audible. Joshua had endured two indignant days of his grilling.

"They think that sending a Negro will help the mission, that Africans will be able to relate more to what we teach," Joshua said.

"If they say they ain't got no problems about you being a Negro, that's a lie from a big bowl of 'em that they just spoonin' you real slow, I'm tellin' you right now. And if they think you can help, they mean they think they can take advantage of you real good."

"They've welcomed me very well," Joshua said, trying to bring the discussion to an end as he pulled out a book and pushed up against the cool wall. He just wanted a quiet evening. "I don't see why you're concerned, since you've seen the endorsements they provided."

"Endorsements?"

"You didn't make it through the whole stack," Joshua said, nodding to the papers next to Marvis.

Marvis leafed through. "Why's your description so long—five pages?" Marvis interrupted Joshua's reading after a while. "And all these references . . ."

"There were a lot of letters of support," Joshua said pridefully.

"The description of Reverend Calloway—it's five lines on a quarter piece of paper. The description of Reverend Ford—six lines on half a piece of paper. They white?"

Joshua's smile disappeared.

"Mmm-hmm." Marvis nodded, claiming victory. "You sure got a few things to learn." He tossed the bundle back on Joshua's bed, unpinning the second to last bit of paper from above his bed in the same motion. *"Ethiopia shall soon stretch out her hands unto God,"* he said, beginning another of his lectures.

———

Finally, he had time to himself again. Joshua sighed with relief as he stood the next night on deck. The sound of the waters brushing up against the hull echoed into the night, and a cool breeze stroked Joshua's cheek as he stared up at a star-filled sky, every inch and crevice adorned with twinkling reminders of the greatness of the world and his smallness in it. Leaning against the deck railing, Joshua looked out into the dark night. Nothing but faintly rippling ocean stretched in every direction. Each time he walked onto the *Amissa's* deck at night, Joshua became enveloped by the gentle canopy of the sky, the communing silence all around him. He relished the feeling of solitude—just he, the stars, and his prayers. Only the gentle lapping of the waves against the side of the ship reminded him that life pressed forward.

Like the previous nights, Joshua took in all the sights. The ship would soon reach Lisbon, their first stop before arriving in Africa. Now, as he looked out into the blackness, he wondered what his ancestors had looked like, walking barefoot through mounds of furrowed soil, planting and reaping crops and gathering reeds for woven baskets. He imagined them walking by the waterside, carrying firewood home in the evening. Somehow it seemed real now. He was going to the land of his grandfather's father. As Joshua looked down at the placid waters and back up at the velvet black sky, the stars flickered, cutting a brilliant image into the sky—a long-winged bird with pearl-colored talons. It was so beautiful. He looked down at the pinpricks of moonlight on the waves that paved an aisle from the horizon to the ship. The sight made him pause: the pinpricks so many, as if reflecting all his kinfolk buried at the bottom of the sea.

That thought sent a chill through him. He imagined the lines of chained captives, led daily onto slave ship decks. The way Lucius described that vile slave passage, he could understand why some captives had jumped to their deaths rather than face what might await in the New World. It was hard to fathom why their dreams of freedom hadn't drowned with them. Battered and gutted, those hopes had somehow managed to bob on the water's surface and now swam in his own hopes and dreams.

You think you can transport blackness? Joshua tried to blot out Marvis's words from the night before. Why did he indulge Marvis, answering his questions about his ministry, his family, and Darius? The bright wings flickered again, looking in the sky like a bird with its feet tied down with twine, trying to set itself free. For a long moment, Joshua couldn't turn his eyes from the sight.

With only the sound of waves in his mind, Joshua pulled a wooden cross from his pocket, the one that Darius had made. Joshua could still see the image of Darius sitting on a stump, fashioning the cross with two wood strips from a sturdy cove tree. He'd bound it securely with two bent nails, hanging it on a boot string; then he gave it to Uncle Nate for his birthday. Like a proud father, Nate carried it to church for years, returning it to Darius just before he went off to the War, to remember the family by. It was the first thing the commander had returned after Darius was killed.

Joshua wondered what Darius had thought as he crossed this very sea, making his way to battle near the Rhine. The thought pained him. Darius was probably so filled with pride to serve as a Negro combat soldier in the War. But he must also have felt such fear. Joshua hoped it hadn't hurt, whatever had happened to Darius. A familiar sadness washed over him—his October sadness, he used to call it. So many of the young Negro men had died in the same autumn battle. No October had passed since then that hadn't brought the memories of sadness back to Joshua's mind.

As he looked out at the ocean, Joshua rubbed his fingers over the ridges of the cross in his hands. He'd found it in his suitcase, tucked between wind-dried blankets. Lu had clearly tucked it there, next to the newly knit gold sweater she'd made, which spoke a hundred unuttered words. Joshua tried to imagine Lu removing that cross with quivering hands from their living-room wall, where it had hung like a medallion ever since the War. She'd barely said a word to him in the hours before he left. But when he'd bounced down the porch stairs toward Reverend Watson's car with his last bag in hand, Lu had steadied herself against the wooden porch rail, looking at him with that stunned expression, wet disbelief—the same expression she'd had on her face the day the messenger had brought the news about Darius. Joshua would never forget the messenger's cold eyes, pale green against paler white skin. He had acted as though the cause was hardly worth the trip to deliver the news, but what he'd handed to Lu in that pressed pulp carried the words that shattered her world. She held that paper in a stunned silence, then crumpled it as if to damn it, tearing into her own flesh with her anger. Then her tears came streaming down.

Joshua's guilt welled again as he thought of it—traveling so far, for so long. He would fare well in South Africa, though—he knew it. He closed his eyes, trying to clear his mind and be still for a moment. Soon he heard that familiar soft song rising over the waters, as if it had been gently mixing in the foaming waves. It felt like a singing of his soul. He smiled as the voice crested and lifted upwards, calling with a flawless low pitch, its long notes held for full values. Joshua squeezed his eyes tighter, letting the music resound, savoring the singing world around him. With the splash of each successive wave against the hull, the voice echoed within itself, calling forth like a young child's cry, a woman's moan, a man's call—all at once, until the voices numbered a thousand. Wide-eyed, Joshua pulled back from the ledge as the haunting sounds grew louder. Lucius was right—it did feel like a return to the Continent.

You think you transport blackness? Joshua chucked to himself as Marvis's silly question flittered through his mind. Does blackness carry across the ocean? Or would it be suspended at the vessel's gates, sink through the cracks as he crossed the platform, melt into the air in the European sun? Why did he let Marvis make him think about such things? Yet, of all of his lessons, Joshua was still stinging from Marvis's words earlier in the night. He again pondered why.

"This here is something Jesus said," Marvis had explained earlier that evening as he unpinned his very last piece of paper from the wall. It was their last night as roommates, the last night before Marvis would disembark in Portugal. Marvis's eyes seemed to say he'd saved the best lecture for last.

"I'm glad you've read the words of Jesus," Joshua had responded very seriously. Even if Marvis was joking, it was a serious matter. "Which saying of Jesus' is that?"

"A most important one," Marvis said, seeming pleased by Joshua's query. "It's my favorite verse, written in Tswana," he said, waving the paper in his hand. "Must be important if Jesus said it, don't you think?"

Marvis's tone was mocking again. He leaned back on his elbows and continued. *"Jesus said to the crippled man by the river, 'Will thou be made whole?'"* Marvis's eyes danced as he looked up from his paper. "You know that story? By the pool of Bethesda—the crippled man had waited more than thirty-eight years to be healed? Jesus asked that crippled man the simple question *Will thou be made whole?* And you know before he asked, Jesus knew the answer—who wouldn't want to be made whole if he'd waited so long to be healed? And I also suppose you remember what Jesus said to him?" Marvis's voice deepened. "You should know it."

As he stared out at the night, Joshua felt himself flushing at the memory now. Of course he knew. Why had he simply sat quietly, letting Marvis continue? Marvis had repeated the words of Jesus again clearly, saying each word distinctly, as if Joshua had never heard them before. *"Crippled man, will thou be made whole? Then rise, take up thy bed, and walk."*

CHAPTER 5

South Africa rose up in the distance against the dimming sky. With brass bells ringing out piercing sounds at the front of the ship, most passengers were already on deck, leaning with clutched hands over the rusted railing to get a closer look as the ship moved steadily past the Twelve Apostles—the small hills clustered at the southern side of Cape Town. Joshua smiled, happy that the Twelve Apostles were the first sights he had seen of the country—maybe this meant his trip would be blessed. The ship moved closer to the city, as Robben Island came into view. Joshua glanced at the travelers around him. Their hearts were beating fast, he was certain, but not as fast as his as he squinted his eyes in the damp breeze, watching the distant land grow nearer.

As the *Amissa* moved closer into northern Table Bay, the stunning landscape took Joshua's breath. The sun had just dipped behind the flat head of Table Mountain, its last rays reaching above that highest point on the horizon, painting the sky in pastel hues—pink, then purple, then blue. Sitting between the mountains of Lion's Head and Devil's Peak, Table Mountain framed the whole landscape as the lights of Cape Town nestled around the mountain bases, twinkling brightly like a jeweled necklace.

The *Amissa* paused beside two other goods ship, far from shore. The waters of the wharf were too shallow to accommodate such large ships. A tug, no bigger than a ferry, floated toward the *Amissa*, coming to carry passengers to shore. "Thank you, Father God," Joshua whispered, heart fluttering, as he joined the line to board the tug. *If only Darius had lived to see this day,* Joshua thought. *If only Lu could see it, she'd be proud.* Lu'd once believed Negroes could achieve anything in America, born as she was ten years after her mother's chains were set free. When she was young, Nate had once told him, the hope in her heart was as bright as the smile on her face. Joshua wished he'd known her back then. He hoped all he would accomplish here might bring that hope back to her eyes.

Officials checked his papers well before letting him board the tug. Once aboard, Joshua held firmly to the ledge as the tug bucked and swayed on the ocean's waves. He thought his heart might burst when it finally reached the gray pier. Stories about Africa waded through his mind, and something deep inside stirred as Joshua stepped on African soil for the first time.

He looked with amazement at the city before him. The stone ridges of Table Mountain towered above the city. As Joshua looked down to the tip of the pier, a mosaic of colors piqued his senses. Taxicabs clogged the streets and people of all colors—red, black, and white—walked to and fro on paved walkways. At the edge of the wharf, the streets were lined with ivory-colored and cobblestoned buildings. Joshua carried his bags toward the street, taking it all in. On the nearest curb, Africans moved feverishly, most of them dressed in dated and worn European fashions. He looked at them curiously as they walked more hurriedly with every movement of the sun farther beneath the mountain's brow. Some carried large burlap sacks on their hunched backs; others carried brooms and crates. Some women and children traveled on wooden penny trams—two-wheeled carts pulled by large-limbed African men, whose muscles strained with the weight. Other women passed by with reed baskets balanced atop their heads. It seemed so odd, Joshua thought, the way the Africans seemed to be rushing from the city, while Europeans clad in gray knickers and long, plaid skirts walked listlessly in and out of shops lining the opposite road side. *The pass laws,* he thought. The curfew for Africans must be nearing.

Joshua surveyed those dainty shops across the street as the smell of beef slabs on open grills mixed with the scents of the sea. There were cafés, gem stores, imported fabric shops, and furniture stores. The bustle reminded him so much of New York, but the low-lying Victorian buildings, Africans walking to and fro, and Indian vendors gave Cape Town a different feel. Joshua tried to look down the road. But it was hard to see far. The nearest two-story buildings were clustered close together, decorated with ornate edifices, verandas on top and on bottom; stretching down the street as far as he could see. As he looked around, his eyes were drawn to a man standing at the edge of the dock, looking directly at him.

"Reverend Clay," the man said with a smile. It wasn't a question, but an observation, as if noticing that Joshua was the only Negro to walk out with that first tug of passengers.

"I'm Reverend Clay." Joshua smiled, feeling a bit nervous. The man came near, shaking his hand briskly, unable to hide his excitement, his smile quickly putting Joshua at ease.

"I'm Reverend Andrew Clement. So good to meet you!" he said with wisps of an English accent. He nodded, still smiling, as if Joshua were everything he'd been told.

"Thank you for taking the time to meet me, Reverend Clement." Joshua smiled back, happy to meet his first missionary representative in the country.

"Please call me Andrew."

"And you, please call me Joshua." He turned toward the bustle around him, waving his hand in the air. "This is incredible!"

"South Africa *is* incredible—in many ways, you'll see." Andrew smiled with cheerful eyes, relishing Joshua's enthusiasm. "Come this way," he said, taking one of Joshua's bags and funneling him through the crowded walkways. "We'll get on the road straightaway and head to the hotel. You must be exhausted."

The kaleidoscope of sounds, sights, and smells transfixed Joshua as they weaved their way through crowds, past Indian vendors frying fish in thick lard and offering bowls of tomato curries. Joshua kept looking for the Africans with pierced noses and tall rings of jewelry around their stretched necks. They were nowhere to be found.

"Are you surprised?" Andrew asked, noting Joshua's expression as they walked along.

"You can tell!"

"What did you expect?"

"This is the first time I've been outside the United States," Joshua replied, feeling quite comfortable in Andrew's presence. Joshua was used to being in the company of whites, with all of the community work he'd done on behalf of Negro rights in Ohio. But he was surprised Andrew seemed so comfortable with him. "I only left the ship once," Joshua continued, "when it stopped in Lisbon. So I suppose I didn't know what to expect here. It just looks so much like the pictures I've seen—"

"Of some parts of England and Germany?"

"Yes! I'd think we were still in Europe," Joshua said.

Andrew smiled, then chuckled. "So true."

He and Andrew soon joined the crowd of vest-suited white men waiting in line for a cab. Africans continued past on the side nearest them, keeping their distance, it seemed, from the shops across the street, moving in the opposite direction from the taxis. They gave Joshua sidelong glances that made him pause. After a few moments, Andrew led Joshua into a shiny black Ford. As they stepped inside, settling into the cool blue seats, the blond-haired taxi driver gazed at them in his rearview mirror, seeming to wonder why a white man had just opened the door for a Negro and seemed to be holding his bag.

"An honorary one?" the cabdriver whispered.

Joshua wasn't sure what he was asking, and couldn't discern from the way Andrew nodded in response. "To the Astel," Andrew replied to the driver. Andrew seemed to keep his eyes averted for a moment, before turning toward Joshua with a rueful look that Joshua didn't quite understand.

As Joshua glanced forward, the driver looked at him again in the mirror and slowly tipped his hat. Tipped his hat! Joshua's mouth nearly dropped. He shook his head faintly, remembering the last time he'd tried to hail a taxi, in New York City. Marvis was right, he now knew. Marvis had insisted that when Joshua was abroad, his blackness would disappear. *They'll know we're American by the sway of our gaits. Abroad, there is little to remind us we are Negroes.* In Lisbon, Joshua had journeyed with Marvis up the narrow side streets into delicate cafés. There, Marvis had proved his point—like Marvis, Joshua had been welcomed as an American, almost with deference in the shops and quaint cafés. It was a welcoming Joshua hadn't expected. And now, also here. *These are good signs,* Joshua thought.

The taxi traveled away from the ocean toward the heart of the city, over the fresh asphalt of Adderley Street, a broad throughway lined with trolleys and large buses. They moved past a crowded open market with cardinal-colored umbrellas covering carts of fresh fruits and breads. Roasting meat scents filled the air again, while five-story Edwardian buildings, with their arches and decorated columns gave the city a distinct European feel. As Joshua observed the bustle of the metropolis, the taxi finally pulled aside just beyond a cramped side street filled with exotic spice scents drifting from nearby tea shops.

As he stepped out, Andrew took one of Joshua's bags. They walked past cluttered shop windows filled with mechanized gadgets and signs boasting MADE IN AMERICA and FROM THE UK! The charm of the cobblestones underfoot and the low hanging eaves overhead created the pleasant feel of a covered market.

Joshua followed Andrew inside a grand-looking hotel, the Astel Inn, where somber-faced women and men each sat alone at their own tables, sipping tea from dainty china cups. They walked beyond the dining foyer into the main lobby, the scent of freshly laid carpets surrounding them. Joshua glanced at the high ceilings, velvet drapes, carefully etched windows, and three-tiered chandelier. He was wide-eyed. He would never have been allowed to stay in a place like this in the United States.

They walked toward a surly manager standing behind the front desk. He was very plump, with a hard, round belly and drooping cheeks, the kind who looks as if he followed every meal with a hearty lager. Joshua tensed at the way that man watched him walk with Andrew, side by side. Trouble was looming, he could tell, by the way that man quickly angled his face down, drooping cheeks wobbling as he seemed to will them away.

"We have no piecework for kaffirs," the manager muttered curtly before they reached the counter.

"I'm sorry?" Andrew said.

"We posted a sign," the manager said, looking at Joshua with buzzard eyes, his tone as pointed as his slick-tipped mustache. He rolled his words as distinctly as possible, their harsh sounds matching the hair curling over the V of his open shirt. He pointed with a stout finger toward a handwritten card posted crookedly to the window. "I suggest you get on back where you came from before someone checks your pass papers."

Joshua scrolled through the long list of reasons why he should drop his eyes and allow Andrew to respond. He ignored the anger stewing inside, looking away as Andrew replied.

"I think you can tell by the way he's dressed, my friend," Andrew said, dropping his tone and narrowing his eyes, "that we're not here to see about a busboy position. When was the last time an African came here looking for a busboy position while dressed in a suit?"

"We don't allow *kaffirs* to stay here—" the manager said.

"I'm here to check in my friend from *America*," Andrew cut him off. "I phoned ahead, to make sure you were quite aware an American would be checking in tonight."

The manager lifted a gnarled hand to wipe his lip.

"If you'd asked him his name, my friend, you could have told by his accent that he's not one of the natives, nor is he a Coloured," Andrew said sternly. "Your papers, Joshua."

Heat rushed to Joshua's face as he pulled his travel papers out on cue. The manager took them, turning them over with hands that defiled them. His lips thinned, as if acknowledging his error. "You're the American Mr. Clay we've been expecting," he said, his tone softened as he scrunched his nose. He kept his eyes cast down as he leafed through his reservation book, as if he still didn't like it. Soon he turned to the wall of message boxes and bronze latch keys behind him, finding a key already wrapped with a tag around it, marked "Clay." When he turned back, the gentleness with which he set the key at Joshua's fingertips conveyed the apology that hadn't quite reached his lips.

"You're not what I was expecting of an American," he said hoarsely, as if that were the best he could muster by way of an apology. "Those bloody Africans—walkin' in here dirty and cupping their hands, asking for work. Give 'em work, and you still can't teach 'em to empty the rubbish bins and change the bedsheets properly." He brushed his lip brow again, as if wiping away the residue of a lie.

"When I'm in error, I admit it," the clerk said. "Didn't mean to mix you up with the *kaffirs* or their like," he said as he scrawled *HW* in broad felt-tip letters over Joshua's hotel docket, in motions that seemed more foul than his words. The manager handed Joshua his docket, marked with damp rings where his fingertips had rested. "Keep that with you while you're here and there should be no problems," the manager said, turning back to the paperwork behind his counter.

Andrew touched Joshua's arm and directed him toward a curved and carpeted staircase. "I've been here several times. The rooms are quite lovely," he said. Joshua felt the heat rushing to his cheeks again. This time his anger was directed toward Andrew, who seemed to treat that whole exchange so casually. Joshua followed him silently up to a polished wood door off a long hall. The door opened onto a sitting room with a rich burgundy settee and long cloth drapes tied on each side of a French window.

As soon as Joshua shut the door behind them, Andrew broached the subject. "You understand what happened downstairs, the distinctions they make here?" Andrew asked, concerned, as Joshua sat down on the settee. Joshua kept his gaze on his bag as he wiped traces of resentment from his face.

"There are whites, Africans, and Coloureds," Andrew went on. "Coloureds are the ones that are of mixed blood—white and African, or white and Indian. Many people won't know what to make of you here. Your skin tone . . ." He raised his eyebrows. "Some people will assume you are African; others will think you are Coloured. Make it clear that you are American, and as the clerk said, you won't have any problems. Negroes from America aren't subjected to the same laws as the natives and the Coloureds."

"Our mission's representatives in America told me I'd be free of segregation practices here," Joshua said, slowly looking at Andrew. "It's still not clear to me why, if the South African government separates facilities for 'whites only,' as they do in the United States. I was told I'd understand once I was here."

"The signs say 'whites only,' but the facilities are separated out for 'Europeans only'—that's what they mean. Africans are thought to be of an inferior culture, not genetically inferior as they insist in the United States," Andrew explained, almost in a whisper. His rueful look told Joshua he didn't condone any of it. "As an American—a European as far as they are concerned—that places you on par with the status of whites here. Just carry your papers with you, and things will be okay," he said as he turned back to the door.

Joshua could see Andrew's good intentions, but he felt stung with humiliation nonetheless.

"I hope you'll relax for the rest of the night, get a bite to eat downstairs. I can answer any questions you have tomorrow when I pick you up. The washroom is down the hallway. Do you need anything before I go?"

Joshua rose and exchanged a handshake, holding Andrew's hand tightly for a moment. "I look forward to seeing you tomorrow," Joshua said very deliberately. Casting his pride aside was all right, Joshua said to himself, because he was determined to attain the goals he'd set by coming here. The shimmer in Andrew's eyes said he understood.

"Have a good night," Andrew said with equal purpose.

As Andrew left, Joshua carried his bag into the adjoining bedroom, placing it on the four-poster bed. Feeling the cool breeze from an appeasing fan light overhead, he opened his suitcase and lifted out another suit jacket. He heard a thud and picked up the wooden cross that had fallen from the suitcase to the floor. Taking a deep breath, he sat down, caressing the cross in his hand. Where had his excitement gone? He sat there for several minutes, too tired to think of hardly anything. Somehow, the cross in his hands brought him comfort. Then his thoughts drifted to his family, his home church, Shantal. He wouldn't get discouraged so quickly, he promised himself, turning back to his suitcase and picking out the clothes he'd need for the morning.

Joshua spent the next morning with Andrew. They took in the sights of the city, driving through upscale, tree-lined neighborhoods, with houses set at long distances from the paved streets, beyond flowering yards. They traveled by taxi up the base of Table Mountain as far as the road would take them. Stepping out on a cliff above the sprawling metropolis, they admired the brilliant vista. Half a world away from America, it was spring in South Africa. The sky was bright blue above a blooming landscape. Andrew pointed down the peninsula to the area in the shining waters where the Atlantic and the Indian Oceans met and mingled. The view made Joshua want to see more. Andrew guided him back through the bustling city, past secondhand bookstores, craft stores, and butcher shops, beyond a cobblestoned cathedral with a towering spire, to a breathtaking fort and castle—a piece of Dutch history in the center of town. They walked by foot down Old Slave Walk, which reminded Joshua eerily of the Malay slaves who had been brought to the country once. They saw the Old Slave Lodge, which had come to serve as the Supreme Court, and peered at the handsome Houses of Parliament, which stretched high behind black iron gates. The city was so different from what Joshua had expected. He wished he could explore it more, but he and Andrew were scheduled to depart that evening on the overnight locomotive to Port Elizabeth.

The locomotive looked quite the same as the ones he'd traveled on in America, Joshua thought when they arrived at the train station, except its shiny black caboose touted a British flag—its red, white, and blue waving proudly in the breeze. For the first time, Joshua was allowed to ride in first class. He tried not to let his face betray how extraordinary this was as he sat across from Andrew in the cabin. As the train lurched forward, slowly gaining steam out of the covered bay, Joshua stared out the window, taking in the passing sights.

"It must be disappointing that the locomotive travels by night," Andrew said.

Joshua nodded. He had hoped to take in more of the South African landscape. But still, he appreciated the opportunity to see a bit of the lush lands before the sky grew too dark. Andrew smiled at Joshua's fascination with it all.

"You seem to have the type of spirit needed here!" Andrew said over the clatter of the train, which rocked gently back and forth as it propelled forward. "Students at Fort Hare will challenge you. Reverend Peter left quite demoralized. Broken, really. He feels he failed. I'm not sure what will come of him now. It's a pity, really. His faith seemed to have ebbed so." Andrew shook his head. "But I have a good feeling about how things will go for you," he said, smiling at Joshua. "Reverend Watson sent us letters telling us he'd spotted you long go. He was so enthusiastic about the brilliant young star he'd found at Wilberforce. Reverend Peter felt so badly rejected at Fort Hare—he says because he was white. Who knows. I'm just glad you agreed to do this, Joshua. You might have what we need to make that mission post grow. Some people here may give you a hard time, but you have support."

His tone caused Joshua to look at him more closely. He sounded as if he had a certain set of people in mind.

"I'm treading on the territory of others a bit, I'm afraid," Andrew continued, responding to Joshua's expression. "Insisting on picking you up and driving you in—some people weren't happy to see me volunteer. I just want you to know you're welcome here. But others will want to take primary responsibility—and credit—for your actions and success here."

"I appreciate your confidence in thinking I'll succeed," Joshua said.

"I'm confident," Andrew nodded assuredly, with a smile that warmed Joshua. Andrew seemed to be everything Joshua had been told—in his late thirties, a committed preacher, humble and warm, who'd already dedicated years in East Africa and the Cape.

"Do they plan, in time, to simply train an African to serve as minister to this Fort Hare mission?" Joshua asked.

Andrew's eyes grew bigger as he scoffed, but he looked quickly as if he wished his reaction hadn't been so forthright. He reluctantly explained. "Most people here and abroad have yet to be convinced that Africans can do the basics—keep a job, count money, keep themselves clean. Those who know better still generally don't want to allow Africans to attain an education. You're . . ." His voice trailed as he stopped himself.

"My choice as a missionary here is as liberal as the mission gets," Joshua said.

Andrew shrugged, seeming embarrassed and choosing not to respond further.

"I admit I don't entirely know what to expect of this experience," Joshua said, trying to ease the moment.

"A challenge! In every way," Andrew smiled.

"I'm ready for the challenge. I aim to keep my spirits high." Joshua smiled.

Andrew nodded, a sure affirmation. He burrowed himself more deeply into the seat, then closed his eyes. Joshua soon followed suit, relaxing back to rest for a while.

"Here we are," Andrew said the next morning, after the locomotive arrived in Port Elizabeth and they traveled by taxi to the city center. The taxi pulled beside a block of parked automobiles. Walking up beside a sleek almond-colored four-door sedan, Joshua smiled, glancing at this newer version of the Ford models that the Hopedale Street boys used to lust after. His mind filled with the memories of the discarded magazines they used to leaf through— shiny Fords, that forbidden fruit they knew they'd never possess. Joshua eyed this one, feeling he knew its every part by heart. A slanted windshield, nickled headlamps, shiny radiator rims, balloon tires, and neatly spoked wheels—a true luxury, this one was. In Philadelphia, only the whites who lived across town could have afforded a car like this.

"All yours," Andrew said.

Joshua looked at Andrew blankly.

"This is all yours for the duration of your stay with us—you must have something to get around in," Andrew said. "Your benefactor, Reverend Roderick Waldron, chose this personally for you. He wants to give you the best chance of succeeding."

Andrew smiled, in a way that lifted Joshua's spirits. Then without another thought and without another care, he placed those golden keys in the tender palm of Joshua's hand. Joshua couldn't say a word.

"You know how to drive?"

"Since I was a kid," Joshua said as coolly as he could. "I drove my uncle's truck whenever he allowed it." A smile edged at his lips. Should he mention that Uncle Nate's rusted blue truck rattled every inch of the way over worn tires, with its bumper barely attached, a lamp tied to its back for night driving, and its bed covered with shovels and soil?

"If you're alert enough to drive, why don't you have a go?" Andrew said.

"I'm alert—I'm just not so sure I'm awake!" Joshua couldn't help laughing.

"You're awake. Get used to it. You're going to be the center of some attention, and of high expectations, I might add."

Joshua stepped into the driver's side, chuckling at the location of the wheel on the right side of the car instead of the left. He hoped he'd be able to maneuver well on the opposite side of the road.

"I'm certain you'll easily get used to driving here," Andrew said as Joshua's hand hovered over the slender ball-headed clutch.

"This might be a little embarrassing." Joshua chuckled with a half smile.

"I'm a good sport!"

Joshua hoped for the best as he ignited the engine and released the brake, pressing the middle pedal to back up. The car bucked, choked, cut off. Joshua squeezed his eyes and laughed.

Andrew held his hat down. "*Maybe* I'm a good sport." He roared with laughter along with Joshua. There was something about Andrew that had already won Joshua's trust. He seemed like an honest, good man. Joshua tried again, and again, succeeding on the third try. As he steered down a main street, through the city center, his confidence bloomed. But just as a broad smile curved across his lips, a police officer waved them aside.

The officer peered in the driver's window after Joshua pulled to the roadside, seeming suspicious of a Negro driving through the city center. Joshua's heart raced, but he did as Reverend Watson had advised, pulling out his papers quickly and handing them through his open window to the officer.

The officer examined the papers carefully as Andrew sat silently, not seeming very concerned. "Good to meet you, Reverend," the officer said, clearing his throat, doing his best to smile, and giving Andrew a certain look. Joshua felt relief that somehow filled him with deep unease.

Andrew continued to guide Joshua through the tree-lined neighborhoods of Port Elizabeth, finally pointing to where he should pull aside. It was fitting that this was the head mission headquarters. Situated on an expansive street graced with Victorian buildings, cast-iron lampposts, and carefully tended flower beds, the cement columns and gables that curled down over the building's verandah gave it a regal look. They stepped out of the car, and Joshua's heart pulsed wildly as they made their way inside.

CHAPTER 6

Joshua walked with Andrew down the woven rug covering the distance of the hallway, toward the bustling sounds flowing from the room at the back of the building. He felt something stir inside, knowing the impression he would make in this first meeting would be important. As they moved down the hall, Joshua glanced at the collection of art sitting on mantels—porcelain pieces painted in Asian designs, paintings, and African curios. What drew his eyes most were the photographs of missionaries at their outposts, carefully strung along the hallway walls like treasures from a plated chest. As they entered the brightly lit lounge, the room buzzed more loudly. Joshua smiled to himself as all eyes turned toward him, the only person of African descent in the room besides the workers circling the room offering juices in frail glasses. Joshua had grown accustomed to settings like this, and he began to scroll through his mind the things he could say to make each of the other ministers feel comfortable with his presence.

"Joshua!" an auburn-haired man said, moving across the room toward Joshua, shaking his hand enthusiastically. "Gentlemen"—he raised his voice before the nearest circle of ministers—"I have the honor of introducing the bright young star from America—valedictorian, student leader, averter of explosions, our dream come true! Sent to us to help save that daring outpost at Fort Hare." The ministers near him all moaned at the same time, shaking their heads at the mention of Fort Hare.

"Ah, so you are the one we have heard so much about," one of the ministers said, reaching for Joshua's hand.

"Welcome to South Africa! You've got your job cut out for you, from what we understand," another minister said.

"The students will challenge you a lot," another one echoed. "Reverend Peter over there"—he nodded toward the back of the room—"you should speak with him. He's who you'll be replacing."

"I'll make a point of it," Joshua responded thankfully, glancing in that direction.

The African workers came closer, eyeing Joshua. He was equally captivated by them, and wished he could speak to each at length. He deliberately said hello to each of them. Their eyes shone at his greeting.

After chatting with several ministers, Joshua noticed one of the few European women in the room, standing half-turned toward him as she conversed with a nearby group of ministers. He was used to this too, as he noticed her examining him from the corners of her eyes. He counted down the moments. Twenty, thirty. She finally turned to him.

"They've taken quite a risk in bringing you here," she said lowly. The unexpected chill in her voice matched the coldness of her eyes. Joshua's mouth almost dropped as her thin lips formed into a little frown. Joshua straightened his back, steeling himself for what would come next. He was so embarrassed, hoping none of the ministers could hear her.

"The others of your lot have behaved so irresponsibly," she continued, making Joshua's anger stir as she spoke a little more loudly, her tone intended to strip him down. She stood there, twisting a long strand of pearls over the lace bodice of her flowered dress. "Do try to make us know we made a wise decision," she said with an icy gaze, before turning her back to him.

Joshua was so grateful his skin was dark enough to hide a flush. None of the other ministers around him acted as if they'd heard a word, but Joshua dropped his eyes. Andrew tugged at his arm lightly, whispering with a chuckle, "Warm woman, wouldn't you say?" Joshua didn't dare share the joke as Andrew chuckled.

"I apologize *for* her," Andrew said, looking at him sincerely. "That's Reverend Waldron's wife."

Joshua's mouth gaped.

"You'll be happy to hear she's not representative of the wives of ministers," Andrew said. "As far as she's concerned, this is a business, one we should succeed in. Try to ignore her as much as possible."

Joshua thanked Andrew.

"Reverend Waldron wants to see you." A young man came to deliver that message. Andrew nodded as if he'd been waiting for the invitation.

"As you know, Reverend Waldron is your benefactor," Andrew whispered. "He has funded many of the new missionaries who have come here recently. He grew quite wealthy years back and is a preacher himself now, you know." They moved toward a gray-haired man standing in a vested suit. Everything about his face was pointed and stern. Reverend Waldron eyed Joshua, with no change in his rigid expression as they approached.

"Reverend Waldron, I'm pleased to introduce Reverend Joshua Clay to you," Andrew said.

"It's an honor," Joshua said, reaching out his hand. Reverend Waldron studied him intently for a moment before extending his own hand. Joshua kept his expression steady.

"I've heard wonderful things about your commitment to the ministry here," Joshua continued, knowing how to keep his voice from faltering in the face of such a lukewarm response. "I have a great deal of admiration for the resources you've dedicated and raised for the effort here."

"And we've heard great things about Reverend Clay, haven't we?" Reverend Waldron said, speaking to the ministers around him. "The letters we've read—he comes highly recommended. Apparently Reverend Clay worked wonders with his congregation in the United States."

Joshua ignored the feeling creeping over him as Reverend

Waldron spoke as if he weren't there, addressing his comments to everyone but him.

"You trained for two years as an associate minister in America?" Andrew asked, as if trying to ease the awkwardness.

"Yes, during school."

"And you were offered your own ministry there at a church? So quickly, that is very impressive," another minister replied.

"I'm sure they're sorry he won't be returning," Reverend Waldron said. "But their loss is our gain. This transitional period is of great importance to our organization, as you all know. We aim to touch lives here with our work. And we believe we are the best group to do so in the eastern Cape. Fort Hare itself is not in the best of conditions. The number of students there has not increased as quickly as its administrators had hoped, and the students can be quite troublesome. Joshua understands the situation he is getting into, if he's read the papers we sent."

Joshua nodded.

"We expect him to help us keep our presence there," Reverend Waldron added.

"I hope to enable the Fort Hare post to flourish. I know that's what we all desire," Joshua said.

"You will of course have a word with Reverend Peter," Reverend Waldron said, finally speaking to Joshua directly, but with a tone that was anything but a suggestion. "It will be important for us to salvage ourselves at Fort Hare. It was a coup that we even secured a spot for our mission there in the first instance. A British mission was going after it aggressively, even though they already have a representative on campus. You shall represent us well."

"Of course," Joshua said as confidently as he could.

"You're a leader now, son," Reverend Waldron said to him. "Write to me periodically and check in with Mr. Garrett at Fort Hare to let us know how you are progressing."

With that, Reverend Waldron turned slightly away, signaling the end to their conversation. Joshua chuckled to himself. *You're a leader now, son.* Reverend Watson had said the same thing. What did they think he was before?

"You will do well to spend a few moments speaking with

Reverend Peter," Andrew whispered, motioning him toward Reverend Peter. "At least learn what went wrong. Be careful what you say to him, though. He's mighty edgy these days."

The warning didn't dampen Joshua's eagerness to finally meet Reverend Peter. He wanted to hear as many details as he could about Fort Hare and the students. But Joshua inhaled deeply as they neared. By the way Reverend Peter was standing as he watched them approach, Joshua thought, this might be an unpleasant exchange.

"I was wondering how long it would take for you to work your way here," Reverend Peter said with a defensive cock in the tilt of his head, his slicked-back red hair faultlessly in place.

"I'm Reverend Clay," Joshua said kindly.

"So you're the one who will prove I have the persuasive skills of a peanut." Reverend Peter shook Joshua's hand limply.

"I've heard you did a remarkable job under very difficult circumstances," Joshua replied gently.

Reverend Peter scoffed, his eyes narrowed. He looked at Joshua almost with contempt. "I'm sorry. Don't misunderstand me—I wish you the best at Fort Hare," he said. "It was simply a trying experience. I'm used to influencing my congregations—you know, bringing home a few lost sheep."

The ministers around Reverend Peter greeted Joshua more warmly, but they fell into an awkward silence, seeming doubtful about what to say in Reverend Peter's presence.

"I've heard it's a difficult congregation," Joshua said. "I'm sure your work has helped pave the way for my work there."

Reverend Peter grimaced, looking at Joshua oddly, as if almost amused to be having this conversation with a Negro. He scratched his neck. "Just be prepared." His tone was sharp as he looked at Joshua. "I don't even think it is a good idea that we decided to keep that post. The students are unruly, they have no interest in doing the things they must to succeed."

"What things would that be?" Joshua asked.

"They must expect, in this climate, that there will be much resistance to educating natives. Most people don't think Africans can learn properly, and there is no demand for skilled natives. The students angry when they feel they have a lack of opportunities, and the backlash—I'm afraid—is targeted our way."

"Even when you sat down with them to try to explain the position of the advisory committee, it didn't help?" Joshua asked.

"It didn't help matters," he said slowly, his spiteful tone rising again. "And that's just the students. The village elders will turn up to your sermons sometimes, and those natives are of a different sort. They never put down those darn rattles." He laughed along with another minister beside him.

"They can be insistent on joyful singing," another minister explained more politely, almost seeming offended by Reverend Peter's remark.

"Our mission tries to teach them about God, to turn them from their witchcraft, and to teach them the civilized way to worship," another added, seeming to take Reverend Peter's side.

"You'll spend your time thinking you're getting through, and then they will begin talking about their witchcraft again," Reverend Peter agreed. "You know, the magic potions they drink, their ancestral worshiping, their multiple gods. Even after you preach to them week after week, and they nod their heads as if you've gotten through, they'll begin worshiping their multiple gods again. Between ancestor worshiping and their witchcraft, if you can get any little bit of information through . . ." He chuckled, shaking his head.

Joshua examined Reverend Peter's face. Where was the love of God? It seemed entirely missing from his words. Joshua swallowed hard as he glanced back toward Reverend Waldron, thinking the same thing. He whisked those thoughts away as quickly as he could. Andrew caught his attention just then, and Joshua smiled. Andrew seemed like a true man of God. Like every institution, Joshua assured himself, there would be a mixture of personalities.

"Well, if the challenge of the people doesn't get to you, I am certain the living conditions will," Reverend Peter said. "There are no amenities there. Running water in an outside well is your luxury. You'll have to go draw water from it every day. There's no electricity, sorry to say. And you'll have to adjust to using the outhouse—it's a nasty affair."

Spoken like a white American from the North, with no understanding of the lives led by Negroes, Joshua thought. He chastised himself as soon as that thought ambled through his mind.

"Outside of the college, there are few paved roads and little access to cars. It's hard to move around, the train only comes infrequently. I'm sure you understand my point," Reverend Peter said.

Joshua and Andrew both kept quiet about Joshua's car. Andrew was right, Joshua thought the car must be a good sign that the mission wanted things to progress better this time. That at least brightened Joshua's mood.

"Do you think the two of us might have an opportunity to speak at greater length about the situation at Fort Hare?" Joshua asked against his better judgment.

Another minister came by just then, touching Reverend Peter on the arm. "May I have a word with you?" that minister asked in a way that seemed too contrived, as if they'd orchestrated the interruption—one trip to the dessert table, one sip of punch, a long walk around the room, back in the nick of time.

"Forgive my cynicism," Reverend Peter said as he excused himself without answering Joshua's question. "Good luck," he said as he walked away.

———————

Dove white clouds hung in the bright turquoise sky as Joshua drove toward the edge of Port Elizabeth with Andrew, en route to Fort Hare. Joshua could feel happiness recede as they neared the city's edges and saw a blighted expanse in the distance where the number of Africans multiplied, as did the measure of forlornness. Joshua glanced to his right, looking across the treeless strip where Africans walked off large dirty buses, stepping over piles of litter. Even from a distance, he could see that this was a land of the brokenhearted. He could sense it in the resignation that curved the backs of those wandering there; that same despondency slowed their gaits and kept their chins downcast. Their hopelessness ambled toward Joshua, wiping a hand to his windows, with a sadness that willed him to stop and open his door. A look of guilt painted across Andrew's face as he followed Joshua's gaze. Such a familiar look, Joshua thought, one he'd often seen among white officials who had supported Negro rights in Ohio—as if Andrew thought this was somehow his fault. Joshua spoke words to put Andrew at ease.

As Joshua drove on, the land became more rustic, with white wooden houses scattered far apart on windswept meadows and cows grazing gently on the land. Any trace of the scents of the ocean had long disappeared as Joshua drove on the open road, the city's buildings no longer in view. He drove down the winding paved path that followed the train tracks, which followed the bends in the river, inland. He felt a growing sense of peace as he drove into the heart of the countryside, as the rolling green hills before him formed a gentle stream out to the horizon. The drive was lovely, Joshua thought, as he kept cresting one hill, gazing to the distance before he drove down that hill, up the next, as if floating on a boat, watching the waves roll ahead.

Everything looked so different from what he expected. The beauty around him seemed strangely familiar. He would never have guessed that God's green earth, on this far side of the world, would look so much like America. He discerned the differences only after a long stretch, when the land became peppered with fan-leaved succulents and giant cactus trees sitting upright on woody trunks, stretching spineless hands toward the heavens. Those plants were so peculiar and stunning, dotting the coarse land all around. Their numbers increased on both sides of the road as broken tar began to line the roadside and a single billboard rose on the hillside, its broad letters proclaiming JESUS SAVES! Joshua smiled, a smile that faded quickly as they passed a dark, ghostly church a mile down the road, the jagged teeth of its broken panes hanging loosely.

"Don't worry, it's not necessarily a sign of things to come," Andrew said, noting Joshua's expression.

After a good hour with no signs of a town, and only a truck or two passing in the opposite direction, the river came back into sight, swelling, and Joshua finally saw the sights he had been expecting. Old men with hunched backs walked barefoot by the roadside, dressed in ocher-dyed cloaks and headbands, holding tall walking sticks. Others, not quite as old, balanced wheelbarrows stacked high with corn and cabbage, moving toward town. Still others maneuvered surefooted donkeys, their manes flopping in the wind as they pulled creaking carts filled with women and children. Young women walked on the roadside, in twos and threes, with babies tied to their backs and reed baskets balanced high on their heads. The sound of Joshua's lone car caused them to look toward them, their smiles and kind movements so recognizable.

Joshua could see goats and rams grazing nearby. Slowly, the first village came into sight. A wooden fence marked the edge of the first homestead, encircling a dozen clay-colored mud huts graced with pointed thatch roofs. Joshua could barely pull his eyes away.

They drove for several more hours, passing several other villages clustered on red earth and grassy hills not far from the roadside. Just as he was beginning to think there wouldn't be a European town for miles, the road dipped into a valley, and the corrugated roofs of a town came into view, sun reflecting from the crosses atop many church steeples. The size of this city, located so far inland, was unexpected.

"This is King William's Town," Andrew explained. "We will be at Fort Hare soon."

Joshua nodded as he gazed at the largest town near Fort Hare, which he'd read had originally been established as a European military outpost. They drove past blocks of double-story Victorian buildings, elegant Edwardian commercial buildings, the post office, the courthouse, and the bustling market on Oxford Street that marked the center of town. After a few minutes more on an open road, palm trees lined the roadside as they descended toward a red-tile-roofed bastion wedged between two hills. Fort Hare. Joshua's heart fluttered again as he drove through open rod-iron gates, following the paved path to the foot of a grassy hill.

"It's beautiful," Joshua said as he stepped out, surveying the campus. Its white-stoned walkway led up a hill to a large cement building. There were only three large buildings that he could see— the other two were set farther off in the distance. Everything here seemed perfectly manicured—the well-mowed lawn, the blossoming trees, the white fence tracing the edge of campus. Somehow the African students helped transform the terrain, bringing it to life with their bustle as they moved and chatted in lively groups. Joshua could sense their youthful determination, which shaped the steel in their backs. Black lampposts dotted the grounds around the students, standing like maces furrowed deeply.

"What's that?" Joshua asked as he looked toward students gathered on a nearby hilltop, just outside a large green tent.

"One of the student societies no doubt," Andrew responded.

Not far from those students, a plump woman with a belt of shells tied around her waist held a sitting circle of students entranced as she danced. They laughed heartily as she sashayed back and forth. Joshua chuckled at the sight.

"That's an *inyanga*," Andrew said.

"A witch doctor?" Joshua asked looking at her curiously.

"Don't call her a witch doctor," Andrew replied. "The villagers consider her to be a traditional healer, a herbalist. They take her healing methods quite seriously."

Joshua nodded. She was different from what he had expected. She wore a headdress, yes, but she was donned in a European-style dress. As they continued up the walkway, Joshua's eyes drifted to the largest crowd of students, who stood enthralled with a young man standing atop an overturned crate. They listened, nodding with concurring sounds as he spoke in a big voice, referring to a newspaper in his hand. Joshua wondered what they found so captivating.

"Reverend Clement, you've arrived!" An enthusiastic voice called for their attention from the bottom of a low hill to their left. A short man, dark-haired and in his fifties, walked toward them with a certain gait, as if he owned every inch of the campus.

"Mr. Pierson Garrett, this is Reverend Clay," Andrew said. "As you know, Reverend Clay, Mr. Garrett is a top administrator at the college here." ᾽

"Thank you for bringing him to campus," Mr. Garrett said with an English accent, shaking Joshua's hand. "I'll take it from here," he said curtly to Andrew, staking his territory in a not so subtle way.

"Joshua, if you need anything, you're always welcome to come visit," Andrew said in a certain tone, as if he thought Joshua would be in touch soon. Joshua wondered what it was Andrew hadn't told him as he waved good-bye and slowly headed toward the main building.

As Joshua walked with Mr. Garrett, he noticed the young leader on the hilltop watching their exchange. The young man quickly moved down from his overturned crate, stepping over a row of low bushes as he forged a path directly to them.

"Hello, Mr. Garrett," that young man said respectfully as he skipped up beside Mr. Garrett, hand outstretched. Mr. Garrett didn't make the slightest pretense of exchanging a greeting.

Dressed in a light sweater and slacks, the young man dropped his hand to his side. "How are you today, Mr. Garrett?" he asked determinedly.

The friction between the two came from only one direction, Joshua noted, as Mr. Garrett simply touched Joshua's arm lightly to move him along.

"Things are going well for the students," Ogenga volunteered, keeping step right behind them, before moving off the stone walkway onto the grass to walk with them again side by side. "We had a productive meeting this morning."

"Good day, Ogenga," Mr. Garrett said.

"Well, who might this be?" Ogenga asked, bouncing in front of Joshua, extending his hand again. "A face I haven't seen," he said enthusiastically.

Ogenga's receding, matted hair looked like he hadn't combed it for weeks, but everything in his demeanor was serious and very respectful. Mr. Garrett's behavior didn't make much sense, Joshua thought. Joshua's arrival was supposed to mark a fresh beginning.

"I'm Reverend Clay," Joshua answered, trying to feign ignorance of the look Mr. Garrett was giving him. "Are you a student?" Joshua asked as he gave Ogenga a hearty hand shake.

"I'm president of the student council, in fact."

"*Oh,*" Joshua said, trying not to look so perplexed as he glanced toward Mr. Garrett, who had walked a few steps down the walkway and turned back, waiting for Joshua. With his medium weight, medium tone, medium height, there wasn't much distinguishing about Ogenga. He was hardly big enough to intimidate anyone, but with those piercing eyes, he seemed like quite a force. The way he squared his shoulders, walked straight-backed, and looked Mr. Garrett directly in the eyes made Joshua observe him more closely. There was a certain openness there, as if Ogenga would gladly have anyone examine everything about him, confident in what they'd find.

A tall young man came jogging up beside Ogenga just then, looking intently at Joshua. "Is this him?" he asked Ogenga. Quite unlike his friend, this young man was dressed in perfectly pressed attire, with well-oiled short-cropped hair, dark skin, and high cheekbones suitable for a king. His towering height—he stood more than a head taller than Joshua—might be enough to scare anyone. But when he spoke, there was a gentleness of spirit, echoing the small eyes that welcomed Joshua.

"You are the new reverend, then?" he asked Joshua this time, a smile lighting his face. "I'm Jovan Mabeza," he said as they shook hands. Jovan moved back beside Ogenga and they both walked with Joshua toward Mr. Garrett.

"We've been looking forward to meeting you. We heard your mission was determined to keep this station alive," Jovan said.

"To make it *thrive*," Joshua corrected him. Both students smiled at his response.

"Reverend Clay has somewhere to be," Mr. Garrett said.

"I am just getting settled," Joshua explained much more politely. "I will be in touch with you and the other students soon."

"You're giving your first sermon tomorrow, we hear," Ogenga said happily as Joshua turned to walk on with Mr. Garrett. Joshua couldn't keep his eyes from smiling. What a determined student. Joshua liked him right away.

"I'm glad you've heard of it," Joshua said. "I hope to see you there. And since you're student body president, I'd like to meet with you and some of the other leaders in another setting—one conducive to getting to know you." Ogenga and Jovan looked at each other, surprised.

"I'm showing the reverend his quarters," Mr. Garrett said sternly enough that Ogenga finally allowed them to walk on without him.

"We look forward to seeing you later," Ogenga said in a definite tone, tapping Jovan on the back as they both jogged back up the hill.

Joshua waited until the two were a distance away, just out of earshot, and then looked toward Mr. Garrett.

"You don't want to start off associating with the troublemakers,"

Mr. Garrett warned before Joshua said a word. "That is a hard road
to nowhere. We want you to build your mission's congregation, that's
true. But those ones aren't amenable to church ways."

That's a bold statement, Joshua thought, *particularly coming from
a man who isn't of the cloth.* He'd need to clarify Mr. Garrett's role relative to his mission. As they continued down the walkway, Joshua saw
a church cresting a low hill near them. Gray and unassuming, a metal
cross topped its tile roof. It looked lonely somehow, quite a contrast
to the rest of the campus.

"That's your mission's church on campus. Quite a forlorn sight,
isn't it?" Mr. Garrett nodded. "It looked just like that every Sunday
when Reverend Peter was here. That's your task—to breathe life into
it."

Joshua nodded as they walked down the curve of a hill in back
of the church, to a row of white houses, each with a lawn set behind
its picket fence. Joshua tried not to let his reaction show as they
continued straight to the largest among them. Twice the size of the
Hopedale Street houses, he could hardly believe the size of his new
home. A large reed basket sat just to the side of the varnished front
door, topped with a broad, tightly tied ribbon.

Mr. Garrett knit his brow as he looked at the basket. "That wasn't
here when I checked on the house a while ago," he said as Joshua
picked it up, glancing at the many wrapped gifts it held, each tied
with a chiffon bow.

"I suppose the congregation would like to welcome you," Mr.
Garrett said.

The lovely gesture brought a smile to Joshua's lips. He followed
Mr. Garrett inside. The wood floors smelled as if they'd just been
scrubbed and waxed. The home was immaculate, with sunlight
flooding through the living room's long windows. As they moved
toward the living room, they passed a long desk nestled beneath a
cross window in an enclave to their right. A typewriter sat there with
a note on its top.

"From Reverend Waldron," Mr. Garrett explained as Joshua
opened the note that read in large handwriting: "So you may write
often."

"That's more than a suggestion," Mr. Garrett commented,

eyebrows raised as he motioned to a stack of long-leafed paper and envelopes on the desk. Joshua wondered when Mr. Garrett had read the note and pondered the emotion he was feeling. There was something about Mr. Garrett that Joshua just didn't trust.

Joshua looked out at the stunning view of the backyard that extended down almost half an acre to a wooden fence marking the edge of campus. The garden looked like the ones Nate would tend on the other side of their hometown, with budding flowers and precisely clipped bushes. His family would never believe this. A single thatch-roofed hut sitting at the far right side of the yard added a nice touch, he thought.

"You will need to hire a maid, someone to help clean for you and iron," Mr. Garrett said as he moved toward the couch. "You can hire a local African woman to work for you. Your monthly stipend is generous; you have more than enough to support it. You'll need the help to keep this place up for entertaining, meeting with administrators, and building those bridges! There are extra rooms for a maid to stay in the back, along with a kitchen; and the larger cooking hut out there is well stocked," he said, pointing to the hut.

"That's a cooking hut?" Joshua asked. He'd assumed it was a guesthouse. "Are the others like it also cooking huts?" he asked, having noticed similar huts near the main campus building.

"Yes, to give the place a traditional look here and there," Mr. Garrett answered as he prepared to leave. "I realize you must be tired. We are greatly pleased to have you join us, and we look forward to having you spread your influence at the right times, helping us inspire the students to follow on the right path. I will come to gather you in the morning, to escort you to your first service. Everyone is quite excited to hear your first sermon."

That bit of news made Joshua feel hopeful.

"Your mission assured me you were made aware of what sorts of issues to address and which to avoid through your sermons," Mr. Garrett said, his chin tilted upward. "I'm sure it will be fabulous."

There was something about the comment that made Joshua ill at ease. He simply nodded, but he let out a sigh when Mr. Garrett finally left. Moving his bags and basket into his bedroom, he flopped down on the large bed set underneath two windows. As he turned over, staring at the ceiling, he searched to understand the feeling that had overcome him. He scrolled the day's events through his mind. Tested, snubbed, warned—all in such a short span. He chuckled, rubbing his temple. This was not exactly the reception he'd hoped for.

But what had he expected? He sighed. Perhaps he'd been foolish to think that he and his mission would be working harmoniously together from the beginning. It would get better. He shouldn't be this tired and discouraged, he told himself. Perhaps he was just weary from the long journey. At least Andrew had seemed very well-meaning. The thought brought a smile to his lips. He took in another deep breath and tried to ease his mind. He'd gotten through worse in the United States. He could still remember the hope he'd had when he had finally been approved for this position. He let his thoughts dwell on that as a tug of determination replaced his discomfort.

He drifted off to sleep for a little while. When he awoke in the darkness, the stillness of the house enveloped him. He felt so alone. Reaching for the lantern beside his bed, he lit it with a match. As he sat back, his eyes were drawn directly to the gift basket. He pulled it next to him. Each small package had been wrapped so delicately, warmth conveyed in the curve of the beautiful bow on top. As he lifted the packages out, one by one, unwrapping them, he smiled at the effort that had gone into preparing it. The gifts were many—a small pouch for carrying coins, a hand-knit scarf, homemade soaps. As he opened each, the discouragement that had lingered with him melted away.

He opened a window next to his bed and heard an owl call out a mellow sound in the night. As he glanced at his backyard, it was so peaceful. The sight of the hut took him back to the images he'd seen at the roadside—the villages and people traveling so peacefully to town. Faintly, he felt the thrill all over again. He could do so much here if he kept his spirits up. "Father God, be with me, give me strength to endure and guide my feet," he whispered. Hunger tugged at his stomach, but he lacked the strength to go look in the kitchen. Everything else could wait until the morning. He had gone over his sermon many times on the ship voyage. He better rest well before the morning. As he lay back on his bed and emptied his mind, taking time again to be still, Joshua heard that familiar voice singing in the distance. It had followed him even here, and the sounds brought him such comfort. *Osukuba ethanda ukundilandela, makazincame, awuth-wale umnqamlezo wakhe, andilandele ke. Kuba othe wathanda ukuwusindisa umphefumlo wakhe, wolahlekelwa nguwo; ke yena othe wawulahla umphefumlo wakhe ngenxa yam, nangenxa yeendaba ezilungileyo ezi, wowusindisa.* The music sounded like a ballad sung softly, as smoothly as if strung over vibrating strings. As he drifted back to sleep, the voice continued gracefully its lovely sonnet with song.

CHAPTER 7

"Normally you would enter from the front, but today it's your introduction to the congregation!"

Mr. Garrett's enthusiasm surprised Joshua. He seemed so different from how he was just the day before. The difference made Joshua feel hopeful for a moment as they stood on the walkway outside the back church doors. Something in his stomach tightened as he heard the singing come to a pause and a congregation member moved near the pulpit to announce their new minister's arrival. A church elder moved next to Joshua to escort him in, as Mr. Garrett stepped aside. Joshua hadn't felt this nervous since the first time he'd delivered a sermon over four years earlier.

The first thing that caught Joshua's eyes as he moved down the aisle was the ivory Jesus hanging on a cross at the church front. As he walked toward the pulpit, he greeted women seated in the right pews and men seated on the left. They smiled and spoke welcoming-sounding words in Xhosa. Old women with thick, taut skin, tanned by the strong sun, tilted their heads back with dignity and reached out their hands to greet him. Men with smiling eyes nodded—some with approval, others seemingly surprised to see a Negro. A gentle feeling washed over Joshua as they eagerly caressed his hand, touching his skin with their rough palms as if trying to feel his soul and smiling at what they found there. Little children tugged at their mothers, pointing at him. Joshua felt buoyed by their welcome and so happy in their presence.

Once he took his seat in the pulpit and others came to a lectern to speak, he surveyed the congregation. Plenty of students were present, dressed in their finest attire. He felt gratified, noting that only two rows sat empty in the back. The church was such a simple building. Bright light streamed through the cross windows, one of the few symbols that marked the threadbare building as a church. Only a broad plank sitting atop bricks served as the pulpit; the preacher's chair and guest chairs were simple wooden seats; folding chairs arranged in two sections around an aisle formed the pews. There was no bronze bird decorating the pulpit, no silver ornaments, no stained-glass windows. Thick wooden beams rested where a finished ceiling should have hung. But Joshua had been in humbler settings. Nonetheless, something seemed missing here. Even considering the dearth of adornments, a notably bleak air filled the room. It perplexed him, given the congregation's enthusiastic greeting.

The choir rose again and sang a well-rehearsed song in English, with deep sounds that somehow lacked soul, though time and again with a change of their inflection, someone would twirl a rattle and Joshua would sense faint traces of joy. Mr. Garrett gave Joshua a disapproving look as his eyes rested on the rattles in an old woman's hands. As the congregation sang long-faced, the stiffness in the air was almost unbearable.

As the choir continued, a young lady slipped through the back church door, drawing Joshua's eyes with her bright smile. The older man by her side, probably her father, seemed to hold her close with his arm wrapped around her. Even at such distance Joshua could see their eyes twinkled at him. He returned their smiles.

"We welcome you, Reverend Clay," an elder said after the choir finished, as he stood before the congregation wearing a worn shirt, slacks, and handmade open sandals. "We realize you are a stranger to our part of the world, Reverend Clay. We celebrate that you would sacrifice to leave your land to be with us. Our homes are open to you. The congregation says welcome."

The congregation said, "Amen," stomping their feet and clapping their hands.

Joshua moved to the pulpit's rostrum. "Thank you for the warm welcome," he said from the heart, feeling something restless stirring inside. Their earnestness touched him. "I thank you for your kindness in greeting me," he said, trying to speak slowly for those still learning English. "This is no sacrifice: it's my honor to come to serve you here. I'm happy to hear your homes are open to me. I look forward to getting to know you."

He shifted his papers and began his sermon, glancing at two interpreters who stood to the sides in the front, repeating his words softly in Xhosa for two sections of elderly people. He hesitated as he began. This felt so odd. When he preached the Gospels back home, he did so freely, with passion beneath his words. Now he looked down at the papers in his hand. He'd spent much time crossing out and editing large portions from one of his popular sermons. *Stress patience, small steps, a willingness to turn the other cheek*. The instructions from his mission flittered through his mind.

He ignored his unease as he wet his throat, continuing his sermon. As he glanced at the congregation now and again, he noticed the elderly closing their eyes from time to time, puckering their lips, drawing their cheeks tight together, trying to distill his words—as if sucking out the goodness of a sweet cherry and spitting out the false pit within. As he continued to speak, students soon cast their eyes toward the windows, moving their fingers in round circles on their Bibles as if no longer listening to his words. He felt his heart sink. At home, he often moved a congregation to tears. They'd rise, one by one, applauding the message and his passion. He received no such response to his words here. As the elderly slowly opened their eyes now and again, they looked at Joshua with forgiving eyes.

After his sermon, Mr. Garrett leaned against the wall in the back, watching the reception as some congregation members stayed to greet Joshua. Many older villagers uttered thankful-sounding Xhosa words; others spoke in broken English. Most of the students had quickly departed, something Joshua noted readily. As the crowds around Joshua cleared, a young man, too young to be a college student, stepped toward him.

"We are glad to have you here," he said with a smile. "It has been many months since we have had a preacher at this church. The Old Man over there"—he pointed—"wishes to speak with you."

Joshua followed him over to the "Old Man," who remained in the same spot at the back of the pews, standing with the posture of royalty next to that young lady. Simply dressed in a tidy white shirt and slacks, he exuded stone-hard confidence that seemed to reflect the respect he no doubt commanded. As Joshua approached him, he could faintly see that this man wasn't holding the young lady beside him, after all. It was she who held her arm steadily around the man's waist, as if quietly propping him up. The man and the young lady both smiled warmly as he approached.

Joshua extended his hand to the Old Man, who ignored Joshua's outstretched hand, hugging him tightly instead. He caught Joshua's chin in his hand, examining his face with care. The blue rings around his irises matched his blue-black skin. "You have turned out well!" the Old Man said like an uncle addressing a long-lost nephew.

Joshua stifled his laughter. *What does that mean?*

"I'm Mr. Maganu. This is Nongolesi, my daughter," Old Man Maganu said as Nongolesi offered Joshua her hand with a gentle movement.

"We thank you for that sermon," the Old Man said. "It was very interesting."

Interesting. Not exactly an enthusiastic word.

"Did you receive the gift basket well?" Nongolesi asked.

"That was from you?" Joshua smiled. He found himself drawn for a moment to the brightness of her smile and the softness of her slanted dark eyes. Her full lips curved into a lovely smile, blooming as she nodded. "The Old Man wished for the community to welcome you well. I placed it on your doorstep on behalf of those in these nearby villages. They all contributed gifts."

"I felt very welcomed," Joshua said. "That was very touching."

Joshua spoke with them for a few minutes. Mr. Garrett seemed to be watching their every gesture and movement, fidgeting a bit and biting his lip the longer they talked on. He finally came to interrupt them.

"Hello, Mr. Maganu," he said with a tone that seemed to dismiss the Old Man. Joshua felt a flutter of anger at the rudeness.

"Good day," the Old Man said, ignoring Mr. Garrett's tone and looking at him with his head tilted upward, as if welcoming a challenge.

"Well done, Joshua," Mr. Garrett said, proceeding to speak about various niceties for a while. Mr. Maganu grew weary of the idle chatting, and politely said good-bye.

"What did the Old Man want?" Mr. Garrett asked as Joshua watched him depart with his daughter.

"Why do you call him Old Man? He doesn't look older than sixty."

"That's just an affectionate term in these parts. Any head of a homestead is called Old Man."

"Oh." Joshua raised his eyebrows. "Well, he asked me over to his home for dinner tomorrow night."

Mr. Garrett paused, nearly frowning. "Well, I suppose he'll fill you in on some of the details around here. He is more fair-minded than some. Be sure to let me know if you have any concerns after your meal with him." Mr. Garrett couldn't mask his concern as he looked over his shoulder back at the Maganus.

———————

Throngs of students loitered near the green tent that was perched again on that nearby hill, reading well-worn pamphlets and engaging in hearty discussions. Some of them waved with broad smiles to Joshua, as he made his way the next morning beyond the main building to another two-story building overlooking the campus. The chink and clank of glasses called out as Joshua walked up a finely carpeted staircase into a dark-paneled room just off the banister.

"Joshua!" Mr. Garrett greeted him with the same enthusiasm he had a few days earlier when Joshua had first arrived. "Welcome to your first advisory committee meeting." He ushered Joshua toward a claw-footed mahogany table that dominated the room. Joshua took a seat next to a few men dressed in suits, near a wall cluttered with oil portraits of some of Fort Hare's European founders, pictured with their thumbs dipped into vest pockets.

"Everyone," Mr. Garrett said as the men in the room glanced at

Joshua over wineglasses, "we are still missing two administrators, but let's start on time. There's much to deliberate."

Joshua's eyes were drawn across the room to the sole African man, in a colorful print shirt, with rimmed spectacles dangling on his nose tip. He seemed happy to see Joshua there, offering a smile. Joshua had been told there were few natives on the advisory committee. *This must be Professor Kabata,* he thought.

Mr. Garrett worked his way through staid discussion points after they all took their seats: They discussed a change in food preparers, the donation of additional beds for new students from the Lutheran Church, the quality of lawn maintenance. "Well, then, to the more sensitive matters at hand," Mr. Garrett finally said, shifting in his seat. "I shall let the rector speak of the demands the students are making—*again*—for curriculum changes."

The rector cleared his throat, then explained the current demands. All of the issues were familiar as they proceeded. Joshua had already been versed in his mission's stance.

"It's clear we will not satisfy these unreasonable demands," the rector stated. "Adding engineering or medical studies would be reckless. There is no external demand for native engineers or scientists. And there is the issue of funding. When we fail to pass natives in those subjects, our reputation will suffer, funding will decrease, and this door to African progress will be closed."

"Even in the unlikely case that we pass one or two of them," another advisory committee member agreed, "when they fail to find employment, we will suffer the same consequences."

"I don't see what there is to discuss here," Mr. Garrett echoed. "Reverend Clay, you're aware of the view of your mission; I was told they have spoken at length with you about these matters."

Joshua nodded. "Our position is in line with what I've heard here today."

Amazement coated Professor Kabata's face. Joshua hesitated, feeling the need to explain. "It seems to me that there is still so much work to be done building up the basic areas of this college. My mission understands and agrees that trying to address such demands isn't worthwhile at this time."

Professor Kabata's expression made Joshua flinch.

"It's amazing to hear you speak with such assurance on this matter, given you've been here less than a week," Professor Kabata said in an ice-cold tone. "Is that your position, or the position of your mission?"

"He has the right to express his opinion, Professor Kabata," Mr. Garrett said, nodding approvingly toward Joshua.

"I will always represent the views of my mission at these meetings," Joshua answered, not wanting his voice to be diminished. "But in this instance, my personal views are also aligned with this perspective. It's the position of my mission that we need to establish a strong reputation before branching into areas where success is not assured," he said. "This school is new and Africans are just getting adjusted to civilization. Give it time, on all sides."

"The students are demanding this change—are you saying they don't know their own desires?" Professor Kabata demanded.

"Professor Kabata, this should be a *constructive* conversation." Mr. Garrett dipped his eyes low.

"I've been shown the single hall this college has," Joshua said gently. "I was taken in its front door, and when I turned in one direction, I was told that little section served as the library. Forty-five degrees to the left, I was told that small section served as the student hall." Many administrators chuckled, nodding their heads. "Another forty-five degrees, and there was a sprinkling of classrooms. This college does not yet seem ready to expand into new areas."

"Which is it—the school isn't ready or the students need time to be civilized?" Professor Kabata seethed. "The students are willing to study in a barn if that's what it takes."

"Reverend Clay is expressing a view consistent with many of us," Mr. Garrett said lowly. A few committee members fidgeted in their seats, uneasy but failing to voice an opinion.

"Have you bothered to speak to the students in forming your position?" Professor Kabata challenged Joshua again in a stinging tone.

"Joshua's point is well taken," Mr. Garrett said, turning his agenda pages over as if preparing to move on to the next subject.

"And how long do all of you intend to pursue this approach?" Kabata asked, turning to Mr. Garrett.

"However long it takes," one of the administrators answered, a little too listfully.

"And if that turns out to be one hundred years on?" Professor Kabata demanded.

"We should vote on whether to change the curriculum. It seems to me minds are clear," Mr. Garrett said. He put forth the motion. It passed, but more members raised their hands to vote in favor of amending the curriculum than Joshua had expected.

"We remind you, Professor Kabata, that voting is confidential— no one outside of this room should know who voted for or against the motion," Mr. Garrett said, leaning across the table, nodding to the other administrators. "And, Reverend Clay, it is a great comfort to know that you understand so clearly the position you must take in order to achieve the results that we all hope for in your mission. When you speak to the students, you must convey the same clarity. You should use your sermons to help them understand that the time is not yet here for such changes. Unlike some of the instructors at this university, you have the capacity to affect change more broadly, by encouraging students to assimilate into a civilized culture. They understand they should attend your mission's church only if dressed in Christian clothes. And the advisory committee supports the view of your mission that the printing of Xhosa Bibles should cease— Bibles should be printed in English only, to encourage natives to learn the English language fully and to be able to worship with us. If you are able to fulfill this role well, the positive impact it will have . . ." He paused. "You understand?"

Joshua nodded.

"And it would also be helpful for us, for the sake of keeping the peace, for you to inform us if you learn of the students planning open revolts. We have seen it all in the past few years—burning pass papers, unauthorized marches through the streets. It reflects poorly on the university."

The room was quiet.

"Reverend Clay?" Mr. Garrett didn't hide his concern at Joshua's silence.

"As a minister, I can't say I'm fully comfortable with that," Joshua said respectfully. "My congregation members must have confidence that they can speak with me freely."

"Well, then, I think we ought to have another discussion sometime soon," Garrett said, taking Joshua's response as a challenge. "With that, gentlemen, I think we are adjourned."

Joshua felt like he'd just been slapped. The advisory committee members seemed to cast aside that last exchange as they made their way to Joshua and welcomed him warmly. As soon as he could, Joshua inched his way toward the door trying to catch Professor Kabata as he walked briskly from the room.

"Professor Kabata, I'm sorry if I have upset you," Joshua said, leaning over the stair railing as he called after him. "Is there a place where we can talk?" He could feel Professor Kabata's anger hovering in the air as he gave Joshua a wintry look, then continued down the stairs.

"Don't be concerned about Kabata," Mr. Garrett said, catching the exchange. "He's never seen eye to eye with the majority of the committee. If you ask me, Kabata's not qualified to sit on the committee."

Hold still in wisdom, Joshua heard Lu's voice ringing in his mind. She'd always say that in a stiff voice. He'd found it odd. She wanted Negroes to be treated as equals, but she always urged such caution, as if she feared the consequences of that yearning, hoping that good deeds alone would create a safe place where justice might prevail.

"*Professor* Kabata," Joshua said, respectfully stressing Kabata's title, "seems like a very incisive man."

Mr. Garrett narrowed his eyes and paused, long enough to make a point. "You know, Reverend Waldron and I are good friends." He let the words linger. "Your mission was so excited when they discovered you and chose you to represent them here. After all, Reverend Watson's endorsement carries much weight around here. He is deeply respected as a clergyman. And oh, he did go on about the young man he'd found at Wilberforce! A young man with an even temper, an incisive ability to preach—a hard worker, one to use prudence. *Prudence,* Reverend Clay. You're what we've all been hoping for, after Reverend Peter failed us so miserably."

Joshua took in a deep breath and forced himself to speak conciliatory words. "I'm hopeful that my presence will allow our mission to grow." He believed those words, but Mr. Garrett made them feel offensive. Joshua decided to change the subject as he turned back to the table and gathered his papers. "You know, the feel of Fort Hare— it feels good. It's like Wilberforce in some ways."

"What ways?"

"The energy of the students. The hopes they have—their determination to change society, to make it better."

"It can border on irresponsible idealism."

"But the underlying sentiment is a good one," Joshua said deliberately. "I understand Africans are not yet at a stage of development where they're ready for bold steps; I've seen the mud huts from the roadways just as you have. But it will help to quell dissension if we at least acknowledge to them that the eventual aim is that they be trained in the professions, even if it is one hundred years out."

"In time, as they mature as a people and are able to handle the responsibilities, those things will come." Mr. Garrett offered a pasty smile.

"When I meet with them, I will express to them the university's intention to make progressive movement toward those longer-term aims. Perhaps that's not being done well."

"When will you meet with the students?" Mr. Garrett asked.

"I'm hosting a dinner for a few of them in a couple of nights. I left it to Ogenga to determine which leaders to bring along."

"You're hosting them where?"

"In my house." *That should be obvious,* Joshua thought.

Garrett snickered. "You don't shy away from danger, do you?"

What does that mean? Examining Garrett's face, Joshua decided not to ask. "I will be in touch with you quickly if any unexpected issues arise," Joshua said.

"We want things to go well here," Mr. Garrett said as he bundled his papers on the mahogany table. "Do make good use of that typewriter and that stationery. I'm sure Reverend Waldron will want to know about your endeavors—*all* of them."

"I've nearly finished drafting my first letter to Reverend Waldron," Joshua responded, knowing he had not mailed it yet because he'd been trying to get the words just right.

"That's a good start," Garrett said, warning him with his tone before he looked away.

CHAPTER 8

Joshua could hear birds chirping outside his window when he finally settled down at his desk the next day to finish writing Reverend Waldron. Their high-pitched two-syllable songs urged him outside. After handwriting the note one last time, he typed the final version.

> *Dear Reverend Waldron,*
>
> *It was a pleasure to meet you in Port Elizabeth. I have found the accommodations in Alice generous, and the welcome of the congregation very warm. I agree, there is much work to do through the ministry here at Ft. Hare. I am optimistic that with hard work this can prove fertile ground for us. I have already made arrangements to meet with several student leaders, and I hope to forge constructive relationships with them. I will keep you informed of how my work progresses.*
>
>

With deep respect and loyalty,

Reverend Joshua Clay
>

Perfect. Joshua folded the letter with a ruler, as precisely as a pleat, and placed it in one of the envelopes stacked at the side of his desk.

He was happy to finally get on the road. The sun had already begun to lower itself in the balmy afternoon sky as Joshua drove down the main road toward the Noni Village—a group of over seventy homesteads including that of the Maganus. Joshua had such a good feeling about the Maganus, and he had learned to trust his instincts. Their warm greeting felt like a promising sign of things to come. He wondered why Mr. Garrett had seemed so concerned.

As he turned off the main road that led to East London onto another paved road heading toward the Amatola Mountains, he caught his breath. A stunning landscape of peaceful meadows stretched in front of him, graced by towering misty blue mountains in the distance. The farther he drove from the main road, the more potholes and broken tar littered the asphalt, as if marking the distance from the nearest town. After a mile or two, he felt a tinge of excitement as he pulled near the outskirts of the Noni Village, the thatched huts of its first homestead perched on the hill to his left.

Joshua parked his shiny Ford on a dusty granite side road and walked toward the wooden fence encircling the closest huts, which nestled together facing the rising sun. As he walked past several young ladies harvesting furrowed corn beds by hand, they smiled. They gleaned their corn skillfully in the afternoon heat, cutting the heads off tall stalks with jointed sickles, bundling them in sheaves, and placing them into woven reed baskets. He wondered if this was how his own ancestors had lived, and how they looked. The thought made his eyes grow wider. He tipped his hat to the young ladies, taking it all in. He entered the homestead's courtyard, the scents of a roasting stew and cloven-footed animals in the air.

A group of barefoot little girls gathered around the courtyard's fence, pointing as he entered and giggling softly. He chuckled at their innocent jesting. Except for their bare feet and tattered clothes, they looked much like Hopedale Street children, running knobby-kneed near him with sunny eyes. He moved toward an elder man sitting with his back to the wall of a mud hut, who smiled toward him and waved him forward.

"*Wamukelekile apha nanhlanje,*" that old man with a toothless smile said from his spot in the hut's cool shade. He paused his skillful work, weaving a book bag with sturdy fibers, to extend a hand to Joshua with a quizzical expression. Most other people around him also paused and stared. The elder man spoke again in Xhosa as he rubbed Joshua's hand kindly, the words clicking across his tongue.

"I'm looking for the Maganus," Joshua said.

"Ahh." The man nodded, narrowing his eyes as he examined Joshua. He snapped his fingers toward a nearby girl, issuing some order to her in Xhosa as she ran past pecking chickens across the courtyard to speak with a woman about Lu's age. Something about that woman touched him as she rose from her knees, where she was smoothing a mixture of mud and dung over the courtyard—to keep it safe from snakes, Joshua had learned. There was something so familiar about her, and so sad, as she turned toward him in a tattered dress the color of a faded rose. She stooped and washed her hands in a metal bin at her feet.

Joshua glanced around as she moved toward him. He hadn't expected a village to look like this. The dung-swept ground felt smooth as cement underfoot, and the beehive huts looked so peaceful.

"*Umfazi Odlakezelayo*, the Raggedy Woman," the old man said, pointing to the woman as she moved slowly on thick ankles.

She studied Joshua's face with her small, sunken eyes, her thick lips finally curling into a faint welcoming smile as she stretched a hand toward him. "You are a stranger to our parts?" the "Raggedy Woman" asked. Joshua was surprised she spoke English.

"My name is Reverend Clay. I'm a minister at Fort Hare."

"Reverend!" Her face lit up. "You come to greet us," she said.

Before he could say a word, she touched his arm, leading him to a cowhide thong chair beside a hearth. She called others nearby to greet him as she touched a kettle on a three-pronged iron holder set just above the fire of a pit and decided it wasn't quite warm enough.

"We are very, very happy you have come this way to greet us and share a meal." She smiled, placing more twigs beneath the kettle. "The other reverend, he never traveled this way to preach at the village. Always we had to travel that distance to Fort Hare." She shook her head. "The littlest ones are off playing, some of the boys are in the fields and others are in school. You will preach here when they return and can hear it well?"

Her warmth touched him, but he was already late. He tried to explain why he'd stopped by. "I'm actually on my way to see the Maganus," he said. "Am I heading in the right direction?"

"We shall feed you well," she said very faintly, as she lifted the lid off a pot set above a second hearth, and a young girl brought a plate and wooden spoon. "We have not had a preacher nearby for some time. At times, we journeyed to Alice to hear that other one at Fort Hare, but many did not like his words," she said, taking the plate and spoon from the young girl.

"*Ucinga ukuba uluhlanga luni?*" a young lady near the Raggedy Woman asked.

"*Likhaladi,*" the Raggedy Woman responded to her.

The young lady seemed to stare at Joshua more intently. "*Hhayi, akalilo,*" she said.

"Are you Coloured?" the Raggedy Woman asked softly.

He knew the question was coming. Everyone he met seemed to ask. "I'm a Negro, an American," Joshua gave his familiar answer.

"Oh," she said, arching her eyebrows. The kettle whistled. "I am *Umfazi Odlakezelayo,*" she said, glancing at him as she fixed ginger tea in a pot. Something in the motioning of her hands made him pause as she sliced the ginger over the hot water and stirred it with a spoon. He glanced around. Somehow she seemed to be the mother figure to all the young children running nearby, a pillar of this community. Joshua's thoughts drifted for a moment to Lu.

"What does your name mean?" Joshua asked as he looked at the woman intently, certain he had heard the elder man incorrectly.

"They call me *Umfazi Odlakezelayo,* Raggedy Woman."

Something in her tone made Joshua narrow his eyes. "Is that the name you were born with?" he asked softly as she handed him a mug of tea.

"My given name was Tahira."

"Shall I call you Tahira?"

His question seemed to surprise her. Something in her eyes answered yes, for they sparkled momentarily, then darkened quickly, as if she had intentionally dimmed the light that had shone there in a fleeting moment.

She pulled out a tin cup and set a calabash next to him. "We have *amasi,* soured milk, also. We have kept the milk there in the calabash for three days. We bring only the best for our guest."

Joshua hoped she hadn't noticed him wince as she poured the thick liquid from a calabash into a tin cup. "Tea is fine," he said.

Guilt tinged his expression. She searched his face, as if wondering whether he had intended an insult. She kept the milk for herself and fixed her own cup of tea also, sipping it slowly. A few young ladies moving back into the courtyard distracted her as they unloaded the sapling branches balanced on their heads onto a larger bundle near the bare frame of a hut. He realized as he watched the rhythm of their living that he had imagined this before incorrectly. It wasn't dark, but peaceful, marked with a set rhythm.

Tahira moved over to the young ladies, sorting through the piles they had brought, seeming to show them which ones were good as she took a long branch that did not seem too thick and bent it into a certain curve, nodding. She pointed out the difference between it and thick, stiff ones, casting those aside.

Joshua's curiosity was piqued. "You're building a new hut?" he asked when Tahira sat back beside him.

"A new *indlu*," she said, nodding proudly.

Joshua made a note for his vocabulary. *Indlu.*

"Beaumont, the stick-fighting champion, a clever one, he is of age," she said with a shine in her eyes. "He is going into manhood now. He must now have his own hut. Soon he will be taken off with the other young boys his age from this village, to learn the ways of men. Then when he returns, his voice shall carry with equal weight as an adult." Her eyes sparkled. "He will receive this *indlu*. When you next come to preach, you will see its walls will be set there very well. Then there will come the top of grass—sewn only once it has been dried just right, and fastened to the frame of the roof. Beaumont will live there until he marries."

She looked around. "Beaumont is that one," she clarified, pointing to a young man, about seventeen, walking back into the courtyard with two oxen behind him. *Beaumont must be her son,* Joshua thought, judging from the shine in her eyes.

"This thing normally the men would help do," Tahira said sadly as she nodded to the young ladies burrowing a few pieces of the sapling branches into the ground to form more of the frame. "*Ubuntu* says all in a community shall assist in building a new *indlu*. It is for the men to plant the branches deep into the mud, and for women to plaster the walls. But now there are few married men with us, only the old men." Her voice dipped low, as if coming from a very dark place. "The others have gone to town. These times have been difficult; there is little money here. The rains have been few, and the crops we have to till on this little land are not plentiful."

The fear in her face pained Joshua. She seemed to be thinking of something broken, breaking still. "God will watch over this community," Joshua said gently. "And I will do what I can when speaking with King William's Town officials to see if there is a way we can help to meet the needs here."

She gave him a look, an expression he couldn't quite read. It bothered him. When she didn't respond further, he surveyed the village more closely. The huts were beautiful, every part of them was made of something natural, from the earth.

"We follow the customs of the ancestors," Tahira said, following his gaze. "Here, where the grass is plentiful, we use branches and thatch, not stone," she said. "Where my mother's Great Mother lived, the huts were stone, but much the same. But then her people settled near the lake some years ago, after the year of the famine. Wild greens grow in this area, and the river flows freely to the nearby lake. It has been our home ever since."

"It's very beautiful here. This is the first village I've visited since arriving."

"Eh?" She smiled, amused. "Beaumont," she then called to the young man as he tied the cattle pen gate shut.

Beaumont walked over, touching Tahira's shoulder with a deep look of love, the bond between them seeming as potent as the cord that must have once bound them together.

"This is our new preacher," Tahira said. Joshua didn't know how to correct her as Beaumont shook his hand enthusiastically. He was only authorized to preach at Fort Hare.

"Your name is very different," Joshua said to Beaumont.

"He's named after a great preacher," Tahira responded as Beaumont beamed.

Several little boys came running through the courtyard then, with their calves wet and their feet muddied. "Help them milk the cows in the *ebuhlanti*," Tahira said to Beaumont, who walked back into the cattle pen with the younger boys. Joshua memorized that new word also. He watched each boy pick up a pail and move near as Beaumont reached under a cow's udder, demonstrating how to pulse the four teats gently. Everything bustled with purpose; two girls sat nearby sorting sugar beans, while others ground corn.

A young girl moved sheepishly toward Joshua, placing in his hands a plate of hot food Tahira had just dipped out.

Joshua tried to explain again that he must be leaving, but Tahira reached over and squeezed his hand, her skin rough against his. "You come to our village; we shall feed you well," she said again, giving him a toothy smile.

They had so little, but were so generous. It moved Joshua. Before he could ask again about the Maganus, the food scents caused him to sit still. Joshua's eyes grew wider as he looked down at the plate in front of him. He could barely believe his eyes as he glanced at the vibrant green collards flavored with onions, the sweet potatoes mixed with dark spices and a thick peppery stew.

"You don't like the food?" she asked, trying to read his expression.

He couldn't speak for a moment. It could have been a meal fixed by his aunts. "It's wonderful," he managed to say. "I would like to bless the meal," he said.

She smiled as they bowed their heads and he said a prayer. Tahira's eyes were bright when she looked up. She nodded and dipped her fingers into the greens, using them to dip up pieces of the potatoes into her mouth. She smiled at him with a motherly look that reminded him of Lu.

"This is *imifuno,*" she pointed to the greens. She seemed to think he didn't like the food.

"Yes, collard greens; we ate this often in my home," he said, following her example and dipping his fingers first into the greens on his plate.

She raised her eyebrows as Joshua savored the flavors. Even the spicing tasted the same as the onion juices dripped over his tongue and the sweetness of the potatoes made him lick his lips. *My family would never believe this,* he chuckled to himself.

"The few people I have met from your land have said they have never eaten these ones," she said.

"Our land is a big place." Joshua smiled as her eyes drifted up to the kink in his hair.

They chatted for a while, until Joshua finished his plate. Before he could say anything, a young lady placed another large plate in front of him.

He took a deep breath and tried not to chuckle. He should have spoken more quickly. "I really must go soon," he said softly as he started to eat the second plate. "I am due to meet the Maganus. They were expecting me a while ago," he explained again.

"Ah, those ones. They are not far. Their homestead is just around the corner," she said. "They are good ones, the Maganus. And they have enough clothes to change into new clothing every day of the Lord's week, and their sleeping mats are raised off the floor. They will keep you well. But you will return to preach to us soon?"

"I would be honored."

After finishing his meal, Joshua stood and shook her hand warmly. He couldn't help smiling broadly. Her hospitality had really moved him. "Thank you for the lovely food," he said, still feeling bad about his reaction to the soured milk, trying to make up for it with his smile.

Tahira called two little girls, both about five years old, speaking to them in Xhosa. "Follow those ones," she said to Joshua. "They will take you to the Maganus."

Joshua followed the two girls out of the courtyard and farther up the hill.

CHAPTER 9

Just around the corner turned out to be a thirty-minute walk across a narrow creek and up a hill. The road didn't extend that far, so Joshua left his car by the first homestead of the Noni Village and followed the two little girls up a wide path across the hillside. The little girls seemed to know every rock and stone on the way. They looked up at him with wondering eyes, giggling to each other and speaking in Xhosa. Finally, they stopped, just as a large thatched roof came within sight. It graced a rectangular wattle-and-daub house. Surrounded by carefully planted pine saplings, the Maganu home welcomed him, even from a distance.

"Hello there," Nongolesi said in a sweet voice from the doorway as the little girls traipsed back down the hill. She happily held out her hand. "Nongolesi."

"I remember your name." He smiled.

"We expected you a while ago."

"I apologize that I'm so late," he said, shaking his head. "I didn't mean to keep you waiting. A kind woman of the Noni Village homestead insisted on feeding me a meal. It was very thoughtful of her, although I'm sorry that it delayed me."

Nongolesi's smile broadened and she chuckled. "I should have warned you that as a foreigner it is very difficult to pass through the villages without the families feeding you well."

Joshua laughed softly. Nongolesi had a delicate charm.

"The Old Man has gone out to check in the fields now. He will be back. Please come, we will wait in the yard."

He followed her to the back of the house, where an older woman was shredding tassels from corn heads spread within the fan of her skirt, the rolls of fat under her arms moving with her hand motions.

"This is my mother," Nongolesi said as the plump woman closed her hands tightly around Joshua's.

"*Molo, wamkelekile ekhayeni lethu,*" Mama Siziwe said, welcoming him with her smile. "We welcome you here."

Nongolesi sat in a thong chair across from the one she offered to Joshua, leaning over a wooden tub of corn heads.

"These we call mealies," Nongolesi said, holding up a head of golden corn, skillfully removing the last of its green outer husk. Holding it over a second bucket, she broke its morsels off deftly with her fingers.

Joshua made another mental note of the new word for his vocabulary. "Thank you for inviting me here," Joshua said. Nongolesi had such a quiet, precise manner, but he sensed she had a very strong will. She worked so harmoniously beside her mother, their movements practically in tandem. He surveyed their beautiful yard.

"Those *izindlu* are for my brothers," Nongolesi said, as Joshua gazed at the thatch-roofed huts across the yard.

"It's very nice to visit your home." He smiled thankfully. "And it's been wonderful to see so much of the countryside so soon after arriving. The walk through part of the village up this hill was beautiful."

"It is good of you to come," she said in a kindhearted tone. "The other preacher never visited us here."

"Reverend Peter?"

She nodded, pursing her lips like she wanted to say more. She shifted her eyes back to the corn in her hands.

"Thank you once again for the lovely gift basket," Joshua said.

Nongolesi's eyes lit up. "We are glad you received our gift basket well. You should know the Old Man had me pick the very best reed basket, instructing that I fill it to its very rim with gifts and more gifts from the many homesteads of Noni, each one to be wrapped very, very carefully."

Her tone made Joshua chuckle.

"Then I had to tie each gift with chiffon strips, and the Old Man checked each one. *That bow is not tight enough,* he'd say. The bows had to poof in full swoops, just right," she said, motioning widely with her hands.

Joshua laughed and Mama Siziwe also chuckled under her breath.

"It was very important to everyone that the basket reflect our hopes for your stay with us here," she said, smiling in a way that warmed him. "We all wish that things will go much better for our new minister."

"I appreciate that," Joshua said, feeling very grateful for the warmth she extended. Something about her seemed so sincere. "Your father is a great educator, I hear."

"He does not teach anymore." She paused briefly. "Though most people outside the government would say he was once a great educator."

"Outside of the government?"

"Those in the government did not like him so much," she said, giving Joshua a certain look.

"Did he run one of the schools?"

"There was one here that he ran, years ago. That building stands empty now."

"He retired?"

"Resigned. He wanted to build a school to teach children to honor our traditional ways," she said, as if others thought there was something very dangerous about that. Her voice grew bright. "It is here now, the independent school they call Ulundi, born of his vision and the hard work of others like Sarah. Before, there was only one high school much farther out. The Ulundi School now continues to grow; students come from far away, traveling by bus as much as an hour each day. Even before the sun rises, they set off and travel this long distance to come to school."

Mama Siziwe nodded, following the conversation.

"Have you met Sarah?" Nongolesi asked.

"Who's Sarah?"

"One of the founders. She is an American like you. A Negro. She comes to the school sometimes."

"No, I haven't met her," he said, telling himself he must try to meet with her at some point. He knew there were some American Negroes in the country, but he'd assumed most were in the largest cities, like Johannesburg. He looked at Nongolesi for a moment.

"Do you teach at Ulundi?"

"I teach English to the children."

He smiled at the way her eyes lit up when she said it. She talked about her students and the merits of teaching mathematics and sciences at the independent school, waving her finger in the air, as if she'd argued her points a hundred times. "Even the girls should learn these," she said.

"Uyayazi ukuba akufuneki uhambe uthetha izinto ezinjalo," her mother reprimanded her.

Joshua wasn't certain what was wrong, but he frowned at her expression as Nongolesi looked away, trying to soften her mother's words. Nongolesi fell silent, giving him an embarrassed smile. She soon moved over to the open hearth in the ground, placing two fresh pieces of wood there to build the fire higher.

"We do not know how long the Old Man will be," she said, glancing over her shoulder at Joshua. "We will prepare a snack for you."

"That's very kind," he said. Smoky wisps sweetened the air as she placed an old metal rack over the pit and placed six freshly stripped mealies there to roast. "So, tell me about your America," she said, sitting back in her chair and glancing in her mother's direction. Mama Siziwe nodded faintly, as if to approve, yet kept her eyes focused on peeling a sweet potato.

"There's a lot to tell. What would you like to know about?" Joshua asked.

"They say America is a great land with no poverty and no hunger."

"Who says?" Joshua chuckled. She made it sound like paradise. "We have some poverty and hunger."

"Well, they say it is made of great big cities."

"Yes, that's true; there are cities there that stretch for miles in all directions, with towering buildings."

Her eyes grew wide trying to imagine it.

"Tell me about the last city you saw before you left," she insisted.

She was so anxious to learn about the world outside of her own. He was drawn to that spirit but looked away for a moment, feeling his eyes had lingered too long on her bright smile. Joshua leaned back into his chair, clearing his mind so he could focus on her question. "New York City." His eyes twinkled, remembering the sights. "Have you heard of it?"

Nongolesi and Mama Siziwe both nodded enthusiastically.

"I hear it is spectacular," Nongolesi said.

"It's known to be the largest and most vibrant city in our country, with all of its great music and dance halls."

"Yes"—she smiled—"we see the American dances here at the movies they show in the city."

That's amazing, half a world away, he thought.

"Africans are allowed to attend the cinema on Sundays at the Africans-only showings," Nongolesi explained, seeing the surprise on his face.

He scoffed, almost inaudibly. *African-only showings.*

"So, New York . . . ," Nongolesi said, prodding Joshua to describe it.

"The last things I saw of New York were its great buildings—they were taller than I had imagined, stories high in the air. And in the ports there, there were great ships from all over the world, gathering the goods we have made to take abroad."

He chatted on. She seemed to enjoy every detail. But Joshua dipped his chin when he remembered how the white women he'd passed in New York City had moved across the street the moment they saw him walking toward them, how difficult it had been to fetch a cab. He didn't see the point of bringing up such things. He continued on, stressing the marvelous things about New York. Something gentle washed over him again as she smiled at his descriptions. He felt somehow like he'd already known her for a hundred years.

"Is that where you are from, New York?" Nongolesi asked.

"Not at all." He shook his head. "That was the first time I'd ever seen it."

She pulled three mealies from the grate after they'd blackened in spots, just the way Lucius would make them on hot summer days.

"We roast corn on the open fire here; it is sweet inside," she assured him. If only she knew how familiar this was.

"I hope you enjoy it," she said, and she handed the piece of corn to him, wrapped loosely in its old husk.

Joshua's eyes grew large as the hot, sweet juice from the kernels dripped over his tongue. The kernels were larger and tougher, but also sweeter than the corn in the USA. Nongolesi smiled at his expression. "It's lovely." He smiled.

"I've seen pictures of the great boats that travel to the United States and Europe," Nongolesi said as she and Mama Siziwe both swallowed a mouthful of corn. "Great boats, 'royal houses afloat,' large enough to be a city. My greatest dream is to one day travel to see the Indian Ocean. Maybe I would see such a boat there on the dock, near Cape Town."

Joshua's smile faded. "You've never seen the Indian Ocean?"

She shook her head.

"Not even from East London?" It was only an hour east.

"It is not always safe to travel with the pass laws," she whispered. "We are banned from most beaches of East London—they are for Europeans only. And that city"—her voice dipped—"it holds many bad memories."

The fear in her voice as she spoke about East London made him almost flush—he wasn't certain why.

"I would like to see the Indian Ocean from Cape Town," she said again, sitting back farther in her chair. "So, tell me about your great trek across the sea," Nongolesi continued.

"Well, I wasn't on one of those luxury ships you've heard of," he said. "I traveled on what they call a goods ship—it transports items that are bartered and sold between countries, but they carry a few passengers also. It was a very dull-looking older ship. My cabin was cramped. They served us thick, greasy food."

"I can't believe this!" She laughed, flinching at the thought.

"It's true." Joshua laughed with her softly, remembering the details. "But the journey was very memorable nonetheless."

"Because you were on the great ocean?" she asked.

He nodded. "It was very beautiful."

"There were times you could not see land in any direction?" she asked as she moved to turn additional mealies on the grate with a fork, shifting their blackened sides upward as they let out a sweet charred aroma.

"Many times—many days," Joshua answered. He smiled at the memory. "It is the strangest feeling. Overwhelming—you look out and all you see is the rolling sea and the shimmer of the moon and stars." He inhaled softly. "But I also had a very eccentric roommate named Marvis—a man I'll never forget." He chuckled.

Joshua heard slow footsteps moving toward them. "Hello there," a deep voice interrupted them from a ways away. The Old Man approached from the fields below with two young boys following behind with long sticks, shepherding cows back into the *ebuhlanti* before sunset. In contrast to the day before, the Old Man was dressed in a traditional animal skin skirt, its leather strips falling gently over his blue-black skin. Joshua quickly wiped the surprise from his face as the Old Man moved with a tall stick toward him. *Some of them need a little teachin' 'bout dressin'.* Lucius's words sounded so silly now. Even dressed like this, the Old Man looked like royalty, his attire as rich as velvet. An even older, equally distinguished man moved slowly with age behind the Old Man.

"We have been awaiting your arrival, Reverend Clay," Old Man Maganu said, extending an outstretched hand to Joshua, his eyes shining.

"My apologies for my tardiness," Joshua said, standing to greet him.

"We figured you must have lost your way. It is difficult for foreigners to find their way here sometimes." The Old Man chuckled.

"The villagers down the road sent two young children to lead my way. I felt very looked after." Joshua smiled warmly.

"Ah, it is the children who often know the best," the Old Man said, nodding distinctly, his eyes telling Joshua he shouldn't forget that. "Children, they are the ones who notice every nick in every rock, every patch of matted sand, and the small puddles along the way. We who have grown older sometimes forget to notice such simple things, to understand this world in simple terms. When you lose your way, remember the children."

Joshua nodded, knowing he was in the presence of an honorable, wise man.

"This is the Great Father of our family," the Old Man said, motioning for Joshua to greet the frail-looking man with sunken cheeks who looked like a walking history book. Joshua felt a chill when the Great Father touched him; his hand's coarseness pulled Joshua back in time, as if he were touching the hand of his own grandfather. *"Lo nguMfundisi omtsha esimthunyelelweyo. Ndiyayazi ukuba usemncinane, kodwa uyathembisa,"* the Old Man said, seeming to explain to the Great Father who Joshua was.

"It's a pleasure to meet you, sir," Joshua said as the Great Father squinted his eyes.

"Walk with me to the fields," the Old Man said to Joshua after exchanging a word with Nongolesi. "We will take supper once Mama Siziwe finishes roasting the chicken. We have killed that one just for you." He smiled.

Joshua couldn't respond for a moment. He hadn't expected the welcome he was receiving. He knew how precious livestock was among the Xhosa. "Thank you for welcoming me so well," he replied earnestly.

The Old Man nodded. "Come see where we live. It is very different from the ways of the Americans, we understand."

Joshua walked with him. A touch of lavender now painted the whole sky as evening set in. They followed the cloven-footed cow marks in the sand past the oak-framed *ebuhlanti*, the thick smell of animals lingering in the air. For a moment, as the Old Man chatted on, Joshua felt a little off balance. There was a familiar cadence to the Old Man's voice and a familiar movement in his hands. Not long before, Joshua had been with Mr. Garrett, and as much as he may have disliked Mr. Garrett, there was a familiarity of European culture that seemed to tie them together. Joshua had expected *that* familiarity, but this . . .

They paused for a moment before the *ebuhlanti,* watching the cattle and goats milling over piles of mealie tassels, their long-haired tails waving away flies.

"Do you know anything about cattle?" the Old Man asked.

"Actually, I know a lot." Joshua chuckled, smiling with remembrance as he looked at the smooth-horned oxen and black cows before him. "My mother's family grew up on a farm in the southern part of the United States. They would send me there in the summers. Their farm was in South Carolina."

"It was plentiful?"

"Very plentiful." Joshua nodded. "We worked long hours in the summer—all day, pruning tobacco." Joshua laughed, shaking his head with the memories. "The cows were about the only thing I looked forward to at the end of the day—those blue-ribbon prize-winning cows—because only the older boys were allowed to milk them. I could finally just rest and watch."

The Old Man chuckled. "Most foreigners who have come to visit have known little about cattle," he said, pleased. "You are a unique one, then. You can appreciate these."

The Old Man spoke about each cow as if it were his child. He knew the history of each one, just as he could recite tales about the *ebuhlanti,* every inch of which held a special memory. This was the center of their home, he explained, the source of its wealth, the place where they prayed. Every bit of soil had been laid with care, and the fig tree outside the pen had been planted in a precise spot. He knew every bush and rock like a mother knows every curve on her child's face. "You see how God has blessed this family," the Old Man said, pointing downhill to the fence marking the end of his homestead.

Fort Hare will look like an oasis. The words floated curiously through Joshua's mind as he surveyed the land. Those were the words his mission officials had uttered, as if by the time Joshua rode through the countryside, saw the surrounding mud hut villages and finally reached Alice, he'd run to Fort Hare, arms swinging, thirsty for a hint of civilization. He looked around. There was so much beauty here, right here in the villages. As they continued downhill toward the mealie fields, they passed two little boys.

"I teach the youngest ones to tend the cattle well," the Old Man explained. "These two boys are the children of a woman in a Noni Village homestead a few miles away. It is best to start them young. That is what went wrong with Nongolesi." The Old Man's voice grew sad. "Nongolesi was always obedient. She always showed respect for our traditions," he said, shaking his head. "But we let her play too long with the little boys. Girls learn to stick-fight with little boys when they are very, very little"—he motioned down with his hands—"but then they must be separated and taught the ways of women. I am at fault, I believe. Now this one we cannot marry off, she refuses. For most women, it would be too late at her age. But men still want her hand. She refuses. That one . . ." Worry filled his expression.

Nongolesi wasn't that old, Joshua thought. She seemed only a few years younger than himself.

The sun dipped beneath the brow of the mountain as the Old Man led Joshua back to the house. The air cooled quickly. Inside, they offered Joshua a seat beneath a cross window at the dining table. They chatted leisurely over another dinner baked in all the flavors of Hopedale Street. The Maganus smiled and chuckled, seeming to know Joshua was probably too full from the meal Tahira had fed him to eat much more. Joshua wasn't sure what he had been expecting, but it wasn't this, he mused to himself. He glanced at the two little boys who ate happily with their fingers. The Maganus were so generous, he thought, for taking in these two additional children to raise while their fathers were off at the mines. Joshua teased a forkful of greens and chatted on.

"You know, you are very different from what we were expecting," Nongolesi said, her eyes drifting to Joshua's hair. "They didn't tell us you'd be a Negro."

Joshua almost chortled as the Old Man's eyes danced at his daughter's bluntness.

"I was very surprised," she said, not noticing her father's expression, "when you first arrived on campus and you stepped out of that shiny car. I had just dropped off the gift basket and you should have seen Ogenga's face—he could hardly believe his eyes! He froze on top of his soapbox. I saw him calculate it out—the other man coming out of the car was Reverend Clement, and the man greeting you was

Mr. Garrett, so you had to be the new preacher. Hardly anything catches Ogenga by surprise." Everyone at the table snickered.

"So, you didn't know I'd be a Negro," Joshua said.

"Or so young," the Old Man added.

Joshua paused, not certain how to respond.

"But it has been nice to receive a young minister," the Old Man clarified. "We have heard about your many successes back home. Mr. Garrett had spread the word that we would be receiving a great preacher."

The words warmed him, but Joshua felt a bit mystified to hear Mr. Garrett speaking so positively of him. "How do you know Ogenga?" Joshua asked Nongolesi.

"He's my brother," Nongolesi said, surprised Joshua didn't know.

"I didn't realize that," Joshua said, thinking about that for a moment. "Your family is truly one that values education," he said, smiling with admiration as he looked toward the Old Man.

"Especially in these times," the Old Man said somberly. "We have heard of Wilberforce and many of the other great Negro schools of America—Lincoln, Tuskegee. Many of the Negroes of your country have helped us to establish the independent secondary school we have here. Seeing their good work made me wish long ago to be an educator."

"I didn't know that so many Negroes had been involved here."

"Enough to have helped bring needed money and contribute to some of the strategies we have adopted in our struggle."

That's why so many of them were deported, Joshua thought. "I understand you were a great educator," he said, changing the subject.

"Until I realized the blackboards of the government schools were doors to a bleak night, eh?" The Old Man frowned. "It led the children into a netherworld, where they were taught to go always to the back door."

Joshua understood his meaning.

"When you were a child, would you play and draw freely?" the Old Man queried.

Joshua nodded, recalling how he'd sit on the porch as Darius helped him color scrap sheets of paper with the rainbow colors of broken crayons, drawing houses, and cities, creating a world.

"One day, I watched the children of the government schools, with their twigs in hand, drawing in the dust," the Old Man explained. "The sand would blow over their marks in the sand, just the faintest wind, and they did not seek to draw again. They no longer sought to create a better world, their hopes and dreams seemed to be no more. That government school they attended taught that the Xhosa had no history before the Europeans came here. It did not teach them pride in who they are. When our children cease to dream a world, we have failed them." The sternness in his voice made Joshua sit still. "No child should be like this, wanting in hope. One of your leaders has said this same thing. You call him . . ." He stabbed his fork in the air, searching for a name.

"Carter G. Woodson?" Joshua asked, his voice splintering with surprise.

"Yes, that one!"

"His writings circulate in East London and Port Elizabeth," Nongolesi said, answering the question in Joshua's expression. "When the Negroes arrive here in the ports, even though the government rarely allows them to disembark anymore, they always find a way to pass their papers and books."

"We agree with this view. The seeds we sow will come back in the future, you see," the Old Man said. "After a good soaking, those ideas the government placed there would have taken root; then the groves they would produce"—he shook his head with wide eyes— "we would soon be finished as a people."

"We have built a school now of our own money," Nongolesi echoed, her eyes as proud as her father's. "We find ways to save our own moneys. Some Negro reverends, some that Sarah knows, have sent moneys to us. You should come see sometime the new independent school, Ulundi—that means "hope". The children would be happy to receive you."

"That is a good idea," the Old Man agreed, with smiling eyes.

Joshua inhaled softly, then surprised himself as he probed. "What have you heard of Reverend Peter, the missionary who left?" he asked.

A thick silence filled the room. Nongolesi bit her tongue.

"He grew very weary of the people," the Old Man said.

"Weary how?" Joshua asked.

"He felt he was having no influence on us heathens," the Old Man said as everyone in the family chuckled.

"No one would attend his sermons," Nongolesi explained. "We have heard he says this is because he was a white preacher. That is not so. He did not try to understand our ways. He never joined us for supper, never came to preach in the villages."

"I do not think he had a bad heart," the Old Man continued. "This place is so different from where he came from, he did not know how to react."

"I hope I am off to a better start," Joshua said.

"You would do well to study with those considered great preachers here," the Old Man continued. "The Brother has touched many, brought many closer to God."

Joshua watched a smile light each of their faces as they thought of the Brother.

"The Brother is accepted among all peoples of this land." Nongolesi nodded. "He wears his black skin with pride; it has never caused him a problem that he is not from this land. People come from far away to hear him. He lives in East London," Nongolesi explained further.

"I'll definitely try to meet with him," Joshua responded, happy to know that another Negro preacher was in the area. Something told him, though, that the Old Man was trying to tell him something. Joshua searched his face. The room fell silent again as everyone cleaned their plates. Joshua glanced out the window. The sky had quickly darkened to coal black, only a bit of light showing as the moon peeked from behind a thin ribbon of cloud.

"You won't make it back to town tonight," the Old Man said, sensing Joshua's concern. "You will stay here tonight. There is a spare room; Mama Siziwe will show you later."

They moved into a warm-looking room with curtains made of bright stripes—yellow, green, orange. Mama Siziwe had already lit a lantern there, which glowed softly. Joshua's eyes were drawn directly to pictures tacked to the top of the walls. Each portrayed a single face, some painted, other sketched in charcoal. Each revealed so much through the tilt of the head, the curve of a lip. He saw a mischievous daughter, a wise man, a proud son in a cowhide skirt, a hopeful girl, a strong pillar of the community holding a long, carved pipe in her mouth, a prideful barefoot woman wearing an ocher-dyed skirt and a shell bracelet. "These are beautiful," Joshua said, taking in his breath as the lanterns cast shadows beneath the portraits all around him.

"My other brother, Mhlobo, drew them," Nongolesi responded.

"He's very talented," Joshua said.

"We discovered Mhlobo's gift when he was twelve," the Old Man said as he helped the Great Father into a cushioned chair. Dark as night, the Great Father sat still and quiet; even so, he provided such a comforting presence. "Mhlobo started to draw designs into the fresh clay of the new *izindlu* we had built. Nongolesi was very mad when she saw the drawings. She said they had labored hard on that *indlu* and she claimed he ruined it."

The tight-knit family laughed at the memory. Mama Siziwe handed a mug filled with tea to Joshua, its sweet scent drifting into the air.

"We had to ask him, are you sure you are of the right clan?" Nongolesi recalled in a teasing voice, a beautiful smile lighting her face. "They only draw this way on *izindlu* in the Transkei," she explained. "We are not of that clan. But our Great Mother, the mother of our Old Man, recognized straightaway that Mhlobo could be useful. She remembers relatives who we were not yet alive to meet. She would describe how one of them looked and Mhlobo would draw pictures—sometimes twenty times before he could get it right. He'd lie out the pictures and she'd point to different versions— take that nose, those eyes, that chin. And soon he would be able to draw the parts into one, and now"—she waved her hand toward the portraits—"we see our ancestors as much as we hear about them."

Joshua nodded, sipping from his cup of tea and settling comfortably into a green cushioned chair, which was covered with a hand-sewn lace runner. As a warm early-summer breeze drifted through the open window next to Joshua, Nongolesi glanced at the reverend, seeming to sense his uncertainty about what he should do. She brought a cardboard-covered book to him. "This was printed in our language, not far from here," she said, handing him the book, a hand-stitched Bible. "Its pages are made from the bark of a marula tree. Have you seen the marula tree?" she asked.

"I'm not sure," he responded as the lantern continued to cast flickering light beneath the sketches of their relatives on the walls.

"The marula tree is the one you see throughout much of this land—it stands erect with a large top of brilliant leaves that feather downward." She motioned with her hands. "We love that tree. Every part of it gives life. The sparrows eat its leaves for food, we make a sweet jelly from the fruit it bears, and even its bark is used for medicines. And now, the paper we make from it provides us this—the marula Bible, that's what you'll hear people call this Bible that they used to print in our Xhosa language."

"A local official ordered the local printer to cease printing marula Bibles, and to only produce Bibles in English in this region," the Old Man stated in a voice that was hard. "The missionaries have failed to protest this policy."

"Many people cannot read well in English. The marula Bible is the one we wish to see printed more often," Nongolesi said, parting its pages. "One day you shall know how to read the Bible in our language," she said, looking at Joshua as she ran her finger across the pages. "This is my favorite." She turned to a precise spot, a glimmer in her eyes as she read New Testament verses. The words flowed like music, effortlessly, the clicking sounds of her language dancing across her tongue. *This is a woman who knows the Bible,* Joshua thought as he watched her expression. She seemed to cherish each word. He realized again how beautiful she was, with her kind eyes and her hair plaited delicately in thin rows. He felt something stir inside.

"You see how beautiful it sounds?" she asked, looking at him.

"It sounds very beautiful," Joshua said softly, feeling uncomfortable, trying not to focus on her gentle smile. His eyes had lingered too long, he felt, dropping his eyes for a moment, thinking of Shantal.

"Perhaps in time you can convince your mission to support the production of marula Bibles again," the Old Man said, probing Joshua.

It was such a simple request. Joshua tensed as a silence floated between them. It bothered Joshua deeply, the words he failed to utter in that moment.

"This one you will need to wait to read until after you learn our language," Nongolesi said, setting the Bible on the low table near her. "But there are many books here, you should choose one." She motioned toward the wooden bookshelves against the wall. They were filled with books, hardback and worn. Joshua walked over and pulled out a hand-stitched one with ink-penned words, its pages tied between thick cardboard pieces.

"That one is a history of the Xhosa in the Transkei," Nongolesi said as she sat down on the sheepskin mat in the middle of the room, leaning over the low table, dipping a fountain pen lightly into an ink jar. She rubbed it gently against the side of the jar before writing on paper.

Joshua sat down with the book in his hands. The tension in the room had faded, he was glad. Why had Mr. Garrett been so concerned about this visit? As the Old Man squeezed his eyes, lost in thought, and Nongolesi quietly penned her work, Joshua sat back and closed his eyes, a smile curving at his lips as he heard that familiar voice calling. It sounded much nearer than in the past, as if it were singing from the low branches of the trees, its voice soft as ruffling feathers, growing louder as the moon's light roamed freely. *Niya kundinqula, nize nithandaze kum, ndiniphulaphule. Niya kundifuna, nindifumane, xa nithe nandifuna ngentliziyo yenu yonke.*

Joshua's eyes drifted back to Nongolesi, who stroked her pen as tenderly as if writing on royal parchment. When she finished the page, she added it faceup to a stack, waving her hand over it to help the ink dry.

"We say that our history is like ants with fat bellies," the Old Man remarked, explaining Nongolesi's work. He had noticed Joshua's gaze. "We must dedicate time collecting and storing honey so that we can feed our nests during a time of famine."

Joshua smiled, wondering if he'd ever sound that wise, sitting in a chair surrounded by his own family. "You have a very beautiful family," Joshua said to the Old Man.

The Old Man smiled, nodding like a man who knew he had been blessed.

"Where is your son, the one who drew these pictures—Mhlobo is his name?" Joshua asked.

The Old Man inhaled deeply, his eyes clouding over. Joshua's throat tightened as the room grew tense again.

"He left for the mines," the Old Man said, his lips tensing. "He wanted to help the family and went off to the City of Gold to live a miner's life. He thought for some reason this land would not keep us well. He wanted to contribute money, but we have always had enough mealies to feed ourselves, and you have seen the many oxen." His tone let Joshua know it was not a subject for further discussion.

The Old Man noted Nongolesi's expression just then—she held her eyes on the Old Man, then dropped them, sitting quietly.

"We are glad Mhlobo has returned from the mines and can be with us again," the Old Man offered softly, as if acknowledging the anger in his previous words and apologizing for them. "A story for the reverend?" the Old Man asked as Nongolesi smiled approvingly. The two little boys in the room smiled excitedly and moved closer to the Old Man's chair. Joshua set his book aside. The room was silent for a moment as the Old Man gathered his words.

"Tell me, people, have you heard?" the Old Man whispered, almost singing the words as he leaned forward. *"Have you heard of that time when the land grew dry, the bellies of the people filled with hunger? Tell me, people, have you heard?"*

Joshua's thoughts drifted as the Old Man spoke. He would always remember how it made him feel as the Old Man spoke words of wisdom. He saw no traces of what he had expected to find here. There were leather skirts, spears, huts, and cow dung, yes. But even the portraits of the Xhosa ancestors dressed in cowhide skirts and loincloths had great dignity. As Joshua's eyes rested on one of the portraits, his thoughts scrolled back in time. He tried to remember every story he'd ever heard about Africa, trying to understand why he had expected things to be so different. He could hardly wait to write his family and tell them about what he was experiencing, about the beauty of the people here.

"Nongolesi, you may choose tonight," the Old Man said as he leaned back, having finished his story.

"Tonight we shall sing the hymn '*Ukholo*,'" she said as she sealed her ink jar, placing her last penned paper faceup to dry. She sat up and sang in a voice kissed by God. Joshua closed his eyes and focused on the tune. Her voice was rich and piercing and full of soul. *This is a woman who knows the Lord*, he thought again. *It isn't possible to sing the words like that and not have encountered the Lord a time or two.* For a while he could not take his eyes from her.

Her family joined her after a few stanzas. They sang on for nearly half an hour before Mama Siziwe motioned the two little children to their feet. The Old Man asked them to offer thanks to the Lord. The sight of them shyly moving together took Joshua back in time to the many nights of his childhood, half a world away, when he and Darius had moved together in just that same way. It was one of the few times Darius would turn serious, as he'd hold Joshua's hand tightly and they'd begin together, speaking so deliberately. He could still hear their voices blending into the stillness of the room on Hopedale Street: *"Now I lay me down to sleep. . . ."* Joshua's eyes dampened with the memory. Now his lips curled in a smile as these two young children held hands. It was an image that stayed with him as the children prayed in Xhosa, in that familiar way, with the placid rhythm of a rhyme.

CHAPTER 10

Joshua placed the last knife and fork beside a plate, finally finishing the table settings. The days since his meeting with the administrators had seemed to pass slowly because he was so anxious to speak with the student leaders at length. As he carefully placed glasses near each plate, he was surprised to find himself thinking about Nongolesi again. She offered such support, even though he hardly knew her. He appreciated the advice she'd given him, prodding him to try earnestly to understand the students' aims. He felt guilty for a moment, knowing he had felt moved by her, and he reminded himself to write Shantal, knowing she was probably awaiting a letter from him. He shook his head, chastising himself when a knock at the door interrupted his thoughts. He mused as his heart pounded a little faster. He wanted this to go well.

Walking to the door, he pulled the chain of his pocket watch, glancing at the time. Fifteen minutes early. He smiled. They must also want to give this a chance. He opened his door to four students. Ogenga proceeded with the introductions as Joshua waved them in happily. Jovan's smile warmed the whole house, but Tumi and Sipho gave Joshua willful glares.

"It goes on, Reverend Clay?" Ogenga asked, looking down the hallway toward Joshua's bedroom.

Joshua nodded. "There are two more rooms in the back," he said, showing them around the house. "Reverend Peter never invited you to dinner here?" Joshua asked. The students snickered together.

"There are laws against that, you know," Tumi said.

"That doesn't apply to a preacher's home." Joshua tried to correct her.

Tumi knit her eyebrows. "Yes, it does." There was such spite in her tone.

"You know, this is bigger than fifteen of the township huts in Ginsberg, where the government's shipping the villagers after declaring their villages white-only areas," Ogenga said, his eyes wide.

"Yes, I've heard about the conditions there," Joshua said gently.

"You haven't seen for yourself?" Sipho said, accusation beneath his curt words as he exchanged a glance with Tumi.

"I've been focusing on getting accustomed to life on campus first," Joshua replied, knowing Sipho was probing. "I intend to visit more neighboring areas soon."

"Well," Ogenga said as he looked down, then met Joshua's gaze, "these are nice borrowed quarters."

Joshua noted his choice of words but didn't respond.

"Nice cooking hut too," Sipho said with a particular slant, glancing out at the traditional thatch-roofed mud hut in the yard.

"I've noticed that the only huts on campus are for cooking. That hadn't escaped me," Joshua said with more of an edge than he'd intended. This wasn't getting off to a good start. "Please come and sit; the food's almost ready." He motioned them toward the dining table at the far end of the main room.

Ogenga flinched as he placed a finger on the carved mahogany dining chair, as if it were too expensive for him to touch. The others laughed at his jest.

"Sorry." Ogenga offered a sincere apology, looking at Joshua.

"I'm glad I can host you all here." Joshua smiled, unoffended, as they sat and he poured lemonade from a pitcher into each of their glasses. A local maid came in with bowls of food. "Thank you," Joshua said to her. They bowed their heads as Joshua blessed the food; then everyone seemed occupied trying to find something to say in the awkward silence.

They managed to chat for a while. Joshua's smile broadened as

Ogenga debated one issue after another with animated gestures. Ogenga was so filled with energy, his eyes looking as if they were always flung wide—as if with every glimpse of the world, he saw something new and was fascinated by it. Joshua found the close friendship he seemed to share with Jovan intriguing. They seemed opposites in many ways. Jovan seemed like a soft-spoken deep thinker, a good listener who spoke sparingly, but when he did speak, he uttered profound words. Jovan chimed in now and again, distilling points. He was impressive.

"We're glad you invited us here," Ogenga said as they finished their plates. "I figured you can't be all bad if you are willing to host the thorn in the side of the administration. What did they tell you— that I am a hothead? A troublemaker?"

"Something not too far from that," Joshua answered, as everyone laughed. "You've certainly built a legendary reputation." Joshua leaned back into his chair, preparing himself for their questions, sensing the topic was about to turn very serious.

"That is a very luxurious motor car they have provided you," Sipho said. "It says a lot, that car."

Joshua noted that wasn't a compliment. Spite hung around Sipho like a cloak, all too conveniently. *There's little way to win Sipho over,* Joshua thought. Joshua had seen others like him crouched in small circles on vacant corners at Wilberforce, always talking about greeting violence with greater violence. "The car gives me the ability to travel the area," Joshua responded, keeping his tone level. "Apparently Reverend Peter had difficulties in that regard."

"So"—Ogenga leaned forward, seeming uncomfortable with the conversation—"you gonna go protest with us, Preacher Man?"

Joshua chuckled aloud, wondering why he was surprised by Ogenga's boldness. They were testing him again, the same way he once prodded administrators at Wilberforce. It felt strange to be on the other side. "What are you protesting?" Joshua asked, wanting to understand them more, as Nongolesi had urged.

"This week, we are protesting a more narrow range of issues than last time," Ogenga said, sitting back with a smile, happy to be asked. "Sometimes we join the townsmen for large protests against pass laws and labor laws. But this week, we are focusing on the right of students to be doctors and engineers." He crossed his arms watching Joshua's reaction.

"I'm sure you know there are restrictions on my activities," Joshua replied gently.

"You think there is something bad about protesting peacefully when we have been so wronged?" Ogenga asked.

Jovan interrupted before Joshua could respond. "Have you visited any of the traditional villages?" Jovan whispered.

Joshua felt as if his face glazed over with guilt. He couldn't pretend not to have noticed that the fabric of the Noni Village seemed to be tearing apart as so many young men had been forced from their families and the community struggled in their absence. He had seen that clearly and remembered vividly the fear in Tahira's eyes. He looked at Ogenga, silent, not knowing how to tread a line in responding.

"What would you have us do in the face of this?" Ogenga asked pointedly. "We intend to go before the magistrate this week."

That was one of those facts Joshua was supposed to report, but he shrugged Mr. Garrett's request away. "I can't join you in a protest; that's not my role here," Joshua replied, shifting in his seat. "But the subject of student protests did come up at the advisory committee meeting."

"Yes, we heard there was an advisory committee meeting," Tumi said in a flat voice. She dismissed Joshua with the same look he had often seen in Shantal's eyes when she'd speak cynically about white Americans.

"No one tried to hide the fact that the advisory committee was meeting," Joshua replied.

"So what did you all decide for us?" Sipho asked. Their eyes met and held for a sour moment.

Joshua dropped his eyes, wiping away any expression that conveyed the dislike he already felt toward Sipho. "No one doubts the validity of your longer-term aims," Joshua replied, addressing his comments to Tumi. "The advisory committee just believes that now is not the time to try to expand the curriculum the way you have requested. With the limited resources . . ." His voice trailed. "Just give this time. Fort Hare is barely twenty years old," Joshua said.

Ogenga looked as if Joshua had just lifted a pair of scissors over his dreams and started snipping. Tumi dropped her fork limply against her cup, letting it call out a thin clank.

"*Ndakuxelele na ukuba uzakufana nomnye lowa?*" Sipho muttered.

"*Mhlambe nangaphezu kwalowa, kuba lona uzenza umuntu omhlophe,*" Tumi said.

"*Andiqondi ukuba sowumqwalasele kakuhle noko,*" Ogenga said coolly, not looking at anyone in particular, just fidgeting with the napkin in his lap.

"*Uyivile na into endiyivileyo?*" Sipho seemed to respond to Ogenga, eyes burning.

"That is what they said twenty years ago," Ogenga finally said to Joshua, his face marked with disappointment. "And what has become of us and this country since then?"

Joshua sat quietly. The pain in Ogenga's voice kept him from responding too quickly.

"My Great Father once had a large plot he farmed farther north, you know," Ogenga said, thrusting a proud chest, looking much the same as when Joshua had first glimpsed him atop that overturned crate. He held firmly the countenance of a man exposed to broad ideas, confident he'd distilled them and stood on sure ground. "They toiled very hard, every day. Their sprawling land stretched far enough to yield all mealies needed for all the winter months. But then the Afrikaners came, each with a wagon, wood for the houses they would build, and two rifles. What do you think became of that land?"

"Now many African homesteads have all been reduced to tiny little reservations, too tiny to yield mealie corn for even half a year," Tumi echoed, her eyes burning. "And now we must sell those mealies to get money for many taxes including taxes for land we are not allowed to own and a government we are not fully a part of. And because there are not enough shillings from the little land we have left, our men are forced to work in the mines for little scraps of money. Our mothers are forced to serve as maids, traveling to and fro on African-only buses. Our families break up. And when we seek to provide for ourselves—now that we cannot sustain ourselves on our own land—to become doctors and lawyers and engineers, we are denied. Yes, Fort Hare helps educate Africans, but not enough, not in all the right ways."

"We are sincere when we say we wish to see change in time," Joshua said earnestly. He understood the urgency in Tumi's tone.

The students were silent. Tumi moved her fork, making little circles on her plate, and then with pursed lips, she touched her fork against her plate again. Ogenga nodded faintly. Joshua pretended not to notice, but it had not been so long since he was once a student—he understood they were communicating among themselves with those faint touches to their plates.

"I understand everything you have said," Joshua said again. "We are on your side, but change can only come over time."

Sipho also touched his fork against his cup lightly.

Ogenga spoke again in Xhosa to no one in particular, just uttering words as he fidgeted with his spoon. He turned to Joshua. "It's interesting how different you are from Sarah."

"The Negro American in East London," Tumi added, her eyes smiling with admiration.

"I've heard of her," Joshua said.

"She's a tough woman. So tough, some didn't know how to react to her at first," Tumi said. "She came and helped lead the fight for these sorts of issues in this region. She has built a secondary school here, one that prepares African students to go to college and trains them for the sciences and engineering."

"I've heard wonderful things about that school, if you mean the independent one outside of East London."

"You should go there sometime," Jovan replied.

"Yes, and while you are at it, take a good tour of East London," Ogenga said. "Enjoy the parts where we cannot travel because we are Africans and the pass laws will not allow it. Go to the white town from which we are banned, and just follow the *Christian* names. Take St. Paul's Road—Paul is in the Bible, yes? Take St. Paul's Road to St. Mark's Road to St. Andrew's Road. Pass by Waterloo Square and the replica of London's Big Ben, and at some point you will come to Milner Road—named after the commissioner appointed to deal with the "African problem". Travel up Queen Victoria Street, visit Rhodes Street. Perhaps even take a look down King Street, named after

Richard King, who was sent to quell the Zulus as they defended their land. Then perhaps find your way to St. John's Road."

The words stung. "What could we do to make you understand our intentions?" Joshua asked, his heart sinking at how bitter the conversation had become.

"What half steps can there be?" Tumi asked.

"They aim to do us in, you know," Ogenga said. "The Afrikaners and the English would not work together before. Now they have united their parties and aim to take what little we have left, bit by bit. Some will think you are supporting this system."

"It's like Sarah says," Jovan agreed. "Many in the administration ask us to be content staring out into the blueness of the sky, having nothing, dreaming nothing, seeking nothing."

Joshua squinted his eyes. "It is not our intention to support a system to keep Africans from progressing," he said. "I invited you here so I could let you know just the opposite. And I will present your views to the advisory committee when I have the opportunity."

"You'll present our views, but you won't support them," Tumi said.

Joshua's lips parted, but he couldn't respond.

"You would do well to stay alert to musty smells where musty smells should not be," Sipho said curtly.

"Is that a local saying?" Joshua asked, frustrated by the opaque language.

"No, but we have a similar one," Sipho said, standing up abruptly as he gathered his jacket from the chair. "*Izinto azisoloko zinje ngohlobo ezibonakala ngalo:* Things aren't always as they seem."

"There is a dance in the Women's Hall. Sipho is going," Ogenga said quickly, trying to explain Sipho's rudeness. "Sipho just wait a minute," he chided.

"I also will be heading over. It is an honor to be asked," Jovan said, seeming to also try to smooth things over. "There are only eleven women here at the college, you know. They just sit back and pick and choose which of us they want."

"That's the way it should be!" Tumi proclaimed.

Joshua inhaled softly, grateful that something had lightened the tension as everyone in the room chuckled.

"You're not going?" Joshua asked Ogenga, trying to act light-hearted.

Jovan chuckled as he stood up, rubbing his hand over Ogenga's receding hair, shaking his head as if to answer on Ogenga's behalf.

"I am too much for those women; they are intimidated by my intellect and haven't worked up the courage to ask me," Ogenga said as they all chuckled on. "We should get going." Ogenga sat up as Tumi moved toward Sipho, who stood near the door.

"I hope we will get together again sometime soon," Joshua said as he walked with Ogenga and Jovan toward the front door. They didn't respond. But as they neared the door, Ogenga's eyes lingered for a moment on the old Astel hotel room docket lying faceup on Joshua's desk.

"Now that you know you're not supposed to invite us Africans into your home, I suppose you'll find another place to meet us next time," Ogenga said, shifting his eyes back to Joshua.

"I don't agree with such rules, that goes without saying," Joshua said, feeling he needed to state that clearly. "But again, I am certain such rules do not apply to ministers. And nonetheless, even if in some parts of the country such rules are enforced, they certainly only apply to white preachers."

"You are an honorary white, so those rules apply also to you," Ogenga said pointedly. Joshua was taken aback by his tone but looked at him blankly. "What did you think *HW* stood for?" Ogenga asked. *"Honorary white,"* he said slowly, letting the words linger, as he handed Joshua the Astel hotel receipt. Joshua's eyes were wide as he looked at the penned letters *HW* scrawled high across the docket. His stomach turned, his thoughts drifting back to the way the hotel manager had scrawled those letters so foully. Heat began to rush to his cheeks.

"I suppose they forgot to tell you some of the finer details about your stay here," Ogenga said, measuring Joshua's response as he continued flushing. "That's the status that American Negroes have when they are allowed to live in this country," Ogenga said.

"I suppose that's their way of saying you've been *civilized*," Tumi said, her eyes burning again. "Otherwise, you too would be told to ride on the broken-down African-only buses. You too would not be allowed to walk freely in the cities, or to walk on the streets named after your Christian saints."

Joshua felt a stabbing inside. He couldn't imagine what could have made him appear more foolish in front of them. Even Andrew hadn't mentioned a word. Joshua knew his expression betrayed what he was feeling. Sipho looked at him with amused pity.

"Again, thank you for the meal," Ogenga said softly, seeming apologetic. The students left Joshua wordless, stinging with humiliation as that *HW* docket burned in his hand.

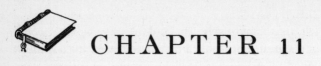

CHAPTER 11

Joshua was still upset when he rose the next day and warmed a kettle of water on the coal stove in his kitchen, preparing a cup of tea. He'd spent time praying, asking God to ease the anger in his heart. He'd also thought long and hard about whether to demand an explanation from his mission, but he didn't see any point in bringing up the matter. What could his mission do about the government's policy? Now at least he understood the rueful looks Andrew had given him when he'd first arrived in Cape Town.

As he dipped a spoonful of sugar into his tea and sank down before his dining-room table, he moved a finger over its smooth mahogany surface, thinking back about the dream he'd just had. He rarely dreamed of Darius, but his restless discontent from the night before had probably spurred it. He replayed that lingering dream in his mind, trying to discern its meaning. He had awoken in his dream to the cool morning air drifting through the open pane of his Fort Hare bedroom window. In his dream, his senses were still dull as he shifted in bed onto his elbows, but he'd felt the unmistakable weight of a stare.

"Preacher Man!" a voice had called to him from across the room.

Joshua had tensed at the sound, turning his eyes toward the light pouring through the window in hopeful bronze shades. A shadowed figure rocked frenetically with a picture of Joshua pulled close; he stroked his hands down each arm of Lu's rocker. He did that so deliberately, Joshua could almost feel the flawless wood beneath his own palms. As a child, Joshua had watched Uncle Nate shave and cut each wood piece precisely, polishing that rocker to a shine for Lu.

"Look at you, Preacher Man! Look at you," the man had said, getting up, his voice full of love. Joshua's throat had tightened and a hundred memories flooded through his mind as he studied the silhouette's curves. Then, as that man stepped out of the shadows, Joshua saw him fully.

"Darius?"

A broad smile spread across Darius's face as he loosened his chin strap, removing his metal helmet. He stood still, letting Joshua study him—his broad shoulders, his proud chin, his hopeful eyes. He looked just as he had the day he left for service, with his nineteen-year-old shoulders squared and every button on his uniform polished to a shine. He then moved quickly to Joshua, swallowing him in a hug. Joshua had longed for one last embrace ever since he was twelve, when Darius had gone off to war. In his dream, Joshua had searched for breath as emotions flooded over him.

Darius sat back, smiling. "I couldn't believe my ears when I heard," he said. "I mean, you always had discipline, but just look at you!" He smiled a crooked smile, one laced with memories. "All grown up! Guess I can't pick fights with you no more."

Darius moved back into Lu's chair, rocking frenetically again before he slowed his motions, looking intently at Joshua.

"I'm sorry I didn't say good-bye before I left," he whispered as he sat in full sunlight, pain registering in his eyes.

Despite himself, Joshua's anger stirred. He felt as if he were twelve again. "Where have you been? They told us you were killed—"

"I know you're angry, I can feel it, Preacher Man," Darius said, voice cracking. "Please don't dwell on that right now. I came to talk with you. I don't have long now," he whispered, biting his lip. "There's something I wanted to say—"

"*Where* are you going?" Joshua's voice rose.

"I know you're gonna do the right thing," Darius said, as if they were the most important words he'd ever uttered.

Joshua felt his heart sinking. "Why don't you have long?"

Darius shifted in the rocker. "I could only come for a minute. I just wanted to tell you, I've been so proud every time I heard 'bout how you're doing—*what* you're doing."

Darius stood up, almost frowning as he turned toward the open window, his eyes burning bright. "Joshua, I know you'll do the right thing," Darius said again, reaching out a hand. And then, in a moment, he was gone.

Joshua took a sip of his tea now, nestling the warm mug in his hands, he pondered the dream's meaning and hoped his emotions would soon settle. Just then he heard the mail carrier slip a letter under his front door. Joshua's smile faded as he opened the envelope, reading the message's single line: "Reverend Waldron acknowledges receipt of your letter." Joshua chuckled. It was as cursory as their conversation, when Reverend Waldron had turned his back to end their exchange. Joshua tucked the note in his coat pocket, prodding himself not to get discouraged, and he headed toward his car. The beauty of the sleek steel brought a smile to his lips again as he stepped inside.

As he drove toward the Ulundi schoolyard, he enjoyed the cleansed smells of nature that the night's rain had left behind. Damp leaves and budding wildflowers perfumed the spring air, and every-thing seemed to crest with the song of birds. The landscape still captivated him as he looked out his car window. He had already writ-ten his family, but his words failed so miserably to capture the beauty here. Joshua's thoughts soon drifted to Shantal again. Six weeks after leaving, he'd finally managed to write her, after penning unfinished letters to her on the *Amissa*. But the letter he'd finally sent was too short, and didn't address what she most wanted to know. His lips tensed. He'd address her concerns soon, he told himself.

He turned onto the road heading toward the Amatolas. Those misty blue mountains were stunning as they towered in the distance above villages that lined both sides of the paved road. Shantal wouldn't appreciate a place like this—she never seemed to share his wonder of God's handiwork. He pondered the strong feeling inside as he allowed himself to dwell on that thought.

He followed the directions the Old Man had provided, driving beyond the farthest Noni Village homestead to the next path off the main road. After a short while, that road came to an abrupt end, as if laborers had simply grown weary and cast their shovels aside. He parked his car on the roadside and set off by foot up an earthen red path, lost in nature as cornstalks towered two feet above him on each side of the path.

After a few minutes, he saw several groups of children walking on the path ahead of him. They moved barefoot in khaki uniforms—some as young as four, others as old as nine—carrying burlap sacks, slates, and bits of chalk. The ones farthest ahead played a game that looked much like hopscotch, leaping over crevices they'd carved into the earth. Every now and again, each child paused, bending to dig their fingers into the damp earth, dislodging creamy-colored stones from their resting spots. Joshua looked at the children curiously. The wet clay seemed to wedge beneath their fingernails, looking like they'd dipped their hands in myrrh. They carried those rocks on their open palms proudly, like jewels on a pillow.

"Hello there," Joshua said to a couple of the children who looked back at him with smiles. A few of them headed back toward him, tussling over who would get to carry his bag.

The one who reached Joshua first took the bag from his shoulder, carrying it like it was a prize. The boy smiled timidly and paused, putting his rock down gently, his eyes marking the spot as if he planned to return and get it again soon. "Good morning, Reverend," he said faintly as he walked beside Joshua, seeming afraid to talk more loudly. He had eyes like Darius's, bright and questioning, and he held a finger to his mouth, as if asking whether it was okay to speak further.

"Hello there. What is your name?" Joshua responded, happy the child knew him as the reverend.

"I am Phumezo, son of Magona. You come to see our school?"

"I'm very excited to see your school," Joshua answered with a smile.

"You will come to lead our morning prayers?" the boy asked, his arm dangling with the bag's weight as he marched alongside Joshua.

"If I am asked, I would be honored to lead a prayer."

"He comes from the land of Sarah," a younger child said definitively to the others, trotting to keep pace with Joshua.

Joshua chuckled at that simple comment as the children skipped across a small stream that flowed from the distant mountains. They laughed as they hopped across the stones, sometimes splashing the cold water.

Joshua followed them, trying to keep from getting wet as he moved across the stones. As he followed them up an incline, he could finally see a flagpole jutting out in the distance. Soon a few iron-roofed brick buildings were within sight. Set beyond a wooden fence on a large grassy compound, the school bustled. A few older girls were running just outside the school gate, their legs flitting under their khaki skirts. As they saw Joshua, they gathered around the open gate, wrapping their arms around each other. They began to sing sweetly for Joshua, moving together, back and forth, stomping their feet up and down in a seamless motion, like a windblown wave across a pond.

> *Ukuba ndihlale endlwini*
> *kaYehova yone imihla*
> *yobomi bam, Ndibone ubuhle*
> *bukaYehova, ndiphicothe etempileni yakhe.*

Their hope-filled song warmed Joshua.

"They sing for you, they are so happy," Nongolesi called out as she strolled toward Joshua from a school building. She moved with such dignity, her face radiant. She watched the children swaying, caught in the song's rhythm, clapping to welcome Joshua. The bravest among them walked forward, extending her hand. "Reverend Clay, we greet you." One after another, with their hair cut short and their uniforms donned proudly, they each came forward to offer him a handshake.

"I never got a reception like this in America!" Joshua said to Nongolesi as she touched his arm.

"The children are very happy you have come."

He smiled at her touch on his arm. There was such a brightness about her; the warmth of her welcome showed in the dimple of her right cheek.

"We are happy to have you," she nodded. Something warm inside stirred as she said it.

Nongolesi looked beautiful, wearing a dark green dress with tiny flower prints. Her hair was braided neatly away from her face again, forming a delicate bun in the back. She motioned Joshua toward the school buildings, where he could smell *imifuno* simmering in the adjoining room as a gentle wind blew through thin cloths tacked over glassless windows.

"The room where the teachers work is there," Nongolesi said, nodding to a room filled with desks and papers. "That one is my desk." She pointed to a desk with an ink jar and a glistening pen.

They walked out into the open schoolyard as a young boy tugged a dangling rope enthusiastically, making the hanging brass bell call forth a penetrating sound. Joshua was anxious to meet more of the children, who had already gathered on either side of the flagpole, boys on one side, girls on the other. They set down their rags and slates as they placed their hands at their sides and lifted their chins to the raised flag.

"It's not the South African flag," Nongolesi whispered to Joshua as a young boy worked the pulley to raise the red-and-green flag to its highest point. "This is an independent school. The government has not bothered us about that flag—not yet."

"Students," a teacher spoke through a white cone, "we gather another day for study. You see the blocks are stacked high." He motioned across the campus to a tall stack of cement bricks. "It will soon be time to construct another building."

The children smiled pridefully.

"We also greet this morning a visitor to our school: Reverend Clay, from the United States of America. He has come to minister at Fort Hare and has come all this distance to see our fine school. We welcome him today." He turned to Joshua. "You will please lead our prayer?"

Joshua smiled and spoke a blessing through the cone as each child lowered their eyes in prayer. A few young girls then led the children in singing several hymns in Xhosa. Their soulful singing went on for fifteen minutes. Joshua's eyes were bright as he turned to Nongolesi.

"Shall I give you a tour of our schoolyard?" she asked, not noticing the admiration in his eyes.

"I'd love to see it," he said as he walked with her. "Did Reverend Peter ever come here?"

Nongolesi gave him a strange smile. "Of course not."

"That was his great loss," Joshua said, responding to her tone. "I may never want to leave."

"That is just what the children are hoping!" Nongolesi chuckled. "They wish that you will come regularly and teach here at our school."

"Teach?" He tried to read her expression. He wasn't certain she was serious.

"There is a great need for more teachers here. Very few of our people have trained to teach. And the children know the presence of an American will help the wealthy English want to give money. Then the children would not need to pay so much to attend."

"I didn't realize they paid to attend."

"A modest amount only, to help sustain the school," she said as she led him to the edge of the school grounds, where one man guided a two-wheeled cart loaded with heavy stones. "This is a *masakhane* school," she explained. "We have made this school with our own hands. Every building has been built through money of the community, by the labor of the people. The stones, we pick them out on the way to school and grind them here. The children bring one each day. They set those ones until the pile gets very high. See there." She walked with him to a large pile of rocks, many colors, big and small. Several older men stood nearby, leaning with hunched backs over thick rods, stirring and dipping a cement mixture from a large bin into rectangular brick molds at their feet.

"It is our future they are building here," Nongolesi said with a shine in her eyes. "And we put all of these buildings to good use. We teach adult students on Wednesday and Thursday afternoons, so that they can learn to read in Xhosa and then in English. And Dr. Nkula comes here and uses a room for a clinic after schools on Tuesdays." She smiled. "We hope to give our young students more resources in time. There are few books here; the students must share. But Sarah has been good in this way. She has helped get moneys for books so we can teach our children better—*even* the girls!"

Joshua was impressed.

"Sarah is a great educator and has also become one of the great storytellers of the region. You'll hear people say, 'That Sarah, she's as grand a storyteller as any Great Mother dressed in her toga, wearing seven layers of colored beads around her neck and a *umbhaco* wrapped high on her head,'" Nongolesi mimicked.

They both chuckled. "Sarah is from your land," Nongolesi said, "but don't let that fool you!"

"Does she teach here?"

"No, she spends most of her time running the independent high school outside of East London. She's the principal," she responded. "Sarah managed to get money from her uncle. He is a minister also. He sends money from the United States. They believe in independent schools, free of the South African government. You will meet her one day, I'm sure."

"This is an amazing undertaking," Joshua said as they stepped closer to the building of classrooms. "It's marvelous to see all the members of the school participating to build this school."

"All members of the *community*," she corrected him. "In two days, you will see old men come from very far, from up in those hills." She pointed in the distance. "Some will sleep in the empty classrooms once the children leave, then rise in the morning to begin to place and seal bricks together. I do not mean to try to convince you to come here often to help teach," she said with a shimmer in her eyes.

He laughed. "Well, it would be very nice to teach here once in a while, but I'd need to ask my mission."

They rounded a corner, stepping into the doorway of a dim classroom with floors smoothed with dung. The class of girls sat behind dual-headed desks, clustered together, four girls to every textbook. The teacher stood before a chalkboard suspended between two wood boards, turning the rotating chalkboard as it whipped about and creaked.

"We have a visitor," the teacher said as he saw Nongolesi and Joshua walk in.

"Good morning, sir," the students said nearly in unison, as they rose. They introduced themselves one by one.

"Will Reverend Clay come to our history class?" the last young girl asked.

"We have our oral history later today," Nongolesi explained to Joshua. "It is an important class where the students recite the stories of the great storytellers, or sing their family anthems. This is how we have shared our history with one another in the past."

He was moved by the invitation. "I'd be happy to," Joshua answered the student.

As Joshua walked with Nongolesi back to the teachers' lounge, she motioned him to her desk. "Here, I'm writing more about the history of our peoples. If you visit our school often, then perhaps you can help us make these into a proper book, with typed letters," she said, touching one of her hand-penned books.

He nodded. "I have a typewriter at Fort Hare."

She smiled broadly.

"Why do I think you are after a lot out of me?" Joshua said, amused by her expression.

"Well . . ."

They both laughed again. "It would be nice to see you often," she said in a way that moved him again. "The Old Man was very pleased to have had you for dinner, and he has asked that I extend to you another invitation. You must come again soon."

"I'd enjoy that," he said.

"You should come on Tuesday, then, just as the sun touches the mountaintop; we shall feed you very well. You can find your way this time?"

"I remember the way." He smiled as a bell pealed the air and students switched classrooms.

"I will wait with you—there is one more class period before the oral history class."

Joshua's heart lifted as she suggested it. He enjoyed spending time with her; he also enjoyed getting to know her and the traditions of her clan. With her, his concerns seemed to melt away. They sat outside of the teachers' lounge on rawhide thong chairs, underneath a thin canvass hoisted on poles that filtered the sun's strong rays.

Joshua could see some children playing a defiant game on the field nearby. The voices of other students carried tunes to them from farther away. In an odd way, the singing reminded him of the voice he'd hear at times. It startled him to realize the words of that voice must also be Xhosa.

"That is the singing period. The students are practicing their hymns for tomorrow morning," Nongolesi explained, interrupting his thoughts.

"It's beautiful," he said, trying to refocus his thoughts.

"So, how is it you have come to be a preacher?" she asked, her eyes filled with questions again.

There was something about her that moved him again. "I was called," he responded, as he reflected on the feelings she was invoking.

"When you were very young?"

"When I was older, actually." He took a sip of water from the cup she'd handed to him. "It's strange, the way it happened, when I look back on it. I carried my aunt Lu's Bible for her on the way to church every Sunday for years, without fully understanding the power between those pages. I didn't truly understand until I was eighteen."

"That's when you were called?"

He nodded.

"How does one feel called?"

He smiled. He hadn't spoken about this since he first headed to Wilberforce. He sat there, shedding multiple husks with a glad heart as he explained. "It was just after the crazy minister on Elm Street preached about joy."

"Crazy minister?"

Joshua laughed. "That's what everyone called him. It was the congregation's way of kidding about the extent of Pastor Johnson's enthusiasm. When he got excited, his body would start bobbing up and down!"

Nongolesi chuckled.

"He preached one Sunday about joy: 'The kind that the world can't give you, so the world can't take it away.'"

"I love the passages in the Bible that speak about joy." Nongolesi smiled brightly. "The one in the Book of Matthew is beautiful, where it says that even though those who follow God may be persecuted, we are the light of the world and we ought not place our light under a bushel, but on a candlestick, to give light to all, that they might see our good works and glorify God."

He was impressed. "Yes, that's what he was talking about." Joshua nodded.

"And that moved you?"

"It moved the crazy minister first." Joshua laughed. "'All those hard times, all those low times, all those worrying nights wondering if there's gonna be food on your table come the mornin' . . . Count it *all* joy!' Then he started bobbing. I could hear the old ladies as they covered their mouths with their fans, whispering to each other— 'The pastor done lost his mind!'"

"Caught in the spirit!"

There was something in Nongolesi's laughter that made Joshua's smile fade. His throat tightened. He felt as if he were betraying Shantal. The thought startled him. He moved his eyes out toward the distance. Shantal had never asked questions like this. That thought startled him even more, as if he'd never fully taken note of it. They had shared so much together, he and Shantal—their aims to make a better future, to fight for greater gains for Negroes. But they talked about his faith so little. Joshua looked back at Nongolesi, feeling as if guilt were streaked across his face.

"So that was the sermon that moved you so?"

Joshua wiped the dampened expression from his face and nodded, forcing a faint smile. "It was that sermon," he said, clearing his throat, trying to relax. "It was like he was preaching just for me. After church that Sunday, I wandered and wandered, and ended up before a pond in a hidden cove, one that I often visited. The sky was dimming by then, and I just bowed down there. And it was unmistakable—I felt an overwhelming sense that I was being told this was what I was to do with my life. It was the first time in my life I thought I could feel God's hand touching me, stroking my cheek, and calling me so clearly. I couldn't ignore it."

"It must feel fulfilling to know you are doing as God intended of you." She smiled. Something about her comment stirred Joshua uneasily. He scrolled her words through his mind again, trying to understand why. He tried to ignore the feeling as they chatted on. Soon the brass bell called out again.

Joshua walked with Nongolesi back to a classroom filled with teenage girls, who smiled at Joshua as he took a seat with Nongolesi at the back of the room. "Thandi is going today," Nongolesi whispered to Joshua as a tall, lanky girl sauntered to the front.

"So you will see now how we traditionally have relayed our history." Nongolesi's smile glowed. She had such pride in their traditions. He wished Nate, Alma, and Lu could experience this too. They were always throwing out the *National Geographics* that pictured Africans in native clothes—if only they could see the pride that filled Nongolesi's face right now.

The other girls laughed at Thandi's dramatics as she hopped up and down, loosening herself up for her performance. Abruptly, she froze in place, opened her eyes wide, then waved her hands.

"Hey, my people, have you heard? Have you heard the stories?" she began, a tune beneath her words. *"Have you seen the boys, the Noni boys now grown old? Have you seen the new sewn huts, heard mamas singing praises? Hey, my people, have you heard the new men singing there?"*

All the girls answered her in English, and several rose on cue, forming a circle as they danced with Thandi, singing next in Xhosa.

"It is the song of the initiates, when the boys leave childhood to become men," Nongolesi said in a quiet voice.

Astonishing. Joshua would never have guessed that the girls would know every word and every step of the men's circumcision song and dance, as if the words were sewn into the fabric of their beings too. They danced pridefully, swaying at the right times, their singing solemn until Thandi placed her hand over her crotch. "Oooooh!" she shrieked, and the room burst into laughter.

"Ziphatheni kakuhle!" the teacher chastised them, but everyone only laughed louder as Thandi kept wincing and limping around with her hand across her crotch.

Joshua and Nongolesi also broke into unstifled laughter. Nongolesi wiped the tears from her eyes as she tried to stop. "This one is cheeky!" Nongolesi managed. "She ought not make fun of the circumcision of the young men."

"Ziphatheni kakuhle!" the teacher said again.

Thandi finally stood still, responding to her teacher's command. "Sorry," she said straight-faced. "We will continue." The girls picked up where they left, solemn again.

"Love your little ones, that they might grow strong." Thandi continued the song of men. *"Sharpen your spear, provide for your wife. Honor your ancestors who have come through trials—the long-ago peoples of this land, who came through the years of hunger, survived the locusts and the thinning cows. Love your young ones, that they might grow strong. So says the word of our peoples."*

———————

As Joshua turned through the courtyard gate, a little girl ran toward a cluster of huts on the far side of the *ebuhlanti,* calling out for Tahira, who emerged from a hut wiping a wet pan. She was again dressed in that faded dress, the one she'd worn a few days earlier. Joshua ran through his mind again all of the ways he had thought to ask her. Her words were still echoing in his mind. *These times have been difficult; there is little money here.*

She smiled as she greeted him and led him beyond the girls peeling sugar beans by one hearth, pointing him to a seat as she prepared a kettle on another hearth. There was something in her hand motions, in the way she wiped the kettle down, that made Joshua's thoughts drift back to Hopedale Street. There was something in the steadfast sureness of her strokes that made him think Tahira served as a village pillar, just as Lu had in their home. He smiled boyishly, feeling she could read his thoughts. They chatted between sips of ginger tea.

"Please forgive me if my question isn't appropriate," Joshua finally managed, "but the other day, you said that you didn't have enough crops to till this year, and the money won't allow you to pay the taxes owed."

She nodded with a frown as she sat next to him.

"I'll have to host guests at my home, at Fort Hare, on occasion. I'm in need of help, just someone to cook and keep the home clean. Fort Hare's administrators have urged me to hire someone. If you need the extra funds, perhaps you'd consider taking a job there. You could work half days, a few days a week . . ." He hesitated as her expression remained unchanged. He didn't really need someone to come by often, but if it would help, he was happy to offer.

"I know you play a big role in this community, so of course you can go back and forth to the village as you need to," he continued. "But you're also welcome to stay in my home when you need to. There are two extra guest rooms there. Yours would be on the far side of the house, with its own entrance—it would be like having your own *indlu* there."

Her lips parted.

"You will need me to cook your meals?" she finally said.

Joshua wasn't able to read her expression. "On occasion," he replied, not certain if she was happy for the offer.

"Perhaps I could travel three times a week and stay overnight when I must be there late."

"I would consider my home to be your home too," he said softly.

"These times have been very difficult," she said intensely. "This offer is very generous. I had not expected to hear such words from you." She searched his face, and whispered almost to herself, "With the moneys, I could pay for Beaumont's schooling. He would not need to suffer in the mines or go to a big city to find work. He could go to school at Lovedale." Her expression told him it was more than she had hoped for. Her sadness hit him with force as he thought back to the images of the African workers he'd seen outside of Port Elizabeth, looking so despondent. He frowned deeply at the memory and understood her fear. By the way she looked at him, he knew he'd done the right thing in asking her.

"If you need time to think about it, to be sure—"

"This job you offer is greater than I had prayed for. I will come to your home on Monday, if the reverend pleases."

"That would be wonderful," he said.

"The reverend will say a prayer?" she asked.

By her tone, she meant a prayer of thanksgiving. She surprised him as she moved to her hut and returned with a marula Bible, offering it to him. He took in a deep breath, rubbing his hand over its cardboard cover. "I don't know Xhosa," he said, embarrassed. He could see her disappointment. "Would you teach me? It would really help me to speak with everyone here in the Noni Village, and I would be able to deliver my sermons much better. It seems some of my congregation have difficulty following all of my words in English." That fact had troubled him more deeply with each passing week.

She nodded, eyes bright, moving her stool closer to him and opening the Bible to a passage she'd marked. Moving her finger across the page as she read the first verse, she translated phrase by phrase. Joshua repeated the words, learning a few full sentences in their native tongue.

> Dear Reverend Waldron,
>
> Greetings from Fort Hare. In recent weeks, I have devoted ample time toward building deeper relations with the students and the residents of surrounding villages. In doing so, I am taking steps to strengthen the approach of our mission among the students and the community here. The students of Fort Hare, who form an important core of my congregation, turned out in good numbers to my first sermon. On the whole, the students seem to embrace an underlying spirituality, but seem to reject the Christian message of the organized church. In the most recent weeks, student numbers have ebbed. Without their presence, attendance at our Fort Hare church will remain low. I intend to continue to acquaint myself with the student leaders here, in the hopes that personal interaction may encourage greater numbers of students to attend our church services.
>
> With your permission, I would also like to minister as often as I can in the local villages, as well as to guide prayers and help in whatever other appropriate way at Ulundi, a local high school. I have already made a tentative commitment to preach at the Noni Village. I believe it is in the interest of our mission that I appear responsive to local needs, as students make no great distinction between the needs of local villagers and their own needs. Please respond at your convenience with your permission to continue forward with such engagements.
>
> My commitment to our success here remains unwavering.
>
> With respect,
> Reverend Joshua Clay

Joshua sat back and read the letter, a satisfied smile curving at his lips. He folded it, precise as a pleat again, placing it in an envelope.

He then reached for his pen and sighed deeply. He'd put off writing Shantal for too long. He tried to relax enough to write freely and to tell her how he really felt about their future. The words simply would not come. Alma's words fluttered through his mind. *Shantal is just who you'll be needin' when you come back to pastor here.* He crumpled the paper in his hand. He'd try again soon.

CHAPTER 12

Another Sunday morning sermon. Joshua steeled himself as he left his home and headed up to the church in the early December morning. He'd been in South Africa seven weeks now and with each week, his congregation had continued to shrink. Most students had stopped attending early on. They'd do exactly what they were doing now: at least ten students sat in their finest clothes, in front of the tent pitched on that hill—the one the student's called Sandile's kop— with their Bibles wide open.

"*Sisithunzela*," he heard a few echo back and forth as he passed by.

Joshua said hello, as always; as always, they offered thin smiles.

The first time this had happened, he'd assumed they were telling each other to head into the pews. Now he knew better. As the choir finished its third song in English, Joshua moved to his pulpit, the pews still half-empty. The handfuls of congregation members present clustered close in the front pews, dust lining the back chairs with an unwelcome haze. Joshua wet his throat as he proceeded, reading out his sermon. He hoped his sadness wasn't apparent as he glimpsed many church members struggling to read the verses he'd cited in English. He labored a moment to flip to the same passage in a marula Bible, speaking a few key points in Xhosa, bringing a smile to the faces of some listeners. He turned back to his English Bible and proceeded on.

He again used his sermon to encourage conciliation and a willingness to wait. The older men and women closed their eyes, as usual, and faintly shook their heads, as if moving his words through a finely netted sifter, threshing out the truth and casting aside all the excess. Every once and again, they'd meet his gaze, looking at him with forgiving eyes, as if they could see past his words to his soul. Mr. Garrett was there too. He'd come from time to time, always sitting in the back pew, arms crossed, raising his eyebrows and glancing around the congregation numbers, clearly not satisfied. At least Andrew sat beside him today and seemed to give Joshua looks of encouragement, while also concentrating carefully on Joshua's words.

After Joshua finished, the choir sang another hymn that somehow seemed hollow. The Old Man and Nongolesi stayed to greet him. Joshua appreciated their support as they spoke heartening words. He felt a bit embarrassed, though, as he seemed to sense the Old Man straining to find words with which to compliment him. Joshua knew how poorly things were going, as the congregation numbers continued to dip. The students seemed to have made up their minds about him. The few students who would show up seemed to read their Bibles for the whole sermon rather than listen to his words, sneaking out from the church as soon as Joshua finished speaking. Even with Old Man Maganu, kind as he was, something disapproving seemed to edge between his words.

"We'll be busy joining the demonstration in East London against the pass laws this afternoon. But you'll come to dinner later tomorrow?" the Old Man asked with a warm smile. Joshua nodded, happy to be asked, though he felt a bit unnerved knowing another protest was planned so soon—political tensions were increasing.

Andrew touched Joshua's shoulder as he prepared to leave with Mr. Garrett. "We will see you in a few hours." He looked at Joshua intensely, seeming to reassure him of his support.

"I look forward to it," Joshua said, and nodded also to Mr. Garrett.

As he watched the Maganus walk across the manicured lawn toward the iron front gate of Fort Hare, Joshua chatted awhile with the last of the villagers. As he finally prepared to leave, he steeled himself again. Just as had happened the past few weeks, when he moved across the walkway toward his home, he could see those very students perched in the same spots they'd occupied on his way in, Bibles still open. This time, he felt a tinge of anger and his cheeks stung, as if the students had reached out to slap him in the face.

Later in the day, they drove toward King William's Town. As Mr. Garrett steered his car, his idle chatter didn't seem to have Andrew fully engaged, and Joshua's thoughts were miles away. He was remembering the smiles on the faces of his congregation members as they finally understood clearly his sermon words once he'd spoken them over in Xhosa. The older congregation members seemed to struggle with English the most. The one group of congregation members who were most loyal, it seemed, was the very group that was most bereft without benefit of marula Bibles.

As Mr. Garrett steered them to the edge of town, past a group of African men gathered before a taxi stand, Joshua strained to look at an African man moving swiftly back and forth across the street on his hands and knees in front of the crowd. His legs beneath his knees dangled lifeless, shriveled like withered vines, their sap no longer flowing. Joshua had seen photos of Africans in this condition in magazines. Most of them had lost their legs to polio. *Atrophy—that's the word they used to describe it,* he thought. Mr. Garrett brought the car to a rest at a petrol station, and Joshua stepped out, still focused on the man who moved on the opposite roadside on all fours, the muscles of his slender arms bulging. That man finally moved squarely in front of the other men, speaking loudly to the crowd.

Joshua couldn't make out his muffled words, but could only watch the man's lips moving and uttering words that held the others enraptured. The memory of his own dream, the one that had so disturbed him before he left America, flowed through his mind. He shrugged that memory away as he continued to watch the crippled man. It was clear he wasn't a beggar, Joshua thought. He spoke too energetically and moved with nimble confidence. The man seemed to sense Joshua was looking. He gazed in his direction then nodded.

Joshua then returned to the front seat, and Mr. Garrett drove them a mile up a tree-lined street to a local official's meeting. They parked before a double-story Victorian with an elegant veranda. They walked through a heavy, polished door across the mosaic of tiles of the foyer. There they exchanged greetings with several local officials. Deliberations began shortly in a handsomely furnished sitting room.

"It is rather unsettling, the frequency with which protests have begun to flare in East London. It seems to me Fort Hare must have some position about whether its students should be free to participate, Mr. Garrett," one of the local officials complained.

Mr. Garrett nodded, while Joshua felt an objection lodging in his throat. A few peaceful protests were hardly cause for restriction.

"We will keep the situation monitored, and take actions if need be to ensure our students are responsible in their actions. Reverend Clay, I'm sure you agree that a stronger stand could be taken, to clarify to the students the counterproductive nature of such protests."

Mr. Garrett seemed to take his reaction for granted, Joshua thought, or perhaps he felt confident he could corner him into a reply of support.

"I have taken the opportunity to meet with several of the key student leaders," Joshua said, feeling nervous about what he should say. He wondered if they could hear him take a deep breath before continuing. "I don't see a reason to restrict student participation in peaceful protests, unless they demonstrate some lack of responsibility." He said it, but he chastised himself for his anemic tone.

Mr. Garrett seemed to sit still for a moment, then cocked his head back and turned away from Joshua.

"We will keep you informed should we believe that any protest is actively being planned by any of our students," Mr. Garrett said to the others, ignoring what Joshua had just said. As the meeting adjourned, Mr. Garrett glanced at Joshua, a deliberate look that warned him not to do such a thing again.

Joshua almost felt as if he now knew every rock by heart. He'd made this journey several times to visit with the Maganus. It was kind of them to invite him again, he thought. As he made his way, he found his spirits lifting. He was thinking of Nongolesi.

"Mama Siziwe went to give the Old Man a drink of water in the fields, Reverend," Nongolesi said as she led Joshua to the backyard and sat back down near a stack of sweet potatoes. She picked up a small knife and continued to peel one.

"Please call me Joshua," he said, feeling he was with a friend.

Joshua reached for another knife right next to her, moving his chair closer to the bucket as he also began to peel one of the sweet potatoes deftly. Nongolesi burst out laughing, her eyes wide.

"What?" Joshua chuckled at her wide-eyed response.

"This is not a man's work," she said, pointing to the sweet potatoes in his hands.

"Someone forgot to mention that to my aunt Lu."

He continued peeling, and she chuckled again, realizing he didn't intend to stop. "I knew there was some reason why I liked you," Nongolesi smiled broadly. "You best not let the Old Man see you do this! He will think I am poisoning your mind."

"If I hear the Old Man, I will put this down right away." Joshua laughed with her.

She smiled, and resumed preparing the potatoes. This was the least he could do, her family had fed him so many times. There was something peaceful about working together with her as he drank in the fresh evening air.

"So how do you feel your mission work is progressing?"

"Well, you saw last week, the congregation is shrinking."

She looked at him, seeming to understand his discouragement.

"Preach from the heart, things will get better."

She seemed to deliberately suggest he wasn't preaching from the heart. He examined her expression but didn't probe her meaning further. Perhaps he simply didn't want to answer the hard question that might follow. He focused on the potato in his hands.

"So what would the evening be like if you were back in America?" Nongolesi asked, looking lovely in a traditional dress.

He smiled. "Well, my aunt Lu would have me do a lot of things to help prepare dinner—chip some ice, fetch some warm eggs from a roadside vendor, pump more water from the well. All of the women of our family would be chatting on about something or other as they helped cook, since they normally finish their jobs by the afternoon.

And Uncle Nate would be on his way back home after a hard day's work."

"These words—*aunt* and *uncle*. Every time I hear them, they sound so strange. We do not recognize such words, you know. They have no meaning here."

"The *uncle* I mean—Nate—is my mother's sister's husband."

"In our culture, my mother's sister is my mother also. My father's brother is my father. My mother's sister's husband, he also is my father."

Joshua chuckled, peeling another potato. "That's complicated."

"It's simple." She smiled, challenging him. "How can you make all of those distinctions—*cousin, uncle. That* seems confusing."

"So how many fathers do you have?"

"Four. The Old Man and Baba, who is no longer living, and the two more brothers of my father, who live in Port Elizabeth."

"Which one is the one who is responsible for your birth?"

"Baba."

"The Old Man isn't your birth father?"

"We don't make that distinction."

Given the closeness Joshua had sensed between Nongolesi and the Old Man, he was very surprised.

"You don't consider your uncle Lucius and uncle Nate to be like your fathers?" Nongolesi asked.

Joshua thought about that for a moment. "If anyone feels like my father, it's my Uncle Nate. I think we are a lot more alike, Nate and I. He gives great advice, sets the responsible example."

"So, he has influenced you more?" she asked as she began dicing the sweet potatoes in her bucket.

"I wouldn't say that, exactly. I've learned from each of my aunts and uncles. Aunt Lu beat the fear of God into me. Aunt Alma inspires me with her kindness, Aunt Waneda with her steady will, Uncle Nate and Uncle Lucius both stressed the importance of education."

"Yes, education and independence are very important."

Her words made him think about Fort Hare and the curriculum.

"How did your uncles convince you education was important?" she asked, pausing her work as he answered.

"You're full of questions."

"You're a different one; I want to know about you." She smiled.

He thought about it for a moment. "I suppose I came to see education as important from simply listening to them talk. Every night, Uncle Nate and Lucius would sit around a narrow table that sat against the kitchen wall or they'd sit in the living room after dinner, and Uncle Lucius would sit there talking about Garvey's message—Marcus Garvey."

"I know of Garvey." She nodded. "His newspapers circulate in the townships of King William's Town and East London. He dreams about how Africans will build their own schools, their own businesses, regain wealth."

"That's exactly what Uncle Lucius would come home excited about," Joshua said, surprised again that she knew so much about America's Negro leaders. "And Uncle Nate also would say work hard and everything will work out."

"So you followed Uncle Nate's advice?"

"To tell you the truth, when I was growing up, I didn't hear much difference between their advice. They seemed to be saying the same thing: work hard, focus, get an education, study, and you'll be able to build a strong home, have chicken every night on your table."

"And so you studied . . ."

". . . and studied. Darius would tease me about that." Joshua chuckled.

"And you went to college straightaway?"

He shook his head. "There have been hard times in America also," he said, knowing that wasn't the popular image of America among South Africans. "The Great War caused such hardships—just like in South Africa. After it ended, I felt I needed to work to help my family. They never asked, but I felt I should contribute. People all around us were losing their jobs. Lu and Nate took me in when my mother died, so I should look out for them also."

"And Darius—he is your brother, then? He also helped out?"

"Darius was my cousin, but in your culture, you would consider him my brother, yes," Joshua said, his smile fading a bit. "Darius wasn't around then. He was killed during the war in Europe," Joshua said softly.

Her eyes dimmed. "I'm sorry, I didn't know that."

"With Darius, I understand what you mean when you say you

make no distinction between cousins and brothers; he was like a brother to me—seven years older and he was the boss." Joshua chuckled. A hundred memories flowed through his mind. "It was like losing my best friend," he whispered. He saw Nongolesi's eyes glaze over as she heard the pain in his voice. Something inside him stirred.

"He was killed fighting?" she asked softly.

"Yes."

She knit her eyebrows. "I didn't know American Negro soldiers had fought in the Great War."

"We served with *pride*," he said, letting the words linger. "It took a lot of effort to persuade the government to let Negro men serve in combat troops, not just as labor troops. Darius went with the 369th Infantry, a Negro platoon. It advanced quickly toward the Rhine and battled the Germans directly. A lot of lives were lost when they came under heavy shelling in a place called Meuse-Argonne. That's when Darius was shot; he died within a week, in October."

Joshua shook his head. "Darius's death hit my family hard. My family hadn't wanted him to join the war effort. Or at least my aunt Lu—Darius's mother—didn't. She didn't trust white men to value his life. My uncle Lucius was opposed only because he didn't think Negroes should be willing to fight in segregated regiments. He supported the aims of the Great War, though—freedom, liberty."

Nongolesi looked at him intensely.

"Anyhow," he said, looking down at his hands as he finished peeling his last potato, "that made it hard to go away to college. Economic times were already hard for Negroes. When white soldiers came back from fighting, they reclaimed a lot of jobs that Negroes had been given. I didn't want to leave with such uncertainty about the future, so I stayed on for five years after high school, working to make sure my family would be okay."

"Five years is a long time to wait if you've been dreaming of college," she said, her eyes large.

Something in her tone made him look more closely at her. "You want to attend college?"

She gave him an embarrassed half smile. "At this point, the Old Man wouldn't hear of it," Nongolesi said.

"Perhaps one day," Joshua said, prodding her to think of it.

She smiled and nodded.

"Had Darius also gone to Wilberforce before the army?"

Joshua laughed heartily. "That would have been far too sedate for my dear cousin. As soon as he turned eighteen, he packed his bags and headed for Harlem—that's in New York City. He wanted to see Marcus Garvey's headquarters and what some people now call the Negro Renaissance. You should have seen the letters he wrote. He loved New York. Then war came, and he made his way into combat."

"Freedom is worth fighting for," she whispered deliberately, letting the words sit between them for a moment.

Joshua nodded. "I brought a few of the letters he wrote me from Europe with me here. When I read them, I can still hear his voice," he said quietly, looking to the distance.

"You should share them in the oral history classes sometime," Nongolesi whispered. "Few of the students know Africans played any role in the Great War. They would be very proud."

He hesitated, then nodded faintly at the thought.

She seemed to search for a way to change the subject, sensing the depth of his pain. "Well, we are glad you have come this long way to be here." She smiled warmly. "So, what of our land? It is said to be one of the most beautiful of lands."

"It is truly amazing," he said, smiling. "But in so many ways, South Africa looks just like America; that's what's so astonishing— the rolling hills, the valleys, the pine trees, the blue mountains. But then as I drive, I see things I've never seen before, like those cactus trees standing tall with wood trunks, cactus branches, and soft red cone flowers. They're such a sight!"

"I love the trees here also." She sounded as if he'd read her mind and she smiled as if confessing a secret. "They remind me to praise God."

"They do?" he said, intrigued by the comment.

"The ones like those cacti, with their hands raised to God in praise."

"That's exactly how they look! Hands lifted, praising." His lips froze for a moment. She could see the world as he did. "So what does that mean, that they're better than the trees with downcast branches?"

"Some of the pines have their hands downcast, yes." She smiled. "But those are pointing down to the earth, marveling at what God has placed here."

He couldn't speak for a moment, as his heart lifted. He let himself dwell on what he was feeling. She could put into words what he had always seen, and seemed filled with the same wonder. He dropped his eyes for a moment, thinking of Shantal again. "So both of those types are better than the ones with straight branches, branches that don't point up or down?" he asked quietly.

"The ones that have their hands outstretched stand in *wonder* of everything above them and everything below," she said, drawing out the words to emphasize her points. "They have extended arms frozen in awe." She stretched her arms out straight with her mouth dropped. They both laughed.

"So all types of trees, they all praise God?"

"Yes, as should everything that has breath," she whispered as Joshua felt his heart grow full.

———————

The next week, when Joshua made his way with the Old Man into the den after dinner, his eyes were drawn directly to two stacks of hardback books in the corner of the room, the moonlight falling softly on them through the window. He knew what they were before he lifted one. He looked toward the old man with guilt etched across his face.

The Old Man settled into his cushioned chair, parting his latest reading book, gazing at Joshua without judgment.

"I wish you to know it was not my desire to make you uncomfortable when I asked you a few weeks ago to consider helping us to have marula Bibles printed."

Joshua was caught off guard by his words. He searched for a response.

"I understand your mission does not wish to see more marula Bibles at this time. Let us not speak of it again," the Old Man said. "If ever you come to believe you have a role with this task, we welcome your assistance."

Joshua sat down, still holding a Xhosa Bible in his hands. "Tahira is teaching me Xhosa," Joshua said.

"Eh!" The Old Man chuckled, his eyes shining. "That's wonderful," he said with such happiness in his voice.

Joshua silently reread the Bible passage Tahira had recently used to tutor him.

"Do you want to try?" Nongolesi asked, having heard the exchange as she sat before her paperwork at the low table.

"Try reading aloud in Xhosa?" Joshua asked.

She, the Old Man, and Mama Siziwe all nodded with the same amused eyes.

"Okay." He chuckled. He began reading, trying to repeat the intonations Tahira had taught, making clicking sounds in the right spots as he pronounced the words.

They all chuckled out loud. "That's good," Nongolesi said brightly. "Most foreigners can't click their tongue at the right time."

"Thank you." Joshua bent forward, playing as if taking a bow.

"There's more than one, you know," the Old Man added.

"More than one what?" Joshua asked.

"Clicking sound," the Old Man answered.

Joshua arched his eyebrows, not understanding.

"There are others, many different types," the Old Man explained as he and Nongolesi and Mama Siziwe each started making different clicking sounds with their tongues—some mellow, some deep, some shallow, some full, some thin. Each was determined by where they placed their tongue on the roof or side of their mouths. Joshua burst out laughing, shaking his head as the Old Man kept clicking.

"Stop, you're discouraging him," Nongolesi said between her laughter.

"You'll get there; you just keep using that one little click you were making." The Old Man chuckled, his eyes still dancing. "People will know what you mean."

It took a moment for the laughter in the room to subside, as Nongolesi wiped a tear from the corner of her eye. Joshua continued to chuckle to himself. As he relaxed back into his chair, sitting still, he heard that beauty-filled voice calling to him again from somewhere nearby. He smiled, then focused on the marula Bible in his hands, becoming lost in his thoughts as he read on.

CHAPTER 13

Joshua drove more quickly than usual on his way to give the good news to Nongolesi, stopping only to pick up three women at the roadside carrying woven baskets filled with fruit and babies tied to their backs. He really had come to enjoy meeting each new villager. *"Molweni. Kumandi ukudibana noni nonkana."* He tried out his most recent lesson as they stepped in the car. Their eyes lit up and they spoke back quickly. He chuckled, letting them know he only knew a little Xhosa. They continued in broken English, looking around his car, examining him with equal ardor. Peculiar clothes, they seemed to be thinking; a slightly softer tone to his skin than theirs, and his hair—their eyes always seemed to focus on the looser kink of his hair.

"Preacher," the woman next to him said to her friend, making Joshua smile. After two months of preaching, word had spread.

After a few more minutes, he dropped the ladies at a village nearby, then returned back to the Noni Village, parking his car at the road's end. He set off by foot on the path's familiar curve, balancing a heavy package in his hands as he moved over the stream's rocks and started up the short incline to the Ulundi School. A smile crept over his face as he imagined Nongolesi's reaction to the news that had made him so happy.

Nongolesi sat at her desk, wiping her pen's curved tip against the ink jar, then pressing it lightly against a piece of paper, comparing her penned words to her handwritten notes. Joshua set his bundle outside and knocked against the lounge door, hardly wanting to interrupt.

"Yes," she said without looking up.

"I don't mean to disturb you."

Her face lit up at the sound of his voice. "I wasn't expecting you," she said happily, wiping her hands against a rag and waving him in.

"This is what I meant before," she said, pointing to two hand-stitched books on her desk, each tied at its rim with twine, their pages yellowed and turned. "You can help with this."

"What is it you're writing so carefully today?" he asked, realizing as he looked at her how happy he was to see her again.

"Our history. The history of our people's journey from the Transkei, as far back as the stories go," she said, moving her hand over the large stack of hand-stitched books. "I have been trying for some time to compile a whole regional history of our peoples. The stories date back sixteen generations!"

Caught by her enthusiasm, he picked one book up gently.

"There is so much to remember. Our ancestors had many trials. The days of the plague of influenza, the years when the locusts came in thick black clouds and destroyed the crops, leaving the people to dig with dirt under their nails, hoping to live off root vegetables. The arrival of the Mfengu. How the House of one of our chiefs was divided when the son of the Right Hand House rose against the son of his Great Wife. The battles against the British. One day, we'll make these into a proper book."

"Actually," he said, knowing he was about to make her very happy, "I brought something that might help." He ducked outside the door and brought forth the object under a thick tarp.

"Your typewriter!"

"I received a response from my mission," he said, setting the typewriter on her desk. "I may preach in the villages, and I can teach and lead prayers at Ulundi once a week."

"Once a week?" She frowned.

"That's good! No other missionary I know has been granted that sort of permission."

"Perhaps they never asked."

His smile faded. "I suppose that could be true, but this is good news. I can accomplish a lot in a single day. It will allow me to get to know the children, and to help out with typing the books." He smiled.

"Yes, this *is* good news," she said, returning his smile. "I'm very happy. When you come, you can spend one of the hours of your day teaching me how to use this typewriter, so when you cannot come—"

"I'll teach you very well."

She reached out and took his hand. His feelings stirred but this time he felt little guilt. He was so happy with the turn of events.

"The children will be so pleased," she said.

"Well, I'm yours for the day," he said with a smile. "So, you'll show me my chores?" he joked.

"The lunch bell will ring shortly. But first I can teach you the way to stir tea, so when you come on your one day a week, you can prepare and have my tea waiting."

"That's one of my chores?" He chuckled.

"You said you wish to serve your congregation well."

"Yes, I did." He laughed. She had her father's sense of humor.

Nongolesi and Joshua shared their good news with the other teachers over lunch and began their first session of typing afterward. Joshua began to type the words from one of Nongolesi's completed volumes as she continued to pen a new book.

"Do you miss home?" Nongolesi asked.

"Yes," he said, not really wanting to admit how much. "And no."

She raised her eyebrows.

"Of course I miss my family. I anxiously wait for each one of their letters. But I don't feel lonely. The people of this region are so warm."

His words brought a smile to her face. "And so you are glad you have come to preach among us?"

"I'm very happy." He smiled. "I've seen so many new things, and so many unexpected things. But it can be frustrating. The students at Fort Hare—I definitely don't seem to be reaching them."

"Give it time. There's much that you have needed to learn about our culture," she said, pausing to sip a cup of water. "Are the peoples here what you expected?"

He looked at her ruefully.

"What's that look?"

He smiled to himself, musing over the fact that she could read his expression. A whole world away, on the other side of the earth, and facial expressions meant the same things. "We hear many different things about Africa in the United States, that's all," he said seriously.

"None of them positive."

"Why would you say that?" He frowned. He hadn't meant to insult her.

"Sarah, the Negro American in East London, has told us some of the stories, about the comic strips in the U.S. that mock our customs and that picture Africans as apes. Sarah says those things taught her to be ashamed."

Joshua's lips thinned as he nodded. He looked away and sighed softly. "I was raised to believe I had no connection to Africa, to that black spot they portrayed so awfully in the books and magazines. I thought of myself as American, so I was never ashamed," Joshua said. "At least, I never thought so until recently." His eyes drifted back to her.

"Many missionaries say they've come to civilize us," she said, pausing her writing. "That's even what they say of Fort Hare sometimes, that many of the European professors think that is what they are doing."

He could tell she was probing. "In America, I spent an extra year training for this position," he responded, even though he preferred not to. "That was the view of the professors who my mission sent to train me during that extra year."

"So this place is different than you expected?" Nongolesi asked.

"Very much," he smiled. "My home church in Philly, my congregation in Ohio—both were filled with such warm people. And I've found that here too. The way your family has welcomed me has been so delightful, Nongolesi. And Tahira also—without a word, she fed me and offered me a place to stay for the night when I stumbled upon her home. It's been a lovely treat. She's come to my home to help out, and will soon be spending more time there. I look forward to that."

Nongolesi smiled at what she seemed to see in his expression. "They still call her Raggedy Woman, you know. They do not do it to insult Tahira, it is just a habit. She has had a difficult life, that one." Pain coated her face. Joshua knew they were a part of the same large village and clan, but he hadn't thought she knew Tahira well.

"She had a husband in Peddie long ago," Nongolesi whispered, "but left him and returned here. It caused her family great shame."

"Why did she leave him?" Joshua looked up from his typing.

"She did not choose him as her husband. She simply wished to choose her own husband. I am like her in that way," Nongolesi said.

Joshua thought he saw fear in her eyes.

"One day, she went to fetch water at the river; a man she had never seen before came and took her for his wife."

"That's allowed. It's a part of tradition here, isn't it?" he asked gently.

Nongolesi nodded. "But I have never agreed it should be allowed. In these days, many more women think as I. But in her day, such words were heresy." Nongolesi shook her head. "This thing she did was considered a great disgrace. The villagers treated her as an outcast. She fled up into the mountains and stayed there for many years, trying to live by herself and tend herself. I know that some people silently went to her, to leave baskets with *izipho zothando*, to help feed her. But they did so without letting her know who they were, so that shame would not also fall on their homes."

Joshua kept quiet. It sounded cruel.

"After some years, the leaders of our village sent word that she should rejoin the village. For two years, she refused; but when the droughts came, she could not care for herself from her little crops, and she returned."

"I'm glad people don't treat her like that anymore," Joshua said. "She's a very kind woman."

"Yes, but if you watch, the villagers feel awkward with her still. They are ashamed of how they once treated her and do not know how to express it. Tahira now plays a big role in leading the village. But there is something about it—you will see. She rarely joins in the smoking of pipes or the passing of beer. She has shown forgiveness, but she has never tried to reestablish the relations that might have been. But she does cherish Beaumont!"

"I thought Beaumont was her son when I first met him."

"In our culture, he is." Nongolesi smiled. "His mother died of influenza. Tahira has since cared for Beaumont as if he is her own. But she is still poor. She had no husband to provide her with cattle, and she has very little land to till. That is why they call her Raggedy

Woman. You think hard on these things," she said, waving her finger again. "Even one so wronged by so many chooses to greet you well. This is something of which we can be very proud."

Joshua agreed. He looked off to the distance, thinking about all she had just said. "The people are so warm here, Nongolesi. I just wish I could reach the students more. It's been very discouraging. Church attendance keeps dropping, more each week as you've noticed."

"You are faring much better than Reverend Peter," she reassured him. "The bad feelings that grew between him and some of the students . . ." She shook her head.

"It's good to hear they're more receptive. But most times, I feel this is a battle I can't win." He sighed, feeling grateful he could share anything with her without worrying she'd judge him.

"Keep trying," she said. "Really. I see how much they respect you."

"Respect!" He laughed, amazed she'd said that seriously. "They sit out in front of the tent near the church as I walk in to preach, reading their Bibles but not coming in to the church for my sermons! And they make a point to be there when I leave after my sermon, still with their Bibles open."

She looked down, seeming saddened by that behavior. "Their faith means much to them," she said, meeting his gaze deliberately. "They have not put away their Bibles, tossed them out along with the discarded pamphlets and rotting leaves. They open those Bibles and read by a candle's light in their dorm rooms every night following a long day's work. That means something. They have been willing to show you their faith. That means something too. They are giving you a chance by showing you that much. They just feel you have not seen things as they really are in this country."

"You sound as though you've heard them talking," Joshua said.

"Ogenga and the other students do not hold in their opinions."

That admission hurt him. "What is it I don't see?" he asked wearily. "They seem to always test me—and they know it's a test I'm always going to fail. They know I can't join them in their protests."

"Maybe they only want you to acknowledge what they face, even if you cannot do much about it. But they do respect you."

He shrugged, then began to type again.

"You are younger than many of them, you know?"

He stopped again, looking at her.

"You are what, twenty-seven?"

"Twenty-eight."

She nodded. "Ogenga is twenty-eight, or somewhere near there. We have not always recorded births and kept track of years of age as you do in America, but Ogenga was born in the year when the Right Hand House of Nkula was formed. Jovan thinks he was born one year prior."

Joshua looked surprised. "I knew that most students worked for a number of years before they came to Fort Hare in order to earn the tuition, but I suppose I never really thought about how old they are."

Nongolesi raised her eyebrows. "Age means much here; it's considered by most to mean more than almost any other factor. When they look at you, they see a young man their very same age, and yet they ask your advice. They give you more respect, I believe, than you can see. That they have overlooked your youth and accepted your status as reverend is very important, even if they do not yet choose to attend more of your sermons."

He leaned back from the typewriter, giving her his full attention. "So, you think I should try harder to see things from their perspective?"

"The situation here—the insult is very, very deep," she said with a flash of anger. "At every turn, the government tells us we are nothing because we are African. They insult our traditions, our families, our history. They have taken the land of our fathers, dug up our sacred burial grounds, destroyed our *homes!* They arrested two of the students who were protesting last week and put them in jail; they are still there. Did you know this? We don't know when or how this will end." There was fright in her eyes. "To the students at Fort Hare, you seem sometimes to see nothing wrong with it."

The anger and disappointment in her voice stung. Joshua felt humbled as he feared the truth in her words.

"Perhaps you just fail to see the situation fully," she said quietly.

"Do you believe I don't fully see it?"

She looked down. "Have you yet been to visit the jailhouses?"

"No."

"If you ever visit there, tell me what you see. I think it is true, some of what they have said," she whispered. "Your eyes have not been fully open. Open them and see more than what you wish to see. I don't mean to speak too boldly to you."

"You haven't spoken too boldly," he said softly. "Thank you for telling me, Nongolesi."

They were quiet for a moment as he began to type again. He thought about her words and flushed.

"How was your last visit at the homesteads of the Noni Village?" she asked, trying to break the awkward silence between them as she continued her work.

"Remarkable," he said, giving her a faint smile to let her know he wasn't angry. "I see Tahira and the others every time I pass through to your home, and Tahira takes the chance to teach me more Xhosa each time, as well as when she comes to my home." The thought brought a smile to his eyes. "I lead a few prayers in her homestead—people from nearby homesteads come to pray with us, but I can't wait to deliver my first sermon at the Noni Village. I'll make arrangements to preach there soon now that my mission has given me permission to do so." He hesitated for a moment. "As much as I enjoy being there, though, when I sit around with the villagers—well, it's not always easy to know what to talk about."

"There's so much!" She smiled broadly. "Everything you have experienced is so new for us. Begin with simple things. But when you tell the stories, you must do it with great animation, with gestures, to make them seem real for those who listen, like they were there."

He nodded with laughter in his eyes. When he was with her, everything around him came into full bloom, even when she had unpleasant things to tell him.

"Tell them about your boat ride, your evenings when Marvis would play his African violin—that famous *nanga*—and about America." She nodded.

He took a deep breath, wishing his time with her wouldn't end.

———————————

Nongolesi's words loomed in Joshua's mind as he returned that night to Fort Hare. He supposed that was because they rang so true—he wasn't preaching from the Bible freely or honoring what he knew to be true, that the aims of the students weren't so unreasonable. He sensed those burdensome thoughts wouldn't fade, he'd one day need to confront them.

The sky dimmed fast. When Joshua finally reached home that night, he picked up another letter that the mailman had slid underneath his front door. He knew the handwriting. Shantal. For some reason, his hand trembled as he held it. He moved to his desk, lighting a lantern and opening the letter with a single stroke of a knife. What was it that told him before he started reading that this would be the last letter he would receive from her? The slant of her pen? The clipped sentences? The pages that numbered more than he would have expected?

He swallowed hard, sitting down as he began reading the first page, a frown clouding his face. His stomach fluttered, and he started down the second page. He wiped his finger to the corner of his eye, and he began the third, then the fourth, his heart pounding. He felt shame flush over him. He had disappointed her, and had hurt her. He set the letter down and stared into the darkness around him.

He gathered his thoughts as he held a pen, hand trembling, and began to write her in return. He should have written her about this before, should have been the one to admit everything he knew he'd never be able to promise her. He wrote now, to apologize, to let her know how much she had meant to him, and to wish her well.

CHAPTER 14

All of the restrictions on his activities as a minister consumed Joshua's thoughts on his drive over to the Maganu homestead on Christmas day. Members of his congregation had asked him just the week before to add his signature to a petition against the pass laws of King William's Town. He could hardly look them in the eyes as he declined. Mr. Garrett had watched the exchange and had questioned him at length about it that Sunday after all the congregation members had returned home. It wasn't Mr. Garrett's actions that most bothered Joshua, though; it was the pure lack of joy during his services. He looked out each week to stale gazes; he was failing to bring any of those listening closer to Christ. That thought made his chest heave, as he took in a long breath. He'd known his time in South Africa would be challenging, but he could scarcely believe things were going so poorly. As the first of the Noni Village huts came into view, he smiled. At least his time in the villages seemed to be well spent, as was his time at the Ulundi School. He could hardly believe he'd been in South Africa over two months already.

He knew his way to the Maganu home very well now. As he journeyed up the last of the footpath, Joshua could see Nongolesi stepping from the doorway of her home, coming to greet him with a sunny smile.

"Merry Christmas," she said.

Joshua felt such peace as he walked closer to her. "Merry Christmas to you," he replied cheerfully. "I have to get used to this"—he said, wiping his brow with a handkerchief—"summer heat on Christmas day!"

"Where you come from . . . ?"

"By this time of the year, it's covered with snow."

"Now that is something different!" She chuckled. "We get snow mostly in June, thin coats only. But some parts of the western Cape get deep layers, we hear."

"Before I arrived, I would never have believed it snowed in Africa," Joshua said, narrowing his eyes. "That's not the image we have of Africa where I come from."

"Well, just prepare when June approaches!" she said, walking him to the door. "You should sit in back," she said, motioning him through to the back of the homestead. "I will fetch tea for you and join you. I still have mealies to finish there."

The home was festive, decorated with recently cut flowers and bowls of fruit and food, in preparation for their family Christmas celebration. Joshua could smell a stew cooking in the kitchen as he walked through to the yard. He was startled for a moment when he saw a young man there, moving with agility on all fours. He paused before a bin of water, removing his gloves and fishing for a rag. Joshua recognized the man from the petrol station, with his legs hanging lifeless beneath the knees. His attention was focused firmly as he untied wooden blocks that were tied with rags around each of his knees. They seemed to provide a sort of shoe for him as he moved on his hands and knees. He loosened the soiled rags from around his knees, soaking them in the bin as he washed his knees down and rubbed a salve over them, soothing a few bleeding scratches. He then tied the wooden blocks back around his knees, fastening them tightly with a fresh set of rags, which he looped carefully through holes forged through the middle of the blocks.

"Hello," Joshua said softly, trying not to startle him.

The man looked unsurprised as he stretched a heavily calloused hand toward Joshua and smiled.

"I'm Reverend Clay."

They exchanged a handshake as the man looked Joshua over. "I believe I saw you near King William's Town," he said plainly. "You looked very lost."

"I wasn't lost," Joshua said, perplexed by the comment. "I was on the way to a meeting with local officials."

The man nodded and pursed his lips. "My name is Mhlobo," he said, smiling after a pause.

"You're Nongolesi's brother?" Joshua asked.

Mhlobo nodded, his eyes probing why Joshua seemed so surprised. He moved back closer to the pail of soapy water, scrubbing his soiled rags, wringing them free of the dried blood and dirt.

"What were you talking about so intensely that day?" Joshua asked, taking a seat and trying not to stare at the flesh beneath Mhlobo's knees. It was a difficult sight, for his withered shins hung limply. "Everyone seemed captivated with your words," he commented, remembering the small crowd that had stretched before Mhlobo.

"The taxi owners fail to pay us," Mhlobo said with a thick voice. "They are white, and they mistreat us. Why, we ask, when we work, do they not pay us our fair share? We need to refuse to work until they pay us our fair share. We are not desperate like the ones who have traveled far to work in the Johannesburg mines." He let the rags soak again and moved back toward a chair, his hands cushioning his brisk movements, power in his every step. Joshua could see he was a proud man; it was clear by the way he perched himself in that chair, sitting up like a full-bodied man, and by how perfectly well-kept he was, down to the oil shining through his short-cropped hair.

Joshua examined his face. He was dark-skinned, with eyes like Nongolesi's, but oddly, something about him at first glance looked so mean. It puzzled Joshua because there had been no meanness in his words, only sternness. Perhaps it was simply the look of a man who'd waged many battles.

"Have you made progress in your requests?" Joshua asked.

"They finally provided for some of our demands," Mhlobo said, speaking with confidence.

"I thought your family had told me you had left for the Johannesburg mines."

Mhlobo's smile disappeared. He dropped his eyes. "This is what the mines of the City of Gold brought me," he said, moving his hand over his shriveled shins. He met Joshua's gaze. "I work in King William's Town now. I must return home to heal when my knees become like this," he said, readjusting the rags around his scratched knees.

"There was an accident in the mines?" Joshua asked gently.

"*Accident* is the word you use when something cannot be helped. It was no accident." Mhlobo shook his head. "They call Johannesburg the City of Gold. That is a dark lie. There, white men judge an African life to be worth nothing. Many men I have watched suffering fates like this in those mines. But those who go think they have little choice but to stay; they need moneys to send to their families who no longer have farms to till." Mhlobo moved back to the pail, to wring the last clotted bloodstains from his rags and set them aside to dry.

"This happened"—he motioned toward his legs again—"when they lowered me down into the mines. It is difficult to not suffer a bad fate there, you should know. If they lower you to the highest levels, it's icy cold there, and you work so hard you sweat in that icy cold, and you can fall sick and die of pneumonia. If they lower you far down, past the tenth level, you are so deep inside the earth, the air cannot circulate freely. It is dark as night and it is hot as you would think hell would be. We crawl on hands and knees, squeezing through tunnels of rocks, with only our head torches to light our way. And we must stay there hours on end. The rocks with gold that we loosen are pulled up from those deep spots, even before we are. The European supervisors load them in large trucks and drive them away, all before they bother to return to get us out.

"A white man who works to collect the gold we mine is paid eighty British pounds for the month; we are paid thirty for the year. If an injury prevents you from returning to work on any day, you lose all of your pay for that month. What means are there for us to protest any decision they might choose?"

The bitterness in Mhlobo's words sent a chill through Joshua. He could see clearly how much Mhlobo had suffered.

"You are a preacher. Where do you suppose those very white supervisors I speak of go on Sundays?" He shook his head as he provided the answer. "To the church that sits not five miles from the mines. And they bless Jesus."

"Jesus would never condone such behavior," Joshua responded. He had never uttered words with such intensity, but he wasn't certain Mhlobo was listening.

"I was asked to go into the deepest part of that mine," Mhlobo continued. "Someone above me failed to set the dynamite right. The rocks tumbled with a roar. That was the end of my legs. My Afrikaner supervisor sent me on a flatbed to a city hospital, but the truck's driver was an Indian man. He took me instead to the clinic of his brother. He can save my legs, he told me. That doctor told me he'd once worked in Kenya, where there were men who had contracted diseases as children, who had kept their legs even though they withered. He told me I could choose to keep my legs. Even though they would turn to this, I would still be free to move, not confined to a chair. You see the choice I have made."

Joshua nodded. "I'm glad God was looking after you."

Mhlobo smiled, a cynical smile, dismissing Joshua's words. "I had never before spoken with an Indian man, not more than a hello as I might have said as I passed one on the street. But on that day, this Indian man said, 'This should not have happened. A black life is worth the same as a white one is worth the same as an Indian one.'"

"Jesus loves all people and values all lives. He stands with those who suffer."

"Is that what you are here to do—stand with us?"

The words silenced Joshua. He felt paralyzed for a moment by the unnerving resentment that stirred inside, a sour resentment toward his mission. He should have been able to answer yes to Mhlobo's question, he realized instead the truthful answer was no, his mission was not allowing him to stand with them. He knew what he felt in that moment would plague him. He frowned as he searched his mind, and searched Mhlobo's face also. Nongolesi joined them just then, not sensing the tension as she began speaking of the Christmas celebration to come.

Joshua enjoyed a feast with the Maganus well into the night. It was a meal with familiar flavors, as fine a meal as he'd ever eaten on Christmas, but his mood had been dampened by his exchange with Mhlobo. He followed Mhlobo and Nongolesi outside, where they joined Ogenga in the circle of a single lantern's light and sat down in chairs. Under the dark canopy of the sky, the stars glimmered low.

"What do you think of how we celebrate Christmas here?" Nongolesi asked Joshua as the lantern light danced.

"It's very special. In many ways, it reminds me of home." Joshua smiled. "My family also celebrates with a great meal and with a church service. But the tributes you make to your ancestors as you recite stories about them—that made the meal feel very special."

"At this time, we must praise them and what they accomplished, for without them we would not be here," Mhlobo said.

"Missionaries have a hard time understanding our current view of the ancestors," Ogenga said. "They say the Xhosa worship multiple gods."

The three siblings chuckled, and Mhlobo looked at Joshua darkly.

"They have not listened well," Nongolesi said.

"We have always believed only in one God, *Qamata,* the one my mother's people—the Zulus—call *Nkulunkulu,*" Ogenga explained. "It is true that in the past our peoples believed that we could communicate with God only through our ancestors who had passed away. If a crop went bad, it was thought that we had acted in some way to cause our ancestors to not carry our prayers to God. In the past, therefore, we would invoke the names of our ancestors in prayer. Some people say this is much like the way Catholics pray, when they pray through the saints. Since Christianity has begun to spread in this land, we now know that we can pray directly to God, but we still wish to honor our ancestors with tributes, through stories we tell to our children on occasions like this."

Joshua sat back, cradling a mug of tea in his hands, trying to listen well.

"Since the missionaries introduced Christianity here," Nongolesi said, "we have always acknowledged that the Bible has helped us understand God, and I accept Jesus Christ as my Lord and Savior. I have not understood why the missionaries still reject so many of our traditions."

Mhlobo nodded. "It is as many suggest, the missionaries have come to our land with a color bar firmly beneath their Christian cloaks. They are willing to bring their Bibles, but always underneath their words is the color bar. We cannot enter their white churches. They do not complain when the government takes our rights away. They tell us that in order to be Christian we must no longer wear our traditional clothes, which they say are heathen, but we must dress as Europeans. They say our ancestors represent multiple gods to us. They have never sought to know our ways."

Mhlobo's biting words caused everyone to pause for a moment, kneading them over. Mhlobo looked sternly at Joshua for a response.

"I've come to see since I've been here at Fort Hare," Joshua said, "that many of the students have already accepted Jesus Christ as their Lord and Savior, and nothing could please me more. I think the trouble some missionaries have here comes because some of your traditional beliefs are so different, they challenge us," Joshua said. "I'm sure there are many of your traditions that the Bible doesn't necessarily contradict, but it doesn't verify them either. So for some missionaries, I'm sure it's less clear what to do with some of those ideas."

"You believe more in their goodness than many of us do." Ogenga snickered. "It has not always seemed that they have had goodness in their hearts."

"Those who try to denigrate our ancestors do not get far," Nongolesi agreed. Joshua sat back and tried to listen openly again. Her conviction was very strong. She quoted parts of the Bible to underscore her points. She knew the Bible so well, had tried to distill it, to understand how Xhosa beliefs and Christianity fit together. He couldn't help smiling. He was drawn to the way she had thought so deeply about the meanings of each verse she quoted, her eye burning brightly and her gestures animated as she spoke of how those understandings fit neatly with some traditional teachings of her people. She explained how many in her family had chosen to cast aside parts of their tradition that did not fit with Christianity well and continued to deeply embrace the many aspects that were consistent with Biblical teachings. Joshua engaged her at length, sometimes making her laugh as he tested her understandings. Mhlobo sat silently beside Ogenga.

As Ogenga changed topics, Joshua relaxed into his chair, admiring the sharpness of Ogenga's intellect. He was impressed by the strong family the Old Man and Mama Siziwe had created. After a few minutes, Joshua's eyes drifted back to Mhlobo. He was startled by the weight of Mhlobo's glare. He could tell Mhlobo had been staring at him that way for a while—an icy, hard, indignant look. Joshua lifted his eyebrows, searching to understand. *What have I done?* Mhlobo seemed to be seething, Joshua could see, and his livid look was directed unmistakably at him. Joshua tried to no avail to find a moment to speak with Mhlobo alone. As he retired to the guest room that evening, something told him this wasn't the end of the matter.

CHAPTER 15

It has been way too long, Joshua thought as he drove many miles past the Noni Village toward the blue Amatola Mountains, which dominated the entire northern view, set high above small villages that lined the roadside. He'd spoiled himself in the United States, always finding a little cut of nature, even at Wilberforce, where he could go for quiet moments to meditate on the direction of his life. He'd been in South Africa for nearly four months, but he hadn't found the time to explore the region to find that special spot, a retreat where he could cast his concerns aside, enjoying God's hand-iwork and reflecting on the direction of his ministry and his life. He'd spent his time well since arriving, he assured himself, taking the time to build relationships with local officials, some of the students, and people in the local villages. But a feeling still gnawed at him. *Always remember to be still.* It was advice that he always tried to heed. Remembering Nongolesi's description of the waterfalls of Amatola, his curiosity had been piqued. It sounded ideal for the purposes he had in mind.

Driving down the paved road toward the mountains, he soon passed the last large cactus tree, standing halfway down the stretch of road, its canopy of prickly branches reaching upward. After a few more minutes, the blue mountains began to look green, and he soon shifted into low gear as his car sputtered up the winding paved incline. On his mile-high ascent up the mountainside, the vista was stunning as he glanced to his right at the villages, with their *ebuhlanti,* cornfields, and farmlands stretching back toward Alice. Halfway up the mountain, he couldn't help stopping his car and stepping out, inhaling the thin, crisp air as he took in the view. He listened. It was so beautiful—the soft wind carried gentle cow moos and sheep cries to him; the crickets chirped in full chorus on the hillside beside him. There was something so peaceful about looking at the slow pace of life here—observing a few young boys with tall sticks under the blazing blue sky, shepherding cattle to rich grazing spots where they grasped fine-leafed grasses, filling their bellies.

After driving farther up the mountain, straight through a low-lying cloud, the thick-trunked pine trees for which the Amatolas were famous surrounded him on every side. He slowed his car as he reached a plateau and the fog thickened around him. The temperature seemed to have dropped considerably at this height. Chimney smoke was in the air, drifting upward from the lines of log cabins that formed Hogsback, a quaint town for loggers nestled at the forest base. Joshua pulled before the first large inn, just beyond a lane of wooden shops, and walked past the blue pickup trucks flanking its entrance.

"Which waterfall are you trying to get to?" the man behind the counter asked in response to Joshua's question.

"I was hoping for something simple—peaceful," Joshua said.

"Thirty-nine Steps," the hotel manager said, nodding. "There are others, like the Madonna and Child Waterfall, but this one, 39 Steps, I think that's the one for you."

Joshua followed the manager's directions, driving ten minutes farther, past the graves of Miller and Donovan, whose headstones noted they'd "given their lives for the benefit of Her Majesty and the Empire, 1894." Joshua took in a deep breath, looking around at the serene pine forests all around. It was hard to imagine that these mountains had been some of the most bitterly contested lands during the Xhosa wars with Europeans.

The paved road soon came to an end, as if Joshua were leaving man's world behind. His car labored over the rough dirt road as he made his way to the gate that sat, as the manager had described, at the base of an earthen red trail. Joshua parked, starting by foot up the cone-speckled path. Painted in a full register of green hues, the sheer range of trees here made Joshua gape—skinny leathery-leaved ones, pea green short ones, and rows upon rows of pines standing in formation. *This is Africa?* Joshua chuckled to himself, barely believing it. He bent his neck back as far as he could, trying to see the tops of the longest-legged timber. He could barely see that high. He smiled at how much this reminded him of his hidden pond cove. The similarities he'd found in this distant land seemed to keep multiplying.

The farther he journeyed up the path the more enveloped he felt by God's handiwork. Wind sounded in the tallest treetops, along with other soaring sounds as the forest's tenants talked to one another. The harmonies of a thick-feathered bird's deep cry, an owl's mellow hoot, and a sparrow's high-pitched chirps rose into the sky. Soon the footpath forked. Joshua took the more narrow path, following the sounds of the river, as lavender-colored wildflowers surrounded him up to his knees, sending their thick jasmine into the air.

The silvery sounds of the river soon grew from a trickle into a tumbling roar as the path moved right alongside the rim of the crystal waters. There Joshua could finally see the river in its fullness. A few steps ahead, a wooden bridge stretched across the flowing stream. He laughed at the tunes under his feet as he stepped onto the bridge and its hollowed rungs called out like drums. From a spot on the bridge, he looked across a stretch of lowlands to his right. There wasn't another man-made object in sight. The sun broke through the fog, which had lifted, forming a high cloud. The sky became brighter, emblazoned, the colors around him turned more vibrant. Even the bees buzzed more loudly. His eyes were wide as he examined all the birds and the flowers he passed. Birds shaped like red robins were fluorescent yellow instead, and the flies and spiders were red, as bright as the berries by the pathway. It was like seeing the world he was accustomed to painted in different hues.

Still seeking the waterfall, he followed the musical sounds of the stream, up a staircase made of the thick roots of a tree that peeked up above the soil. The path turned again into a thin red earthen trail; the trees now dipped their branches low. He worked his way through low-hanging moss coils, until his eyes finally rested upon the water-fall.

The water cascaded gently from a high cliff, and the layers of rock beneath the free-falling stream formed a crystal stairway to the heavens. Thirty-nine Steps. He sat on a rock near the pool beneath the waterfall. He listened to the music of the streams, feeling his soul fill as he looked at the glory of God's creation and breathed in the fresh pine air. He felt such peace, and he sighed deeply as he closed his eyes, trying to sort through his thoughts about his time in South Africa and his ministry.

The thought that vexed him waded through his mind again: He no longer felt like a vessel, at least not for God's Word. He let himself dwell on that thought as he folded his hands into a steeple and prayed about his ministry, the students, the struggle. *Father God, please guide my steps. Please help me to succeed here, Father, for all it means to the natives of this country and to my people back home. Help me to build bridges here. Give me wisdom.*

He opened his eyes, gazing on the water full of light and reflections. He loved being this close to nature, where nothing stood between him and God. No gold-plated ornaments, no paned windows. He sat still, emptying his mind of all thoughts for a moment. Faintly, he heard the voice singing a familiar song in the distance. The same as always, echoing with the singing world around him. The tune brought a smile to Joshua's face: it was so assuring. *Ukuthi, Mabanganilukuhli abaprofeti benu abaphakathi kwenu, kwan-abavumisi benu, ningawaphulaphuli amaphupha enu eniwaphupayo. Ngokuba ndiyazizi iingcinga endizicingayo ngani, utsho uYehova: iingcinga zoxolo, ezingezizo ezobubi; ukuba ndininike ikamva nethemba.* Joshua sat with his hands in a steeple, saying another gentle prayer, praying for guidance, seeking to order his steps.

———————

It took only a few more bleak Sundays with the number of empty chairs in the pews growing before Joshua set off for the Brother's home. Reverend Chandler hadn't sounded surprised to receive Joshua's call and welcomed his visit enthusiastically. As Joshua drove east from Fort Hare toward King William's Town, the sights brought a smile to his face again. Summer had ended, but the sky remained vibrant blue and bright above him. He reflected on his time in South Africa again; he loved so many things about the country—the people were so warm, the setting so beautiful. As his thoughts drifted to the memories of all of the resistance he had experienced to his selection as a missionary—Reverend Watson had needed to push hard to have his selection approved—it disappointed him to know he wasn't delivering. Everyone had assumed he'd have immediate success—his family, his professors, even Reverend Watson. *Reverend Watson here thinks because your skin's a different color from ours, you can help turn that mission around.* He remembered the U.S. head of his mission saying that to him with disdain, preparing to grill Joshua for any hint that he might be sympathetic to encouraging Africans to revolt. Reverend Watson had put his reputation on the line, supporting Joshua strongly. Joshua wiped a bead of sweat from his brow. *Father God, please guide my steps,* he prayed silently. *I want to have success here. Please send me a sign to help guide my steps so that I might know how to best serve You through works that will glorify Your name.*

Joshua inhaled deeply with frustration, and as he drove a few miles down the roadside, he wiped his brow again in the heat. Suddenly a loud blast startled him as his car rocked violently, bucking to the left before it limped to the roadside and sank on a hind wheel. The acrid smell of burned rubber filled Joshua's lungs as he stepped out of his car, wide-eyed, staring at the flat rear tire. He let out a moan as he stood in the middle of a long stretch of road. The last village he'd passed was nearly ten miles back. He looked up the road, trying to measure the distance to the next village, and sighed. Standing in a dip in the asphalt, he couldn't see beyond the hills in either direction. He was certain that the next village was also at least ten miles away. He pulled his hat from inside the car, to provide needed shade, and set off by foot in the direction of East London.

The asphalt was too hot to walk on, seeming to burn right through his soles. Stepping off onto the roadside, he became immersed within God's handiwork again as soft grass cushioned his steps. The crickets called forth in full song, a choir of hundreds that seemed near enough to touch from between the thin meadow blades that billowed in the warm wind.

He mopped his brow at least thirty times before he heard a distant rattle and turned back toward Alice. He could see a plume of dust and dirt rising above the hilltop, moving toward him from the direction of Fort Hare. Relief filled him as an open-backed truck reached the top of that hill and descended toward him. Thank goodness he could get a lift.

That truck seems far too silent, Joshua immediately thought as the truck slowed to a halt in front of him, its driver having noticed Joshua's wave. It lacked the usual banter of men on the way to the fields, or the singing he'd heard from small African buses. As Joshua quickened his step toward it, he saw at least ten young men huddled against railings on the truck bed, their eyes cast to the distance. Each was draped in an ocher-dyed blanket, their bodies smeared head to toe with clay that had dried in a chalky-gray layer. Joshua smiled. The teenagers were young initiates.

The initiates kept their eyes cast away as an African man hopped from the passenger cab and approached Joshua quickly. The man wore a hole-ridden shirt and seemed coated in a thin film of dirt, as if he'd been sweating and laboring in the fields.

"*Kutheni ulapha uhleli wedwa nje mhlobam? Ibiyinqwelo yakho phaya phesheya kwendlela?*" he asked Joshua.

"*Ndimtsha kwelilizwe. Uyakwazi ukuthetha isiNgesi?*" Joshua said, letting him know he didn't speak much Xhosa. He only knew enough to get by in his sermons. "East London?" Joshua asked, motioning his hands down the road.

"The driver in this truck, he can take you to East London," the man replied, scratching his matted hair. "Sit there in the back with the young boys," he said, pointing to the truck bed.

Joshua hopped onto the truck bed, its floor swept as cleanly as any dung-smoothed courtyard. The truck lurched forward as its tires gripped back onto the asphalt. The young initiates tried to erase the smiles that edged at their lips quickly as they looked at Joshua, seeming to ponder who he was, and seeming prideful to have someone see them rubbed in their white clay, the sign that they had been circumcised and were passing from childhood. Each young man seemed to wear nothing at all underneath those blankets, their muscled arms showing clearly from beneath their blankets and the sweaty smell of their bodies wafting strong. They stared silently out into the distance, with guarded stillness, as the truck bounced up and down, the cedar of the truck bed rattling all around them.

"Nibhekaphi nonke namhlanje?" Joshua spoke some of the Xhosa he'd learned, but the initiates kept their gazes averted. They only smiled more fully when passing African buses that slowed as they approached, their drivers pressing long on their horns, honking in triumph, just like the men at the roadside who cheered as they saw the truck approaching, waving their sticks high in the air. Joshua smiled at the revelry. His eyes soon rested on a familiar face.

"Beaumont, hello there!"

Beaumont turned his eyes farther away.

The truck came to an abrupt stop as Joshua noticed the man in the passenger seat staring into the back at them through the window cut in the truck's cab. That man stepped out of the cab swiftly and marched back to the truck bed, barking orders to the young men, then climbed up to sit next to Joshua.

"These ones are not allowed to speak at all, unless we instruct them so." He chastised Joshua as the truck lurched forward, back onto the pavement.

Joshua nodded apologetically as the rattling cedar rang out again. He sat quietly for a long stretch, until the truck turned off the main road, proceeding up a winding side trail.

"Are we going to East London?" Joshua spoke over the rattling cedar.

"Soon, soon." The man waved away Joshua's concern. "We must drop these ones first."

"They're going to a village in these hills?"

The man laughed heartily. "No village is so far from the river! It's their time, these ones," he said, as if Joshua should know all of the details. "We are just coming back from the river. We are teaching these ones the ways of men. We will take them back into the hills, away from all others in the villages, to their circumcision lodge— their *iibhuma* where we will teach them about their duties and responsibilities as men and heads of their future homes. Where is it you come from, my friend?"

"The United States."

"Europe!" the man said, scratching his matted hair again.

"That general direction."

"Very far away! Welcome to our land. What brings you here?"

"I'm a minister at Fort Hare."

"Ah," he said with a glimmer in his eyes, "it is well that we have strong places to worship. Tell me, my friend, you remember your time?"

The truck came to a stop just then, and the driver stepped out, issuing orders in Xhosa like a commander to cadets as the young men filed out of the truck with twinkles in their eyes, their clay-coated bodies flashing from beneath their blankets as they hopped down from the truck. The cloud of excitement moved with them as they jogged up a trail toward several huts in the hills.

"This driver shall carry you very well to East London." The man waved Joshua into the truck's cab.

"This European does not know the rites of men!" the matted-haired man said to the driver, teasing Joshua as he waved good-bye and set off behind the initiates.

"From Europe!" the driver said with a grin as he drove down the road to East London." So how do your boys turn to men in Europe, then?"

"We don't quite have the same sort of ceremony as you."

"Eh? Only once in a life will a young boy take this step to manhood. We take them off into these hills, they stay there for six weeks or more and we will teach them to be strong, to provide for their families, to be good fathers. With the circumcision and these teachings, this marks their passage to manhood, and when they return to their villages, the community will feast—a feast fit for kings! You must join us at the *umgidi* when we celebrate the return of the initiates at the Noni Village."

Joshua could only image the reaction of his mission if he dared. But he thought about it for a moment longer. What harm would there be? "I hope to attend," Joshua responded cautiously.

Soon Joshua could see the Victorian buildings of East London's city center looming in the distance. As the driver approached the outskirts of town, they turned onto an open strip of land, a large clearing where buses clustered together and Africans crossed the dusty paths slowly. This was an area much like the one he had seen at a distance when he had first begun his drive from Port Elizabeth—the one that had brought a rueful look to Andrew's face. Joshua felt his own frown etching deeply as they drove closer to the crowds. As they stopped amid the clamor, Joshua's throat went dry. The chafing despair overwhelmed him.

Joshua stepped from the truck, thanking the driver and turning as instructed toward African taxis lined in the distance. Young boys ran up to him with large cardboard boxes hoisted on their shoulders, trying to hawk their lime green bananas, pumpkin seeds, and squat tangerines. Joshua looked at their tattered clothes and pulled coins from his pocket, choosing several tangerines. Seeing his money, other boys ran beside him, offering greens and corn. He bought small amounts from many of them, tucking the fruit and vegetables in a sack. Something in him stirred as they walked away from him with parted lips, as if wanting to know how he could afford so many purchases. His lips parted also at the look on their faces, because to them so little money seemed like so much.

As he walked among those in this land of the brokenhearted, avoiding puddles of urine and gullies of dirty water that spotted the dusty paths, his heart sank further. Only black faces lingered here. Palpable resignation curved the backs of those who walked off the African-only buses. He'd rarely seen such destitution. He moved beyond hodgepodge market stands made of cardboard and past women breast-feeding their babies as they sat on blankets at the curbside. He passed beyond beggars stained in their own bile, and as he walked through the field of buses to a line of makeshift taxis, he stepped toward the one in front with its passenger door open.

"I'm just going to meet Minister Chandler," Joshua said in a tone he barely recognized. The sights around him had shaken him.

"The Brother!"

"You know him?" Joshua asked, barely able to turn his eyes from the destitution around him.

"You will do well to know the Brother." The African driver grinned. "He is one of the great preachers of our land."

CHAPTER 16

The African taxi driver carried Joshua to a quiet neighborhood of wattle-and-daub houses with iron roofs, one of the nicest neighborhoods he'd seen in the segregated township on the outskirts of East London. Its modest houses were built close together, with tiny spaces of tended grass decorating each home. Joshua stepped onto a handwoven mat with hopeful letters scrolled high. SIBUYE, it read. He'd already learned that term, the students would use it often—"we are one."

Joshua found himself unexpectedly greeted by a woman with long brown hair that dipped into a neat ponytail over her back, faint gray traces showing here and there. Her mahogany eyes were warm and smiling as she opened the door widely, extending a lightly perfumed hand. "We've been expecting you," she said with an accent he now recognized as Afrikaner. "I'm Lydia. I will let my husband know you've arrived."

The Brother wears his black skin with pride. That's what Nongolesi had said, Joshua remembered as he recalled her words. *An African man married to an Afrikaner?* He tried not to let his surprise show as she guided him to the sitting room, moving with the carefree posture of the once-privileged, hair swaying with the confident lilt in her walk. She left to get her husband. Joshua stood near a sofa covered with a quilt made with pieces of African kente cloth, sewn together with Scottish blue cloth and fabric with a traditional Indian design. Bound together with thick threads, the collage somehow blended with the portraits on the wall—an Indian man with his child, a Scottish dancer, an African mother carrying water home for a meal.

Joshua walked over to a spinet against the wall, gazing at a picture of a twenty-years-younger Lydia on top, her hair gelled in place, falling in broad locks around her face. The photograph captured the slight curve of her lips, a window to her soul as she seemed to chuckle at the intended prim moment.

"He tells me to bring you in," Lydia whispered from the doorway. Joshua followed her to a study draped in more deep African colors and Scottish blues. The curtains were drawn tightly, two lanterns providing the only glow in the room. Intensity filled the air as Jovan hunched over a desk in the middle of the room, writing quickly in a workbook. A distinguished-looking white man, in his early fifties and dressed simply in a white shirt and gray slacks paced in the corner, gripping a watch tightly in his hand. His shoulders were rounded, his brow knit, as if he carried the weight of many battles. Joshua's eyes were drawn directly to the large cross hanging around his neck.

"Time," the pacing man said as Jovan looked up at him and moaned.

"Well?" the man asked, his eyes hopeful.

"There were two I did not understand well. We did not cover those subjects," Jovan replied.

"As we knew there would be—at least two or three subjects that we would not cover," the pacing man said with reassurance as he touched Jovan's arm lightly. "You can miss three and still pass. But we still have some time before the exam. I'll try to find other sources for you to study."

"Darling, this is Reverend Clay," Lydia said.

"Ah, do come in," the man said with a broad smile. "I'm Reverend Beaumont Chandler." He stretched a hand toward Joshua. Joshua concealed his surprise, the best he could, as the Brother looked at him with piercing eyes, as green as the most verdant grass. There was something so serious about his face, so determined, as crow's-feet fanned out from the corners of his eyes, seeming too deeply etched for a man his age, the fleshly signs of struggles waged.

"Hello, Jovan, I didn't expect to find you here," Joshua said awkwardly.

"Hello, Reverend Clay," Jovan replied, seeming equally surprised.

"We're just finishing up," Reverend Chandler said with an accent. "Jovan, I shall look this over," the Brother said, waving the workbook like a precious passport. "We should meet in three days time. I'll meet you at the bus station. Will your money hold up enough to pay for another trip?"

"Sure, I just can't have any more beer nights with the boys."

"Well then!" The Brother let out a boisterous laugh, and Lydia chuckled also. Lydia parted the curtains, letting daylight in.

"Thank you, Brother," Jovan said as he nodded to Joshua, then departed.

"I'm pleased to meet you here. We're very glad you have come to visit. Do have a seat," the Brother said, motioning Joshua to a cushioned chair that welcomed Joshua as warmly as the Brother had.

"We heard there was much ado in the attempt to get a new preacher for Fort Hare," Lydia said, standing next to the Brother as he sat across from Joshua. "Would you like some tea?"

"I don't want to put you to trouble."

"It's a pleasure," she said, leaving the room.

"So, tell me, Reverend Clay, why have you found your way here with us today?"

"Please call me Joshua."

"And you may call me Brother."

"Well, I'd like to think it's not a bad start, but turnouts at my mission's church on campus have been low. I was advised to speak with you."

"Advised by whom?"

"Old Man Maganu," Joshua said.

"Ah, yes, a man of much wise advice."

"Yes." Joshua smiled. "That he is."

"Well, I'm glad he encouraged you to come visit. So, Joshua, why were you surprised when you came in here just now?"

Joshua hesitated a moment. "I hadn't expected to see Jovan here."

"A little work, my friend, just a little work. Was that all?"

Joshua gave him an embarrassed smile, wondering if he should answer fully. "Okay, I had assumed you were African, or a Negro from America," Joshua said softly.

"Is that so?" the Brother chuckled.

"Many Xhosa refer to you as the Brother."

"That they do," he said, letting his words linger. "I'm from Scotland, actually," he said. "I've been here in South Africa for over twenty years. This is my home now."

Joshua nodded.

"So, Joshua, we are glad to find your mission has not turned away from Fort Hare. And they've sent a young minister to try to revitalize things. You weren't at all worried to replace Reverend Peter, the one who ran away?"

Joshua smiled at his words.

"You know he must have been running from something," the Brother responded to Joshua's expression.

"I hear different stories in different places."

"And what do the officials of your mission say?"

"Heathen intransigence—the students and villagers rejected him."

The Brother laughed boisterously. "Is that so?"

"What do you say?" Joshua probed.

"I say he was running from something."

"What would that be?"

"That's for you to tell me. You're out there, not I."

Lydia came in with the tea; she handed Joshua a porcelain cup, while the Brother wrapped his hands around a battered tin cup. His hands were rough and wrinkled with age that didn't quite show on his face, except for those lines of intensity etched around his eyes. Lydia sat next to the Brother, taking a sip from her cup.

"So, you've been having difficulties already?" Lydia asked, looking at him with equal curiosity.

"It's a half-filled church heading toward a third-filled," Joshua responded honestly.

"And on the first day?" the Brother asked.

"It was full."

"With students or those from the community?" the Brother probed.

"Both."

"And now?"

"Mostly the community."

"Old or young?"

"Older."

"And on meeting with the students? Did you meet with them early on?"

"On my fourth day on campus."

"Why not on the first?" the Brother asked in a stern voice.

"I was preaching."

"Why not on the second?" Lydia chimed in.

"I was meeting with the advisory committee."

"Ah—and did they know you were meeting with the advisory committee?" the Brother asked.

"Yes," Joshua said hesitantly. "They already knew when the administrators were scheduled to meet. And I also mentioned it to the students over dinner."

"Well, that could explain a large part of your problem," the Brother said, arching his eyebrows as he set his tin cup down on the table in front of him.

"It seems they've made up their minds about whom you intend to serve," Lydia agreed.

Joshua's eyes darkened. "I didn't know it was either-or."

"Now you know," Lydia said. "That's how many perceive it, anyhow."

"I know some of those activists," the Brother said in a reassuring tone. "Jovan is one. He speaks with his pen, mind you, but he and those I've met around him are not ones to prejudge others harshly. Not that I have seen. Perhaps this misunderstanding can be reversed with ease."

"It probably can if they think you're genuine." Lydia nodded.

"And how do I convince them of that?"

The Brother took a deep breath, running a hand through his thinning sandy brown hair, wisdom seeming to show with every missing hair on his head.

"Well, what exactly are you preaching about as you preach to them?"

"The basics, about the Christian principles of the need to forgive, to turn the other cheek, and a willingness to wait for change."

The Brother's eyes were dancing with something, Joshua couldn't quite tell what. It didn't seem positive. "That's an interesting choice, given the circumstances your congregation is facing—being stripped of all political rights, of their land, of their wealth."

"There are restrictions—or rather, recommendations—from my mission about what I should focus on with this congregation."

The Brother scoffed under his breath and his lips thinned. Lydia remained silent, taking another sip of tea.

"There are ways to rectify this," the Brother continued after a moment. "You're just starting up a hill, when they would have given you a chance to walk down one instead."

"And what do you advise?" Joshua asked.

"Be careful what you preach," the Brother replied.

"What do you mean?" Joshua questioned.

"Try, Joshua, to understand the needs of your congregation," the Brother said. "Open your heart and mind to them and the circumstances of their lives. Don't just give them a message sent by a missionary organization too distant to care about them."

"You think I've been making that mistake?"

"Most do," he said. "I did." There was no embarrassment in his admission. Joshua respected his candor. "I've learned quite a bit in the time I've spent here. I've learned to get to know my congregation members, to really look each in the face and see the *person,* their hopes, their fears." The Brother's voice grew fiery. "My advice to you— learn to listen. To your congregation members, yes. But most important of all, learn to listen to hear what God wants you to preach. Go where God would have you go, and be still long enough to discover God's Will." He tapped his finger on the table before him. "Be willing to follow God's Will. He will tell you what He wants you to say to His people."

Joshua flinched at the suggestion that he wasn't already following God's Will. But something inside stirred at the words, a feeling that plagued him as the Brother continued—he knew the Brother had simply voiced a concern he'd uttered to himself many times now.

"Would you like to come to my service tomorrow?" the Brother asked.

"I must preach at Fort Hare tomorrow," Joshua replied.

"Why don't we begin working on this straightaway?" the Brother suggested. "I can send one of my associate ministers to Fort Hare to preach in your place. It sounds, my dear reverend, as though they won't miss you much out there either way."

Joshua smiled faintly at his bluntness. He sensed the Brother's sincerity. He seemed to be a very trustworthy man. "Well, I can't say no then," Joshua replied, casting his pride aside.

"In the meantime," the Brother said happily, "there's someone I'd like you to meet. If you don't mind, that is. Do you have a few moments?"

"Of course."

"You'll take him to meet Nokwe and Sarah?" Lydia guessed.

"Indeed," the Brother said, gathering his sweater and bag and pecking his wife on the lips.

"I'm not certain whether Nokwe will be home at this hour," the Brother said as he set off with Joshua on foot. "But you can speak with Sarah until he returns. She's a force in her own right."

"Sarah—she is the American?"

"You've heard of her?"

"From the children at Ulundi. From the Maganus. From folks on the street in King William's Town."

The Brother laughed and nodded.

"They keep talking about her school. She's married to the famous leader Nokwe?" Joshua asked, surprised.

"The very one. Quite a man he is, to be able to gallop into your country and woo a woman of her stature. They didn't know each other long before she agreed to join him here."

Joshua could hardly imagine—a Negro American woman married to one of South Africa's most prominent leaders. He wondered what she would be like.

Joshua and the Brother conversed easily during the half-hour walk through the neighborhood. It wasn't until that moment, as he watched the Brother chatting, that he realized how distant he felt from many ministers in his own mission. He was glad to have found ministers in the country with whom he felt some kinship. First Andrew, now the Brother. The Brother seemed genuinely interested in him, asking about his family, his years at college, his journey over to Africa. He was, like everyone else, highly amused to hear the tales about Marvis and his insistent schooling of Joshua during the voyage over.

"Have you ever heard the word *sisthunzela?*" Joshua asked. He wanted to understand what the students always muttered to each other as he passed them with their Bibles open on his way to deliver his sermons. He had not felt comfortable asking anyone else.

"It translates as not dead, if I am correct," the Brother replied. "Where have you heard that?"

"Just around campus," Joshua said plainly, though he knew his face wore a different expression.

The Brother was silent for a moment, seeming to understand where Joshua might have heard it. "I suppose it might refer to a state of bondage—of someone not quite dead, yet not fully alive." The Brother inhaled, easing the awkwardness by changing the subject. "So, you've heard of Nokwe?"

"The man with an intellect like a raven and a voice of thunder," Joshua said.

"Indeed, the man is legendary! He's a worldly man—he's traveled to London to agitate for Africans. He's met men of African descent from around the world. He says now he understands this is bigger than South Africa, this struggle we are waging against racism. He envisions a world in which we all live hand in hand, all colors of man and woman, hand in hand as equals. He *is* impressive."

They strolled a few more blocks, to a tin-roofed home set a few feet from the dusty road. A honey-colored Negro woman with high cheek-bones, deeply set eyes, and thin lips opened the door with a broad smile. Her skin seemed to shine, as if she'd spent the day with her face turned to the sun, tanning it to a deeper glow. She was dressed in an African design, a necklace of bright beads strung on black twine, her hair shaved close like the local schoolgirls.

"How is East London's most beautiful principal, my dear?" the Brother stepped forward, hugging her.

"*Le ndoda ikhangelekayo iyandithuka!*" she responded with a low commanding voice.

"Ouch!" the Brother replied, looking toward Joshua. "She gets on me for referring to her as beautiful, let alone calling her 'dear.' I do it merely to get her riled up."

She laughed.

"I wanted to bring the new missionary from Fort Hare to meet you, Sarah," the Brother said, turning to Joshua. The Brother didn't seem to notice Sarah's smile disappear. "Reverend Clay, please meet Sarah Nokwe."

She offered Joshua a limp hand, her coolness keeping him speechless. The Brother didn't seem to notice that either as Sarah ushered them inside her bright, tidy home. They walked over smooth floorboards past hallway shelves covered with books—*Pilgrim's Progress,* a Xhosa Bible, two hand-sewn books labeled XHOSA FOLK TALES. They blended well with the wall decorations displaying African artifacts and hopeful paintings of African mornings, with the sun coming out of a dark place. In the far corner hung a framed newspaper clipping from a North Carolina newspaper. IS HE HUMAN? it read underneath a photo of an African man standing in chains on a slave auction block.

"Do you have time to stay for tea?" Sarah asked the Brother as Joshua's eyes paused on the clipping.

"I can't stay long, my dear; I must minister to some patients in the African hospital today, but I do hope you have a few minutes for Reverend Clay."

"Have a seat," she pointed the men to a sofa. Sarah gathered the papers strewn across the coffee table in the middle of the sitting room, tying them with a piece of twine, misty-eyed, as if rolling up a dream for a short while. "Just reviewing the plans for our school's expansion." She smiled as the Brother looked at her curiously.

"You received the money from America?" the Brother asked.

"Indeed!"

"My dear!" He hugged her. "You do work miracles." Joshua could hear the depth of his happiness.

"Thank you for helping us write the proposals." She touched his arm as they both took a seat.

Sarah's manners spoke of a privileged upbringing that few Negroes had known. Joshua had not known what to expect, but he was impressed. Her presence could fill a room. She had a sharp mind and a piercing gaze—Joshua could see why Nokwe would have been moved by her. The three of them talked on for a little while about the expansion of her independent secondary school. The Brother soon excused himself, preparing to leave.

He held each of Sarah's hands in his, like cherished gifts, kissing her good-bye. Joshua noted as Sarah walked to the door the picture on her mantel, showing her in front of a college sign in cap and gown, her long hair falling softly as grass down her back. When she returned and took her seat, a chill filled the air again.

"So, you hope to speak with my husband to discuss your experiences at Fort Hare?" Sarah asked without a hint of enthusiasm.

Her tone made him hesitate, but he gave her a brief explanation of the difficulties he'd encountered. She listened, looking more at her teacup than at him, her lips tensing up. She finally looked directly at him, tilting her chin upward, inhaling slightly as if trying to soften the words to come. "Do you hate them because they are African?"

Joshua's mouth dropped. He replayed her words through his mind a second time. From her expression, he knew he hadn't misunderstood. Sarah set down the half-eaten cookie in her hand. His silence only made her more mad.

"Let me ask it another way," she said, her anger out of proportion to whatever impression he might have already made. "Do you *despise* your congregation members? Does it offend you when you see African women walking barefoot with babies tied to their backs; do you flinch when you see African men in their hide skirts; do you cringe at the thought of their *amasi,* that soured milk? Do you hate them because their traditions are different from ours?"

Her words stung. Joshua squinted his eyes.

"Either you hate them because they are different, or you *respect* them. I am not hearing that you respect them."

"Reverend Clay!" a voice called out. Joshua couldn't have been happier for the interruption as Nokwe came gliding through the front door. "I ran into the Brother a short while ago; he said you'd come to visit." Nokwe smiled broadly as Joshua rose to exchange greetings.

"You will stay with us tonight, then?" Nokwe asked, sitting down with them.

"I'm afraid I can't," Joshua said, knowing Sarah had probably just winced at the offer. He didn't dare glance toward her. "My car is sitting halfway up the road to King William's Town with a flat tire. I should be leaving quite soon to retrieve it. I was told I could fetch a spare tire in the city. But I hope I will be able to meet and speak with you at greater length sometime soon."

"We will certainly arrange that," he said earnestly. "We're sorry you can't stay much longer, but you'll be joining us for church with the Brother in the morning?"

"I look forward to it."

"And for supper tomorrow evening?" he asked, raising his eyebrows in an invitation. Joshua felt wrapped up by Nokwe's sunny smile. He was everything Joshua had imagined from the descriptions he'd read in African newspapers—a handsome, energetic, sharply dressed man, with bright eyes and flawless dark skin. Everything about him seemed so sure and confident, the sign of a natural leader.

"Our home is always open," Nokwe said as Sarah stood wordlessly, collecting some cups and saucers from the far end of the low table.

"Let me help clear the dishes," Joshua said, surprising himself. Sarah's hostility had left him ridden with a feeling that he didn't want to linger.

A slight chuckle escaped Sarah's lips as she looked at Nokwe's expression. "He's an American, darling—it's permissible." She turned to Joshua with a smile for the first time. "A man helping with the dishes isn't quite standard within Xhosa culture," she teased. "I'm still working on my husband."

They all shared a laugh, and Joshua followed Sarah into the kitchen with a handful of dishes, setting them gently onto the counter. Sarah kept her eyes fixed on rinsing the dishes in the tin bin on the kitchen table.

"I'm sorry if I offended you, Sarah," Joshua said, his heart continuing to sink as she looked at him, lips pursed. She was the first Negro he'd met here. Of all the people with whom he should have felt a kinship, she should have been the one. They were talking to each other as two who shared a common past and a common culture.

"Your question took me by surprise," he said as an apology.

She looked back at him with such angry eyes.

"I have met many missionaries," she said slowly, "white *and*

Negro." Her breath lingered on the words. "They come here to try to 'civilize' Africans. And what does civilize mean to you, Reverend Clay? They've done such a job on you, and you don't even know it. You look at Africans here and you see what they want you to see. You act here the way they want because you don't even try to think for yourself."

"I can't understand your attitude or these questions," he said, his voice rising a pitch.

"Why aren't you with the AMEs?"

"Because I'm not a member of the African Methodist Episcopalian denomination."

"The AME church, in my experience, produces the only Negro missionaries who come here with their heads clear. Are you saying you support their aims, but you're just not in their denomination?"

His temper was beginning to stir. "You know I attended Wilberforce, so of course I support their general aims; but I'm also saying I haven't taken the time to assess their aims as missionaries because I'm not a member of their church."

"Strong schools, economic independence, control of their communities, full equality—that's what they stand for. And what does your mission stand for?"

"My mission is here to spread God's Word, nothing else. We're not here to take political stances."

She laughed, shaking her head. "That's not possible! By your very presence in this country and your choice not to support the battle for freedom, you *are* taking a stance." She took in a frustrated breath, wiping her hands on a kitchen rag. "Negroes who participate in organizations like yours are usually worse than the whites in such organizations. You come here filled with so much shame about your own blackness, hoping to help erase and blot out the root of it, and all you do is cause a great deal of hardship to the Africans of this country in the process." She set the rag down, pausing for a while, seeming to wonder if she should say more. She shook her head, turning toward the kitchen door. "I'm sure my husband is wondering what is taking so long," she said, moving back into the sitting room.

CHAPTER 17

"What makes you so confident?" the Brother's voice peaked as he walked down the aisle between the pews, speaking directly to his congregation. "What makes you feel entitled to dignity, to respect? I know what you should say. Say 'I am because I AM.'"

Even the hair on his head refused to be harnessed. It bounced up and down with every nod as he paced up and down the front of the church, standing on the same plane as the church members, who sat squeezed together as the church brimmed over wall to wall. The symbols of their purpose surrounded them—African cloths hung on the walls, runners stitched with Indian weave, adornments with English designs. The congregation had welcomed each other at the start of service with hearty handshakes, and they had stretched their hands to Joshua with equal warmth. Joshua relished the sight as the Brother's associates—one white, one African, one Indian, each bearing a cross—led the opening prayer. The congregation stood, hand in hand, as they said the soulful prayer. Then they spent an hour in joyous song, energized, rattling pebbles within hollowed gourds echoing off the four walls. Some congregation members tapped their palms freely against the taut skin of tambourines, jingling the slender discs in their slots. Others clapped their hands or stomped their feet, the whole congregation swaying to the rhythm of the music.

The Brother stepped backward and forward as he spoke, excited to preach. He stood in front of a sign bearing the words of Galatians: THERE IS NEITHER JEW NOR GENTILE . . . FOR YE ARE ALL ONE IN CHRIST JESUS. He paced again the length of the modest church, to another sign that seemed to bear the same words in Xhosa.

"You want to know the source of my strength, the foundation I stand on, why I am so certain I deserve dignity, equality, respect? If anyone asks you, say, 'I AM made me, so I am! I can turn to the pages; I can point to the words,'" the Brother said, pointing to Exodus 3 as he shook the Bible in his hand.

"The Lord said if they want to know my name, tell them my name is I AM. Tell them I AM sent you. He told Moses, I've read the words— meant for the Gentiles, meant for the Jews. *Akusekho mYuda namGrike; akusekho khoboka nakhululekileyo; akusekho ndoda nankazana; kuba nina nonke nimutu mnye, nikuKristu Yesu. We are One in the Spirit. We are One in the Lord.* I have felt the Spirit. If you want to know why I'm so certain, I say I am because I AM. And because I AM, I am. I AM! So I am because I AM, so I am!"

Even Joshua couldn't help laughing along with the congregation as the Brother continued repeating the phrases. "This one is crazy with the truth!" he heard a woman in the choir say between her laughter. It was impossible not to be caught up in the Brother's passion. Seeing him move his congregation like this made Joshua's thoughts drift back in time. There had been a time when he moved congregations like this too, back in America. There had been a day when Joshua felt God flowing through him, using his words to touch others. Memories unspooled through his mind. His face dipped into a frown as he asked himself what had changed. He didn't like the thoughts that flitted through his mind. The words of the Brother drew his attention again.

"In the face of every insult. In the heat of every fight," the Brother went on, "With the Bible, you stand on the Word of God. Proclaim it out loud: 'I am because I AM!'"

After church, Joshua traveled back to Sarah's home, to enjoy a flavorful meal. It was a pleasure to be in the company of Nokwe. The Brother had described him well, when he called Nokwe a visionary leader. Among the things that impressed Joshua was Nokwe's vision of

creating a South Africa in which the cultures of all groups are cele-
brated. Sarah barely exchanged a glance toward Joshua, but she didn't
object when Nokwe invited him to stay after dinner with the others,
to sip tea and chat leisurely in the sitting room.

"You've had quite a day," Nokwe said with a soft smile to Joshua
as he studied him from across the room. "Now you see, the Brother can
preach! People come from far away to hear him. He's considered one
of the best preachers in the eastern Cape. And his church—he started
it in a small vacant room in an Indian shopkeeper's building."

Lydia smiled as she joined the two of them, having overheard
Nokwe's comment. "When Beaumont left his mission, they predicted
he would flounder. If they could have, they would have shipped him
out of the country by now," Lydia said. "But he knew how the system
works. He'd been here long enough, so he changed his citizenship
before he broke from his mission. As a British citizen, he was entitled
to stay, and plus he was married to me by then."

"So from this little room, his church grew," Nokwe said, sitting
back in his chair.

"And grew and grew!" Sarah joined in, sitting next to Lydia on the
longest couch, the two holding hands like schoolgirls. "People
donated all of the materials to build that church we sat in this morning. Even now, it bursts at the seams."

"I'm so proud of my husband—I can barely hide it." Lydia beamed.
"Oh, I've shamed my family. First, in not mourning the dissolution of
my first marriage. Then for the decision to marry this heretic. But I
have never once regretted following Beaumont to fight for the right
things. Can you believe when he first began, they called it Beaumont's
Folly?" Lydia added. "They said he'd never gain more than ten people
to attend his church, with its message of unity."

"And now, every week they attend—people of every background,
the rainbow children of God hearing about the love of God. They love
the message," Nokwe said.

"And they love the messenger," Sarah added. "The Word is burning in his soul."

"It's a sight to behold—black and white, yellow and red—hand in
hand. Whenever I get weary," Nokwe said, squeezing his eyes tightly,

"it takes only one more trip to the Brother's church, and I remember what it is I fight so hard for."

Sarah passed tea around, pouring it as a sweet chamomile smell drifted forth. The Brother took a seat near Joshua's chair.

"We must toast." Nokwe raised his teacup as if it were a wineglass. "To old friends, and to *new* friends," he said, smiling toward Joshua.

They raised their cups and each took a sip.

Somehow, oddly, Joshua felt a comfort in this company that he had not yet experienced with any member of his mission. Except for Andrew, that is. Joshua relished the evening, enjoying hours of political and cultural discussions, feeling as if he were among old friends.

"So tell us, Joshua," Nokwe asked, "are you as committed to the cause of Negro liberation as Sarah?"

He seemed to use the word *Negro* to refer to both Americans and Africans. Joshua nodded, not certain what sort of response he should give.

Nokwe looked toward his wife. "Did you tell Joshua how we met, Sarah and I?"

"This gallant man," Sarah said, smiling at Nokwe, "we met across the sea, you know. I thought it very odd, at first, that this African man had journeyed to the United States to find a wife. But then, they explained it to me, how Negro political leaders in America were assisting him in his fight in South Africa with funds and advice. Nokwe believed it was important to have a Negro American for a wife, one who by her experiences could understand the black struggle in its fullness, understand that this struggle crosses many seas.

"Some highly regarded friends told me about Nokwe and tried to convince me I'd be his perfect wife. A wife!" She laughed. "And to a man I'd never met before. I was nearly thirty and I had no intention of marrying. I loved Africa from the books I had read, the people I had met. But the thought of leaving America . . ." Her voice drifted. "But then I met Nokwe, chatted with him over dinner, attended his political talks, and I was impressed. It was spring, change was in the air." She crossed her arms and rocked a bit with the sweetness of the memory. "And before he left New York, he proposed. His vision of the future, of the possibilities—it moved me. His description of the needs of his people—our people now—the education they needed, what I could bring . . ." She took in a deep breath, as if reliving the weight of the decision she made. "He seemed so confident I'd respond soon, and respond well." She smirked at him as he smiled.

"They're very related, you know," Nokwe said to Joshua. "The two struggles, I mean. What you are fighting for in America, what we are fighting for here, it's the same."

Joshua didn't respond. He didn't need to. The Brother chimed in, speaking about the Bible, and its support of liberation. Joshua's thoughts wandered then as he observed everyone in the room. He felt so honored in their presence; the causes they were fighting for were so noble. He had such a strange feeling, one that told him he was at home among them; with them, he felt a kinship. He took in a deep breath with that thought, sensing it was a feeling that would linger on.

———

Joshua took a moment to rest from proofreading some of the pages he had set firmly in typed letters earlier that week at the Ulundi School. The papers were almost ready to be bound into a book. Nongolesi was right—the history of the Xhosas was rich and deep. The more he helped the school to record the histories, the more he appreciated the effort of the school to pass that history on. He sat back farther in his chair in the Maganu's living room, the lantern flickering low. Mama Siziwe filled it with more paraffin. He was so happy that the Old Man continued to extend invitations for him to join them. The Maganus felt like his family away from home. That notion made him chuckle to himself as he remembered the Old Man's words that first day they'd met. *You turned out well.* The memory brought laughter to Joshua's eyes.

As the Old Man chatted with Nongolesi, Joshua's thoughts drifted to the letter he'd read that morning from his family. Every time a letter from them arrived, his heart lifted. He missed them more than he could say. He had been glad to hear that things were still going smoothly at work for them amid the turbulent economic times. He was also surprised to read their response to his last letter. They said they wished they could be with him in Africa to see all of the new sights he'd described—quite a change from their worries before he'd left America. They'd even written that several of the traditions he'd described were ones they'd grown up with—the soured milk, the roasting of corn. That made him smile. When they raved on about how many resources their home church had received from Joshua's mission, in honor of Joshua's service, he'd set the letter down for a moment, inhaling deeply. Five months since he'd arrived, and things weren't going well for him at Fort Hare—church attendance was still dwindling. What if he failed and had to return to the U.S. early? The flow of those resources to his home church would end. For a few moments, he couldn't get that thought from his mind.

"We are going to have some mealies outside, if you like," Nongolesi said.

Mhlobo and Ogenga had joined the family for this Sunday meal. Joshua was happy to see Mhlobo again for the first time since Christmas Day nearly three months earlier. Their conversation might have been sour then, but Joshua still hoped to get to know him better. Joshua followed Mhlobo and Ogenga outside, helping them place logs into the hearth as Ogenga set them afire underneath a metal grate. Hounds called their attention to the *ebuhlanti*. Ogenga and Mhlobo went to ensure there wasn't any trouble, leaving Joshua and Nongolesi alone for a moment.

"Thank you for encouraging me to meet the Brother," Joshua said, as he sat back in a thong chair. "I finally met him."

Nongolesi smiled. "He is greatly admired—you can see why?"

"I can see why." Joshua smiled. "His church is inspirational, the way he draws people from all backgrounds. It was exhilarating to be there." He looked away for a moment. "It was a little troubling also."

"Why?"

Nongolesi sounded so concerned. Joshua realized again how much he appreciated her support.

"Because the more I have preached here at Fort Hare, the more it bothers me knowing some of the policies my mission supports, like their stance on the distribution of marula Bibles." He spoke softly, almost as if afraid for anyone else to hear. "The whole point of my being here is to bring people to Christ. And how can I do that if they can't read His words?" He shook his head. "I suppose my role can also be to try to persuade my mission to adopt better policies where the policies need improvement."

"You'll find your way," Nongolesi assured him. She looked at him with such certainty and such deep emotion, it fortified him.

"I must thank you also," she said softly.

"For what?" Joshua smiled as he gathered his sweater around him in the fall chill. In a month or so, winter would begin in earnest, and it would be too cool to sit out at night and chat, so Joshua tried to enjoy the evening.

"Thank you for being willing to come and help us at Ulundi," Nongolesi responded. "Your presence means more than you can know." Her facial expression moved him. He had grown closer to her in the last few weeks. She always knew what to say to strengthen his determination to keep trying at Fort Hare, and to make him feel his work at the Ulundi school made a difference. And she was so supportive of his ministry. He'd never met a woman who moved him as she did. He narrowed his eyes, trying to blot out what he was feeling in that moment, reminding himself she was a member of his congregation.

"The children are wonderful," Joshua replied. "The work you are doing there is very important. Every moment I've spent at Ulundi has been a pure pleasure." He smiled. "I'm just glad to be of use. It's still rather discouraging at Fort Hare, but I'm giving it time. My family commented on how I seemed so happy in my last letter to them."

She beamed. "When you speak of them I can see you miss your family. One day, you will not need to leave your family, because you will be the head of it. They will go where you go."

Joshua smiled at the words. "And you, why are you not married?" He chastised himself the moment he'd said the words. Curiosity had gotten the best of him.

"You've been talking to my father. He's been complaining again."

Joshua chuckled at her tone. "No, no, I just wondered."

"Men know not to come too close." She chuckled. Then her tone grew serious. "They know I will signal a man when I am ready. I was ready once, though, long ago. When I was five."

"Five?" He chuckled.

"Yes, and I let a little boy from another village kiss me. Right on the lips."

"But you didn't marry him?" Joshua joked.

"Baba saw and had the boy's father whip him with a thin stick, and

I was confined to our *indlu* for a week." She laughed. "Both Baba and the Old Man were very concerned, thinking I would grow to be too friendly toward men. Now the Old Man thinks they were too hard on me back then, and that is the reason I have not married. At least, that is the reason he points to *this* week."

"And what was it last week?" Joshua laughed at her tone.

"I went to Lovedale and that high school ruined my respect for womanly duties."

Her facial demeanor made him laugh harder. "What was it the week before that?"

"That week, he said he should have taught me greater obedience in the home so I would have learned to be more dutiful to a man. There are many reasons he invents why I have not married. Always he thinks of a new one. Every week, another new one."

"So the boy who kissed you, he is the only one you would have married?"

"I wouldn't have married him; I just liked that one little kiss," she joked. Then she answered seriously. "I shall marry when I meet the right man."

"And what will the right man be like?"

"I will know him when I meet him."

He pondered his feelings for a moment. For some reason, her answer disappointed him. He didn't know why.

"I suppose I think the same thing—I'll know when I meet her," he said softly, talking more to himself than to her. "She'll be a strong Christian who believes in serving God and in building a home that honors God. She'll be warm, someone who takes pride in Negro accomplishments, but who can also see beauty in people of all races." His lips froze for a moment, the words seeming to sit in the air. He knew who that sounded like. He could paint her face in bright colors on a canvas, with finely plaited hair, gentle slanted eyes, deep ebony skin, and a dimple in her right cheek. The thought startled him, his heart growing full at the same time. Nongolesi shifted her eyes to the distance; Joshua couldn't see her expression. Relief floated over him as Ogenga and Mhlobo moved back toward them from the *ebuhlanti*. He was glad for the interruption. But Joshua felt unnerved as he noted Mhlobo's angered expression, which was focused squarely on him.

CHAPTER 18

The pencil in Joshua's hand touched the paper almost of its own accord the next day as he jotted a few ideas down on a blank page, but he found it increasingly difficult to mold his sermons the way his mission wanted. He leaned over his desk, looking out the window of his home, seeing more clusters of new freshers traipsing across the campus, their strides telling him they were even more fiery than the students of the year before. The tempo of change filled the air, building toward a crescendo—one that would bring about what? Joshua didn't know, but he sensed it wouldn't be good.

He looked back at the paper, stroking a dull blade gently, freeing more of the pencil's lead tip, the wood shards curling in tight swirls. He prodded himself to cross out words that seemed too bold, pausing, reading, and shaving the wood pencils again. An urgent knock on the front door startled him.

"What is it?" he asked as he opened the door, alarmed by the steady pounding. Mhlobo moved right past Joshua on all fours. Ogenga followed apologetically a few steps behind.

"We have come to see you," Mhlobo said in a thick voice, moving straight past Joshua to his living room.

"Is something wrong?" Joshua asked, taken aback by his tone.

"We have come to have words with you," Mhlobo repeated more sharply.

Joshua couldn't speak for a moment. He glanced at Ogenga, who stood silent next to his older brother.

"Please sit and let me get some tea for you," Joshua said.

"We have not come to share tea," Mhlobo said, sounding as if the offer were an insult. "We demand that you end the insults directed on our home."

A hundred thoughts fluttered through Joshua's mind; he tried to discern what Mhlobo could be referring to. He looked back blankly. "If I've done something—"

Mhlobo moved deftly onto the couch, and Ogenga sat beside him quietly. "We have seen that you have eyes for Nongolesi," Mhlobo said.

Joshua's lips parted.

"Has my father not opened his home to you, killed his fattest chicken from the yard, offered you the finest foods from our home?"

"Yes, of course he has," Joshua said, his brow knit, barely able to gather his words before Mhlobo waved his hand in the air, hushing him.

"Has he not offered you milk from the finest cow, provided a place for you to rest at night? And you, in turn, have disrespected our family, brought shame upon our house."

It took a moment for Joshua to realize his mouth now hung open. He recovered enough to take a seat across from Mhlobo. "What have I done?" he asked, trying to make Mhlobo understand his earnestness.

Mhlobo perched himself up farther on the sofa, sitting up so straight that even though his lower legs dangled lifelessly, he held a posture that made it clear only his legs had been crippled. "We see the way you look at Nongolesi," he said, breathing deep. "We are told by the teachers at the Ulundi School that you arrive early to the school to speak with her. You take her to sit and talk in the open—in view of the schoolchildren."

Joshua's voice splintered. "I've enjoyed speaking with Nongolesi, just like I've enjoyed getting to know you and learning about your experiences."

"You stroke her cheeks."

"She was crying!" Joshua said, remembering the one time he'd wiped the tears flowing down Nongolesi's cheeks.

"I find no joke here," Mhlobo seethed.

"One of the men of the villages had been killed in the mines," Joshua explained. "I stroked her cheek to wipe her tears away, that was all."

"You dishonor our family," Mhlobo said so lowly, Joshua's heart sank. "This must end."

"You are not to go off alone with Nongolesi at the school," Ogenga said gently, trying to soften Mhlobo's words. "If we hear you've done that again, the family will send someone again."

"And you are not welcome to enter into our home," Mhlobo added, words that stabbed at Joshua's heart. "Until you return with an offer of *lobola*, you should not journey back to our home."

Joshua steadied his thoughts. It took a moment for him to gather his words. "You know I'm grateful for the warmth your family has shown me," Joshua said. "I had thought over these months I had come to know both of you somewhat. I had thought you would realize I am just learning your customs. If you have come to know me even a small bit, you know I never intended to insult a family that has been so kind to me and has opened its doors to me from the first moments I arrived here." Joshua knew the hurt rang in his voice.

"You are not to enter our home again until you intend to negotiate the *lobola*," Mhlobo said firmly, as if Joshua hadn't said a word. Mhlobo moved swiftly from the couch. Ogenga closed the door behind them as they left.

Joshua hadn't felt such a wind of coldness in his home since arriving. He felt so empty as he sat alone remembering his stroke of Nongolesi's cheek—on the day they'd both sat beneath the shade of the berry tree, sipping the tea she'd prepared for them. He recalled their talks at school, their time chatting in the teachers' lounge. He hadn't realized that behavior was seen as disrespectful. He brushed his hand over his brow, exhaling to relieve his frustration. He sat by himself for nearly half an hour, barely recomposing himself before another knock pounded on his front door. A dark chuckle escaped from his throat as he prepared to greet Mhlobo again.

He opened the door, caught unaware as Tahira stood before him, shoulders shuddering with her sobs, her face streaked with tears.

"Tahira"—he reached for her arm as she steadied a large basket with a few disheveled clothes thrown inside.

"Sorry to disturb you again, Reverend." Ogenga's voice drew Joshua's eyes a few feet away, where he gathered items that had fallen, placing them back in Tahira's basket. An apology was written across Ogenga's face as he gazed at Joshua. Was that guilt about what had just happened with Mhlobo, or about returning so soon after their sour exchange, Joshua wondered.

"I ran into her on my way back to the village," Ogenga said. "She was rather upset and said she was due to meet you later. I thought I should bring her here."

"Please come in, sit down." Joshua touched Tahira's arm, but she barely moved as sobs formed deep in her throat.

Ogenga prodded her to the couch. "They've taken them to Nocno," she managed to say, her eyes fixed on Joshua. *"Baza kubab-ulala etolongweni,"* she said more frenetically.

Joshua pulled his chair closer to her and touched her hand.

"What is she saying?" Joshua asked Ogenga.

"The women of Noni Village needed thread to sew the wedding cloak for one of the young ladies. They sent another young lady into town to the general store to fetch it, and she was arrested, taken to the King William's Town jail for breaking the pass laws as she didn't have her pass papers with her. Three of the old ladies marched down to that same store, tearing their pass papers right in front of its owner! Mr. Donovan called the police and the three old ladies were arrested on their way back to their bus stop. They pulled them, screaming, into a police car—many people saw it. They even beat one with a baton."

"The police beat an elderly woman?"

"That is what is being said in every homestead from here to King William's Town. They let the young lady go, but the women have been taken to Nocno, the jailhouse. There is no one to speak on their behalf to get them out. We are trying to reach Nokwe in East London."

"What can I do?" Joshua asked as he handed Tahira a handker-chief.

"Go to Nocno. Plead as Nokwe would," Ogenga said a little too quickly.

Words got caught in Joshua's throat as he shook his head. "Ogenga! You make these suggestions—you know I can't do that."

"These are old ladies! They did nothing wrong," he pleaded. "They are frightened, and whole villages are outraged. When the young boys return from school later, do you think they will just hear and do nothing? Just see what sort of eruption there will be then. All you must do is go and ask for their release. You're a preacher; they will listen."

A silence drifted among them. Tahira didn't move her eyes from Joshua. The handkerchief sat still in her hands, her tears flowing freely down her cheeks. Joshua lowered his eyes, sighing audibly.

"Tahira"—Joshua asked her to understand—"as a minister with my mission, I'm not supposed to do anything political."

Tahira twisted the handkerchief in her hands, her tears stream-ing more quickly. Joshua took the handkerchief from her hands, wiping the rivulets from her cheeks.

"We only ask that you go and make the request. If they say no, just leave. At least you tried. It can make a big difference in what happens next," Ogenga pleaded again.

Joshua clenched his jaw, angered by the situation Ogenga had placed him in. He closed his eyes, feeling a pulsing in his throat as he said the words: "I'll go." He was too incensed to say anything else.

Joshua gathered his coat and walked briskly toward his car, his anger trailing in the air as Ogenga skipped to catch up to him.

"How do I get to Nocno from here?" Joshua asked, temper flar-ing.

"It will be difficult for you to find the jailhouse if you don't know the way."

"Ogenga!" Joshua said, astonished at his boldness.

"I promise to stay in the car," Ogenga said with a stone face. "You will not find it unless I show you," Ogenga said again. Against his better judgment, Joshua let him come along.

The afternoon was filled with thick, dark-bellied clouds, reflecting the mood of all around them, as if the sky would soon weep. "I thought there was a jailhouse in King William's Town," Joshua said after they got on the open road toward East London.

"There is, a smaller jail. By taking the old ladies to the big jailhouse in East London, they're trying to make a point. Nocno is a harder place to be."

Joshua shook his head. "Why do you call it that?"

"Can you hear the sound?" Ogenga enunciated it again as they drove down the hilly path. "*Noc-no.* It is the sound the sickles make as the prisoners are put to forced labor all hours of the day and night. It is a sort of hell, that place. Many die at Nocno—they're found hanging by rafters, but no one believes they have taken their own lives. Tahira thinks maybe you can get the women out before they are killed."

Joshua's eyes were wide as he looked at Ogenga, knowing he was quite serious. As they reached the outskirts of East London, Ogenga guided Joshua down a fork in the road, where they soon faced stretches of open land—a desolate land with hardly a plant as far as he could see. As the paved road came to an end, Joshua saw a large brick building a distance away, at the edge of a cliff facing East London. Cranes, tractors, and dump trucks surrounded it.

"Stay here," Joshua said as he slowed his car a distance away from five police cars parked at the wire gate entrance. One lone officer sat in the open door of a patrol car. He stood up as Joshua's car approached.

"You said you'd stay here," Joshua said. Ogenga nodded, sulking in the passenger seat. Joshua moved toward the officer with his travel papers in hand, shoulders squared, not flinching as the officer moved toward him.

"I'm Reverend Clay from Fort Hare," Joshua said.

"You don't look like any reverend I know," the officer said, ignoring Joshua's extended hand.

"Would you like to see my papers?"

He didn't respond as he took the papers from Joshua's hand.

"I'm here to secure the release of a few women who were taken into custody this morning near Alice."

The officer scoffed under his breath, stepping back to the building toward a guard holding a rifle in the compound doorway, exchanging a few words. The entrance guard disappeared into the building, leaving the first guard standing near the doorway, arms crossed, drawing a circle in the sand with his toe. Joshua pulled his coat more closely around him in the cold wind. Trying to avoid more trouble, Joshua kept his distance, listening to the tractors rattling as they moved rubble across the compound. The long wait made Joshua's temper begin to simmer as his heart raced at the same time; he wondered what they were up to. He wet his throat. The first officer finally moved toward Joshua having received instructions.

"We're making sure there's plenty of room," that officer said, nodding toward the cranes as he walked straight past Joshua, handcuffs jingling. He muttered over his shoulder, "You can go in now."

They weren't going to provoke him, Joshua told himself as he walked up the steps toward a slender man in a dark suit who stepped into the complex's door.

"I'm Reverend Clay from Fort Hare," Joshua greeted him, his chin held firm.

"I'm Warden Johnson," he said, smoking a cigar. "Who is that *kaffir* you have out there?" He nodded toward Ogenga.

"The *young man*," Joshua said, "is a student from Fort Hare. He simply showed me the way here."

The warden's eyes grew larger, taking Joshua's words as a challenge. "You better make sure that *kaffir* stays put," he said.

"Ogenga has already assured me he will."

"Sit," the warden said, pointing to a chair in the hall as he moved inside, leaning against the wall. He squashed the bud of his cigar, pulling another from his pocket, cutting and lighting it. "So, you're here to pick up those three old *kaffirs*."

"I am here for the three elderly African women you brought here this morning for protesting peacefully."

"For disturbing the peace," the warden said in a biting tone. "Haven't you heard, Mr.—"

"Reverend Clay."

"That's right, a preacher." He laughed, squinting his eyes. "They haven't learned their lessons yet, have they? And where is that accent from, Reverend Clay?"

"The United States," Joshua said.

"Well, you'll do well to learn that in our country, breaking pass laws—trespassing in the white city where *kaffirs* aren't allowed unless we've given them special permission—is a crime. They will be punished. And tearing pass papers is not going to be tolerated."

"Each of those women is old enough to be my grandmother," Joshua said gently. "One of them has been very sick recently."

"Yes, they are quite old. Only a little life left in them, I'd say. I wouldn't think a wise man would find it worth the bother to come fetch them."

The words began to stir Joshua's anger. "I'm here to see to their safe return. All of the villages from Alice to ten miles away have heard about this—they are aware the women were brought to Nocno. You've made your point. It's not in anyone's interest for this to flare up."

The warden sucked on his cigar and blew the smoke toward Joshua's face. "You're brazen, Reverend Clay."

He took his time, puffing on his cigar, looking down the hallway as a line of African men were led, handcuffed, and heads bowed as they walked single file to a room in the back. "Come," the warden said, bright-eyed, as if he'd just had a great idea, "let me show you our illustrious East London jail."

Joshua didn't move.

"Would you like to leave with your *kaffirs*?"

Joshua rose and followed. The warden led him through two sets of metal gates, each clanking shut behind them as two guards stood on either side, rifles in hand, with stony expressions. They entered the room where the single file of African men now stood naked, backs turned to the wall, standing over clothes puddled at their feet. The prisoners steeled themselves against the shouts of officers, stiffening their shoulders to absorb the brunt of the batons swiped at them. The warden, seeming to enjoy the expression on Joshua's face, moved down the hall, waving for Joshua to follow.

The warden walked with a certain taunt in the motion of his legs;

Joshua asked himself how much of this he would tolerate. They moved down a hallway with thick steel doors flanking each side. When the first hallway gave way to a second strip, the warden pulled out a chain of keys and touched them to the long bars of the doors, one after another as he continued down the corridor, calling out perverted tones. The sounds sent a chill through Joshua as his thoughts drifted back to Lucius's haunting details about the rattling sounds of chains during slave voyages to America.

"The sound is music to my ears!" the warden said, chuckling over his shoulder.

At the end of that corridor, the warden opened a door onto a space large enough to be a classroom. "Our chapel," he said. A large cross hung directly across from them, and curved rows of folding chairs were dispersed evenly throughout the room. "Your mission has paid for this, if yours is the one of Reverend Waldron. Your excess donations provide us with chairs for the strip-down rooms, desks for our junior wardens."

"Mr. Johnson, this has been enough."

"Just one more stop," the warden said over his shoulder.

Joshua reluctantly followed him into an open courtyard made of cracked cement.

"Look at these glorious grounds," he said, waving at the courtyard that opened onto a cliff, with a view of East London in the distance. "We are expanding, growing. Soon we will be able to accommodate many more of the *kaffirs*. Life terms will pose no problem. But then again, many of them will never live out a life term. Many of them go mad in here, you see. They beat their heads against walls, hang themselves from rafters. It's a pity, really," he said as he tossed his cigar to the ground, squelching it with a turn of his shoe. "Come round this way, this is the best part."

At the far side of the courtyard, tucked behind a wall, were rows of African men dressed in khaki shorts and caps, the clothes of little boys. They knelt on scraped knees before metal bins on the ground, their assigned numbers printed on their breast pockets. The silence was striking as officers walked behind them, looking over their shoulders as they, like the men of the Ulundi School, spooned a cement mixture into brick molds. They met Joshua's gaze when the guards weren't looking. In those moments, Joshua understood so clearly the beliefs and views and conviction of the students he had come to know at Fort Hare. All Joshua saw as he looked at these men were the fathers who should have been rocking their children to sleep, the sons whose mothers wept for them at night, students who should have been at Fort Hare, and men too elderly to harm anyone. He glanced to a group of Indian men farther off, dressed in long pants with no caps, laboring in the same way.

"These are our enablers." The warden smiled. "They're helping us to expand. The most efficient system uses cheap labor, and as you know, the cheapest labor is free."

Joshua felt his whole body run cold. He wasn't sure if the warden knew the particular chord those words struck.

"It's ingenious. They make the bricks for us to use; we're able to bring in more of their friends. Or do they refer to them as their *brothers?*"

Joshua felt heat rushing to his cheeks.

"The civilized don't want to mingle with the heathen. *Kaffirs* have no place here in our country, except the place we assign to them. As an educated man, who sees the logic and the ease of expansion, I trust you will teach the *kaffirs* in your congregation to behave." He turned to a guard. "Show the kind reverend the three *kaffir* women we herded in this morning. I trust they've had time to glance out and wave hello to their sons and husbands."

Joshua could feel redness in his eyes as he signed the paperwork for the three women. They came out, walking slowly with age, and sat on a bench. Dressed in simple dresses and turbans around their hair, they held their chins high. Joshua touched each of their hands, and simply said, *"Izinto zizawulunga,"* telling them things would be okay. Even though they steeled their chins, he saw the fear they tried to hide in their eyes. Something close to hatred shone in his eyes as he turned toward the overseer's desk to finish the paperwork for their release.

Joshua walked ahead of the ladies back to his car. The three women crowded in the back, in spite of Ogenga's urgings that one of them could sit in front. Joshua walked past the car and kept his face turned to the distance. Something inside made him feel ashamed and angry and sick. He didn't try to mute those feelings. They pierced

every part of his soul, thoughts that would not go away: Everything
the warden had said was true. He knew in his heart, those were
words of truth—funds from his mission supported this jailhouse.

He could sense Ogenga peering from the open passenger door,
waiting for him to return. After a few minutes, Joshua slipped back
into the driver's side. He kept his eyes to the distance for a while, his
disappointment so great in his own mission that he feared the
expression showing on his face. He finally glanced back at the three
women, to assure them they would be going home now. They
huddled closely together, holding hands in a chain that would not be
broken. Their chins remained steeled, but Joshua could see their eyes
welling with tears. Worse than how he felt about his mission in that
moment was how he felt about himself—he was so separate from
those women; he wasn't standing with them fully. Ogenga kept quiet,
as if he knew Joshua needed time. As Joshua slowly put his key into
the ignition, he felt as if a veil had just been lifted, his eyes now
opened. He turned slowly to the passenger seat, with the benefit of
second sight, and finally saw Ogenga.

———————

Joshua spent nearly an hour praying, trying to rid himself of his
anger and sorting through his thoughts after he returned from
Nocno. As he sat still at his desk, he closed his eyes and listened to
the echoing of his soul—that voice sang from not far away, such a
strident song. *Osukuba ethanda ukundilandela, makazincame, awuthwale umnqamlezo wakhe, andilandele ke. Kuba othe wathanda
ukuwusindisa umphefumlo wakhe, wolahlekelwa nguwo; ke yena othe
wawulahla umphefumlo wakhe ngenxa yam, nangenxa yeendaba
ezilungileyo ezi, wowusindisa.* Joshua sighed. He'd done what he
could, he assured himself: after seeing to it that the three women
returned safely to the Noni Village, he'd spent time there urging
everyone to use caution. Now he tried to mete out a measured
response in a note, scrawling in the lantern's dim light.

> Dear Reverend Waldron,
> I visited the East London jailhouse this afternoon. I thought it best to
> inform you of this. In an unfortunate incident, the King William's Town

police arrested three elderly women from the Noni Village this morning, in a baseless act that threatened to incite a backlash in the villages. In traveling to Nocno, I chose to take an action that I believed would be most prudent and help avoid the eruption of unnecessary violence in this area. The authorities released the women upon my request. It is my belief that this matter is resolved and tensions in the villages will calm over.

The warden at the East London jail, however, made a disturbing allegation, insisting that our mission contributes to the maintenance of the jailhouse. Certainly, the presence of a chapel in that institution stands as an admirable tribute to the works of our mission. I believe it is unwise, however, for our mission to persist in allowing excess moneys from donations to be used for whatever the jailhouse chooses, which the warden says has included purchases for guardsmen and furnishings.

I do not wish to overstep the bounds of my duties. However, this allegation puts our mission in the most negative light. If this is true, it rightly looks to Africans in this region as if our mission is propping up this jailhouse, which is known for holding Africans arrested for peaceful protests. If by chance you find the assertions of the warden to be true, it is my hope that you will take every action as you are able to end such uses of any excess mission donations.

Yours loyally,
Reverend Joshua Clay

A knock called at his door as he finished.

"You don't need to knock when you come here now, Tahira," Joshua said, letting her in. "This is your home also."

She looked tired—as tired as he—as she moved with heavy steps to the couch.

"You're a good one, *Makinda*. I owe you much," Tahira whispered, sinking into the sofa. He'd never seen her look so weary.

Joshua moved the lantern to the living room table and sat across from her.

"You don't owe me anything," Joshua said, running a hand across his brow. "The elderly women of our village shouldn't have been put in jail. And in Nocno . . ." He shook his head, his eyes burning again.

She hesitated at his words. He wondered why. "Yes, this was a great offense to *our* village," she said. "If we had asked the other preacher, the one before you, he would not have journeyed there. Protesting in such a way is wrong, he told us—Christ instructs the African to turn the other cheek."

Joshua scoffed audibly, closing his eyes. Using Christ's words to excuse injustice, the very notion turned his stomach. It made as much sense as permitting mission funds to contribute to strip-down rooms. "I'm very tired," he whispered.

"I will leave you."

Joshua sat as the lantern light flickered low, too tired to replenish its oil. He closed his eyes, searching for peaceful thoughts.

"Has *Makinda* eaten?" Tahira asked softly, pausing on her way to her room beyond the kitchen.

"What is *Makinda?*"

"You—a young bird. Have you eaten, *Makinda?*"

He smiled, wondering what had caused her to name him "*Makinda.*" "I hadn't even stopped to think about eating."

"I will slice some bread for you. You will have it with butter and tea."

He looked at her gratefully. When she returned with a teapot, he slumped down in a chair next to the dining table.

"It's been a very long day," he said, chuckling sourly, lines of worry etching themselves into his brow. He considered his words before he spoke again. "This morning, even before you came, Mhlobo and Ogenga came by and demanded that I never return to their home." He stretched his neck and rubbed it, his eyes growing full. Repeating the words aloud, he realized how much their words had pained him. Tahira poured the tea wordlessly, seeming to avoid his gaze. She just kept pouring, measuring out cream and sugar. Her silence made him examine her face.

"They said I have eyes for Nongolesi, so I am not welcome in their home again until I return with *lokola.*" He took the cup she offered.

"*Lobola,*" she corrected him. There was an edge to her voice. She wiped crumbs from the table with a clean cloth.

"What are they talking about?" he whispered, looking at her intently. He could barely read her expression in the darkness of the room.

She lifted her chin upward, the same prideful way the three old women had at Nocno, as if preparing to weather an insult. She placed sliced bread near him and turned coolly back to the kitchen.

"Tahira, do you know what they mean?" he asked. "I'm sorry." He apologized for the irritation in his tone. "I'm in a foul mood. But there's something you're not telling me."

She gave him as stern a look as he'd ever seen. "You must give *lobola* to marry Nongolesi."

He nearly choked on the laugh that bellowed from deep inside. "Marry Nongolesi!" He grew quiet when her expression didn't change. She was serious. He squeezed his eyes shut. How could this day get any worse? "Nongolesi and I are just good friends," he said, looking at Tahira squarely, as if answering another accusation.

"Mmm," she said, nodding her head, lips pursed as she shook the rag in her hand at him. "I too have seen. I too have seen you have eyes for Nongolesi."

Joshua's lips froze as he stared with astonishment at Tahira. She kneaded the cloth as if she thought she had said too much. She held her chin up, nonetheless, and stepped toward the kitchen.

Joshua dropped his eyes. "Nongolesi is a beautiful woman," he said, stopping her. "It would be hard for any man to fail to notice that. She's a warm and smart and dedicated woman." His eyes twinkled as the words passed over his tongue, and he wiped away the look he knew was on his face. "But I had a girlfriend until recently and I don't need to become involved with anyone else so soon. And Nongolesi is also a congregation member, and I would not date a congregation member because it would cast a doubt on how seriously I am taking my missionary work. I've never thought about Nongolesi as more than a friend."

Tahira stayed silent, an expression of disappointment on her face. *Disappointed at what?* "You should speak freely, Tahira; this is your home also. What are you not telling me?" he asked softly.

She loosened the cloth in her hand, nearing the table. "It is an offense to a family if you court a woman in her family home," she said. "It seems to many that you have eyes for Nongolesi. And yet you have visited her in her family home on many occasions. You show no respect for her father."

"Tahira, they invited me to their home," Joshua said.

"Even so, to speak with Nongolesi as you have . . ."

"I'm not courting Nongolesi," Joshua said. She hadn't seemed to hear him.

"You have spent much time with her. Tradition is that you should fetch her at the river. That is our way."

He looked at her blankly.

"When she goes to fetch water in the early mornings, or in the evenings, you must meet her at the river and court her there, out of the sight of her parents. There is a fear that if a young man spends time with the unmarried woman he has eyes for at her home, she will fall pregnant."

"Tahira! I'm a minister, for goodness' sake!"

"It is tradition that men court women by the river." Her tone was harsh.

Joshua couldn't respond; he was too stunned to be insulted.

"If you are to show respect," she continued, "you must never let a father know you are seeking his daughter if you do not have *lobola*. You must give many cattle to marry Nongolesi. The offer of *lobola* is a sign of respect, to honor the family. It shows that a young man values the young lady's family and her ancestors. It is also our way to ensure that a young man is fit and capable of providing for his chosen woman and the children she will bear. Until you gather the needed *lobola*, you must spend time with Nongolesi only at the river. You must court her properly, write her a poem also. When you have secured the *lobola*, only then can you go to her father's house. Then this thing shall be set right."

Silence filled the room. Tahira waited for his response.

"I didn't realize how people viewed my actions," Joshua whispered. "Nongolesi's father never said anything about this."

"I'm sure he tries to be understanding about your behavior, but Mhlobo believes you should know our ways by now."

"I'm not courting Nongolesi," Joshua insisted again. "But thank you for letting me know how people have viewed my actions."

Tahira left him then, her lips still tight, as Joshua sat alone in the darkness. He hadn't felt so alone since he'd first arrived, nor was he certain he'd ever felt so tired.

CHAPTER 19

Joshua headed with Andrew to a local missionary meeting at a church in King William's Town. He wished the meeting hadn't come on the heels of his Nocno visit. He was still in such a sour mood. As Joshua pulled his shiny Ford in front of the church, he wondered for a moment why he'd never bothered to visit this church. He'd seen no reason to he supposed: It was for whites only. While driving past on many prior occasions he had never dwelled on why its cobblestone structure was so tall and elegant, its cross-crested steeple adorned in gold. But now he caught his breath as he walked through the church doors, stepping into the stunning sanctuary with red velvet carpet, deep-colored paned windows, polished mahogany pews, and a dove-crested rostrum. It was, after all, funded by the same benefactors who funded the Fort Hare church. His wide-eyed indignation startled him. He had assumed all the mission churches in South Africa were like that of Fort Hare, sparsely furnished, modestly built. He glanced at Andrew, who seemed to read Joshua's mind as he shook his head. They moved silently toward a group of ministers clustered in the front. As Joshua sat on the front pew bench. He nodded to Mr. Garrett, who sat a few seats away, representing Fort Hare.

The ministers discussed the usual topics. No Bibles should be printed in Xhosa in the region for the foreseeable future, but they would increase the number of Bibles printed in English. An objection lodged in Joshua's throat. Efforts would be redoubled to bring villagers into the churches to learn proper ways to worship, ensuring they wore European clothes. Joshua dropped his eyes, pondering the burning sensation on his hand, as if he were holding that *HW* docket again. Marvis's words floated through his mind. *You think you can transport blackness?* What was blackness? The tint of the skin, the hue of the soul, an ache for freedom that crosses the sea, a tussling voice that refuses to fall silent? The official moved on to the last topic. No public stance would be taken on the issue of forced relocations of villagers to Ginsberg. This time, when he felt a steady throbbing in the base of his neck, Joshua spoke.

"I've been in the country nearly six months now," Joshua began, "and it's been my pleasure to have come to know the people living near Fort Hare. Many of our mission's policies seem less than ideal when considering how best to minister to the needs of local villagers. I would like to see this mission change its stance on the policy of Xhosa Bible distributions, as a start. It is difficult, especially for the elderly of the local villages, to read in English. Of those who can read, they have learned Xhosa best." Joshua smiled and shuddered at the same time, amazed to hear his own voice in Mr. Garrett's presence.

"Is there anything else you'd like to register your dissent about while you're at it, Reverend Clay?" Mr. Garrett asked.

Joshua ignored the cynicism of his question and willed his voice to sound again, to carve out words in the expectant silence. "There are other matters on which I believe the position of our mission needs reconsideration," Joshua said diplomatically. "At the present time, I would like to voice most strongly my view about the Xhosa Bibles. In my view"—Joshua doubled the thickness of his tone—"we are placing the desire to have the villagers learn English above the imperative to spread God's Word."

"I would also like to make my disagreement with the current approach clear," another minister spoke up. "This isn't on the agenda tonight, but we should make a point to put it there for our next meeting."

Mr. Garrett looked toward Joshua in the way he often looked at Ogenga. Joshua nodded toward the group and requested the matter be considered during the next discussion.

On the road back to Fort Hare, Andrew sat quietly. "I assume you disapproved of my comments in church," Joshua finally said as he steered the road back to Alice. Glancing at Andrew, Joshua wet his throat, expecting stern words.

"I often feel"—Andrew began in a whisper to the distance—"as if working for our mission is working against God." Andrew slowly turned toward Joshua, the shadows under his eyes etched deeply, as if he could hardly imagine he'd just uttered those words aloud. His lips thinned, and he sighed heavily, glancing out the window again. He remained silent for the rest of the drive.

The Brother walked into Joshua's home, dressed as usual in simple slacks and a pressed shirt. He slowly unfolded his preaching robe on the couch. Joshua could feel the depth of the warm relationship the Brother shared with Tahira when she greeted him.

"How is Beaumont?" the Brother asked.

Tahira's eyes lit up. "He grows very strong. His time for manhood is here," she said proudly.

"Yes." The Brother squeezed his eyes and smiled. "And I shall attend the celebration of the circumcised initiates when they return," he said happily. "Beaumont has grown into such a lovely young man, Tahira; you've raised him so well."

She beamed at his words, thanking him for the compliment as she took his robe to iron. If you were to judge a man by his treatment of others, Joshua thought, the Brother was truly a jewel. He had a way of making everyone he met feel loved. The more Joshua grew to know him, the more honored he felt in his presence. He was certainly grateful for how the Brother had opened his home and given him advice as he tried to find his way. They'd spent many evenings exchanging tales about their earliest days as ministers. Joshua even shared his uncertainties about his work with his mission. The Brother had become a trusted friend.

"Please have a seat," Joshua said, happy to finally welcome the Brother into his home. The Brother sat on the sofa, pulling the cross around his neck from underneath his shirt.

"I like to keep it close so I can feel it at all times." He smiled as

Joshua looked at him running his finger over the cross. The Brother seemed lost in his thoughts for a moment. "I heard there was quite a commotion the other day," the Brother said.

"A protest gone bad."

"Did I hear correctly—they put old women in Nocno?"

Joshua nodded.

"So, the rumors are true. The intransigence of the government is growing by leaps and bounds! The local villagers are indignant, you know. Let's just hope things will die down now." He shook his head for a moment. "Thank you, by the way, for getting those women out of Nocno. I realize that you were treading a thin line. Your mission won't be pleased," he said as he pulled his Bible out of his bag and leafed through it to a set page, examining the notes he'd written on a piece of paper.

"Sometimes it's necessary to straddle lines," Joshua said.

"Sometimes it is necessary to *cross* them," the Brother said, looking up sternly, raising his eyebrows. "Are the women okay—they're unharmed?"

"They're fine, just a little shaken and very angry."

"Well, we can be grateful at least that they're unharmed."

"The government will only respond with more violence if there's any more taunting of the pass laws," Joshua said. "The students get so angry, asking me why God stands still in the face of troubled times like this."

"I don't believe it is God who is standing still," the Brother said in a low voice.

Joshua's thoughts lingered on the Brother's comment as Tahira returned, handing the Brother his robe.

"My dear, you do treat me so very kindly," the Brother said to Tahira.

"Pleasure." She smiled at his charm.

The Brother stood to put on his robe. Joshua waited for Tahira to leave before he mustered the words. "What do you think of the Xhosa concept of *Qamata*?"

"Ah, a complicated topic," he said as he adjusted his robe. "You have found yourself wrestling with this already?"

"I don't know what to say when I hear someone speak as if *Qamata* and Jehovah are one and the same," Joshua whispered.

The Brother looked at him intently, sitting back down. This was important, that's what those fierce green eyes said. He leaned toward Joshua, giving the matter his whole attention. "The fact that you are wrestling with this already is a good sign, Joshua. A *very* good sign." He twiddled his thumbs for a moment, as if he didn't know where to start.

"Many of the European missionaries who came here," he began, sitting back, "especially the wave that came over forty years back—those missionaries came here explicitly to help build the British empire. Explicitly, Joshua—they made no pretense of their purpose. Anything non-European was deemed backward." He rubbed the cross around his neck again. "Once you try to understand Xhosa customs, it is no easy matter to try to understand how all of their customs and traditional beliefs fit with Christianity, precisely because not all of those traditions and beliefs are at odds with Christian beliefs, you see. As far as I know, the Xhosa have always believed in only one God."

The Brother paused for a moment. "We sometimes tend to become confused, thinking that only things European are Christian, when, in fact, we as Christians can learn something from Africans. Don't assume that only things European are Christian. The one thing we know with certainty is that the ultimate revelation of God is through Jesus Christ. Anything inconsistent with the teachings of Jesus Christ should be changed. But the fact is that many Xhosa beliefs do not conflict with Christian teachings; so as you try to assess how their beliefs fit together with what we must teach as ministers, let the Bible be your guide."

Joshua raised his eyebrows.

"Ah, you doubt," the Brother responded. "Where does it say that God has revealed Himself only to the Europeans? I must have missed that, son. Please show me where it says that exactly." He scooted his Bible across the table to Joshua. "Where does it say, 'Thou shalt only wear trousers like those designed in Europe if you are to come into a church and worship Me'? 'Thou shalt not use tambourines when you sing praises to Me'? 'Thou shalt not perform the circumcision dances'? Please, Joshua, minister to me."

Joshua lowered his eyes, a little surprised by the intensity of the

Brother's reaction. The Brother leaned over and scribbled on an envelope in the middle of the table. "Tell me, Joshua, what is God like?" he asked as he jotted down some words with a pencil and turned the paper facedown on the table. "How would you describe God?"

"God is merciful and forgiving," Joshua said, inhaling deeply. "God will grant you peace in a world of chaos."

"What else?"

"God will bless you when you don't deserve a blessing, and He will open doors for you just in time. He plans ahead for you, and He will carry you through hard times."

There was a shine in the Brother's eyes as he looked at Joshua. "Yes, that is God." He motioned for Joshua to read the note on the table.

Joshua picked the envelope up from the table. The Brother had written those same traits in tall print across the envelope.

"When I first arrived in South Africa," the Brother explained, pointing to the envelope in Joshua's hand, "the Xhosa used those very words to describe *Qamata*, the Great Spirit, to me."

Joshua took in his breath, remembering the way Tahira had described *Qamata* when she first arrived at his home and thinking to Nongolesi's many descriptions also. He pursed his lips.

"You don't seem entirely convinced, so please tell me, how do you know God exists?"

"Because I experience Him," Joshua said softly.

"How do you experience Him?"

"When I pray, I receive a feeling, sometimes it's overwhelming, a feeling of empowerment and of peace, and I sense oftentimes what God wants of me, as if He is speaking to me in words I can't hear out loud. But I know nonetheless. And I often feel His presence."

"And where is God?"

"Everywhere," Joshua said. The moment he said it, he understood the Brother's point.

"So, do you presume that the Xhosa people in this land have never experienced God? Does that make any sense?"

Joshua nodded slightly. He whisked away any hints of defensiveness, letting his mind dwell on the Brother's words. "Yes," he responded, "if God is everywhere, the Xhosa must have experienced God."

"And if they have experienced God, how strange is it to think that they might have given a name to God by which to call Him?"

The wind drifted from Joshua. He squeezed his eyes tight and ran the back of his hand across his brow.

"And if you haven't figured it out already," the Brother said, "it was around this time that Reverend Peter ran away."

Joshua squeezed his eyes shut and sat back in his chair, feeling no need to say anything. "Before I came here," he finally responded, "I was told the Xhosa worship multiple gods. The representatives of my mission who trained me—all of them told me that."

"Before Christianity was brought here to South Africa, the Xhosa considered God to be so revered, so *almighty,* that they did not believe they should pray to Him directly. They prayed instead to their ancestors, calling on them to take their requests and concerns to God. That does not mean that the Xhosa believed in multiple gods or that they thought their ancestors possessed power to make the sun shine and the clouds rain. The Xhosa will tell you that when Christianity came, they were thankful for the ability to understand *Qamata* better, to read His Word and know that because of Jesus Christ they are saved and they can pray to God directly. I do not believe we have brought to them a new God, but we have shown them the Way. In what we preach, we must make it clear that Jesus is our Lord and Savior. That is what I mean, let the Bible be your guide."

Joshua became lost in thought. "So many of my congregation members already seem to understand Jesus is our Lord and Savior. So if we aren't here primarily to teach them that, why are we here?"

"That is for you to question, Joshua, and you *should* be questioning that. You may not like the answers you get back. What is this all about? No drums, no dancing, no traditional clothes, no hand clapping. The Bible says, *Wisdom cries out,* and so if you love the Lord and wish to dance down the aisle because of the joy you feel, why say it should not be so?"

Joshua was half listening now. He felt overwhelmed.

The Brother was quiet for a while as he relaxed back into the sofa and gazed through the long paned windows to the manicured backyard.

"God communicates with all of us, I know that to be true. I have full faith, Joshua, that you will find your way here. And you know, as do I, you can only find your way by going where God asks. Have you prayed, asking God to guide you?"

"Of course," Joshua said.

"And has He provided you that guidance?"

"I can't say I have heard clearly, no."

"What happened?"

"I'm not sure what you mean."

"After you prayed for guidance?"

Joshua shook his head and chuckled, not quite knowing what the Brother was suggesting.

"Think back to anytime recently when you asked with all of your heart for guidance on this matter," the Brother prodded.

"There have been many times."

"Name one."

"When I was on my way to see you for the first time," Joshua said.

"What happened when you asked?"

"My tire burst and I was stuck on the roadside!" Joshua joked. "Was that a sign?"

"What happened after your tire burst?"

"I came to see you," Joshua answered, shrugging his shoulders. "After I got a lift in the back of a truck from some men driving initiates to their circumcision huts in the mountains."

"You were in the back of a truck with initiates?" The Brother got wide-eyed and roared with laughter.

"What are you suggesting? You're saying that was the guidance?" Joshua laughed, not certain if the Brother was joking.

The Brother raised his eyebrows as he kept shaking his head. "I can't answer that for you," the Brother said, finally straight-faced again. "But be aware, if God is seeking to guide you, your heart and mind must be open to it."

Joshua was quiet with those words.

"I must say that being here, in South Africa, has been an exhilarating experience for me," the Brother said softly. "I find it reassuring that the Xhosa have experienced God as I have. That makes God all the more real to me. And what a great God He is. Do you think it is a coincidence that this great God of ours, when He gave His only

begotton Son, gave Jesus in a land located where three races meet—
at the junction of Europe and Asia and Africa? Is it coincidence that
the Bible describes Jesus as bronze with hair like wool? My dear
Joshua," he said, leaning forward and pointing his finger in the air,
"if you rolled into one every living man on this earth—from the
darkest Negro to the palest white man—what would that person
look like? Bronze skin with hair like wool! God is with all of us, for
all of us." He thumped his finger on the table and sat back, rubbing
his fingers over his cross again. "With all of our problems, and all of
this strife among the races, God loves all of us." He closed his eyes
and whispered, "Knowing that, Joshua, brings me peace."

"I spread the word that you'd be preaching today," Joshua said to
the Brother as they headed up the hill to church a while later. "I hope
the turnout will be decent. It hasn't picked up much since I first
came to see you, but things are going better for me among the
villagers."

"Just give it a little time. If you stay on the right path, they will
come to your sermons" the Brother said.

The morning was rather cool, a reminder that winter was nearing. Joshua looked at the familiar tent, perched in its normal spot at
the top of Sandile's kop. Several students sitting with their Bibles in
front of it paused their chattering as they caught sight of the two
preachers. They rose and moved toward the church, but slowed
before the back church doors, as if their passage was blocked. Joshua
was alarmed for a moment.

"Go ahead and organize yourself," Joshua said, leading the
Brother to the side entrance to his office at the front of the church.
"Let me just make sure there's no problem in the pews."

Joshua prepared himself for what he might see as he peeked
through the doorway leading from his office to the pulpit. Perhaps
someone had fallen? Someone was ill? His lips parted as he peered
in, barely able to believe the sight. The church was filled, wall to
wall. People had squeezed their chairs tightly together, making room
for others to stand or sit by the walls: the young, the old, students,
mostly Africans, some Indians, and some Coloureds. Joshua had last

seen some of the students at his first sermon, when, a few minutes into his ministering, their hopeful looks were replaced with cheerless gazes as they seemed to wait politely for his lecture to end.

"It's brimming over," the Brother said without looking up from his notes when Joshua joined him in the church office.

"Yes, it is," Joshua said, feeling embarrassed by the obvious sign of his own failings.

"Just old friends coming to visit," the Brother explained. "I used to preach here on occasion, when I was posted out this way. I'm glad to have touched many hearts with God's Word."

Joshua could hear the choir rising on cue. They sang in Xhosa, an upbeat song, and he was surprised as he heard gourds rattling and hand cymbals clicking. The congregation clapped to the beat, lifting their voices as one into the air, singing more loudly as the Brother and Joshua walked in from the side room to the pulpit. Choir members, wearing bright African cloth, smiled broadly as the Brother too joined in the singing.

Joshua glanced around the little church. It didn't matter in God's eyes where his children bowed their heads to pray, he knew. But this church was funded from the same purse as the church for whites he'd just visited in King William's Town. Joshua shook his head, remembering its grandeur. The bleakness of this church compared to that one had been intended to say a certain something, he thought. He no longer denied what that something was.

When the song came to a close, Joshua spoke from the rostrum. "We welcome here today Reverend Beaumont Chandler—"

The congregation sang out again, clapping their hands, even before Joshua could proceed with the introduction. Their eyes shone as they looked at the Brother with the sort of expressions conferred to a man who had refused to ignore their tribulations, who had spent his life sharing their suffering, castaway by choice. It was humbling to watch. Joshua glanced back at the Brother, who seemed to be meditating as he hugged his Bible close. He motioned the Brother to the rostrum when he looked up. The Brother called out a warm hello and smiled at the congregation's joyous response. The congregation finally fell quiet, preparing to hear him speak—a silence broken only by a baby's cry.

"*Ungavi kakubi ngenxa yesikhalo sabantwana,*" the Brother said as the crowd applauded and stomped their feet. "Don't feel bad about the cry of those babies," the Brother translated. "Their cries are like music to my ears, for it lets me know this community will go on and on, and with it, the love of the Lord shall grow!" The congregation stomped and applauded to the words again.

"*NguYehova umkhanyiseli wam nomsindisi wam, ndiya koyika bani na?*" the Brother continued. "I have come today to speak to you about a very important topic, one that is central to affirming our Christian principles." He shifted his weight as he glanced back at Joshua, his eyes twinkling. Joshua wondered what he was up to.

"I would like to preach to you today about rising, taking up thy bed, and *walking.*"

Joshua had to stifle his laughter. He'd told the Brother on several occasions about Marvis's lectures and the ship voyage across the Atlantic. Joshua nodded. It was a fitting topic. *Thank you, Lord,* Joshua prayed silently. *Thank you for such a shining example of Your love and of Your work.*

After the sermon ended, Joshua ushered the Brother outside the church to greet congregation members. The Brother had dared to touch on the very themes Joshua's mission had instructed him to avoid, and the congregation seemed to bask in his words.

Nongolesi joined the long line of those waiting to have a word with the Brother. Joshua's heart lifted as he saw her, feeling his guard melting as she neared and he looked in her gentle eyes. He still saw her each week at the Ulundi School, but he kept their interactions as distant as he could. As she moved in front of him now, he quickly wiped away the smile curving on his lips, feeling as if everyone had noticed the expression. But Joshua felt captivated by her beauty, the faint dab of perfume on her wrist filling his lungs as he shook her hand. He kept his expression flat, turning his eyes away from her quickly, letting her know she should move on. She froze for a moment, the look on her face making him wince. She moved on to greet the Brother.

"That was a fine sermon." Ogenga moved behind Nongolesi, greeting Joshua but addressing the Brother more enthusiastically as more students gathered around them. "I'm always very moved when I hear you speak. It is always inspiring to see how the Scripture empowers us to rise and walk, and is on the side of those seeking dignity and liberty."

"Brother, do come again," another student said.

"At Reverend Clay's request, I shall be happy to visit from time to time." The Brother nodded to Joshua respectfully.

"Brother, I know a young student from Peddie, he is very clever indeed," Ogenga said anxiously. "His mind is sharp. Since Jovan is almost done with his special studies with you, I had hoped you might have time for another student—"

"I have another student already," the Brother said. "But Sarah will be free again shortly; perhaps she can take him. Or perhaps Reverend Clay—"

"Hello, Reverend," the students said to Joshua awkwardly.

". . . Perhaps Reverend Clay will be able to take our young friend from Peddie under his wings," the Brother said.

Joshua wasn't certain what they were speaking about. Andrew pulled Joshua away before he could probe.

"I'm glad you invited me today," Andrew said to Joshua, moving with him away from the students. "I always enjoy listening to the Brother." Andrew smiled as he watched the Brother chat easily with admiring students.

"I used to preach that way," Joshua murmured.

"What happened?"

Joshua was startled by Andrew's question. He hadn't realized he'd made his comment aloud. He felt exposed for a moment, not having intended to broach this subject. He took in a deep breath, deciding to answer. "I came to Africa."

Andrew arched his eyebrows, prodding for more of an explanation.

"I changed the way I preached because my mission told me I should before I came to Africa," Joshua answered more fully.

"You bought into an idea," Andrew said.

"That makes it sound so innocent," Joshua scoffed under his breath.

"No, it's not innocent," Andrew said in a tone that made Joshua examine his face. Andrew shifted his eyes away, looking at the Brother. "It's an idea that contradicts everything Jesus stood for," Andrew said quietly.

CHAPTER 20

Rain danced in the leaves, sending crisp perfume into the air. As the morning's showers slowly tapered, the sun peeked through the clouds and birds began to chirp to each other from the scattering of trees. Joshua had made his way to the Noni Village on time, but he wasn't certain if he'd still be preaching. In the homestead where Tahira lived, there was no place to deliver his sermon except for outdoors, in the makeshift worship area the villagers had created near a splintered cross, worn from the weather, that they'd staked into the village's highest hill. Ever since Reverend Peter had stopped preaching at Fort Hare, they had gathered among themselves on Sundays to sing praises there, and they would often journey to hear Joshua. He was pleased to come to them for a change. As he made his way inside the courtyard, Tahira offered him a chair within one of the huts.

"They are still preparing for your sermon," Tahira said as she handed him a mug of tea, that she'd warmed over a hearth dug in the center of the hut's earthen floor.

"With the rain, I wasn't sure if I'd still be preaching," Joshua said, peeking through the hut's opening at the clouds. "How will the villagers know whether we will still be having church?" he asked, knowing some of them were miles away.

"One of the elders will send a signal," she replied as she spooned water from the barrel beside her to fill the teapot again.

"What sort of a signal?" Joshua asked, still not understanding.

Tahira looked at him, amused. "The signal they always send in the village to let others know our prayer meetings should soon begin," she replied.

Joshua let the topic rest, as he leafed through his Bible, reviewing his notes, and practicing the verses he would cite in Xhosa from a marula Bible. He was tired of flipping back and forth between the two Bibles, wishing silently the two could be combined into one.

In spite of the rain, the village was bustling. Joshua heard young ladies moving to and fro, carrying buckets of mealies and beans. If the weather cleared, this would be the day of the return of the initiates celebration. Excitement hovered in the air. Just then, a crisp beat called out, startling Joshua. He looked through the hut's doorway, to see an old man sitting outside pounding a taut-skinned drum, hitting its head with brisk close-fisted beats, one thick stroke followed by two quick ones, over and over for nearly a minute. The drum's baying silenced all other sounds, even the birds seemed to be still. When the drummer finally stopped, silence lingered for nearly a minute. *So that's what Tahira meant!* Joshua turned back to his sermon notes. Then in the distance, he heard another persistent beat, another thick pounding of a drum. Its deep pitch seemed to answer them back from two miles down the path. When it stopped, the lands fell silent again. Joshua was astonished, and smiled. There was somehow such a beauty to this. More beautiful still when he heard yet another drumbeat answer them from a faraway hill, even farther away than the second.

When the talking drums finally ceased, Joshua moved to the edge of the courtyard nearest the roadside. Leaning over its wooden fence, he could see people beginning to walk from a couple of miles up the road, moving along the roadsides from villages closer to the mountains. Some led donkeys pulling gray carts filled with elderly men and women. Some mothers followed, holding the hands of their toddlers. One man hobbled on a wooden leg. Joshua was so moved as he watched them make their way to the Noni Village, smiling broadly when they saw him. He shook their hands, one by one, as they made their way into the courtyard. After thirty minutes, enough of them had gathered to begin. They sat on blankets and palm leaf mats in a semicircle around the cross. Some of the women started singing in Xhosa from their hearts, shaking their tambourines and rattles.

Every voice lifted, ringing with such beautiful harmonies. Joshua was so moved by the expressions on their faces. A young girl drew his attention, motioning to him from a few feet away. She dared to move closer and whispered to him, "That young girl there, she wishes to come, but she does not have the proper clothes." She pointed toward another little girl standing barefoot near a hut dressed in a traditional cloak and cowhide skirt, while most other villagers wore dated European fashions.

Joshua moved toward her as the singing continued. Her eyes grew large, as if expecting a reprimand. "Please join us," he said gently. She motioned her hand at her skirt. "Wherever God's house is, that is your house too," Joshua said very deliberately. "Wherever they worship God, you can come as you are." The smile that lit her face said more than her words ever could.

She moved toward her friend, sitting beside one of the village Mamas. With *amaqhiya*—headdresses—knotted on their heads like crowns, the women sang on, their joy ringing through.

———

It was early afternoon when Joshua finished his sermon, traveling with some young boys to shepherd goats to thick-leaved pastures. He had decided to attend the celebration for the return of the circumcised initiates. From what he had been told, he didn't foresee anything about it that would conflict with his role as a missionary. He was excited to experience his first traditional celebration. Most everyone from the Noni Village would attend, and the air of excitement continued to grow. Joshua headed back early from helping the young boys, knowing that the women would be hurrying to hoist the roof onto Beaumont's new hut, finishing it before nightfall when the celebration would begin.

Tahira looked at Joshua with questioning eyes as she steadied herself on top of a rickety ladder against the newly plastered mud walls, preparing to help tie the thatch down on top. The women had already bound the thatch grass with ropes, sewing the thick strands sturdily. Joshua rolled his sleeves upward as he walked toward them.

"I thought you said this was a man's work?" Joshua smiled, answering her expression. "You might as well put me to good use."

He was pleased by her surprised look and the smile that stretched across her face. "There is another ladder there." She pointed. "This is heavy," Tahira whispered, seeming grateful for the presence of a young man strong enough to help tie the roof firmly in place.

When they finished an hour later, Tahira helped rub aloe into the scratches on Joshua's hands and arms. He didn't mind the abrasions—the work had been a pleasure.

The preparations for the night's feast continued. Joshua could smell the scents of a thick peppery stew and lamb's meat roasting over an open fire in the middle of the courtyard. Several young women stirred pots full of spinach, corn, and sugar beans. The Old Man, Mama Siziwe, Mhlobo, and Ogenga arrived at the homestead an hour before the celebration began, each dressed in traditional attire. By then, the courtyard was filling with families from all parts of the village, some in traditional dress, some in European styles; they clustered chatting in groups cheerfully. The Brother and Lydia were chatting among them.

No one seemed to mind the chilly air of the early-winter night. It was an unusual time of the year to hold the *umgidi,* but the villagers had timed it to occur before a few of the new men would need to travel to begin work in the Johannesburg mines hundreds of miles away. The coming-out celebration for the initiates meant so much, especially now.

As soon as the sky fell dark, village elders lit a few lanterns and struck matches to the many large candles hoisted on tall sticks that formed a circle on the outskirts of the dung-smoothed courtyard. Joshua heard drumming begin. Three elder men pounded an incessant rhythm that beat hard against Joshua's chest. A ceremony master, dressed in a traditional cloak with a tall spear and an anklet that jiggled loudly, moved to the center of the courtyard, announcing the beginning of the festivities. The crowd fell silent expectantly, and a procession of elder men dressed in brightly colored costumes and jeweled masks paraded through the court entrance. The donkey hair of their masks blew in the gentle wind as they formed a circle before the onlookers and froze, in perfect time with the drums, before all leaping at the same time as the drumming resumed. They moved in a flamboyant dance to the beat, with animated gestures, denoting the procession of the ancestors. They danced deliberately, pausing close to wide-eyed young children. The praise singers followed, recounting the stories of the ancestors represented there.

It felt like such a solemn occasion. Joshua relished the sights—the living history before him, the vibrant sounds, the pride in family. The maidens of the village came dancing in next. Nongolesi was there, dancing with other young ladies in a single line, in a tribute to the new men of the village. Joshua felt as if many eyes were drifting his way, trying to watch and read his expression. He tried to keep his eyes from focusing on Nongolesi's elegant gestures as she moved in tandem with the other ladies. Dressed in traditional *umbhaco*, with *amaqhiya* around their hair, they chanted a song together. They were a beautiful sight. *She* was a beautiful sight.

All fell quiet again as the men and women depicting the ancestors moved to the edges of the courtyard and the master of ceremonies took center stage, calling out long-awaited words: *"Oronta batshile, namakhwenkwe khange abheke umva. Busele emva ubuntwana babo. Amakhwenkwe alishumi adlulile ebukhwenkweni. Konke kulungile."* The crowd cheered calling out ululations as a young boy whispered a translation to Joshua: "The initiate huts have been burned and the boys have not looked back. They have turned from their childhood and have passed to manhood. All is well."

Joshua smiled. Silence lingered for a while, in another very expectant pause, before the drums called out again, this time in a deep manly rhythm, a warrior's song. A broad smile spread across Joshua's face even before the new young men danced with bold steps through the courtyard. The pride and love and hope of the community were palpable; Joshua could practically touch them. Dressed in palm leaf skirts and masks, with bare feet and beaded anklets, the new men moved in a line through the entrance, their bodies cleansed of all white clay, signifying they had washed away their childhood.

Now they were smeared with red ocher, marking their return as *amakrwala*, new men.

With their determined steps and firm expressions, and the necklaces with ornate beadwork hanging in layers on their chests, the *amakrwala* were a sight. Holding spears upright, they stepped forth in unison, leaping together, stomping their feet at the same time, clapping hands, beginning a chant filled with the promises they had made to honor their families and their history. The sheer beauty of the celebration took Joshua's breath. As they continued their animated dance, their intricate footwork well practiced, pride seemed to grow among the bright-eyed onlookers. Several of the girls observing from their mats mouthed along to the traditional chant's words. Joshua glanced from them to the shining eyes of several old men, trying to read their expressions. Were they remembering their own initiates' celebration? Or was that a look of pride, knowing that even under such hard times, the village had raised such strong young men? Joshua's gaze fell on Mhlobo just then, whose darkened eyes caused Joshua to pause. Mhlobo's fearful eyes shifted from the young men to the older ones, seeming to note the absence of men in between—the husbands and fathers who were off at the Johannesburg mines, not to return at least for nine months. Joshua understood.

The celebration continued on as each new man was formally reintroduced to the village. Joshua felt he was beaming as proudly as Tahira when Beaumont stepped forth. At the conclusion, jubilation was still in the air and lines formed around several three-pronged pots as the feast began. Nongolesi moved with a group of teachers toward Joshua as he waited with others to fill his plate with food. Joshua glanced back at Mhlobo, who had stern eyes on him. But Mhlobo nodded, as if it were okay. Nongolesi was in a group, Joshua thought, that probably made a difference.

Nongolesi smiled faintly as Joshua began speaking with the teachers near her. Joshua tried to tell himself he wasn't feeling anything special toward Nongolesi, but he was. And when his eyes lingered on Nongolesi, her beauty struck him again. He knew what drew him was much more than her bright eyes and smile. He realized so clearly how much he'd missed their talks. She looked at him somewhat sadly. He quickly turned his gaze away.

The adults sat cross-legged in small circles on grass mats, enjoying the finest food the women of the village could have prepared. Joshua joined one of the groups as they passed *amasi* in a special beaded calabash around the circle. Tahira sat across from him, looking Joshua's way as the calabash of soured milk reached him. Joshua pretended not to notice as he took a long, deep swig, letting the milk's coolness perk his senses. It poured thickly over his tongue, its flavor lingering. It was delicious. He'd rarely seen Tahira smile so broadly.

Joshua enjoyed chatting with those closest to him. Long after the children were put to bed, Joshua could see the pride of the new men, who for the first time could join in the storytelling after the initiates' celebration. As the adults sat in a circle, some of the older women pinched tobacco from beaded pouches into long-stemmed pipes, puffing the fragrant clouds into the air. Finally, the chosen elder moved to the center of the circle. Joshua had been looking forward to this. Nongolesi's Great Father had been chosen to impart wisdom to the new men as a conclusion to the night's celebration. The silver-haired old man sat on a carved wooden stool, wearing a traditional *isibheshu* and wrapping a wrinkled hand around his walking stick. His hollow cheeks seemed to pulse for a moment as he prepared to speak. The crowd sat silently with anticipation, with only the faint movements of goats in the cattle pen audible. A young boy next to Joshua prepared to whisper an English translation to Joshua as the old man spoke slowly and deliberately, in a raspy breath.

> *Hey, my people, have you heard?*
> *Have you heard the story?*
>
> *Of the people of this land*
> *where you sit in grace today.*
>
> *They have sung a pulsing song*
> *that we might hear, might see.*
>
> *Look back across sixteen seas*
> *Of mothers, sons, fathers, daughters.*
> *See the labor of their love,*

the fields they sowed,
the soils they tilled,
the fruits they bore,
to fill your soul.

When the land was parched,
when cornstalks withered,
when earth's fruits failed to bloom,
your ancestors still rose
from homes with care,
standing before that rising sun.

They labored till daylight set,
that you might dream, be free.
Think back to those days long past,
Of the honor in their hearts,
the love in their hands.

The blood they shed for you
was not bled and splattered,
that you would live in waste,
no hope, no joy, no tomorrow.

Rise up on your weary legs.
Pray to God for strength.

Every life has its challenge.
Each of you must face your charge.
Remember your ancestors
across the sixteen seas.
And say "I too will stand
my chin held firm,
my gaze fixed high,
within God's grace,
amid God's love,
facing ever still,
that rising sun."

"You will sleep in my hut tonight, *Makinda*," Beaumont said after Joshua led a prayer among the remaining family members to bless the end of the initiates' celebration. Joshua could see Beaumont's radiant expression as he led the way to his new hut. The women had finished adorning it and had swept its floor smooth with mud and dung. Beaumont untied a sheepskin mat with thick fleece from a rafter above them and motioned Joshua toward two blankets near a log-filled hearth dug in the hut's floor.

"This one they have made for you, that you may come visit often," Beaumont said with a shine in his eyes as he handed the sheepskin mat to Joshua.

Joshua smiled. Their warmth always touched him. The mat smelled freshly cured. Joshua rolled it out in the same manner Beaumont had rolled his own onto the smooth floor. Beaumont then blew out the lantern, wisps of smoke carrying the bittersweet smell of paraffin into the air. As Beaumont lay in the dark, Joshua could still feel his excitement, as if he were relishing an experience he did not want to end.

"I'm glad you could come, *Makinda*," Beaumont whispered.

"I wouldn't have missed it," Joshua said, turning on his mat toward Beaumont, making out only his shining eyes. "You know, we're all so proud of you." He could see Beaumont smile.

As Joshua lay underneath a single wool blanket, he thought about Nongolesi again. He could tell by her expression tonight that she too missed the budding friendship they had shared. He pondered why he was reluctant to court her by the river. He had told himself for too long that he simply did not care for her as more than a friend, but he knew that wasn't true. Perhaps he cared too much about what others thought, just as he had with Shantal. In that moment, he willed himself to stop betraying his own heart.

As he heard Beaumont's breaths grow louder, as if he were now sleeping, Joshua glanced around in the darkness. It was easy to forget this house was a hut. Its walls were solid, plastered perfectly smooth with mud and dung—the work of many days of hard labor. Though the night was cold outside, it felt just like he was inside a cement house, warm and cozy. Joshua lay still for a while, listening to the muffled sounds of the last women putting away mats outdoors. He heard the animals in the *ebuhlanti* and the crickets chirping farther off. He relished the warm comfort and peace of this community around him. As he thought about the day's events, he wondered how his mission had managed to believe that the traditions he'd seen today conflicted with missionary teachings. He didn't like any of the thoughts that skirted through his mind as he thought about that more deeply. *Father God,* Joshua said in silent prayer, *Please help me to serve You well, and to have the courage to take the right steps.*

He lay still again, reflecting on the words of his own prayer and what they meant. Then, as he listened to the whispering night, he relished the serene sounds he had longed to hear. He closed his eyes, wanting the music to stay in his mind forever. He could only recognize some of the Xhosa words, but the singing brought him peace as the voice sung nearby so gingerly: *Osukuba ethanda ukundilandela, makazincame, awuthwale umnqamlezo wakhe, andilandele ke. Kuba komnceda ntoni na umntu, ukuba uthe walizuza ihlabathi liphela, waza wonakalelwa ngumphefumlo wakhe?*

CHAPTER 21

June's fall weather had quickly turned colder, as Joshua began his seventh month as a minister at Fort Hare. He reached over to his church office window, closing its wooden shutters to block a raw wind blowing through it, but he kept the curtains pulled back, enjoying the white light flowing through the thin layers of clouds that filled the sky. Joshua sat back and thought about his ministry. Things were beginning to go better; attendance had picked up ever since he had helped retrieve the Noni women from Nocno, even more so after his Noni Village sermon. He had enjoyed delivering the sermon in the Noni Village, and promised himself to go more often to tend to the needs of the villagers as much as he could. With every passing week, though, he became firmer in his belief that his church was hindering his efforts to bring people to Christ. What the villagers needed most, especially the older ones, was to read the Word in their own language. He could see the logic in the Old Man's views. He sighed, realizing it would be very difficult to sway his mission. If they truly sought to spread God's Word, they should eventually support this stance, he thought. He promised himself to continue to try to persuade them.

As he parted his Bible to begin to feed his mind for his next sermon, he marked the same verses he wished to cite in a marula Bible. His Bible was so worn—torn at its bind, its pages hanging loosely—that he still found it difficult to turn quickly between it and the marula Bible during his sermons; he always seemed to fumble. He ran his hand over the binding, wondering how he would be able to mend it. That thought swam through his mind again—he wished the two Bibles were one. Just then, a bashful knock called at his office door.

"Come in," he said, trying to see through its ajar opening at who stood there. His heart beat faster for a fleeting moment as Nongolesi walked through. Their eyes met and held. He couldn't say a word, he was so surprised by her boldness in visiting him alone. As she took a seat, he realized there was nothing more that he wanted in this moment than to have a chance to speak with her again, like they used to. His heart had never felt so full. After seeing her at the initiates' ceremony, his feelings for her had refused to settle or be brushed to the back of his mind. Joshua could only imagine what Mhlobo would have to say if he learned about this.

Nongolesi smiled, a gesture that seemed a little forced, and seemed to pretend not to notice the awkward silence. "We have not seen you often," she said. "I wanted to make sure you are keeping well."

Joshua kept from his face any look that might encourage the visit. "How is the Old Man?" he asked, hoping his steady tone sufficiently hid what he really felt.

"He keeps well, but I have never seen him like this," she whispered.

The pain in her eyes made him lean toward her. "What's wrong?"

As her eyes brightened, seeing his genuine concern, Joshua's heart sank. It was as if she had doubted he really cared.

"He does not seem to sleep well. He travels far to try to build support against the forced removals. He believes the forced removals will soon come close to Alice. I have never seen him so worried. Perhaps it is my imagination, but he seems to tire much more easily. I do not have a good feeling about it."

"Is there anything I can do?" Joshua's voice trailed a bit, as he remembered Mhlobo's warning to him not to visit their home.

She shook her head. "He will let us know if there is something we should do." She kneaded her hands. "He is sorry to have missed your sermons in the past two weeks," she said. "But we tell him of your sermons when he returns from his trips. He hears. He criticizes."

They shared a laugh. Her directness was refreshing. "I value his wisdom and insights," Joshua said. He looked around, shrugging. "I'm sorry I can't offer you tea—the office here isn't equipped."

The crooked smile that decorated her face made Joshua hesitate, then chuckle as he realized the double meaning of his comment.

"I've trained you very well." She smiled.

Joshua's emotions welled with so much love, it made his heart ache. His eyes were wide with that thought. *Love.* He had tried to ignore how much he'd missed her. Seeing her made the loneliness more real. He dropped his eyes for a moment. When he looked back at her, he knew his eyes were asking her to leave.

"I can't stay long," Nongolesi said, seeming uneasy in what she saw as he looked at her. She fidgeted with the purse in her hands. "I just wished to make sure you are keeping well."

He nodded, knowing he was disappointing her by not saying more.

"I also wished to ask whether something is wrong," she said softly.

His throat tightened. "What do you mean?"

"We do not speak much at school or after church as we once did."

"Nothing is wrong." He shook his head, keeping his eyes blank.

She clenched her jaw and lowered her eyes. "Mhlobo told me he came to see you weeks ago," she said, staring at her hands. She looked back up at him with damp eyes. "You needn't listen to what he says," she whispered.

He didn't dare say what he felt, and he couldn't find other words.

"I must be getting back home." She rose, seeming embarrassed by his silence.

Joshua followed her quick movements to the door, feeling heat flushing his face. "Nongolesi." He touched her arm gently. He could sense her hurt.

"I'm sorry if I haven't been a very good friend lately," he said, feeling so much guilt. "Nothing is wrong," he said as flatly as he could.

She looked at him, deep into his eyes, and her lips tensed at what she saw. His heart sank at her expression. When she left, her eyes were still sad. Joshua tried to steady his thoughts, the twisting in his stomach telling him he had not done the right thing.

———————

After another hour, Joshua returned to his home, still thinking of Nongolesi. As he closed the front door behind him in the early afternoon, he felt so alone, the stillness in the house so overwhelming. He tried to whisk away the hollow feeling he felt, as he placed the package he'd just found on his front steps onto his desk. The handwriting on the address was Lucius's. It made him smile. Lucius never sent packages. Joshua certainly hadn't been expecting this one. As he peeled it open, he wished he could stop thinking of Nongolesi.

He pulled a book from inside brown paper wrapping. Thin and perfectly square, it was the shape of a child's book. The title scrawled across it read *Black Boy in the Jungle.* The cartoon on its cover pictured a barefoot jet black little boy. Wild-eyed, flat-nosed, with bloodred lips and devilishly pointed hair, it seemed intended to mock Africa. Joshua uttered an incredulous sigh as he sat down at his desk to read the letter tucked inside.

A smile curved at his lips as he recognized Alma's handwriting. She went on about how proud they were of his accomplishments. He scoffed. If only they knew. She went on, as always, about Lucius, complaining this time that he'd been prancing around the house ever since they'd received Joshua's first few letters about Africa. He kept bragging that he'd been right all these years about the lies they told in America about Africa, she reported; he kept saying over and over, "They done a job on us"; then he'd sit in his spot in the center of the living-room couch, pulling another book from Harlem to teach them about what others had to say. The image made Joshua chuckle. He could see it so vividly.

The writing then changed abruptly to Lucius's, who spelled the way he spoke, in broken English. He explained the book enclosed was the latest one the white education officials had instructed the local elementary school to use to teach Negro children. *What is more vicious,* Lucius had asked in capital letters, *than making Negro children read this book as an example of their history?* He'd underlined his question several times. Joshua realized there was a time when he'd have rolled his eyes at Lucius's ranting. This time, he thumbed through the book carefully.

The monkey-people in the deep, dark jungle were pictured walking in and out of African-looking huts, wearing African-looking clothing. The Old Man's words floated through Joshua's mind, the ones he'd spoken months ago. *The seeds we sow will come back in the future. After a good soaking, those ideas the government placed there would have taken root—we would soon be finished as a people.*

A knock at the door interrupted Joshua's deep thoughts.

"I was beginning to think you weren't home."

"Were you knocking long?" Joshua asked, embarrassed, as he welcomed Mr. Garrett in and gathered his jacket to keep him warm.

"For the past five minutes." Mr. Garrett looked at him strangely.

Joshua gave him an apologetic look, but didn't offer an explanation, as he headed with Mr. Garrett to King William's Town. The sky was still brilliantly blue, but was now laced with full-bodied clouds. As Joshua drove down the open road, he took in the winter landscape, noting that few of the trees had lost their leaves; most were evergreen, with cactus trees standing tall among them. As they made their way to the matinee, he wondered why Mr. Garrett was uncharacteristically silent. He'd gone on at length two weeks earlier about this musical play they would attend with several regional leaders—the Tarzan production taking South African society by storm. It was no coincidence, Joshua assumed, that Mr. Garrett had first invited him to attend the play shortly after Reverend Waldron had probably received his letter urging him to reconsider the mission's jailhouse donations. He assumed the invitation was their way of trying to loop him closer in, to keep an eye on him.

"By the way," Mr. Garrett finally began as Joshua steered up and down the dips and ascents of the hilly road, "a few weeks ago, Reverend Waldron mentioned you seemed unsettled by a trip to the East London jailhouse. We thought we'd give this some time. You

haven't written him about it again, he said, so he supposes the matter
is at rest."

"I was very unsettled," Joshua said, ignoring the hint of accusation in Garrett's tone. He wasn't much in the mood to tolerate a
thinly veiled warning.

"You shouldn't have been there in the first instance," Mr. Garrett
said sharply, having waited for Joshua to say more. "Reverend
Waldron wasn't pleased. But we are all prone to errors in judgment.
Just know in the future, that is not your place."

"Mr. Garrett, my mission established a chapel at Nocno. I will
feel free to go there, and perhaps even to minister there unless my
mission tells me directly I cannot." The authority in Joshua's tone
seemed to surprise Mr. Garrett.

"I think you would be asking for trouble."

Hold still in wisdom. Lu's words echoed through his mind as
Joshua pulled his car aside near the brightly colored double-story
theater, happy the drive had come to an end. They moved with a
strained silence beneath the ornate awning, entering a handsome
lobby beneath high ceilings with European murals that seemed as
elegant as the marble beneath their feet. Their heels clicked across
the floor as Andrew caught Joshua's eye, standing in a semicircle with
some local officials.

"I was hoping I'd see you here!" Andrew's eyes lit up as he pulled
Joshua aside. "How was your sermon in the village?" He smiled
hopefully.

"Much better than I'd expected." Joshua smiled back. "I felt at
home, and I was warmly received."

"That's great," Andrew said, happiness cracking in his voice.
"Well, the play will begin soon, but let's fetch a cup of tea afterward,
and you can drop me 'round later at the train station. I want to hear
all about how things are going at Fort Hare."

"I'd like that," Joshua responded, feeling pleased that he would
have someone to confide in.

They took their seats at the call of a bell. The lights dimmed, the
long velvet curtains parted, and a line of European performers
dabbed in black makeup proceeded onto the stage, hopping one
behind the other in a parody of an African dance. Joshua felt his

stomach pinch as they moved center stage, wielding long, curved knives in the air. They jumped and pranced and froze, cowering as they stumbled upon a phonograph, feigning trepidation of the music floating forth as the needle caressed the disc. The audience roared. Joshua thought he'd explode, his stomach now turning fits. He lifted his chin and narrowed his eyes, feeling Andrew growing indignant also as the first act proceeded and the performers began mimicking voodoo rituals. Perhaps what made Joshua's heart sink the most in those moments was knowing that when he'd first arrived seven months earlier he'd have seen nothing wrong with this. Now, indignation kept Joshua's feet anchored in place. But as he felt his face still flushing, heard his breathing grow loud in his ears as his heart pounded mercilessly, he lifted to his feet and moved to the aisle. Mr. Garrett was speechless as Joshua moved past him, walking out, not stopping to look back.

"Joshua," he heard a voice call as he was halfway across the lobby.

Andrew scurried up beside him, touching him on the arm. "I thought we were going to have tea?" he said, wiping his hand through his brown hair and looking at Joshua knowingly.

Joshua examined his face.

Andrew nodded, and Joshua smiled slightly. They proceeded to Joshua's car.

Joshua could hear the kettle humming on the stove in the kitchen, near Tahira's room, as he walked back through his front door later that night. Speaking with Andrew always buoyed his spirits, though he didn't always know what to make of where Andrew stood on the issues he wrestled with. As Joshua passed his desk just beyond the doorway, the light of a single lantern across the room flickered on the child's book that Lucius had sent, drawing his attention to its position tucked between his Bible's pages. He hadn't left the book there.

Tahira came out from the kitchen, wiping her hand on a towel. Her lips tensed as she followed Joshua's gaze toward the book.

"Would *Makinda* like a cup of tea now?" she asked, ignoring Joshua's expression.

He tried to wipe the shame from his eyes. "I apologize for this," Joshua said softly, pointing to the book. "I didn't mean to leave it out. My family was upset about it and sent it to me to see."

Tahira lowered her chin, her lips still thin, but her eyes softened, telling him she accepted the explanation.

"I will fix tea for you," she said.

Joshua moved over to the dining table, kneeling by the hearth nearby to light a small fire to warm the room. He took his jacket off as the room slowly warmed.

"I'm glad you were able to set time aside tonight so we could talk," Joshua said as Tahira sat down. He pulled a box out of the burlap sack, unwrapping the box of cookies he'd purchased in King William's Town. Tahira's eyes smiled as she glanced at the box.

"I just wanted to take a few moments to say thank you," Joshua said.

The smile that extended to Tahira's lips meant more than he could say.

"That's why I asked you to have tea tonight," he continued. "I feel I don't say it enough. It's been delightful having you here, Tahira. You've helped make this place feel like a home." He enjoyed the happiness that glimmered in her eyes with his words.

"I heard you talking to one of the women in your village, saying you had never had cookies like these and that you thought they looked lovely. I hope you'll like them," he said.

"Thank you, *Makinda*," she said, bowing her head a bit as she took the box gingerly from his hands and opened it, trying not to damage its clear wrapping while removing its cover. "Oooh," she said as the lines around her eyes seemed to ease; she looked girlishly at the many colors of the cookies—strawberry, vanilla, chocolate. She leaned the box toward him. He pulled out a chocolate one. She picked out a strawberry one and bit in, seeming surprised that it was fluffy. She chuckled as a crumb fell down her chin.

Joshua smiled broadly at the sparkle that graced her eyes for a moment, but her eyes quickly darkened again in their familiar way.

He always hoped he could make her smiles linger longer. They rarely did, except for when she spoke of Beaumont.

"I want to thank you also for your advice," Joshua said at last. "I've thought a lot about what you said about Nongolesi a few weeks ago. Your words were very wise. I've seen Mhlobo in the city since he came and told me not to visit their home again. I apologized to him. He seems to believe me when I say I never intended to insult his family."

"That will help set things right," she replied, chewing more slowly.

"I've taken care not to spend time alone with Nongolesi at the school, or to speak with her alone after church," he said, expecting her to nod approvingly. She didn't. By now, he knew how to read the tenseness of her lips and the silence that was now following. Tahira lowered her tin cup from her lips.

"I have seen you have eyes for Nongolesi," she said sternly, disappointment in her eyes as the firelight flickered gently.

"Yes, I understand how people viewed my interactions with her," he said, surprised by her reaction. "I'm hoping my actions now will help correct those impressions."

Tahira set her cup aside, staring at the light reflecting from its sides. When she finally met his gaze again, she looked at him with forgiving eyes. He knew he shouldn't speak.

"When I was young," she said after a few moments, her voice thick with remembrance, "young and beautiful"—her eyes sparkled for a moment, playfully—"all the young boys would flirt with me, and say, 'I shall make you my wife.' But there was one who caught my eye. A handsome one, and a stick-fighting champion. He won against the chief's son!" she said, her eyes bright. "He would visit me at the river. We came to be in love. He wished to marry me, but I did not think he had means to keep me well. In my heart, I wanted to marry him. But we worried about what others would say if my family accepted a small amount of *lobola*. We chose to wait one more year so he could secure more *lobola* before he approached my father.

"Then one day"—her voice deepened—"when I trekked to the river, I was grabbed from behind. My heart was leaping. You have heard our saying *Intliziyo yam yayivuya ngokwenene*—'My heart leaped to the sky.' But when I looked at the hands around my arms, my heart feared. I could see it was not the one I loved, but another I had never seen, from a village nearby. He covered my mouth that I would not scream, and he whispered in my ear, 'We will send word to your father that you are married.' My heart sank," she said, her voice cracking. "This was our way. He had done nothing wrong. But this one I did not love." Her broken words lingered in the air.

"He took me to his village and tied me to the central pillar of his hut. The older women came and told me, 'Look, girl, you are of age, you must get married.' All day and all night, they kept me there, until I said I would give it a try. He never beat me, and I bore his child. Two months later, the child died, and I fled back to my village. I did not love that one. I could not stand his touch. My family never forgave me for the transgression. I was forever considered *umabuy ekwendeni,* one who deserted her marriage. Some consider this act worse than when an unmarried girl falls pregnant, a great disgrace," she said, as if chastising herself. The lines around her eyes stretched more deeply, as if the pain had never gone away.

"That one I loved was told never to come near me. And I was to have no contact with young girls anytime," she said. Her lips quivered. "They said I would teach young girls naughty things. I was never to marry again, I was not fit to be a wife or mother. And from that time, I was to play a role of *inkazana,* the one men go to, who will lie down with them to take care of their needs when their wives swell so large with a child that they cannot share the sheets with them any longer. 'This thing I will not do!'" she said, thrusting her hand in the air. "And so I left this village for many, many years."

The pain in her voice made Joshua sit still.

"He died, that one I loved—Natonde—during the years when influenza killed many. He sent word, in the days before he passed. The message a young boy delivered: 'Natonde loved Tahira,'" she said, her eyes wet. She sat for a moment, nodding her head, as if considering the words again. *"Think,"* she whispered as she looked at Joshua so intensely. "Think what would have been if we had followed our hearts."

Joshua's eyes were wet. He was now so much more aware of the depth of her sorrows. Tahira sat wordlessly with her memories. He tried not to think about his own struggles, his own desires to heed the callings of his heart. "I understand," Joshua responded in a quiet voice. "I'm very sorry for the pains you have suffered, Tahira."

Sitting with her in the stillness, the fire crackling softly, he wasn't sure what to say, until Tahira's eyes were drawn to another sack on the corner of the table.

"That's also for you," he said hesitantly, not certain if he should give it to her right then. "It's a part of the gifts I wished to give to you tonight."

Her eyes smiled as he handed it to her. She opened the sack, then looked up, startled.

"Ogenga told me you lost your Bible the day the three women were taken to Nocno. I had wondered why we've been practicing with your friend's Xhosa Bible."

As she lifted a marula Bible from the sack, she gasped.

"I located a merchant in town who still has a few Bibles like this, written in Xhosa. I purchased this for you." The look on her face made him so happy.

"My Bible was not like *this*," she said, rubbing her hand against the gold-crusted pages and the soft leather cover.

"I'm glad to be able to give this to you."

She took a deep breath, as if never before touching such a luxurious book. She opened the Bible to its middle, handing it to Joshua. He cradled it in his hands, brushing the soft pages between his fingers. He frowned as he looked at the Xhosa on its pages. He shook his head. "You know my learning isn't coming quickly."

"You're making good progress, and you can learn more. We will practice more often. Xhosa is a beautiful language, this one."

"It's very beautiful," he said earnestly. "I've never asked you, do you have a favorite passage?"

"Would you like me to read it to you?" She smiled.

"I'd like that very much."

She took the Bible from his hands, reclaiming a precious jewel. She moved the lantern closer, cocking her head to the side slightly, mouthing the words silently for a moment—the gesture caused him to stiffen and think back in time, thousands of miles away. It oddly reminded him of that dream he'd had months ago, the night before he left for Africa. He was startled for a moment. Then Tahira spoke out into midair, cherishing the words as they clicked across her tongue.

"*Kuba wenjenje uThixo ukulithanda kwakhe ihlabathi, ude wancama uNyana wakhe okuphela kwamzeleyo, ukuze bonke abakholwayo kuye bangatshabalali, koko babe nobomi obungunaphakade.*" She looked at Joshua, seeming to think he should recognize the rhythm. He pursed his lips and shook his head.

For God so loved the world," she translated the Word, letting the words dance over her tongue, "*that He gave His only begotton Son.*"

Joshua lowered his eyes. He should have recognized that rhythm.

"*That whosoever believeth in Him,*" she continued, "*should not perish, but have everlasting life.*" The intensity in her voice stirred deep feelings in him, and Joshua closed his eyes, letting the words fill him as she continued reading the words of the Apostle John.

"*Kuba uThixo akamthumanga uNyana wakhe ehlabathini, ukuze aligwebe ihlabathi; wamthuma ukuze ihlabathi lisindiswe ngaye. For God sent not His Son into the world to condemn the world; but that the world through Him might be saved.*" Her voice cracked. She paused, then continued in her own words. "It means that even though this life is so difficult, and we have been made to suffer so much, God loves us."

The pain in her voice made Joshua open his eyes. She was no longer translating the words directly, but telling him what the words meant to her.

"For God so loved the world," she said, rocking back and forth slightly. "He lets us know that even though foreigners have come here and despised us, laughed at the dung in our hands, the huts we build, our soured milk—that in spite of all these things, God loves us." Her voice broke again, her hand tightened around the Bible.

Joshua's heart raced. How could he have been so wrong? His mind filled with that one question, asked over and over again, feeling as though every mistake he'd made since his arrival sat painted across his face in bold colors. He looked at Tahira's worn dress, soiled in spots, her dark skin, the kinked hair peaking beneath her turban, her stout nose. It was as if the pain had been sitting somewhere deep inside him, pouting with its legs crossed, waiting to stand up and be heard. Joshua measured the kink of his own hair in the curl of hers, saw the fullness of his own lips in the plumpness of hers, the blush of his pigment in the hue of hers. He looked at her as a child would. He hadn't known how deep his soul was until the pinprick of pain began to spread from a depth he could barely comprehend, and welled inside, on fire.

"*Ke lowo uyenzayo inyaniso uyeza elukhanyisweni, ukuze imisebenzi yakhe ibonakalaliswe; ngokuba isetyenzelwe kuThixo,*" she read on as he diminished further in the holy place she had created. "Even though these things have made life for us *so* hard"—she looked at Joshua, pointing her index finger to a precise spot, pressing it firmly onto that life-giving pulp—"*God loves us.*"

Joshua raised his hand to wipe a tear from the corner of his eyes as he heard clearly the words she had not said, *God loves us, Joshua, even if the missionaries do not.* Did she realize she was stabbing at his heart? The lines on Tahira's face stretched long as heated shame flushed over him.

"That even though this world is so hard," Tahira whispered, almost to herself, "*God loves us.*"

She looked over to him then, her eyes wet. He measured his every breath, felt a pulsing in his neck, and tried hard to keep tears from streaming down his cheeks. It took a few moments, but he finally managed to speak the word caught in his throat as he uttered a low and gasping, a faint and humbled, "Yes."

Joshua awoke in the middle of the night. This night was worse than all of the ones that preceded it in the prior weeks, ever since he had visited Nocno. His talk with Tahira had cast dark shadows in his mind, troubling him more than he could express. She had touched a ripe chord. Ever since he had traveled to Nocno, his nights had been restless. Each night, he'd awaken in the twilight, sometimes only for an hour, sometimes longer. He would stretch an arm behind the back of his neck, staring into the darkness, willing his mind to empty of all thoughts. But his eyes would burn in those midnight hours. This time, as he rolled over on his side and inhaled deeply, he allowed himself to dwell on the images of the jailhouse, of the play, of Tahira as she pointed at that precise spot in the Bible. A thought strode through his mind, and he did not try to whisk it away this time: He was on the wrong side of the fight. That thought, which emerged firmly from the shadows of his mind and finally stood tall, caused an uneasy feeling that would not go away. He searched his mind, trying to understand how he had come to this point. The love he used to be filled with—God's love—where was it? He hadn't felt it fully for so long.

He lifted himself out of his bed at the first sign of a brightening sky, when all but the sparrows seemed to be sleeping, and he made his way past the small villages lining the roadside, up the winding road cut into the mountainside, across the cone-scattered pine trail. Only upon reaching the wooden bridge, with the jasmine and pine scents thick in the air, did he pause long enough to take in the sights well. The top branches of the pine treetops flopped in the high wind like the manes of wild horses, and ravens called to one another in deep voices as they flew from crown to crown. Looking across the lowlands that stretched in front of him from that spot on the bridge, he realized the fogs were not cast thick. His gaze reached a sweeping distance as he saw what was often hidden beneath the low clouds of this land: rows upon rows of pines, which stretched above the emerald mountains all around him. Beyond them, the peaks of bluer and more distant mountains stood proudly. On days like this, with no veil of mist to block the vista, Joshua could see clearly that in this spot, nature truly enveloped him as healing waters trickled down the mountainside.

Joshua rubbed his hands against his arms to warm himself in the early June air, pulling his coat more tightly as he proceeded up the root stairs and rested before that shimmering pool beneath the waterfall. He shivered a bit in the winter chill. As he knelt beneath the crystal stairs, he unfolded the letter in his pocket and reread it. It had just arrived from Reverend Waldron. They had no intention of changing the policy about mission donations to the jailhouse. Joshua exhaled heavily, rubbing his hand on his temple. He understood that the growing sense of unease he felt was intended to tell him something.

As he tried to quell his unease, Joshua's thoughts floated back to that place he'd imagined a hundred times before. Why had his grandfather and the other slaves always gathered before the red riverbanks beneath the blue mountains? Perhaps it was safer to gather far from the slave quarters. Or perhaps they had sought the same peace that he found here. He opened his Bible, that very one that his grandfather had once held, tracing his fingers across the mud stains left there by those slaves who'd prayed by the riverside to be set free. He turned to a few pages he'd marked—he read parts of First Samuel and the Psalms, reading in the Bible about the use of tambourines and the singing and dancing with joyful songs at religious ceremonies. Next he turned to First Corinthians and Psalms 150, to read the same about cymbals. *What is this all about? You should be questioning that. . . . What is this all about? No drums, no dancing, no traditional clothes, no hand clapping.* The Brother's words echoed in his mind. The Brother was right: Joshua didn't like the answers he had received to that question.

As he brushed his hand over the cover of his Bible, his mind drifted back in time again. What had his grandfather read, Joshua wondered, as he had held this very Bible to the moon's light, in order to call each word with care. What words comforted him in that midnight hour, filling his heart with hope enough to place one foot in front of the other with a firm belief in a better day? He wished he knew the answer now. His family had sacrificed so much for him. All of the indignations his aunts and uncles had suffered, all of the long hours they had labored, so that he might get to this day, have the opportunity to prove the worthiness of the Negro. Every action he took would have its consequence. That was precisely the problem.

As the sun's light filtered more strongly through the trees and glistened on the crystal pool before him, Joshua bowed his head, praying. As he finished his prayer, he moved to a patch of smooth grass, relishing the peace and stillness. The voice sang again. This time he tried to memorize every Xhosa word he recognized. *Ezam izimvu ziyaliva ilizwi lam, ndibe nam ndizazi, zindilandela; mna ndizinika ubomi obungunaphakade; azisayi kutshabalala naphakade; akukho namnye uya kuzihlutha esandleni sam. UBawo, ondinike zona, ungaphezu kwabo bonke; akukho bani unako ukuzihlutha esandleni sikaBawo. Mna noBawo sibanye.* The sound was so close, so wistful, he wasn't certain if it were anything more than the yearning of his own heart. When the singing ended, he looked around. With dew pearls glistening on the leaves, he seemed to see history all around him. The sunlight brushed every dewdrop with a tiny scarlet hue, which lay like the shed blood of those who had fought and lost here. The warrior's cries seemed to rustle through the wind; widows' tears seemed to trickle in the waters. The feeling inside told Joshua all he needed to know. He willed himself to heed that feeling—when it came to marula Bibles, when it came to forced relocations, when it came to Nongolesi. He closed his eyes faintly, opening them again to the world around him. The needles of every pine tree seemed piqued, the flowers staked firmly to the ground. Perhaps the answers had been with him all along.

———————

Joshua returned home well after dark, when the moon was set high in the sky. He felt he had begun to sort out many matters that had troubled him, simply by taking the time to be still. As he entered his home, which lay dark and quiet, he lit a lantern so he could attend to the first order of business. His hand trembled as he picked up the latest letter from his family, rereading it slowly. He sank down into the chair beside his desk and picked up *Black Boy in the Jungle,* centering it in the moonlight that drifted through his window. Of the many things he felt were first steps to order his direction, this was among the most important. Taking his time, he examined each disparaging cartoon in that child's book again. It was so similar to the ones he grew up with. The monkey-people it portrayed were supposed to be African, and ignorance filled their expressions. Joshua's thoughts drifted to the clipped newspaper article that hung in Nokwe's home. *Is he human?* Part and parcel of the same thing, he thought—a thought that sent a chill through him.

As he glanced back at the book and paused, he heard that voice still singing, a tune sung on eighth notes, its hard, deliberate accents forming a compelling tune. With the pulsing song in his ears, Joshua read by the light of his lantern, rubbing his hands over the pages of the children's book, wanting to feel them fully, to know them for what they were. He read on into the night, healing his splintered soul, thought by thought. Hours later, when he reached the last page, he sighed deeply. Opening the book back to its first page, he began examining it again.

CHAPTER 22

It had been a week since Joshua had prayed in the early morning hours at 39 Steps. Since then, he'd kept his prayers focused every day on discerning the right steps to take as a minister. As he did, he found his thoughts drifting more often to his memories of the Nocno jailhouse. The prisoners had sat there, staring off into the blueness of the sky, with empty, unthoughtful gazes, before turning their eyes back to their tasks of setting cement into brick molds. They seemed to have lost all hope in their lives and in their futures. In their eyes, Joshua had seemed to see the very brokenness that Tahira so feared when she spoke of the villages and the fate they were suffering as they lost their strong young men to the mines of Johannesburg. Finally, on a quiet morning Joshua moved to his writing desk, pressed his pencil to a clean sheet of paper, and started writing a new sermon. Every time the words of his mission leaders echoed in his mind, trying to guide his words, he chased them away, letting his words flow freely.

Joshua pulled that sermon out later in the afternoon, when the warden stepped into the door of the East London jailhouse, pulling his cigar from his mouth.

"As minister of Fort Hare, I am authorized to use the chapel," Joshua said coolly, waving the sermon in his hand. "I appreciated your tour of the facilities, and I'm heartened to see my mission has done such good work helping to build and maintain the chapel. I want to make sure we put it to good use." Joshua kept any twinkle of ridicule from his eyes. His tone was respectful, but they both understood. The warden simply turned his back and walked away as a guard led Joshua to the chapel.

In many ways, Joshua was surprised it was so simple. The guards alerted some of the inmates that they were free to attend an evening sermon. As the room filled with over forty men, mostly African, some Indian, Joshua greeted each. He led the men in the local hymns he had learned. Many of them seemed to know the words; the others soon followed the choruses. As the singing took on a life of its own, with the prisoners clapping to the words, Joshua felt his heart might burst, knowing each stanza helped renounce the rattle of their chains during the day. As he clapped and sang along with them, a man in the front row caught his eyes. Joshua's hands froze. He looked just like Nate. Another sitting a few rows back also caused him to hesitate. He looked like Lucius. Joshua inhaled deeply and had to stand back for a moment as the men kept singing a chorus from the heart. He could barely conceive of what he was thinking and feeling in those moments, as if these men fed his soul much more than he nourished theirs. He was happy to stand with them. As he began his sermon, he told them that this was their chapel and they should use it even if there ever came a day when he could no longer visit. That night, for the first time in months, Joshua slept peacefully through the night.

———————

A few more trips to his crystal stairs and Joshua felt a sense of direction, a rightness of purpose that had somehow been missing before. He promised himself he'd go to the jailhouse often, once a week if he could, until his mission forbade it. Now, as he drove down the road on his way to see the Old Man, the birds formed two successive V shapes in the sky. They somehow reflected his mood.

Joshua had sent ahead to receive permission to visit the Old Man. As he made his way up the path to the Maganu home, he smiled as the July sun peeked through thick clouds. Spring was on the horizon. As he neared the Maganu home, the Old Man greeted him with a warm smile.

"What has inspired this?" the Old Man asked with a tenderness in his voice. There was no negative judgment underneath his words, no questioning why Joshua had hesitated so many times before to help their cause.

"I don't agree with the policy to produce Bibles only in English," Joshua replied. He had thought through carefully what lines he felt he could straddle. This was one of them. In some ways, he was mystified it had taken him eight months to say those words to Mr. Maganu.

"It's that simple?" the Old Man asked.

"I wish I had realized earlier it was that simple," Joshua said. "I—"

The Old Man waved his hand, stopping Joshua, shaking his head as if no apology were needed.

"It's important that the people can read this Bible in their own language, so they can understand it more fully," the Old Man said. "It is harder for anyone to refashion its messages for false purposes when you understand the words well."

Joshua nodded, and gratitude overwhelmed him as the Old Man accepted the wad of cash Joshua provided to help fund the printing of marula Bibles. "As I am able, I will work with other ministers to devote funds to printing Bibles in other languages also. Only a few districts in the region have tried to cease such printing, I understand. If we spend our stipends carefully, we can save money and every few months we can gather that money together to help ensure people in the villages can secure Bibles that they can read well."

There was a look in the Old Man's eyes that fortified Joshua, and the feeling inside let him know he was on the right track.

Later that evening, Joshua dwelled on his decisions, on the thin line he'd chosen to tread. If his mission discovered his actions, he couldn't predict the consequences. But he knew by what he was feeling that he was moving steadily in the right direction. He couldn't understand, then, why he failed to mention his troubles to his family as he penned another letter at his desk. He ended his letter by telling his family how happy he was that they were receiving greater resources from his mission. As he penned his words, he shaded his eyes. The last thing he ever wanted to do was fail them or cause them shame. He stared at the letter for a moment, then signed it, and prepared to mail it in the morning.

As Joshua prepared to leave the teachers' lounge, Nongolesi emerged from her classroom at the call of the bell. Joshua's heart lifted as their paths headed toward each other. From a pinprick in the center of his heart, a brightness welled, and he knew he would no longer want to cast it aside. Nongolesi made his heart sing. It was that simple, and the implication clear.

She saw him and averted her eyes. It had been over two months since Joshua had tried to distance their relationship. He knew she was hurt, but she didn't let it show in her demeanor. "How are you?" she greeted him, forcing a happy tune into her voice.

"You look tired," she said with concern. "I'm sure you've done a full day's work with the typing. You should rest." Nongolesi pulled her sweater closer around her as a cool wind blew.

"It's a labor of love," Joshua said, hoping she would not leave quickly.

"Are you going to the cricket game later—the big game between Lovedale and Fort Hare?" she asked.

"I've heard the students speaking of it—"

"You should go."

"I've never been to a cricket game," he said, happy that she was even bothering to mention it.

"Well, this game is a very special one." She gave him a smile that made his heart melt. In that moment, he couldn't understand why he had hesitated to allow himself to acknowledge how much he had grown to care about her. Right now, every hesitation vanished, nothing had ever felt better than to be spending time with her. He hoped he would be able to speak with her at length so he could honor what he'd promised himself during his last trip to 39 Steps—he'd finally tell her how he felt about her.

"All of the young Africans who have made it to these schools—Lovedale, Fort Hare—they will all be at this game. And the atmosphere—the air, the energy! It's a big celebration. Your presence would mean a lot; it would make the students feel you are a part of them."

She was always so supportive of him, even when he didn't deserve it. "I just hadn't given it much thought," he said, trying to focus on what she was saying. So many thoughts were swimming through his mind. "Will you be at the cricket game?" he asked with a hopeful look in his eyes, which seemed to catch her off guard.

"Of course, I wouldn't miss it. There is always a gathering in the aftermath, when Fort Hare celebrates."

"They're so sure they'll win?"

"They *always* win," she said. Shaking her finger, she joked, "And you better tell all of your students you think they will win!"

He laughed. The more he grew to know Nongolesi, the more he saw with clarity how much his relationship with Shantal had lacked. He'd known all along his relationship with Shantal had never felt completely right, but his time in South Africa when he needed a pillar of strength, a woman who could grow with him in faith—he knew that person wasn't Shantal. Things felt so different with Nongolesi.

"The students will go to the restaurant in Alice afterward. The Old Man would never allow me to go there, not even for that celebration. But you should go."

"If the Old Man disapproves, I probably shouldn't."

"He disapproves only because I am a woman. There is no liquor there. It is a respectable place for a preacher to go. The students go there to eat and talk and gloat!"

He smiled. "I'll look into it. Nongolesi, thank you."

Her face brightened as he said those words, and his heart filled again. She smiled back, a bittersweet smile, as she turned and walked toward the teacher's lounge.

Joshua took Nongolesi's advice and attended the cricket game. He even joined the students afterward as they traveled into Alice to share a meal at a local restaurant. The students at Joshua's table had at first looked at him with lifted brows, their expressions soon melting into gentle smiles. He'd made a constant effort to meet with students, but never so informally. Joshua sat with them for a while, talking about nothing. . . . And everything. *It's a start,* he thought.

He looked forward now, a day later, to speaking with Ogenga at greater length. "Studying hard?" Joshua asked Jovan as he walked through the kitchen door of their sparsely furnished dormitory. No paint on the door, no food on the counters, only a modest wooden table with four chairs in the center of the dusty unfinished floor.

"I'm protesting," Jovan replied, looking up from his writing with his brow furrowed. He leaned back from the kitchen table. "I'm surprised to see you here."

"Ogenga invited me around."

"He's in his room." Jovan smiled, seeming happy to hear that news. "You can go upstairs and fetch him."

Joshua walked up a creaking set of stairs that sounded as if they'd soon give way. As he reached the top, he could see light coming from a room right off the stairs. Joshua moved to the cracked door and knocked softly. He could see a lantern dangling from the bedroom's ceiling as Ogenga sat on his bed against the wall, on top of a colorful quilt. The only other piece of furniture appeared to be a bedside table. Joshua's eyes lingered on the Xhosa Bible that sat on top of it.

As he jumped to his feet, Ogenga caught Joshua's surprised eyes lingering on the Bible. "What have I done?" He opened the door wide.

"Nothing." Joshua laughed. "I thought you invited me around?"

"So soon?"

"I can come back in a month or two."

"Very funny." Ogenga smiled. "You're welcome here," he said very purposefully, though his eyes probed for more of an explanation. "Did you see Jovan downstairs?" he asked, moving past Joshua and motioning him to follow back down the stairs. "He won't believe you came by our dorm."

"He's down there," Joshua said from a few steps behind. Ogenga paused midway down the stairs, ushering Joshua in front of him.

"I think he said he was—protesting?" Joshua said as he walked back through the kitchen door to find Jovan still hunched over a piece of paper.

"I can hold the pen as effectively as a gun," Jovan said, having heard Joshua's comment. He looked up from his paper.

"He writes for *Imvo,* the African newspaper in these parts."

"I'm impressed," Joshua said. "I didn't know they published student writings."

"He's one of the most eloquent thinkers around," Ogenga bragged. "They publish him often."

"It's good to think about different ways of living, the best that the world offers," Jovan said with lively eyes. "There are so many ideas right now."

"What are you writing about?" Joshua asked.

"Pass laws," Ogenga guessed, turning a chair backward, sitting on it while resting his chin on top of its curved back. He leaned to the side, pulling another chair out, inviting Joshua to sit down.

"I've already sent that one off. This one is more"—Jovan paused, squinting his eyes and grinning—"philosophical."

"Oh, no!" Ogenga kidded as Joshua took a seat.

"This is about *ubuntu,*" Jovan said.

Ogenga raised his eyebrows and nodded approvingly. "That's a great choice."

"*U-bun-tu.*" Jovan pronounced it again, blowing the word gently through his lips. "The word itself sounds brilliant. 'I care about my brother and myself'—that's how it translates, in words and in spirit," he said, tapping his pen in his hand. "I am asking to what degree the system of Europeans is compatible with our basic belief in *ubuntu.* Your society seems so individualistic. It seems that you don't care sometimes about the man next door to you," he said, looking at Joshua.

"So you advocate what?" Ogenga asked.

"I don't really take a stance. I simply say we must think this through very carefully. Times are changing. And we must change."

"But we should control that change," Ogenga said, sitting up straight and tapping his hands on his chair. Ogenga was getting that bright-eyed look again, the one that often accompanied his finger-pointing chatter. He truly loved ideas.

"We will do well to take the best of what is new," Jovan said, nodding. "We have always done that. When the Mfengu came, we embraced some of their concepts of how to till the soils. Our music, it is said, some of it comes from the peoples in the east of Africa."

"So the broad idea is to respect our past *and* to choose the path that will honor the future," Ogenga said.

Jovan nodded, leaning his chair on its hind feet, tapping his pen on the table. "It's in the details that the difficulty comes. This is such a dark period we are in—a dark period of our history," he whispered, lost in his thoughts for a moment. "But we will make it through this. You don't just throw sixteen generations away."

"Jovan wrote about the pass laws last week," Ogenga said to Joshua. "Students and workers are going to protest the laws soon in East London. Many Fort Hare students will join in those protests."

"The school may expel you if you go," Joshua said hesitantly.

Ogenga met his gaze. "We want the government to stop plucking the grapes from our yard and giving them all away. Fighting with a pen, we fight that way. Fighting with our feet, we will fight that way also."

"We're not of the mind that anyone should be made to leave this land," Jovan agreed. "But this country, it is for all of us. There's a place for these peaceful things. But you must be willing to do what it takes. We are preparing to bring forth change through many means, like what the Brother helps us to do—educate ourselves to provide for ourselves. Perhaps you will help us, like the Brother suggested when he preached here."

"And how is the Brother helping you?" Joshua asked.

"He teaches us," Jovan said.

"Teaches what?" Joshua probed.

"The subjects you and the advisory committee believe we don't need," Ogenga said, his tone sharp. "Jovan is studying to be a doctor. Fort Hare won't adequately provide courses. But the Brother sees value and he tutors students. Jovan will soon take South Africa's national exam on his own, without the full benefit of formal training, but if he passes, he will be awarded his first degree in medicines. Then he'll go abroad to train to be a doctor. The Negro colleges in the USA are willing to train him. Tuskegee has already trained students from Africa before him. And when Jovan comes back as a doctor, he will be able to live free from the moneys of the government. Some whites who see the system is wrong will come to Jovan for services. As he gains greater resources, he can use those resources to help others follow that same path."

"I never said I thought you should not be doctors and engineers," Joshua said. "My mission simply believes that it must come with time."

"*Your mission?* I thought that was your view too," Jovan probed.

Joshua looked down for a moment, but met their gaze as he responded. "I wouldn't say that's the way I see things. . . ."

Jovan and Ogenga stared at him, lips parted, then exchanged glances with each other.

"*Ndikuxelele ukuba yena ulungile. Unenthliziyo enthle, kwaye nenyaniso uyayibona,*" Ogenga said to Jovan.

"*Andidingi kuqinisekiswa. Ngabanye ababemthandabuza,*" Jovan responded.

"Hey!" Joshua laughed, knowing they were talking about him.

Ogenga turned back to Joshua with a piercing look. "We know of the struggle for equality the Negroes are waging in the USA," he said. "Marcus Garvey has written of it in his newspaper, and Negroes from your country, like Sarah, speak of it. You support that struggle there, in your country, and the many different means that have been necessary to protest for change?"

"I worked hard in an effort to bring about greater equality when I was in college." Joshua nodded. It was a subject dear to him.

"How?" Ogenga asked.

"I ensured that our training at Wilberforce was the best, that the government devoted funds to bring good professors to us, that we would have good opportunities to gain employment in the communities around us, and that laws were applied as justly as possible to Negroes."

"By organizing protests?"

"Sometimes," Joshua answered, seeing disappointment register in their eyes. He knew where this was going.

"So I must ask you—you must have a reason," Ogenga said. "Why not here? Why do you not support the same here?"

Joshua tensed up as Ogenga held his gaze firm. What would his mission expect him to say? In this moment, he didn't really care. He addressed them in a quiet voice. "I'm not afraid to admit when I'm wrong. And I am saying that my views are not what they once were."

Ogenga and Jovan exchanged glances again. After a moment, Ogenga turned back to Joshua. "Perhaps we're getting somewhere with you, *Makinda*."

As Joshua drove down the familiar road in the direction of the Amatolas a couple of weeks later, he glanced out his window as a few young ladies walked across the meadows with clay pots hoisted on top of their heads, their arms swinging listlessly as they chatted on their way back from fetching water at the riverside. He knew that Nongolesi and her friends had probably just arrived at that very same river on this late-winter day, and his heart grew full.

"I don't believe I'm going to do this." He laughed to himself as he drove down an unpaved side road that ended about a quarter mile from the river. Parking his car at the roadside, he set off by foot the rest of the distance as the gentle sounds of the river grew louder. The grass was soft underneath his shoes, cushioning his every step as he walked through a cluster of trees. He could soon hear young women laughing as they dipped their pots into the river. The trees thinned and he glimpsed Nongolesi with two other young ladies by the river. They laughed together as they gently rinsed their clay pots, then filled them to the brim with cold water. Joshua took a deep breath, feeling like he was about to dip his feet into those very same crystal waters.

"Nongolesi," he said just loudly enough for his voice to carry through the last trees as he moved the final steps into full view. Nongolesi and the young ladies looked in his direction, getting wide-eyed at the same time. Nongolesi froze with a smile lighting her face for a moment. The other two girls gathered their belongings quickly, scurrying inland as they glanced back at Nongolesi with smiles.

Nongolesi looked beautiful, dressed in a traditional *umbhaco*, her hair wrapped in a matching orange *iqhiya*. She stood happily for a moment, then seemed apprehensive. "You were just walking through this part of the neighborhood?" she asked, trying to break the awkward silence as Joshua moved toward her.

"It would be much easier if I could say yes," he said, not knowing fully how she would react. "But I came here for a special reason."

"What is the *something special*?" she asked.

"You." His heart sank a bit when she failed to smile. She stepped back toward the river, tipping her pot into the water, taking her time to rinse and fill it again.

"I had hoped for some time you would come here," she said slowly as she turned back to him. "You didn't."

The look on her face pained him. He moved closer to her, feeling nervous. It had taken him so long to muster the courage, he wouldn't get discouraged now. The cold water grazed his hand as he took the pot from her. "I'll gladly carry this for you," he said. She remained quiet.

He considered all the things he wanted to say—he'd thought them all through—but he knew none of them would serve as adequate excuses for his behavior. "I needed time, Nongolesi," he said earnestly. "I know I've hurt you over the last couple of months."

She lifted her chin as he said those words, but didn't respond. "You know there was someone special back in America," he said. "I had to deal with that, to sort it out in my heart." He felt better as he saw her stiffness melt, and he saw forgiveness in her eyes. She wiped away a tear that had teased at the rim of her eyes, giving a half smile.

"It was easier to see you at your father's home," he said, looking at her intensely. "Well, I suppose I should say it was easier to see you at your father's home until Mhlobo let me know he'd have my hide."

She laughed softly. "You made him very angry," she said, smiling.

"I hope you know I would never intentionally insult your family. I didn't realize my actions would be taken that way, and I apologize. Do you have a few moments? Can we talk here?" He held his breath, waiting for her response.

She nodded and his heart grew full. They walked over to the rocks near the riverside, sitting and talking for a long while. Joshua cherished the way she made him feel as they talked on into the late afternoon.

CHAPTER 23

Everyone in the church looked to Joshua as though they'd just swallowed a fluffy, sweet-feathered canary. Sitting in his pulpit seat, parting the pages of his Bible, a smile curved at the edges of Joshua's lips. Given their expressions, he was certain they'd already heard the news. He could practically hear them whispering behind their hands, *Joshua trekked to the river to greet Nongolesi!* The truth was, he didn't mind what anyone thought or said. He had returned to the river every day over the past week, and he'd never been happier.

The choir rose and sang, a Xhosa hymn sung freely. The bleakness he'd once felt in the church had long since disappeared ever since he began to preach more freely. He nodded as they rattled the gourds and tambourines he'd supplied the choir with a few weeks earlier. The joy in this place! He enjoyed the services so much now, relishing the sights of the expressive-colored clothing his congregation now felt free to wear, the traditional attire and *amaqhiya* many women of the villages wore, and the smiles on the faces as mamas began to dance in the aisles, swaying to the tambourine-laced music. Joshua welcomed also the fire in his belly, the one he'd missed so much during his first months of preaching in South Africa. He savored the feeling of the Lord's love flowing through him, feeling as if he were only a funnel for Someone much greater than he.

He smiled as he looked down at his Bible now. It bulged in his hands, twice the size it once was. He felt twice as blessed. Having seen Joshua's Bible holding together with loose threads, one of the Noni elders had offered a broad toothless smile, assuring Joshua that he could mend the torn binding of his Bible while sewing it together with his marula Bible. He explained the work could be undone, if Joshua didn't like it—the covers would remain the same; only the side binding would need to be expanded to sew the two Bibles together. Joshua had explained the importance of his Bible, its history, the mud stains on its cover. The man's eyes had twinkled: he understood. Joshua had nervously watched the man's work as he labored for hours, cutting and stitching the two, attaching Joshua's original mud-stained cover on the front and back of the new combined books, using fresh leather to secure it all at the bind. The Book he now held in his hands was beautiful.

The choir finished its last song. Joshua moved to the pulpit, preparing to minister about the unifying theme of Corinthians. *"Kuba thina sonke sabhaptizelwa mzimbeni mnye ngaMoya mnye, nokuba singama Yuda, nokuba singamaGrike,"* he said flawlessly, reading from a Xhosa chapter. *"Nokuba singamakhoboka, nokuba singabakhululekileyo . . . ukuze kungabikho kwahlukahlukana emzimbeni, kubekho ukunyamekelana kwamalungu ngakunye; kuthi, nokuba lilungu elinye eliva ubunzima, avelane amalungu onke; nokuba lilungu elinye elizukiswayo, avuyisane amalungu onke."*

His congregation members nodded brightly. Joshua flipped back to the English version of the words, interpreting the Xhosa ones he'd just uttered. "We are all One in the Spirit; there should be no division in the body of God's children. They will know we are Christians by our love."

———————

Joshua was still glowing from the strong reception to his sermon as the church bells rang out on the hour later that day. He took his seat along with the other advisory committee members as Jovan made his way into the dark-paneled administration room. Mr. Garrett pointed Jovan to a wooden chair at the lone end of the long table around which the rest of the committee was gathered. Jovan sat silently, eyes downcast.

"We have only one point to discuss at this special session today: our recommendation to the administration of the expulsion of Jovan Mabeza," Mr. Garrett said, clearing his throat. "The rector will review the charges."

"Last weekend," the rector said, "during the dance in the women's hall, the chaperon noted inappropriate and ungentlemanly behavior on the part of Mr. Mabeza, who knows there is a strict policy with regard to interacting with the women on campus. In the instance of dancing, there must at all times be at least a foot in between the man and the woman. The dance chaperon noted that Mr. Mabeza openly danced sternum to sternum with a young lady named Mazi, flouting established rules."

The advisory committee members tried to mold their lips into the frowns they seemed to think Mr. Garrett expected.

"Mr. Mabeza, what do you have to say for yourself?" the rector asked.

"I made a tremendous mistake, sir," he said, shoulders slumped. Joshua nearly chuckled at his feigned remorse.

"I appreciate that the college has allowed me to stay on as I have completed extra studies on my own for my medicine degree," Jovan said. "I should have exercised greater care. I have not wished to put my status at the college at risk, sirs."

"You knew about the guidelines, did you not?" the rector asked, leaning back into a tall-backed chair.

"Yes, sir, but I had been to cinema not too long ago—the cinema in King William's Town, where they show the American movies. The dancing I saw influenced me, sir, and I forgot myself at the women's dance."

"Is she even your girlfriend, this Mazi?" Mr. Garrett asked indignantly.

"She is now, sir."

The room burst into laughter. Even Joshua chuckled along, knowing Jovan hadn't intended the comment as a joke.

"There is nothing funny here," Mr. Garrett fumed as the men kept on laughing.

"It seems to me that Mr. Mabeza was unduly influenced by external sources and regrets his subsequent actions," Joshua said. Disbelief coated Professor Kabata's face. "Are you sorry for what you have done, Mr. Mabeza?" Joshua asked.

"I am very sorry, Reverend," Jovan said.

"Will it happen again?" Joshua asked.

"No, Reverend Clay, never again," Jovan responded.

Professor Kabata leaned toward the table. "He has had no previous breeches of college rules," he chimed in as Mr. Garrett's forehead began to shine.

"And he has been an exemplary student in all other ways," Joshua said, meeting Mr. Garrett's gaze. "Expulsion is too severe a response. We should send a sign, perhaps subjecting him to a limited curfew for the next month, but his status should not be placed in jeopardy."

Most members around the table nodded at the authority of Joshua's recommendation. Mr. Garrett squinted his eyes as Professor Kabata grinned. After a few more comments, the committee members recommended a strict curfew instead of expulsion. Jovan's eyes shone toward Joshua as he walked out of the room.

"You look beautiful today," Joshua said to Nongolesi a few weeks later, after he made his way back to the river. He noticed she was clothed in a dress he'd never seen before, her hair plaited in a new design. She sat on her knees next to the river's bank, twining a blade of grass between her fingers.

"That is nice of you to say," she responded, barely able to conceal the shine in her smile. "But I'll have you know my mother forced me to go with her to town to secure this dress." She looked at the river. "Everyone heard about your trek to the river. I don't know how." She smiled to herself. "My mother has thought for some time that I had feelings for you. *There's hope here.* That's what she was thinking when she heard about your trek; I could see it in her eyes. And the Old Man can hardly contain his happiness," she said, rolling her eyes.

Joshua chuckled.

"So here I am, wearing this new dress my mother bought me with my hair done especially for you. I'll have you know I prefer my dresses made with bright-pattered fabrics, if they are the ones cut in European style. And I like our traditional dresses in bright colors also. But look at this dress," she teased, waving her hand over its flat solid color.

"It's lovely," he said.

"My mother thought it was the best new one she could find. She is plotting with the Old Man now." She looked at him, shaking her head playfully.

Joshua laughed at her tone. "You didn't need a new dress to catch my eye," he said.

She chuckled. "This place is so beautiful," she said, looking out at the clay riverbanks as water gently gushed past. A cool August breeze blew. She reached to put on her sweater.

"I love it here also," Joshua said as he moved from the tree stump a few feet away and sat next to her. "I look forward to speaking with you. It's become the highlight of my week."

She plucked the blade of grass, smiling broadly, rolling the blade in between her palms.

"There's something about the river; its waters sound like music," she said. "And the colors on the water—I have always believed that God lets images reflect on the water because the world is so beautiful, he wants to see it twice."

Joshua smiled. Her words made him pause.

"*Makinda,* you've seemed a bit down lately. Is something wrong?"

He took a deep breath. "There's been a lot of things weighing on my mind."

"What things?"

"The students, mostly. All the things they want me to do to push for curriculum changes. The advice they seek about their protests. I'm glad that my church services are nearly full now, but the requests students are making . . ." He let out a sigh. "I don't know where my ministry fits in, or *if* it can fit in. It's hard to know which way to turn." He looked at her, hoping she'd say something gentle. He hadn't been so frank about his concerns with anyone else.

"How was it when you preached at home?"

"A lot easier. I suppose I simply understood the situation better there. In most situations I faced in Ohio, you could bring both sides together, black and white, and build bridges."

"And things are not that way here?"

"It's not that they're so different. There were times back home when we had to hold a protest or two—times when that was the only path to change. But I was free to engage in such matters there. Here, my hands are tied. 'The bright young star with an even temper from Wilberforce'—that's who they recruited. I'm simply supposed to bring more people to God. How can you bring more people to God if you're indifferent to their suffering?"

"You'll find the right way," she said softly, without a doubt in her tone.

He moved closer to her, touching his hand to her cheek. He held his lips to hers softly. Her breath caressed his cheek as he moved away to look at the smile that had appeared on her face. He kissed her again. It felt brilliant and consuming, as if she had milk and honey under her tongue. The perfume of the flowers peaked as he savored her kiss again.

It had been nearly two months since Joshua had begun to court Nongolesi, so Joshua knew Ogenga must have heard about his treks to the river, but Ogenga hadn't mentioned a word. He and Ogenga continued their relationship as it had been for months, sharing meals in the mess hall, debating topics in the dorm rooms, and chatting as Ogenga mingled after church. Ogenga had begun to feel like a trusted friend. Now, as Joshua steered his car down a hill and pulled up another on the road from East London back to Alice, he glanced in the rearview mirror at the backseat loaded with the books they'd secured for the latest students who would begin special studies with Joshua and Professor Kabata. Joshua hadn't taken biology since the course in college, but he remembered a thing or two and had happily agreed to tutor a student.

As he and Ogenga laughed and chatted on, exchanging stories about the challenges of student government, Joshua mused at how much they had in common. But as they reached the top of a hill and gazed down the stretch of road ahead, they both caught their breaths at the same time.

Ogenga cursed at the tractors and trucks lining the valley, beside a local village. Women walked slack-shouldered with heavy steps on the roadside, carrying sacks with their belongings. Old ladies were shouting angrily nearby, and young children everywhere seemed to be crying.

A frown glazed over Joshua's face. He could hardly believe his eyes. "The local officials promised they wouldn't pursue any removals here," Joshua said under his breath. The Old Man had been right as he feared the relocations would reach closer to Alice. Joshua drove to the heart of the clamor. "Please stay calm, Ogenga," Joshua pleaded, following Ogenga's gaze to the tractor that was demolishing a mud hut near the roadside. He could feel Ogenga's temper flaring. "We don't need for things to get worse. You'll stay here?" Joshua asked; Ogenga nodded.

Joshua stepped from the car. A cluster of men in plain clothes who stood by guided the work. They looked at Joshua with their arms crossed as he neared, glancing at his shiny car and back to him. "Just what do you think you're doing?" a stone-faced officer said to Joshua, his lips forming a thin line above a deep-clefted chin.

"My name is Reverend Clay of Fort Hare," Joshua responded. "I spoke with the commissioner last month and he told me there would be no removals in this area. The relocations were only authorized south of King William's Town, past the river. This is not south of King William's Town. This isn't permitted, and you and I both know that. The magistrate told me that if we ran into problems, we would be free to file a cease and desist petition."

The officer laughed, squinting his eyes. "Perhaps you haven't been around long enough to know, Reverend, that we will have the final say, petition or no petition," the cleft-chinned man said.

"I will be filing a cease and desist petition, and I will see you shortly, when I return with the paperwork from the magistrate." Joshua hoped they could not tell that his heart was racing. "Be prepared to defend your actions when the magistrate asks why you acted in direct contravention of the decisions laid out last month. You and I both know that Fort Hare is well funded by benefactors you don't want to make unhappy. As a minister of Fort Hare, my voice will carry weight with them. If you carry on here, you'll be asked to account for your actions."

Joshua stepped back to his car, taking a deep breath. He glanced in his rearview mirror as he pulled back onto the road, seeing the men exchanging words. The cleft-chinned man slowly waved the tractors to stop. "I think they're listening," Joshua said, somewhat surprised. "It's too late to file today," he said, glancing over at Ogenga, "but I'll go to East London tomorrow to make sure a petition is filed. I'll call Nokwe."

"When?" Ogenga asked, his eyes red.

"First thing in the morning. I'll be up before the sun. And I'll arrange to get a message to Nokwe tonight."

"Why call Nokwe?" Ogenga asked.

Joshua looked at him. They both knew he couldn't sign the petition himself. If his mission found out he'd done such a thing . . . Joshua couldn't finish the thought.

"I'll go with you tomorrow," Ogenga said, not pressing Joshua to answer.

Joshua stopped his car when he reached the hill's peak, stepping out and looking toward the village. The tractors had paused their work. Joshua nodded. "Ogenga, just have faith that we can use the offices of the magistrate to do as local officials have promised. Forced relocations won't be allowed here."

"You think that order will change anything?" Ogenga said to Joshua in a bitter tone.

"Some of the government officials are on our side."

"We'll see what your friends and that piece of paper will do. That village will be gone within three weeks."

Joshua and Ogenga arrived at the covered platform just as the 7:00 A.M. locomotive rocked into the center bay, spurting a black cloud into the air. It let out a piercing high-pitched whistle while a red, white and blue British flag boasted proudly on its black caboose. As the locomotive came to a stop, with dust clouds hovered above it, Africans disembarked from the very last cars, and whites unboarded from the front.

"All the special treatment you've been getting may be obscuring your view of life here," Ogenga said as they made their way to the third-class cabins for Africans. Joshua was never surprised anymore by Ogenga's directness. The smell of burning coal hovered in the air as they joined the line of Africans six cars down, mostly women, who stepped single file into the car. Joshua followed Ogenga, wincing at the stench flowing from the urinal to their left as they made their way down a cramped hallway searching for a cabin with space. Finally finding one, Ogenga slumped down on the soiled seat next to Joshua, across from two young African men dressed in tattered clothes. Ogenga had been unusually quiet on the drive to the station, and again now, his thoughts seemed far away. Perhaps he was thinking of the exchange awaiting them at the magistrate's office.

Joshua greeted the two men, who stared back at him with wrinkled brows.

"Are you Coloured?" the one on the right asked after a while, after the train had pulled out of the station, rocking back and forth as it gained speed.

Joshua smiled slightly. He would always be asked this question, he'd decided, as long as he was in South Africa. "I'm African, like you," Joshua responded. He could sense a smile curving across Ogenga's face.

"What is this accent you have?"

"I'm also from the United States."

"Ah!" both men said at the same time, over the loud rattle of wheels.

"That is very, very far away. We have heard of this land." The man on the left nodded.

"I have wanted to go to the United States," the man on the right said. "We have heard it is the land filled with riches and ample food. You like it there?"

"My family is there. I like it. The country has some problems, but they're getting better."

"And there is no hunger?" he probed further.

"There is hunger in some parts," Joshua replied.

"One day, I will save enough money to move there," the man on the right muttered, looking out at the hills rolling past.

"How much is it," his friend on the left chimed in, "to rent an apartment in America?"

"In some places, twenty dollars a month," Joshua replied.

"And are they big? Larger than the government *izindlu*?" the same man asked.

"Much bigger," Joshua said.

"They have electric lights?"

"In many parts of the country—in the big cities—the houses and apartments have electric lights," Joshua said.

"And how much to hire a car? Cars here, they are very expensive."

"You can buy an old one for forty dollars. That type of car would be about eight years old—the kind you have to crank in front to start up," Joshua said.

"Do you have a car in America?"

"My uncle does."

"Uncle?"

"Married to my mother's sister," Joshua said.

"Your father?" The man on the left seemed to correct him.

"Yes, my father," Joshua said.

"And how much is it for a girlfriend for a night?"

Joshua's lips froze; he tilted his head to the side. "I don't think I know what you mean." He fumbled, hoping he was misunderstanding.

"A girlfriend for a night . . ."

Joshua felt Ogenga tense up.

"You know, you meet a woman," his friend on the right tried to help explain. "You go up to her and say, 'I love you, I love you.' And you ask her how much money she will want for spending the night with you."

Joshua's mouth dropped, and Ogenga sat up, crossing his arms.

"In my country, that's called prostitution," Joshua said plainly. "It's against the law."

The men shrugged, exchanging questioning glances.

"One day, we shall go to America," one of them said again; the two men nodded to each other.

Ogenga leaned over and whispered to Joshua. "I told you this locomotive ride would show you how we live." Ogenga gazed out the window, trying to appear as if he weren't speaking about the two men across from them. He leaned back into Joshua's ear. "To them, that was like asking about the cost of a loaf of bread. They have little money to support their families because the government has taken their land, so they travel away from their families—nine months out of the year—to the Johannesburg mines. And how do they meet their needs?" He motioned toward his groin. "You know this?"

Ogenga's eyes were burning.

Joshua nodded.

"The government encourages this, sets up the whorehouses right outside of the miners' hostels. If they don't die of TB, they will die of syphilis, or worse yet return to their villages to spread diseases to their wives, who will bear sickly babies. This is what we mean when we say the white man has broken our families. Perhaps it is real to you now."

Joshua looked out the window. He didn't want to hear more. He tried to focus instead on the details he would provide Nokwe with as he filed the petition.

———

Joshua stroked the razor blade against the tip of his pencil one more time as he sat before his desk three weeks later. He silently willed himself to turn his attention away for a short while from the building tensions on campus. Instead, he focused solely on the gentle touch of the lead against the paper as he wrote sweet words. He scratched a few out, reflected a little longer, and continued writing. It was a balmy September day and his mind was filled with pleasant thoughts of Nongolesi. He had met her so many times by the river in the last few months. As he continued his drafting, he marveled at the remarkable things the last year had brought. As he sat remembering what it felt like to leave the port in New York, when he'd wondered what life in South Africa would bring, he knew he certainly hadn't expected this.

From the corner of his eyes, he could see a smile playing at the edges of Tahira's lips as she cleaned the dining table nearby. As he sank more deeply into his desk chair, trying to get the words just right, he scratched his temple with frustration. Tahira chuckled under her breath.

"I see that smile!" Joshua glanced over his shoulder, knowing Tahira was enjoying this. She'd been watching him struggle like this every day of the previous week.

"Anything I can do for the reverend?" she asked, barely stifling her laughter.

"My future rests on this." Joshua teased her back, but only half-jokingly.

"The reverend writes well."

"I just hope I write well enough!" he said.

"You may read it to me if you need ears, *Makinda*." She turned to him as she wiped the mantel with a feather duster.

He chuckled, knowing her offer was sincere. She cared about him deeply, just as she would have for a son. The thought made him smile. "I don't dare subject you to this," he said, "even though I know you'd be inclined to be kind."

"The reverend writes well," she assured him again.

Joshua gathered the blank sheets together, squaring their edges against the table, took another deep breath and started his composition again on a clean sheet.

The crystal waters trickled softly over slick stones. Joshua could hear the stream's gentle music as he walked toward the bank. He had a cool, peaceful feeling as he walked the familiar distance from his car. A spring wind blew and leaves rustled faintly as he made his way through the thinning trees. Nongolesi lingered listlessly at the water's edge, moving as gracefully as a butterfly in flight. She was dressed again in an outfit he had never seen, one with a traditional African design. As she leaned and dipped her hand into the healing waters he could nearly feel the dampness on his own hand. Seeing her kneeling by the clay bank with a pot next to her, his thoughts drifted to that faraway place and time he'd imagined, when his grandfather had gathered with those of different tribes, trying to speak a common language as they motioned to their Bible and prayed. He smiled.

Nongolesi playfully retraced her steps and sat on a bed of bright grass. She turned with an expectant smile as she heard his movement.

"Hello, Nongolesi," he said softly as he sat beside her. The air was warm and fresh and the flowers poured out their perfume as he pressed his lips against her hand in a tender kiss. She smiled and looked again to the river. "This place is so beautiful. I say that every time I see you here, don't I?"

He chuckled. "Yes, but I'm struck by the beauty here also. It fills me up every time I come to a place like this."

He turned, facing her more directly, and said with a smile in his eyes that he couldn't hide, "I've been working on something."

She looked at him, as if she knew what it must be. He reached in his pocket and pulled out a sheet of paper.

"A poem?"

She beamed as he nodded.

"One written especially for you, a result of many hours of toil. I've gone through every pencil in my home, every eraser, every leaf of paper. . . ."

"You play!" She laughed.

"I toiled very hard," he said. "Just ask Tahira! I wanted to get this as right as I could. I am actually very nervous about this, you know. I'm a preacher and you have me nervous about speaking out loud!" He chuckled as he unfolded the piece of paper.

She smiled as he held up the page, as if he were about to read. But then he handed it to her. "This is for you, to always remember this by. I don't need the paper to read," he said very deliberately.

Her hands seemed to tremble as she took the paper. She seemed moved by his intensity. He turned so he was facing her directly, feeling the gentle wind off the water stroking his cheek. She tucked the piece of paper beside her as he took both of her hands in his.

"This is the best I could do," he said.

She nodded as he began to recite the words he'd written with such care.

> In a moment of stillness,
> I think of you,
> the one whom God has brought to me,
> my love,
> my sweet Nongolesi.

You have helped me to see
the music in the meadows and the trees,
the brightness in the sunshine,
the promise in the sunset,
the love in every flower's bloom.

I long for the joy of your laughter.
I wish for the warmth of your smile.
I hope for the love in your eyes.

My heart is painted in gladness.
Dimness recedes to light.

Like sun rays on the mountain's breast,
dewdrops in the trees,
you fill my heart with gladness;
I am strong and wise and free.

I think of you with waking eyes,
with profound wonder and
with great surprise.

Please always know
my love is true.
It is deep.
It is pure.
Will ever be

So strong,
so sure,
so enduring.
The greatest torrent
could never wash it away.

As he finished, he held his breath as Nongolesi sat perfectly still. In the curve of her smile and the tear running down her cheek, Joshua could see everything he needed to know.

CHAPTER 24

"I'm glad we have a chance to speak at length. And again, I apologize for interrupting you. I should have called," Joshua said, noting that he had interrupted the Brother as he was sitting on his porch, starting down another Bible passage.

"I'll meditate on the Word again later in the day," Reverend Chandler responded, always making him feel welcomed. "Is there some special reason you've come to visit? You seem preoccupied," the Brother asked as he walked into his house, toward the door of his study.

Joshua took a moment and mustered the words. "Well, I do have a question—you seem to know the area well. Where can I purchase some cattle?"

"You want to purchase cows?" The Brother laughed.

"A fair number of them. Cows and oxen."

"Your mission pays you very well." The Brother laughed, taking a few steps inside his study toward the window overlooking his tiny backyard. "They pay very well indeed, if I have heard correctly. I know you give money to community needs, but I take it you eat well on that stipend. Why would you feel it necessary to buy a fresh source of meat? Are your taste buds so demanding?"

"It's useful to have oxen and cows. You know they're valued in this area."

"There is a man to the south who has fallen upon hard times; his cows are thinning and he will sell them at a low price. But, of course, you might offer him a good amount, to help him out."

"I would be happy to help him out, regardless," Joshua replied. "But I actually need plump oxen and very productive cows—ones that will produce a lot of milk."

"Plump, affordable, productive cows? What's gotten into you, my dear reverend?" The Brother laughed again, looking out his window to his yard.

"What is that smile?"

"Why would a young unmarried man like you," he said, turning toward Joshua with laughter in his eyes, "a young man without a family to feed, need cows and oxen? It doesn't make any sense! There's not even an *ebuhlanti* in your yard."

"We'll build one."

"Who's *we*?"

"This is important." Joshua squinted, knowing the Brother was joking with him now.

The Brother turned away with a smile on his face, twiddling the freshly cut flowers on his mantel between his fingers as he gazed out his window. "Perhaps I can help you if you state the matter more directly?"

"I think you already know," Joshua said, laughing to himself at the Brother's response.

The Brother kept his gaze cast outward; he squeezed his eyes and smiled broadly as he relished the words that rolled across Joshua's tongue.

"I need to secure some *lobola*."

———————

Driving two miles beyond the outskirts of East London, the Brother guided Joshua to a trusted local herder. "You didn't realize that everyone knew you loved Nongolesi? It was written in broad letters all across your face, lingering down your ears like pearl earrings, cloaking you like a warm blanket." He laughed. "Whenever she came near you, your eyes would get big. And when you tried not to let your eyes grow big, your chest would well up. And when you tried to keep your chest from welling up, you'd start to knead your hands with longing."

Joshua shook his head. "It's amazing what others can see." He couldn't say much more. He glanced out the window. "You know there was someone special in my life before I left America."

"You told me, but you spoke of her—I am forgetting her name. . . ."

"Shantal."

"Oh, yes. But you see, you spoke of Shantal with admiration, with intense respect, but not with deep love, my dear reverend. You told me you felt you couldn't talk in depth with her about your ministry, that somehow she lacked faith. Disinterest, isn't that what you called it?"

"Detached."

"It seemed to me that every time you looked at Nongolesi, you saw a glimpse of the face of God, what God would want for you. The way she studies the Bible, tries to weave it into her every choice, her every action. The way she teaches these ways to little children. She's a beautiful woman, Joshua. I'm glad you had the courage to follow your heart. It can be hard sometimes. It was hard for me when I met Lydia."

"Why? She's such a lovely woman."

"It's quite different from your situation, really. Lydia showed me the extent to which my own heart had hardened against the whites of this country. It had become increasingly difficult for me to view any Afrikaner without judgment. It seemed like a pure evil—to travel to this land knowing that your purpose was to exploit those who lived here, to denigrate them, relegate them, exploit them, mock them. To take their land by force and set about robbing Africans of a means to sustain themselves, all the while living in luxury." He shook his head as he slowed the car near an intersection to allow an *ibhasi* to pull past.

He continued forward after the small bus pulled through the intersection. "When I met Lydia, a woman born of one of the most pungently racist Afrikaner families in the country, all I could see were those evils, not her person. But then I felt her precious kiss on my cheek one day—thanking me for the work I had done at an orphanage." His eyes got big. "And I felt the love. But . . . it took some time for me to sort through all of that. She's a bold woman.

Bold enough to stand up against her family's wishes. Even her walk is so filled with hope. And she bears the insults that are levied against her by Africans who prejudge her when they hear that Afrikaner accent drift through her lips." He shook his head. "In the face of that, she just squints her eyes and flashes a smile that says she will persist regardless. I love her spirit."

"So, you followed your heart."

"Yes," the Brother said. "Many of the Europeans who came of their own accord did so with bad intent. But those born here, they became a part of something they had no part in creating. It doesn't, by any means, excuse their inaction against the unjust of this land. But with Lydia, I relearned what I had once known—not to judge anyone, white or black, from their backgrounds or their color. Kindness doesn't have a color. And what color is love? I accepted my love for Lydia, and, ahh, my dear reverend, my life has been so much more enriched! You will have as lovely a home with Nongolesi."

"Her father hasn't said yes yet."

"He will. He knows you are an honorable man." The Brother slowed his car as they approached a junction. "This is it," he said, looking straight ahead as he parked his car and stepped out, heading toward a small village. "We shall find ourselves some plump, affordable, productive cows!"

Mhlobo seemed to see Joshua and his negotiation party coming first as they walked up the familiar path to the Maganu home, hats in hand. Jovan and two elder village men had agreed to lead Joshua's part of the *lobola* negotiation. Joshua wiped any hint of surprise from his face as he watched Mhlobo move toward him on his hands and knees, dressed in a traditional cowhide skirt, his bare chest decorated with a beaded necklace. Joshua had only seen Mhlobo in traditional dress once, at the initiates' celebration. Joshua didn't think it odd, until Ogenga walked out dressed the same way, with a crooked smile on his face, holding a traditional spear in his hand. The smile on Ogenga's face broadened as he watched Joshua take note of the attire. Joshua inhaled deeply and almost laughed out loud. He was in for a hazing.

As Jovan had predicted, the Maganu men offered Joshua and his negotiation party an abundant dinner, with the seasoned meat of a freshly killed lamb and the best that the Maganu harvest had to offer—mealies, greens, yams, pumpkin seeds. They ate and chatted, idle chatting that made Joshua grow more nervous with each passing minute. Finally, after Joshua had cleaned his plate twice, the Old Man waved a young girl to clear the table. The room was filled with silence as she moved the last plates from the table and brought out some ginger tea, leaving the men alone for their talks.

"We are glad you have come to visit," the Old Man said from his position across the table from Joshua, with the Great Father and another elder man seated on each side of him. They too had donned traditional clothing, with bare chests and naked feet. "Is there something else?" the Old Man asked Joshua.

Jovan had coached Joshua well. That was his cue. The Old Man would not utter any more words; the negotiation had begun. Joshua himself could utter only one last response before the representatives of each party took over the negotiations. "Yes," Joshua answered, knowing this would be the last he would be able to speak unless a question was asked of him. "I have come here to ask to marry your daughter, Nongolesi."

The Old Man squinted his eyes and fell silent, according to tradition, as the elders in the room continued the conversation.

"*Lona, UNongelesi, wakwala ukutshata kwakude kudala. Kutheni ufuna ukutshata intombazane edudelweyo nguJambasi?*" the Great Father asked from his seat to the right of the Old Man.

"This one, Nongolesi, has refused for years to be married." A younger man translated for the Great Father. "And many consider her too old. Why is it you wish to marry a woman so far beyond her time?"

"I love Nongolesi." Joshua kept the answer simple.

The young man translated Joshua's response.

"*Kutheni uthanda lo?*" the Great Father asked.

"Why do you love this one?" The young man translated again as Nongolesi's grandfather narrowed his eyes, prodding Joshua.

Joshua said words from his heart. "I love the woman that she is. I love her strength. I admire her love of God and her devotion to family. She is what I had hoped for in a wife."

He saw the Old Man's eyes twinkle at the words, but the Old Man kept his lips pursed.

"It should be understood that when Nongolesi marries," an elder to the Old Man's left said sternly, "that following in the tradition of our people, her family name shall remain Maganu. She will also take this," he said, motioning to a tall, carved spear, "the spear of her father into her home. This spear is the symbol that should you mistreat her, her clan always stands with her. You will be called to account for your actions."

Joshua nodded, silent in the face of the words.

"We had heard word that you had inquired about cattle in East London," the elder said. "So this request from you does not come as a surprise. We have had time to consider whether we would entertain such an offer of *lobola* from you."

Joshua tensed at his disapproving tone.

"There is one among us who has great concerns, who questions whether we should accept your offer," the elder continued. "Mhlobo does not believe you respect our traditions."

Joshua's heart sank as he glanced toward Mhlobo.

"When you came here nearly one year ago," the elder continued, "you supported the ideas that we must dress as the Europeans, worship as the Europeans, turn our back on sacred traditions. Is this not true?"

"One year ago, I had not yet come to know the peoples of your country," Joshua said, keeping his voice steady. "I respect your traditions. I had hoped that my respect for your traditions had become clearer in recent months."

His response didn't seem to move them.

"If you are to marry Nongolesi," the elder continued, "we must be satisfied that you understand our traditions and respect the works of our ancestors, who have given their labor and their lives that we might live well."

The Maganu party conferred among themselves in Xhosa for a moment, and Joshua tried to read Jovan's reaction to what they were saying. Ogenga smiled faintly from beside Mhlobo.

"We will consent to this marriage, only after Mhlobo has expressed confidence that you will do right by Nongolesi," the elder said to Joshua. "Mhlobo wishes to take you to the Transkei, to the heartland of the Xhosa peoples, over which our ancestors crossed to get to these green hills here. He wishes to take you there to be certain of what is in your heart. Do you agree to travel with him there?"

Joshua, surprised at the suggestion, glanced at Mhlobo, who looked back stone-faced. "I agree," Joshua replied.

Silence lingered in the room for a moment.

"What offer do you have of *lobola*?" the elder asked in a stiff voice.

Joshua's heart lifted at those words, and Jovan and party members took things from there. As they concluded the negotiations, Mhlobo looked at Joshua, holding his gaze; a grin then spread across his face.

———

A week later, the Old Man nodded his head proudly as Joshua used Mhlobo's stick to herd each ox and cow into the Maganu family's *ebuhlanti*. The cattle, with their thick bellies, moved slowly, swollen udders wobbling. All of the men of the homestead surrounded the *ebuhlanti*, along with Joshua and his envoys, who had negotiated the *lobola* amount. The Maganus had agreed to accept twelve heads of cattle; Joshua delivered fifteen. As each cow and ox passed through the gate, the Old Man nodded his head proudly, knowing only a man who could provide well for his daughter could afford to give so much cattle. With that, the engagement was nearly sealed, even if the wedding date might be postponed until Mhlobo approved.

That evening, the men of the homestead walked back out toward the *ebuhlanti*. With the pungent smell of goats and oxen in the air, the men lit small fires in four pits dug at equal distances around the pen. Joshua glanced back toward the house and could see Nongolesi and the other women watching as the men gathered in the *ebuhlanti*, kneeling down together. The Old Man bent down on one knee, his right hand clutching his carved walking stick firmly, and called out words to their ancestors, letting them know of the engagement, then praying to Jesus Christ to bless the future of their family, the bride and the groom.

Ogenga then led a goat by the rope around its neck, preparing to kill it so that they could roast it for the celebratory meal. Pushing it down on the ground, the Old Man sat open-legged on top of it, using its horns to hold its head down. He retrieved a long, sharp knife, its handle carved with an intricate design. Squeezing his legs tightly to hold the goat still, Old Man Maganu said proudly to all of the men gathered there, "We ask God to help us bless this day and we feast to bless this special occasion." With one smooth motion, he slit the goat's throat, its blood spilling over his hands, forming a puddle on the ground.

The low clusters of bushes dotting the Transkei's sprawling green hills looked from a distance just like the kink of Ogenga's nappy hair. Mhlobo and Joshua couldn't stop kidding Ogenga about it as he sat in the backseat of Joshua's shiny Ford, his head held high. Joshua still didn't know why Ogenga refused to comb his hair. He was always well kept in every other way. He supposed it was some form of a protest.

Joshua glanced out the window, amazed at the beauty of the land around him. South Africa was so diverse! When they first set off from East London, lush green scenery had stretched before them, with blooming meadows blowing in the spring breeze, the scents of the Indian Ocean still in the air. Within an hour, as Joshua drove inland, they passed over long-legged bridges, over free-flowing rivers, and the landscape on each side of the newly tarred road had transitioned to golden fields with towering eucalyptus trees, stretching up the hills as far as he could see.

The three men chatted on easily, but each time Joshua glanced over his shoulder at Ogenga, he found the sight so odd, the way Ogenga held his drum so tenderly in his lap. He'd never seen Ogenga or Mhlobo use a drum. He shrugged it off as they drove past thatch-roofed villages nestled close to the roadside, a few miles apart from one another. Joshua could see mothers walking across their dung-swept courtyards, bringing their young children home for a meal. He smiled at the sight. It reminded him so much of the journey with Reverend Watson on his way from Philadelphia to New Jersey. There he'd seen blond-haired mothers calling their children home to eat, their skirts fluttering in gentle winds. The scenes hadn't seemed to change, only the colors.

They soon found themselves on a winding road cut steeply into tan mountains, taking them farther inland. After a mile-high ascent, Joshua felt his stomach curling, his legs feeling hollow as he drove higher up into cactus-peppered mountains. "Keep attention!" Mhlobo would joke every time Joshua turned his head to take in the view, seeing the villages below grow so small.

After another hour, the terrain transitioned to a thirsty, barren land, with cacti standing twice as tall as any man and a few brown shrubs scattered in lonely rows. For miles, there wasn't a sign of a village in any direction—no travelers by the roadside, no animals in the fields—as if the parched lands couldn't sustain an ounce of life. After another hour, when they saw a river trickling in the distance, they came upon another village.

"We should rest for a while," Ogenga suggested, knowing Joshua must be tired.

Joshua pulled aside at the edge of a homestead.

Everything here was tranquil and slow. Men walked nearby in traditional *izibheshu* and cow skin skirts, carrying their walking sticks as boys tended cattle peacefully in the fields. In this barren land where the Xhosa and Zulu peoples met and mingled, the dress was a bit less familiar, and the villagers coated their faces with clay to protect them from the scorching sun. The huts, with their high thatched domes, were painted in two tones, not just one; their upper walls were the color of earth and their bottom halves stained white. In the same way, the Xhosa and Zulu tongues blended here. Even though Mama Siziwe was Zulu, Ogenga and Mhlobo hadn't retained much of her language. They found it hard to converse with the old men here, who motioned for them to sit as they offered them swigs of water. They sat and drank from a beaded calabash, passing it among them as Ogenga and Jovan spoke in broken sentences about the crop yields, the new taxes due, the forced relocations. Joshua found his heart sinking as he glanced around. They were in the middle of nowhere, and still the government's policy was taking its toll. The community seemed to strain with so few young men around.

As they traveled on, they drove so far inland that there was nothing around them but wind-sculpted cliffs, angular crags polished by strong gales, and the few plants that could survive the sun's sweet assault. As they pulled atop another mountain, Joshua looked down upon a valley. It was breathtaking. Oceans of golden land stretched to the horizon in neatly formed crests and troughs. The sun, dipping toward the horizon, colored the whole sky pink. It was difficult to discern where the sky ended and the golden sand began.

"This is where we are heading," Mhlobo said as they descended toward the level plane. Mhlobo pointed to a slender stick figure in the distance, which took on more definite shape as they drove closer. It was a tree—an odd-looking one at that. It stood by itself in the midst of the parched land, with no other vegetation around it. What made it such a sight was its blooming green crown, Joshua thought. By itself in a sea of dried sand, yet thriving as if surrounded by silver streams. Something about it was so peaceful, solitary but somehow not lonely, as it stood thick-trunked and flouting a leathery canopy that lifted in a bouquet to the sky. There was little in the landscape to obstruct the image of its hands raised to heaven. As the sun continued to set, it became a silhouette against the darkening sky.

They traveled across the valley as peacefully as sailing across a sea, finally pulling aside a short distance from the tree. Mhlobo struggled to move from the car; Ogenga helped him move down. Mhlobo stretched his arms, happy to take in the sights around him. After such a long drive, Joshua was thrilled also to step out, taking in deep breaths of the desert air, relishing the brush of thistles and sand beneath his feet.

Ogenga retrieved the drum, blankets, and food as Mhlobo dug a small pit a few yards from the tree. Ogenga placed a few logs there, and Mhlobo set them on fire to keep the trio warm as the temperature dropped with the onset of nightfall. They sat back quietly eating some of the food Nongolesi had packed. Joshua tried to survey the land again in the dimming light. The seas of sand around him stretched as peacefully as the waves of the Atlantic, as far as his eyes could see. Joshua thought back to his journey across the ocean. Joshua thought of Darius just then. It was October again, a whole year after he had departed for South Africa. He would never have imagined himself here, his eyes graced with another type of sea. Ever since Darius's death, October had been a month of sadness; now it seemed marked by hope.

There was little wind in this valley of brambles. The sky darkened quickly, a crescent moon soon lanced the sky. The lantern, low with paraffin, burned less brightly as the night wore on. Joshua paused, taking it all in. The darkness enveloping them became velvet thick. There was something peaceful in the deepest, darkest black of that night, as silver stars shone above them. Soon that voice called from somewhere not too far away. It sang so solemnly. Joshua smiled and continued eating in the cool night beside Mhlobo and Ogenga.

"I suppose you are wondering why we have come here," Mhlobo finally said, his tone serious.

"Partly so that you can see the heart of Xhosa lands, to see this place where our ancestors once lived," Ogenga said softly.

"And partly so you can see what is becoming of us," Mhlobo said, finishing the thought. "Even in this distant place, you see the government's effects here. You saw there were few young men in that village we passed not long ago. Those women have no one to protect them. All the young men have been forced to go work in the mines. Those women will only see their husbands again when some concubine sends their dead body back for them to bury. And all the while, they are left to care for their sickly babies," Mhlobo said. "I held one such baby in my arms once. Its limbs sagged and its eyes looked poisoned, and I asked what the future of our people will be. It would be a miracle if that sickly child lives, and if it lives, what of its children? Do you understand? This is what we are fighting."

"I understand," Joshua said softly. "I know that when I first arrived, I took positions that I now believe to have been wrong. I'm not ashamed to admit it—just the opposite. I'd be ashamed if I were still defending those views."

Joshua's definite tone seemed to satisfy Mhlobo.

"I see the truth about much of what you have been saying all along," Joshua continued. "But it is still going to take me time to understand what I should be doing here. The position I have with my mission makes it difficult for me to respond as I would under other conditions."

Ogenga folded his hands in his lap and looked down for a moment. He looked up slowly. "Everyone has seen that you have changed. When you first arrived, students used to ask—I mean you no offense—if we must change, whether we would wish to be like you or like Sarah."

"And they said Sarah," Joshua said. That was obvious.

"They said they hoped to remain true to themselves," Mholbo said deliberately, letting the words sit in the air. "But if they had to change, they wished to be like Sarah rolled up with the Brother, as one. Sarah is strong and believes in fighting for what is right. She says, 'I am the one who was sent away, whose roots were clipped, who was taught to be ashamed, and taught to always use the back door. But I have learned how to fashion tools, to cast iron into a fire, to forge even sharper pliers, and I have fixed those broken tendons, those roots that once held me firm.' That is a source of her strength," he said proudly.

"But sometimes she speaks with racism in her words," Ogenga said. "The Brother—never. He loves the Lord, and he believes all peoples are one. We would wish to roll the two into one."

Joshua was moved by the sentiment. He nodded.

"People believed you were secretly ashamed of us," Ogenga said. "They do not say that anymore."

"I'm glad they can see a change." Joshua said quietly.

"We are not that different, you and us," Ogenga said. "From the histories we hear of your land, and of the slaves taken to America—the slave masters taught their history meant nothing; they broke their families, taught the slaves to speak only in the master's tongue. Such things help give birth to the mind of a servant."

Mhlobo took in a deep breath, agreeing. "And that too is what we are fighting," he added.

They were all quiet for a while, pulling their wool blankets around their shoulders.

"There is another very important reason why we have traveled to this place," Mhlobo said. "That you might see *Isihlahla Sethemba*," he said, looking toward the proud tree in front of them." He scooped his hand into a little loose sand, cradling a dusty hand full of hope. "This is what I call the 'Tree of Everlasting Hope.' As a child, this was one of my favorite spots. We would journey here once every few years. The Old Man wished to teach us about our history. This tree has taken on new meaning for me as I have come to understand this dark cloud that hangs over our history.

"Maybe there had been others where this tree stood, and when the dry winds came, the roots of those other trees were not deep enough to touch the streams flowing beneath these dry lands, and so they withered away. Or maybe a seed from a tree plucked by a plunderer found its way back to its native land, learning to flourish by developing roots strong enough to tap the rivers beneath these sands. In either instance, this tree could not have blossomed in times of harsh winds and drought except for its deep roots. But it thrives, does it not?" Mhlobo smiled as Joshua nodded.

"One day, its seeds will spring forth and take root as well. Until then, it remains proof of streams in the desert, eh? Can't you see?" Ogenga asked Joshua.

"I see." Joshua thought about the words as a faint wind blew.

In the quiet, Ogenga stoked the fire and gave Mhlobo a mischievous look. Mhlobo reached for the drum.

"We *also* had to get you alone," Mhlobo said, caressing his hand over the shell of the drum, a crooked smile on his face, "to teach you the groom's dance."

"Oh, no!" Joshua laughed as they both stared at him expectantly. "I don't dance." Joshua shook his head.

Mhlobo and Ogenga both chuckled.

Joshua hadn't danced since Darius had stood with him by their pond's rim, teaching him the latest jigs. Joshua must have been eleven back then, and he had never been able to move like Darius could. He'd only try the dance steps in that hidden cove, where no one else could see. Darius would tease him, chuckling at his awkwardness, prodding him to try again.

Mhlobo looked at Joshua seriously. "It's tradition," he said.

"Really, Mhlobo, I don't dance. . . . I can't dance!"

"The groom must dance the special groom's dance at his wedding," Ogenga scolded.

Joshua protested. "I'm sure there's some way we can—"

"Do you intend to marry Nongolesi?" Mhlobo interrupted, arching his eyebrows high. He smiled broadly.

"Yes," Joshua said, feeling outnumbered. He started chuckling. They had him just where they wanted him.

Mholbo looked at him steadily as he threw his arm wide, popping a closed fist over the drum, letting out a deep sound that echoed from the hills.

"Look . . ." Joshua tried to protest again.

Mhlobo hit the drum once more, and it uttered another crisp sound. "If you wish to marry Nongolesi . . ." Mhlobo said, waving Joshua up.

"You're intent on getting me yet." Joshua chuckled under his breath as he stood up.

"You start with your right foot," Ogenga said.

Joshua stood up, moving his foot to the right spot, stepping in line with Ogenga.

CHAPTER 25

The sky was just dimming to a deep blue when Joshua and Mhlobo arrived back at the Maganu homestead after dropping Ogenga off at Fort Hare. Joshua was happy to step from his car and stretch his aching body as they made their way up the path toward the Maganu home. "You've returned well!" Nongolesi called out with a smile as she moved through the front door, helping to carry Mhlobo's bags into the house. Joshua could smell a stew boiling as he moved to the backyard to greet Mama Siziwe, who was weaving a basket as a few mealies roasted over the fire.

Mama Siziwe caressed his hand. "We are glad you returned well," she said in a dry voice, her eyes a bit red.

"Where is the Old Man?" Mhlobo asked, concerned by the strained look in her eyes.

"He rests in the back," Mama Siziwe said.

"He is weak?" Mhlobo asked.

"He will join us for supper," she offered as if to assure Mhlobo, but she looked much more somber than usual. Something in her eyes seemed to frighten Nongolesi.

"In the past few weeks, he has tired much more quickly," Nongolesi said softly. "He was getting better but now he cannot even walk to the fields to check the work of the boys. He rests here and reads during the day, not much more. His energy is sapping quickly."

"Have you taken him to see a doctor?" Joshua asked as he moved next to Nongolesi and stroked her arm.

She nodded. "We tried. They acted as if they could not help."

"Perhaps he just needs to rest," Joshua said gently.

Just then, Joshua heard a rustle against the door as the Old Man walked toward them, his head held high, his smile shining even though his body curved into his walking stick as he moved. He offered Joshua a firm embrace. Joshua tucked his arm around the Old Man, helping him stand up. He found himself saddened by seeing the Old Man so weakened, a strong spirit trapped in a failing body.

"I thought I heard voices here," the Old Man said in his raspy voice. "We had hoped you would return well."

"Old Man, you should be resting," Mama Siziwe said sternly as she walked over to lead him back inside. "You will go rest in the living room."

Joshua sat down in a thong chair as Nongolesi sat in another, reaching into a basket of mealies and peeling one slowly. Her worried eyes followed Mama Siziwe and the Old Man as they walked back into the house. Joshua sat next to her and began peeling a corn head, knowing it would make her laugh.

"You know you're not supposed to do this work." She chuckled.

"I will just be a stubborn American and ignore the rules one more time." He flashed her a smile as he pulled back the tassels and placed the bare corn head in a separate basket. She held out her hand, which he covered with his in a warm caress, making her smile more deeply.

"So how was this great journey?" she asked.

"It was incredibly beautiful," Joshua answered.

"Mhlobo, it was beautiful?" she asked.

"We experienced many new things on the journey." Mhlobo nodded from his spot near the hearth with a broad grin that made Joshua laugh.

"I knew he'd be up to something." She looked at Joshua. "You must have known that he and Ogenga were in cahoots together. Are you all right?" she teased.

"I survived," Joshua said as Mhlobo excused himself to change clothes before supper.

"His tone is different." She smiled at Joshua. "Perhaps he feels he worked on you well."

"He did!" Joshua laughed. "And what a beautiful countryside, Nongolesi. The people of the Transkei are so kind."

She nodded, and seemed lost in thought for a moment as she turned back to the mealie in her hand, stripping another methodically as she hummed to herself and then sang a soft song. Joshua's eyes grew larger with every additional syllable.

Niya kundinqula,
nize nithandaze kum,
ndiniphulaphule.

Her tune sounded as if it had rolled right off the water, merged with the whites of the waves, drifted from a faraway hill—as peaceful as a sparrow calling forth in the wind.

Niya kundifuna,
nindifumane . . .

"What is that you're singing?" Joshua was startled by the urgency in his own voice.

"You look as if you have seen a ghost!"

He chimed in with the words. "*Xa nithe nandifuna ngentliziyo yenu yonke; ndifumaneke kuni; utsho uYehova.*"

Nongolesi's eyes grew large. "How do you know Baba's song?" she whispered, her hands frozen around a mealie.

"What did you call it?"

"The song of my father. He used to sing it to us. He said an angel had sung it to him in his dreams. The song sets words from the Bible to music. 'Remember the words of our Lord, *And ye shall seek me, and find me, when ye shall search for me with all your heart.*'" She provided the translation. "Where did you hear this?" she demanded.

Her reaction startled Joshua. He hesitated for a moment, gathering the words to explain. "I hear this song sometimes at night. When the sun sets. When the wind is still but the leaves continue to rustle. When the rains come lightly. I think of it as a song of my heart."

"For how long have you heard this sung?" she asked, as if she could hardly believe his words.

Joshua had never stopped to think about that. He tried to think back to the first time. It was well after he started college. He searched his memories carefully. "I think I heard it the first time during the extra year I spent at Wilberforce," he answered. Thinking about his answer, he nodded. "Yes, I think that was the first time."

"I don't know how that's possible," she said, lowering her eyes. "Baba played that song for us, plucked it on his *nanga*. I have never heard it sung any other place. How could you know it?"

Joshua couldn't manage a word at first. He sometimes forgot that the Old Man wasn't Nongolesi's natural father, but her uncle. He wished he had been able to meet her natural father, Baba. His eyes dampened as he tried to understand what she was saying.

Nongolesi's eyes were red. She quickly gathered the corn heads in her reed basket and moved into the house.

Joshua could hear Nongolesi exchanging words with Mhlobo in the back room. He didn't say a word as he joined them at the table and shared dinner with the family. The Old Man guided the conversation, asking about the journey, the harvests they saw, whether the people appeared well fed. Nongolesi hardly looked in Joshua's direction. He hadn't meant to offend her.

"I should probably be going, and get back home," Joshua said after supper.

"It's too late to drive these roads," Nongolesi replied. "You should stay. Is it okay?" she asked the Old Man, who nodded.

Joshua's heart eased hearing those words from Nongolesi, and he thanked the Old Man for his generosity.

"You will wake early tomorrow so that we may discuss the wedding date." The Old Man smiled toward him.

Joshua glanced toward Mhlobo, who also nodded and smiled.

Joshua should have been happier than on any day in his life, now that the Old Man had fully consented to their marriage. But the distance Nongolesi had put between them dampened the moment. As Joshua moved to the den and sat in a chair at the far side of the room, the evening was filled with familiar sights. Mama Siziwe lit two lanterns, which cast their long shadows underneath the portraits on the wall. Nongolesi carefully recorded the history of her people on her parchment, and Mhlobo perched himself up in a thong chair near the Old Man, both of them squeezing their eyes together, enjoying the gentle breeze blowing through the open window next to Joshua.

Joshua parted his Bible to the passage Nongolesi had quoted from Jeremiah, and he silently read the full passage. *Then shall ye call upon me, and ye shall go and pray unto me, and I will hearken unto you. And ye shall seek me, and find me, when ye shall search for me with all your heart. . . . I will turn away your captivity. . . .*

He closed his eyes for a moment. Faintly outside, from some-place nearby he heard that gentle song. Joshua looked toward Nongolesi. She seemed to sense his gaze, tightening her lips, but she kept her eyes focused on her writing. Mhlobo simply gazed outside, his expression unchanged. The Old Man sat with his eyes shut. Joshua gathered his voice.

"I hear the singing," he said quietly, as Nongolesi looked at him.

"What do you hear?" Mhlobo asked. He seemed to speak for Nongolesi, as if she had instructed him to probe.

"The song I often hear. A song of my heart—that's what I've named it."

"The voice you hear, it sings different songs?"

"It seems to be the same words I think, but it's sung to different tempos sometimes."

"What are the words?" Nongolesi asked in a whisper.

"I don't know what all the words mean, but I can sing most of them, I've heard the words so many times." He took a breath and sang along with the voice, his baritone blending with its alto, mixing into a sweet melody the fullness of which only he seemed to hear. "*Osukuba ethanda ukundilandela, makazincame, awuthwale umnqamlezo wakhe, andilandele ke. Kuba othe wathanda ukuwusindisa umphefumlo wakhe, wolahlekelwa nguwo; ke yena othe wawulahla umphefumlo wakhe ngenxa yam, nangenxa yeendaba ezilungileyo ezi, wowusindisa.*"

Mhlobo sucked in his breath, his eyes full. A smile curved at the lips of the Old Man as he opened his eyes and Mama Siziwe looked on peacefully as Joshua sang the words. Nongolesi's eyes dampened and like the rest of her family, she slowly nodded.

Joshua had waited anxiously for his wedding day to come. On the eve of his wedding, he tried to take it all in. It was one of those moments when he simply paused in wonder at the blessings God had brought to him. He had never imagined when he first set foot on South African soil that he would have found the woman who filled his heart as Nongolesi did. He could hardly have conceived that fourteen months later he would marry the love of his life. This time in the USA he would have been celebrating Thanksgiving. But now he had something different to be thankful for. As his guests arrived at his home on the eve of his wedding, the night became consumed with the celebration that Ogenga had organized according to tradition. The elders walked in, some in cotton shirts and dark pants, others in traditional skirts that their wives had sewn together from oxen skin. They joked together, sang, told stories into the night. Elderly men told Joshua tales about marriage, and younger ones came to joke with him about the carefree life he would leave behind. Slowly, the men from more distant villages rose to return home before the last *ibhasi* departed from Alice. Others waited longer, knowing they could walk the distance home. As the night passed, the numbers filtered down to Joshua and those in his wedding party— Jovan, Ogenga, and Professor Kabata.

By the time Joshua was ready to drift to sleep, he was certain that Nongolesi's family was halfway through their long journey by foot from their home to his, walking along the roadside, by the river, across the meadows. Xhosa weddings normally took place in the homestead of the groom's father, he knew. But for this one, his home would have to suffice. As everyone else drifted to sleep, Joshua turned on his own mat and looked out of his living-room window into the darkness. He tried to imagine what Nongolesi's family looked like as the men led the way, carrying all of Nongolesi's earthly belongings in a wooden cart drawn by a donkey across the damp earth. He could practically see them steadily whipping the cloven-footed animal to ensure they made good time, while Nongolesi walked behind them, surrounded by women of her family and village. He pictured Nongolesi, with the bright eyes of a bride, naked except for a wool blanket wrapped around her, her nakedness a sign according to tradition that she was leaving one life behind and entering into a new one. He imagined the feel of the grass and mud beneath her bare feet, weeds sweeping against her shins, rough wool against her flesh, and the night's chill teasing at the edges of her blanket as she walked beneath the stars and moon.

He wished he could share it all with her. Ogenga had told him how their family had slaughtered one of their finest cattle the day before to announce to their ancestors that Nongolesi was moving on to a new life, and prayed that Jesus would watch over them. For the first time in her young life, Ogenga told him, Nongolesi had entered into her family's cattle pen, her father by her side as she said good-bye to her home and prayed again to God. As Joshua imagined it all, he longed to have his own family with him. He wished with all his heart that Lu, Nate, Lucius, Alma, and Waneda could have been present to share this day. He knew his family was so happy for him. They'd sent him long letters and gifts to share with Nongolesi, writing that they were certain she must be a remarkable woman. He'd written back, promising they'd meet Nongolesi one day. As his mind drifted back to the thoughts of his wedding, Joshua's heart filled with anticipation, and he slowly drifted to sleep.

Joshua was still sleeping lightly on his mat in his living room, near members of his groom's party, when stray dogs barked from the edge of his yard, at the very bottom where the fence marked the edge of the campus. The baying sounds cut through the crisp dawning sky. He woke up promptly, his slumber so light with excitement. As he rubbed the sleep from his eyes, Ogenga sat up near him, nudging Jovan awake.

"They've arrived. It's begun," Ogenga said excitedly as Jovan smiled broadly.

Joshua nodded, understanding that the bride and her company had arrived and were settling at the edge of his yard, underneath the large pine trees clustered at the far slope of the lawn. It was still fairly dark, but Joshua could make out their figures as they settled themselves underneath the trees. After the sun slowly rose, he knew Nongolesi would step into the middle of a circle of elderly Noni women, who would surround her as she dropped the wool blanket from her shoulders to her heels, stepping into her bridal *umbhaco*. At that moment, the young Noni girls would begin to sing and dance, first underneath the trees, then out on the lawn in full sight, and the day's festivities would begin in earnest.

By the time the sun was bright, the groomsmen had all washed themselves down and were finishing their preparations. Professor Kabata returned to Joshua's house. Soon Sarah, Lydia, and Tahira arrived, all dressed in the same brightly dyed *umbhaco,* their hair swept underneath beaded headdresses. Joshua had never seen Tahira dressed so elegantly. She always saved every shilling of money he gave her for Beaumont's college education. "You look so beautiful," he said to them all, but touched Tahira's arm in particular. Nokwe and the Brother, stepping inside right behind the ladies, agreed.

On this promising day, everything around them was blooming in hopeful blushes, and Joshua's senses were ablaze. Jovan prepared some bread, butter, and soured milk for breakfast. Everyone laughed when Joshua couldn't eat a bite. After Joshua slipped into his bedroom to change into his wedding clothes, he peeked through his bedroom window. He saw many members of his congregation there, and Andrew sat so peacefully among them. Joshua's lips curved into a broad smile as he watched Sarah, Tahira, and Lydia move from inside to the middle of the yard, beginning to dance to a soft drumbeat. Joshua had been so moved when they had volunteered to fill the role of the women in his family, performing the traditional dances on his wedding day. He knew they'd have to keep dancing until Nongolesi's family consented to send forth the bride, which could take at least half an hour. He never thought he'd see Tahira dance! He could barely stop chuckling at the sight. He was also very glad his relationship with Sarah had grown strong. Joshua watched them finish the first dance, laughing as they motioned toward Nongolesi's family. He heard the women of Nongolesi's family scoff loudly, shouting in a jovial tone that the dancing wasn't good enough, that they must try again before they would send forth the bride. He also heard laughter from his living room, as the men of his party watched happily.

Joshua took a deep breath and quickly checked in the mirror one last time to make sure his shirt and dark pants looked well pressed. He then pulled a traditional blanket around his shoulders. As he rejoined his party in his living room, the Brother pat him on the back. "The time is almost near." The Brother smiled warmly, as he prepared to deliver the ceremony's opening prayer.

They both looked back into the yard, hearing Nongolesi's family refuse to send the bride forth again. Tahira, Sarah, and Lydia resumed their dancing. It was quite a sight, the three of them blending their steps together. He could tell they'd practiced together many times. As he glanced around his home, he took it all in again. There was so much happiness here, as if everyone believed this marriage would truly be blessed.

Finally, the women of the Maganu home nodded, and Tahira, Sarah, and Lydia stepped back into Joshua's living room, laughing the whole way. Joshua gave them each a hug. Tahira, with such love in her eyes, stroked his arm just then.

"Thank you," Joshua said to Tahira. "If it weren't for you, I may have never seen this day."

She nodded and lowered her eyes as she turned back to the others. Finally, after the Brother led the guests in prayer outside, they were ready: Joshua walked out with his groom's party, the grass cool under his bare feet. They stopped near the small cattle pen that Jovan and Ogenga had helped build to hold the cow the Maganu family would give to Joshua, to supply the bride with milk until she bore her first child. Just then, Joshua saw Nongolesi sitting on a palm leaf mat surrounded by her family; she was dressed beautifully in a white *umbhaco* and a beaded white *iqhiya* wrapped around her hair. Her neck was graced with a long beaded necklace that hung in an intricate design. Her face lit up as she saw the look of pleasure in Joshua's eyes.

Two drums called out, spreading far their deep insistent sounds as Mhlobo and another drummer played the same song to which Joshua had practiced in the Transkei. The bridal party and the groom's party formed two long lines across from each other, dancing and singing according to their tradition. Joshua chuckled to himself. *If only my family could see me, they wouldn't believe this.* He was dancing! Everyone present seemed to be tickled by the sight too, and Ogenga couldn't hide his broad smile as Joshua lifted his feet, stomped, clapped, and swayed with his party at the right times. Joshua couldn't have imagined a happier day.

After a long while, both parties were seated, enjoying the dancing and singing of the best performers of the nearby villages. The Old Man came forth after they finished, dressed proudly like many villagers, in a traditional brightly dyed cloak, with colorful beads decorating his neck and chest. The strips of his leopard skin skirt underneath fell over his thighs as he moved with the assistance of his wife in front of the pen to announce that the *lobola* had been paid and all was well.

The Old Man's favorite African minister from Port Elizabeth moved before the onlookers to lead the ceremony. "*Silapha namhlanje ngenjongo ephakamileyo, ukudibanisa indoda nenkosikazi kumtshato ongcwele phambi kukaThixo, phakathi kwezizalwana, nezihlobo,*" he spoke pridefully. "*Lemini yanamhlanje iyakuba yimini esikelelekileyo ebomini balamadoda nalamakhosikazi. Umtshakazi nomyeni mabaze ngaphambili.*"

Joshua stood up and stepped before the minister as an elder woman handed Nongolesi the Old Man's spear, the one she would take into her new home.

Joshua's heart swelled as Nongolesi stepped beside him and he finally took her hand in his. In the weeks prior to this day, he had grown so lonely for her. Since his first trek to the river, he'd grown accustomed to sharing her company several days a week. But shortly after he had returned from the Transkei and Mhlobo had approved the marriage, things changed. Nongolesi had sent Joshua a special set of beads, the *ucu,* as a sign of her full acceptance of his proposal. Her family held a celebration, with young girls dancing to mark the occasion, and Nongolesi had then sent a note to Joshua inviting him to her family's home, where she showed him the engagement gifts she had steadily received from friends and women from the villages. All were made with care—blankets to keep warm in, baskets to carry food in, thick pots to cook in, fragrant soaps, the many symbols of well wishes for their future. But shortly after that, the elder women of her village had taken Nongolesi off to a secret place, pampering her and teaching her the secrets of her new role as a wife. Joshua was not certain when she had returned to her home, but he had not seen her for weeks. He was grateful now to caress her hand lightly, wishing again that his family could be here. Nongolesi smiled back at him, but then she winked with a warning as she twisted her father's spear in her right hand. The onlookers burst out in laughter. *Thank you, Lord,* Joshua thought as he chuckled also. *Thank you so much, for blessing me with such a wonderful woman.*

"We have come this day to witness a blessing from the Lord, our Father God," the minister continued in English. "We will join today in marriage Nongolesi Maganu and Joshua Clay. They shall become one flesh. Mr. Maganu, what is it you have to say today?"

The Old Man stepped forward, with such a shine in his eyes. "We find Joshua Clay a strong and admirable young man. He is fit to marry our daughter. We accept him as a son into our family. We welcome him as our own."

As the Old Man returned to his family, the minister proceeded. "It is fitting that you will each present to the other a ring in the presence of God and of these witnesses, to symbolize the vows of marriage you will now exchange. Remember that these rings are perfect circles," he said, raising the rings he had just blessed. "Just as each ring is unbroken and whole, so too will your lives, your home, and your marriage be encircled by the perfect love of God. Joshua, present this ring to your bride, repeating after me," the minister said as he handed the ring to Joshua.

Joshua happily repeated the words as he placed the ring on Nongolesi's finger. Tears rolled down her cheeks. "*I give you this ring and I declare in the presence of these witnesses that I take you, Nongolesi Maganu, to be my wife. I will always love you, and I will be faithful to you until death shall part us.*"

As an elder woman held Nongolesi's spear, Nongolesi placed a ring on Joshua's finger, repeating the same vows. They knelt together as the minister administered communion for the two of them. They broke bread and sipped wine together, saying a prayer aloud.

"I now pronounce you man and wife," the minister affirmed as they stood together and family and friends clapped and called out ululations. "Joshua, you may salute your bride," the minister said as the two shook hands according to tradition. Then Joshua pulled Nongolesi close, his hand on the small of her back, and kissed his wife.

CHAPTER 26

"So, it's done," Ogenga whispered as Joshua rounded another hill and they caught sight of trucks lining a long stretch of road between King William's Town and Fort Hare. Jovan groaned as they looked at dust plumes hovering high in the air as a tractor turned one of the last huts to rubble. Crow's-feet etched themselves more deeply around Joshua's eyes as he pulled aside where women and men clustered together, clutching as many of their belongings as they could carry. Only three months had elapsed since his wedding, but building political tensions had displaced the serenity he'd felt during that blissful occasion. Despite it all, Joshua had hoped the magistrate officials had spoken honestly when they'd assured him again that no further relocations would occur near Fort Hare.

Ogenga and Jovan stepped out before he did, moving swiftly toward the moans audible from a distance, near the last huts still standing. Joshua's heart beat wildly as he followed them a few steps behind. One woman called more frenetically than the rest, beyond a flatbed truck. Joshua knelt beside her, trying to soothe her with his words as Ogenga and Jovan surveyed the scene.

"*Jonga benze ntoni*," she said with bloodshot eyes, tears flooding her face. With a hopeless expression, she looked from Joshua to Ogenga to Jovan.

"They have shot a man," a frightened young girl echoed, pointing a ways away.

Ogenga and Jovan moved quickly as Joshua followed them farther into the crowd, his heart pounding again. They all breathed out at the same time, relief washing over them as he saw a man sitting on the ground, handcuffed, a bullet wound in his leg wrapped in soiled rags. *Just a minor wound,* Joshua thought, moving his hands to his temple, so grateful. But his heart sank again as he heard a moan from farther away, a sound as deep as death. Joshua braced himself for what he'd see. A short distance away, a man lay facedown in a puddle of blood.

Ogenga moved toward that fallen man, burying his head in his hands. That moan called out again. Joshua turned to see two young girls with tear-streaked faces standing a few steps away. He moved over to them, trying to turn their faces from the scene. The younger one shrieked, backing away when he held out his hand to her.

"Where is your mama?" he asked, trying to soothe them. The older girl, about eight years old, shook her head, tugging on Joshua's coat as if asking him to shield her. The younger girl backed away quickly.

"Come, darling," he said to the younger one, but she only cried louder. The older girl grasped at Joshua's pocket so hard, a letter fell from it. It was another curt letter from Reverend Waldron. Joshua picked it up as she rubbed her crying eyes. Slowly, the older girl bent down, opening her tear-stained fist when she straightened back up, laying what she'd picked up in the palm of Joshua's hand. His wooden cross. Joshua hadn't felt it drop. For a few moments, he couldn't take his eyes from it, frozen by the image of the child's hand that had just placed it there. He lifted his gaze to look at her, and for a fleeting moment, the world disappeared. All he could see was he and she, her fear and the shaven cross. His lips parted, but words did not come.

The younger girl came forward quickly, trying to tug the older girl away. But the older girl stood firm, stepping closer to Joshua.

"I couldn't hear you," he said after she mouthed voiceless words. She gathered as much breath as she could, her faint voice barely audible over the clamor. She pointed back toward the police officers standing near the fallen man. Speaking in halting one-syllable words graced with the simplicity of a child's eyes. She spoke words he knew he could never turn his mind from again: "How is it we serve the same God?"

––––––––––

Joshua tossed all night long. As he turned over in the twilight hour, Nongolesi stared back at him. "I didn't mean to wake you," he apologized.

"You didn't," she said. He'd never seen her eyes so sad. He held her close for a moment. They both feared it. The future. The thought made him so angry. What should they expect next? As much as he wished to ignore it, as much as he avoided saying it out loud, he knew as did she that the Noni Village might be next.

The next day, he rose early and Nongolesi joined him as he drove to Ginsberg, the township to which the government had relocated Africans from their homesteads in this region. He drove far beyond the plush neighborhoods and Victorian plazas of King William's Town, up the single dusty road to the township, wondering the whole stretch why he had not yet visited this place. The township wasn't far away. The truth came to him quickly as the bleak sights came into view, images that would burn in his mind. They drove up the segregated hill, rows of dilapidated cement huts for Africans to their left, larger brick houses with tin roofs for Coloureds to their right. As they drove deeper into this land of heavy steps and blood-shot eyes, the faces of the brokenhearted were everywhere—on the children who played the best they could between urine puddles spotting the path, on the grown men who loitered by the roadside. Joshua's stomach twisted as he moved around the car, holding Nongolesi's cold hand close as she stepped from the car.

"What has become of us?" The tremble in Nongolesi's voice pierced him.

As they walked downhill, his eyes fell on an astonishing view. King William's Town stretched before them, its Victorian buildings painted in pastel hues, sun reflecting off its many church steeples. Directly in their view also stretched the Amatola Mountains, the land of waterfalls and valleys, lush and green, the highest peaks in the distance appearing blue. The sight was peaceful and beautiful and majestic and cruel. That most bitterly contested land, the ones Xhosas had been forced from, sat as a daily reminder of all that was taken from the people now living in this blighted haven. Anger glazed Nongolesi's face. She seemed to be thinking the same thing.

Joshua knocked on the opening of the nearest government-erected *indlu,* its metal frame poking from beneath chipped cement. From inside the darkness, an old woman looked at Joshua, nodding with no particular enthusiasm as he introduced himself. This one *indlu,* Joshua could see, functioned the same as four once had in the villages. An older woman lay covered on a table she was using for a bed, just inside the door. A shelf stood in the back covered with pots and cups. Every other spare space was cluttered with chairs and clothes. Nongolesi lowered her eyes.

Joshua felt so ill prepared as he tried to speak words to bring hope here. Nongolesi wiped her tears as they moved to the next hut, past old men sitting on overturned pails, cradling half-empty beer bottles between their knees with hands that had once woven book bags for the children. As they rubbed their hands over the rounds of the bottles and lifted them to their lips, Joshua's eyes were wide with all that had been shattered here. The men paused briefly to greet Nongolesi and Joshua with breath that shamed them. Joshua wondered what occupied their minds then—these men—as they simply stared out into the blueness of the sky.

"Reverend," a young boy said to him as he looked up the hill in his direction. "Mama wishes to speak with you."

Joshua approached an old lady sitting before another *indlu;* she seemed to be looking out with such despair. "You have seen this place," she said in a splintered tone. "We will die here."

"I have this community in my prayers," Joshua said emphatically as he met her gaze. "We are working to see that the relocations end and that you might live in better conditions."

"We'll fight hard," Nongolesi echoed.

"Several people have spoken to us about helping to open a church here. We will do so," Joshua said, thinking back to conversations he'd had about this with Sarah and Nokwe. Nongolesi nodded beside him. "I will come to preach here often. And when this church is built, we will also use it to school the children."

The woman's eyes reddened. She simply looked as if she'd grown unaccustomed to speaking with hope of the future.

"The young children can grow strong and we can prepare them for a better future in a church and in a school," Nongolesi said, responding to her expression.

The old woman continued to stare at them, the grim shadows in her face growing longer as her eyes shifted to the children playing near ditches. A tear rolled down her cheek.

"What are you up to?" Joshua asked curiously as Nongolesi swirled a glass of milk from the bottle the milkman had delivered earlier. Joshua was happy to see her smiling again. The last month since the removal of the last village had cast a somber cloud over everything and everyone. Joshua had found the courage to do the unthinkable—he signed his name to a petition to restore the village land to the people. He also filed a petition with Andrew and the Brother, asking the magistrate to issue further orders preventing other forced relocations in the area. It was only a matter of time before his mission found out. He'd worry about the consequences later, Joshua told himself.

The strain of the tensions was taking its toll on everyone. Even the Old Man continued to grow more weary. Each loss of additional rights and land caused the Old Man to redouble his efforts, while growing sick under the strain. To see Nongolesi smiling so fully meant so much at a time like this. Joshua arched his eyebrows, moving closer, wondering what she was up to as she gazed so intensely at the milk in her hands.

"I'm getting used to its taste—it's different from ours," Nongolesi said.

Joshua knew that she could not drink the milk of his home. According to tradition, until she became pregnant with their first child, she could only drink milk from the cow her family had given to him shortly before their wedding. As soon as the thought fleeted through his mind, his eyes grew fuller. She beamed back.

"You look surprised!" She chuckled as he hugged her tightly, rubbing his hand over her belly. "I have been happy to have you as my husband, but did you think I was growing fat with happiness alone?"

He felt as if he were smiling as he'd never smiled before. He couldn't wait to write back home.

They shared the day together, choosing to cast aside any reason to worry or fret. They strolled through the yard, dreaming about the future family they might have. Even that, though, was punctuated by silent, somber moments as they each seemed to wonder what sort of world their child would inherit. After supper, Joshua relished the time to lie on the living room sofa and listen to Nongolesi's soft breaths as she leaned against him and he stroked her hair.

"What will you want to call this one?" Nongolesi finally broke the peaceful silence. "When you rub my stomach like that, I know you are thinking of this. Your eyes drift and get happy."

He smiled. She knew him so well. "I'm just very happy the baby is coming."

"And if it is a girl, what shall we call her?"

"Nongolesi."

She laughed hard. "No, we will call her by another name."

"I haven't thought of any other name."

"We will see when the child is born. It is a custom to name the child after an important event or thing of beauty. One in our village is called Umangaliso—Miracle. Another is called Umnyama—Rainbow," she said as she nestled in closer against Joshua. "Well, if it is a boy, what shall we call him?"

Joshua shook his head. "Do you have a boy's name you like?"

She paused for a long while. "Darius."

The suggestion made him sit perfectly still. She always seemed to know his deepest thoughts, even his unspoken dreams. She turned slightly so that she could see his face.

"That's not a very African name," he said, trying to hide what he was feeling. "It doesn't follow the tradition here."

"There will be other children, God willing. We can follow tradition then," she said, seeming to understand what he felt.

Joshua wasn't sure how he'd become so blessed with a woman

like this. She understood, and he was grateful. "If it is a boy," he said softly, nodding, "yes, I would like to call him Darius."

With political tensions rising, Joshua knew the overwhelming peace he'd felt as he settled into married life with Nongolesi could only last a short while. Only six weeks had passed since the forced removals near King William's Town, but the tempo of defiance among the students and villagers kept increasing. After a few days of basking in Nongolesi's news about the baby, an urgent knock sounded at his front door. Joshua examined the envelope the messenger handed him, direct from mission headquarters. *This can't be good*, he thought, *a note sent by messenger and not by mail*. The telegram's single line read, "You are to report to mission headquarters on Thursday of next week."

Joshua remained standing in front of his desk, too unsettled to sit down. He rubbed his hand against his brow, sighing. *This isn't a surprise*, he told himself. He'd known he'd been treading a thin line lately, especially after signing another cease and desist petition. But the depth of his own foreboding still unsettled him. Another knock on his front door, which still stood ajar, interrupted Joshua's thoughts.

"I wasn't expecting you," Joshua said, smiling faintly as he opened the door fully and greeted Andrew. He felt a little embarrassed, realizing Andrew might have seen the worried expression painted a moment earlier across his face. Andrew stared at the note in Joshua's hand, then held up his own.

"So, we've both been summoned, it appears," Andrew said.

Joshua was too stunned to respond.

"We might as well travel there together," Andrew said in a tone intended to assure Joshua.

They reached Port Elizabeth a day before their meeting with mission officials, with just enough time to rest overnight after completing the long drive. It felt so odd to return to the headquarters with Andrew under these conditions. The last year and a half had brought such changes. Somehow, as they pulled in front of the mission headquarters, the building looked so different than it had before—smaller, a little too exquisite, a little too removed. They walked off the woven carpet into the silent room at the end of the long hall.

"Come in, gentlemen." A mission official motioned them to two chairs placed side by side at the opposite end of the long table, across from six officials.

"Reverend Clay, you have put us in an impossible situation," the leader among the officials said after reciting a long list of his offenses. "Reverend Clement, it goes without saying that you should know better; your actions in signing the cease and desist petitions in King William's Town are equally intolerable. We had hoped to wait until Reverend Waldron returned from abroad to deal with this, but he may not be returning for five months and at this rate we shouldn't wait until then. Having heard about that last petition, we cannot allow this to continue. Do either of you deny what we have heard about your actions?"

Andrew responded in a thin, measured tone, apologizing, then assuring them he'd conform more closely to mission guidelines. Somehow there were shadows between them in those moments, he and Andrew. Joshua's breaths grew shallow as Andrew spoke, the air seeming so thick it was difficult to breathe. Joshua reminded himself to square his shoulders and to look them directly in the eyes as Andrew finished. He swallowed hard as the officials turned their piercing eyes toward him. Keeping his voice steady, he explained his position, his voice growing stronger with each breath. The stern faces looking back at him didn't move. After conferring in low tones among each other, they dismissed Joshua and Andrew, instructing them to return the next day to receive the committee's decision.

Time had rarely seemed to pass so slowly—more slowly still as Andrew explained to Joshua his decision to acquiesce to their demands, for now, in order to continue his work in the villages. "Sometimes you must make compromises to gain a little," Andrew said. Joshua's conscience now resisted that notion. Joshua tried to assure himself on that restless night that the officials understood how much he'd done to build up attendance at their mission's services. Congregation numbers at Fort Hare were swelling. Perhaps they'd give him latitude.

"You have a choice to make, Reverend Clay," the missionary leader said when they reconvened. The committee directed its full attention to him this time. "We have entrusted you with a tremendous honor. You appear to have severely abused it. It is our decision, contingent upon the final approval of Reverend Waldron when he returns, that you may continue to preach at Fort Hare."

Joshua sighed quietly, and Andrew seemed to smile.

"On three conditions," the mission official continued, his voice dipping low.

Joshua held his breath.

"One, you refrain from helping with any further distribution of Xhosa Bibles. Learning English is an integral part of assisting Africans to assimilate into civilization. We fully support the distribution of Bibles, as you know. But you will distribute English Bibles only."

Joshua winced as he thought about the members of his church who so struggled to read the Word from English Bibles.

"Two, you will limit your preaching at the East London jailhouse to once a month. You have caused no small amount of ill will with the warden. We will leave it to Reverend Waldron to determine if your activities there should cease entirely."

Joshua touched his hand to the hot spots on his cheeks, trying to sketch that scenario in his mind. He felt the room darkening around him as he prepared for their last demand.

"Finally," the official went on, "you will refrain from any further endorsements of efforts to end forced relocations."

Joshua's breaths grew short, his heart racing as he thought of the village huts turned to rubble, and of the faces of the disheartened now living in Ginsberg. He rubbed a damp hand on his slacks, searching for his response. *I can do this,* he told himself, ignoring the pulling inside. He shifted uneasily, looking at Andrew, who stared back blankly.

"I may still preach in the Noni Village and in Ginsberg?" he asked the official.

"Until such time as Reverend Waldron makes a final decision on this."

Joshua's stomach turned with the words he uttered. "I agree," he whispered, his heart sinking with the weight of his own words.

―――――――――

After a few stops to visit with other missionaries in the field, Joshua and Andrew had been gone nearly ten days by the time Joshua returned back to Fort Hare. As he traveled with Nongolesi to the Maganu home he only had a short while to relay to her what had happened. Nongolesi led him into the hut where the Old Man lay; the Old Man insisted on resting in the nearest hut in their yard. It seemed to bring him peace to lay within those mud-plastered walls that were topped with carefully sewn thatch, in the traditional manner of his ancestors. As Joshua moved to his bedside, the Old Man seemed to be a ghost of the man he once was, barely able to lift his hand around Joshua's arm. The Old Man's struggle to stop the forced relocations had seemed to take a physical toll, as if he thought each successive failure had been his fault. He kept pushing himself harder, traveling to muster support in the region for efforts to halt the relocations. The strain of watching their way of life fall apart had worn on him heavily. Joshua was astonished with how much weight he'd lost. A rash had now broken out across his brow. Whatever ailed him seemed to be sucking his life away.

The Old Man motioned for Joshua to sit beside him on a stool; he was barely able to get a word out of his dry throat. Joshua said a prayer aloud, blessing the Old Man, who seemed so comforted by his presence. The Old Man pulled Joshua's face toward his lips just then, slowly mouthing words that seemed so important to him. "Nongolesi," he said with dust in his voice, "I have long worried for that one. I do not worry anymore for that one or the family to come." His eyes were smiling.

Joshua's eyes welled. He should have felt such peace and pride at the words. Instead, a sense of betrayal shuddered through him; he was troubled by the compromise he'd made in Port Elizabeth. The Old Man was looking to Joshua now, as if to say he believed Joshua would carry forward in the right path and ensure the safety of the family. "I will treat your daughter well, and I will honor the children we bear together," Joshua said hoarsely.

The Old Man seemed to wonder why Joshua trembled, and he stroked his hand, closing his eyes as if trying to feel the truth in Joshua's words. Joshua felt so much shame in that moment. He could barely move as the Old Man opened his eyes again, smiling at what he thought he'd sensed in Joshua, his eyes shining so deeply. The Old Man drifted quietly back to sleep.

"I have told Mama Siziwe you will drive me to the nearby village. I sent for an *inyanga* to prepare to come," Nongolesi said, as Joshua emerged from the hut.

"Nongolesi!" Joshua's voice rose an octave.

"It's tradition." Nongolesi's temper flared. "The surgery won't be able to get the medicines to us straightaway, that's what they said. They meant they won't have extra medicines for an African until next week. This *inyanga* can help, I know it. An *inyanga* knows his health can be restored only if strengthening his mind and soul as well. The one I have called, Zalinda, is known as the great healer of diseases."

Her conviction softened Joshua's response, and Andrew's words to him long ago echoed through his mind. *Don't call her a witch doctor.* Joshua had learned that some of the *izinyanga* were much more like herbalists, having learned to use tree bark, roots, and herbs to treat ailments. He searched Nongolesi's face and chose to trust her judgment.

They didn't exchange a word as Joshua steered two villages away to the home of the *inyanga*. Zalinda, that middle-aged woman he'd seen long ago at Fort Hare, came toward the car. She was wearing a bright-print European-style dress; a hollow oxen horn hung around her neck. Zalinda sat in the backseat, a young boy beside her, chatting on as they drove back toward the Maganu homestead. "I am a *healer,*" she went on, as if she needed to explain this to the foreigner in the car. "Whether you are ill or whether you are healthy has more to do with this," she said, moving her fingers up to her temple. "What you believe, the health of your mind, matters. Your spirit must be right for you to be cured, not simply healed, and to be rid of sicknesses." Something about her words rang so true.

When Zalinda finally moved beside the Old Man, who lay half

conscious on the bed, she touched her fingers to his forehead gently, then promptly took a seat on a stool next to him. "Move that rug," Zalinda said, pointing to the rug at the foot of the bed. Nongolesi rolled it up, opening a stretch of floor in front of Zalinda. Spreading her legs wide, Zalinda emptied a pouch into the fan of her dress. She scooped the contents in her hands, examining them to ensure she had all she needed. Zalinda puckered and blew over the charms in her hands, gently throwing them out on the floor before her. The ivory, black, and gray stones fell among the large feathers and animal teeth. In an easy motion, Zalinda swept off the stool, kneeling down, taking a closer look at how the charms had clustered together.

Joshua chuckled faintly under his breath, and gave Nongolesi a sour look.

"Do not make a sound!" Zalinda hushed him. She collected her rocks, feathers, and bones, seeming very unsatisfied. Mixing and blowing on them once more, she tossed them again. "Just as I thought," she said, satisfied that time. "This illness is not great. We will make him very well soon."

She swiftly pulled two small bags and two tiny calabashes from her pouch, spreading pinches of herbs from them onto a plate. She mixed the thin-leaved herbs with some furry ones, followed by ones shaped like tiny dried sticks. "These are the famous *muti* from the mountains of Ukholo. These I will have him drink," she said, mixing them together with her finger in a large mug of water. Mama Siziwe helped the Old Man take a few sips, wiping the water that dripped on his chin.

"Have him drink this same mixture in the morning and for two more days," Zalinda said to Mama Siziwe. "By the fourth day, he should be well. I will pray to our Lord that it will be so. You must pray also that the Lord our God will watch over you and allow this *muti* to work well."

The young boy who had accompanied Zalinda lifted a small drum and began to play a determined rhythm. Zalinda stood in the middle of the room, smiling broadly as she began to dance, sashaying her hips right to left. "We shall make him well!" she proclaimed, jiggling the shells strapped on her belt and anklets deftly to the drumbeats as she waved her hands in the air, humming to the heavens. Even before she departed, Joshua knew that her presence alone had lifted the Old Man's spirits. He could see it in his eyes as they had opened faintly and shone brightly as she wiped her hand across his brow. It was as if he were watching a symbol of their past draw on the wisdom of the ages as she poured the *muti* down his throat.

―――――――――

"Without our *izinyanga*, we would have perished long ago," Nongolesi said to Joshua four days later as she stood next to him, peering into her father's hut as he sat up, talking again. The rash on his forehead had cleared. Joshua nodded, thinking back to that first day he had arrived at Fort Hare, seeing Zalinda on the hillside before the students. Perhaps that is what they had found so captivating— the traditions Zalinda was helping them to bring forward, even as the world around them changed. They must have found that inspiring.

The Old Man seemed to hear their movements, and he slowly motioned Joshua and Nongolesi into his *indlu*. He kissed Nongolesi on her forehead and motioned for Joshua to come close. He wrapped his fingers quickly around Joshua's wrist as if he urgently needed to tell him something.

Joshua lowered his ears to the Old Man's lips. The Old Man sucked in a raspy breath, then breathed out. "*Inyanga!* Ah! Uh-huh!" He grinned broadly, chuckling hard as he shook a finger at Joshua.

Joshua laughed, shaking his head. They had been right about the skills of the best *izinyanga*; Joshua felt no shame in saying so.

"Now you know the ways of our people." The Old Man nodded, patting Joshua's hand. Joshua made a mental note to himself to thank Zalinda as soon as he found the chance.

CHAPTER 27

After being away for so long, Joshua was anxious to attend his church's service again. He'd only missed two Sundays, but he already missed spending time with his congregation. And with the Old Man regaining his health, there was so much for which to give thanks. Nongolesi told Joshua they'd already made arrangements for the service because they hadn't known when he'd return from Port Elizabeth. He thought it odd when she claimed she couldn't quite remember the name of the guest preacher. She simply prodded him to relax and enjoy attending the service.

As he walked hand in hand with her now, seeing familiar faces entering the pews, he felt his heart swell. If he hadn't fully realized it before, he knew now how much he'd missed his congregation over the past weeks. He waved to the young couple he'd just joined in marriage, to the woman he'd prayed with as she lay ill a month ago, to the student who'd experienced difficulties in school. The thought of ever being forced to leave them weighed heavily. He moved his free hand over the wooden cross around his neck. He'd been wearing the cross Darius had fashioned ever since he'd returned from Port Elizabeth and had gone to see the Old Man. He wanted, like the Brother, to always feel it close.

As they moved nearer to the church, its silence seemed peculiar. Nongolesi raised her hand to silence his questions as she walked with him to the front entrance, then led him through the front of the church. The whole church rose in applause. Joshua was almost too stunned to respond as one of the students moved to the front and playfully waved Joshua to his pulpit seat. The church chuckled at her motions.

"We are here to welcome Reverend Clay back after two long weeks," the student said with a smile. "We had feared he might be taken from us. You see he has returned." Church members stomped their feet. "Reverend Clay has served us very well. And now that we hear he has had a dose of an *inyanga,* he is really one of us!" The whole church laughed and stomped their feet again as Joshua chuckled to himself. Nongolesi beamed from the front row.

"We wish today to welcome you back," the student went on. "On this day, you will not preach, but we will sing praises, and more praises, to bless our Lord and to ask that in hearing these songs we all will be strengthened during these hard times."

Joshua's eyes dampened. The choir rose, dressed as had become their custom over the last few months, in bright dresses and shirts, some in traditional *umbhaco* and *isibheshu.* Joshua smiled as the choir held up their tambourines, rattling them freely, singing one song after another. He could hardly have imagined a more beautiful sound.

Joshua cherished the sense of peace that lingered with him after that worship service. As he made his way across campus the next day, he also reflected on how his life in the past few weeks had been filled with such valleys and peaks. He had so much to be grateful for, but there were so many more battles to wage. The thought made him sad, sad for what he'd promised in Port Elizabeth. As he made his way from the administration building back to his home, his eyes fell on the tent gracing Sandile's kop, crowning it like an emerald pointing toward the sky.

Students nodded to Joshua as they ducked under the tent's parted flaps and moved inside. Joshua narrowed his eyes as he neared, chuckling to himself as he followed an impulse, tucking inside the tent behind the students. The tent seemed larger inside than it appeared outside. He gazed over clusters of folded chairs forming semicircles where students chatted with one another; some held pamphlets and thin worn books; others, to his surprise, held their Bibles open while engaged in animated chatter. On the farthest side, a man dressed in a checked shirt lingered with students. Joshua sat down on a chair nearest the tent's opening and observed.

Tumi surprised him as she walked up to him, staring at him intently. He had spent very little time with her since she'd come to dinner with Ogenga well over a year and a half earlier. There was skepticism in her eyes, as always.

"How was the exam?" he asked.

"Your prayer worked," she said coolly.

"You did well!" He smiled.

She nodded, a smile curving at her lips. "It might even inspire me to go to church more often," she said half-jokingly.

"It would be wonderful if that were the effect," Joshua said very seriously. "I believe in your talent."

She seemed unprepared for his kind words. Her smile curved fuller. "Well, you know this will be the talk of campus later tonight. Reverend Clay came inside the tent!"

"It is useful for me to understand what is feeding your minds."

"The truth."

"You think the truth is here?" Joshua asked.

"Various bits of it. We funnel through the best ideas of what we hear from other lands, we compare it to what our ancestors have taught, and, yes, we find the truth here."

"And who is your friend across the way." Joshua nodded to the checked-shirted man. "This is the infamous Xolile?"

"The very one."

"Is he all that they say?"

"He is a great orator, like the Brother. His ideas are very different, though. He talks of socialism and Russia. Some of his ideas are much like our own—take care of your brother, for it is right. But many of his other ideas"—she smiled—"it is like he invents them as he goes along."

"Like what?"

"The idea that class is what will determine our future, and that race is not relevant to our struggle. That message does not get far."

"So why do you say there is truth here?"

"Some of the ideas we discuss here are honorable. The other ideas that have no worth, we cast those aside, just like we cast aside those false ones that you missionaries bring."

"The Bible has no false ideas."

"Yes, but missionaries can, can they not?" she asked with a stone face.

She probably didn't realize the feeling her words stirred in him. Joshua lowered his eyes, then looked at her directly. "Yes, they can. And when they do, they do great harm to the message we seek to put forth."

"You are not as bad as the rest. Or at least you have become much better than they."

He smiled broadly. "Is that a compliment from Tumi?"

She laughed, realizing that she had just spoken a kind word about him in an unguarded moment. "No," she said, trying to wipe away any traces of her smile as she walked away, shooing him with her hands. He chuckled as she turned back with a smile and said again, "No!"

———————

The July sun had already blessed the land and faded behind the mountain's brow. Joshua found peace in all the blushes of evening that graced the mid-July sky as he walked off his restless energy at the edge of the road on his fifteen-minute journey to the only restaurant serving Africans in Alice. The air was raw with winter, in full force now. Mud sloshed gently beneath Joshua's soles as he gathered his coat tightly in the breeze. His thoughts focused firmly on Jovan. Joshua had grown so close to the students in the past year, coming to understand fully their hopes and dreams. He couldn't have admired Jovan more as the young man pursued so relentlessly his goal of passing the national exam to receive an undergraduate degree in medicine. Jovan had studied with the Brother for nearly two years now, and Joshua admired his determination, as he tried to secure his degree without much benefit of formal training. Jovan had already received an offer of a scholarship from Tuskegee Institute, the Negro university in the United States, where they would help prepare him further for medical school. Joshua felt such pride knowing so many Negroes in America understood the importance of the struggle in South Africa. Jovan's results had been released earlier in the day, and the whole campus was buzzing, hoping that Jovan had passed. Joshua had kept Jovan in his prayers all week long, hoping he would fare well. *He'll do it,* Joshua assured himself. Several Fort Hare students had managed the feat in the past few years and had traveled to America to train to become doctors.

As Joshua walked through the restaurant's double-door entrance, the restaurant fell silent, buzzing again when the students realized it wasn't Jovan. With the muffled sounds of a sultry blues song playing on a phonograph at the back of the room, Joshua nodded hello to various students. The sole Alice restaurant to serve Africans was humble, with plain tables scattered across unvarnished floors and a few intimate hanging damask lights. Joshua was surprised to see Sarah sitting at a center table next to the Brother, Ogenga, Sipho, and Jovan's girlfriend, Mazi. Sarah was leaning toward Ogenga and Sipho, engaged in a consuming chat. Joshua made a note to speak to her further about his work building the Ginsberg church and school. The Brother leaned away from the table, his brow deeply furrowed as he kneaded a newspaper in his hands. Joshua had never seen him so tense. As Joshua neared their table, he saw Sipho glance toward the Brother with approval in his eyes. It was one of the few times Joshua had ever seen Sipho look at a white man with anything other than contempt.

"Preacher Man!" Ogenga said when he saw Joshua, extending his hand. "My brother has come to pray for me." The whole table laughed.

"I *always* pray for you," Joshua said, making them all chuckle again. He exchanged a quick embrace with his brother.

"A gin and tonic for the preacher," Ogenga called to a waitress as everyone laughed.

"And to think that after all this time, I had thought you and I were getting somewhere," Joshua said as he removed his winter coat and took a seat in the chair Ogenga had pulled out next to him. He was glad to see Ogenga back in bright spirits, now that the Old Man's health was recovering. He knew how much Ogenga had appreciated his prayers for the Old Man. The constant trips Joshua had made to look in on the Old Man had seemed to give Ogenga strength to continue his work among the students even while he remained so worried for his father.

"Well, I suppose you've made your way here for the same reason we have," the Brother said.

"I was just in the neighborhood," Joshua said, circling a finger around the rim of the glass of water the waitress poured for him.

"So was I," Sarah added jokingly.

"I thought he'd be back by now," Joshua said, shifting in his chair as he took a swig of cool water.

"If he isn't back soon," Ogenga replied, "that's not a good sign."

"Are you nervous?" Sarah asked the Brother, rubbing her hand on his arm.

"Not more than any of you. I have faith in Jovan; I just want him to get what he deserves," the Brother said. He brushed a hand over his forehead, as if he were sweating in the cold night.

"You've done a brilliant job tutoring him," Ogenga assured the Brother. "If he doesn't make it now, he'll try again. You know he's not one to give up."

"They should have passed him the first time," Sarah said under her breath.

They chatted for a while, and the room fell silent again as the double doors rattled. The buzz resumed again as Lydia walked in. She stood in back of the Brother's chair, wrapping her arms around him, planting a kiss on his cheek. "The car's right outside, *ja,*" she whispered in his ear. "Jovan will pass his exams. We'll celebrate. I'll get you home to rest," she assured him. Her support of the Brother brought a smile to Joshua's eyes.

They spoke for a while, until they heard a bit of clatter outside as the doors opened again. Ogenga lifted his newspaper in front of his face as Jovan ambled through, shoulders stooped. Everyone pretended to engage in conversation.

Jovan headed directly to the cook's counter, barely looking at anyone. "I sure could use a mealie beer right now," Jovan said to the cashier, loud enough for Joshua to hear. The cashier only shook his head. Jovan ordered a sandwich. Slowly, Jovan surveyed the room. Ogenga's eyes grew dark as he tried to read Jovan's expression. Jovan caught his gaze and approached with a frown. Jovan stood between his girlfriend and the Brother.

"All of you here at once. Am I missing a party?" Jovan asked plainly.

Sarah stretched her lips into a deliberate smile, as if preparing to appear upbeat in the face of bad news.

"How are you feeling?" the Brother asked, studying Jovan's expression.

Jovan looked down. "I really wish this"—he raised the glass of water in his hand—"was a mealie beer. I could use one tonight," he said as he moved his eyes to meet the Brother's gaze, "to *celebrate!*" A smile lit across his face.

The Brother stood and hugged Jovan and the room burst into cheers as the students read the meaning of the embrace. The students rose to their feet, pounding their fists against the tables, clapping and cheering. Jovan reached for Mazi, who was crying. He squeezed her tightly as the students broke out in a song.

Joshua took a few steps back from the table, taking in the sight. He still had not forgiven himself for being on the wrong side of the fight for so long. But his happiness for Jovan made his heart so full. Joshua was so proud of him.

The cheers were followed by more jubilation, and another song. Joshua imbibed the hopes and dreams of the students as they swayed to an anthem full of the faith that the past had taught:

> Nkosi sikelel'i-Afrika
> Maluphakanyisw' uphondo lwayo,
> Yizwa imithandazo yethu,
> Nkosi sikelela, thina lusapho lwayo . . .

The anthem had been written so recently, but it seemed inscribed on each of their hearts. The students sung it like a hymn, sending the sounds deep into the night. Locking arms and rocking back and forth, they chanted over and over, *Izinto ziza kutshintsha!*

"*Makinda*," Ogenga called from a few feet away, "*Izinto ziza kutshintsha!* Things will be different."

Jovan moved toward Joshua to give him a hug. "I know you'll help someone else get here," he said to Joshua, as if to assure Joshua that he believed he now stood with them. All the differences between them seemed to melt away—reverend, student, American, South African. Joshua looked at Jovan, this man of ambition who was nearly his age.

"You deserve this and so much more, Jovan," Joshua said.

More hands pounded on tables again, refusing to pause, as the students demanded a speech. Jovan moved swiftly atop a chair, holding his water as if it were champagne, beginning his charmer's banter. Joshua chuckled; he hoped the sight would remain inscribed in his mind. Joshua touched the Brother on his shoulder to say good night.

"Come with us, *Makinda*," Ogenga called back to him. "We will be out all night; this is the time for us to go into the fields, singing praises and more praises!"

"I'll pray for you." Joshua chuckled, smiling at Ogenga as he departed.

———————

"I didn't expect to see you here," Sarah said a couple of days later, greeting Joshua as he took a seat in the chair of her principal's office.

"I mentioned the other night I would drop by to speak with you about the church and school we are building in Ginsberg," he said.

She nodded, as if she hadn't been fully convinced he would follow through. She set aside the book in her hand, *Up from Slavery,* giving him her full attention.

"Is that required reading here?" He nodded toward the book.

"Very much so," she said, smiling.

"Well, I will enjoy your input about what books and resources we should gather for our school. Nongolesi and I have used much of our savings to purchase building materials. The Ginsberg children have already gathered piles of rocks—larger than you can imagine!"

She chuckled. "I *can* imagine."

"They're so enthusiastic and full of hope."

"The church and the school represent their future," she said.

He nodded and inhaled softly. She was right. The preparations for the building was having the effect Joshua had intended, spreading hope through all of Ginsberg. Even older men who had sat idly for months, no longer lifted tarnished bottles of bitter beer to their lips while staring out at the blue sky. Instead, they had begun to help smooth the ground and crush the rocks into a fine powder needed to make cement.

"We want the church and school to be finished as soon as possible. Nongolesi has developed detailed plans for the grounds. And Old Man Maganu is gaining strength again—he has helped rally the support of the men of Ginsberg. They are willing to work hard to ensure we can build the church as quickly as we can."

"Does your mission support this move?" Sarah asked.

"I was told I could continue to preach in Ginsberg, and this doesn't interfere with my ministering duties elsewhere. I can't see why contributing to a local effort to build a church and to help educate local children should pose a problem for them." He said that flawlessly, but he knew he was doing more than just contributing to the effort. And his mission might have something to say about that.

Sarah raised her eyebrows, knowingly, then smiled at him. "Well, as you see"—she waved around, gazing out her window—"I have a lot of experience with building an independent school."

Joshua gazed out at the three buildings of classrooms.

"I'm proud of you, Sarah," he said without a hint of embarrassment. The words made her pause, and then she smiled, a smile that filled his heart.

"I was speaking to some of the craftsmen of Nongolesi's village, and they tell me they can erect a building in seven weeks if they have all of the materials on hand. We begin laying the bricks in their molds shortly, so we hope to begin setting the walls within the month. Any input you have we will appreciate."

She nodded with cheerful eyes as he unwrapped a series of ground plans for her to examine.

# CHAPTER 28

On the way back from East London, Joshua was occupied with heavy thoughts. In the nearly four months that had passed since he'd returned to Fort Hare from Port Elizabeth, he'd abided as best he could to the agreement he'd made in Port Elizabeth, turning his ears from the faint voice inside that urged him to work more explicitly with the Old Man and local leaders to help prevent any further relocations. He kept thinking of Andrew's words. That's what Andrew had done—he also had chosen to compromise on this matter. Joshua had taken stands on so many other important issues, it should be okay, this choice. But faintly, he never seemed convinced of his own reasoning.

Only when he returned to Ginsberg—joining hands with the men and women of the township, stirring the same barrels of cement that they did, casting the bricks into their molds with the same ardor, working with Nongolesi and the Old Man to finalize the church plans—did he feel in some peculiar way that his soul was resting. In the past few months, he had taken the time to preach a sermon in Ginsberg each week, following his Fort Hare sermon, delivering messages of hope and redemption. Both services were very well-attended.

Why can't I be satisfied with that, he wondered. Why had he chosen to take such a risk now? He shook his head, knowing something about Ogenga's tone, as he asked Joshua to drop him to a last-minute protest in East London, had prodded Joshua to answer yes. Joshua was scheduled to travel to East London to gather supplies for the new church in Ginsberg anyhow. But in a pulsing truth, he knew that was just an excuse; he also knew his actions could be interpreted as directly supporting that evening protest.

What bothered him now, as he returned from East London, driving slowly in the August showers, was a sense of foreboding. From the scene in East London, he was certain something fiery was brewing. He felt so uneasy as Ogenga and his friends had stepped out of his car, but Joshua hadn't found the voice to urge them to reconsider.

Others, those closer to the planning, seemed to sense also there would be something different about this protest, something much more ominous. He'd heard students murmuring about it, insisting that Jovan shouldn't attend. The whole community hoped that Jovan would depart safely for the United States. Joshua's heart brightened, at least for a moment, as he thought of the promising opportunities that awaited Jovan at Tuskegee. But his sense of foreboding about the protest still refused to vanish.

He felt such relief when he reached home that night: no telegram had been slipped under his door. Perhaps his nerves had flared for no reason. His thoughts were still heavy, though, as he lit a lantern near his desk and reread a letter from his family. He was so happy to receive another note from them. They raved on again about the resources their church had received from his mission. *We knew you'd be a success, Joshua,* Alma had written and underlined that compliment several times. He supposed this depended on what she meant by success. Wiping a hand over his neck, Joshua considered the words again. A success? He blew out the lantern and slipped into bed next to Nongolesi. She lay facing him in the dark. He kissed her gently on the forehead and ran his hand across her stomach. She was nearly seven months pregnant now, and Joshua was filled with excitement every time he imagined the child they would bear and raise together. She stirred beside him; he put his arm around her and drifted to sleep.

Later that night, Joshua's heart pounded mercilessly. Wiping his fingers lightly to rub the sleep from his eyes, he felt his throat pulsing as the knock on the door kept on, loud and urgent. His thoughts were fraught with fear as he opened the front door and a freshman mouthed the words he'd dreaded hearing one day: Ogenga had been taken with other protesters to Nocno.

Joshua'd rarely felt so helpless or so remorseful about a decision. Two weeks later, he set off for the Nocno prison and moved through three successive gates, each one screeching shut behind him as the guard led him to a spartan room of brick walls and dusty floors. Nocno had finally granted Joshua permission to see Ogenga. He flinched at the sight of Ogenga's black-and-blue face as another guard led Ogenga to a seat in the visiting booth on the other side of the speaking glass.

Ogenga seemed different somehow, Joshua thought, as he sat looking at him through the thick slate of glass between them. Joshua prayed it was only a temporary change, for the light in Ogenga's eyes had dimmed. "Are you okay?" Joshua whispered to his brother. He couldn't wish away the wave of guilt overwhelming him as Ogenga touched a finger to his swollen eye, trying to ease the pain.

"I'm okay," Ogenga said, speaking through the mesh-netted hole in the glass. "They will say I stumbled and fell." He chuckled darkly.

"I will come to see you as often as I can," Joshua assured him, knowing his visits would be allowed only because he was a minister. No one else in the family had yet been allowed to see Ogenga. "We're trying hard to get you out of here."

The look in Ogenga's eyes pierced Joshua. Ogenga shook his head, expressing his belief that those were futile acts. He sat still for a moment, collecting himself. "*Makinda,* the warden comes by every day," he said finally. "He comes to whisper in my cell about what he calls his good news." He looked down at his hands, his lips trembling at the cruelty of the term. "You know, I never imagined what it would be like to be here," he said, wiping his lip. "They have posted a wood fence at the edge of the cement courtyard and they say, 'You now live in your new *ebuhlanti.*'"

"You will make it through this," Joshua whispered. "The magistrate has not made a ruling yet. Many protestors have made it out of situations like this."

"Ah, the good news," Ogenga said. "That's what I was saying. The warden comes every day, every night, to tell me this news, ever since he put me in a dark room by myself, at the far end of the jail, for ten days. Ten days." Ogenga laughed. "No light. No one to talk to. There was only darkness." His voice splintered. "He said he put me there so when I came out I would hear him well. His words were 'You're an educated man.' And he got the most sinful smile on his face."

"That's what he said to you?"

"I'm an educated man," Ogenga repeated, "and the warden says that will seal my fate here. He says the government now realizes it is the educated African who is the true threat to society. Because of my education, I will never be permitted to leave this place." The look in Ogenga's eyes frightened Joshua.

"The warden has no authority to keep you here, only the magistrate can decide that," Joshua said, touching his hands to the glass between them. "And you're not alone, Ogenga," he said more firmly. "We will keep fighting to get you out."

Ogenga shifted in his seat again. "I've asked God for strength. I've prayed to the ancestors that they seek this on my behalf also." He lowered his eyes and was quiet for a moment. "Did you prepare a Psalm for me?"

"As you requested," Joshua said, opening his thick Bible to the pages he'd marked.

"Each time you come—"

"Every time, I will prepare to read a Psalm with you," Joshua said. He turned to a precise page. "This is Psalm twenty-seven." He began reciting it from memory. "*NguYehova umkhanyiseli wam nomsindisasi wam . . .*"

Ogenga smiled, hearing Joshua speak so well in Xhosa. "You speak so well now, you keep getting better," he said, smiling.

Joshua nodded and Ogenga's eyes were cheerful for a moment.

"Let me read with you," Ogenga said.

Joshua knew the words by heart, so he held the Bible up to the glass, taking a moment to wipe a circle of thick dust on the pane so Ogenga could see the Xhosa words clearly. They sat there, viewing each other face-to-face, reciting the words together.

Joshua's thoughts still lingered on Ogenga a week later, even as he walked with Jovan toward the dock in the distance, where they could see the Brother, Lydia, and Sarah sitting silently on a bench, each lost in thought. Joshua recognized the saddened hush around them. The grim crackdown in East London following the last student protest seemed to take its toll on everyone. He tried to shift his thoughts, speaking enthusiastically with Jovan about all that awaited him at Tuskegee. Sarah turned toward them just then. Her face lit up, as did those of the Brother and Lydia, as they rose to greet Jovan.

"Well, this is it, the great adventure begins," the Brother said, hugging Jovan tightly, as he might have hugged his own son. "Well done, Jovan. I know you'll do well in America."

"You have the addresses I gave you?" Sarah asked.

Jovan pat the breast pocket of his jacket, smiling broadly. "Close to my heart. My new family in New York—I can't wait to meet them." He hugged Sarah tightly also.

"Lydia"—Jovan turned toward her, putting his arm around her gratefully—"thank you for all of the encouraging words, the good food, the support. Take care of this one, huh?" he said, nodding toward the Brother. "Make sure he sees a decent doctor now and again so he can keep well until I can return and provide him with superior care." He grinned, making everyone chuckle.

"*Makinda.*" Jovan turned to Joshua as a shipman on the wooden platform called "All Passengers" through a large cone. Joshua smiled, thinking of all Jovan had ahead of him at Tuskegee. "You sure I should mention your name?" Jovan asked. "I hear professors in all the Negro colleges know each other, so even though you went to Wilberforce, the professors at Tuskegee probably know about you. Sure I'm not going to get chastised for having fraternized with naughty Joshua from Wilberforce?"

"You foiled my trick." Joshua laughed as they embraced. "Try not to get into too much trouble over there."

"I should be saying the same to you." Jovan smiled, making Joshua chuckle. *So true.*

Jovan's eyes grew damp. "You look after Ogenga," he said. Joshua nodded.

"It wasn't your fault," Jovan said, as if he were watching the lines of sadness in Joshua's face furrow themselves more deeply. "You couldn't have known he'd end up in Nocno." He paused, until Joshua nodded. "When I write to you," Jovan continued, "tell Ogenga what I say. They don't always give letters to prisoners. My letters will probably not make it to him."

"I will. You have my word," Joshua said.

From farther out on the ocean, the luxury liner let out three blows of its horns, and Joshua could see that the double-decked tug had reached the dock, ready to carry passengers to the ship. White South Africans lined up at the tip of the pier, and the shipman carefully tied a rope between two poles behind the last of the second-class white passengers, marking a clear divide before calling the Africans to line up behind them. Joshua, Lydia, the Brother, and Sarah all seemed to mutter under their breaths at the same time.

"I am going out like this"—Jovan nodded toward the segregated line—"and I shall be returning like this. Little will have changed in five years' time, I'm sure. But *Ngenye imini!* One day!" He looked at them as they echoed the words back.

The sight of Jovan moving toward the segregated line made anger stir in Joshua, and it fortified his impulse to continue to press harder in the ways he could to bring change for his congregation. Jovan joined the African section of the line, waving to Joshua and the others as he smiled broadly and disappeared onto the tug.

Joshua's thoughts remained on Darius for days after his dream.

"Preacher Man!" Darius had whispered in Joshua's dreams, from across his Fort Hare bedroom as the sun lifted over the horizon, casting a lovely morning hue throughout the room. "Preacher Man!" he whispered more deliberately. In his dream, Joshua's heart sank as he awoke, recognizing the contours of the voice. Lifting onto his elbows, Joshua had squinted his eyes in the bright light pouring through the window and braced his heart. This would be short-lived, he knew: Another short exchange and then Darius would vanish again. Joshua studied every inch of Darius's face again, which shone with brightness. Darius sat perfectly still, as if reading Joshua's every thought. After a moment, Darius lifted his eyebrows and looked Joshua straight in the eyes, flashing his broad charmer's smile. Joshua's eyes welled as happiness showered over him; a tear rolled down his cheek as his lips curved into a smile.

"How you doin', Preacher Man?" Darius said softly.

Joshua couldn't stifle a dark laugh. "How am I doing?" He shook his head, sitting up fully, swinging his legs over the edge of his bed. "I think it's fair to say I'm getting a little beaten up down here."

"Who you allowin' to beat you up?"

Joshua noted his wording. Just like Darius. He hadn't meant those words as a criticism, just a challenge. In his dream, Joshua fought back his urge to reach out and touch Darius, fearing he'd disappear.

"I don't know which way to turn," Joshua said, never taking his eyes off Darius, who moved toward him, blocking the brightness of the sun as he passed in front of the window. For a moment, all Joshua could see was his dark silhouette—his squared shoulders, his proud chest. Darius swallowed Joshua in a tight hug again, lingering in the embrace, as happiness flooded to every nerve in his body. Joshua's eyes grew wide though, as he felt moistness against his chest. He pulled back, running a hand across a scarlet line that quickly grew into a puddle of blood on his nightshirt. His eyes were instantly drawn to the gaping hole in Darius's chest.

"Darius!" He let out an anguished moan as the room closed in around him. He touched Darius's open wound. As that crimson blood soaked his trembling hands, his heart sank, knowing finally that it must have hurt, whatever had happened to Darius. His eyes darkened, and he still trembled as he measured Darius's expression. Joshua saw no pain there, no bitterness, not even a remorseful pout.

"It don't hurt anymore," Darius said. "You know how I died in the war, Josh. But it hasn't hurt for a long while."

"Why was it so important?" Joshua's voice rose an octave, his anger directed fully.

"I asked you not to stay angry, Josh," Darius said, his voice also rising.

"We are still trying to understand *why*. You didn't even ask if it was okay. 'We'll always be here for each other.' Isn't that what you'd always say? 'We'll make a better way in this world together, Joshua.'"

"I know you think I let you down," Darius said lowly.

"Lucius warned you what would happen—they'll throw you right out front; they won't try to spare your life."

"I know I hurt all of you."

"And what about Lu? There hasn't been a day in our house since they came to tell us you were gone when she has smiled, really smiled."

"You think I don't know I broke Ma's heart?" Darius's temper finally flared. "You think I don't see her there when it's late at night and y'all are sleepin', when she turns from Pa and cries. She still cries." His voice cracked. "I know she didn't want me to go, Joshua. And I know she worked hard to build us strong. But I wanted to be *free*."

"Are you free? Are you free now, Darius?"

Darius's eyes burned. "You think I don't wish I could reach out my hand and stroke her hair and say, *I love you. Ma, I love you—you didn't do anything wrong*."

Joshua pulled farther from Darius, and blood streamed down from Joshua's hands, pouring from his own searing wounds. He looked up with so much anger as he touched his hands together, trying to stop the trail of blood. He couldn't even look at Darius anymore. He looked down, squeezing his hands as tightly as he could, but the blood flowed freely. Darius smoothed his own hands over each of Joshua's, so softly. Joshua looked him in the eyes again.

"I know you think I let you down, Joshua," Darius said again, this time peacefully. "But I've had time to think." He shook his head as if he'd considered the matter a thousand times, his eyes full. Joshua's eyes grew larger as Darius moved his hands away and Joshua held his dry hands up, his wounds healed. Darius's wounds had disappeared too.

Darius stood and stepped closer to the window. He spread two fingers wide in a perfect V. "Don't you see?" Darius asked, looking at Joshua so intensely, a placid smoothness to his tone as he held that

V steady. "It's not here or there. It's here *and* there. It's one; we're one." His eyes shone with a burning rightness. He flashed his fingers again in a second V, as broadly as he could stretch his fingers. "Haven't you seen by now?"

Joshua averted his eyes, knitting his brow, trying not to understand.

"I know I hurt Ma and all of y'all." Darius's voice dipped low as he stepped back toward the sunlight. As he turned back from the open window, his face shone brightly as he searched Joshua's face. "But I've had plenty of time to think—that's what I came to tell you, Joshua." He whispered the words he had come to say: "Preacher Man, Reverend man, if I had to, I'd do it again."

Joshua went numb, too stunned to move for a moment; then his soul filled with peace. He wiped a tear as he looked back at Darius, who whispered the words that set Joshua's heart free as he faded back into the sun. "Preacher man—*Joshua*—I'd do it again."

As Joshua sat at his desk now, tallying the money Andrew had collected to purchase additional marula Bibles, he thought back to that dream and somehow it brought him peace at a time when everyone around him was so ill at ease. Nongolesi's fidgeting called his attention to the dining room. She'd tried her best to eat well because of the baby, but her appetite had failed her many times lately. She'd make circles with her spoon in her stew at dinner, pushing her bowl away with a frown after a while. Tahira had also become distant, her voice weak, her temper short anytime she overheard Joshua talking with Andrew about Ginsberg. He didn't need to ask; he didn't even want to. He knew what worried them so: Month by month, week by week, the relocations were moving closer to the Noni Village.

Mustering all his strength, Joshua kept preaching messages of faith and fortitude. His trips to see the children of the Ulundi School filled him with hope, as did his work building the Ginsberg church and school. Not a week passed now without making substantial progress toward finishing the Ginsberg church. There had been one delay after another, as they ran short of supplies or funds. But as he labored with the other men of the township, crushing rocks and laying more bricks in their molds, the children would gather near, their gazes graced with hope. It kept his determination strong.

Joshua reached across the desk, opening the letter that had just arrived from Philadelphia, penned in Alma's handwriting. This letter differed from all the others; it lacked the signatures of the other Hopedale family members. She alone had signed it. He sat and read her words. She complained that Lucius was spending more time than ever around Liberty Hall; she said he'd come home speaking of things that would upset the family. Lucius had been saying, she wrote, that people were beginning to murmur that another war in Europe was coming. Her penmanship had become unsteady as she wrote that they could not imagine, after all the hard times, that there might be more troubles. *But Lucius comes home and talks about Double V—"Victory at home and abroad."*

That phrase drew his eyes. *Double V,* like Darius's fingers in his dream. Joshua too had heard the murmuring about the tensions in Europe and the possibility of war. His lips parted as he read on. Lucius was saying that Negroes should send their sons to fight, this time in desegregated troops. She finally wrote out the heart of her concerns: She couldn't see how Joshua could become involved, since he was a preacher. *But you know this aunt of yours always worries about you,* she wrote, ending her letter.

Joshua realized how differently he reacted to this letter than he would have two years earlier. He, like his family in America and those around him, would each have to decide how many sacrifices they were willing to make to forge a steady path to a better tomorrow. He inhaled deeply, scratching his temple. He rubbed his fingers across the cross on his neck. As he nestled further in his seat, he folded the letter and tucked it away, promising himself not to read it again. He closed his eyes, sitting still. And as he knew it would, the voice called to him from someplace nearby so gracefully. *Osukuba ethanda ukundilandela, makazincame, awuthwale umnqamlezo wakhe, andilandele ke. Kuba othe wathanda ukuwusindisa umphefumlo wakhe, wolahlekwelwa nguwo; ke yena othe wawulahla umphefumlo wakhe ngenxa yam, nangenxa yeendaba ezilungileyo ezi, wowusindisa.*

———————

Joshua could only draw circles in the sand outside the Maganu family home so many times before the restlessness became unbearable. He and Nongolesi had been staying at the Maganu home during the last week and a half as her birthing time neared. He wiped his sweaty palms on his trousers, his heart racing, as he sat in front of a low fire burning in a small pit, adding warmth in early September's morning air. Joshua rose and paced again, laughing at himself out loud.

"Always, men pace," the Old Man said, chuckling. "No matter where in the world, that is what we hear—thousands of miles away and all men pace at times such as this."

Joshua heard Nongolesi cry out a few times in the clear morning air, each of her moans cutting at Joshua's heart. The cries made the Old Man wince too, but the Old Man seemed much more filled with anticipation for the child that would soon enter the world.

"Just sit; she'll be okay," Mhlobo said, prodding Joshua to sit down.

Joshua couldn't stand it anymore. He ignored Mhlobo's words as he shot through the house to the bedroom door.

"*Amadoda mawangangeni kweli gumbi!*" one of the old women said from the far side of the room. "Men must stay out!"

Old women from the village lined the dim room's walls, with nothing threatening in the clutch of their wicker sticks. According to their tradition, if a birthing mother cried out in childbirth, she should be silenced with steady thrashing. But each woman here held their sticks almost in a tribute to tradition, offering Nongolesi nothing but words of encouragement. The smiles on their faces reflected the memories of ages, of the children who had brought new life into the village time and time again. They looked on with wonder, as if seeing it all again for the first time. The calls of the midwife guided Nongolesi, who was drenched in sweat and grasping a side of the bed.

Joshua could sense the history between Mama Siziwe and Nongolesi as Mama Siziwe sat caressing Nongolesi's arm. With every grunt Nongolesi uttered, another tear rolled down Mama Siziwe's cheek. And with every moan Nongolesi let out, another drop of perspiration formed on Joshua's brow.

"*Kuacha siku hizi,*" another woman repeated a few more times, and one of the women finally pushed Joshua back out of the room.

After pacing for a few more minutes, Joshua finally sat down, burying his head in his hands. Just then, he thought of Lu and his family back home. They had sent him letters of congratulations when he had written about Nongolesi's pregnancy. Alma kept sending more notes with advice on raising an infant. He smiled, since it was so much like her. It was hard to accept that his family had been absent for so many important events in his life.

The sun had risen far above the mountaintop when Joshua finally heard one last long moan and then silence. His eyes grew full as a high-pitched cry from meek lungs called out in a new world. The Old Man and Mhlobo each awoke from their naps in chairs nearby. Joshua headed straight past them into the room. Nongolesi was crying as Mama Siziwe wiped a damp rag across her forehead and gave her a glass of water.

Nongolesi swallowed slowly as one of the villagers massaged her stomach, relaxing her back down. Joshua moved next to Nongolesi, softly stoking her hair as another woman removed the bloodied rags at the edge of the bed. He glanced up as a woman returned to the room, having washed the baby. The baby had settled down and lay quietly in the villager's arms. Joshua could never have imagined the wave of emotion he would feel the moment he set eyes on their first child.

"You have a son," the midwife said to Joshua as she handed the baby to Nongolesi. The child's eyes seemed welded shut, but the baby smiled, as if responding to the soft feel of his mother's flesh.

"Little Darius." Nongolesi held him up, weeping as she looked at the baby. Joshua beamed as she placed the child in his arms. Joshua cradled the infant closely. The little fingers. The tiny toes. The curly, wet hair. The gently slanted eyes. Joshua thought his heart would burst. He could hardly believe the miracle he held in his hands. He couldn't peel his eyes away. "Little Darius." He was a pure marvel.

———————

As he brought Nongolesi back to their home and helped to tend to his new child, the joy Joshua had felt holding his son lingered with him. After a week, he felt freer to leave their home for a while, long enough to speak with a class full of twelve-year-olds. The boys were smiling expectantly as he moved to the front of the Ulundi School classroom. Their smiles provided a welcome reminder of why he had just chosen to break his promise, signing another petition Nokwe had prepared to submit to the King William's Town magistrate, requesting that the villagers be allowed to return to their land wherever possible. Joshua took a deep breath as he thought about it: It wouldn't be long before his mission found out. Somehow, that no longer mattered.

The teacher reminded the class that Joshua had come to share his brother's letters about the Great War. Joshua glanced across the room as they welcomed him warmly with their clapping. He took a seat, moved by their enthusiasm, and he began recounting the history of Africans in America, about the discriminations and brutalities they had faced, and about the long debate the community had gone through when deciding collectively whether they would encourage their young men to fight in the Great War. The students sat with frozen lips, their eyes squinting as they took in all of the information. One boy interrupted Joshua, raising his hand high.

"Yes?" Joshua pointed to him.

"What was your brother like, Reverend? Why would he wish to fight in the Great War, in spite of the sufferings of Negroes?"

Joshua sensed many of them were wondering the same. He described Darius—his hopes, his courage, and his commitment to work for equality. "He was filled with the belief that by helping America to spread its ideals abroad, we could also help to secure them at home. It would be a Double Victory," Joshua said. Those simple sentences summed it up. "But his letters can tell you more than I can about his spirit," Joshua said, lifting the yellowed sheets of paper from a tattered envelope. He could hear Darius's voice every time he read these letters; they always brought back such memories. Now more than ever, he understood his cousin's convictions, and had even come to share them. He took a deep breath and read aloud, in the shining tone that would have rung in Darius's voice had he said the words himself: *"Joshua, you'll never believe what this is like. We neared the Rhine today. . . ."*

# CHAPTER 29

Joshua knew something bad awaited him just around the corner when he'd passed Mr. Garrett a few days earlier, who walked with an extra skip in his step, too cheery, as he smiled that well-worn smile Joshua didn't trust. So he took a deep breath as he answered the knock at his door the next morning, swallowing hard when Reverend Waldron stared back at him. Word hadn't yet reached Joshua that Reverend Waldron had returned to the country from his fund-raising trip abroad. It was mid-October now; Reverend Waldron had probably been back in South Africa for a few weeks, Joshua figured. Reverend Waldron sucked in an irate breath, moving past Joshua without a greeting, standing firmly near Joshua's desk with an expression that Joshua had dreaded. By the way he looked, Joshua knew this wouldn't be pleasant.

"I've received a phone call from the warden at the prison, *again*," Reverend Waldron said with a face of steel, his icy stare enough to strip Joshua's confidence if he let it.

Joshua straightened his back and looked Reverend Waldron directly in the eyes, like Lucius had taught.

"Sir, the chapel is funded by our mission. I have felt free to preach there because it hasn't interfered with my duties at Fort Hare and the prisoners need to be ministered to. They are experiencing unjust imprisonments and have benefited from my sermons."

"You incited the prisoners."

Joshua paused, taken aback that Reverend Waldron was accepting the word of the warden before speaking to him fully about the matter. "I simply lead songs and prayers, and give short sermons. My visits never last more than an hour. And I have refrained from preaching in the jailhouse more than once a month ever since our mission instructed me as such in Port Elizabeth. But with your permission, I would like to resume my ministry more often there."

Reverend Waldron warned Joshua with his eyes. "Consider yourself to have been told firmly you are not to preach again at the jailhouse."

Joshua turned and walked toward the window of his living room.

A young man Joshua had hired to help around the house stepped in from the yard and noticed Reverend Waldron was visiting. "Shall I bring some *amasi*?"

"Yes, and two cups, please," Joshua responded.

"Did you submit another petition to local authorities?" Reverend Waldron asked in a tone that was thick and cold.

With his back still to Reverend Waldron, Joshua closed his eyes. He'd known it wouldn't take long for Waldron to hear. He turned again to face Reverend Waldron directly. "I submitted it. They ignored it, as they always ignore those petitions. They're moving ahead with forced relocations near Alice."

"That's not the point."

Joshua's eyes burned.

"I said that's not the point."

"What is the point, sir?"

"Our mission leaders explicitly barred you from that sort of activity," he said, his voice rising.

Joshua sighed heavily, knowing Reverend Waldron was looking for a convincing apology. The young man returned to the room, placing a pitcher and two mugs on the table. "Would you like soured milk, sir?" Joshua asked.

Reverend Waldron was livid. Joshua wasn't sure whether he was mad at the choice of beverage or his failure to apologize. "Sir, the petition was received. The petition was rejected. That is the end of the matter," Joshua said, sighing.

"Your behavior—and your attitude, I might add—is a source of serious concern, Reverend Clay. Was it not enough, the warning we issued to you in Port Elizabeth? We let you know from the *beginning*," he said, tapping his finger hard against Joshua's desk, "that we could not afford trouble with this mission. I dare say I think you've forgotten why you are here."

"Sir, the Fort Hare church has never been more vibrant. The church is filled, every Sunday. The congregation is receiving and embracing God's Word," Joshua said. Reverend Waldron looked at Joshua as if he were missing the point again. "I have succeeded in spreading God's Word and bringing people to God; I thought *that* was why I was here."

"With members showing up in animal skin skirts." Reverend Waldron looked at him with contempt. He took a step toward Joshua, preparing to drive some point home, when he looked out the window, his eyes growing large. "What is that?" His voice rose another octave.

"A cow in an *ebuhlanti,* sir," Joshua said, steeling his back as he met Waldron's gaze.

"I can see it is a cow," he said, the words seething through his lips. "*What is it doing here?*"

"It's tradition that a young married woman drink milk from her own cow until she has her first child," he said in a tone that implied Reverend Waldron should have known that. "It is tradition to keep the cow even after the first child is born, as a gift from the bride's family."

"Reverend Clay, this is a missionary house."

"Yes, it is," Joshua said slowly, letting his words speak a hundred more.

"You are to take down that byre, and take that cow—"

"Reverend Waldron, I mean you no disrespect," Joshua interrupted. "But that's *my* cow, sir."

Everything Joshua left unsaid turned Reverend Waldron's ear tips red, his whole face following, turning bright crimson. The way Reverend Waldron shook the hat in his hand, Joshua knew he'd just stepped over a line. The Reverend Waldron's anger lingered well after he departed.

Joshua sat down, moving his hands over his face. He was shaken.

"Are you all right, Reverend?" the young man asked, peeking back through the kitchen door.

Joshua nodded, willing himself to chase from his mind the fears of what Reverend Waldron would do next. He looked back through the window at his cow, its swollen udder, its blooming teats, its tail flopping listlessly in the wind. He mused to himself: it was a beautiful sight. He gathered his coat, heading to secure additional building supplies for the Ginsberg church.

————————

Reverend Waldron summoned Joshua to Port Elizabeth one more time. Joshua had no difficulty finding his voice this time, when the mission committee demanded he explain himself.

"As ministers, we have a mandate to stand for justice," Joshua said, keeping the timbre in his voice strong. He said his words deliberately. "I do not believe we can in good conscience remain silent on the matter of forced relocations—it threatens the way of life of the people here, and we need to make it clear that the policy runs counter to creating a South Africa in which all of the races live harmoniously, as equals. If we seek the betterment of our congregations, I cannot see how I can remain silent as their entire way of life is destroyed."

Reverend Waldron's eyes darkened; he seemed too stunned to respond momentarily. "Reverend Clay," he said lowly, recovering after a moment and sounding indignant, "you know very well we don't support forced relocations; we simply take no political position on the matter."

"Sir, I believe taking no political stand is taking a stance."

This was his last chance, they told him. Joshua knew they had not removed him simply because the Fort Hare mission had never been so well attended. Joshua listened, nodding at the right times, ignoring the impulse that grew stronger to resign and to find some other way to stay in the country. He thought of his congregation, his deep desire to support their needs. He held his tongue because he knew there would be no other way to stay in the country.

Joshua was drained by the time he arrived back home in Fort

Hare in the late afternoon a few days later. As he stepped from his car, Nongolesi came to the doorway with heavy steps, tears streaming down her cheeks.

"What is it?" he asked, frightened by the look on her face.

"We've received word they've begun the relocations in the Noni Village," she said, barely getting the words out. "The Old Man has gone to East London to try to secure support to stop this."

Joshua could hardly believe the words. "I'll go. Please stay here, Nongolesi."

"I have to see it for myself," Nongolesi said in a voice he barely recognized.

"We won't be able to do anything to stop this," he said, squinting his eyes.

Nongolesi nodded, still insisting on coming. They left Little Darius with Tahira as they drove toward the Noni Village. They were silent as they rounded a hill and the familiar thatched hut roofs were not in sight. As they drove farther, they could see the flattened land where Tahira's homestead once stood. It took Joshua's breath away. He wasn't sure if he touched Nongolesi's hand to console her or to steady himself.

Joshua drove past the rubble of Tahira's old homestead up the road that once lay at the edge of the Noni Village, to the spot where he normally parked his car, and his stomach curled as he saw that the path now continued much farther into the hills. Weeds were cast to the side of the road, and tractor trails blazed ahead of them, forging a path toward the Maganu family home.

The cleft-chinned officer whom Joshua had seen far too many times greeted him as Joshua stepped out of his car. They walked around the crumbled walls of the Maganu home that was still half-standing. Nongolesi stooped and picked up the scattered sketches of her ancestors that had once graced their walls, as many as she could find, as tears streamed down her face. Joshua busied himself also, gathering as many hand-stitched books as he could find. He was speechless in the face of the tractors and trucks parked all around to help finish demolishing the Maganu home. He stood for a moment, looking at the sight, bereft of words.

"Didn't I tell you—petition or no petition, I'd get my way, in all of this area," a voice said to him, almost in a whisper.

Joshua turned toward the cleft-chinned man as he waved the workers aside. They were done for the day.

———————

Joshua froze in bed in the twilight hour, as Nongolesi pushed up on her elbows beside him, and they held their breaths at the same time. Joshua tried to steady his mind, tried to comprehend how this could be happening a second time as an urgent knock persisted on his front door. He moved with a knot in his stomach, bracing the lantern in the darkness as he opened the door to a young African boy standing on the front step, out of breath. Nongolesi's eyes harbored the same fear that Joshua felt as she followed his hurried movements, holding Little Darius tightly. She waved the young boy to the couch, offering him a glass of water, which he clutched and gulped quickly down, wiping a drop from his lip as he steadied his breathing.

"What is it?" Joshua's heart raced.

"Sorry, Reverend, sir." He stumbled over the words, his voice faltering. "I was sent to give you word that they've taken several students to Nocno. And Beaumont, of the Noni Village, is near death in hospital."

"What happened?" Joshua's voice sank low.

"After they destroyed Noni homesteads, the students came from Lovedale, Fort Hare, the villages, even some of those who live in Ginsberg—they all journeyed to King William's Town to stand there in those streets and protest, all of them so angry," the boy continued. "The police came, their dogs were let loosed, and several students were pushed to the ground and beaten. Beaumont was so angry for what they did to the Noni Village—"

"Why is Beaumont in the hospital?" Joshua asked sharply.

"He too was beaten but escaped and rode with friends to the houses of King William's Town, the houses of the whites. They lit a match there to a guesthouse. He did not flee from the fire quickly enough; the police found him and did not stop those from the houses from strapping Beaumont to a tree and whipping him until every part of his body bled. You would not recognize him. The bandages are soaking through, there is so much bleeding. They do not expect he will live."

Just then, Joshua heard a rustle as Tahira moved back against the wall to steady herself. He hadn't heard her come into the living room from her bedroom in the back of the house. She shrieked as she slowly comprehended the words. Little Darius began to cry.

"I will stay with Little Darius," Nongolesi said, her expression as astonished as Joshua's. "Take Tahira quickly."

Joshua drove Tahira to King William's Town as quickly as he could. It was pure darkness on the road, except for the small space his headlights cut onto the road a few feet at a time. Joshua kept his eyes intently focused, driving carefully in the silent car. Tahira stared out into the darkness numbly, her lips trembling. The road seemed to stretch forever. As they finally walked into the hospital for Africans, several Noni Village women rose long-faced from their blankets on the floor to greet them. The fear in their faces, as they shook their heads, warned Joshua not to let Tahira see Beaumont.

The Brother walked out of a hospital room just then, with the same expression on his face. "You should not see Beaumont like this," the Brother said to Tahira.

"I must see my son," she said.

Tahira clutched Joshua's arm as he moved toward the room from which the Brother had just emerged. The room seemed to darken as Tahira dug her fingernails into his arm, gasping for air; Joshua also sucked in his breath. Beaumont was covered with blood-soiled bandages, his face swollen. Joshua felt so empty, and too afraid to try to comprehend the depth of hate that could have produced this. Tahira bent double, letting out a cry from deep in her throat, then fell to the ground, swinging her arms, calling out in Xhosa, cries, curses, and more cries. She struck her fists out at Joshua and the Brother as they tried to calm her.

It was some time before they were able to get Tahira to rest on a mat outside Beaumont's room. She drifted into an uneasy sleep. "Beaumont will not be long for this world," a villager whispered. Joshua frowned as Tahira's eyes open just then. She had heard those words.

Joshua returned to Beaumont's side, while the Brother too sat beside Beaumont. The Brother brushed his hand through his hair, a tear rolling down his cheek as he looked at this young man, whom Beaumont's mother had named after him, whom he'd known since the day he was born. Joshua reached for the Brother's hand, and together they prayed with all their strength that God's Will would be done.

In the early morning, a doctor asked the two ministers to leave as he examined Beaumont. The doctor emerged from the room, looking hopeful. "He may hold on," he repeated a few times. Joshua's eyes lit up and he quickly looked for Tahira. Many Noni women lay sleeping on the floor, covered with their blankets. He looked over at them again. "Where is Tahira?" he asked one of the few women who sat awake.

Pure anger registered in her eyes. "Tahira could not stand the sight," she replied.

Joshua returned home to let Tahira know the hopeful news.

"Tahira never returned here," Nongolesi said, her eyes clouded with worry.

Joshua didn't know what to think. He headed up to Ginsberg to see Tahira's family members who had been resettled there. They told him the same thing.

Joshua had barely slept a wink since Beaumont had been taken to the hospital. He couldn't. Every creak of the house at night made him jolt awake; he kept hoping Tahira was making her way back through the door. It had been nearly six days of waiting. He'd driven back to Ginsberg daily to inquire if anyone had heard anything. Finally, he asked her relatives about her days, years ago, when Tahira had refused a role of *inkazana* and had fled into the mountains. They sent a young man to show Joshua the way to that place in the hills.

The skeletons of new wood houses rose up where the Noni Village once graced the land. The sight sent a deep flash of anger through Joshua as he drove to the road far in back of the new homes, and followed the young man by foot up the narrow dirt path into the hills, the sun blazing strong above. It took nearly an hour of walking and calling out before they saw Tahira in the spot where she had once lived alone. She was lying under a tree, her bruised ankle swollen. She lay stiff, feeling nearly lifeless, as Joshua cradled her and tried to wake her from her wearied slumber. He could hear faint breaths slipping through her lips and she opened her eyes ever so slightly.

"Go back to the main road to get help," Joshua said to the young man, panicked. Joshua wondered how long she'd been there—she looked famished, her throat dry as she tried to form a word.

Joshua struggled by himself to carry her toward the main road as the young man hurried back down to the main strip. Joshua could only move her slowly, resting every so often. With every pause in his journey, he held her and stroked his hands against her arms, as if trying to keep the blood flowing through her veins.

"Tahira, please try to make it," he pleaded.

That song was loud in his ears as he cradled Tahira's limp body. Baba's song. It called out more loudly than he had heard in so long, with a haunting tempo in a cold, dark pitch. Joshua carried Tahira another fifteen minutes and paused again, patting her cheeks after he rested her down. She seemed so weak. He feared if she fell into another slumber she may never again wake. If only he hadn't let her go to see Beaumont. If only he had tried to intervene in the protest, prodded the students to reconsider. If only he had taken a stronger stand with officials, maybe the forced relocations could have been prevented and Tahira's homestead would still be standing. Joshua sat and rocked Tahira, who faintly opened her eyes again. His heart filled with joy at her movement, until he looked into her eyes. There was nothing but darkness there. He tried to tell her that Beaumont was getting better. She didn't seem to hear.

The flame in Tahira's eyes slowly dimmed, and she seemed to fade into herself. Joshua thought he could hear her unspoken words, thick words from a tried soul. And as he continued to speak to her, she looked past him as if looking at someone else. In that moment, she stayed perfectly still, but her eyes smiled. As she fixed her eyes back on Joshua's face, there seemed to be nothing in between them in that moment. Not age. Not country. Nothing. Her eyes told him that nothing he had failed to say during the two years she had known him mattered anymore. *It was okay,* that is what the light in her eyes said, because she was in unchanging hands. He could feel it, he could see it. In that moment, Tahira's face glowed—glowed with such a brightness—and then, with a smile, she was gone.

Joshua's lips froze, disbelieving. He couldn't move; the magnitude of his failures had never weighed more heavily. He knew that in Tahira's eyes he should have found forgiveness. He felt only his own condemnation, lost by his own steps in the midst of an endless dusk, with no sun, no stars, no velvet to the darkness. The faint voice still sang in the distance a dark-pitched song intended just for him, Baba's Song sung on splintered chords.

What does God do? Joshua wondered. *What does He do when He brings you to that moment—when He has called you and led you and tested you, and you know you are being tested, and He builds your trials to a point and asks you to utter a word, the right word, and your lips part, but the wind doesn't rise?*

The voice in the distance faded, in a decrescendo, but as the words melted away, Joshua heard each one clearly. *Ezam izimvu ziyaliva ilizwi lam, ndibe nam ndizazi, zindilandela; Ezam izimvu ziyaliva ilizwi lam, ndibe nam ndizazi, zindilandela; Ezam izimvu ziyaliva ilizwi lam, ndibe nam ndizazi, zindilandela.* The voice dulled further still, until Joshua could no longer hear the remnants of its aching broken song.

The sky was midnight blue, but Joshua knew every step by heart as he made his way by himself up to 39 Steps. Joshua hadn't remembered a thing after he had lost Tahira. He must have sat for hours rocking her lifeless body until he had felt a young man's hands trying to pry his arms from Tahira. He had felt so numb when he returned to his home to retrieve his Bible. Now, as he moved up the footpath, all he noticed was the silence that surrounded him. There was barely the chirp of a cricket or a call of an owl. There was no Baba's song. There was only the rush of water over the creek's bed, and the stilted smell of jasmine. He didn't rest until he reached the pool at the base of 39 Steps. He sank down on his knees, the wetness of the morning showers creeping up his slacks. The wind gently stroked his cheek. He prayed into the night, and in the darkness, he found light.

As night turned into morning and the sun began to shimmer on the pond, Joshua thought back to that dream, nearly two years ago now when he'd watched his own image sink in a world turned upside down. As he moved through the mud and slush, taking a seat on a nearby rock, he knew now that dream had been no mistake. He opened his Bible and read by the early-morning light, reading one thin page after another as he worked his way through the Gospels, confirming everything he'd known all along. As the sky dimmed again to a dreamy twilight, he prayed again to God, the Lord of his silent tears. *Forgive me, Father.* Those words alone echoed in his mind again and again, knowing his feet, drunk with the wine of the world, had strayed from God.

The next morning, as his skin soaked up the sun's pulsing rays, he lost himself again in prayer. *How is it we serve the same God?* The words once asked of him echoed in his mind. He continued to meditate on his readings, rubbing his hand against the mud stains of his Bible. There was no song except the one that flowed forth from within his heart. He sang it out loud, dwelling on each word. *Osukuba ethanda ukundilandela, makazincame, awuthwale umnqamlezo wakhe, andilandele ke. Kuba othe wathanda ukuwusindisa umphefumlo wakhe, wolahlekelwa nguwo; ke yena othe wawulahla umphefumlo wakhe ngenxa yam, nangenxa yeendaba ezilungileyo ezi, wowusindisa. Kuba komnceda ntoni na umntu, ukuba uthe walizuza ihlabathi liphela, waza wonakalelwa ngumphefumlo wakhe? Niya kundifuna, nindifumane, xa nithe nandifuna ngentliziyo yenu yonke; ndifumaneke kuni; utsho uYehova. Ndiya kukubuyisa ukuthinjwa kwenu.*

He prayed to walk forever shadowed beneath God's hand and he penned the most important words he might ever write. When he finished, he looked back over the Gospels. Jesus riding humbly on a donkey, placing his hand on the untouchables, breaking bread with the poor, healing the weak. The answer had been with him all along. He felt a sense of peace, a weight of chains being lifted and of talons set free. On that second night, when his thoughts were clear, he gathered his Bible and walked down the rooted steps with such certainty, as if a lamp were strapped firmly to his feet. His ordered steps led him down the narrow trail. He smiled as the bridge played out pleasing music as he moved across its rungs with the force of two men.

CHAPTER 30

Only a board or two creaked as Joshua made his way down the wooden planks of the hallway to his bedroom. He heard the gentle sounds of Nongolesi sleeping as he opened the door. She brought a smile to his face. He stood over the wooden crib and listened for a moment to Little Darius's peaceful breaths. He lifted his son, wrapping his arms around him tightly, and moved quietly to the living room. He gently parted a window curtain, light from the October moon filtering softly through the trees, and looked at his son—the little slanted eyes that shone like dark pearls, the scrunched-up little nose, the kinked hair, his little chest moving up and down. He was so beautiful. Little Darius opened his shining eyes a little more widely, his wet lips curving into a smile as he curled his fingers around Joshua's thumb. Baba's song rang from inside Joshua's soul so clearly. He danced with Little Darius as he softly sang that song, understanding the importance of each word. After a time, he gently placed Little Darius back in his crib and moved back to his writing table.

That thought preoccupied his mind again as he sat and unfolded the sermon he'd written beneath the crystal stairs. *If in that moment, when God brings you to that special place and time, and the wind doesn't rise through your lips, God should forsake you, just as you have Him,* he thought. He closed his eyes, wishing with all his soul that he could feel such punishment. But he understood that God believed in second chances; every morning was a cheerful invitation to reorder his steps. And he also knew God would call again and build things up to a point and ask him to utter the right words. Carefully, he penned a letter to his family. He had never wanted to bring shame upon his family, but what shame they would or would not feel because of his decisions this night no longer mattered, he knew. He composed the second page, and then the third, preparing to mail it in the morning. He finally slipped into bed to get a short nap before speaking with Nongolesi and heading to the church in the morning.

"*Makinda* has a heavy heart." That's what Nongolesi had told him the villagers had been saying in the days he'd been gone before the waterfall. *They are so right,* he thought as he walked through the back church doors, up the aisle toward his pulpit. Joshua touched the hands of his congregation members as he moved toward the front. The church was crowded. He shook the hand of a Mama from the Noni Village, whom an *inyanga* had just healed. He embraced the hand of the new student whom the Brother had begun to tutor. He nodded toward the young couple across the room who had just born a new daughter. They all reached out to him with knowing caresses, as tender as that first day he'd entered this church. Today, he felt as though he were walking naked underneath a blanket. As he stood in the pulpit, the silence in the sanctuary was broken only by the sounds of a congregation member shifting in his seat and the sound of Joshua opening his thick Bible on the rostrum. Joshua's eyes drifted to the Brother, Andrew and Nokwe, who sat together, and to Sarah and Lydia, seated across the aisle. He was glad they had received his message in time. He spotted the Old Man, who nodded toward him, and Mama Siziwe, who narrowed her eyes, as if she knew what would soon transpire. The rest of his congregation members faintly nodded their heads, but seemed to be holding their breaths.

Joshua wiped a bead of sweat from his lip, thinking of Tahira as his eyes grew full. He cleared his dry throat, preparing to speak words that would further heal his splintered soul. As he gazed into the eyes of his congregation members, a mountainous weight melted away. He felt again the strength of two men merged into a gracious whole.

"*Luvuyo nethamsanqa ukubasendlini yeNkosi yethu kwakhona, ukuhlulelani ngelizwi lakhe elibalulekileyo,*" Joshua began, using words he'd learned well over the past year. "I thank the Lord for this glorious day that the Lord has made. I thank Him also for the opportunity to preach before you once again. It is truly an honor." He watched heads nod in response.

"I want to continue today on the theme the Brother preached about so well some months ago," he started slowly, the timbre strong in his voice. "The Brother preached it so well, about *Rising, taking up one's bed, and walking.* About the man before the pool of Bethesda. As we all know, that crippled man made up his mind that he wanted to be made whole. He rose; he took up his bed; he walked, as Jesus commanded and empowered him to do. All of us as we embark on our Christian journey will relate to the story of the crippled man before the pool of Bethesda. Sooner or later, we come to that critical juncture where we must rise, take up our bed, and walk. Does anyone here know what I mean?" He took in a breath as they nodded their heads and uttered concurring sounds. Andrew's eyes were shining.

"It's a wonderful thing to rise and walk, to be empowered, to know that the love of the Lord, the rightness of the Lord, is underneath your every step. I feel that since I've come to South Africa, I have been challenged to understand what it means to seek God's voice, to rise and to walk. And it's a wondrous experience. It's amazing when you feel the thrill of the new movement, the new activity of your limbs. You can see it in the toddler who first rises and puts one foot in front of the other. A pure triumph rings in that child's eyes. You can imagine it also in the crippled man, whose legs were once withering, fading to nothingness, as he watches them grow thick again, throbbing with new life.

"Since coming here, I've begun to walk, taking joyous steps like a young babe. One foot in front of the next, in front of the next," he said, walking down from the pulpit. "And I smiled for the journey, as I know many of you have done during your own journeys." He looked at Sarah just then, whose eyes had misted, and to several old women near her, who sat quietly listening to his every word.

"But as you become caught up in the thrill of the new activity of your throbbing limbs," he said, moving farther up the aisle, "it is easy to forget an important fact. It's so basic you can forget it—simply rising and simply walking is not the end of the story, for we will not always be treading on level ground."

Joshua could see his words registering with the congregation as heads nodded again. "The ground everywhere isn't smoothed over, swept clean with cow dung, safe from snakes and clear of any lingering holes. And as I have traveled on my own journey here, I have found, not a pit, not a pothole, but a mountain standing in my way. It's large, it's rugged, and I've found myself on its backside."

He moved back toward the front of the sanctuary, so he could see the expressions of his congregation more fully. "On the backside of a rough mountain. Does anyone know what that's like? I've been in your lovely country—our lovely country—for just over two years now. And I know now that there is only one right answer to the dilemma you face when you find a mountain in your path. Sometimes God is the One who has put that mountain there. Sometimes, someone more sinister worked to pile it high. But in either case, there is only one right answer."

Looking up and down the aisles, Joshua felt so renewed, like a blooming flower blessed by heaven's tears, poking its petals through layers of fallen wood. "This is perhaps what you wouldn't stop to think about when you have heard the story of the crippled man before the pool of Bethesda," he said, his eyes burning brightly. "We see that crippled man rise. We see him take up his bed. We see him walk. But just because God empowers us, it does not mean we will have the *spirit* we will need to rise to the occasion during hard times. In those times, you need another spirit with you. Just like God's servant Caleb. The Bible provides all the answers, you see. So when I look at a mountain in my path and I don't know what to do, I know I'll find an answer in the Good Book. And for this, I turn to Caleb, the loyal servant of God, who was sent to spy out the promised land. In the Book of Numbers, it tells us that when Caleb saw that promised land, he saw also that he would not be able to capture it easily. But he did not flee from the task at hand. He responded with the one right response: Don't try to find a river that might flow around your mountain when the riverbeds all around you are dry. Don't try to pray all night that in time a tunnel might be bored through your mountain. And certainly do not turn off from the right path and hop onto one more convenient regardless of where it might lead.

"The right answer is to place one foot in front of the other, in front of the other, and scale up that mountain. Right up the backside. Clinging on to every jagged rock. Pull up against the backside. Take the bruises and the scrapes that you will encounter on the way up. And you see, for me, this is *personal*," he said with a fiery voice. "I feel ever since I was selected as a missionary, and the entire time I've been here, God has been asking me, *Joshua, do you hear My voice? And I humbly admit before you that I refused to hear the question. God has been asking me, *Joshua, what are you going to do about this mountain? Joshua, are you following Me?*"

He saw a tear roll down Sarah's cheek, and the Brother had closed his eyes and was nodding. "I lacked the courage to face that question squarely," Joshua continued. "I have fallen short of taking actions that would fully glorify God. But God is a gracious God, and He granted me the time to reflect on the Word, to decide what I was going to say in response to that most important question.

"I love my family back home in America, and I know some of them may be disappointed by my decisions today. But I've watched villages that have stood for years demolished in fifteen minutes. I've seen schools torn down, voting rights taken away, burial grounds unearthed, innocent men hauled to prison, women left bereft of their husbands while cradling sickly babies.

"The Bible says, *Ye shall seek me, and find me, when ye shall search for me with all your heart. . . . I will end your captivity; I will restore your fortunes*. All of this, if you will seek the Lord *with all your heart*. And what did I see when I finally looked, with all my heart? The answer is written all over the Bible. Two full days before a waterfall, I read and reread the words of the Gospels. *The meek shall inherit the earth. Blessed are they that walk in the way of the righteous*. God did not write, *All are one in the eyes of the Lord, except the Africans*. God did not say, *I have come that you might have life and joy, except for the Africans*. God did not say, *I am on the side of those fighting for freedom and righteousness, except for the Africans*. And so I must ask, if God is in me, where would God want to stand? What would Jesus seek to do?

"My answer today is the only answer a Christian should give. I have *another* spirit with me, and because of that, I know we are all God's children. That God loves you." As he turned to Sarah, he said his words deliberately. "That I am African, and He loves me." He nodded toward the Brother. "That we are worthy because I AM made us."

He moved back to the pulpit and ran a finger across the cover of his Bible. "I will not run from the mountain that has been placed in my path. I will serve my Lord with all my heart and climb right up the rough side of that mountain. And so when faced with that most important question, I say before you all today, the only answer that is the right answer, as Caleb said in that age long past, *Ndinike ezo ntaba! Ndinike ezo ntaba!—Give me this mountain!*"

The congregation burst into applause, their eyes shining, as Joshua repeated the phrase again. It brought a smile to his face as the Brother squeezed Sarah's hand, and Andrew nodded, wiping away a tear. "God is with those who say, *We are One in the Spirit; we are One in the Lord; we are all the children of God.* And so I must also say on this day, in my most critical hour, that I resign as a minister of this mission at Fort Hare." A rumble traveled through the room. He let the murmuring quiet down.

"I cannot continue to serve a mission that chooses to stand on the wrong side of a battle for justice," he said. "I cannot condone a mission that says through its actions that we are *not* One in the Spirit, that God is not love. A mission that—in the face of injustice—does nothing, says nothing, and in doing nothing, says it's all right. I cannot free my hands to do God's work when they're clutching a false truth. Today I am making my choice known. As for me and my family, we're going to serve the Lord. And we have a struggle to wage."

He stepped from his pulpit with the strength of two men.

Joshua motioned everyone to the dining table, rolling up his sleeves. Nongolesi and Mama Siziwe fixed tea for everyone seated at the dining table in Joshua's mission house. Everyone seemed quiet, not knowing what to say in the minutes after his sermon.

"I'm very proud of you, my son," the Old Man said, breaking the silence as Mama Siziwe and Lydia nodded beside him. "It takes great courage to stand tall in a time of crisis. You have done that with your words today, and you should be proud of the example you have provided to all who witnessed this today."

"That was quite a sermon," the Brother agreed, looking at Joshua from beside Lydia with as much pride as Joshua saw in the Old Man's eyes. Andrew sat silently across from the Brother, looking at Joshua with what he thought was approval, though he looked troubled as well.

"With a sermon like that, word is going to spread quickly," Nokwe said. "Your mission officials won't want you around the students after a sermon like that."

"You know they're going to come for you?" Sarah whispered, echoing her husband.

"We were up early this morning; Nongolesi and I are already preparing to move from this house," Joshua said. "I'm sure they will file the paperwork for my deportation with the magistrate as soon as they hear about the sermon. They'll just need to wait for approval from the magistrate," Joshua said.

Joshua looked intently at Nongolesi who sat down beside him. She kept her expression even, but he knew how much his decision was affecting her.

He had woken her early before heading to the church. "I'm asking you," he had said to her.

"You're my husband," she had responded to his question. "Where you go, I will follow," she had said, but her eyes had been wet. He knew she was trying to hide her pain.

"Nongolesi, I didn't expect I would be leaving South Africa like this," he had said to her. "They will probably force me out of the country and never permit me back. And if you leave with me, they may not ever permit you back. We had never talked about that possibility. Your whole life has been in South Africa, all of your family is here. I'm asking you, and you can tell me when you are certain and you are sure. I'm asking you if you will go with me to America."

"Where you go, I will follow," she had responded again.

Nongolesi finally looked at him now as she set her teacup down. She smiled faintly and nodded to say she was okay.

"Where will you go when you move from this house?" Sarah asked.

"To Ginsberg," Joshua replied.

Nokwe smiled approvingly, and the Brother nodded.

"After all, it is tradition for our community to build a hut for a newly wedded couple." Nongolesi smiled, trying to lighten the mood. "We did not need a new hut all of those many months ago, but now!"

They all chuckled.

"Ginsberg may prove to be a bit of a tinderbox," Sarah warned.

"With the direction of events in the country, what location wouldn't?" Joshua asked. The room fell quiet with that somber recognition. "Our presence is needed in Ginsberg."

Nokwe nodded. "I've been there many times. The weight of the despair there . . ." He closed his eyes as if he couldn't find the words to express his thoughts.

"Just so you know, we will be moving over tomorrow. We've packed most of our belongings already. We'll need a ride—we're leaving the car behind," Joshua said, looking at the Brother.

"All the symbols of your status will be gone," Sarah observed.

"Stripped down to nothing," Joshua replied.

"God loves to strip something down to nothing in order to build it back up in a new light. You're on a good path," the Brother said softly. Joshua smiled at the words intended to soothe him. The Brother was quite a friend.

"Let's make good use of the time you have left with us, Joshua," Nokwe said with a certain urgency. "With your experiences in America, whatever you can share with us about the strategies that are used in your country to protest and make gains, whatever you can do at the schools—"

"We'll make good use of the time. We have already accelerated the completion of the church and school in Ginsberg. There've been delays in finishing it, but we should have it completed soon. The books will arrive for the children next week. After that, I will have time to speak at length with you about the strategies we have used back home."

Joshua asked everyone to join hands so he could say a prayer for their futures and the future of the country. As he looked around him at the circle they'd formed, he felt so blessed. "We have many reasons to give thanks," he said as he spoke to God from his heart.

———————

The morning sun began to filter through the thin curtains Nongolesi had tacked over the paneless windows of their *indlu* in Ginsberg. When Joshua awoke, his heart soared with the feeling of dawn in him. He looked around their tiny home and felt such peace, as if gazing at floating lily pads outstretched on a pond, sun shimmering all around him.

It had been a few days since the Brother had dropped Joshua and Nongolesi off to their new home. Their government-built *indlu* sat toward the top of a row of other huts, next to the one Mama Siziwe and the Old Man now shared. The Old Man had left for Port Elizabeth, to spearhead a larger regional effort to build support among Africans and the English for peaceful organized protests. It had been difficult to say farewell to him. Both Joshua and Nongolesi understood they could be deported at any time. It had been a long and tearful good-bye. Mama Siziwe would soon leave to join the Old Man in Port Elizabeth for a long period of time. Joshua was glad that he and Nongolesi could spend time with Mama Siziwe during this period, to help quell her fears.

From his visits to Ginsberg, Joshua knew their hut would be small and dilapidated, its entirety half the size of his Fort Hare bedroom, with peeling walls and water puddles forming beneath the leaks in its roof. He knew too that it could be quite possible to sit in the government *indlu's* darkness and grow old with anger, to fade away in this building that seemed intended as a mockery of traditions. Built with materials that couldn't weather the faintest showers, the peeling cement of the *indlu* showed the steel shell beneath, clearly telling who was beholden to whom.

Neighbors had dropped off a sheep's skin mat to welcome them, along with a bowl of fruit, a few tin pots, and a calabash for soured milk. Mama Siziwe had placed candles in the corner for them. And with the bright orange and yellow fabric a few women had dropped off, Nongolesi managed to make the *indlu* look like a home, tacking the curtains with hand-painted daisies over the sill openings. At night, when all the township had gone to sleep, Joshua would lie awake for a while, with joy-filled thoughts. He felt peace every time he closed his eyes here, or sat down on the dung-smoothed floor, or stripped naked as he showered with the other men in a row of open stalls outside, not caring that the open showers had been meant to humiliate them. It only strengthened their resolve.

The first order of business had been to finish the church in Gins- berg, which sat on the highest spot on the hill. There hadn't been a day since Tahira had died that Joshua hadn't thought of her. Her memory made him work harder. Block by block, as Joshua worked with other men to lift and plaster the bricks in place, he came closer to forgiving himself for all the mistakes he had made.

The church was nearly finished. Now Joshua had a sense of peace as he opened his Bible and prepared a sermon he would deliver that evening at the request of villagers. He was all the more excited, knowing in a few days he'd mark the opening of the church and school with a sermon before the children.

Joshua rode an African-only bus to the stop a few blocks from Liberty Hall in East London. As he walked into Liberty Hall, he noted it was a shell of a building, with only a few paned windows and a proud red, green, and black flag hoisted over its entrance. He smiled to himself as he walked underneath the main archway with the words ONE GOD, ONE AIM, ONE DESTINY etched there.

He looked across the large room cluttered with folding chairs and tables and a long makeshift stage at its front. It was just as he imagined Garvey's Liberty Halls looked in the United States. As he scanned the room, looking for the Brother, the beauty of the scene touched him. Muslim clerics, Jewish rabbis, and other clergymen in robes stood among plain-clothed men and women. He saw Nokwe and Sarah immersed in a serious-looking conversation at the far side of the room. He had to look twice as his eyes locked on Andrew leaning over a table and speaking to a group with the comfort of a man who'd been here many times before. Andrew froze a moment when he caught Joshua's gaze.

Joshua took in a breath as Andrew slowly excused himself from the table, and moved toward him. Joshua couldn't utter a word.

"Welcome," Andrew said with sincerity in his eyes. He paused when Joshua didn't respond. "Joshua, you know I feel much the same as you about all of the things that are going on in this country," he said, answering the look on Joshua's face.

"Why didn't you tell me?" Joshua asked, trying to wipe away the feeling of betrayal.

"That I'd been here many times before?" Andrew asked. Andrew touched Joshua's arm earnestly. "While I have expressed to you my discomfort with our mission, I did not feel comfortable telling you any more about my own actions." He could see Joshua wasn't satisfied with the response. "Joshua, you are here under special circumstances; unlike me, the consequences for you will be grave if our mission finds out about you even being here. The most they can do to me is ask me to leave the mission, not the country. I did not want to influence you unduly."

Andrew turned and looked back at the room. He nodded at the view. "This sight is beautiful, and I am glad you are here."

Joshua could feel his anger melt away. Just then, the Brother came over with two rabbis and a Muslim cleric, beginning the introductions.

CHAPTER 31

Joshua looked at his watch ticking slowly. He paced back and forth across the *indlu* in the bright daylight filtering through the curtains, glancing at the drawings of their ancestors that he and Nongolesi had tacked to their walls. "Time," he finally called out.

The African student hunched over a small table in the center of the room and moaned, setting his pencil down.

"How do you feel?" Joshua asked.

The young man from Peddie sat back, brushing his hand over his brow. He chuckled as if overwhelmed by his own feelings, then flashed a grin. "Not bad. I think it is okay." He nodded with surprise.

"I'll check your work against the answers." Joshua smiled back. "I know you did well!" he said in an encouraging tone as the young man stood up.

"You're going to pass that exam. You're ready—I can feel it. We'll do another mock exam next week, and we'll keep preparing."

"Joshua," a voice called softly from the entrance to his *indlu*.

"Andrew!" Joshua greeted him with surprise. "Please come in, I was just finishing with my student Kolela."

Kolela and Andrew shook hands. "Reverend Clement is a minister in this region," Joshua said to Kolela. "And Kolela," he continued, turning to Andrew, "is studying to pass the national exams in biology so he can travel to the United States to become a doctor."

Kolela tried to hide his smile as he moved toward the door. Joshua and Andrew walked with him to the edge of the row of huts, encouraging him to keep up his studies as Kolela waved a grateful good-bye and he headed down the hill.

"Welcome to my new home," Joshua said, waving his hand in the air as Andrew surveyed his surroundings. "Would you like to come in for a cup of tea?"

Andrew seemed embarrassed as he looked over Joshua's *indlu*. "It's a big transition," he commented as he gazed at the peeling walls.

"A good transition," Joshua corrected him.

Andrew nodded knowingly. "Don't bother with tea. I came to just visit for a short while."

They sat on thong chairs in front of the *indlu,* looking down the hill as small children played on the unpaved paths. As they ran around with confident smiles, playing a defiant game, Joshua smiled. He rubbed his sore hands and wrists, which had been scratched again and again as they had hurried to finish the church and school. They'd already begun to teach the children there. Seeing how bright the children's hopes for the future had grown warmed Joshua.

"You seem to have accomplished a lot here," Andrew said, looking back to the church, complete except for a few minor touches.

Joshua smiled. The church was the biggest gift he could possibly bestow before leaving. "Before I saw you the other night, I thought you might frown on my decision to quit our mission and relocate here," Joshua said.

Andrew shook his head and sighed, a guilty sigh. "Now you know better," he said, scratching his temple. "It took a great deal of courage for you to make that decision." He looked to the children and beyond to King William's Town, seeming uncertain about something. The doubting frown made him look so young. He brushed his hand through his brown hair, trying to find the right words.

"I wanted to just apologize again—I didn't mean to hide from you the depth of my misgivings about our mission. My intention was not to be deceitful." He shifted in his seat, and looked at Joshua directly. "The longer I have stayed in this country"—he closed his eyes a bit—"the harder it has been to reconcile my faith with conditions and the mandate we have been given by our mission."

Joshua was surprised to hear such a frank confession, even after seeing Andrew at Liberty Hall.

Andrew sat back. "I fear I am right behind you, Joshua." He chuckled, as if he could hardly believe he'd admitted it. "It may not be long before I too make the same choice you have. And I envy you—you seem to have made the decision with such a strong spirit, as if you haven't a single doubt about your path."

"I'm very certain," Joshua said in a tone that made Andrew's eyes widen. Joshua could see how much he was struggling. "But it took a lot to get here," Joshua said, feeling as if crow's-feet were stretching across his face.

Andrew examined his expression. "I know you must miss Tahira. I understand losing her was a tremendous loss for you."

Joshua nodded and looked to the distance, unable to reply further.

"I'll be going to the march in East London in a few days," Joshua said after a while. "Several clergymen will be leading the next major demonstration against the government's policies of forced relocations and the revocation of African voting rights. You're welcome to join me for the last planning meeting, or during the march."

Andrew lowered his eyes. "I am many things," he said with disappointment, "but ready for that step, I am not. I hope you can understand, Joshua."

Joshua studied his face. From the moment he had arrived, he sensed so much goodness in Andrew. "We all have to respond in our own way, in our own time," Joshua replied without judgment.

Andrew stood up. "I will check in on you again soon."

"I hope I'll still be here." Joshua smiled; Andrew's eyes grew sad. "If they . . ."

". . . deport me," Joshua said, finishing his sentence.

"I hope you will find a way to stay in touch."

Joshua was moved by the intensity of his tone; Andrew acted as if he were losing one of his closest friends.

"You're an honorable preacher, Joshua, a true man of God, and I know your ministry will bring forth good fruit, no matter where you are."

Hearing those words lifted Joshua's spirits. There were so many times in South Africa when he had failed to be a true man of God, he thought. They embraced, and Andrew stepped back toward his car. Joshua was quite sure that would be the last time he would see Andrew.

The African-only bus dropped Joshua at the foot of the path near Reverend Msomi's home. Old sedans and trucks lined both sides of the street for nearly two blocks. There was something about the sight of car after car that made him understand the determination he'd feel in Mr. Msomi's home even before he walked through the door. The most affluent and powerful African men seemed gathered from all parts of the region.

The house was filled with the young and old, the keepers of a pulsing hope who were scrawling their dreams in broad letters on canvases. Young men and women were scattered on the far side of the floor, writing with pens and dipping brushes into paint, and seeming to see their future in every extra drop of paint and ink they laid on protest banners. *Sibuye,* they wrote on the placards, *we are one.* Other signs read *Nikosi sikelel'i-Afrika.* The makings of an uprising were palpable.

Joshua's eyes were drawn to Mhlobo, who was drawing on the tallest placard in the room. As Joshua neared, his eyes grew wider at the portrait that Mhlobo had drawn carefully there. It pictured many images of Jesus, each with His hands outstretched. The Jesus on the far right was black; the one on the far left was white. Another was golden-colored, another copper-skinned. Their images overlapped and melted into one another, until they met in the Jesus in the middle. Joshua blinked and could barely imagine how Mhlobo had managed to make them all look exactly alike, except the skin color— even the one in the middle who stood with welcoming eyes, bronze with hair like wool. "Mhlobo," Joshua said, his breath nearly taken away.

"I've been working on this very long." Mhlobo smiled, his look saying that this was his most important piece of work.

"It's amazing work," the Brother said as he walked up next to Joshua, gazing down at Mhlobo's handiwork. "I'm glad you came.

Please sit with us," the Brother said to Joshua, looking at him with the love of a proud father. He steered Joshua toward a table.

"It's going to be quite an event tomorrow," Reverend Msomi said as he leaned into the others at the table. "It's a unity protest, so it won't just be students. There will be elderly people from homesteads, young men, doctors, those clergy who are willing to join us." He nodded as Joshua took a seat beside the Brother. "The police won't be happy to see ministers and rabbis and clerics there endorsing the effort. It's intended to be a peaceful protest, but we have to be prepared that things might fall out of our control."

Joshua nodded along with the others.

"Welcome, Reverend Clay," Reverend Msomi said. "I was just telling the others that some clergymen will be leading this march. But you are not obliged to be with us at the front of the line."

"I will be there with you at the front," Joshua said.

The others looked at him, then smiled.

———————

The sound that stood out the most was the rhythmic flapping of the flag as the wind blew its red, green, and black fabric against the building next to them. Joshua was amazed that a crowd so large could be so silent. When he first arrived, everything around him had buzzed. The trail of marchers extended several blocks, numbering in the thousands. Many of those protesting came with their placards strapped around them with twine. Several men hoisted Mhlobo's placard of the many Jesuses high in the air. As the gathering crowds grew more full, the anticipation seemed to rise. Facing the sun, Joshua took a deep breath. He felt as if a new day had dawned. The throngs of people squeezed more closely together in the street as Nokwe called through a cone, "We march on!" With his simple command, they slowly forged a straight path ahead, singing and marching toward the victory that stood on the horizon.

Joshua helped lead the crowd along with the other clergymen, some African, some Indian, some Coloured, some Afrikaner, some English, some Jewish. It was a beautiful sight as they walked hand in hand, a rainbow of colors. *Will I ever be involved in anything more important than this?* Joshua asked himself. *Lord, I thank you,* he prayed silently, *for giving me the strength to be on the right side of this fight.*

The excitement of the crowd quickly turned to silence as they heard police vans moving up adjacent streets toward them. Everyone stood frozen, holding their breath. The vans came into full view then, their engines idling. The church leaders held the crowd back, hoping not to provoke the police.

Joshua saw a single officer step out of one of the vans, his gun jiggling in its holster as he walked toward them. He stopped a distance away and turned to the police vans behind him, motioning them forward. The crowd clutched hands more tightly in that first moment and sang out their freedom song, their voices lifting higher than the revving engines; then the police rifles lifted, without a single call of warning, and Joshua heard the first shots ring out.

Everything seemed to blend together—the screams, the bodies thrown against him as people ran from the gunfire. Joshua kept searching for Nongolesi. She was his only thought in those minutes. Why hadn't he insisted more strongly that she stay home? After a few moments, he found her crouching low behind a steel barrel. He covered her with his body and they could hear the trucks moving past them, shots still ringing out. Tears were streaming down Nongolesi's face. She squeezed her eyes shut as the shots finally came to a close.

Joshua felt numb. He could barely believe they fired on unarmed protesters. When he finally stood up, his heart pounding wildly, he could hear the Brother saying in a thin voice, "Jesus." Flush-faced, rocking back and forth with his hands pressed together in prayer, the Brother was bending over four bloodied bodies. Joshua put his arm around the Brother, consoling him. He heard sobs then and more moans from nearby as others dared to emerge into the middle of the road. Joshua had to steady himself as he looked at the scene around him. Reverend Msomi was holding a bloodied rag to his right arm, a look of astonishment coating his face as he also looked at the bodies strewn across the street.

Joshua glanced back to see the Brother standing red-faced, walking near the bodies. "Sweet Jesus," the Brother said again.

The morning downpour tapered to a sprinkle and the sun began to peak through the clouds. Birds began chirping in the trees that were planted near a couple of *izindlu* on the nearly barren hills of Ginsberg. Joshua ran his finger across the articles he'd found tucked in his bag as he began slowly to prepare to pack. Negroes were hurting missionary work in Africa, inciting Africans to protest for greater rights, the South African newspaper had claimed in 1921. He had never dreamed, when he first journeyed here, that he'd be among the number to be sent back home in "shame." He tucked the article away, without any notion of regret. He bundled his notes and his Bible, preparing to deliver his first sermon, which would inaugurate the new church and the school.

Each day Joshua awoke to find himself still in Ginsberg, he said a prayer of thanksgiving. He was surprised his mission's leaders had not come to remove him yet. It was probably a delay in the deportation paperwork, he mused. But he was grateful, so grateful, to see the dedication of the church and school on this Christmas Day of 1936. He expected most residents of Ginsberg would try to attend. He'd made a special point to invite the Coloureds from across the divide. This church was for every one of God's people. He had prepared a special sermon just for the children—one, he hoped, they would hold in their hearts as long as they had breath. Knuckles rapped against the entrance to his *indlu*.

"We've come to give the reverend a surprise," a young girl said in a sweet voice as Joshua moved to the door. He looked at her questioningly.

"If you're ready a few minutes early, *Makinda*," Mhlobo said from a few yards away, "we would like you to see a present we have been working on for you. You should see it before you dedicate the building and give your sermon." He nodded, a twinkle in his eyes.

Joshua smiled. What could get Mhlobo smiling like that? He gathered his Bible and a small paper with notes and headed with them to the church. He saw Nongolesi and Beaumont standing near the pew doors with a few more villagers; they all had broad smiles.

"What is this?" He chuckled, taking in Nongolesi's expression.

She was beaming as she waved him through the side door to the pews. He loved the feeling every time he walked into the church—it was so cozy and inviting. He could still smell the plaster from the setting bricks. It only took a moment before an object on the wall across from him caught his eyes. One of the young boys from the village walked next to it, preparing to undrape it on Mhlobo's command.

"We want to make sure you know we will never forget you, what you have done here," Mhlobo said in as serious a voice as Joshua had ever heard. The room was filled with emotion as villagers and some of the children surrounded him. "This is to show you we will never forget how it is we have this church and this school and to let you know we will use this church and school to raise our children well."

The young boy tugged away the drape, and Joshua's lips froze as he looked at the painting on the canvas that hung within a hand-carved frame. It had been painted so intricately. It was the portrait of a Bible, a thick one, bound in black leather, parted at John 3:16. Seeing the mud spots drawn carefully on its sides sent a chill through Joshua. The mud spots trailed across the two parted pages—the one on the left that was in Xhosa, and the one on the right that was in English—as sunlight poured through a window in back of the Bible in hopeful shades of bronze, illuminating the Truth in both languages. Joshua's eyes clouded over.

Joshua could hardly utter a word. His whole two years here seemed to stare back at him from the painting. Nongolesi hugged him deeply, but he wasn't sure that even she understood everything he was seeing as he looked at the portrait. "Thank you so much," Joshua whispered.

"It will always grace this church to remind us of the minister who helped to spread God's Word and to build this church," Beaumont said, seeming to speak for all the other young people of his village who stood nearby. Joshua's eyes welled.

The congregation members began to gather early, an hour before the sermon would begin. Even several of the men who'd sat for months on end sipping beer gathered there looking at the church as if daring to hope again. Joshua prepared to address the children first, before the adults would also join them. He spoke the words he hoped would stay with them forever. He said a silent prayer as he thought of Tahira and began his sermon citing John 3:16, explaining about their inheritance and their rights as God's children.

Soon the adults also filled the pews, most of them African, and some of the Coloured from across the dirt divide. They all looked around the new building with such pride. He could see it in the way they thinned their lips and nodded their heads. He looked back at them with equal pride as a few of the African men began to lead praise songs, clapping and shaking their tambourines. It wasn't long before one of the village Mamas stepped out into the aisle and lifted her skirt so she could dance more freely. She brought back a memory from half a world away. Nothing could have brought a brighter smile to Joshua's face as he felt joy fill the room.

As he stood again, to address the families nestled together, he shared their sun-ripened hope and preached a passionate sermon. *Never forget God's love,* he told them. Their smiles assured him that many would remember these words and call upon them in a midnight hour.

CHAPTER 32

Everyone knew they'd come for Joshua. As the December summer sun grew stronger and shades on the ground stretched fuller, two sedans pulled up the main road of Ginsberg, brushing aside skinny dogs in their way. The children crowded around the cars defiantly as several men stepped out.

Joshua and Nongolesi had already packed, but they took their time collecting the last of their belongings from their *indlu*. Joshua tried to tick off a list of things he had wanted to ensure he'd done before they left. It was hard to concentrate and think of them all. But most important, he'd already given to Mama Siziwe a thick wad of money, from the sale of his watch and other belongings, for her to tuck away and use in times of trouble. As they moved their bags outside their hut, Mama Siziwe's eyes were heavy. She wasn't ready for this moment.

Tears were streaming down Nongolesi's face. "Tell Mhlobo and Ogenga I will write as soon as we reach America," Nongolesi said as she hugged Mama Siziwe tightly. Nongolesi wouldn't even be able to hug the Old Man good-bye one more time.

As Joshua hugged Mama Siziwe, he realized how deeply he would miss them all. It tore at his heart, the idea that he may never be allowed to return to the country to visit the people who had become his family. Joshua held Nongolesi's hand tightly as she moved with Little Darius into the backseat of the first sedan.

Joshua felt no need to ask forgiveness for the words he was about to utter as he gathered his breath, wanting to say them well as he moved closer to Mr. Garrett and whispered them. The eyes of the onlookers grew wide as Garrett's ear tips turned red, soon followed by the rest of his face. Joshua looked him in the eye and nodded, letting the words sink in. Then he took his seat next to Nongolesi.

It didn't show in her face, but Nongolesi's clenched fist was cold and trembling, reflecting the depth of her sadness as the sedan shook against the gravel, pulling onto the road out of Ginsberg. The second sedan trailed behind them. Nongolesi gazed out the window at the children who filled the path behind the cars as they rolled down the hill. She turned back to Joshua, whispering words he needed to hear: "I am happy to be with my husband."

Joshua caressed her hand warmly and kissed her on the forehead, touching his hand also to Little Darius's face. He turned back to Ginsberg, taking heart as young children gathered at the roadside, locking arms and swaying in a dance of triumph, taunting the drivers as they passed by, as if to tell them they had not given up. Joshua kept his eyes on Ginsberg until they were far beyond the last hut.

———

Joshua stood later on the deck of the Cunard, gazing out at the peaceful sky. As soon as she'd heard his deportation was final, Sarah had arranged to secure tickets for them on the luxury liner, that royal city afloat. From its deck, he glanced back, to take a last look at South Africa. The sun had already blessed Table Mountain and had disappeared beneath its brow, and the land was becoming a silhouette against the darkening sky.

"I thought you'd be here." Nongolesi interrupted his thoughts.

He wrapped his arms around her and Little Darius, who she cradled in her embrace. Joshua felt relieved by how at peace she seemed to be as they passed Robben Island and stared back at the twinkling lights of Cape Town. The ship moved south, past the Twelve Apostles, soon shifting its bearings, gathering steam to head northward back up the Atlantic.

"I thought you were going to rest," he whispered in her ear.

"I also wanted one last look," she said, looking at Africa as the ship sailed farther away.

"We'll return again one day."

She didn't respond to his comment, but he could feel her tense up at his words. She bowed her head down a bit as if tears were about to flow freely again.

Joshua stood behind her and tried to hug her more tightly. The cool summer-night wind blew off the waters, and her body stopped trembling under his warmth. They didn't say another word for a long while as they watched the land of Africa slowly pass from view. Joshua would never forget his time in South Africa. So many images floated through his mind as he watched the dark masses of land pass from sight, curved like camels moving in the night. How could he have ever imagined the richness of what he was to experience when he first set foot in South Africa? He remembered the shining face of the Brother as he shouted out, "Because I AM!" His heart grew full as he remembered Tahira, pressing her finger hard to the blessed evidence in her hands. He took heart remembering Jovan's victory of gaining his degree and heading to America. He was fortified remembering the chants of the students, vowing that things would be better. He held close to his heart the memory of Ogenga and Mhlobo sitting before the Tree of Everlasting Hope, his reminder that there are streams in the desert.

Joshua felt a tremendous weight, leaving his congregation and his family behind. Ogenga was still in jail; Joshua frowned deeply with worry that his brother may never get out. And as his thoughts drifted to his family in America, he flushed when he imagined their disappointment. By now, they had lost the support of his mission, and they would be bereft of those funds as the depression wore on. He tried to picture how they had reacted when learning that he was being deported. He hoped most of them would come to understand and support his reasons for resigning. As he thought back to Ginsberg, he only hoped that his presence had been like a stone thrown into a puddle, leaving hope-filled ripples in its wake. But still he worried about the country he was leaving. When Africans finally secured freedom, would *ubuntu* prevail? The families torn apart, would they heal? His concern was only matched by thoughts about the Negroes of his own country. *It's one; we're one.* Darius's words rang clearly in his mind.

Nongolesi began to hum Baba's Song as she kept her eyes cast on the stars that graced the sky and the ripples of the water. That song had remained within Joshua's soul. It rang in his ears as clearly and as beautifully from within him as it once had when he'd heard it sung from afar in stillness. *Ndifumaneke kuni; utsho uYehova. Ndiya kukubuyisa ukuthinjwa kwenu* . . .

Joshua stayed with Nongolesi on deck until the African continent faded on the distant horizon, and the Atlantic Ocean became the only view in sight. By then, the sky had turned as black as the deepest desert night. Joshua looked down at the placid waters. The pinpricks of moonlight on the waves paved an aisle from the horizon to the ship. Just as on his journey to Africa, those pinpricks numbered so many, like the number of his kinfolk buried beneath the sea. Joshua nodded, this time so much more knowingly. The shining stars flickered just then, their brightness cutting an image into the sky. It was meant only for his eyes, he knew, and a smile curved at Joshua's lips as he looked at its wonder—a long-winged bird with pearl-colored talons, picking itself up, setting itself on a trackless ascent, flying freely.

JOSHUA'S BIBLE: XHOSA TRANSLATION OF THE VOICE SINGING

This is a translation of the song that Joshua hears.

SONG Part 1
Jeremiah 29:12–14
Then shall ye call upon me, and ye shall go and pray unto me, and I will hearken unto you. And ye shall seek me, and find me, when ye shall search for me with all your heart. And I will be found of you, saith the Lord: and I will turn away your captivity . . .

Niya kundinqula, nize nithandaze kum, ndiniphulaphule. Niya kundifuna, nindifumane, xa nithe nandifuna ngentliziyo yenu yonke; ndifumaneke kuni; utsho uYehova. Ndiya kukubuyisa ukuthinjwa kwenu.

Jeremiah 29:8 and 11
Let not your prophets and your diviners, that be in the midst of you, deceive you, neither hearken to your dreams which ye cause to be dreamed. For I know the thoughts that I think toward you, saidth the Lord, thoughts of peace not of evil, to give you an expected end.

Ukuthi, Mabanganilukuhli abaprofeti benu abaphakathi kwenu, kwanabavumisi benu, ningawaphulaphuli amaphupha enu eniwaphu-

payo. . . . Ngokuba ndiyazazi iingcinga endizicingayo ngani, utsho uYehova: iingcinga zoxolo, ezingezizo ezobubi; ukuba ndininike ikamva nethemba.

SONG Part 2
John 10:27–30

My sheep listen to my voice; I know them, and they follow me. And I give them eternal life: and they shall never perish, neither shall any man pluck them out of my hand. My Father, which gave them me, is greater than all; and no man is able to pluck them out of my Father's hand. I and my Father are one.

Ezam izimvu ziyaliva ilizwi lam, ndibe nam ndizazi, zindilandela; mna ndizinika ubomi obungunaphakade; azisayi kutshabalala naphakade; akukho namnye uya kuzihlutha esandleni sam. UBawo, ondinike zona, ungaphezu kwabo bonke; akukho bani unako ukuzihlutha esandleni sikaBawo. Mna noBawo sibanye.

SONG Part 3
Mark 8:34–36

If anyone would come after me, he must deny himself and take up his cross and follow me. For whoever wants to save his life will lose it, but whoever loses his life for me and for the gospel will save it. What good is it for a man to gain the whole world, yet forfeit his soul?

Osukuba ethanda ukundilandela, makazincame, awuthwale umnqam-lezo wakhe, andilandele ke. Kuba othe wathanda ukuwusindisa umphe-fumlo wakhe, wolahlekelwa nguwo; ke yena othe wawulahla umphefumlo wakhe ngenxa yam, nangenxa yeendaba ezilungileyo ezi, wowusindisa. Kuba komnceda ntoni na umntu, ukuba uthe walizuza ihlabathi liphela, waza wonakalelwa ngumphefumlo wakhe?

ABOUT THE AUTHOR

Shelly Leanne has won the 2004 Honor Award in Fiction from the Black Caucus of the American Library Association for this debut novel, *Joshua's Bible*, which has also been a Black Expressions "Member Favorites" book and earned a starred review from *Booklist*. A recipient of a Fulbright Scholarship, the Du Bois Institute Fellowship, and the Carter G. Woodson Fellowship, Shelly Leanne has spent time living in South Africa, Trinidad, and England, and teaching in rural Kenya. She served as a Harvard University faculty member from 1997-2001, where she taught about human rights and about South Africa. A graduate of Harvard and Oxford University, she now resides with her husband in the Los Angeles area. You can contact her via her Web site, www.joshuasbible.com.